WATER-MELON

MARIAN KEYES

Reprinted in Arrow Books, 1999

11 13 15 17 19 20 18 16 14 12

Copyright © Marian Keyes, 1996

The right of Marian Keyes to be identified as the author
of thies work has been asserted by her in accordance with the Copyright,
Designs and Patents Act, 1988

First published in the United Kingdom in 1996 by Poolbeg Press

· This edition first published in 1997

by Mandarin Paperbacks and reprinted 10 times

Arrow Books Limited
Random House UK Ltd
20 Vauxhall Bridge Road, London SW1V 2SA

Random House Australia (Pty) Limited
20 Alfred Street, Milsons Point, Sydney,
New South Wales 2061, Australia

Random House New Zealand Limited
18 Poland Road, Glenfield,
Auckland 10, New Zealand

Random House South Africa (Pty) Limited
Endulini, 5a Jubilee Road, Parktown 2193, South Africa

Random House UK Limited Reg. No. 954009

A CIP catalogue record for this book is available from the
British Library

Papers used by Random House UK Limited
are natural, recyclable products made from wood grown in
sustainable forests. The manufacturing processes conform to
the environmental regulations of the country of origin

Printed and bound in Germany by
Elsnerdruck, Berlin

Acknowledgements

The first person I want to thank is my editor Kate Cruise O'Brien. Kate "discovered" me when I sent some short stories to Poolbeg, purely on spec, and immediately there was a magic between us. She believed in *Watermelon* before I did, before it was even written! She has been so lovely to me, very protective, incredibly enthusiastic, always full of praise, sensitive with any suggested changes or corrections, not to mention being very kind and hospitable and a good friend.

And, of course, huge thanks must go to Mr Poolbeg, Philip MacDermott, and all his wonderful staff. Philip has been so welcoming and kind and all his staff have worked so hard and sensitively on *Watermelon*. I'd like to say a special thanks to Brenda for the great cover, Nicole for the meticulous typesetting, Breda for organising my marketing and publicity and Kieran for his patience with my contract.

Thanks to Mam and Dad, who have always been there for me. They are two of the most selfless and genuinely decent people I have ever met. And thanks to my wonderful brothers and sisters, Niall, Caitriona, Tadhg and Rita-Anne, all so beautiful and gifted and unique.

Thanks to Charlotte and Niall for patience, tolerance and support above and beyond the call of duty. Also thanks to both of them and to Kirsten for the compassion and kindness they've shown to me. Thanks to Belinda, my guinea pig, for all the encouragement and enthusiasm.

Thanks to Eileen for so much. For her gentleness, her unjudgemental friendship and the meticulous work she did on my contract.

Thanks to Ailish, for her enthusiasm and energy and for the friendship she's shown me over the years.

Thanks to Louise for the great loyalty, love and friendship she's given to me.

Thanks to Conor, Patricia and Alan for everything, especially for January 1994. There aren't words to convey my gratitude.

Thanks to Liam, for the good example and the great crack.

Thanks to Jenny for *everything*. She's done so much for me, I don't know where to start. So I won't.

Thanks to the wonderful Albyn. Meeting her has been such a gift.

Thanks to Maureen Rice for her gorgeous quote.

Thanks to the staff of the Rutland Centre and to the people who were "inmates" when I was there. Thanks to all the great people I've met in the rooms of Alcoholics Anonymous.

And finally, thanks to my beloved Tony, my tame pedant! For his admiration, for bullying me into working when I didn't want to, for his practical advice, for laughing when I wrote something funny and for making me so happy.

For Mam and Dad

Prologue

February the fifteenth is a very special day for me. It is the day I gave birth to my first child. It is also the day my husband left me. As he was present at the birth I can only assume the two events weren't entirely unrelated.

I knew I should have followed my instincts.

I subscribed to the classical, or you might say, the traditional role fathers play in the birth of their children. Which goes as follows.

Lock them in a corridor outside the delivery room. Allow them admittance at no time. Give them forty cigarettes and a lighter. Instruct them to pace to the end of the corridor. When they reach this happy position, instruct them to turn around and return to whence they came.

Repeat as necessary.

Conversation should be curtailed. They are allowed to exchange a few words with any other prospective father pacing alongside them.

"My first," (wry smile).

"Congrats . . . – my third," (rueful smile).

"Well done," (forced smile – is he trying to imply that he's more virile than me).

Feelings do tend to run high around this time.

Or they are allowed to fling themselves on any doctor who emerges exhausted from the delivery room, covered in blood up to his elbows, and gasp "Any news doctor???" To which the doctor might reply "Oh God no man! – sure she's only three centimetres dilated." And your man will nod knowingly, while understanding nothing other than the fact that there is still a fair bit of pacing to go.

He is also allowed to let a spasm of anguish pass over his face when he hears the agonies of his loved one within. And when it's all over and mother and child have been cleaned up and mother is in a clean nightdress and is lying back against the lacy pillows looking exhausted but joyful and the perfect infant is suckling at her breast, then, and *only* then should the father be permitted to enter.

But no, I gave into peer pressure and agreed to be all new age about it. I was very doubtful, I can tell you. I mean I wouldn't want any of my close friends or relatives at the removal of . . . say . . . my appendix. Humiliating! You'd be at such a disadvantage. All these people looking at you, at places of yourself you'd never even seen before, not even with a mirror. I didn't know what my large intestine looked like. And by the same token I didn't know what my cervix looked like. And nor did I want to. But half the staff of St Michael's hospital did.

I felt at a great disadvantage. That I wasn't doing myself justice.

To put it simply I was not looking my best. As I say, a humiliating kind of a business.

I'd seen enough macho inarticulate lorry drivers

on the telly, a tear in their eye, a catch in their voice, struggling to tell you about how being present at the birth of their child was the most pro . . . prof . . . pr . . . pr . . . deep! thing that ever happened to them. And I'd heard stories about beer-slugging jock rugby-players who invited the entire team around to watch the video of their wife giving birth.

But then again, you'd wonder about their motives.

Anyway James and I got all emotional about it and decided he should be there.

So that's the story of how he was there at the birth. The story of why and how he left me is a bit longer.

Chapter One

I'm sorry, you must think I'm very rude. We've hardly even been introduced and here I am telling you all about the awful things that have happened to me.

Let me just give you the briefest outline of myself and I'll save details like, for example, my first day at school until later, if we have the time.

Let's see, what should I tell you? Well, my name is Claire and I'm twenty-nine and, as I mentioned, I've just had my first child two days ago (a little girl, seven pounds, four ounces, totally beautiful) and my husband (did I mention his name is James?) told me about twenty-four hours ago that he has been having an affair for the past six months, with – and get this – not even his secretary or someone glamorous from work, but with a married woman, who lives in the flat two floors below us. I mean, how *suburban* can you get! And not only is he having an affair but he wants a divorce.

I'm sorry if I'm being unnecessarily flippant about this. I'm all over the place. In a moment I'll be crying again. I'm still in shock I suppose. Her name is Denise and I know her quite well.

Not quite as well as James does obviously.

The awful thing is she always seemed to be really nice.

She's thirty-five (don't ask me how I know this, I just do. And at the risk of sounding very sour grapes and losing your sympathy, she does look thirty-five) and she has two children and a nice husband (quite apart from my one, that is). And apparently she's moved out of her flat and he's moved out of his (or ours, should I say) and they've both moved into a new one in a secret location.

Can you believe it?! How dramatic can you get? I know her husband is Italian but I really don't think he's likely to kill the pair of them. He's a waiter, not a Mafia stooge, so what's he going to do? Black pepper them to death? Compliment them into a coma? Run them over with the dessert trolley?

But again, I seem flippant.

I'm not.

I'm heartbroken.

And it's all such a disaster. I don't even know what to call my little girl. James and I had discussed some names – or, in retrospect, I had discussed them and he had pretended to listen – but we hadn't decided on anything definite. And I seem to have lost the ability to make decisions on my own. Pathetic, I know but that's marriage for you. Bang goes your sense of personal autonomy!

I wasn't always like this. Once I was strong-willed and independent. But that all seems like a long, long time ago.

I've been with James for five years, and we've been married for three years. And, my God, but I love that man.

Although we had a less than auspicious start, the

5

magic took hold of us very quickly. We both agree that we fell in love about fifteen minutes after we met and we stayed that way.

Or at least I did.

For a long time I never thought I'd meet a man who wanted to marry me.

Well, perhaps I should qualify that.

I never thought I'd meet a *nice* man who wanted to marry me. Plenty of lunatics, undoubtedly. But a nice man, a bit older than me, with a decent job, good-looking, funny, kind. You know – one who didn't look at me askance when I mentioned "The Partridge Family", not one who promised to take me out for a night in McDonalds just as soon as they were finished their Inter Cert (or their GCSEs, for any non-Irish people that may be reading), not one who apologised for not being able to get me a birthday present because their estranged wife had taken all their salary under a court maintenance order, not one who made me feel old-fashioned and inhibited because I got angry when he said that he'd screwed his ex-girl-friend the night after he screwed me ("My God, you convent girls are so *uptight*"), not one who made me feel inadequate because I couldn't tell the difference between Piat d'Or and Zinfandel (whatever that is!)

James didn't treat me in any of these unpleasant ways. It seemed almost too good to be true. He liked me. He liked almost everything about me.

When we first met we were both living in London. I was a waitress (more of that later) and he was an accountant.

Of all the Tex-Mex joints in all the towns in all the world, he had to walk into mine. I wasn't a *real* waitress, you understand, I had a degree in English, but I went through my rebellious stage rather later than most, at about twenty-three. Which is when I thought it might be a bit of a laugh to give up my permanent, pensionable wellish-paid job in Dublin and go off to the Godless city of London and live like an irresponsible student.

Which is something I should have done when I *was* an irresponsible student. But I was too busy getting work experience in my Summer holidays then, so my irresponsibility just had to wait until I was good and ready for it.

Like I always say, there's a time and a place for spontaneity.

Anyway, I had managed to land myself a job as a waitress in this highly trendy London restaurant, all loud music and video screens and minor celebrities.

Well to be honest, there were more minor celebrities on the staff than amongst the clientele, what with most of the staff being out-of-work actors and models and the like.

How I ever got a job there at all is beyond me. Although I may have been employed as the token Wholesome Waitress. To begin with I was the only waitress under eight feet tall and over five and a half stone. And although I may not have been model-material, I suppose I had a certain, shall we say, natural kind of charm – you know – short shiny brown hair, blue eyes, freckles, big smile, that kind of thing.

And I was so unworldly and naive. I never

realised when I was coming face to well-made-up face with the stars of stage and television.

More than once I'd be serving (and I use the word in its loosest possible term) some table of people (and I also use that word in its loosest possible term) when one of the other waitresses would elbow me (sending scalding barbecue sauce into the unfortunate groin of a customer) and hiss something like, "Isn't that guy that you're serving whatshisname out of that band?"

And I might reply, "Which guy? The one in the leather dress?" (Remember, these were the eighties.)

"No," she might hiss back, "the one with the blond dreadlocks and wearing the Chanel lipstick. Isn't he that singer?"

"Er, is he?," I would stammer, feeling untrendy and foolish for not knowing who this person was.

Anyway I loved working there. It thrilled me to the middle-class marrow of my bourgeois bones. It seemed so decadent and exciting to wake at one in the afternoon every day and go to work at six and finish at twelve and get drunk with the barmen and busboys afterwards.

While at home in Ireland my poor mother wept bitter tears at the thought of her daughter with the university education serving hamburgers to pop-stars.

And not even very famous pop-stars, to add insult to injury.

I had been working there about six months the night I met James. It was a Friday night, which was traditionally the night the OJs frequented our restaurant. OJ standing, of course, for Office Jerks.

At five o'clock every Friday, like graves disgorging their dead, offices all over the centre of London liberated their staff for the weekend so that hordes of pale, spotty, cheap-suited clerks descended on us, all wide-eyed and eager, looking for the stars and to get drunk, in any order you like.

It was de rigueur for us waitresses to stand around sneering disdainfully at the besuited clientele, shaking our heads in disbelieving pity at the attire, hairstyles etc., of the poor customers, to ignore them for the first fifteen minutes or so of their visit, swishing past them, earrings and bracelets jangling, obviously doing something far more important than attending to their pathetic needs and finally, after reducing them near to tears with frustration and hunger, to sashay up to the table with a huge smile, pen and pad at the ready. "Evening Gentlemen, can I get you a drink?"

It made them so *grateful*, you see. After that it didn't make a blind bit of difference if the drinks orders were all wrong and the food never came at all, they still left a huge tip, so lucky did they feel to get our attention bestowed on them.

Our motto was "Not only is the customer always wrong, he is likely to be very badly dressed into the bargain".

On the night in question, James and three of his colleagues sat in my section and I attended to their needs in my normal irresponsible and slapdash fashion. I paid them almost no attention whatsoever, barely listened to them as I took their order and certainly made no eye contact with them. If I had I might have noticed that one of them (yes, James, of course), was very handsome, in a black-haired, green-eyed, five-foot-tenish kind of way. I should have looked beyond the suit and seen the soul of the man.

Oh shallowness, thy name is Claire.

But I wanted to be out the back with the other waitresses, drinking beer and smoking and talking about sex. Customers were an unwelcome interference.

"Can I have my steak very rare?" asked one of the men.

"Um," I said vaguely. I was even more uninterested than usual because I had noticed a book on the table. It was a really good book, one that I had read myself.

I loved books. And I loved reading. And I loved men who read. I loved a man who knew his existentialism from his magic-realism. And I had spent the last six months working with people who could just about manage to read *Stage* magazine (laboriously mouthing the words silently as they did so). I suddenly realised, with a pang, how much I missed the odd bit of intelligent conversation.

Because I could raise the stakes in any conversation on the modern American novel. I'll see your Hunter S Thompson and I'll raise you a Jay McInerney.

Suddenly the people at this table stopped being mere irritants and took on some sort of identity for me.

"Who owns this book?" I asked abruptly,

interrupting the order-placing. (I don't *care* how you want your steak done.)

The table of four men started. I had spoken to them! I had treated them almost as if they were human!

"I do," said James and, as my blue eyes met his green eyes across his Mango Daiquiri (even though he had, in fact, ordered a pint of lager), that was it, the silvery magic dust was sprinkled on us. In that instant something wonderful happened. From the moment we really looked at each other, even though we knew almost nothing about each other (except that we liked the same books) (oh yes – and that we liked the look of each other), we both knew we had met someone special.

I maintained that we fell in love immediately.

He maintained nothing of the sort and said that I was a romantic fool.

He said it took him at least thirty seconds longer for him to fall in love with me.

Historians will argue.

First of all he had to establish that I had read the book in question also. Because he thought that I must be some kind of thick model or singer if I was working there as a waitress. You know, in the same way that I had written him off as some kind of sub-human clerk. Served me right.

"Have you read it?" he asked, obviously surprised, the tone of his voice actually implying "can you read at *all?*"

"Yes, I've read all his books," I told him.

"Is that right?" he said thoughtfully, as he leant

11

back in his chair, looking up at me with interest. A lock of his black silky hair had fallen across his forehead.

"Yes," I managed to reply, feeling slightly nauseous with lust.

"The car chases are good, aren't they?" he said.

Now, I should tell you here that there were no car chases in any of the books we were talking about. They were serious profound books about life and death and similar matters.

"Jesus!" I thought in alarm, "handsome, intelligent *and* funny. Am I able for this?"

And then James smiled at me, a slow, sexy smile, a knowing kind of smile, totally at odds with the pin-striped suit he was wearing, and I swear to you, my entrails turned to warm ice cream. You know, kind of hot and cold and tingly and . . . well . . . like they were dissolving, or something.

And for years afterwards, long after the initial magic had worn off and most of our conversations were about insurance policies and Lenor and dry rot, all I had to do was remember that smile and I felt as if I had just fallen in love all over again.

We exchanged some more words.

Just a few.

But they were enough to let me know that he was nice and clever and funny.

He asked for my phone number.

It was a sackable offence to give a customer my phone number.

I gave him my phone number.

When he left the restaurant that first night, with

12

his three cronies, a blur of briefcases and umbrellas and rolled-up copies of the *Financial Times* and sombre-looking suits, he smiled goodbye at me, and (well, I say this with the benefit of hindsight. It's very easy to foretell the future when it's already happened, if you know what I mean) I knew I was looking at my destiny.

My future.

A few minutes later he was back.

"Sorry," he grinned, "what's your name?"

As soon as the other waitresses found out that a suit had asked for my phone number and, worse again, that I had actually given it to him, I was treated like a pariah. It was a long time before I was invited round again to their squat to snort cocaine, I can tell you.

But I didn't care. Because I had really fallen for James.

For all my talk of independence, I was actually a very romantic person at heart. And for all my talk of rebellion, I was as middle-class as you could get.

From the first time we went out together, it was wonderful. So romantic, so beautiful.

And I'm sorry to do this to you but I'm going to have to use a lot of clichés here. I can see no other way round it.

I'm ashamed to tell you that I was walking on air. And I'm even sorrier to have to tell you that I felt like I'd known him all my life. And I'm going to compound things by telling you that I felt that no one understood me the way that he did. And as I've lost all credibility with you I might as well tell you that I didn't think it was possible to be this happy. But I won't push it by telling you that he made me feel safe, sexy, smart and sweet. (And sorry about this, but I really must tell you that I felt that I had met my missing other half and now I was whole, and I promise that I'll leave it at that). (Except perhaps to mention that he was a right laugh and great in bed. Now I mean it, that's *all*, positively *all*.)

When we first started going out together I was waitressing most nights so I could only see him when I finished work. But he would wait up for me. And when I came round, exhausted, after hours of dishing up char-grilled whatever to the people of London (or the people of Pennsylvania or Hamburg, if I'm to be more accurate) he would – and I can't believe it to this day – he would bathe my aching feet and massage them with Body Shop peppermint foot lotion. Even though it was past twelve and he had to be at work helping people to fiddle their tax returns, or whatever it is that accountants do, at eight the following morning, he still did it. Five nights a week. And he would bring me up to date on the soaps. Or go to the twenty-four hour garage for me when I ran out of cigarettes. Or he would tell me funny little stories about his day at work. I know that it's hard to believe that any story about accountancy could be funny, but he managed it.

And it meant that we could never go out on Saturday nights. And he didn't complain.

Weird, huh?

Yes, I thought so too.

And he would help me to count my tips. And give

me great advice about what to invest them in. Government bonds and that kind of thing.

I usually bought shoes.

Shortly after this I had the good fortune to be sacked from the waitressing job (a silly misunderstanding involving me, several bottles of imported lager, a "dinner-in-lap" scenario and a totally unreasonable customer who had absolutely no sense of humour. Anyway, I believe his scars faded almost completely.)

And managed to secure another position with more regular hours. So our romance proceeded on a more traditional timetable.

And after a while we moved in together. And after a bit longer we got married. And a couple of years later we decided to have a baby and my ovaries seemed to be game and his spermatozoa registered no complaint on that score and my womb had no objection so I got pregnant. And I gave birth to a baby girl.

Which is where you came in.

So I think we're pretty much up to date here.

And if you were hoping for, or expecting some kind of awful gory depiction of childbirth, with talk of stirrups and forceps and moans of agony and vulgar comparisons with excreting a four stone sack of potatoes, then I'm sorry to disappoint you.

(Well all right then, just to humour you, take your worst period pain ever and multiply it by seven million and make it last for about twenty-four hours and then you have some idea what labour pains are like.)

Yes, it was scary and messy and humiliating and

quite alarmingly painful. It was also exciting and thrilling and wonderful. But the most important thing for me was that it was over. I could kind of remember the pain, but it no longer had the power to hurt me. But when James left me I realised I'd rather go through the pain of a hundred labours than go through the pain of losing him that I felt then.

This is how he broke the news of his imminent departure to me.

After I held my baby in my arms for the first time, the nurses took her away to the baby ward and I was brought back to my ward and went to sleep for a while.

I woke up to find James standing over me, staring down at me, his eyes very green in his white face. I smiled up at him sleepily and triumphantly. "Hello darling," I grinned.

"Hello Claire," he said formally and politely.

Fool that I was, I thought he was being grave and serious as some kind of mark of respect. (Behold my wife, she was delivered today of a child, she is woman, she is lifegiver – you know, that kind of thing.)

He sat down. He sat on the edge of the hard hospital chair, looking as if he was going to get up and run away any second. Which indeed he was

"Have you been to the baby ward to see her?" I asked him dreamily, "She's so beautiful."

"No, I haven't," he said shortly. "Look, Claire, I'm leaving," he said abruptly.

"Why?" I asked snuggling back into my pillows,

16

"you've only just got here." (Yes, I know, I can't believe I said that either, who *writes* my lines?)

"Claire, listen to me," he said, getting a bit agitated. "I'm leaving you."

"What?" I said slowly and carefully. I must admit he had my attention now.

"Look Claire, I'm really sorry, but I've met someone else and I'm going to be with her and I'm sorry about the baby and everything and to leave you like this, but I must," he blurted out, as white as a ghost, his eyes bright with anguish.

"What do you mean by you've 'met' someone else?" I asked bewildered.

"I mean that . . . well . . . I've fallen in love with someone else," he said looking wretched.

"What do you mean, another woman, or something?" I asked feeling as if I'd been given a blow to the base of my skull with a cricket bat.

"Yes," he said, no doubt relieved that I seemed to have grasped the basics of the situation.

"And you're *leaving* me?" I echoed him disbelievingly.

"Yes," he said, looking at his shoes, at the ceiling, at my bottle of Lucozade, at anything other than my eyes.

"But don't you love me anymore?" I found myself asking.

"I don't know. I don't think so," he replied.

"But what about the baby?" I asked, stunned. He couldn't possibly leave me but he especially couldn't leave me now that we had had a baby together. "You've got to take care of the two of us."

17

"I'm sorry, but I can't," he said. "I'll make sure that you're taken care of financially and we'll sort something out about the flat and the mortgage and all that, but I have to go."

I couldn't believe we were having this conversation. What the hell was he talking about, flats and money and mortgages and crap? According to the script we should be cooing over our baby and gently arguing about which side of the family she got her looks from. But James, *my* James, was talking about leaving me. Who's in charge around here? I'd like to complain about my life. I distinctly ordered a happy life with a loving husband to go with my new-born baby and what was this shoddy travesty that I'd been served up instead?

"Jesus, Claire," he said, "I hate to leave you like this. But if I come home with you and the baby now I won't ever be able to leave."

But wasn't that the whole idea, I thought bewildered.

"I know that there's no good time to tell you something like this. I couldn't tell you when you were pregnant, in case you lost the baby. So I have to tell you now."

"James," I said faintly, "this is all very weird."

"Yes, I know," he agreed hurriedly. "You've been through a lot in the last twenty-four hours."

"Why were you at the birth, if you planned to leave me the minute it was over?" I asked him, holding his arm, trying to get him to look at me.

"Because I promised," he said, shaking my hand off his arm and not meeting my eyes, looking like a chastised schoolboy.

"Because you promised?" I said, trying to make sense of this. "But you've promised me loads of things. Like to cherish me and to love me till death do us part."

"Well, I'm sorry," he mumbled. "But I can't keep those promises."

"So what's going to happen?" I asked numbly. I didn't for a second accept a single word of what he was saying. But the band keeps playing even though no one is dancing. I was having what to all intents and purposes might appear to the impartial outside observer to be a conversation, with James. But it wasn't a conversation at all because I didn't mean anything that I said and I didn't accept anything that he said. When I asked him what was going to happen, I didn't need an answer. I *knew* what was going to happen. He was coming home with me and the baby and there would be no more of this nonsense.

I think I almost felt that if I kept him talking and with me he would realise how silly he was being to even think of leaving me.

He stood up. He stood too far away from me for me to be able to touch him. He was wearing a black suit (we had often joked in the past about him wearing it to oversee receiverships and liquidations) and he looked grim and pale. And in a way he had never looked more beautiful to me.

"I see you're wearing your undertaker suit," I said bitterly. "Nice touch."

He didn't even attempt a smile and I knew then that I had lost him. He looked like James, he

19

sounded like James, he smelt like James, but it wasn't James.

Like some fifties science-fiction film, where the hero's girl-friend's body is taken over by an alien – it still looks like her on the outside (pink angora sweater, sweet little handbag, bra so pointy it would take the eye out of a spider, etc.) – but her eyes have changed.

The casual observer might still think it was James. But I knew from looking at his eyes, my James had left. Some cold unloving stranger was in his body. I didn't know where *my* James had gone.

Maybe he was in the alien spaceship with Peggy-Jo.

"I've moved most of my things," he said. "I'll be in touch. Take care of yourself."

He turned on his heel and quickly left the ward. In fact, he almost broke into a run. I wanted to run after him but the bastard knew that I was bed-bound courtesy of several stitches in my vagina.

He was gone.

I lay in my hospital bed, very still for a long time. I was stunned, I was shocked, I was horrified, I was disbelieving. But in a very odd kind of way, there was something I did believe about it. There was something almost familiar about this feeling.

I know it couldn't be a feeling of familiarity, because I had never been deserted by a husband before. But there was definitely something there. I think there's a part of everyone's brain, certainly mine, that keeps look-out on some rocky outcrop high in the hills, waiting for signs of danger. And it signals back to the rest of the brain when trouble is afoot. The emotional version of "the injuns is coming". The more I thought about it, the more I realised this part of my brain had probably been flashing mirrors and sending up smoke signals like crazy over the past months. But the rest of my brain was with the wagon camp down in the pleasant verdant valley of pregnancy and didn't want to know about impending danger. So it completely ignored the messages it was sent.

I'd known that James was miserable for most of the time that I was pregnant, but I had put that down to my mood-swings, my constant hunger, my raging sentimentality, where I cried at everything from *Little House On the Prairie* to *The Money Programme*.

And of course our sex life was drastically curtailed. But I had thought as soon as I had had the baby that every thing would be back to normal. Except better, if you see what I mean.

I thought that James's misery was just as a result of my being pregnant and its attendant side-effects but, looking back, maybe I had ignored things that I shouldn't have.

So what was I to do? I didn't even know where he was staying. But some instinct told me to leave him alone for a while. Humour him. Pretend to go along with it.

I could hardly believe it.

Leaving me, indeed! My normal reaction to feeling hurt or betrayed was to go on the warpath, but somehow I knew that it wouldn't do me any good at all in this situation. I had to stay calm and sane until I could decide what to do.

One of the nurses squeaked past me in her rubber-soled shoes. She stopped and smiled at me. "How are you now?" she asked.

"Oh fine," I said willing her to go away.

"I suppose your husband will be in to see you and the baby later," she said.

"I wouldn't bet on it," I replied bitterly.

She gave me a startled look and moved away quickly, over to one of the nice, civil, polite mothers, clicking her pen and throwing me nervous glances.

I decided to ring Judy.

Judy was my best friend. We'd been friends since we were eighteen. We had come over to London together. She had been my bridesmaid.

I couldn't cope with this on my own. Judy would tell me what to do.

I cautiously and gingerly levered myself out of bed and, as quickly as my episiotomy would permit, I made my way to the pay-phone.

She answered the phone immediately.

"Oh hi Claire," she said. "I was just on my way over to see you."

"Good," was all I said.

God knows, I *wanted* to bawl crying and tell her about James allegedly leaving me, but there was a queue of women in pink towelling dressing-gowns behind me waiting to use the phone (no doubt to ring their devoted husbands) and, against all the odds, I had *some* pride left.

"Smug bitches," I thought sourly (and irrationally, I must admit) as I limped back to bed.

As soon as Judy came I knew that she knew about James. I knew because she said, "Claire, I know about James". Also because she didn't arrive with a huge bunch of flowers, a bigger smile and a card the size of a kitchen table with storks all over it. She looked anxious and nervous.

My heart sank to my boots. If James was telling other people, then it *must* be true.

"He's left me," I said dramatically.

"I know," she said.

"How could he?" I asked her.

"I don't know," she said.

"He's fallen in love with someone else," I said.

"I know," she said.

"How do you know?" I asked her, pouncing on her for the information.

"Michael told me. Aisling told him. George told her."

(Michael was Judy's boyfriend. Aisling worked with him. George was Aisling's husband. George worked with James).

"So everyone knows," I said quietly.

There was a pause. Judy looked as if she would like to die.

"Then it must be true," I said.

"I think it is," she said, obviously embarrassed.

"Do you know who this other woman is?" I asked her, feeling lousy about putting her in such an awkward position, but I had to know, and I was too shocked to ask James before he left.

"Er, yes," she said, even more embarrassed. "It's that Denise."

23

It took me a minute to realise who she was talking about.

"WHAT!" I shrieked. "Not nice Denise from downstairs?"

A miserable nod from Judy.

It was just as well that I was already lying down.

"That *bitch*!" I exclaimed.

"And there's more," she mumbled. "He's talking about marrying her."

"What the hell do you mean?" I shouted. "He's *already* married. To me. I hadn't heard that they had made polygamy legal in the last day or so."

"They haven't," she said.

"But then . . . " I trailed off bewildered.

"Claire," she sighed despondently. "He says he's going to divorce you."

As I said, it was just as well I was already lying down.

The afternoon ebbed away, along with Judy's patience and any hope that I might still harbour.

I looked at her in despair.

"Judy, what am I going to do?"

"Look," she said matter-of-factly, "in two days you'll be getting out of here. You still have somewhere to live, you have enough money to feed yourself and the baby, you'll be going back to work in six months, you've got a new-born child to look after and give James some time and eventually the two of you will sort something out."

"But Judy," I wailed. "He wants a *divorce*."

Although James seemed to have forgotten one big fact. There is no divorce in Ireland. James and I were married in Ireland. Our marriage was blessed by the Fathers of the Church of Our Lady of Perpetual Succour. Although a fat lot of good it had obviously done us. So long, Succour.

I was at a total loss. I felt alone and afraid. I wanted to pull the blankets over my head and die. But I couldn't because I had a poor defenceless child to look after.

What a start in life she was getting. Less than two days old and already she'd been deserted by her father and her mother was on the verge of cracking up.

For the millionth time I wondered how James could do this to me.

"How could James do this to me?" I asked Judy.

"You've asked me that about a million times," she said.

So I had.

I didn't know how James could do this to me. I just knew that he had.

Up to now I suppose that I'd thought that life doled out the unpleasant things to me in evenly-spaced bite-sized pieces. That it never gave me more than I could cope with at one time.

When I used to hear about people who had cumulative disasters, like having a car-crash, losing a job and catching their boyfriend in bed with their sister all in the one week, I used to kind of think it was their fault. Well, not exactly their *fault*. But if people behaved like victims that they would become victims, if people expected the worst to happen then it invariably did.

I could see now how wrong I was. Sometimes

25

people don't volunteer to be victims and they become victims anyway. It's not their fault. It certainly wasn't my fault that my husband thought that he'd fallen in love with someone else. I didn't expect it to happen and I certainly didn't *want* it to happen. But it had happened.

I knew then that life was no respecter of circumstance. The force that flings disasters at us doesn't say "Well, I won't give her that lump in her breast for another year. Best to let her recover from the death of her mother first". It just goes right on ahead and does whatever it feels like, whenever it feels like it.

I realised no one is immune from the cumulative disaster syndrome. Not that I thought that having a baby was a disaster. But it could certainly come under the heading of upheaval.

I'd thought I was so in control of my life and if, God forbid, anything ever did go wrong with myself and James that I would be able to devote my full time and energy to fixing it. I didn't quite expect to be dumped within twenty-four hours of giving birth to my first child, when my energy levels were at an all-time low and my vulnerability levels at an all-time high.

Not to mention being as fat as the fool that I so obviously was.

Fat arse never won fair James.

Judy and I sat on the bed in silence, both trying to think of something constructive to say. Suddenly I had the answer. Well, maybe not *the* answer, but *an* answer. Something to be getting on with for the time being.

"I know what I'll do," I said to Judy.

"Oh thank God," I could feel her thinking fervently. *"Thank God."*

And like Scarlett O'Hara in the last few lines of *Gone With The Wind*, I said plaintively, "I'll go home. I'll go home to Dublin."

Yes, I agree with you. "Dublin" doesn't have quite the same ring to it as "Tara", but what would be the point in me going home to Tara. I knew no one there. In fact I had only ever passed through it about twice on my way to Drogheda.

Chapter Two

Judy collected me from the hospital a couple of days later. She had booked me and my baby on a one-way flight to Dublin. She took me home to pack some things.

I had heard nothing from James in the meantime. I was stumbling around in a grief-sodden daze.

Sometimes I simply couldn't believe it. Everything he'd said to me seemed like a dream. I couldn't really remember the details, but I could remember the feeling. That sick feeling that something was very wrong.

But sometimes the loss would make a guest appearance.

It would invade me. It would take me over. It was like a physical force. It knocked the life out of me. It took my breath away. It was savage.

It hated me.

It had to, to hurt me so much.

I can't really remember how I spent those couple of days in hospital.

I can vaguely remember being bewildered when all the other new mothers talked about how their lives had now altered forever, how it would never be just oneself ever again, the problems of having to adjust their lives to fit in with their new baby and all that.

But I couldn't see what the problem was. Already I couldn't imagine life without my baby. "It's you and me, sweetheart," I whispered to her.

The fact that we had both been abandoned by the man in our lives probably sped up the bonding process. Nothing like a crisis to bring people together, as they say.

I spent a lot of time sitting very still, holding her.

Touching her tiny, *tiny* little doll's feet, her perfect pink miniature toes, her tightly curled up little fists, her velvety ears, gently stroking the delicate skin of her incredibly small little face, wondering what colour her eyes were going to be.

She was so beautiful, so perfect, such a miracle.

I had been told to expect to feel overwhelming love for my child, God knows, no one could say that I hadn't been warned. But nothing could have prepared me for this intensity. This feeling that I would kill anyone who so much as touched one of the blonde wispy hairs on her soft little head.

I could understand James leaving me – well actually, I couldn't – but I *really* couldn't understand how he could leave this beautiful, perfect little child.

She cried a lot.

But I can't really complain because so did I.

I tried and tried to comfort her, but she rarely stopped.

After she cried for about eight hours solid on the first day and I had changed her nappy a hundred and twenty times and fed her forty nine thousand times I became slightly hysterical and demanded that a doctor look at her.

"There *must* be something terrible wrong with her," I declared to the exhausted looking youth who was the doctor. "She can't *possibly* be hungry and she's not" (I sniggered slightly as I said this) "'soiled', but she won't stop crying."

"Well, I've examined her and there's absolutely nothing wrong with her, so far as I can see," he patiently explained to me.

"But why is she crying?"

"Because she's a baby," he said. "It's what they do."

He'd studied medicine for seven years and that was the best he could come up with?

I wasn't convinced.

Maybe she was crying because she somehow sensed that her Dad had abandoned her.

Or maybe – major pang of guilt – she was crying because I wasn't breast-feeding her. Maybe she deeply resented being fed from a bottle. Yes, I know, you're probably outraged that I didn't breast-feed her. You probably think that I wasn't a proper mother. But, long ago, *before* I had my baby, I had thought it would be permissible to have my body returned to me after I had lent it out for nine months. I knew that I wouldn't be able to call my soul my own now that I was a mother. But I had kind of hoped that I might be able to call my nipples my own. And, I'm ashamed to say that I was afraid that, if I breast-fed, I would be a victim of "shrunken, flat, droopy tit" syndrome.

Now that I was with my gorgeous, perfect child

my breast-feeding worries seemed petty and selfish. Everything really *does* change when you give birth. I never thought I'd see the day when I'd put anyone else's needs before the attractiveness of my tits.

So if my little sweetheart didn't stop crying soon, I was going to consider breast-feeding her. If it made her happy, I'd put up with cracked nipples, leaky tits and sniggering thirteen-year-old boys trying to get a look at my jugs on the bus.

Judy, baby and I arrived home. I let us into our flat and, even though James had told me he was moving out, I still wasn't prepared for the bare spaces in the bathroom, the empty wardrobe, the gaps in the bookshelf.

It was so awful.

I sat down slowly on our bed. The pillow still smelt of him. And I missed him so much.

"I can't believe it," I sobbed to Judy. "He's really gone."

My baby started to cry also as if she felt the emptiness too.

And it was only about five minutes since she'd last stopped.

Poor Judy looked helpless. She didn't know which one of us to comfort.

After a while I stopped crying and slowly turned my tear-streaked face to Judy. I felt exhausted with grief.

"Come on," I said. "I'd better pack."

"Fine," she whispered, still rocking me and the baby in her arms.

31

I started throwing things into a holdall. I packed everything I thought I would need. I was all set to bring a pile of disposable nappies the size of a small south American country, but Judy made me leave them behind. "They *do* sell them in Dublin too," she gently reminded me. I flung in baby bottles, a bottle warmer with a picture of a cow jumping over the moon on the side of it, soothers, toys, rattles, babygros, little socks the size of postage stamps, everything I could possibly think of for my poor fatherless child.

As I was now a single parent family I was obviously overcompensating. "I'm sorry, darling, I've deprived you of your father because I wasn't clever or beautiful enough to hold onto him, but let me make it up to you by showering you with material goods."

Then I asked Judy to give me back a couple of nappies.

"What for?" she demanded, holding them tightly to her.

"In case we have an accident on the plane," I said, trying to grab them from her.

"Didn't they give you any sanitary towels in the hospital?" she asked, sounding shocked.

"Not if *I* have an accident, stupid. If the *baby* has one. Although strictly speaking, it wouldn't really be an accident, would it?" I said thoughtfully. "More like an occupational hazard."

She doled out three nappies. But reluctantly.

"You know, you can't keep calling her 'the baby'," said Judy. "You're going to have to give her a name."

"I can't think about that just at the moment," I said, starting to feel panicky.

"But what have you been doing for the past nine months?" Judy sounded shocked. "You must have thought of *some* names."

"I did," I said, my lip starting to tremble. "But I thought of them with James. And it wouldn't feel right to call her one of those names."

Judy looked a bit annoyed with me. But I was on the verge of tears again, so she didn't say anything further.

I hardly brought anything for myself apart from a handful of baby books. Why would I bother, I thought, now that my life is over.

And besides nothing fitted me any longer.

I opened my wardrobe and recoiled from the disgusted looks all my little dresses gave me. There was no doubt about it. They were all talking about me.

I could almost see them elbowing each other and saying "Look at her, the size of her. Does she honestly think that dainty little size tens like us would have any truck with that size fourteen body she's dragging around? Small wonder that her husband ran off with another woman."

I knew what they were thinking.

"You've let yourself go. And you always said that you wouldn't. You've let us down and you've let yourself down."

"I'm sorry," I explained cringingly. "I'll lose weight. I'll be back for you, I promise. Just as soon as I'm able."

Their scepticism was palpable.

I had a choice of wearing my maternity clothes or a pair of jeans that James had left behind in his haste to get going. I put on the jeans and caught sight of my revolting overweight body in the bedroom mirror. God, I was horrific! I looked as if I was wearing my big sister's Michelin Man suit. Or worse again, I looked like I was still pregnant.

In the few weeks before I gave birth I was absolutely enormous.

Completely circular. The fact that the only thing that fitted me was my green wool smock, coupled with the fact that due to continuous nausea my face was always green, gave me the appearance of a watermelon who had put on a pair of boots and a bit of lipstick.

Now, although I was no longer green, I still looked like a watermelon in every other respect. Like a watermelon that could have done with a course of iron tablets.

What was happening to me? Where had the real me and my real life *gone?*

With a heart that wasn't the only heavy thing about me, I went to ring the taxi to take us to the airport.

The buzzer rang. I took one last look around my living room, at the gap-toothed shelves, the shiny new unused baby intercom up on the wall (the *waste!*), the hillock of abandoned nappies on the floor.

I closed the door behind me before I could start crying again.

Firmly.

Yes, I know. Fairly unsubtle symbolism. Sorry about that.

Then I realised that I was missing something. "Oh Jesus," I said, "my rings." I ran back in and got my engagement and wedding rings from my bedroom. They had been on the dressing-table for the past two months because my fingers were so fat and swollen that I couldn't wear them. I jammed them onto my hand and they just about fitted me.

I caught Judy giving me a funny look.

"He's still my husband, you know," I said defiantly to her. "Which means that I'm still married!"

"I didn't say anything," she said affecting an innocent expression.

Judy and I struggled down in the lift, juggling bags, holdalls, handbags and a two-day-old child in her carry-cot.

And that's another thing they don't tell you about having a baby! The manuals should say something like "It is imperative that your husband does not leave you in the first few months of your child's birth, as otherwise you will have to carry everything yourself".

Judy was hoisting everything into the taxi when I saw, with horror, Denise's husband coming up the road. He must have been on his way home from work.

"Oh Christ," I said, ominously.

"What?" asked Judy in alarm, her face red and sweaty from her exertions.

"Denise's husband," I muttered.

"So what?" she said loudly.

I was expecting some kind of terrible emotional scene from him. As I said, he was Italian. Or I was afraid that he would suggest some kind of alliance between me and him. Something along the lines of "my enemy's enemy is my friend." I *certainly* didn't want that.

My eyes locked with his and I felt, in my guilty and fearful state, that I knew exactly what he was thinking. "It's all your fault. If only you had been as attractive as my Denise, your husband might have stayed with you and I would still be happily married. But no, you had to go and ruin everything, you fat ugly cow."

"Fine," I thought, "two can play at that game."

I stared back at him, returning his thought messages. "Well if you hadn't married a husband-stealing, home-wrecking floozy, if you had married a nice decent girl, none of us would be in this mess."

I was probably doing the poor man a terrible injustice. He didn't say anything to me. He just looked at me in a kind of sad and accusatory way.

I hugged Judy goodbye. We were both crying. For once my baby wasn't.

"Heathrow, Terminal One," I said tearfully to the taxi driver and we swept away from the kerb, leaving Mr Andrucetti staring bleakly after us.

As I struggled down the aisle on the Aer Lingus plane, I bumped against several irate passengers with my bag of baby supplies. When I finally located my seat a man got up to help me stow my bags. As I smiled my thanks at him, I automatically wondered if he fancied me.

It was so awful. That was one of the things I really liked about being married. For a couple of years I was off that horrible merry-go-round of trying to meet the right man, finding out that he was already married, or living with another man, or pathologically stingy, or read Jeffrey Archer, or could only have an orgasm if he could call you "mother", or any one of the thousands of character flaws that weren't immediately obvious the first time you shook his hand and smiled into his eyes and got a warm buzzy feeling in the pit of your stomach, that had absolutely nothing to do with any non-prescribed drugs that you might or might not have taken earlier in the evening, and thought to yourself, "hey, this could be the one."

Now I was back in the situation where every man is a potential boyfriend. I was back to a world where there are eight hundred exquisitely beautiful women to every one straight single man. And that was even before we start weeding out the truly hideous ones.

I looked at the helpful man properly. He wasn't even that attractive. He was probably gay. Or, more likely, this being an Aer Lingus flight, he was probably a priest.

And as for me, a deserted wife, with a two-day-old baby, the self-esteem of an amoeba (that much?), two stone overweight, the arrival of post-partum depression imminent, and a vagina ten times its normal size, I was hardly a prize catch myself.

The plane took off and the houses and buildings

and streets of London circled away below me. I looked down as the roads and streets of London got smaller and smaller. I was leaving behind six years of my life.

Is this how a refugee feels? I wondered.

My husband was down there somewhere. My flat was down there somewhere. My friends were down there somewhere. My life was down there somewhere.

I had been happy there.

And then the view was obscured by cloud.

More of that unsubtle symbolism. Sorry again.

I sat back in my seat, my baby on my lap. I suppose I must have looked just like a normal mother to all the other passengers. But, and the thought struck me quite forcibly, I wasn't. I was now a Deserted Wife. I was a statistic.

I had been lots of things in my life. I had been Claire the dutiful daughter. I had been Claire the scourge of a daughter. I had been Claire the student. I had been Claire the harlot (briefly. As I said, if we get the time, I'll fill you in). I had been Claire the administrator. I had been Claire the wife. And now here I was being Claire the deserted wife. And the idea did not sit comfortably with me at all, I can tell you.

I had always thought (in spite of my professed liberalism) that deserted wives were women who lived in corporation flats, that their husbands, pausing only to blacken their eye, left with a bottle of vodka, the Christmas Club money and the children's allowance book, leaving them behind weeping, with a huge mound of unpaid utilities bills, a spurious story about walking into a door and four dysfunctional children, all under the age of six, joyriders to a man.

It was a humbling and enlightening experience to find out how wrong I had been. *I* was a deserted wife. Me, middle-class Claire.

Well, it would have been a humbling and enlightening experience if I hadn't been feeling so bitter and angry and betrayed. What was I? Some kind of Tibetan monk? Mother bloody Teresa?

But I did realise, in some funny way, through the self-pity and the self-righteousness, that some day, when all this was over, I might be a nicer person as a result of it, that I would be stronger and wiser and more compassionate.

But maybe not just yet.

"Your father is a bastard," I whispered to my child.

The helpful gay priest started.

He must have heard me.

Within an hour we began the descent to Dublin Airport. We circled the green fields of north Dublin and, even though I knew that she couldn't really see anything yet, I held my baby up to the window to give her her first view of Ireland. It looked so different from the view of London we had just left behind. As I looked at the blue of the Irish sea and the grey mist over the green fields, I had never felt worse. I felt like such a failure.

I had left Ireland six years ago, full of excitement about the future. I was going to get a great job in

London, meet a wonderful man and live happily ever after. And I *had* got a great job, I *had* met a wonderful man and I *had* lived happily ever after – well at least for a while – but somehow it had all gone wrong and here I was back in Dublin, with a humiliating sense of déjà vu.

But one major thing had changed.

Now I had a child. A perfect, beautiful, wonderful child. I wouldn't have changed that for anything.

The helpful gay priest beside me looked very embarrassed as I cried helplessly. "Tough," I thought. "Be embarrassed. You're a man. You've probably made countless women cry like this too."

I'd had more rational days.

He made a fairly lively exit once we landed. In fact he couldn't get off the plane fast enough. No offers to help me unstow my bag. I couldn't blame him.

Chapter Three

And so to the baggage reclaim department!

I always find it such an ordeal.

Do you know what I mean?

The anxiety starts the minute I get to the arrivals hall and stand at the carousel when I suddenly become convinced that all the nice, mild-mannered people that I shared a plane journey with have turned into nasty luggage thieves. That every single one of them is watching the carousel with the express purpose of stealing my bags.

I stand there with a narrowed suspicious face. One eye on the hatch where the bags come out and the other eye darting from person to person, trying to convey to them that I'm wise to their trickery. That they've picked the wrong person to mess with.

I suppose it would help matters slightly if I was one of these well-organised people who somehow manage to stand near the start of the carousel. But instead I'm always down at the far end, squinting and standing on tip-toe, trying to see what's coming out of the hatch and when I finally see my bag emerging I'm so afraid that someone will steal it that I can't stand patiently and wait for the carousel to deliver it to me in due course. Instead I run the length of the

41

arrivals hall to catch it before someone else does. Except that I usually find it impossible to breach the tightly-knit cordon of other people's trolleys. So my bag sails serenely past me and circumnavigates the arrivals hall several times before I'm able to grab it.

It's a nightmare!

This time, to my surprise, I managed to secure myself a place quite near the hatch.

Maybe people were being nicer to me because I'd got a baby about my person.

I knew she'd come in useful.

So I waited at the carousel, trying to be patient, jostling with all the other people who had just got off the flight, buckling at the knees every so often as a fellow passenger delivered a killer blow to the back of my ankles with his trolley.

I made eye-contact with as many people as possible, hoping to convince them not to steal my bags. Isn't that the kind of advice criminologists give you? You know the stuff I'm talking about. That if you've been taken hostage you must befriend your captor. Make eye-contact with him, so that he realises that you're a human being and so is less likely to kill you.

Anyway. I'm sure you know what I mean.

Nothing happened for ages.

All eyes were trained on the little hatch for the first glimpse of our suitcases.

Nobody spoke. Nobody even dared to breathe. Then suddenly! The noise of a carousel starting up!

Great!

Except it wasn't our one.

An announcement over the tannoy. "Will passengers recently arrived from London on flight EI179 proceed to carousel number four to reclaim their baggage."

This, in spite of the fact that the screen above carousel two had confidently assured us for the last twenty minutes that the baggage would shortly be making an appearance there.

So a mad scramble to carousel four. People shoving and pushing as though their lives depended on it. And this time no one seemed quite so bothered about the infant in my arms.

As a result I was at the very end of the new carousel.

And for a while I was all right.

Calm even.

I tried to look determinedly cheerful as one by one the people around me rescued their bags.

No one in their right mind would want to steal some bags full of baby clothes and bottles, I told myself.

And I'd got full confidence in the ground staff of Dublin Airport not to divert my bags to a flight going to Darwin.

Or Mars.

But when the only thing left on the carousel was a set of golf clubs that looked as if they had been there since the late seventies and they had passed me for the fourteenth time and my baby and I were the only human beings left in the arrivals hall and the tumbleweed had started blowing past me, it was finally time to read the writing on the wall.

"I knew they'd get me one day," I thought, feeling sick. "It was only a matter of time. I bet it was that old cow with the rosary beads. It's always the quiet ones."

I began to run up and down, my baby in my arms, frantically searching for an official. Eventually I found a little office with two fairly jovial looking porters within.

"Come in, come in!" one of them invited me as I hovered uncertainly by the door. "What can we do for you on this fine wet Irish afternoon?"

I launched into my story of my stolen bags and carry-cot. I was nearly in tears again. I felt so *victimised*.

"Don't worry, missus," I was assured. "They're not stolen. They're only lost. I'll find them for you. I've got a hotline to St Anthony."

And sure enough, about five minutes later he returned with all my luggage. "Are these yours, love?" he asked.

I assured him that they were.

"And you're not going to Boston?"

"I'm not going to Boston," I agreed as evenly as I could manage.

"Are you sure?" he asked doubtfully.

"Quite sure," I promised.

"Well someone seemed to think that you were, but never mind. Off you go now," he laughed.

I thanked them and hurried towards the "Nothing to Declare" channel.

I rushed through with my trolley and my baby and my retrieved luggage. My heart sank as one of the customs men stopped me.

"Easy, easy," he said. "Where's the fire? Have you anything to declare?"

"No, I haven't."

"What's that you've got there?"

"It's a baby."

"*Your* baby?"

"Yes, my baby."

My heart had nearly stopped beating. I hadn't told James that I was leaving. But had he guessed that I would come here? Had he told the police that I had kidnapped our child? Were all the ports and airports being watched? Would they take my baby away from me? Would I be deported?

I was terrified.

"So," the customs man continued, "you have nothing to declare but your genes." He guffawed heartily.

"Oh yes, very good," I said limply.

"A great wit, our Mr Wilde," said the customs man conversationally. "A venerable gentleman."

"Oh absolutely," I agreed.

"You gave me a terrible fright," I smiled at him.

He assumed a sheriff type stance and drawl.

"That's OK, ma'am," he winked. "Jest doin' mah job."

It was nice to be home.

Chapter Four

I rushed out into the arrivals lounge. On the other side of the barrier I could see my mother and father waiting for me. They looked smaller and older than they'd looked the last time I saw them, six months ago. I felt so guilty. They were both in their late fifties and had worried about me from the day I was born. Well, from before the day I was born, if I'm to be quite accurate, because I was three weeks overdue and they thought they'd have to send a welcome committee in to get me.

I've heard of people being late for their own funeral but I have the unusual distinction of being late for my own birth.

And they worried about me when I was six weeks old and had colic.

And when I was two years old and wouldn't eat anything but tinned peaches for an entire year. They worried about me when I was seven and doing really badly at school. And they worried about me when I was eight and doing really well at school and had no friends. They worried about me when I was eleven and broke my ankle. They worried about me when I went to a school disco and had to be brought home blind drunk by one of the teachers, when I was fifteen. They worried about me when I was eighteen and in my first year in college and never went to any lectures. They worried about me when I was doing my finals and was never out of a lecture. They worried about me when I was twenty and split up with my first true love and lay in a darkened bedroom crying for two weeks. They worried about me when I gave up my job and went to London to work as a waitress when I was twenty-three.

And here I was nearly thirty, married with a baby of my own and they were still having to worry about me. I mean it wasn't very fair, was it? Just as they'd taken a big sigh of relief and thought, Thank God, she's managed to land herself a fairly respectable man, maybe we can let him worry about her from now on and get on with the business of worrying about her four younger sisters, I had the audacity to turn around and say, Sorry folks, false alarm, I'm back and this one is worse than any of the other things I've forced you to worry about.

No wonder they were looking a little bit grey and cowed.

"Oh thank God," said my mother when she saw me. "We thought you'd missed the flight."

"I'm sorry," I said and burst into tears again. And we all hugged each other and they both cried when they saw my baby, their first grandchild.

I really would have to give her a name soon.

We negotiated the maze that is the car park in Dublin Airport. Proceedings were delayed slightly when my father attempted to leave by the Pre-Paid exit, when he hadn't, and all the cars backed up behind him had to reverse to let him out. He lost his temper slightly and so did another driver, but let's not dwell on that.

When we got out on the road we drove for a while in silence. It was a very strange situation. My mother sat in the back with me and she held the baby and rocked her gently. I wished that I was still a baby and that my mother could hold me and make me feel so safe and that everything was going to be all right.

"So Unlucky Jim fecked off," my father said abruptly.

"Yes Dad," I said tearfully

My father had never really liked James. My father is the only man in a house full of women and he craves male company, someone to talk to about the football and that kind of thing. James didn't play enough rugby and knew far too much about cooking for his liking. It didn't matter that my father did all the housework in our house, cooking was a different matter, women's work, he called it. But the last thing he wanted was to see me unhappy.

"Now look, Claire," he said in a voice that I recognised as the "I'm about to make a speech concerning emotional issues, I'm not used to doing it and I'm very uncomfortable doing it, but it has to be done and I do actually mean it" voice. "We're your family and we love you and this is always your home. You and the baby can stay with us for as long as you like. And . . . er . . . both your mother and I know how unhappy you are and if we can help in any way just let us know. Ah . . . er . . . right," and accelerated, mightily relieved that he'd got that out of the way.

"Thanks Dad," I said, crying again. "I do know it."

I was immensely grateful. It was wonderful knowing that they loved me. It was just that it was no substitute for losing a man who was my soulmate, my best friend, my lover, my one reliable thing in an unreliable world.

We finally reached home. It looked just the same. Why shouldn't it? Life, against its better judgement, goes on. And it smelt just the same. It was so familiar, so comforting. We carried the bags and carry-cot up the stairs to the room that I shared with my sister Margaret all my life until I moved to London. (Margaret, twenty-six, sporty, outgoing, clean-living, living in Chicago, working as a para-legal, married to the only boyfriend she ever had). The room looked really funny, because no one had stayed in it for so long. Some of Margaret's shoes were on the floor, but covered in dust. Some of her old clothes were still hanging in the wardrobe. It was like some kind of shrine.

I flung a few of the bags on the floor, I set up the carry-cot and put the baby in it, I put the bottle-warmer with the picture of the cow jumping over the moon on the side on to the dressing-table, I sat on the bed and kicked off my shoes, I put my books on the shelves, I left my make-up bag spilling over on the bedside table. And in no time at all the place looked like a pigsty.

There, that was miles better.

"So, who's here?" I asked Mum.

"Well, just us and Dad at the moment," she said. "Helen is at college, she should be home later. God alone knows where Anna is. I haven't seen her for days."

Anna and Helen were my two youngest sisters. They were the only ones still living at home.

My mother sat with me while I fed the baby. After I had winded her and put her back to sleep, my mother and I sat quietly on the bed, saying nothing. The rain stopped and the sun came out. The smell of the wet garden came in through the open window, and the sound of the breeze blowing through the branches of the trees. It was a peaceful February evening.

"Will you eat something?" she finally asked.

I shook my head.

"But you must eat, especially now that you've got the baby to look after. You have to keep strong. Will I make you some soup?"

I winced involuntarily.

"From a packet?" I asked.

"From a packet," she gently agreed.

"No, really Mum, I'm fine."

Perhaps I'd better explain. The ability to cook skips a generation. I could cook. Ergo my daughter wouldn't be able to. God love her. What kind of start in life was she getting? And by the same token my mother couldn't cook. My mother and culinary delights were not the best of friends. In fact, it would be fair to say that my mother and culinary delights were barely on nodding terms.

Nightmarish memories of family dinners came

flooding back to me. Was I out of my mind? What the hell had I come home for? Did I really want to *starve* to death?

The next time you have to lose a lot of weight very quickly – that two week sun holiday? your sister's wedding? a date with the office hunk? don't bother joining Weightwatchers or try to subsist on Lean Cuisine, or fiddle around with powdered meals. Just come and stay in our house for a couple of weeks and insist that Mum cooks for you.

Seriously, there's plenty of space, you can have Rachel's room. You'll be skin and bone at the end of the two weeks. Because no matter how hungry you are you still won't be able to bring yourself to eat anything that my mother makes.

I'm amazed that none of us was ever hospitalised for malnutrition when we were younger.

My siblings and I would be summoned for our evening meal. We would all sit down and stare silently at the plate in front of us for a few perplexed moments. Finally one of us would speak.

"Any ideas?"

"Would it be chicken?" says Margaret doubtfully, poking it tentatively with her fork.

"Oh no, I thought it was cauliflower," says Rachel, the vegetarian, rushing off to gag.

"Well whatever it is, I'm not touching it," says Helen. "At least you know where you are with cornflakes," and leaves the table to get herself a bowl.

So by the time my mother sat down at the table and told us what it was ("it's colcannon, you ungrateful brats"), we would all have released ourselves from the dinner-table on our own recognisance and would be foraging around in the kitchen cupboards trying to find something vaguely edible.

"Margaret," my mother would call, knowing that Margaret was the most dutiful of all of us. "Wouldn't you even try it?"

And Margaret, being a good girl, would lift a sliver to her lips.

"Well?" my mother would ask, hardly daring to breathe.

"You wouldn't give it to the dog," Margaret would reply, honesty being another of her virtues, alongside obedience and bravery.

So after several years of tearful evening meals and ever-increasing breakfast cereal bills, my mother, to everyone's eternal relief, decided to stop cooking altogether.

So, if any of her daughters or her husband told her that they were hungry, she'd take them silently by the hand and into the kitchen. She'd say "behold the upright freezer full of frozen convenience foods", and flinging wide the freezer door, with several flourishes exhort them to survey the myriad delights within. Then she'd cross the kitchen with the would-be diner and say "All hail the microwave. My advice to you is to befriend these two machines. You will find them invaluable in your fight against hunger in this house."

So now you realise why I was so reluctant to take her up on her offer of soup.

But the wonderful thing about my mother not

cooking or doing any housework is that it meant that she had plenty of time for the truly important things in life. She watched an average of six soap operas a day and read about four novels a week, so she was expertly placed to give her daughters advice on their broken romances.

She was no stranger to romantic tragedy.

Especially if it was Australian.

For example, she was there when Skip (illegitimate son of Brad and some nurse he had an affair with when he was in Nam) was married to Bronnie (half-sister of Wayne and Scott) and Bronnie got pregnant and Skip started having an affair with Chrissie. Naturally, Jeannie (step-daughter of Chrissie) found out and told Mrs Goolagong (no relation). Mrs Goolagong confronted Skip over a couple of tinnies and some tucker in the Billy Can and it turned out that Skip was feeling really excluded by the pregnancy and all Bronnie could talk about was the baby. Mrs Goolagong put his mind at rest. Skip ended it with Chrissie, made it up with Bronnie, Bronnie had a beautiful baby called Shane, and Chrissie went back to the Northern Territory, with her dog Bruce. (I believe that Mrs Goolagong was subsequently sacked from the Billy Can for having the aforementioned tinnies and tucker while she was on duty, but that's another story.)

We sat there in the darkening room, listening to the sound of my baby breathing contentedly.

"She's so beautiful," Mum said.

"Yes," I said and started to cry quietly.

"What happened?" Mum asked.

"I don't know," I said. "I thought everything was fine. I thought he was as excited about the baby as I was. I know that the pregnancy wasn't easy. I was always sick and I got fat and we hardly ever had sex, but I thought that he understood."

And my mother was so good. She didn't give me any of that nonsense about men being . . . well . . . different from us, dear. They have . . . needs . . . dear, in the same way that animals do. She didn't insult me by assuming that James left because we hadn't had sex while I was pregnant.

"What am I going to do?" I asked her, knowing that she no more had the answer to that than I did.

"You've just got to live through it," she said. "That's all you can do. Don't try to make sense of it, you'll drive yourself mad. The only person who can tell you why James left is James and if he doesn't want to talk to you, you can't force him. Maybe he doesn't understand it himself. But you can't change the way he feels. If he says he doesn't love you anymore and does love this other woman, you've got to accept it. Maybe he will come back, maybe he won't, but either way, you've got to live through this."

"But it hurts so much," I said helplessly.

"I know it does," she said sadly. "And if I could make it go away, you know I would."

I looked down at my little girl asleep in her cot, so peaceful, so innocent, so safe and happy now and felt an unbearable anguish. I wanted her to always be happy. I wanted to hug her and hug her and never let her go. I never wanted her to feel the rejection and loneliness and shock that I was feeling now.

I wanted to protect her always from pain. But I wouldn't be able to. Life would see to that.

Just then the door opened, jolting us both out of the misery that we had sunk into. It was my youngest sister Helen. (Helen, eighteen, scraped into first year in university by the skin of her small white even teeth to do something incredibly useful like Anthropology, History of Art and Ancient Greek, long black hair, slanty cat eyes, always laughing, extremely badly behaved and loved by most people, especially the men whose hearts she broke by the truck-load. I think the phrase "Bold as Brass" was coined especially for her).

"You're here!" she shouted as she burst into the room.

"Here, give me a look at my niece," she screeched. "Isn't it gas! Imagine me being an auntie. Was it awful? Is it really like trying to shit a couch? Tell me, I've always wanted to know, what do they boil the water and tear the sheets up for?"

Without waiting for an answer, she thrust her face right into the carry-cot. The poor child started to cry in terror. Helen picked the baby up out of her cot and held her under her arm like a rugby player just about to score the winning try for Ireland.

"Why's she crying?" she demanded.

What could I say?

"What's her name?" she asked.

"Claire hasn't decided on a name just yet," said Mum.

"No, I have," I said, deciding to add to the general confusion.

I looked at Mum. "I've decided I'm going to call her after your mother."

"What!?" screeched Helen, in horror. "You can't call her Granny Maguire. That's no name for a baby."

"No, Helen," I said wearily. "I'm going to call her Kate."

She stared at me for a moment, wrinkling up her beautiful little nose, as realisation dawned.

"Oh I *see*," she said, laughing.

And then she muttered, not quite under her breath, "Well, that's still no name for a baby."

She handed the baby back to me, rather in the manner that farmers pass two stone sacks of potatoes from their truck to the greengrocer. That is, clumsily, carelessly, with scant regard to the welfare or comfort of the potatoes. Then, to my horror she said, "Hey, is James here? Where's James?"

She obviously didn't know.

I started to cry.

"Jesus," she said, shocked.

"Why's *she* crying?" she demanded of my mother.

My mother just stared dumbly at her. She couldn't answer her.

Would you believe it? She was crying.

Helen stared in baffled disgust at three generations of Walsh women, all crying.

"What's *wrong* with all of you? What have I said? Mum, why are you crying?" she said in exasperation.

We just looked at her, huddled together on the bed, tears rolling down our respective faces, newly-christened Kate roaring like a train.

"What's going *on*?" she said in frustration.

Still we sat there. Still we said nothing.

"I'm going downstairs to ask Dad," she threatened. But then she bit her lip and lingered by the door as she thought about it. "Unless he's going to start crying too."

Finally Mum managed to speak. "No, don't go anywhere, love," she said, stretching out her hand to Helen. "Come and sit down. You haven't done anything."

"Then why are you crying?" asked Helen, reluctantly returning to the weeping bed.

"Yes, why are *you* crying?" I asked my mother. I was just as curious as Helen about why my mother was crying. Had her husband just left her? Did her nappy need changing?

I didn't think so, so why the tears?

"Because I was just thinking about Granny," she sniffed. "And how she didn't live to see her first great-grandchild. And it's lovely that you've called the baby after her. She would have been glad. And honoured."

I felt so guilty. At least *my* mother was still alive. Poor Mum, Granny had only died last year and we all missed her so much. I hugged Mum and baby Kate, both of them crying.

"It's such a pity," mused Helen wistfully.

"What is?" I asked her.

"Oh you know, that Granny wasn't called something nice like Tamsin or Isolda or Jet," she said.

I don't know why I didn't kill her there and then.

But for some reason it was very hard to get cross with her.

And then she turned her attention to me. "And why are you crying?" she demanded of me. "Oh God, I know, I bet you've got that post-natal depression thing. There was a thing in the paper about a woman who had that and she threw her baby out of a twelfth-storey window and then she wouldn't open the door when the police came and they had to break the door down and she hadn't taken the bins out for weeks and the place was disgusting and then she tried to kill herself and they had to put her in an electric chair. Or something." Helen told with relish, never one to let annoying little details like hard facts interfere with the telling of a good bloodthirsty tale.

"Or maybe they just locked her up, or something," she admitted reluctantly, trailing off.

"Anyway, is that what's wrong with you?" she demanded cheerfully of me, back on track. "Just as well we don't live on the twelfth floor, isn't it Mum? Otherwise it'd be splatted baby all over the patio. And Michael would give out shite about the mess."

Michael was the ill-tempered, work-shy, superstitious octogenarian who came in about twice a month to "do" our matchbox of a garden, in his own highly scientific fashion. The wrath of Michael was a fearful thing to behold. As was Michael's gardening. On the rare occasions that he actually did any gardening, that is. My father was far too frightened of him to sack him. In fact the whole family was terrified of Michael. Even Helen was quite subdued around him.

I remembered the afternoon the year before when

my poor mother stood, freezing, in her apron (which she wore purely for the sake of appearances) in the garden, nodding desperately, smiling tightly, far too afraid to leave, as Michael explained, in great detail, with inarticulate grunts and frighteningly wide-sweeping gestures with the shears how, for example, if the hedge was trimmed the wall would fall down. ("You see, it needs the hedge for the support, missis") Or how if the lawn was cut all the grass would wither and die. ("The germs gets into the grass, in through the cut bits, and it all just ups and dies on you").

My mother finally made her way back into the kitchen, where she tearfully banged utensils as she boiled the kettle for Michael's tea.

"The lazy old bastard," she sobbed to myself and Helen. "He never does anything. And he made me miss *The Flying Doctor* and *Countdown*. And the grass is up to our knees. I'm ashamed of my life of it. We're the only house in the neighbourhood with a jungle of a garden. I've a good mind to spit into his tea!"

A tearful pause. A count of three.

"May God forgive me," she quavered. "Helen, leave those Jaffa Cakes alone! They're for Michael's tea."

"Why does Michael get Jaffa Cakes when you hate him and all we get are horrible Digestives?" asked Helen loudly.

Good point, I thought.

"Shush," said my mother. "He'll hear you."

Michael was at the back door at this stage,

removing his impeccable wellingtons. You could have eaten your dinner off them.

"I mean, you don't hate us," Helen continued querulously. "And we don't get nice biscuits and *you hate Michael*," (the last three words delivered very loudly and in the direction of the back door) "and he gets lovely ones. Oh hello, Michael, come in and have a biscuit." She smiled sweetly at him as he limped into the kitchen, conspicuously holding his back, as if it ached from the rigours of his labour.

"Evening," he grunted, looking at me suspiciously. He obviously thought it had been me talking about him. No one ever suspected Helen with her angelic innocent face.

The fools, the fools.

"Will I pour your tea?" my mother asked him obsequiously.

But later that evening I heard my parents arguing in the kitchen.

"Jack, you'll have to say something to him."

"Look, Mary, I'll cut the grass myself."

"No, Jack, we pay him to do it. So he should do it. Giving me all that nonsense about grass catching germs! He must take me for a right bloody eejit."

"All right, all right, I'll talk to him!"

"Or maybe we should just concrete the whole thing over. And then we'd have to sack him."

But Dad never "talked" to Michael. And I happened to know for a fact that he cut the grass himself, the day Mum went to Limerick to see Auntie Kitty, and told my mother a bare-faced lie about it.

And from time to time Helen asked my mother that, if she promised never to cut the grass, would my mother buy Jaffa Cakes specially for her.

Helen was right. If a baby was "splatted" (is there such a word?) all over the patio, Michael would indeed give out shite at the mess.

But it wasn't going to happen.

Although if Kate didn't stop crying soon, I'd have to reconsider that.

"No, Helen," I explained to her. "I don't have post-natal depression. Well, I don't think I do. Not yet, anyway."

Christ! That was all I needed.

But before I could tell her about James leaving me, my Dad came into the bedroom.

We were going to have to start moving some of the furniture out into the landing if the visitors continued to arrive at this rate.

"Hijack," we all chorused.

My father acknowledged this greeting with a smile and a bow of his head. You see, my father's name was Jack and, in the early seventies when hijacking was the popular news item, (since overshadowed by child abuse), an uncle from America greeted my father with the words "Hi Jack." My sisters and I nearly did ourselves an injury with mirth. It never failed to raise a smile.

Well, perhaps you needed to be there. "I've come to see my first grandchild," announced my Dad. "Can I hold her?"

I handed Kate over to Dad and he held her expertly. Immediately Kate stopped crying. She lay placidly in his arms, clenching and unclenching her little starfish hands.

Just like her mother, I thought sadly – putty in men's hands.

I really would have to nip this in the bud with Kate. Get some self-respect, girl! You don't need a man for your happiness! Every other mother would be reading their little girls stories about engines that could talk, and wolves that meet their comeuppance, I would read my child feminist diatribes instead, I decided.

Out with *The Little Mermaid* and in with *The Female Eunuch*.

"When are you going to give her a name?" asked Dad.

"Oh, I just have," I told him. "I'm going to call her after Granny."

"Lovely," beamed Dad.

"Hello, little Nora," he said to the pink bundle in a sing-song baby voice.

Helen, Mum and I exchanged stricken looks.

Wrong granny!

"Er no Dad," I said awkwardly. "I've called her Kate."

"But my mother isn't called Kate," he frowned in confusion.

"I know Dad," I faltered. (Oh Christ, why was life so fraught with pitfalls?) "But I've called her after Granny Maguire, not Granny Walsh."

"Oh I see," he said a bit coldly.

"But I'll call her Nora for her second name," I promised cringingly.

"No way!" interrupted Helen. "Call her something nice. I know! How about Elena? Elena is Greek for Helen, you know."

"Shush Helen," admonished Mum. "It's Claire's baby."

"You always told us we had to share all our toys," said Helen sulkily.

"Kate isn't a toy," sighed Mum.

Really, Helen was exhausting.

However, as she had the attention span of a saucepan, that is, absolutely none whatsoever, she turned her attention to other things.

"Hey Dad, can I have a lift to Linda's?"

"Helen, I'm not a chauffeur," replied Dad evenly and tightly.

"Dad, I didn't ask you what you do for a living. I *know* what you do for a living. I simply asked you for a lift," Helen said in a very "I'm prepared to be reasonable about this" voice.

"No Helen, you can bloody well walk!" exclaimed Dad. "I honestly don't know what's wrong with all you young people. Laziness, that's what it is. Now, when I . . . "

"Dad," Helen interrupted him sharply, "*please* don't tell me again how you had to walk three miles to school in your bare feet. I really couldn't bear it. Just give me a lift," and she gave him a little cat smile from under her long black fringe.

He stared at her in exasperation for a moment and then he started to laugh. "Oh all right then," he said, jingling his car keys. "Come on."

He handed Kate back to me.

The way a baby should be handed back.

"Night, night, Kate *Nora*," he said, with perhaps a little too much emphasis on the "Nora." I didn't think he had quite forgiven me, yet.

Dad and Helen left.

Mum, Kate Nora and I remained on the bed, savouring the silence occasioned by Helen's departure.

"Now," I said sternly to Kate, "that was your first lesson on how to treat a man, courtesy of your Auntie Helen. I hope you took lots of notice. Treat them like slaves and, sure enough, they'll behave like slaves."

Kate stared wide-eyed up at me.

My mother just smiled inscrutably.

A smug, secret smile.

A knowing kind of a smile.

The smile of a woman whose husband has done the hoovering for the past fifteen years.

Chapter Five

And so to bed.

It felt very odd to be going to sleep in the bed that I had spent my teenage years in. I had thought that those days were gone forever.

Déjà vu.

But I could have done without it.

And it was kind of weird to be kissed goodnight by my mother when I had my own child in the cot beside me.

I was a mother, but I didn't need Sigmund Freud to tell me that I still felt like a child myself.

Kate stared open-eyed at the ceiling. She was probably still in shock from her encounter with Helen. I was a bit anxious about her but, to my surprise, I actually felt quite tired. I went to sleep quickly. Although I'd thought that I really wouldn't be able to sleep at all.

Ever again, I mean.

Kate gently roused me at about two a.m. by crying at about a million decibels. I wondered if she had gone to sleep at all. I fed her. Then I went back to bed.

I went back to sleep but, a few hours later, I jolted awake again, filled with horror. Horror that had nothing to do with the exuberantly flowery Laura Ashleyesque wallpaper, curtains and duvet cover that surrounded me and that I could dimly see through the darkness.

Horror that I was in Dublin and not in my flat in London with my beloved James.

I looked at the clock and it was (yes, you guessed it) four a.m. I should have taken comfort from the fact that approximately a quarter of the Greenwich Mean Time world had just jolted awake also and were lying, staring miserably into the darkness, worrying about everything from "Will I be made redundant?", to "Will I ever meet someone who really loves me?" to "Am I pregnant?".

But it was no comfort.

Because I felt as if I was in Hell.

And comparing it to someone else's Hell doesn't make the pain of my one any less.

Sorry to be bloodthirsty about this but if one is having one's leg sawn off with a rusty hacksaw, one doesn't take comfort from the fact that the person in the next cell is being nailed to a table.

I sat up in bed in the dark.

Kate slept peacefully beside me in her pink carry-cot.

We were like night watchmen. Taking it in shifts to stay awake. At least one of us seemed to be awake at any given time.

Although the resemblance ended there because I couldn't say – well, at least not with any sincerity – "Four o'clock and all is well."

My stomach lurched with the horror of it all. I

couldn't believe that I was in my parents' house in Dublin and not in my flat in London with my husband. I felt that I must have been out of my mind to have left London and left James to another woman. I had just abandoned him!

Had I gone completely mad? I had to go back. I had to fight for him! I had to get him back!

How had I ended up here?

I had taken some wrong turning into a parallel universe where things still looked like my life, but it was all evil and sinister and wrong.

I *couldn't* be without James.

He was part of me.

If my arm had fallen off I wouldn't have said, "oh let it be for the moment. It'll come back if it's meant to be. No point in forcing it. It might only drive it away." After all, it was my arm and James was much more a part of me than any old arm.

I needed him a lot more.

I loved him a lot more.

I simply couldn't be without him.

I wanted him back. I wanted my life with him back. And I was going to get him back. (And get him on his back.)

(Sorry, that was flippant and vulgar.)

I was panic-stricken.

What if I had left it too late?

I should never have left.

I should have stood my ground and just told him that he and I would be able to work things out. That he couldn't possibly love Denise. That he loved me. That I was too much a part of him for him not to love me.

But I had admitted defeat and delivered him into Denise's cellulitey (but they were!) arms, without any kind of protest.

I had to speak to him now.

He wouldn't mind me ringing him at four in the morning. I mean, this was James we were talking about here. He was my best friend. I could do *anything* and James didn't mind. He understood me. He knew me.

And I would fly back to London with Kate in the morning. And my life would be fixed.

The last week would be forgotten. The break in our lives would be mended seamlessly. The scar would fade. Only if you looked very closely would you ever see it.

Everything would be straightened up and righted. Everything would be back on course. The way it was always meant to be.

It had all been a terrible mistake, a messy mix-up, but no permanent harm has been done.

All's well that ends well, isn't that right?

I know what you're thinking.

No, really, I do.

You're thinking, "She's gone mad."

Well, maybe I had. Maybe I was deranged with grief.

You're thinking, "Have some self-respect, Claire."

But I'm afraid that I'd realised that my marriage mattered more to me than my self-respect. Self-respect doesn't keep you warm at night. Self-respect doesn't listen to you at the end of each day. Self-respect doesn't tell you that it would rather have sex with you than with Cindy Crawford.

This wasn't just some teenage schoolgirl romance that had gone wrong. He hadn't asked another cheerleader to the Prom. This wasn't about *romance*.

This was about love.

I loved James. He was part of me. This was too good to just let go.

Even if the captain of the football team asked me to go to the Prom with him instead, and I could wear my new dress and hold my head up high and salvage my pride, it didn't matter. I still had to get James back.

I struggled out of bed, fighting my way through the acres of wincyette nightdress that my mother insisted that I wear. When I had fled London I had forgotten to pack a nightdress. And when my mother discovered this she tartly informed me that no one was sleeping naked under her roof. "What if there was a fire?" and "That might be how they do things in London, but you're not in London now." So I had a choice of wearing a pair of Dad's paisley pyjamas, or borrowing one of Mum's huge, Victorian, floor-length, high-collared, fleece-lined flowery nighties. How the woman ever managed to get a man to impregnate her even once, never mind five times, while associating with such garments was beyond me.

They would dim the ardour of a fifteen-year-old Italian. By the time that any man had wrestled successfully with the yards of fabric and was lucky enough to uncover some human flesh he would be far too exhausted to do anything about it.

I chose the nightdress over Dad's pyjamas

because the huge quantities of fabric in the nightdress made me feel waif-like and skinny and cute. Whereas Dad's pyjamas were alarmingly and depressingly snug.

All feelings are relative, I'd decided. I was wrong to feel fat. I was not too fat. There was nothing wrong with me. It was just that the rest of the world was too small. There was no need for me to change. All I needed to do was to change the world around me. Simply make everything around me about fifteen percent bigger than it was now – clothes, furniture, people, buildings, countries – and suddenly I would be the right size again!

Make that twenty percent. Then I could feel positively fragile.

Everything, I was quickly realising, was just a question of *proportion*.

Everything was good or bad, fat or thin, big or small only by comparison with what surrounded it.

So keep your smart remarks about my nightdress to yourself. There was method to my madness (well, at least to that particular aspect of it). I happened to know what I was doing. Emaciated, that's how I felt. Skinny and floaty and girl-like.

It took me about ten minutes to get out of bed and, when I finally managed to stand on the floor, I nearly garrotted myself by standing on the back hem of the nightdress, thereby pulling the front collar upwards, tightly and violently onto my throat, in a vice-like grip.

I coughed and choked a good bit and Kate started to move and fret restlessly in her cot. "Oh don't wake up darling," I thought frantically. "Don't cry. There's no need. Everything's going to be all right. I'm going to get your daddy back. You'll see. You hold the fort here."

And miraculously she calmed and settled and didn't wake up. I tiptoed out of the dark room and out into the landing. The huge nightdress swirled roomily around me in a pleasing manner as I went down the unlit stairs. The phone was downstairs in the hall. The only light was from the street lamp outside the house, which shone through the panes of frosted glass in the front door.

I started to dial the number of my flat in London. The noise of me dialling echoed in the silence. It sounded like rifle-fire in the stillness of the sleeping house. "Jesus," I thought shakily, "the McLoughlins from three houses up will be over to complain about the noise."

There were a couple of clicks as the phone in Dublin connected with the phone in an empty flat in a city four hundred miles away.

I let it ring. It might have been a hundred times. It might have been a thousand times.

It rang and rang, calling out to a cold dark empty flat. I could imagine the phone, ringing and ringing, beside the smooth, unruffled, unslept-in bed, shadows from the window thrown on it as the lights from the street streamed in through the open curtains. Open, because there was no one there to close them.

And still, I let it ring and ring. And slowly hope left me.

James wasn't answering.

Because James wasn't there.

James was in another flat. In another bed.

With another woman.

I was crazy to think that I could have got him back just because I wanted him back. I must have been out of my mind to have thought that I could just ignore the fact that he was living with another woman. He had *left* me, for God's sake. He had told me that he loved someone else.

Slowly, sanity returned.

Temporary insanity had come a-calling and I had shouted "Come on in, the door is open." Luckily Reality had come home unexpectedly and found Temporary Insanity roaming the corridors of my mind unchecked, going into rooms, opening cupboards, reading my letters, looking in my knickers drawer, that kind of thing. Reality had run and got Sanity. And after a tussle, they both had managed to throw out Temporary Insanity and slammed the door in his face. Temporary Insanity now lay on the gravel in the driveway of my mind, panting and furious, shouting, "She invited me in, you know. She *asked* me in. She *wanted* me there."

Reality and Sanity were leaning out of an upstairs window, shouting "Go on, get going. You're not wanted round here. If you're not gone in five minutes, we'll call the Emotions Police."

I suppose any psychiatrist worth his salt would have said that I was In Denial. That the shock of James leaving me so suddenly was too great for me to assimilate. That I simply couldn't accept it or cope with it. It was easier for me to pretend that nothing bad had really happened and, that if I pretended that everything could be fixed, it actually would be.

I sat on the floor, in the cold, dark hall. After a long time I hung up the phone.

My heart, which had been beating frantically, returned to normal. My hands stopped shaking. My head stopped pretending and fantasising.

I wouldn't be going back to London in the morning.

My life was here now. At least for the moment.

I felt wretched.

After all the exhilaration of thinking I could speak to James and just kiss everything better, I was left with the biggest, emptiest sadness I had ever felt. Sadness as big as a continent. As deep as the Atlantic. As empty as Helen's brain.

My feet started to get cold.

Although I felt as weary as a person a thousand years old, I felt that I would never be able to sleep again.

The pain of the loss I was feeling was too great to let me sleep. And I desperately wanted to sleep. Anything to stop this feeling.

How I wished that we had a neurotic mother. One who kept sleeping pills and Valium and anti-depressants by the crate-load in the medicine cupboard in the bathroom.

As it was she acted as if we were prospective candidates for the Betty Ford clinic if we asked for two Paracetamol for our sore throat/stomach ache/broken leg/perforated duodenal ulcer. "Offer it up," she would say. "Think of Our Lord suffering on the cross." Or "What would you do if painkillers hadn't been invented?" To which she might receive the reply, "Being nailed to a cross would be a day at the races compared to this earache." Or "You can scourge me at the pillar any day of the week if you take away the pain in my tooth."

This, of course, would put paid to any chance, however slim, of extracting drugs from my mother. Blasphemy was high on her list of unforgivable things.

Or how I wished that my sister Anna still dealt drugs. What I wouldn't have given for a tab of E right then.

As it was, the chances of procuring even an alcoholic drink were unpredictable. Neither of my parents drank very much. And they kept very little alcohol in the house.

No, I mean it. This was not a policy decision of theirs. This was not a stance they took. This was something that happened to them.

Even when they *tried* to keep alcohol in the house they still, in actuality *kept* very little alcohol in the house, thanks to myself and, more recently, my sisters.

Our motto seemed to be, "No percent proof too large or too small. All beverages considered." Anything from raw Poteen to cherry brandy to Babycham and everything in between was grist to our particular mills.

In my younger days, those halcyon days before I discovered what alcohol could do for me, we had a full, if eclectic, drinks cabinet.

Purest Polish vodka jostled shoulders with litre bottles of Malibu. Bottles of Hungarian Slibovitch behaved as if they had every right to stand next to a bottle of Southern Comfort. There was no cold war in our drinks cabinet.

You see, Dad was forever winning bottles of brandy or whiskey at golf. And Mum would occasionally win a bottle of sherry or some kind of girlie liqueur at Bridge. People brought us presents of bottles of fancy drink when they went on holidays. Our next door neighbour brought us back a bottle of Ouzo from Cyprus.

Dad's secretary brought us the Slibovitch when she went on her holidays Behind The Iron Curtain. (This was in 1979 and myself and my sisters all thought she was really daring and brave and questioned her at length on her return as to whether she had witnessed any violation of the human rights of the Hungarians. "Is it really true? Do they still have to wear flares and platforms?" we asked, our eyes round with horror. While Margaret, ever practical, wanted to know what the exchange rate was for a packet of chewing gum. "How many packets would I need before I could buy a house?" Honestly, that girl had vision.) Anna won a bottle of fluorescent yellow banana schnapps at the St Vincent de Paul Christmas raffle. Someone else came by a stray bottle of apricot schnapps.

Bit by bit our alcohol collection grew. And, as my parents barely drank and we children hadn't started yet, our drinks cabinet overfloweth.

However, those happy days were no more.

I'm sorry to report that when I was about fifteen, I

discovered the delights of alcohol. And quickly came to realise that my pocket money was not going to stretch to accommodating my new-found passion. With the result that I spent many an anxious hour, looking over my shoulder, as I siphoned off small amounts from the various bottles in the cupboard in the sitting-room.

I decanted them into a small lemonade bottle I had procured as receptacle for the concoction I would make. I was afraid to take too much from any one bottle, so I would choose from a wide spectrum of drinks. And put it all into the one lemonade bottle, you understand. With scant regard to what the final product tasted like. My priority was to get drunk. And, if I had to drink something that tasted disgusting to do so, then I would.

I spent many a happy hour, after drinking the mixture of, (let's just say), perhaps sherry, vodka, gin, brandy and Vermouth (Auntie Kitty had brought us the Vermouth from her trip to Rome), joyfully inebriated, at whatever disco I managed to bully or hoodwink my parents into letting me go to.

Great days. Glorious days.

To avoid any awkward and embarrassing scenes with my parents I would replace whatever I had taken from each bottle with a corresponding amount of water. What could be neater, I thought.

However, like those delicate plants that are overwatered and die, I managed to also overwater a lot of alcohol. A bottle of vodka, in particular.

My day of reckoning finally came.

One Saturday evening, when I was about

seventeen, Mum and Dad had the Kellys and the Smiths over for drinks. Mum and Mrs Kelly happened to be drinking vodka. Or so they thought. However, thanks to my efforts over the previous eighteen months or so, what was once Smirnoff was now more or less 100 per cent purest, unadulterated water, untainted by the merest hint of alcohol.

The rest of the party had the good fortune to be drinking actual alcohol.

So, as Dad, Mr Kelly, Mr Smith and Mrs Smith got louder and redder and chattier and laughed at things that weren't remotely funny, and Dad told everyone that he didn't declare all his income to the tax man and the Smiths revealed that Mr Smith had had an affair last year, and that they nearly split up but they were making a go of things now, Mum and Mrs Kelly sat stiff and poker-faced, smiling tightly as the others guffawed with laughter.

Mum found nothing even remotely amusing in Mrs Smith spilling her Bacardi and Coke (I didn't really like Bacardi, so its alcoholic content was pretty much intact) all over the good sitting-room carpet, but Dad was highly entertained by it. Mirth abounded. All except for the vodka drinkers.

The penny dropped with my mother the next day.

The bottle of vodka was sent for and subjected to several tests. (As in, "Here, smell that. What does that smell like to you?" "Nothing, Mum," *"Exactly!"*)

Results from the makeshift forensics lab set up in the kitchen showed that the bottle of vodka had indeed been tampered with. Tampered with repeatedly, in fact.

There was a tearful scene between myself and my parents. Well, my mother, at least, was tearful. But with embarrassment and rage. "Oh, the shame of it," she wailed. "Inviting people over and offering them drinks and giving them watered down stuff instead. I could die! How could you? And you took the pledge and promised not to drink until you were eighteen."

I was surly and sullen and silent. I hung my head to hide my shame and my fury at being caught.

Dad was silent and sad.

A purge ensued. The drink was all rounded up and incarcerated. Detained without trial in a secure cupboard that had a key. Only Mum knew where that key was kept and, as she said herself, she would rather suffer the torments of the damned than reveal its whereabouts.

Naturally it was only a matter of time before myself or one of my sisters figured out how to pick the lock.

A type of guerrilla warfare ensued with my mother forever seeking new hiding places for the rapidly diminishing supply of drink. In fact Helen swears that she heard Mum on the phone to Auntie Julia, who is an alcoholic, asking her to recommend good hiding places. But this has never been corroborated, so don't take it as gospel.

But Mum was only ever a tiny step ahead of us. No sooner had she found a new place for her cache, than one of us would find it. In the same way that new antibiotics have to be constantly invented to combat new and resistant strains of bacteria, so Mum had to constantly invent new hiding places.

Unfortunately for her they never stayed new or hidden for long.

She even tried sitting down and reasoning with us. "Please don't drink so much. Or at least please don't drink so much of mine and your father's drink."

And the answer she usually got, uttered more in sorrow than in anger I have to say, would be something like, "But Mum, we like to drink. We are poor. We are left with no choice. Do you think we *enjoy* behaving like common thieves?"

Even though Margaret, Rachel and I had left home and could afford to support whatever bad habits we chose, Helen and Anna were both still living at home and were bone-crunchingly skint. So the battle continued.

And what was once a proud and noble drink collection was now a tatty and raggedy and depleted few bottles, travelling nomadically round the wardrobes and coal buckets and under the beds, looking for a safe haven. Long gone are the full and sparkling bottles of spirits with recognisable brand names. All that remain in their stead are a sticky bottle of Drambuie, covered in fluff, with about a centimetre left in the bottom, or half an inch of Cuban vodka (honestly, there is such a thing. Obviously the right drink for the ideologically sound Comrade in Cuba) and the almost full bottle of banana schnapps, which Helen and Anna have both declared that they would rather die of thirst than drink.

I continued to sit on the cold floor in the dark hall. I really felt as if I needed a drink. I would even have drunk the banana schnapps if I'd known where to find it. I felt so unbearably *lonely*. I toyed with the idea of waking my mother up and asking her to give me a drink, but I felt really guilty at that idea. She was so worried about me, if the poor woman had managed to get to sleep I couldn't in all conscience wake her.

Maybe Helen could help.

I wearily climbed the stairs to her bedroom. But when I crept into her room her bed was empty. Either she had spent the night at Linda's or else some young man had got very lucky. If she had spent the night with a man, his suicided body would probably be found in the morning, with a note beside it saying something like "I have achieved everything I ever wanted to do in life. I will never be as happy as this ever again. I want to die on this note of ecstasy. PS She is a Goddess."

Then, as if I wasn't feeling awful enough, I was suddenly gripped with a panicky fear that something terrible had happened to Kate.

That she'd had a cot death. Or choked on vomit. Or suffocated. Or *something*.

I raced back to my room and I was so relieved to find that she was still breathing.

She was just lying there, a wrinkled, pink, fragrant bundle, her eyes screwed shut.

As I waited for my breathing to return to normal and for the sweat to evaporate from my forehead I wondered how other parents coped. How did they let their children out to play with other children? Didn't they panic every time they were away from their child for more than five minutes?

I was finding it hard enough now. How the hell

would I cope when she had to go to school? There was no way I could be expected to just abandon her like that. The school would have to let me sit at the back of the classroom.

Now I *really* needed a drink.

Maybe Anna was home.

I dragged myself over to her room and quietly opened the door.

The fumes hit me when I had the door opened about an inch.

The alcohol fumes that is.

Bingo!

"Thank God," I thought. I'd obviously come to the right place.

Anna was curled up in bed, her long black hair spread out all around her with what looked like a Big Mac box on the pillow beside her.

"Anna," I whispered loudly to her and shook her a bit.

No response.

"Anna!" I whispered, a good deal more loudly this time and shook her shoulder vigorously.

I turned on her bedside lamp and shone it into her face, Gestapo style. Wake up!

She opened her eyes and stared at me.

"Claire?" she croaked disbelievingly.

She looked really quite frightened, as though she thought she might be hallucinating.

And as this was Anna, it was quite possible.

That she was hallucinating, that is.

Fond of the mood-altering substances, if you follow me.

The poor girl. As far as she knew I was four hundred miles away, in another city, in another life. But here I was manifesting myself in her bedroom in the middle of the night.

On the scrounge, to add insult to injury.

"Anna, sorry to disturb you like this but have you anything I could drink?" I asked her.

She just stared at me.

"Why are you here?" she asked in a little frightened voice.

"Because I'm looking for a bloody drink," I said exasperatedly.

"Have you a message for me?" she asked, still staring at me wide-eyed.

Oh Christ, I thought in annoyance.

Anna loved anything to do with the occult. There was nothing she would like more than to be possessed by the devil. Or to live in a haunted house. Or to be able to foretell disasters. She was obviously hoping that I was some kind of paranormal phenomenon. Either that or she was drunker than usual.

I had a good mind to tell her something awful.

Like "Yes Anna, beware! Your crop will fail." Or "Yes, Anna, beware!" (the "beware!" bit is important) "your pail is leaky and you will lose the milk that you carry to market." or "Yes, Anna, beware! do not cut the branches from the hawthorn tree."

The fact that Anna had no crop, no milk to carry in any leaky pail to any market or wasn't within ten miles of a hawthorn tree wouldn't have bothered her in the slightest. She would still have been completely delighted with her supernatural visitation.

"Yes Anna," I said, deciding to humour her but at the same time feeling a bit foolish. "They have sent me. I've been sent to get the drink."

"In my rucksack," she said faintly.

Her rucksack was flung on the floor with one shoe (what had happened to the other one?), her coat, a carton with some chips left in it and a can of Budweiser. I had difficulty opening the bag as two helium balloons were attached to the cord. Anna had obviously been to some kind of party.

I nearly cried with relief when I found a bottle of white wine in her bag.

"Thanks Anna," I said. "I'll repay you tomorrow." And left.

She was still looking dazed and frightened. She nodded dumbly. "OK," she managed to mumble.

I checked Kate. She was still sleeping peacefully.

I had half-expected her to be sitting up in her cot, with her arms folded, demanding to know where the father I had promised her was. But she was just asleep dreaming baby dreams, about pink clouds and warm beds and soft people who smell nice and lots to eat and lots of sleep and lots of people who love you.

And never having to queue for the loo.

I took the bottle of wine downstairs to the kitchen and wearily opened it. I knew I would feel better after having a drink. Just as I was pouring myself a glass of wine, Anna appeared at the kitchen door, rubbing her eyes, looking confused and anxious, her long black hair strewn around her white face.

"Oh Claire, it really is you. So I didn't imagine it," she said, sounding half relieved, half disappointed. "I thought I might have the DTs. And then I thought you might be a vision. But I thought if you were a vision that you would appear in something nicer than Mum's awful nightdress."

"Yes, it really is me," I smiled at her. "Sorry if I gave you a fright. But I was dying for a drink." I went over to her and put my arms around her. It really was lovely to see her.

Anna looked a lot like Helen, little white face, slanty cat eyes, cute little nose.

But the resemblance ended there. For starters I didn't want to kill Anna about twenty times a day. Anna was a lot quieter, a lot sweeter. She was very kind to everyone. She was also, unfortunately, very vague and very ethereal. More than once I'd heard her name being mentioned in the same sentence as the phrase "away with the fairies."

Well, I suppose I had better be perfectly frank with you. There's no getting away from the fact that Anna was a bit of . . . well . . . a bit of a hippie, I suppose.

She never really had a proper job. And she always seemed to be going to rock festivals. Every time I rang from London and asked after Anna, my mother would say something like "Oh Anna's gone to Glastonbury," or "Anna's in Lisdoonvarna," or "Anna's got a job in a bar in Santorini."

And there were days – bad days admittedly – when Mum might say "how the hell would I know how Anna is? After all, I'm only her bloody mother."

She got jobs intermittently. Usually in wholefood restaurants. But they never seemed to last any length of time. Well, neither did the restaurants either, for some odd reason.

She claimed the dole.

She, as I have mentioned, sold drugs. But only briefly. And in the nicest possible way.

No honestly.

She never hung around school gates trying to sell high-grade heroin to eight-year-olds.

She just sold the odd bit of hash to her friends and family. And doubtless made a loss on it.

She made jewellery and occasionally even sold some.

A precarious kind of existence, but she didn't seem too bothered by the insecure nature of it.

Dad despaired of Anna. He called her irresponsible. And, of course, the blame for Anna's instability was laid squarely, if not particularly fairly, at my door. Dad said that I had hightailed it (his word) to London at a time when Anna was at a very impressionable age and I had given her the idea that it was perfectly acceptable to give up a good job and go off and work as a waitress. What kind of role model was I? he asked me.

Dad desperately tried to mould Anna into a responsible, tax-paying citizen. He managed to get her a job in an office working for a construction company.

Apparently someone owed him a favour.

It must have been a very large favour.

It was a mistake to try to force Anna to work in an office. Like trying to squash a round peg into a square hole. Or wearing your shoes on the wrong feet. Unpleasant, uncomfortable and almost certainly doomed to failure.

It was a disaster.

Anna was like an exotic flower, used to tropical climes, suddenly thrust into a damp cold country. How could she possibly survive? She could only fade and wilt, her beautiful bright petals withered and brown, her delicate perfume gone.

Administrative work wasn't quite where her talents lay. She was too imaginative and creative to knuckle down to something as tedious as filing.

And too stoned to do it right.

One Monday morning her boss, Mr Sheridan flung a cheque on her desk and said, "Send that to Bill Prescot with a compliment slip."

Luckily her boss intercepted the post before the cheque went out with a letter written by Anna which said, "Dear Mr Prescot, although I have never met you, I believe that you are a very pleasant man. All the builders speak highly of you."

Mr Sheridan wearily explained to Anna that sending a compliment slip did not actually involve complimenting anyone.

She lost track of the time every lunch hour because she had found a swan's nest at the canal near the office and would spend ages watching the birds and cooing over the eggs. (And rolling and partaking of several joints also, if the rumour-mongers are to be believed).

But the day she suggested changing the filing system for the construction workers, so that instead of organising them by their surname, she would do it by their Astrological Star Sign instead, Mr Ballard the office manager decided that he had had enough.

Favour owed by the managing director to Jack Walsh, or no favour owed by the managing director to Jack Walsh, that girl had to go.

Although Anna protested that really she had only been joking, (she said, laughing, no doubt making things worse for herself, "Honestly, how could we possibly consider filing them by their star sign. I mean, we don't even know their rising sign"), her P45 was promptly issued. Anna found herself once more without gainful employment.

Dad was furious and mortified with embarrassment. "What goes on in her bloody head?" he thundered. "Do you know, I'd nearly swear she's on drugs."

Honestly, for an intelligent man, there were times when he was alarmingly naive.

And Anna's only other real brush with gainful employment was when she was still at school and the career guidance teacher asked her what she wanted to do with her life. Anna told her that she wanted to be at one with the elements. And then couldn't understand it when she was put on a two-week placement with a company that manufactured the insides of kettles.

Once she had established that I wasn't a psychic phenomenon, Anna, though disappointed, decided to make the best of the situation.

"Pour me a glass of that too," she said, gesturing at the bottle of wine, so I did, and we both sat down at the kitchen table.

It was about five a.m.

Anna seemed to find nothing remotely strange at the lateness or, more accurately, the earliness of the hour.

"Cheers," she said, raising her glass to me.

"Yes, cheers," I replied hollowly. I drained the glass in one go. Anna looked admiringly at me.

"So what are you doing here?" she asked conversationally. "I didn't know that you were coming. No one told me . . . well I *think* no one told me," she said a bit doubtfully. "I haven't been home in about a week."

"Well, Anna, it was a bit of a sudden decision," I said sighing, as I geared up for a long tortuous explanation of my tragic circumstances.

But before I could, she interrupted me abruptly.

"Oh my God!" she said, suddenly clapping a hand to her mouth.

"What?" I demanded, feeling very alarmed. Was the corkscrew hovering in mid-air? Had a banshee's face appeared at the window?

"You're not pregnant anymore!" she exclaimed.

I smiled in spite of myself.

"No, Anna, I'm not. Can you figure it out?"

"You've had a baby?" she asked slowly.

"Yes," I confirmed, still smiling.

"Jesus!" she screamed. "Isn't that fabulous!" And flung her arms around me. "Is it a girl?"

"Yes," I told her.

"Is she here? Can I see her?" Anna asked, all excited.

"Yes, she's in my room. But she's asleep. And if

you don't mind I'd prefer not to wake her. Not until I've finished this bottle of wine, anyway," I said morosely.

"Well fair enough," conceded Anna, pouring me another glass of wine, one alcohophile to another, "Get that inside you. I suppose it's a long time since you've been allowed to drink alcohol. No wonder you're knocking it back."

"Well, it is a long time since I've been able to have a drink. But that's not why I'm so desperate to get drunk," I told her.

"Oh?" she asked me quizzically.

So I told her about James.

And she was so gentle, so sympathetic, so unjudgemental and, in her own flaky way, so wise, that I slowly started to feel a bit better. A little bit calmer. A little less weary. A little more hopeful.

I suppose the bottle of wine had also better get a mention on the credits. It played a small but not insignificant part in the lifting of my spirits. But it was mostly thanks to Anna.

She murmured stuff like "If it's meant to be, it's meant to be" and, "We're all being taken care of, even if it doesn't feel like it at the time" and, "There is a plan for all of us" and, "Everything happens for a reason".

Hippie type talk. But I found it very comforting.

And at about six o'clock, just when the birds were starting to sing, we abandoned the kitchen, leaving the table strewn with glasses, the well-and-truly empty bottle, the cork, the corkscrew, an overflowing ashtray and wrappers from a packet of biscuits (yes,

Digestives. Mum still didn't buy Jaffa Cakes for us) which Anna had eaten.

Dad would be getting up in an hour to make breakfast for himself and Mum. He would deal with the mess, we reasoned. He liked to do things, we agreed. He needed to feel needed.

We slowly climbed the stairs, our arms around each other, and I fell into bed, feeling sleepy and relaxed and calm. Anna spent a few minutes gazing in wonder at Kate and then insisted on getting the two helium balloons (which she had misappropriated from the party she had been to, along with the bottle of wine) and tying them onto Kate's carry-cot. Then Anna kissed me goodnight and tiptoed out of the room. I went straight into a deep, dreamless sleep.

Kate woke me fifteen minutes later screeching for her breakfast.

I fed her and then staggered back to bed.

Just as I was drifting back to sleep I heard Dad getting up. A few minutes later I heard him pounding up the stairs shouting to my mother, "Your daughters are drunken pups!" (They were always her daughters when they lost jobs, didn't go to Mass, stayed out late and dressed indecently. They were his daughters when they passed exams, got degrees, married accountants and bought houses). "Drinking all night and lying in bed all day! Am I supposed to clear up the mess in the kitchen?"

Dad had obviously discovered the remains of our little "early house."

Mum wailed plaintively, "Oh no, they've found the drink again. I thought they'd never find it out under the oil tank. Now I'll have to find a new place to hide it."

After a while this commotion died down. Just as I was hoping against hope that I might catch an hour or two of sleep, someone started ringing at the front door. Naturally, this was quite alarming because it was only seven-thirty in the morning. I heard Dad open the door and engage in conversation with a man's voice. I strained to hear what was going on. Could it possibly be James? I felt such a surge of hope that it nearly hurt.

Then there was the sound of Dad running up the stairs. He shouted to my mother, "There's a madman at the front door with a shoe. He wants to know if we own it. What'll I do?"

There was a perplexed silence from my mother.

"I'm going to be late for work with all these interruptions this morning, you know," Dad told her, as if it was her fault.

I started to cry with disappointment. It wasn't James at the front door. I knew exactly who it was.

"Dad," I called tearfully, "Daaaaaad!"

He stuck his head round the door. "Morning love," he said. "I'll be with you in a minute. I'll make you some tea. It's just that there's a lunatic downstairs and I'd better get rid of him first."

"No, Dad," I told him. "He's not a lunatic. He's a taxi-driver. Wake Anna. I bet it's her shoe."

"Oh, so she's finally bothered to come home, has she?" shouted Mum from her room.

Dad went off to Anna's room muttering "I might have known Anna would be involved in this."

Anna was duly roused. And it turned out that the man at the front door was the taxi driver who had dropped Anna home in the early hours of the morning. When he'd finished his shift he found a shoe in the back of his car. And was now travelling, in the manner of Prince Charming, round the houses of the young women he had delivered home during the night, trying to match the shoe to the young woman. Anna was indeed his Cinderella.

Anna gave effusive thanks. The taxi driver left. Anna went back to bed. Dad went to work. I closed my eyes. Kate started to cry.

So did I.

Chapter Six

Wet and windy and miserable. For the first two weeks that I was home it rained every day. Apparently it was the wettest February in living memory.

I would wake in the middle of every night to the sound of the raindrops cracking and spattering at the window, drumming and pounding on the roof.

The weather made everyone miserable.

Luckily I was suicidal anyway.

In fact the weather made me feel slightly better. It seemed like Fate's way of evening up my miserable life with everyone else's happy life, if you know what I mean.

Anna and Helen lounged moodily around the house, staring longingly out the windows, wondering if it would ever stop.

Mum talked gloomily about building an ark.

Dad tried to play golf while up to his knees in water on a flooded golf-course.

I was the only one who didn't mind the torrential rain.

It suited my mood perfectly.

I didn't care if I couldn't go out.

I would have been happy never to have gone out again.

I spent hours just lying on my bed, staring at nothing, Kate beside me in her cot, while the rain poured down outside, steaming up the windows, turning the garden into a quagmire.

My mother would bounce into my room each morning and fling back the curtains, on another grey, sodden day, and say "Well, what's on the agenda for today?"

I knew that she was only trying to jolly me out of my misery. And I tried to be cheerful. It was just that I was so tired all the time.

She would then offer to make me my breakfast but as soon as she left my room I would drag myself over to the window and close the curtains again.

I didn't neglect Kate. Really, I didn't.

Well maybe I did.

To my eternal shame Mum brought her to the baby clinic. Mum drove to the supermarket and bought mounds and mounds of disposable nappies and baby formula and Sudocreme and talc and bottle steriliser and everything else that Kate needed.

In fairness to me, I didn't abandon Kate entirely. I *did* take care of her in lots of ways. I fed her and changed her and washed her and worried about her. Sometimes I even played with her. I just couldn't seem to do anything that involved leaving the house for her.

Not because I didn't love her. I loved her more than anything else in the universe. There is nothing that I wouldn't have done for her (except, as I said, leave the house). But I didn't seem to have any energy left for me.

Getting dressed was such a huge undertaking that I never managed it. On the rare occasions that I did get out of bed I put one of Dad's golfing jumpers on over Mum's nightdress and wore a pair of hiking socks. I would genuinely *intend* to get dressed properly. But later.

As soon as I've fed Kate, I would say.

But after that I would be so exhausted that I would have to lie down for a while and read a few lines of an article in *Hello*. It was a measure of how depressed I was that I would even consider living in a house that had a copy of *Hello* in it. I could barely concentrate enough to read. I would look at the pictures of totally obscure and minor Royalty, photographed in their "sumptuous" homes and wonder if they were happy.

And what that felt like.

And then I would idly think that no one could be happy living in a house with those horrible baroque chairs and ancient tapestries and pictures. Or married to Prince Whoeverhewas, who was fat and bald and had false teeth and was at least twelve times the age of the former "exotic dancer" whom he had taken as his wife. He only came up to her waist.

After lying down for a while I might have to go to the loo. I would spend about half an hour trying to summon the energy to go to the bathroom. It was as if I were made of lead.

Once I got to the bathroom it was all I could do to stagger back to bed again.

I'll just lie down again for five minutes, I would promise myself, and then I really will get dressed.

But by then it would be time to feed Kate again.

And after that I would have to lie down again, just for five minutes . . .

Somehow I just never got round to it.

If only I was left alone to sleep forever I would be all right. That's what I thought. But people kept bothering me.

I was lying in bed one afternoon (I don't know why I say one afternoon. It's not as though it wasn't a regular event) when a Neanderthal-looking young man carrying a hammer strolled into the room.

My initial reaction was that I had been cooped up too long and had started to hallucinate.

Then Mum burst in all breathless and anxious.

It turned out that the young man had come to fit a baby intercom between my bedroom and the living-room. Mum had watched him like a hawk downstairs but when she had gone to answer the phone he had escaped and made his way to my room.

Mum rushed over and forced me out of the bed as though it was the middle of the night and she was a group of secret policemen who were about to take me away and torture me. I still have her finger marks on my arms. My God, but she'd be lethal with an electric cattle-prod.

You see, she thought that I might give the intercom man impure thoughts if he had to work in close proximity to me while I was still in my nightdress so it was a matter of acute urgency to get me moved as quickly as possible.

In addition to my displacement troubles with the

intercom man Helen never gave me a moment's peace. Most mornings she would stand in the bedroom doorway and look at me lying prostrate on my bed, and bellow, "Your breakfast is ready. And last one down the stairs is a big fat smelly pig!"

In an instant she would be gone, thundering back down the stairs to the kitchen, while I limply tried to tell her that I was a big fat smelly pig already. Therefore her challenge meant nothing to me.

Well I was big and fat, that was for sure. Very watermelonesque. Well, at least I had been when I arrived in Dublin. I couldn't be certain now as I hadn't looked in a mirror or tried on any clothes since the day I left my flat in London.

I was most certainly smelly. There was as much chance of me climbing Mount Everest as there was of me washing my hair.

I did have the occasional bath, but only because my mother organised the whole thing.

A combination of persuasion and coercion.

She would fill the bath with steaming and fragrant bubble bath so that I would smell of kiwi-fruit and papaya. She would put huge soft towels on the heated towel rail for me. She would offer me a loan of her lavender body-lotion (ugh, no thanks). She would threaten to report me to the authorities for being an unfit mother. Kate, she told me, would be put in a foster home.

So I would have a bath every day or so.

Grudgingly.

But perhaps I wasn't a pig. I honestly couldn't remember the last time I had eaten anything. I was never hungry. The thought of eating something scared the life out of me. I knew that I wouldn't be able to. I felt frozen. As if my throat was blocked up and I wouldn't ever be able to swallow anything.

I couldn't believe that this was happening to me. Because I'd always had a very robust appetite. When I was pregnant, it was better than robust, more like steel-reinforced. I spent my teenage years praying desperately to be anorexic. I had no truck with the idea that anorexics were poor, sick, misfortunate girls. I thought they were as lucky as could be, with their protruding hip-bones and their lean thighs and their waif-like air.

I never lost my appetite, no matter what the occasion. Exam nerves, job interviews, wedding day jitters, food poisoning – nothing short of death made the slightest difference to my ability to eat like a racehorse. Whenever I met a thin person who would trill, "Oh, silly old me, I simply forget to eat," I would stare at them with ill concealed bafflement and bitterness, feeling unglamorous and lumpy and bovine. The lucky bitches, I would think, how could *anyone* forget to eat. I had an appetite – what an untrendy and shameful thing to have.

Because when the world ends and we have shuffled off our mortal coils and we're all in Heaven and time ceases to exist and we are pure of spirit and have eternal life, which we will spend contemplating the Almighty, I will still need a KitKat every morning at eleven o'clock.

But I would console myself with the thought that these skinny people were probably lying through their teeth. They were really raging bulimics or taking amphetamines or having liposuction every weekend.

And now, for the first time in my life, I was not hungry. In fact I was appalled at the idea of having to eat.

I didn't care. I got no thrill out of it whatsoever. If only I had felt like this when I was seventeen. I would have thought that I was one of the chosen few.

But I was too weary and miserable to care.

The days dragged on. Sometimes I would get out of bed and take Kate downstairs to watch an Australian soap opera with Mum. I would have a cup of tea with her and then I would go back to my room.

Helen continued to plague me. Three days after the baby intercom was fitted she tiptoed very elaborately into the room. "Is that on?" she mouthed, pointing at the intercom.

"What?" I asked crossly, looking up from my copy of *Hello*. "No, of course it's not on. Why the hell would it be? Kate is here and so am I."

"Fine," she said, "fine, fine." With that she doubled over with mirth. She sat on the bed, shaking with laughter, tears ran down her face. I sat and stared at her with ill-concealed distaste.

"Sorry," she said, wiping her eyes and trying to assemble herself. "Ahem, right, sorry, sorry."

"What's going on?" I asked as Helen sat up straight.

"I'll show you now," she promised. "But you're not to make any noise."

She went over to the intercom and switched it on and started to say things into it in a croony, sing-songy type of voice. "Anna," she crooned, "ooooooohhhhhh, Aaaaaaannnnaaaaaa."

I stared in fascination. "What on earth are you doing?" I asked. "Shut up," she hissed, as she turned the intercom off. "I'm giving Anna a psychic experience, d'you see?"

"What do you mean?" I asked, totally baffled.

"That space-cadet Anna is in the living-room and she doesn't know about this intercom, so she'll think she's hearing voices," explained Helen impatiently. "Now, would you shut up."

She started with her singing and crooning again. She told Anna that she was her spirit guide and that she was to be especially nice to her sister Helen and all kinds of other stuff. She spent a good half hour kneeling on the floor, wailing and whispering into the intercom.

For several days after that, every time anyone was on their own in the living-room, Helen would come straight up the stairs and into my room, where she would spend ages telling the person that she was their subconscious or their guardian angel or whatever and that they must be especially nice to their sister/daughter/friend (tick as appropriate) Helen.

She continued to do it long after everyone knew that the disembodied voice was Helen, and blithely ignored her.

It meant that I didn't get a moment's peace.

The disappointment nearly killed poor Anna.

Still the rain bucketed down. The canal burst its banks. Roads were impassable. Cars were abandoned in flooded lanes. I heard about all these things from other people. I never left the house.

I thought about James all the time. I would dream about him. Lovely dreams where we were still together. And when I woke up I would forget, for a few minutes, where I was and what had happened. I would be bathed in a gorgeous warm fuzzy happy feeling. And then I would remember. It was like being kicked in the stomach.

I had heard nothing from him. Absolutely nothing. I really had thought that after a week or so he would contact me. Just to see how I was or at least how Kate was. I couldn't believe that he had no interest at all in Kate, whatever about me.

The saddest thing of all was that he didn't even know her name was Kate.

I rang Judy when I'd been back in Dublin about five days. I asked her if James knew where I was and held my breath. Hoping and hoping that she would say that, no, he didn't know. That would at least explain why he hadn't contacted me. But she said, sadly, that James did know. Then, though it tore me apart to do so, I asked her if James was still with Denise. Once again, she said yes.

I felt, not that I was crying inside, but that I was bleeding inside. Bleeding to death.

I thanked Judy, apologised once again for putting her in such an awkward position and hung up the phone. My hands shook, my forehead sweated, I felt sick at heart.

There were times that I felt that James really would come back, sooner or later. That he had loved me so much that he just couldn't stop loving me overnight. That it was just a matter of time before he appeared on the doorstep, distraught with remorse, beside himself with guilt, wondering if he had left it too late to reclaim his wife and child. And, in that case, that it might be an idea to get out of bed and wash my hair and put on some make-up and wear some decent clothes, in honour of his imminent arrival. But then I remembered what a contrary bastard Fate is. The more hideous I looked, the higher were the chances that James would arrive out of the blue.

So I stayed in the nightdress, the golfing jumper and the hiking socks. I wouldn't have known what lipstick was if it jumped up and bit me.

I often felt like ringing him. But it always happened in the middle of the night. I would be gripped by terrible panic at the enormity of my loss. But I had no idea how to contact him. I hadn't been able to humble myself sufficiently to ask Judy for the phone number of the flat he was sharing with Denise. I could have rung him at work during the day, but the anxiety and the desire to talk to him never really came upon me in the day-time. I was really very glad about this. What good would ringing him do? What could I say to him?

"Do you still not love me? Do you still love Denise?" To which he would reply, "No to the first question, yes to the second. Thank you for your enquiry. Goodbye."

Time passed. Slowly, very slowly, my feelings started to change. The landscape of the desert changes very gradually as little breezes lift grains of sand and move them, sometimes a few feet, sometimes miles and miles, so that at the end of the day, when the sun sets, the face of the desert is completely different from the landscape it had in the morning when the sun rose on it. In the same way, tiny little changes happened in me.

But they were nearly too small for me to notice them as they were happening.

It wasn't so much that the lead weight of hopelessness had left. But something else had arrived. Ladies and Gentlemen, put your hands together and give a warm welcome to Humiliation.

Yes, I started to feel humiliated.

What took you so long? I can hear you saying.

Well, sorry chaps, but I had a major backlog of Loss and Abandonment in my in-tray.

A little twinge of humiliation at first. An odd little feeling one day when I wondered how long Judy had known about James and Denise. That feeling expanded like a balloon until humiliation was nearly all I felt. I smarted with it. I was raw with it. My soul blushed with it.

Who had known about James having an affair? I wondered.

Had all my friends known about it and talked about it among themselves and agonised about telling me?

Did they say things like, "Oh we can't tell her now, not when she's pregnant."

Did they look at me with pity?

Did they thank God that at least they could trust their husbands or boyfriends?

Did they say to themselves, "The one thing Dave/Frank/William would never do is have an affair. He mightn't do any housework/give me enough money/ever discuss a problem, but at least he wouldn't be unfaithful."

Did they look at me and sigh huge sighs of relief and say, even while feeling guilty, "I'm so glad it's her and not me."

I was so angry. I wanted to shout at the world, "You're wrong! I thought I could trust my husband! I thought he was too goddamn *lazy* to have an affair. But he did have one. And so could Dave/Frank/William. Maybe they're already having one. Or have had one and now it's over. Maybe when your husband went to France for the rugby he had sex with someone there. You don't know. Anything is possible. Ask not for whom the bell tolls. Because let me tell you right here and now, it tolls for thee."

When I thought about Denise I cringed. When I thought about herself and myself exchanging pleasantries about the weather and me complimenting her on how well she was looking and telling her how my pregnancy was going and thinking that she was so sweet and nice, when all the time she was having sex with my husband and making him fall in love with her, I wanted to travel back in time and grab myself by the scruff of the neck and drag myself, protesting, away from the conversation with Denise and admonish myself, like a mother to a naughty child, "Don't speak to that horrible woman."

And then I wanted to get Denise and beat the living daylights out of her.

I was deeply mortified and embarrassed by the thought that everyone else knew about James and Denise when I was blissfully unaware.

I didn't want to be thought of as a victim. But I felt so pathetic. So foolish. So deeply, deeply humiliated.

I started to feel extremely angry with James.

The humiliation arrived gradually. It sidled its way in and one day I turned around and it was there, grinning at me. "Hi there," it said, all bonhomie and familiarity, as though we were old friends. "Remember me? And I'm sure my friend Jealousy needs no introduction."

I can't believe that it took three weeks for me to start feeling jealous. I had always thought that, if a man that I loved slept with someone else, jealousy would be the immediate and overwhelming feeling. But it was way down the list in this particular case, limping home furlongs behind Loss, Loneliness, Hopelessness and Humiliation.

I hadn't been so much thinking of James as being with Denise. Just more that he wasn't with me. My loss, rather than her gain.

Overnight that changed.

I was with my mother one afternoon when she put a video on. Some film that was supposed to be a romance, but it was really an excuse for pornography. She was engrossed in it, and "tut-

tutted" energetically. I tried to pay attention to it and feed Kate at the same time. I kept losing track of the plot. "Who's that he's having sex with now? Is that the woman from the lift?"

"No, silly," said Mum. "It's the woman from the lift's *daughter*."

"But I thought he was found in bed with the woman from the lift," I said, confused.

"Yes, he was," explained Mum kindly. "But he's being unfaithful to her now, with her daughter."

"The poor woman from the lift," I said sorrowfully.

Mum gave me a sharp glance. Oh God, no, I could feel her thinking in alarm. Was I going to start crying? I bet she was sorry that she didn't get out something innocuous like *The Amityville Horror* or *The Texas Chainsaw Massacre*.

I watched the two people on the screen, having sex, enjoying themselves at the cost of the woman in the lift's happiness. I suddenly thought of James and Denise in bed.

They do this, you know, a voice in my head told me.

They go to bed together. They have sex. They lose themselves in their passion for each other. She touches him. She sleeps with his beautiful body and his delicious skin and his silky black hair. She can wake up and watch him sleeping, his spiky black eyelashes throwing little shadows on his face.

What are they like together, I found myself wondering. What way does he treat her? What's he like when he's with her?

Does he gently scrape his stubbly jaw across her face, in the morning, the way he used to do to me and then laugh at my shout of outrage, his even teeth showing very white in his handsome face?

Does she go to sleep with her head on his muscular chest, her arm thrown across his stomach, his manly arm around her neck, smelling the faint scent of Tuscany from his lightly tanned skin, the way I used to?

Does he wake her in the morning by trailing his hands along her thighs, the way he used to with me, and instantly turn her on, the way he used to with me?

Does he pin her down in bed, his hands holding her arms above her head, his legs locking hers, grinning down at her, leaving her deliciously helpless as he moves slowly against her, driving her mad with desire, the way he used to with me.

Does he kiss her with an icecube in his mouth, turning her mouth cold and her body hot with desire, the way he used to with me?

Does he gently bite the curve of her neck and shoulder and send shivers of lust through her whole body, the way he used to with me?

When she wakes up in the morning is her first thought, "Jesus, he's beautiful and he's in bed with me." Because mine always was.

I was insane with jealousy.

Or do they do it differently, I wondered. Is she different from me in bed? Is she better? What's her body like? Has she a smaller bum, bigger tits, flatter stomach, longer legs? Is she really adventurous and does she drive him crazy with passion?

I wondered all this even though I knew Denise and could have answered most of those questions myself. (Smaller bum? No. Bigger tits? Yes. Flatter stomach? Unlikely. Longer legs? Hard to tell. We're probably neck and neck).

She didn't act or behave like a sex-kitten. She had always seemed so nice and well . . . *ordinary*, I suppose, but now in my head she was Helen Of Troy or Sharon Stone or Madonna.

I was being torn apart with jealousy.

It was like having a burning spiky ball in my chest that was sending out green poisonous rays all over my body, choking me so that I could barely breathe.

My head was filled with pictures of what I imagined they were like together in bed.

I just couldn't bear the idea of him desiring her. It filled me with powerful and impotent rage. And fury. I felt like killing them both. I felt like sobbing hysterically. I felt ugly with jealousy. Disfigured with it. I felt my face was twisted and green with it.

It's such an ugly emotion. And it's so utterly pointless. And it has nowhere to go.

If you lose someone or something, you feel a loss, then after a while, you fill in the hole in your life and the loss gradually gets smaller and smaller and eventually goes away. There's a point to the pain. There's a reason and a direction.

But there was nothing to be gained by me feeling jealous. And I wouldn't have minded but the jealousy was caused entirely by myself. It was my own imagination that was causing me the pain.

It was the emotional equivalent of me picking up a razor and cutting open my arm, or my stomach, or my leg. Jealousy was self-mutilation. It was as painful and as pointless.

And I was feeling the pain, not because something had happened to me, but because something hadn't happened to me. Why did something that was going on between two other people and didn't involve me in any way hurt me so much?

Well I was damned if I knew.

I just knew that it did.

Chapter Seven

The time that followed is still referred to in our house as The Great Terror. Helen alludes to it even now by saying something like "Do you remember the time when you started behaving like Adolf Hitler and we all hated you and wished that you would go back to London?"

The change in me was terrible.

It was as though someone had flicked a switch.

I went from feeling sad and lonely and miserable to explosive rage and jealousy and desire for revenge on Denise and James. I fantasised about terrible disasters befalling them.

I wasn't being offensive to anyone when I went through the phase where I spent my time lying on my bed, barely able to summon the energy to speak because my grief was so great. I was a bit boring, I suppose, and not much use for hoovering and other household chores but other than that I couldn't be faulted.

But now I was like a madman on the rampage. I had so much anger and hatred in me and the person who should have been receiving the brunt of it, i.e. James, wasn't there. So my family, who were innocent bystanders, who, in fact, were trying to help me, ended up being shouted at and having their doors slammed in his stead.

When I first returned from London there was a dignity to my suffering. I felt a bit like a Victorian heroine who had been disappointed in love and had no choice but to turn her face to the wall and die, albeit beautifully, surrounded by smelling salts, from her grief. Like Michelle Pfeiffer in *Dangerous Liaisons*.

Now I was more like Christopher Walken in *The Deerhunter*. Psychotic. Crazed. A danger to myself and others. Walking round the house with a mad look in my eyes. Rooms full of conversation falling silent when I entered them. Mum and Dad watching me fearfully. Anna and Helen leaving rooms when I arrived.

I wasn't wearing battle camouflage and didn't have a belt of bullets slung across my chest and wasn't carrying some kind of fearsome looking automatic weapon and didn't have a grenade in my pocket. My face wasn't smeared with dirt (although on reflection it might have been. The baths went by the board completely during this terrible time). But I felt as powerful as if I had all those things and I was treated with as much fear as if I did have them.

The Great Terror started the day I watched that video with Mum. (I won't go into the details of what happened there. I'm too ashamed of myself. And anyway the video shop agreed to drop the charges. It was totally true what the assistant said. They only stock the videos. It was no reflection on their personal opinions or morals. I was just a little bit overwrought at the time).

The Great Terror continued for several war-torn

days. Anything could trigger a tantrum in me, but especially romantic scenes on the television. My head constantly played a video of James and Denise in bed together. When I saw other loving couples on television I was pushed to overload.

Luckily I saw no loving couples in real life or I might not have been responsible for my actions. Mum and Dad certainly didn't behave like a loving couple. The most romantic thing my father said to my mother from one end of the week to the next was, "Will we go to the Freezer Centre on Thursday evening?"

Helen had a steady stream of young suitors through the house but she made cruel, teasing fun of them and their puppy-like devotion. Which pleased me in a grim, cold kind of way. As for Anna, well that's another story, to be told another day.

I cried an awful lot during this time. And swore. And threw things.

As I said, television usually upset me. I'd see a man lean over and kiss a woman and immediately the green fire of jealousy would rush through me, excruciating energy would fill me. I would think of James. And I would think of my James with another woman. For a second it would just be a thought in the abstract, as if he was still with me and I was being silly and imagining "worst possible" scenarios. And then I would remember that it *had* happened, and that he *was* with another woman. The realisation hurt just as much each time. The tenth time it happened it was as awful and as shocking and as sick-making as the first time.

So I might throw a book at the television, or some shoes at the wall, or Kate's bottle at the window. Or really anything handy or close by at all would be thrown at a nearby surface. Then I would eff and blind like a fishwife and stomp from the room, slamming the door so hard that slates probably fell of the roof. It got so bad that when I thumped into the sitting-room and the television was on, Anna or Helen, or whoever was there, would flick the remote control and quickly change the channel from whatever they were watching to something inoffensive like The Open University programme on applied physics, or a documentary about how fridges work or a gameshow where all the contestants had obviously had lobotomies. (An example of their stupidity, "What's the capital of Haiti?", "Em, would it be 'H'?"

"What's on?" I would growl at them.

"Oh, err . . . , just this," they would reply nervously, indicating the television with a flutter of their hands.

We would all sit there in silence, pretending to watch whatever programme the remote control had found for us, me giving off palpably frightening vibes, Anna or Helen or Mum or Dad sitting stiffly, afraid to talk, afraid to suggest changing channels and wait for a decent interval to elapse so they could leave and continue watching their programme on the small television in Mum's room.

And when they would get up and start sidling to the door, I'd pounce on them. "Where are you going?" I'd demand. "You can't even bear to be in the

113

same room as me, can you? It's bad enough that my husband has to leave me but imagine my own family treating me like this."

The poor victim would stand there awkwardly, feeling shamed into not leaving but definitely not wanting to stay.

And hating me for it.

"Well, go on then," I'd tell them viciously. "Go."

Because I was so terrifying no one, not even Helen, had the courage to tell me that I was being incredibly selfish and, in the vernacular, a right little bitch. I held the whole family to ransom with my wild tempers and unpredictable mood-swings.

Kate was the only one I treated with any respect. And even that only happened occasionally.

Once when she started crying I shouted sharply at her, "Shut up Kate!" Quite unbelievably, she stopped immediately. The silence that followed sounded almost stunned. Try as I might I haven't been able to reproduce that tone of voice since. I've practised with all kinds of different inflections, like "Shut *up* Kate," or "Shut up *Kate*," or, "*Shut* up Kate," but it makes no difference. She blithely continues to bellow, no doubt thinking "Ha! You might have frightened me once, for about a nano-second, but you can be damn sure it won't happen again."

I had so much energy. My body wasn't big enough to contain all the energy that flowed through me. I went from having no energy to having far too much of it. I had no idea what to do with it. I felt as if I was going to explode with it. Or go mad with it. I was torn because I didn't want to leave the house but

I felt as if I could run a hundred miles. That I would go crazy if I didn't. I had the strength of ten men. During those awful couple of weeks I could have won gold medals in the Olympic games in any sport you care to mention.

I felt that I could run faster, jump higher, throw farther, lift heavier, punch harder than anyone alive.

That first night that the jealousy kicked in, I drank half a bottle of vodka.

I bullied Anna into loaning me fifteen pounds for it and Helen into going to the off licence for it.

Anna would have willingly gone to the off licence for me.

And Anna would have willingly come back from the off licence for me.

But when, is the question.

She might have reappeared in a week with some vague story about how on the way to the off licence she met some people in a transit van who were going to Stonehenge and how she thought it might be nice to join them. Or how she had some strange out-of-body experience and lost a week.

I could have told her that there was nothing strange about it. That if she went over to her boyfriend Shane's flat and smoked a lot of drugs that was what generally happened. And that the correct name for it was an out-of-your-head experience, not an out-of-body experience.

Not that it was an easy battle to win with Helen. "I'll drown," she grumbled, the weather still being inclement.

"You won't," I assured her grimly, through gritted teeth, my tone of voice implying, "But it would be no trouble at all to arrange."

"It'll cost you," she told me, changing tack.

"How much?"

"A fiver."

"Give her another fiver," I ordered Anna.

Money changed hands.

"That's twenty that you owe me now," said Anna anxiously.

"Have I ever reneged on my debts before?" I asked Anna coldly.

"Er, no," said the poor girl, far too frightened to remind me that I still owed her for the bottle of wine that I "borrowed" from her first night that I was home.

"And where are you going?" I asked Helen imperiously.

"Upstairs to change into my Speedos."

When Helen returned from the off licence, a long time later, drenched wet and dripping water everywhere and complaining loudly, she handed me the litre bottle of vodka, which was in a soaking wet bag.

Change from the fifteen pounds was not asked for.

Nor was it offered.

By the time I discovered that the bottle had already been opened and about a quarter of it was missing, Helen was long gone.

As were her chances of making it alive to her nineteenth birthday.

My vengeance would be a terrible and awesome spectacle to behold, once I got my hands on her.

I was not a woman to be trifled with.

In spite of the vodka I still couldn't sleep. I roamed the house from room to room late at night when everyone else was asleep. Carrying the bottle and my glass. Looking for somewhere that I felt safe. Hoping to find a place where those horrible pictures would stop running through my head. But my jealousy and hatred kept me awake. It kept prodding at me and I couldn't settle to anything. I couldn't find any peace.

In desperation, I thought that perhaps if I tried a different bed or a different room that I might be able to sleep.

I went into Rachel's old room. (You know, the room that you'll be staying in when you come on your starvation week). I turned on the light.

The room had that same ghostly feeling that my and Margaret's room had had when I first arrived back from London. The feeling that no one had slept in there for a long time. Although clothes still hung in the wardrobe and posters were still on the wall and a plate was still under the bed.

I came across the exercise bike and the rowing machine that Dad had bought about nine years ago in an enthusiastic but short-lived attempt to get fit.

There they were, on the floor of Rachel's room, covered in dust, looking old-fashioned and creaky and cobwebby, a far cry from the exercise bikes and rowing machines of today, with their computer programmes, their video screens and their electronic calorie counters.

I looked at them affectionately, prehistoric and all

that they were, and memories came rushing back in waves.

The excitement the day the van delivered them!

Dad, my sisters and I were thrilled.

Mum was the only one who wasn't excited. She said that she couldn't understand what all the fuss was about.

That she had no need to go courting pain and suffering. That she already had a surfeit of that in her life, what with being married to Dad and mother to the five of us.

The rest of us were beside ourselves.

We all clustered round oohing and aahing as the chrome and metal machines were unloaded and installed in the conservatory.

We all held great hopes and high expectations from the machines. As we thought that we would have bodies like Jamie Lee Curtis (she was very *in* then) from the briefest contact with them, naturally demand to use them was high.

Dad also said that he wanted a body like Jamie Lee Curtis. Mum didn't speak to him for a week.

We all jostled and fought to use the machines in the beginning.

Like a wartime munitions production line they were in use round the clock.

There were always queues.

And let's just say people didn't always behave honourably and respect the queueing system. All manner of gazumping and gazundering going on.

More than one tear was shed and more than one harsh word was spoken in the pitched battles about who was next.

We especially loved the bike. Margaret, Rachel and I were obsessed with the size of our bums and thighs.

There wasn't that much interest in the rowing machine because we were so young that we hadn't even realised that people get fat upper arms.

Margaret and Rachel and I spent the best part of our teenage years standing with our backs to full-length mirrors, almost breaking our respective necks as we tried to swivel our heads round without moving our bodies to see what our bums looked like from the back.

Asking each other anxiously, "What does my bum look like? Really big or just mediumly big?"

We wasted so much time torturing ourselves and worrying about the size of our bums.

Every pair of jeans that we ever bought or tried on had to be assessed for its bum-reducing qualities. Every shirt or jumper or jacket was similarly appraised to see how good it was at covering said bum.

The obsession with the largeness of our bums was matched in intensity only by the obsession with the smallness of our chests.

It was so sad!

Because we were beautiful.

We had such lovely figures.

And we had no idea.

Rachel used often to say that she wished that she had lived in olden times. Around the time of the famine, to be precise. She once said wistfully to me, "Imagine how skinny we'd be if we had to live on stones and grass for a few months."

I'd have paid very large sums of money indeed to have the body that I had then.

And then that made me think in alarm, "Jesus, will a day come when I look back at the body I have today and wish that I still had it?"

Maybe I should have started to enjoy the way I looked, bad and all as I thought it was. Because one day I'd wish I looked like that again.

Although I couldn't possibly imagine ever being that desperate.

Naturally the novelty with the exercise bike and the rowing machine wore off very quickly. A combination of accidents and disappointed expectations.

Although Helen was only nine, she decided that she alone knew how the rowing machine worked. She assembled us all for a demonstration. To impress us, she set the weights far too high and then attempted to lift them without doing any warm-up exercises. She promptly pulled a muscle in her chest.

And caused an almighty fuss.

The poor creatures who suffered at the hands of the Spanish Inquisition didn't screech and carry on as much as Helen did.

She claimed to be paralysed down one side, the only thing that relieved any of her symptoms was huge quantities of chocolate and round-the-clock attention.

Helen was Helen from a very early age.

According to her the pain was unbearable. She asked Dr Blenheim to put her out of her misery. The rest of us also found her pain unbearable and agreed that she should indeed be put out of her misery.

But Dr Blenheim said there was some kind of law

against doing this.

Murder or wilful manslaughter or something I believe he called it.

Dad assured him that we preferred to call it a mercy killing.

A mercy for the rest of us, that is.

And what's more, that we wouldn't report him, but Dr Blenheim still couldn't be persuaded to do it.

And, as none of the rest of us ended up looking even remotely like Jamie Lee Curtis, in spite of all our exertions, we felt a little bit let-down and disappointed and decided to get our own back on the bike by ignoring it.

After a while even Dad stopped pretending to use the machines. He muttered something vague about having read an article in *Cosmopolitan* about too much exercise being as bad for you as none at all.

I had read the article in question myself. It was actually about compulsive exercisers, truly sick people, people who were nothing at all like Dad.

But as far as Dad was concerned he had a cast iron excuse. He was perfectly justified in abandoning the bike and the rowing machine.

He used the *Cosmopolitan* defence whenever Mum made a lot of noise about how much the machines had cost and how she had never wanted him to buy them and how she had predicted that this was exactly what would happen etc.

So the two machines were sadly discarded and left to gather dust, along with the pink leg-warmers and pink and blue twisted sweatbands that we bought to look good on them.

In fact Margaret and I had even bought Dad a pair of pink legwarmers and a sweatband. He wore them once to entertain us. I think there's still a photograph of it round somewhere.

So I was very surprised when I almost tripped over the bike and the rowing machine in Rachel's room.

I hadn't seen them in years. I had thought that they would have long ago been exiled to the Siberia that is the garage along with the SpaceHopper, the pogo sticks, the roller skates, the skateboards, the game of Kerplunk!, the Trivial Pursuit, the swing-ball, the squash rackets, the clackers, the Chopper bikes, the Teach Yourself Spanish tapes, the mini-bridge, the fibreglass canoe and the thousands of other toys and diversions that enjoyed a period of brief but fierce popularity, not to mention causing countless rows, in our family before they fell from favour and their appeal faded and they were cast into the outer darkness, to live with the coal and the lawnmower and the screwdrivers.

I was very glad to see them.

If a bit taken aback.

They were like old friends that I hadn't seen in years and that I had bumped into somewhere totally unexpectedly.

I can see now with the benefit of hindsight what I really needed was a punchbag. So that I could have worked off some of the terrible anger that I felt towards James and Denise.

But in the absence of a punchbag, and the fact that the current legislation forbade me from using

Helen's head, the discovery of the bike and the rowing machine was a Godsend.

I somehow realised that a little bit of physical exercise might be the one thing that would stop me going round the bend and exploding with jealousy and resentment.

Either that or vast quantities of alcohol.

So I put down my bottle and my glass on Rachel's dressing-table and climbed up on the bike, tucking the nightdress under me. Yes, I was still wearing one of Mum's nightdresses. Not the same nightdress that I started wearing the night I arrived back. Things hadn't got that bad. I hadn't sunk that low. But a nightdress that was definitely from the same stable.

Feeling a bit foolish (but not that foolish. After all, I had a half bottle of vodka under my belt) I started to cycle. And while the rest of the house slept I cycled and sweated. And then for a while I rowed and sweated. And then I got back on the bike again and cycled and sweated a bit more.

While James slumbered peacefully somewhere in London, his arm thrown protectively over Denise, I cycled like a madman, in a bedroom that still had posters of Don Johnson on the wall, hot, angry tears pouring down my puce face.

I couldn't help but feel sorry for myself at the poignant juxtaposition.

Every time I pictured the two of them in bed together I cycled even faster, as though if I cycled hard enough I'd get away from the pain.

When I thought of her touching his beautiful

naked body I would get another spurt of furious sickening energy and I pushed my body even harder.

I was afraid that I would kill someone if I stopped cycling.

I hadn't exercised in months, had done nothing strenuous in ages (apart from give birth to a child) but I didn't get tired or even get out of breath.

The harder I pushed myself the easier it got.

I felt as if my thigh muscles were made of steel (and they definitely weren't, let me assure you).

The pedals whizzed round in a blur. I felt as if my legs were lubricated, they worked so easily. It was as if someone had oiled my joints.

I cycled faster and faster until eventually the tight hard knot in my chest started to unravel. A feeling of calm settled on me.

I was able to breathe almost normally.

When I eventually clambered down from the bike, the handlebars slippery from my sweat, my nightdress sticking to me, I felt nearly elated.

I went back into my room and lay down.

Kate eyed my scarlet face and my soaking nightdress, but didn't seem particularly interested.

I put my burning face on the cool pillow and knew that now I would be able to sleep.

I woke up very early the next morning. I even beat Kate to it. In fact in a neat reversal of roles I woke her up with the sound of me crying.

"Now you see what it's like," I thought as I sobbed. "Is it any way to start the day?"

The spectres of jealousy and anger returned.

They had stood over me as I slept, looking down

at me. "Should we wake her now?" one consulted the other.

"All right," said Jealousy. "Would you like to do it?"

"Oh no, why don't you?" said Anger politely.

"It would be my pleasure," said Jealousy graciously. Then grabbed me roughly by the shoulder and shook me awake.

And I woke to the horrible picture in my head of James in bed with Denise.

The bitter rage was back, coursing through me like poison.

So while I fed Kate, I finished the rest of the vodka and then went back into Rachel's room and got back up on the exercise bike.

If there was any justice in the world I should have been as stiff as a poker after my exertions the previous night. But the one thing that I had learnt over the past month was that there wasn't any.

Justice, that is.

So I wasn't as stiff as a poker.

I spent the next week or so eaten up by anger and jealousy. I hated James and Denise. I terrorised my family without even realising that I was doing it. And when things got too much for me I climbed aboard the bike and tried to cycle away some of my terrible rage. I also drank far too much.

I owed Anna a fortune.

Helen was charging me extortionate amounts for going to the off licence for me.

And the forces of supply and demand dictated that I had no choice but to pay her.

I was a buyer in a seller's market.

She had me, so to speak, over a barrel.

I could either pay her or go myself.

And I couldn't face leaving the house yet.

Therefore I paid her.

Or rather, because I had no hard cash myself, Anna did.

I had every intention of paying Anna back, but in my own time. I wasn't particularly worried about the impact I was having on Anna's cashflow.

But I should have been.

I mean, she was only on the dole.

And she had a mid-weight to heavy drug habit to support.

But I only cared about myself.

I was kind of half-drunk most of the time. I thought that I'd numb the pain and anger by getting drunk. But it didn't really help. I just felt sort of lost and confused. And then when I sobered up, in the few minutes it would take for me to drink my next drink and for the effects to hit me, I would feel horribly depressed. Really, really bad.

I never thought I'd hear myself say it but drink really isn't the answer.

Drugs, maybe.

But not drink.

It was only when I accidentally overheard a conversation between Mum, Helen and Anna that I realised how awful I was being.

I was just about to go into the kitchen when I caught the sleeve of my jumper (well, *Dad's* jumper) on the knob on the cabinet in the hall.

While I extricated myself I heard Helen talking in the kitchen.

"She's such a bitch," Helen was complaining. "And we're afraid to watch anything on telly that has people kissing in it or anything, in case she goes ballistic."

Who were they talking about, I wondered, but perfectly prepared to join in the character assassination, no matter who the unfortunate person was. That's how mean and bitter I was.

"Yes," Anna said, joining in, "I mean, yesterday when we were watching telly she threw the vase that I made for you for Christmas at the door, just because Sheila told Scott that she loved him."

"Did she?" asked Mum, sounding outraged.

I realised, with a shock, that they were talking about me. Well, it must have been me. I was the one that had thrown that horrible vase at the door.

The bloody cheek of them!

I stood quietly at the door and continued to eavesdrop like the horrible person that I had become.

"I really can't believe it," Mum went on, sounding shaken to the core. "And what had Scott to say about that?"

"Oh Mum, can't you forget about *Down Drongo Way* for five minutes," said Helen sounding like she was going to cry with frustration. "This is serious. Claire is behaving like a monster."

Well, maybe I am but I learnt everything I know from you, my dear, I thought, acidly.

"It's nearly like she's possessed!" continued Helen.

"Do you think she might be?" asked Anna with

127

great excitement, obviously ready to whip out her Filofax and give them the name of a good exorcist ("I hear he's great. All my friends use him").

"Look girls," said Mum gently, "she's been through an awful lot."

Yes, I bloody well have, I silently agreed, standing frozen at the door.

"So have a bit of sympathy. Try and have a little bit of patience. You can't imagine how awful she must feel."

No, you most certainly can't, I mutely concurred.

A silence followed.

Good, I thought, that's shamed them.

"She broke your Aynsley ashtray last night," mumbled Helen.

"She did what?!" said Mum sharply.

"Yes, she did," confirmed Anna.

You quisling! I thought.

"Right," said Mum decisively. "She's gone far enough."

"Ha!" said Helen triumphantly, obviously speaking to Anna. "I told you that Mum hated that crappy old vase that you made for her. I knew she was only pretending to like it. Why else would she not care about Claire throwing it at the door, but she did care about her Aynsley ashtray?"

Time I left, I thought.

I quietly went back upstairs, feeling shaken.

A strange feeling had come over me.

I later looked it up in my emotional reference book, and identified it.

There could be no doubt about it.

It was definitely Shame.

Later that evening, while I was lying on my bed drinking cider, I had a visit from my Dad.

I was expecting it.

This is what used to happen whenever I misbehaved when I was younger. Mum would discover the indiscretion or misdeed or wrongdoing or whatever.

She would then send in the heavy guns by telling Dad.

He knocked quietly and then stuck his head round my bedroom door, looking distinctly sheepish.

It was a long time since he had had to do this. No doubt Mum was behind him, in the landing with an electric cattle-prod, hissing "Get in there and tell her. Put the fear of God in her. She won't listen to me. She's afraid of you."

"Hello Claire, can I come in?" he asked.

"Sit down Dad," I said indicating the bed, and hastily stashing the half-drunk bottle of extra-strong cider in my bedside locker.

"Hello, my favourite grandchild," he said to Kate.

I didn't catch her reply.

"Well!" he said, trying to be jovial.

"Well," I agreed dryly. I was not making this easy for him.

I was feeling a horrible mixture of feelings. A combination of shame, mortification, embarrassment at my childish behaviour, defensiveness at being told off, resentment at being treated like a child and a realisation that it was time that I stopped behaving like a selfish bitch.

Dad sat down heavily on the bed, crushing an empty beer can that he hadn't noticed nestling in the duvet.

He retrieved it from under him and held it up to me sadly.

"What's this?" he asked me.

What does it look like, I felt like asking him, feeling all guilty and fifteen again.

"It's a beer can, Dad," I mumbled.

"Imagine how this makes your mother feel," he said, going for the guilt jugular. "You lying in bed and drinking beer on your own and during the day."

That's nothing, I thought in alarm, hoping to God that he didn't suddenly fling himself on the floor and notice the two empty vodka bottles under the bed.

I was overcome with panic and shame. I could barely wait for him to leave. The poor man didn't know the half of it. I had to get rid of the two bottles before he did the hoovering on Friday. He would be bound to come across them then.

But then again, maybe he wouldn't.

Brevity seemed to be his by-word when it came to the hoovering.

No such thing as moving objects, like chairs for example, and cleaning under them.

Or even objects like books or shoes if I was to be honest with you.

Or even tissues or safety pins, if I was to be completely frank.

He came from the "why clean under it when you can just clean around it" school.

Out of Dad's sight, out of Dad's mind.

What the eye didn't see, the hoover didn't grieve for, as it were.

So perhaps the empty vodka bottles could slumber peacefully under the bed and remain undisturbed and undiscovered for decades.

But nevertheless I decided that I was going to throw them out anyway.

I was ashamed and mortified by the way I had been behaving. I was being selfish and irresponsible.

"You're being selfish and irresponsible," said Dad.

"I know," I mumbled.

I felt sick with guilt.

And what kind of mother was I being to Kate?

"And what kind of mother are you being to Kate?" he asked.

"A crap one," I mumbled.

The poor child, I thought, it's bad enough that her father has abandoned her.

"The poor child," said Dad. "It's bad enough that her father has abandoned her."

I really wished this mental echoing would stop.

"Drink never drowns anyone's sorrows," sighed Dad. "It only teaches them how to swim."

You might think that this was a very profound and true thing that he'd just said.

So did I.

The first eight hundred times I heard it.

But now I recognise it for what it really is. It's the first line, the opening paragraph, in Dad's "The Evils of Drink" lecture.

I heard it so many times in my teenage years that I could practically recite it myself.

It's a mug's game, I thought.

"It's a mug's game," said Dad sadly.

And God knows, I don't want to end up like Auntie Julia.

"And, God knows, you don't want to end up like Aunt Julia," said Dad, wearily.

Poor Dad, Auntie Julia was his youngest sister and he had to bear the brunt of most of her alcohol-related crises.

When she would lose her job because she was drunk at work, the first thing she did was to ring Dad.

When she got knocked down by a bicycle because she was wandering the road drunk late at night who did the police ring?

That's right.

Dad.

It's money down the drain, I thought.

"And it's money down the drain," he said heavily.

Money I don't have.

"Money you don't have," he continued.

And it'll destroy my health.

"And it'll destroy your health," he advised.

It'll ruin my looks.

"It solves nothing," he concluded.

Wrong! He forgot to tell me that it'll ruin my looks. I'd better remind him.

"And it'll ruin my looks," I reminded him gently.

"Oh yes," he said hurriedly. "And it'll ruin your looks."

"Dad, I'm sorry for everything," I told him. "I know I've been really mean to everyone and a worry to you all, but I'll stop. I promise."

"Good girl," he gave me a little smile.

I felt as if I was about three and a half all over again.

"I know it can't be easy for you," he said.

"It's still no excuse to behave like a bitch," I admitted.

We sat in silence for a few minutes.

The only sounds were of Kate snoring happily – maybe she was as glad as everyone else that I'd had my comeuppance – and me sniffing back tears.

"And you'll let the girls watch their programmes on the telly?" Dad enquired.

"Of course," I snivelled.

"And you'll stop shouting at us all?" he asked.

"I will," I said hanging my head.

"And you won't throw any more things?"

"I won't throw any more things."

"You're a good girl, you know." He half-smiled at me. "No matter what your mother and your sisters say."

Chapter Eight

After Dad had given me my pep talk the previous evening he kissed me – awkwardly mind you – but it was still a kiss, and without being able to look me in the eyes he told me he loved me.

Then he gently shook Kate's soft pink little foot and left the room.

And I lay on my bed for a long time thinking about what he had said. And what I had overheard Mum and my sisters saying earlier.

And some kind of change came over me.

Some kind of peace entered my soul.

Life goes on.

Even my life.

I had spent the last month releasing myself on my own recognisance from life. The excessive sleeping, the drinking, the exercising, the not washing myself. They were all things I had used to keep life at bay.

Because living without James and with rejection was just too terrible.

I didn't want my life.

Well, not that version of it anyway.

So I had decided to do without a life altogether.

But life was an irrepressible kind of a chap and no matter how much I tried to pretend that he wasn't there he kept poking his head through any gaps in my defences and trying to get me to play with him.

"Oh *there* you are," he would say exuberantly, as bouncy as a rubber ball, as I lay on my bed alone drinking vodka and orange, the ever-present copy of *Hello* by my side, "I've been looking everywhere for you. Hey, that doesn't look like much fun. Come with me and we'll find some other people and have a conversation and a bit of a laugh."

"Oh fuck off and leave me alone," I would reply. "I'm fine as I am. I don't want to talk to anyone else. But as I'm talking to you could you get me a bottle of Smirnoff if you're passing an off licence."

But after Dad's talk I decided that I had to start living again.

And I had to stop thinking just of myself.

I had to do it.

And I would be able to do it.

I still loved James very much. I still wanted him back. I was still heartbroken. I still missed him like a limb. I would probably still cry myself to sleep every night for the next century.

But I was no longer crippled by my loss.

I had been cracked across the ankles by the cricket-bat of James's infidelity and betrayal. It had sent me crashing to the ground, leaving me lying there gasping with pain, unable to stand up.

But I was only bruised.

Badly, mind.

But, contrary to first impressions, nothing was broken. Now I was clambering painfully to my feet and seeing if I could still walk.

And, though I was limping badly, I discovered to my joy that I could.

I'm not saying that I didn't feel jealous. Or angry. Because I did.

But it wasn't so bad. The feeling wasn't as big. Wasn't as powerful. Wasn't as horrible.

Put it this way. I still wouldn't have turned down the chance to punch Denise in the stomach or to blacken James's eye but I no longer entertained fantasies of sneaking into their secret love nest and pouring a huge vat of boiling oil over their sleeping bodies.

Believe me, this was progress.

So bloodied and bowed, but not *as* bowed, I decided to relaunch myself on the world with the minimum of fanfare.

As I drifted off to sleep I counted my blessings.

Well, that's not exactly true. I didn't actually *count* them. I didn't say to myself "well that's five blessings that I have. Now I can go to sleep happy."

But I did think about the good things in my life. And this was a radical and major departure from the way I had been thinking for the past month.

I had a beautiful daughter.

I had a loving family. Well, I was sure they'd be loving again just as soon as I stopped behaving like an anti-Christ.

I was still youngish.

I had somewhere to live.

I had a job to go back to in five months.

I had my health (Bizarre – I never thought I'd hear myself say that this side of ninety).

And most of all, and I'd no idea where it came from, but I had some hope.

I slept like a baby.

Actually I did nothing of the sort.

Did I wake every two hours roaring like a train, demanding to be fed or changed? No I did not.

But I slept very peacefully.

And that was plenty to be going on with.

I would love to be able to tell you that the next morning when I woke up the rain had stopped and the clouds had been chased away and the sun had come out on a brand new blue-skied day.

The sunny day reflecting my sunny mood, if you will.

The black rain clouds gone, just like my black gloom clouds, as it were.

I think there may even be a song about it.

However real life isn't like that.

It was still drizzling.

But what the hell.

I woke at the usual crack-of-dawn time and fed Kate.

I gently probed my feelings, the way you probe the gum around a sore tooth with your tongue. And I was delighted to discover that my mood hadn't changed from the previous evening. I was still feeling alive and hopeful.

It was absolutely thrilling.

I went back to sleep and woke again at about eleven. There was a bit of a fuss going on in the shower room. Apparently Helen had discovered a lump on her breast and was screaming blue murder.

Mum came running up the stairs and after a consultation I heard her telling Helen angrily, "Helen, that's not a lump on your breast, that *is* your breast."

Mum thumped back down the stairs muttering to herself. "Frightening the life out of me, putting the heart crossways on me like that . . . I'll kill her."

Helen got dressed and left for college.

And I had a shower.

I even washed my hair.

And then I tidied my room.

I fished the two empty vodka bottles out from under the bed. And picked up the empty cans of extra strong cider and the cartons of orange juice and I put them all in a plastic bag for the rubbish.

Next I rounded up all the glasses I had used over the past couple of weeks and assembled them in military formation to be brought downstairs to the dishwasher. I picked up the pieces of the glass I had broken by flinging it at the wall one particularly upset and drunken night and wrapped the shards in an old newspaper.

And most symbolic of all I threw out every copy of *Hello* in the room.

Several hundred "sumptuous" homes condemned to the rubbish in one fell swoop.

I felt cleansed and purified.

I no longer wanted to read crappy magazines. I would put myself on a strict diet of *Time*, *The Economist* and *The Financial Times* from now on.

And just once in a while I would glance at the copy of *Marie Claire* that Dad bought every month, ostensibly for Helen and Anna, but which he really bought for himself.

He absolutely loved it. Although he dismissed it as womanly rubbish. Frequently we would stumble upon him surreptitiously reading it. While he neglected his household chores, I might add.

Often he would be found engrossed in some article, maybe about female circumcision or compulsive sexual behaviour or the best methods of removing the hair from one's legs, while the carpets remained unhoovered.

Finally, after mulling it over for about a month I decided that I would get dressed.

And would you believe it when I tried on the pair of James's jeans that I had worn over on the plane from London they no longer fitted me.

What I mean is they were far too *big*.

That's what living on a diet of vodka and orange for a month does for you.

(But don't try this at home.)

So I went into Helen's room to raid her wardrobe.

Because, by God, she owed me.

She'd bled me dry over the past two weeks or so with her extortionate demands for "expenses" for going to the off licence for me.

Fond and all as I was of Anna I didn't want to wear one of her long shapeless frocks, all bells and mirrors and tassles.

In Helen's room, on her chair, along with a huge mound of pristine, totally untouched, very expensive textbooks I found a lovely pair of leggings.

Very flattering. They made my legs look long and slim.

Never mind flattering.

Downright miraculous, more like.

If the man who made them ever wanted to be canonised I'd rate his chances highly.

In her wardrobe I found a beautiful blue silk shirt.

And would you believe that was very flattering also. It made my skin look very clear and my eyes look very blue.

I looked at myself in the mirror and got a shock of recognition.

"Hey, I know her," I thought. "It's me. I'm back."

For the first time in months my reflection looked normal. I didn't look like a watermelon with legs because I was no longer either great with child or as fat as a fool. And I didn't look like some kind of escapee from a mental institution, all uncombed hair and voluminous nightdress and deranged aspect.

It was just me, the way I remembered myself.

I drenched myself in Helen's Obsession, even though I hated it and, after satisfying myself that there was nothing else of hers that I could help myself to, I went back to my room.

I even put on some make-up. Just a little bit.

I didn't want Mum ringing the police to report a strange woman intruder on the premises.

Then I leaned over Kate's cot and introduced the new me (or rather the old me) to her.

"Hello darling," I cooed. "Say hello to Mummy."

Before I could apologise to her for looking such a mess for the first month of her life, she started to scream crying.

She obviously had no idea who I was.

I didn't look or smell anything like the person she was used to.

I shushed her and calmed her down. I explained to her that this was actually the real me and the other woman who had been looking after her for the past month was an evil impersonation of her mother.

She seemed to find this a reasonable enough explanation.

And then I went downstairs to see Mum who was watching television.

"Hi Mum," I said, as I came into the sitting-room.

"Hello love," she said glancing up from *Home and Away*.

Then she swivelled round doing a double take that nearly gave her whiplash.

"Claire!" she exclaimed. "You're up! you're dressed! You look beautiful. Isn't this great!" And she got up from the couch and came over to me and gave me a huge hug. She looked so happy.

I hugged her back and the two of us stood there like idiots, grinning, with tears in our eyes.

"I think I'm getting over it," I said shakily to her. "At least I think I'm starting to get over it. And I'm sorry for being such a bitch. And I'm sorry for worrying you all so much."

"You know you don't have to apologise," she said gently, still holding me by the arms and smiling into my eyes. "We know it's been awful for you. And we just want you to be happy."

"Thanks Mum," I whispered.

"So what are you going to do today then?" she asked cheerfully.

"Well, I think I'll watch the end of this with you," I said indicating the television. "And then I'm going to cook the dinner for all of us this evening."

"That's very nice of you Claire," said Mum a bit doubtfully. "But we all know how to work the microwave."

"No, no," I protested laughing. "I mean I'm going to actually cook a real dinner for you all. As in, you know, go to the supermarket and buy fresh ingredients and make something from scratch."

"Oh really," said my mother and a faraway look came into her eyes. "It's a long time since a real dinner was cooked in that kitchen."

She said it in the manner that some wise ancient old crone from a legend might say, "Oh it be many a long and luckless year since a tall strong young man from the McQuilty clan broke bread under the same roof as a young man from the McBrandawn clan that we didn't hear the clash of steel on steel, and the streets didn't run with the blood of brave young warriors," – or something similar.

It was on the tip of my tongue to say that a real dinner had *never* been cooked in that kitchen, at least not while it was the ancestral family home of the Walsh clan, and while Mum was at the helm of the nourishment ship, but I stopped myself from saying it just in time.

"It's no big deal Mum," I told her. "I'll just do some pasta or something."

"Pasta," she breathed, still with the faraway look in her eyes, as if recalling another life, another time, another world. "Yes," she nodded, some kind of recognition appearing in her eyes. "Yes, I remember pasta." (She was still using the sort of voice where you would expect her to say "aye" instead of "yes".)

"Jesus!" I thought in alarm. "Has she been so traumatised in the past by her encounters with cooking that this suggestion has unhinged her totally?"

"So is it all right if I borrow the car to go down to the shopping centre to buy some stuff?" I asked her, feeling a bit nervous about it.

"If you must," she said faintly, resignedly. "If you must."

"And can I borrow some money? I've only got Sterling," I asked her.

"They take credit cards," she replied quickly. The mention of money had returned her abruptly from whatever twilight world she had been inhabiting for the last few minutes.

It's not that she's stingy, you understand. Far from it. But years of struggling to feed five children and two adults on a limited budget makes for good husbandry. Being careful with money is a hard habit to break.

Or at least so I was told.

I actually had had no first hand experience of it.

She gave me the car keys and we put Kate on the back seat in her cot.

Mum stood on the step and waved me off as if I was going away forever, instead of just down the road to Superquinn.

But it was a bit of an adventure. I hadn't left the house in weeks. It was an indication that I was on the mend.

"Have a good time," she said. "And remember, if you change your mind about making the dinner, don't worry. No harm done. You won't be letting any of us down. We can have the usual. No one will mind."

Why did I get the idea that she didn't want me to cook anything, I wondered as I drove away.

I had a really lovely time in the supermarket, strolling the aisles, pushing my trolley, with Kate in a sling on my front. Buying the provisions for myself and my child, playing happy families, even if it happens to be happy single-parent families.

I bought another twenty tons of Pampers for Kate. Mum and Dad had been so good buying all the baby provisions while I had been prostrate with either grief or alcohol. But it was time for me to be responsible. I would be the one who took care of Kate from now on.

I flung all kinds of frivolous and exotic food into my trolley. Galia melons? Yes, I'll have a couple of them. A box of hand-made fresh cream chocolates? Why not. A bag of highly overpriced glamorous lettuces? Go right ahead.

I was having a great time.

Hang the expense. Because I was going to pay by credit card.

And where did the credit card bills get sent to?

That's correct. My flat in London.

So who was going to have the responsibility of paying it?

Right again.

James.

I smiled at other young and not-so-young mothers who were also doing their shopping.

I must have seemed just like one of them. A young woman with a new baby. With absolutely nothing to worry about except perhaps the possibility of not getting a full night's sleep in the next decade. There was nothing to indicate that my husband had left me.

I no longer carried my humiliation like a weapon.

And I didn't resent anyone else their perfect life. I didn't hate every other woman in the world whose husbands hadn't left them.

How did I know that the woman whom I exchanged smirks with over the avocados was blissfully happy?

How did I know that the woman whom I gently jostled as I got my bottle of Honey and Mustard dressing off the shelf was completely free of all concerns?

Everyone had their own worries.

Nobody was perfectly happy.

I hadn't been singled out specially by the Gods for misery to descend on me.

I was just an ordinary woman with ordinary problems, doing her shopping, among other ordinary women.

I passed the alcohol department and I caught a glimpse of rows and rows of bottles of vodka, glittering and shimmering, silver light glinting off them. Almost as though I could hear them all calling "Hey Claire, over here! Pick me, pick me! Can we come home with you?" I instinctively turned my trolley in that direction.

And then turned it away again.

Remember Auntie Julia, I told myself sternly.

And Dad was right. Lying in bed drunk was no life. It solves nothing.

With an awful shock I realised that I might be finally grown-up.

I was *agreeing* with Dad's "The Evils of Drink" lecture, instead of sniggering and scoffing at it.

Of course, I had been warned that this day might finally dawn, but I was still unprepared for it.

If I didn't watch out my next step would be to squint at the television when *Top of the Pops* is on and say "is that a boy or a girl?" about the singer. Or say "why can't they write songs with tunes to them anymore? Because that's not a song, that's just noise."

A little bit shaken I cruised the frozen desserts aisle.

When I was pregnant I used to eat frozen chocolate mousse by the truck-load. In fact it used to really annoy James.

So I thought I'd get myself one for old time's sake.

And as a mark of defiance.

I held Kate up to show her the rows and rows of boxes of chocolate mousse.

"Meet the family," I said.

I took out a box and held it for her to see.

"You see that," I told her. "Without that you probably wouldn't be here." She looked at it with her round blue eyes and reached out her fat little arm to touch the condensation on the box. Obviously something in her blood was calling out to the chocolate mousse, something as old as mankind, recognising something that had befriended her mother through rough times.

I went and paid, gaining a lot of pleasure from the astronomical amount that James would be charged on the credit card.

And home we went.

On the way we stopped at the bank and I changed my Sterling to punts. As soon as Anna got home I was going to give her back every penny that I owed her. At least now she could pay her dealer. And thereby continue to have an intact pair of kneecaps.

Chapter Nine

I had to ring the doorbell when we arrived back home as I had left without a key. Mum answered.

"I'm home," I said to her. "We had a great time, didn't we Katie?"

Mum watched me as I carried plastic bag after plastic bag into the kitchen.

She circled me suspiciously while I unpacked the groceries onto the kitchen table.

"Did you get everything you needed?" she asked tremulously.

"Everything!" I confirmed enthusiastically.

"So you're still going ahead with this idea of making them their dinner?" she said, sounding on the verge of tears.

"Yes Mum," I told her. "Why are you upset about it?"

"I really wish you wouldn't do this," she said anxiously. "You'll give them notions, you know. They'll expect cooked dinners all the time after this. And who'll be expected to do it? Not you, that's for sure. Because by then, you'll have swanned off back to London and I'll have to deal with their whinging."

Poor Mum, I thought. Maybe I was being insensitive, showing off my fancy cooking in her kitchen.

She paused while I cheerfully put some fresh pasta on a shelf in the fridge. "Are you listening to me?" She raised her voice, as her view of me was blocked by the fridge door.

"They're perfectly happy with the microwave stuff," she continued. "Did you ever hear the expression 'if it ain't broke, don't fix it' – And what's that?" she demanded, pouncing on a cellophane bag of fresh basil leaves, and poking them suspiciously.

"That's basil, Mum," I said, swishing past her, to pack some pine kernels away in the cupboard.

"And what does that do?" she asked staring at it as if it were radioactive.

"It's a herb," I replied patiently. Poor Mum, I understood how insecure and threatened she was feeling.

"Well it can't be much of a herb if they couldn't even put it in a jar," she declared triumphantly.

She might be feeling insecure and threatened, but she had still better watch her step, I thought grimly.

And immediately I regretted it. I was feeling, hell, almost happy. No need to be mean to anyone. No need to get cross with anyone.

"Don't worry Mum," I told her apologetically. "I'm not making anything special. They probably won't even notice the difference between this and the frozen stuff."

"Maybe today you won't make it as nice as you usually do," she said wheedlingly.

"Maybe I won't," I agreed kindly.

I started opening and shutting cupboards, searching for utensils for making the pesto sauce.

It soon became apparent that despite our fridge freezer and our microwave, in all other respects our kitchen was The Kitchen That Time Forgot.

It was as though I had gone Alice-like through a murky mirror or been washed by a freak flashflood into some lost valley that was completely untouched by the outside world.

In one of the cupboards there was an enormous heavy beige ceramic mixing bowl, with about an inch of dust on it. It was probably a wedding present when Mum got married nearly thirty years ago. And it looked as if it had yet to be used.

There was a charming artefact of a hand whisk that could have been from the Bronze Age or could be even older. It was in marvellous condition, considering its great age.

There was even a cookbook that was printed in 1952 with recipes that included powdered egg in the list of ingredients and faded sepia tinted pictures of heavily decorated Victoria sandwiches.

Positively prehistoric.

It wouldn't have surprised me in the slightest if a couple of dinosaurs lumbered through the kitchen door, had a slice of bread and butter and a glass of milk while standing at the counter, put their plate and glass in the dishwasher, nodded civilly to me and lumbered out again.

I thought with a pang of loss of my well-stocked kitchen in London. My liquidiser, my food processor that could do everything bar tell funny stories, my juice extractor, not just a citrus fruit one, mind, but a proper juicer. I could certainly have done with them now.

"Haven't you got anything at all that I could use for chopping?" I asked Mum in exasperation.

"Well," she said doubtfully, "how about this. Would this be any good?" she said anxiously offering me an egg mandolin, still in its box.

"Thanks Mum, but no." I sighed. "What am I going to use to chop the basil?"

"In the past I've usually found that one of these works quite well," she said now in a slightly sarcastic tone, obviously a little bit fed up with my pretentious antics. "It's called a knife. I'm sure that if we ring around we could find a shop in Dublin that stocks them."

Suitably humbled I accepted the knife and started to chop the basil.

"And what exactly are you making?" asked Mum, who sat watching me looking half resentful, half fascinated, as if she couldn't believe something as outlandish as cooking was going on in her kitchen.

"A sauce to go with the pasta," I told her as I stood chopping. "It's called pesto."

She sat there silently, just looking at me as I worked.

"And what's in that?" she asked after a while, obviously hating herself for asking.

"Basil, olive oil, pine kernels, Parmesan cheese and garlic," I told her calmly and matter-of-factly.

I didn't want to panic her.

"Oh yes," she murmured, nodding sagely, knowingly, as if she encountered such ingredients every day of her life.

"First of all I chop the basil very finely," I told her,

in the same manner that a surgeon uses to explain to his prospective patient how he will perform the triple by-pass.

Gently, thoroughly, dispelling any mystique.

("First of all I break your sternum")

"Then I add the olive oil," I continued.

("Then I open up your ribcage")

"Then I crush the pine kernels, from the bag here," I told her, rustling the bag.

("Then I borrow some veins from your leg – have a look on the chart here")

"Finally I add the crushed garlic and the parmesan cheese," I finished. "Simple!"

("Then we sew you back up and in a month's time you'll be walking two miles a day!")

Mum seemed to take all this information calmly in her stride. I must say, I was proud of her.

"Well go easy on the garlic," she told me. "It's hard enough to get Anna to come home as it is. We don't want the poor little vampire to think we're picking on her."

"Anna's not a vampire," I laughed.

"How do you know?" asked Mum. "She certainly looks like one a lot of the time, all that hair and those awful long purple dresses and that desperate make-up. Would you not have a word with her and try to get her to smarten herself up a bit?"

"But the way she looks is the way she is," I told Mum as I put the chopped basil into a saucepan. "It's Anna. She wouldn't be Anna if she looked different."

"I know," sighed Mum. "But the go-heck of her. I'm sure the neighbours think we don't clothe the child at all. She looks like a tinker. And those boots! I've a good mind to just throw them out on her."

"Oh no Mum, please don't do that," I said anxiously, thinking that Anna would break her heart without the Doc Martens she had so lovingly painted with sunrises and flowers.

I must admit that I was also slightly concerned about whose shoes Anna would wear if hers were thrown out.

I feared for mine.

"I'll have to see," threatened Mum darkly. " And now what are you doing?"

"I'm adding the olive oil," I told her.

"What did you buy oil for?" she demanded, obviously thinking that she had a right bunch of idiots for daughters. "There's a bottle of oil that I use for the chips. You could have used that and saved yourself the money."

"Err . . . thanks. I'll know the next time," I told her.

There was really no point in trying to explain to her the difference between, on the one hand, extra extra virgin Tuscan cold-pressed prime olive oil and, on the other hand, Flora oil that had been recycled about ten times and had little bits of blackened, charred chips floating it.

I might be unnecessarily pretentious when it comes to food, but Goddammit, you can go too far in the other direction too.

"Right!" I said. "For my next trick, I will, without the aid of a safety net, grate the Parmesan cheese."

I took the hunk of cheese out of the fridge, where

it was obviously terrorising everything else in it. The packets of sliced plastic easi-cheese were shrinking against the back wall of the fridge, frightened out of their wits by this exotic new-comer.

But grating the cheese was easier said than done.

I searched high and low but there wasn't a grater to be found.

Eventually I located a grater of sorts. It barely belonged to the genus "grater". It wasn't even one of the round ones that at least stand by themselves, never mind an electric one. It was just a little piece of metal with ridges on it.

And you would have to be a more dexterous person than I am to be able to manoeuvre the lump of cheese and grate it successfully on this contraption.

My hands kept slipping and I would grate a goodly portion of my knuckles along with the cheese.

Mum tut-tutted as I blasphemed and then she started sniffing in alarm as the characteristic aroma of the Parmesan cheese filled the kitchen.

A commotion broke out in the hall. The sounds of voices and laughter. Mum glanced at the clock hanging on the kitchen wall.

She did this although the clock hands had stood at ten to four since the Christmas before last.

"They're home," she said.

Dad brought Helen home from college most evenings, so they arrived home together. He did this in spite of the fact that he had to drive about ten miles off his normal route to collect her.

Helen burst through the door, looking absolutely beautiful. In fact, even more beautiful than usual, if that could be possible. There was a kind of radiance around her. Even though she was just wearing jeans and a jumper she looked exquisite. Her hair long and silky, her skin translucent, her eyes glowing, her perfect little mouth in a charming smile.

"Hi everyone, we're home," she announced. "Hey, what's that awful smell? Phew! Did someone get sick?"

We could hear the sounds of people talking in the hall. Dad was talking to someone with a male voice.

We obviously had company.

My heart did an involuntary little somersault. I still hadn't stopped hoping for James to arrive unexpectedly on the doorstep. However the male voice was more likely to belong to one of Helen's friends.

Although it would be more accurate to call them Helen's slaves.

Even though I knew I was being silly to think that James might just appear out of the blue I still felt a pang of disappointment pierce me when Helen said "Oh, I brought a friend home with me. Dad's showing him where to hang his coat up."

Then she looked at me. "Here!" she shouted. "What are you doing wearing my clothes? Get them off this minute."

"Sorry Helen," I stammered. "But I had nothing else. I'll buy new ones and you can borrow them all."

"You can be bloody sure of it," she said darkly.

And she left it at that.

Thank God! She must be in a good mood.

"Who's this lad that you've brought?" asked Mum.

"His name is Adam", said Helen. "And you're to be nice to him because he's going to write my essay."

Mum and I started to assemble our facial features into expressions that were both welcoming and compassionate. Another poor boy had fallen for Helen. His life was to all intents and purposes over. Everything in his future was tainted and ruined.

All he had ahead of him now was an existence of misery and despair, which he would spend pining for the fair Helen.

Mum and I exchanged glances. Like a lamb to the slaughter, we were both thinking.

I went back to grating the cheese and my knuckles.

"That's Mum," said Helen's voice, obviously introducing the doomed Adam to Mum.

("Flee! Flee for your life! Save yourself, Adam, while you still can," I felt like telling him)

"And that's Claire over there," continued Helen. "You know, the one I told you about. The one with the baby."

Thank you Helen, you little cow, I thought, for making my life sound like some kind of dreary inner-city kitchen-sink drama.

I turned around, ready to smile kindly at Adam and extended my hand, reeking of Parmesan and with its pulped knuckles.

And got a bit of a shock.

This wasn't one of Helen's usual callow youths.

This one really was a man.

A young one, I grant you.

But undeniably a man.

Over six foot tall and very sexy.

Long legs. Muscly arms. Blue eyes. Square jaw. Big smile.

If we had a testosterone-ometer hanging on the kitchen wall the mercury level would have gone through the ceiling.

I was just in time to see him giving Mum the firmest handshake of her life.

He then turned his attention to me. Out of the corner of my eye I saw Mum shaking her crushed hand and surreptitiously inspecting her wedding ring to see if it had been bent out of shape by the strong grasp.

"Err, hello," I said, feeling flustered and confused. It was a long time since I had encountered such a strong concentration of manliness.

"Nice to meet you," he smiled at me, holding my mutilated hand gently in his huge one.

My God, I thought, feeling a bit overwhelmed, you know you're getting old when you start noticing how young-looking all the gorgeous men are.

I could hear Helen's voice, but it seemed to be coming from a long way away. It was drowned out by the roaring sound of all the blood in my body rushing to my face to make me blush in a way that I haven't done since I was fifteen.

"Seriously," she was saying. "There's an awful smell of puke."

"That's not puke," Mum was saying knowledgeably. "That's the smell of the Palmerstown cheese. You know, for the presto sauce."

Chapter Ten

Dinner was a bit of an odd affair, because we were all slightly taken aback by Adam.

Helen has always had hordes of men (although it's more accurate to call them boys) in love with her. A day didn't pass that the phone didn't ring with some stammering youth on the other end of the phone making enquiries as to his chances of taking Helen out.

And the house had a steady stream of male visitors. Their invitation to tea usually coinciding with the breakdown of Helen's stereo, or Helen's desire to have her room painted or, as in this case, Helen needing to have an essay written and Helen having no intention of doing it herself.

And the promised tea rarely materialised on completion of the task.

But none of them had been like Adam.

They were usually a bit more like Jim.

Poor Jim, to give him his full title.

He was lanky and skinny and went around wearing black all the time and all year round. Even at the height of Summer, he wore a long black overcoat that was miles too big for him and big black boots. He dyed his plentiful hair black and never looked me in the eye. He didn't talk much and when he did it was usually to discuss suicide methods. Or to talk about singers from obscure bands who had killed themselves.

He once said "hello" to me and gave me a kind of sweet little smile, and I thought that I had misjudged him but I later discovered that he was blind drunk.

He always carried a decrepit copy of *Fear and Loathing in Las Vegas* or *American Psycho* in the torn lining of his black overcoat. He wanted to be in a band and kill himself when he was eighteen.

Although I thought he must have extended the suicide deadline because he was eighteen the Christmas before and I hadn't heard that he had died yet and I'm sure I would have.

Helen absolutely hated him.

He was always ringing her and, whenever he did, Mum would speak to him on the phone and lie through her teeth as to Helen's whereabouts. She would say something like "No, Helen's missing, presumed drunk," while Helen stood in the hall looking at Mum, waving her arms frantically and mouthing "Tell him I'm dead."

After Mum had hung up the phone she would shout at Helen.

"I'm not doing any more lying for you. I'm putting my immortal soul in peril. And why won't you talk to him? He's a nice lad."

"He's an asshole," Helen would reply.

"He's just shy," Mum would say in his defence.

"He's an asshole," Helen maintained, louder this time.

On occasions like Valentine's day or Helen's birthday, at least one bunch of black roses would be delivered from him. Handmade cards would come in the post with very graphic pictures of shattered hearts and blood, or a single red teardrop. Terribly symbolic.

There was a time when you couldn't go into our kitchen without finding Jim in there, still wearing the long black coat and talking to Mum. Mum had become his best friend. His only ally in his quest to win Helen's heart.

Most of Helen's would-be boyfriends spent far more time with Mum than they ever did with Helen.

Dad hated him. Possibly even more than Helen did.

I think he felt disappointed by Jim.

Because Dad was so starved of male company he had hoped to do a bit of male bonding with Jim, what with Jim being a more or less permanent fixture in the kitchen along with the washing-machine or the bread-bin.

One evening he came home from work and as usual found Jim sitting in the kitchen with Mum. Helen went straight to her room as soon as she heard that Jim was on the premises. Dad sat at the kitchen table attempting to talk to Jim.

He said "Did you see the match?"

Jim just looked at Dad completely blankly. The only match Jim looked like he knew anything about was a self-immolator's or a pyromaniac's one.

So that was the end of that.

Now Dad also thought Jim was a dead loss.

He said that Jim should put his money where his mouth was and stop just talking about killing himself and actually get on with it.

Mum said that Jim was really a little pet, once you got to know him.

And that it was a sin to encourage someone to take their own life.

It felt as if Jim was always around. Whenever I came home from London he seemed to be drooped over the kitchen table, with a little black cloud hovering over his head, carrying his air of tragedy around with him like a briefcase.

But I always said "Hello Jim" to him. At least I was polite.

Even if he totally ignored me.

Then I discovered why he had been ignoring me.

On my second day home from London the doorbell rang and I went and answered it and found a haircut wearing a big long black coat standing on the front doorstep.

I wasn't sure whether he had come to see Helen or Mum but Mum was out so I called Helen.

"Helen, Jim's at the door."

Helen came down the stairs looking puzzled.

"Oh hello Conor," she said to the gloomy youth on the step.

She turned to me.

"Where's Jim?" she asked.

"Well . . . here . . . isn't he?" I said, a bit startled, indicating the boy in the long black overcoat.

"That's not Jim, that's Conor. I haven't seen Jim in about a year. I suppose you'd better come in, Conor,"

161

she said ungraciously. "Oh and by the way that's my sister Claire. She's home from London because her husband left her."

"Nice one Claire," she hissed angrily at me as she herded Conor into the sitting-room. "I've been avoiding him for the last month."

There is no doubt but that she will burn in Hell.

At least that explained why Jim ignored me every time I said "Hello Jim."

Because it wasn't Jim at all.

But it looked just like him.

Then every time I saw Jim, I would say "Hello Conor."

Apparently I was still wrong.

His name was William.

But he was the absolute image of Jim and Conor.

But Adam was a different proposition entirely from Jim and his clones.

Handsome, intelligent(ish), presentable . . . you know, *normal*! He had one or two social skills, didn't look as if he would crumble into dust if he was caught in a direct ray of sunlight, and could do more than just stare glassy-eyed at Helen and dribble.

After he had shaken hands with us all he then said politely to Mum, "Can I help you to set the table?"

Mum was very taken aback. Not just at the offer of help. Which was indeed remarkable in itself.

But at the suggestion that we set the table at all.

You see, people tend to fend for themselves at meal-times in our house and eat their dinner in front of the television watching *Neighbours* instead of at the kitchen table.

"Erm, no that's all right thanks Adam, I'll do it."

And looking slightly bemused she did just that.

"You're in for a treat tonight," she said girlishly to Adam. Honestly, it was so embarrassing. A grown woman and she was behaving like a starstruck teenager. "Claire has made the dinner for us."

"Yes, I heard that Claire was a great cook," he smiled at me, throwing me into pleasurable confusion. He really shouldn't smile at me like that while I'm draining the pasta, I thought, as I nursed my scalded hand.

I wondered who had told him that I was a great cook because I was sure that it certainly wasn't Helen.

Maybe he was just being charming.

But, hey, what's wrong with that?

"All right ladies and gentlemen, please take your seats for this evening's performance," I called out, indicating that the dinner was ready.

Adam laughed.

I was pathetically pleased.

There was a general shuffling and scraping of chairs as everyone sat down.

Adam looked totally incongruous as he sat at the table, completely dwarfing his chair, looking ridiculously square-jawed and handsome.

It was a bit like having Superman in your kitchen or having Mel Gibson drop in for a cup of tea.

I took my hat off to Helen, she'd picked a beaut this time.

Adam's wholesome good looks were a welcome change from Jim/Conor/William's lank misery.

In a couple of years' time he'd be completely devastating.

I placed the salad that I had prepared in the centre of the table. Then I put the pasta and sauce on plates and brought them over to the diners.

The arrival of the food threw Mum, Dad and Helen into a bit of a quandary. The fact that it was home-made made Dad and Helen suspicious.

Quite rightly.

God knows they had every reason to be suspicious after the ways they had suffered in the past. I suppose it was too reminiscent of all Mum's disasters.

And naturally Mum was only too happy to foment trouble. If she encouraged them to refuse point-blank to eat it, it would mean that I wouldn't cook any more dinners and the old order would be restored, thereby letting her off the hook.

When Helen's plate was put in front of her she made noises as if she was vomiting. "Uuuugggghhhh!" she said, staring in disgust at her plate. "What the *hell* is that?"

"Just pasta and sauce," I said calmly.

"*Sauce?*" she screeched. "But it's *green*."

"Yes," I confirmed, not for a second denying that the sauce was green. "It's green. Sauce can be green, you know."

Then Adam came to the rescue. He was tucking in with great gusto.

I suppose he was one of those penniless students

who can go for months without getting a square meal and so would eat just about anything.

But he was acting as if he was enjoying it. And that was good enough for me.

"This is absolutely delicious," he said, charmingly cutting through Helen's histrionics. "You should really try it, Helen."

Helen glared at him, "I'm not touching that. It looks revolting."

Dad, Mum and Helen stared, with held breath, their faces frozen with horror, at Adam, as he swallowed a mouthful of food, obviously waiting for him to die.

And when, after about five minutes, he was still alive and not rolling around on the floor, like a victim of the Borgias, screaming to be put out of his misery, Dad ventured a try.

Now, I would love to be able to tell you that one by one every member of my family picked up a fork and despite their earlier prejudices were won over to my fancy cooking. And that we all hugged each other and with wry smiles and self-deprecating shakes of our heads freely admitted how wrong we were. A bit like some American sitcom.

But I can't do that.

Helen, with great shudders and contorted face, noisily refused to touch it, in spite of the beautiful Adam giving it his seal of approval,

She made herself some toast.

Déjà vu, or what.

Dad ate a little bit and declared that no doubt it was lovely but that his tastes were humble. That he couldn't possibly appreciate such exotic and sophisticated food. As he said "I'm a simple man. I never even tasted lemon meringue pie until I was thirty-five."

Mum also ate a little bit but with a martyred air. She made it very clear that to waste good food was a sin.

Even horrible food.

Therefore she ate it. Her attitude seemed to be that we were put on this earth to suffer and that this dinner was sent to her as some kind of penance. But that given the choice between climbing Croagh Patrick with a broken leg or finishing her plate of pasta, she would rather start lacing up her mountaineering boots any day of the week.

But at the same time she was hard pressed to contain her glee at Dad and Helen refusing to eat it.

Every so often she would catch my eye and it was obviously a bit of a struggle for her to maintain her poker face.

Though she would rather have died than admit it, she was thrilled.

Then Anna arrived home.

She wandered into the kitchen looking very pretty in a rather ethnic, ethereal kind of way, all trailing scarves and long crocheted see-through skirt and colourful jewellery. She had obviously met Adam previously.

"Oh hi Adam," she said breathily, obviously delighted, flushing with pleasure.

Does he always make every woman he comes into contact with blush, I wondered.

Or was it just our family.

Somehow I suspected not.

What hope could there be for a man so young who had such an intense effect on women? He could only grow up to be a complete and total bastard.

Expecting women to weep, faint, scream and fall in love with him as easily as breathing.

He was far too handsome for his own good.

A disfigurement or two wouldn't have gone amiss at all.

Spare the spots and spoil the man.

"Hi Anna." He smiled at her. "Nice to see you again."

"Er yes," she muttered, blushing even more and knocking over a cup. The insides of her eyelids were probably bright red at this stage.

I sympathised. I probably didn't have one intact blood vessel left in my face after my Adam-induced blush earlier. Every capillary in my cheeks had burst like bubbles coming to the surface of a glass of champagne.

Conversation wasn't exactly scintillating at the dinner table. Helen, never the hostess with the mostest at the best of times (unless we include the hostess with the mostest rudeness), had picked up a magazine (it was actually a copy of *Hello* – how had that one got through the net, I wondered) and read through dinner.

"Helen, put down the magazine," Dad told her sharply, obviously embarrassed.

"Shut up Dad," said Helen in a monotone, not even looking up.

But every now and then she would look up at Adam and give him a witchy little smile. He would look at her, totally enchanted, and after holding her gaze for a little while, smile back at her.

You could have cut the sexual tension with a breadknife.

Anna, never a candidate for the *Late Late Show* at the best of times, seemed to be completely stuck dumb by Adam, such was her awe.

Anytime he addressed a question to her, she just simpered and giggled, hung her head and acted like some sort of village idiot.

It was quite annoying, to be honest with you.

He was only a man, and a very young one at that, for God's sake. Not some sort of deity.

Mum and Dad pushed their food nervously around their plate. They didn't talk much either.

Dad made a brief stab at talking to Adam.

"Rugby?" he murmured at him, as if he was in a secret society and he was trying to find out if Adam was a member also.

"Sorry?" said Adam, looking quizzically at Dad, desperately trying to figure out what he was trying to say to him.

"Rugby? Prop maybe?"

"Em, er, sorry, but what do you mean?"

"Rugby? Do you play it?" Dad decided to lay his cards on the table.

"No."

"Oh," Dad sighed like a deflating balloon.

"But I like watching it," said Adam gamely.

"Ah pshaw!" said Dad, practically turning his back

on him, making his disappointment felt with a dismissive wave of his arm.

And that, I suppose, was the end of that fledgling friendship.

For some reason I felt that it was my responsibility to talk to our visitor. Maybe it was because I had got used to being in civilised society, where guests were treated like guests. Where, if someone invites you to dinner they don't throw you in with a crowd of strangers and completely ignore you.

If I'd said it once, I must have said it a thousand times, but it beat me how Helen got away with behaving the way she did.

"So you're in Helen's class in college?" I asked him with false brightness, desperately trying to kick-start some kind of conversation.

"Yes," he replied. "I'm in her anthropology group."

And that seemed to be the end of that topic.

He continued to eat.

He continued to live.

Dad continued to marvel.

Adam was a pleasure to watch. There was something so healthy about him. He had an enormous appetite and he was so appreciative. "This is really delicious," he said, smiling at me. "Any chance of some more?"

"Of course," said Mum coquettishly, almost knocking over her chair in her haste to serve him. "I'll get it for you. And would you like another glass of milk?"

"Thanks very much, Mrs Walsh," he said politely.

He was so nice. And I'm not just saying that because he was the only one who ate the dinner I made.

He was so boyish in a manly kind of way.

Or perhaps he was so manly in a boyish kind of way.

Well, whatever it was it was very attractive.

But even though he was alarmingly good-looking I felt very relaxed with him, because I knew that he must be only about eighteen or so. Although he looked and behaved with a lot more maturity.

To be honest, I nearly felt a little bit jealous of Helen, landing herself such a hunk.

I remembered vaguely what it was like to be young and in love.

But I told myself not to be so silly. I'd fix things with James. Or else I'd meet someone else as nice.

(Nice??!!, I thought, in alarm. Did I just say nice? That was hardly the right word to describe James at that moment.)

But Adam, the hero, saved the conversation.

Mum asked him where he lived.

This is part of a routine enquiry and is the first question in a set of two that Mum religiously asked gentlemen callers.

The second question involved finding out from the young man what his father did for a living.

And thereby assess the approximate wealth of the family just in case Helen happened to marry into it. And so that Mum would have a rough idea of how much she would be expected to spend on the "mother-of-the-bride" dress.

But Adam managed to head Mum off at the pass and avoid being asked to produce a recent copy of his father's payslip by entertaining us all with snippets of his life story.

Apparently he was from America. Both his parents had recently returned to New York so he lived in a flat in Rathmines.

Although both his parents were Irish and he had lived in Ireland since he was twelve, he still looked American.

It must be something they put in the air in America, I thought. Fluoride, or something, that made them grow so big and beefy.

It was definitely one in the eye for the crowd that said genetics take precedence over environment.

If he had spent the first twelve years of his life in Dublin instead of New York he would have been only five foot five, instead of six foot two. He would have had white freckly skin instead of faintly olive skin. He would have had wispy mousy hair instead of sleek black hair. He would have had a weak nondescript jaw instead of a square granite jaw.

That was obviously what a lifestyle of eating pastrami on rye, bagels with cream cheese and lox, drinking sodas and beers, watching the ball game, calling jam "jelly," calling jelly "jello," calling crisps "chips," calling chips "fries," calling people 'Mac' even when it wasn't their name and having storm doors and a deck on your house did for you.

Adam amused us all with stories of what it was like for him when he first moved from New York to

171

Dublin. And how the native children welcomed him by calling him "fascist imperialist Yank" and acting as though he was personally responsible for the US invasion of Grenada, and beating the crap out of him for calling tomatoes "tom-ay-toes" and for calling his mother "Mom" instead of "Mammy."

And how the native children would scoff and sneer at his Americanisms. As poor Adam said, "I didn't know that I was saying things the wrong way."

Apparently the other boys would say things like,

"Hey, Micko, what time did you put the garbage in the trash can on the sidewalk?"

"Ten of eleven, Johnny, or maybe it was twenty of eight."

Cue for raucous laughter.

And how, when he tried to defend himself by beating up some of the native children he got called a bully because he was so much bigger than the other boys.

We all nodded sympathetically, sitting round with our elbows on the kitchen table, looking at Adam, our hearts breaking for the poor lonely twelve-year old boy who couldn't do anything right. You could have heard a pin drop. The mood had suddenly changed from a lighthearted one to a sombre one.

Even Dad looked on the verge of tears.

He was obviously thinking, "He mightn't play rugby but that's still no way to treat the lad."

Then Adam turned the full force of his attention onto me.

He twisted round in his chair and fixed me with an intense look.

In a funny way, he made me feel as if I was the only person in the room.

He was so eager and enthusiastic about everything. Like a little puppy. Well, like an enormous puppy, actually.

There seemed to be no cynicism about him at all.

So this is what it's like to be young, I thought.

"So, Claire, tell me about your job," he said, "Helen tells me that you've got a really important job working for a charity."

I bloomed under the warmth of his interest, like a flower in the sun and started to tell him.

But before I could Helen interrupted, "I didn't say it was important," she said sourly. "I just said it was a job. And anyway she had to give it up when she had the baby."

"Oh the baby," he said. "Can I see her?"

"Of course," I said delighted, but wondering why Helen was being so nasty.

Why she was being even nastier than usual, I mean.

"Kate's asleep at the moment but she'll be awake in about half an hour so you can see her then."

"Great," he said, looking at me.

Honestly, he was gorgeous. His eyes were a kind of navy blue. And he had the most beautiful body.

I thought this purely from an objective point of view.

He's my sister's boyfriend, so it's all right for me to admire his beauty just aesthetically speaking, as it were.

I felt a bit like a wise old woman admiring the

handsome young men. Realising how gorgeous they were while acknowledging that my day of dalliance with them was long gone.

He was so tall and he looked so sexy even thought he was just wearing a pair of faded jeans and a grey sweatshirt.

For dessert I produced the chocolate mousse which was greeted with a great deal more enthusiasm than the dinner was. The jostling and scuffling that broke out between Anna, Helen and Dad for the biggest piece was nothing short of shameful, and us with a visitor in the house.

But Adam just laughed good-naturedly.

After a while I took him to see Kate.

We tiptoed into the room.

"Can I hold her?" he asked reverently.

"Of course," I smiled, very touched by his awe.

I thought it was the sweetest thing I ever heard that such a big tough man wanted to see my baby.

Sort of like a huge burly lorry-driver crying at country and western songs. Incongruous and touching.

I handed Kate gently to him and he took her and held her gingerly.

She didn't even wake up.

The idiot!

What kind of daughter was I rearing?

Being held, for the first time, by a beautiful man and she slept through it.

It made such a beautiful picture. The huge young man holding the perfect little baby.

"What colour are her eyes?" he asked.

"Blue," I said. "But all babies have blue eyes first. Then they usually change to another colour."

He continued to stare at her with an expression of wonder on his face.

"You know, if you and I had a baby its eyes would definitely be blue," he mused, sounding almost as if he was talking to himself.

I jumped with shock.

I could hardly believe my ears!

Was he flirting with me?

I felt a surge of rage.

I had thought he was so innocent and nice. A sweet young man.

The *nerve* of him!

Not only was I old enough to be his mother. Well, very nearly. But he was here with my *sister* and was doing a very good impression of being her boyfriend.

Had he no respect?

No sense of decency?

But I was wrong. I looked at him and our eyes locked for a minute. I could see that he was really deathly embarrassed.

He definitely knew that he had made a faux-pas.

He looked so young and afraid.

Like a naughty little boy.

The room was full of tension and embarrassment.

"Well I'd better get back to Helen and the essay," he said hurriedly, practically flinging Kate back in the direction of her cot, and rushing from the room without a second glance.

I sat on the bed feeling a bit funny.

Was I feeling foolish for overreacting?

Was I feeling sad at my cynicism for just jumping to the wrong conclusion?

Was I feeling . . . God Forbid . . . *disappointed?*

No, I decided. Definitely not disappointed. But certainly a bit foolish.

You've been away from men too long, I told myself sternly. You'd better get back into circulation. So that the next time you meet an attractive one you won't be jumping to any ridiculous conclusions.

But at the same time I must admit that I was slightly piqued by the way he reacted at the suggestion that we have a baby. There was no need for him to look quite so horrified.

God, but it was typical.

In time honoured tradition I had gone from being furious at the suggestion that he did fancy me to being furious at the suggestion that he didn't fancy me, in about thirty seconds.

Being rational was never my strong point.

I mean, I might well be an "older woman" but I wasn't exactly The Bride of Dracula. I'd have him know plenty of men found me attractive.

Well, I was sure there must be some somewhere who did. There were three billion people on this planet. Out of that lot I was sure I could have rustled up a few poor misfortunes who liked the look of me.

The nerve of the guy. Just because he happened to be extremely good-looking didn't give him any right to make me feel like a horror.

And I might not have been quite as beautiful as Helen.

In fact I wasn't even remotely as beautiful as Helen.

But I was a kind person.

Not that anyone ever fancied someone because they were a kind person.

If that was the case Mother Teresa would have to fend them off with sticks.

But however.

I fed Kate and put her back to bed.

Then I went downstairs to Mum.

I passed Helen's bedroom on the way and the door was firmly shut.

The pair of them were obviously well ensconced in there.

Essay writing, indeed!

Mum and Dad might have bought that line, but I've used it enough times myself to know what it really means.

But at the same time if they were having sex, they were doing it very quietly.

Not, of course, that I was listening at the door or anything.

And not, of course, that it had anything, in the whole wide world, to do with me.

Helen could screw whoever she liked.

As indeed, could Adam.

Nothing, as I say, at all, to do with me.

With great purpose I watched television with Mum.

Much later we heard Helen and Adam in the kitchen.

Then we heard her saying goodbye to him.

He stuck his head round the door and thanked us for the lovely dinner and said that he hoped to see us again soon.

Mum and I smiled our goodbyes at him.

"Lovely polite lad," said Mum, in a satisfied fashion.

I didn't answer her. I was thinking that he didn't look too dishevelled for someone who had just been having sex. And wondering why I cared.

Chapter Eleven

After Adam left, and Helen had sent him out into the wet and wild March night to make his way home to Rathmines, she closed the front door behind him and came into the television room and sat down with Mum and me.

"He seemed like a lovely lad," said Mum approvingly.

"Did he?" said Helen distantly.

"*Lovely,*" said Mum emphatically.

"Oh don't go on like you usually do," snapped Helen irritably.

There was a little bit of an awkward pause.

Then I spoke.

"What age is Adam?" I asked Helen casually.

"Why?" she asked without looking away from the television screen. "Do you fancy him?"

"No," I protested, blushing hotly.

"Oh really?" she said. "Everyone else does. The whole of college does. Mum does."

Mum looked a little bit taken aback and startled and like she was about to hotly defend herself. Before she could, though, Helen started talking again to me.

"And you looked like you fancied him. Giggling

and smiling at him. You're worse than Anna. I was mortified."

"I was being *polite*," I insisted.

I really felt annoyed.

And embarrassed.

"You weren't being polite," she told me tonelessly still looking at the screen. "You fancied him."

"Helen, for God's sake, did you expect me to ignore him and not talk to him?" I asked her angrily.

"No," she said coldly. "But you didn't have to be so obvious about fancying him."

"Helen, I'm a married woman," I said, raising my voice at her. "Of course I didn't fancy him. And he's much younger than me."

"Hah!" she shouted back at me. "So you do fancy him. You're just afraid that he's too young. Well don't worry, because Professor Staunton is married and she's in love with him and got drunk and was crying in the bar and saying she'd leave her husband and everything. We were all in fits laughing. And she's *ancient*. Even older than you!"

At that Helen jumped up and ran out of the room, slamming the door thunderously behind her. No doubt dislodging the last few remaining slates from the roof.

"Oh God" sighed Mum wearily. "It's like a bloody relay race around here. No sooner does one daughter stop behaving like an anti-Christ than another one starts. How did you all get to be so temperamental? You're like a pack of Italians."

"What's *wrong* with her?" I asked Mum. "Why is she getting all touchy about Adam?"

"Oh, I suppose she's in love with him," said Mum vaguely. "Or at least she thinks she might be."

"What?!" I asked aghast. "Helen in love? Are you out of your mind? The only person Helen is in love with is herself."

"That's a very unkind thing to say about your sister," said Mum looking at me thoughtfully.

"Well I don't mean it unkindly," I explained hurriedly. "I just mean that everyone's always in love with her. It's never the other way round."

"There's a first time for everything," said Mum wisely.

We sat quietly.

Mum broke the silence.

"Anyway, she was right."

"About what?" I asked her, wondering what she was talking about.

"You *did* fancy him."

"I did *not* fancy him," I said indignantly.

Mum turned to me with raised eyebrows and a knowing look.

"Don't be ridiculous," she scoffed. "He was *gorgeous*! I fancied him myself. If I was twenty years younger I'd give him a run for his money."

I said nothing.

I was feeling a bit upset.

"And what's more," Mum continued. "He fancied you. No wonder Helen's nose is out of joint."

"That's crap!" I protested loudly.

"It's not," said Mum calmly. "It was obvious that he fancied you. Although, then again," she continued doubtfully, "I thought he fancied me too. Maybe he's just one of those men who makes every woman feel beautiful."

Now I was feeling very confused indeed.

"But Mum," I tried to explain. "I'm married to James and I love him and I want to fix my marriage."

"I know that," she said. "But maybe a little fling is exactly what you need. To get your self-confidence back. And to get your feelings for James in perspective."

I stared at Mum in horror. What was she talking about?

This was my *mother* for God's sake. What on earth was she doing encouraging me to have a fling, and me a married woman. And with my younger sister's boyfriend, of all people.

"Mum!" I said. "Get a grip. You're scaring me. I mean, I'm not eighteen anymore. I no longer think that the best way to get over one man is to get under another!"

Too late, I realised what I had said.

I could have bitten my tongue off.

Mum looked at me with narrowed eyes.

"I don't know where you heard a vulgar expression like that," she hissed. "But it certainly wasn't in this house. Is that the way they talk in London?"

"Sorry Mum," I mumbled, feeling mortified and ashamed but at least back on familiar territory.

I sat on the couch beside her feeling awful.

How could I have said something so crass?

Or rather, how could I have said something so crass in earshot of my mother?

Talk about foolish.

"Well," she said after a while in a more conciliatory tone. "We'll say no more about what you just said."

"OK," I said, feeling relieved.

Thank God! I was just about to start packing my bags for my move back to London.

"Anyway," she said. "He's twenty-four."

"How do you know?" I asked her amazed.

"Aha," she winked at me, touching her nose. "I have my sources."

"You mean you asked him," I said. I knew my mother of old.

"I might have," she said coyly, giving nothing away.

"So you see," she continued, "he's not too young for you at all."

"*Mum,*" I wailed in anguish. "What's this all about? Anyway I'm nearly thirty and he's only twenty-four. So he's still far too young for me."

"Nonsense," said Mum briskly. "They're all at it. Look at Britt Ekland, always being photographed with that fellow that's young enough to be her grandson. Although maybe he is her grandson. And that other floozy, the one that goes round with no clothes on, what's her name?"

"Madonna?" I ventured cautiously.

"No, no, not her. You know the one. She has a tattoo on her backside."

"Oh, you mean Cher," I told her.

"Yes that's the one," said Mum. "I mean, she must be my age if she's a day and look at the way she carries on. None of them a day over sixteen. I

183

suppose Ike must have been the last man she was with that was older than her."

"Ike?" I asked her, my head swimming slightly.

"Yes, Ike. Her husband," said Mum impatiently.

"No Mum, I don't think Cher was married to Ike. Cher was married to Sonny. Ike was married to Tina," I told her.

"Who's Tina?" she asked me, sounding baffled.

"Tina Turner," I gently explained.

"What's she got to do with anything?" said Mum, sounding outraged, looking at me as if I'd gone completely mad.

"Nothing at all," I tried to explain, feeling that I was fast losing any grip on this conversation. "It's just that you said that Cher and Ike . . . Oh never mind, never mind. Just forget it."

Mum sulkily muttered to herself that she didn't have to forget anything. That I was the one who had brought Tina Turner into the conversation.

"Stop being cross, Mum," I told her, in a placatory fashion. "I get your point. I see what you're saying. Adam isn't too young for me."

I glanced nervously at the door as soon as I had said this. I half expected Helen to come bursting through and shout, "I knew you fancied him, you horrible old age pensioner."

And then attempt to strangle me.

She didn't. But the fear still lingered.

"But anyway Mum," I continued, "the age question aside, aren't you forgetting a couple of other vital points? Like, the small fact that Adam is Helen's boyfriend."

"Aha!" she said, holding up her index finger and going all sage-like and wise-old-womanly on me. She practically put on a black headscarf and developed a squint, "but is he?"

"Well why else was he here?" I asked, reasonably, I thought.

"To help her to write her essay," said Mum.

"And why would he do that if he's not her boyfriend? Or at least if he's not making a damn good attempt to be," I asked again, reasonably, I thought.

"Because he's a nice person?" said Mum.

But she sounded a bit doubtful.

"Anyway," I said, "it was obvious that he really fancied her."

"Was it?" she said, sounding genuinely surprised.

"Yes," I said, quite emphatically.

"But even if he is her boyfriend, he won't be for long," predicted Mum.

"Why do you say that?" I asked, wondering what other information she had gleaned from the beautiful Adam.

"Because of the way Helen is," said Mum.

"Oh," I said disappointed. So she had no further gems on Adam to impart.

"Helen just wants to make him fall for her. Then she'll torment him for a while. And then she'll discard him," said Mum. "She was always like that. Even as a child. For months before Christmas she'd be pestering us for this doll and that bike. And the turkey wouldn't be even eaten before she had broken every single thing that Santa brought her. She wasn't happy until she had destroyed everything. Dolls' heads and legs and bicycle chains and saddles all over the place. You'd break your neck on them."

"That's not a very nice way to talk about Helen," I said, echoing what Mum had said to me earlier.

"Maybe not," said Mum, with a sigh. "But it's the truth. I love her and she's a good girl, really. She just needs to grow up a little bit. Well a big bit, I suppose."

"But you said that Helen might be in love with Adam," I said.

"I said that Helen might *think* she's in love with him. An entirely different proposition," she said.

"And even if she is in love with him, although if you ask me I think she's too immature to be capable of it," continued Mum, "it would do her no harm at all to be dealt a little bit of hardship by life. She's had everything far too easy. A little bit of heartbreak goes a long way. I mean look at how good it's been for you. It gives you humility."

"So you want me to have a fling with Helen's boyfriend to give me back my confidence and to give Helen a bit of humility," I said, finally thinking that I had grasped what Mum was saying to me.

"Good God," said Mum, annoyed. "You're making me sound like that one out of *Dynasty*. Playing God with people's lives and all that. It sounds very cold-blooded when you say it like that."

"I'm not saying that I want anything to happen exactly," she continued. "But I really did feel that Adam was very attracted to you. And that, if he is and if anything was to happen, and if you survive Helen's attempts on your life – by Jingo, there's an awful lot of 'ifs' there – then maybe you should just let what's going to happen happen."

"Oh Mum," I sighed. "You've made me all confused."

"I'm sorry sweetheart," she said. "Maybe I've got it all wrong. Maybe he doesn't fancy you at all."

But of course it will come to no surprise to you to hear that I didn't like her saying that either.

I've had enough, I thought.

"Well I'm off to bed," I said.

"Sweet dreams," said Mum, squeezing my hand. "I'll be in to kiss Kate goodnight."

And off I went.

I went to my bedroom and got ready for bed. My nightdress was obviously in a right huff with me. It didn't take kindly to being neglected and left at home while I wore Helen's leggings and shirt to the Shopping Centre. I got a right ticking off.

I was your friend, it told me. I saw you through the rough times, it reminded me. You're fickle and nothing but a foul weather friend. The minute things pick up, and you start feeling a bit more normal, you just discard me, throw me over.

Oh shut up, I thought, or I'll never wear you again. And then you really will have something to give out about.

I had more important things on my mind than disgruntled nighties and their grievances.

As I lay down I realised that I hadn't really thought of James in about three hours.

This was an absolute miracle.

All in all it had been a most unusual day.

Chapter Twelve

The following day dawned bright cold and blustery.

I know this because I was awake at dawn.

It was a typical March day.

The rain had finally stopped.

But there's absolutely no symbolism in this fact.

Lets face it, the bloody rain had to stop sometime.

After I had given Kate her bottle, I sat with her on the bed as I winded her. It was fast becoming clear to me that although I had been lucky enough to be dragged out of the mire of misery, this new found liberation brought with it certain responsibilities.

Yesterday had been very nice.

Really good fun.

But, and the thought came to me unbidden, there's more to life than having fun.

The little man in my head with the sandwich board, which normally says "The End Is Nigh", was today proclaiming "There's More To Life Than Having Fun."

He works for my Conscience department.

I hate him.

The miserable bastard.

He's always showing up with his board and ruining things on me, especially when I'm shopping, proclaiming weighty things like, "You Have Four

Pairs of Boots Already" and "How Can You Justify Spending Twelve Pounds On A Lipstick."

He would completely ruin my shopping. Either I wouldn't buy the item in question. "I'm sorry," I would stammer, as the assistant paused putting the shoes into the box and fixing me with a murderous stare. "I've changed my mind."

Or else I would buy it but I'd feel so guilty about it that all the enjoyment would be gone.

Anyway today the miserable old killjoy reminded me that I had to do a lot more with my life than swanning around a supermarket introducing Kate to boxes of frozen chocolate mousse. What kind of value system was I giving her?

Or making dinner for my family. Or getting odd little crushes on my sister's boyfriend.

I walked over to the window with Kate in my arms and we stood looking down at the garden that Michael so lovingly didn't tend.

I was feeling a bit like a man who is just about to face a firing squad.

A bit on the pensive side.

It was time for me to face the music.

Time to be grown-up and responsible.

Something I've never been any good at.

At the first hint of any trouble in my life, Responsibility goes and locks itself in the bathroom of my brain, refusing to come out. No matter how much Duty and Obligation try to cajole him and persuade him. He stays firmly barricaded in there, sitting hunched on the floor until all the trauma and drama have passed.

I had to address various questions.

Horrible ones.

Involving money and custody of our child and the marital home.

And I swear to God it was so painful. My brain winced as I considered each subject.

This was the first time since I had watched James's back as he walked out of the hospital ward that I had looked at the practicalities of splitting up with him.

Like, should James and I meet to consider selling our flat?

Should we share out our possessions equaliy between the two of us?

That would be extremely amusing.

For example would we drag our three piece suite out into the middle of the room and saw the couch in half, and take a piece each with all the foam and stuffing spilling out, plus a matching chair?

You know, that kind of thing.

I honestly didn't know how we were going to divide most of our possessions. Because they didn't belong to me and they didn't belong to James. They belonged to the elusive third party, "us."

The person or energy, or whatever you want to call it, that was formed by the union of James and I. Which was much more than the sum of its parts.

How I wished I could find the missing "us."

If only I could track it down and lure it back with offers of all these wonderful possessions. Like some awful third-rate game show host.

See that lovely television.

It's yours. Now will you stay?

Have a look at the fine fitted kitchen.

Beautiful isn't it? Well it can all be yours if only you'll come back.

Though I suppose you wouldn't get anything like a fitted kitchen on a third-rate game show.

You'd be lucky to get your bus fare home.

But I wished that it could be as easy as that to get the James and Claire "us" back.

Or if all I had to do would be to put an announcement on the evening news that says something like "Would the James and Claire 'us', last known to be touring the (let's just say) Kerry area please contact the Gardaí in Dublin for an urgent message."

But it looked like the "us" wasn't just missing. It was dead. Killed by James.

And it died intestate.

In theory the state inherits all the possessions belonging to "us."

In practice, of course, nothing so surreal and ridiculous as that was going to happen.

Now pass me that saw, would you?

You see I firmly believed that there was only one way to deal with unpleasant situations – and what was my current situation if not unpleasant? And that was to take a deep breath, face them fairly and squarely, look them in the eye, stare them down and show them who's boss.

Grasp, as it were, the nettle.

Swallow, if you will, the medicine.

If anyone was to ask my advice on how to cope with something that they were dreading, that was exactly what I would tell them to do.

I really believed very strongly in this.

And perhaps one day I might even take my own advice and actually do it.

You see, although I honestly did believe that this was the best way to approach nasty situations I had never had the courage to do it.

I was a master of avoiding unpleasant tasks.

I could have procrastinated for Ireland.

Captain Claire Webster, nee Walsh, Chief Procrastinator, reporting for duty, Sir!

My motto was "always put off till tomorrow what you are supposed to do today. And if you can manage to avoid doing it until next week, then so much the better."

A nice pithy little motto, encapsulating a lot, I liked to think.

To sum up my attitude let me just tell you that I don't think I had ever, in my whole life, done the washing up on the actual night of a dinner-party.

I always promised myself that I would.

That waking up, with a hangover, to filthy plates and a kitchen that looked like a battle-ground was too horrible to contemplate.

But you know what it's like.

The end of the evening has rolled around and the

table is strewn with half-full dishes of melting Baked Alaska, which I have more or less abandoned.

Now I must say, in my defence, that up to this point I am usually a model hostess, positively dancing attendance on my guests, ferrying plates and dishes and cutlery to and from the kitchen as though I was on a conveyor belt.

However my sense of hospitality decreases in direct proportion to the number of glasses of wine that I've had.

So by dessert and coffee time I am usually far too relaxed (all right then, far too drunk, if you will insist on calling a spade a spade) and no longer feel any need to clear the table.

If the table had collapsed in front of me under the weight of the uncleared crockery I would have just laughed.

If my guests wanted a clean table I'm afraid that they'd have had to do it themselves.

They knew where the kitchen was.

Were they waiting for a gilt-edged invitation?

In the middle of the table there always was a completely untouched bowl of fruit.

I mean, what's the problem? Fruit is lovely.

I *always* bought fruit and no one ever ate it. Protestant dessert, Judy called it. My friends said that it was bad enough for me to insult them by offering them something like a banana or an orange for dessert. That their idea of a decent dessert, nay their *only* idea of a dessert, was something positively bursting with saturated fats and refined sugar and double cream and alcohol and egg whites and cholesterol.

The kind of dessert that your arteries contract an inch or two just from looking at.

I was sure that they developed such attitudes in their deprived childhoods.

They probably had to have jelly and custard after every dinner for about twenty years.

God knows, I sympathised. I too had been to that jelly hell.

But to expect them to peel and eat the said piece of fruit with a knife and fork was tantamount to me ordering them from my house and telling them never to return.

So the upshot was that I always bought fruit and my guests always never ate it. If you follow me.

And the view of the table was always obscured by about a thousand glasses, several of them overturned, with their contents, be it white wine, gin and tonic, Irish coffees or Baileys, fast spreading out and intermingling and making friends with each other on the table cloth, forming little seas around the islands of Saxa salt, which some conscientious poor soul (usually James) had thrown down to halt the trail of devastation wreaked by the advancing hordes of spilt red wine.

And I would be on my twenty-second Sambucca and reclining on the two back legs of my chair, or sitting on James's knee telling anyone who'll listen how much I love him.

I had no shame.

My sobriety was less than judgelike but I was at one with the universe. And somehow I usually found that I was really far too mellow and relaxed to think about cleaning.

"It's no bother at all," I would slur, grandiosely waving away drunken offers of help and sending the ash from my cigarette flying into the bowl of cream, or down the front of James's white shirt, (I usually started smoking at this stage in the evening, even though I no longer smoked). "It'll take me ten minutes at the most in the morning."

And the saddest thing of all was that I almost believed it at the time.

And, fool that I was, I never stopped hoping that the washing-up fairies would come in the middle of the night and blitz the place. You could keep the new pairs of shoes. And the money under my pillow. Just wash my kitchen floor.

Every morning after a party I staggered down to the kitchen and for a second I paused with my hand on the kitchen doorknob and had a beautiful warm fantasy that when I flung wide the door that the place would be gleaming, the sun glinting off the polished surfaces, all the cups and plates and bowls and pots and pans scrubbed and put away (in the correct cupboards. I wanted these fairies to be smart as well as hard-working).

Instead, as I gingerly picked my way through the debris, I was hard pressed to find even an unbroken glass for my much-needed couple of Disprin, never mind a clean one.

And while we're on the subject of dinner-parties I'd like the answer to a couple of questions.

Why, at dinner-parties does someone always tear all the paper off the labels on all the bottles of wine, so that when you come down in the morning the table is covered with little annoying sticky scraps of paper that adhere to everything?

Why do I always use the butter dish as an ashtray?

Why does at least one person always say, usually fairly late in the evening I must admit, "I wonder what Dubonnet and Guinness would taste like?" or "What would happen if I lit my glass of Jack Daniels?"

And then proceed to find out.

Just for the record, the Guinness causes the Dubonnet to curdle in the most disgusting fashion and the Jack Daniels goes up like a Kuwaiti oil well that even Red Adair would have his work cut out to contain, and singes and blisters the paint on the dining-room ceiling.

So now you know.

I really wouldn't advise it.

But if you really have to do it, try not to do it in your own house.

Let some other poor idiot have to get out the step-ladder and the dust-sheets and the rollers and brushes.

To be fair to James – although why should I, the bastard – he was always very good about housework and especially about cleaning up after said dinner-parties. He never got as drunk as I did, so at the very least he was in a fit condition to move most of the carnage from the dining table to the kitchen so that in the morning one room was fairly presentable. Apart from, of course, the Jack Daniels scorch marks on the ceiling. But at least I knew I could paint over them.

Again.

I had some paint left after the last dinner-party.

And the inevitable couple of hungover bodies usually to be found in an unshaven and dishevelled state (and that's just the women) on the living-room couch. In fact they were nearly harder to get rid of than said scorch marks on the ceiling. Or the cigarette burns on the carpet.

Lying around for half the day, groaning and demanding cups of tea and Paracetamol and saying that they'll vomit if they move.

Anyway I was doing it again.

Procrastinating, that is.

I was doing everything to avoid doing what I should do.

Trying to make myself think about the practicalities of no longer being with James was like trying to make myself look directly at the sun on a really bright day.

Hard to do either.

And they both made my eyes water.

I suppose I'd better think about the custody of Kate problem. Although was it a problem? James hadn't shown the slightest bit of interest in her. And, after all, he was the (boo, hiss!) adulterer. And because of this, what with him being the wrong-doer and everything, I supposed custody would be automatically awarded to me.

But instead of feeling triumphant about it, I didn't even feel relieved.

This was no victory.

I wanted James to care about our child.

I wanted my child to have a father.

I would have much preferred for James to bring me to court and indulge in bitter slanging matches and slander me by calling me a lesbian, or a woman of low morals (no grounds for slander there, I'm afraid) or whatever. Because, by trying to get custody of Kate by blackening my name, he would at least be caring about her.

I hugged Kate fiercely. I felt so guilty. Because somehow, somewhere, without me even knowing that I was doing it I had messed up and because of that, poor Kate, innocent little bystander, had to do without her Dad.

I just couldn't understand James.

Didn't he have any curiosity at all about Kate?

I couldn't make sense of it.

Was it because Kate is a girl?

If the baby had been a boy would James have tried to make a go of things with me?

Who knew?

I was just trying to make sense of a senseless situation.

And what about our flat?

We had bought it together and it was in both our names. So what did we do?

Sell it and split the proceeds?

Me buy out his share and live there with Kate?

Me sell James my share and let him live there with Denise?

No way!

Whatever happened I was not letting James move another woman into the home that I had made.

I would rather have burnt the place to the ground first.

Well maybe not to the ground. I had no specific bone to pick with the people who lived on the two floors beneath us. Why should they lose their homes just because my husband was moving his fancy woman, his doxy, into the family home.

But I certainly wanted to burn the flat to the floor. Gillian and Ken, the people who lived directly below us, would have had to put up with a flame or two licking their ceiling.

Over my dead body.

You know, anytime I'd heard people saying that passionately I just thought that they were being all Mediterranean and hot-blooded. That they were just playing to the camera and overreacting.

And I knew that I'd said it myself thousands of times but I'd never really meant it until that minute. But I meant it, really meant it then.

Over my dead body, would he move Denise into my home.

And what about money? How on earth was I going to manage to support Kate and myself on my salary?

I barely knew how much I earned.

Other than it was damn all compared to what James earned.

That it was his salary that had kept us afloat since we'd been married.

So now I was going to be poor.

I felt as if I'd wandered out onto a balcony and suddenly realised, to my horror, that there was no ground at all beneath me. Just lots and lots of limitless, empty space for me to fall through.

The thought of being without money was terrifying.

I felt as though I was nothing.

That I was just this faceless woman afloat in a big hostile universe with absolutely nothing to anchor me to anything.

Loath as I am to admit it, I felt less of a human being without my husband and his fat salary.

I hated myself for being so insecure and so dependent. I should have been a strong, sassy, independent, nineties woman. The type of woman who has strong views and who goes to the pictures on her own and who cares about the environment and can change a fuse and goes for aromatherapy and has a herb garden and can speak fluent Italian and has a session in a flotation tank once a week and doesn't need a man to shore up her fragile sense of self-esteem.

But the fact is I wasn't.

I would like to have been.

And maybe I would become one.

It looked as if I'd have no choice.

I'd been pretty much presented with a fait accompli.

But at that time I was more of your fifties wifely type.

I was perfectly happy to be a home-maker while husband went out to earn the loot.

And if husband was prepared to share the

household chores as well as earn the lion's share of the loot, then so much the better.

I suppose I wanted to have my cake and eat it.

But then again, what were you going to do with your cake if not eat it?

Frame it?

Use it as a draught excluder?

Put it in to scent your knickers drawer?

That must surely be one of the most stupid sayings I've ever heard.

How were James and I going to separate the funds from our joint bank account? It was going to be like trying to separate Siamese twins. Ones that were joined at all the vital organs. The heart and the lungs and the liver. It would be impossible.

I would have nearly given up all rights to the money to save all the inevitable wrangling. The only thing that was stopping me from writing off any money of mine in the bank account was the idea of James spending it on Denise. Buying her flowers and theatre tickets and fancy underwear. I was sorry, but I could see no way that I could let money of mine subsidise such a scheme. I was opposed to it on principle.

It was morally wrong.

Besides, I'd seen a really nice pair of shoes yesterday in the shopping centre and I wanted them for my own.

I can't describe the feeling of immediate familiarity that rushed between us. The moment I clapped eyes on them I felt like I already owned them. I could only suppose that we were together in a former life. That they were my shoes when I was a serving wench in Medieval Britain or when I was a princess in ancient Egypt. Or perhaps they were the wench or the princess and I was the shoes. Who's to know? Either way I knew that we were meant to be together.

And I had no immediate access to funds. Therefore I had to lay claim to my money in England.

Sordid and unpleasant as it might be.

My head swam slightly at all this.

Kind of like the way it had swum the night before when Mum started her Cher and Ike conversation.

Little did I think, the warm April day three years ago when I married James, that our union would end in such a way.

That something that started out as such good fun and so full of hope and excitement could end in heartbreak and legalese.

That I would be dealing in so many clichés.

Arguing about money and possessions.

I'd always thought that James and I would be different. That even though we might be married that there was no reason that we had to act it, Goddammit!

That fun and love and passion would always be the most important things to us.

I'd vowed that there would never come a day when I would walk into a room and say to James, without even looking at him, "The tiles in the bathroom are coming loose. You'd better take a look at them."

Or, again giving him but the most cursory of

glances, "I hope you're not thinking of wearing that jumper to the Reynolds's dinner."

The same way that I'd vowed not to be the kind of woman who determinedly ate her way round the kitchen table finishing her children's leftover dinners.

Or the kind of woman who addressed her husband directly as "Daddy". Not in the "No darling, leave the razor, that's Daddy's" sense. Although I'm not too keen on that either.

But in the "Will we get ice cream now, Daddy?" sense. As if your husband and yourself had ceased to mean anything to each other any longer in your own right. That you no longer existed as people. All you were now was parents of children. Your lover was no longer your lover. He was simply the other parent of your children.

I had promised myself that I would never turn into everyone's mother.

Fine women and all as they no doubt are.

I was amazed how arrogant I had been.

And how naïve.

What on earth had made me think I would be any different?

Hadn't I realised that thousands of women before me had made a pact with themselves never to lose the magic in their marriage?

The same way that they fiercely promised themselves that they would never let their grey hair show, would never let their breasts droop, would never get wrinkles.

But it still happened.

Their will wasn't strong enough to fight the inevitable, to reverse the waves of time.

And neither was mine.

I lay Kate back down in her cot while I went to have a shower. I was obviously really getting to grips with this living business, I thought to myself proudly.

"Cleanliness," I told Kate, feeling very self-righteous, feeling that I was a Good Mother, "is next to Godliness."

"And I'll tell you what Godliness is when you're a bit older."

In the shower I couldn't stop thinking about James. Not in a maudlin or bitter way. Just remembering how great it had been. Really, even though he had hurt me in a way I never thought he would I couldn't forget just how brilliant it was with him.

When I first met James and we were out with other people, I would watch him across a room, talking to someone else. I would always think to myself how sexy and handsome he looked. Especially if he was looking all serious and accountant-like. That always made me smile. He looked as if he was no fun at all.

But, let me tell you I knew differently.

And it gave me such a thrill to know that when the party or whatever had ended that my man would be coming home with me. I wanted it always to be like that.

I had seen enough married women get fat and unattractive and speak to their husbands as if they were handy-men. And it made me very sad.

What was the point in being married if all the

magic was gone? If your only points of contact were the state of decay and disrepair of your dwelling place? Or how badly your children were doing at school?

You might as well be married to a Black and Decker drill. Or to a text-book on child psychology.

Anyway, I still couldn't make any sense of it.

I loved him.

I had wanted it to work.

I had tried very hard to make things beautiful.

Actually that wasn't true at all.

I didn't have to try hard at all to make things beautiful. They just were beautiful effortlessly.

Well I'd thought they were.

I thought that all the searching for The Right Person was over for both of us. I had met a man who loved me unconditionally. Even better than the unconditional love that my mother had for me, because unfortunately that unconditional love had certain conditions attached.

And he'd made me laugh in the same way that my sisters or my girl-friends could make me laugh. But it was even better because I didn't usually wake up in the same bed as my sisters or my girl-friends.

So the opportunities for having a good laugh with James were far more plentiful and in far nicer places.

And about far nicer places too, I suppose.

You know, I thought if anyone was going to have an affair that it would be me.

Not that I thought that I *would* have had one, if you know what I mean.

But I was always the loud rowdy one who was regarded as great fun.

And popular opinion held James to be the sensible reliable one.

Quiet, self-contained, as steady as a rock.

That's the trouble with men who wear suits and reading glasses and who fix you with a sincere gaze and say things like "Well in a period of low inflation, a fixed rate mortgage is your best bet," or "I would sell the treasury stock and buy Government equities," or some such similar statement.

You get hoodwinked into thinking that they're as dull as ditchwater and as safe as houses.

And I suppose that even I did a bit with James.

I felt that I could behave or misbehave in any fashion that took my fancy and that he would smile tolerantly on me.

He was amused by me.

No, not amused. That sounds sort of patronising and disdainful.

But he was certainly entertained by me.

He really thought I was great.

And I, on the other hand, felt very safe and secure and protected with James.

The very fact that I knew I could make a show of myself and James would still love me ensured that I *didn't* make a show of myself.

I didn't get drunk very often any more.

But even in the days when I did and I would wake up the next morning with a pounding headache and cringing from the few snippets of what

I could remember of the previous evening, he would be so sweet.

He would laugh kindly and get me glasses of water and lean over and kiss me on my throbbing forehead as I lay like a corpse in the bed and say soothing things like "No, sweetie, you weren't obnoxious. You were really funny," and "No, darling, you weren't overbearing. You had us all in stitches," and "Your bag will turn up. It was probably under some coats at Lisa's. I'll ring her now," and "Of course you can look those people in the eye again. I mean, everyone was plastered. You weren't the drunkest by any stretch of the imagination."

And on one really awful occasion, my worst "morning after" ever, I think – the promises to never drink again were thick on the ground that morning I can tell you – "Hurry up angel, your hearing is at nine-thirty. You can't be late because the solicitor said your judge is a right bastard."

Now look, wait a minute. Just let me explain. Please hear me out.

Yes, I was arrested one night but it wasn't because I did anything illegal. I was simply in the wrong place at the wrong time. I just happened to be somewhere that just happened to be an unlicensed drinking club. I had no idea that the people running the place were doing anything criminal.

Apart from the price they were charging for the wine.

And the jackets the bouncers were wearing.

The jackets alone deserved ten years solitary confinement.

I don't know how I managed to get mixed up in it. All I know for sure is that drink was taken and spirits were high.

When we saw the policemen entering the club and everyone started hiding their drinks under their tables, Judy and Laura and I thought it was brilliant fun.

"Just like prohibition," we laughingly agreed.

I decided that I would tell my favourite joke to some of the policemen, which is the one that goes: How many policemen does it take to break a lightbulb? The answer being, of course, none. It fell down the stairs.

And one of the policemen took great umbrage at this and told me that, if I didn't behave, that he would arrest me.

"Arrest me then," I smiled up at him saucily and extended both my wrists for him to put the bracelets on. I obviously hadn't come to terms with the fact that these were real policemen and not just strippograms.

So no one was more surprised than I was when the policeman did just that.

Of course I realised that he was only doing his duty.

I bore him no grudges. I wasn't bitter.

The bastard.

I must admit that I was very, very taken aback.

I tried to tell him that I was just a suburban, middle-class young woman. That I had even managed to get a man to marry me and that *he* was an accountant. I told him all this to let him know that

I was on the same side as him. Righting wrongs and fighting injustice and all that.

And that by arresting me that he was throwing everyone's stereotype of a drunk and disorderly person into disarray.

So off I went in the squad car, peering tearfully out the window at Laura and Judy.

"Call James," I mouthed at them as I was driven off.

I knew that he would know what to do.

And he did.

He bailed me out and got me a solicitor.

And I don't think I have ever, ever in my whole life been so frightened.

I was convinced that I would have a confession beaten out of me and I'd be jailed for several lifetimes and I'd never see James or my friends or family again.

I'd never see blue sky again, except from the exercise yard, I thought feeling intensely sorry for myself. I'd never wear nice clothes again. I'd have to wear those horrible prison sack dresses.

And I'd have to become a lesbian. I'd have to become the girl-friend of Missus Big so that she'd protect me from all the other girls and their Coke bottles.

And I already had a degree and it was no big deal.

And I'd have to start smoking again.

And I was no good at doing an Australian accent.

I was distraught.

So when James came to the police station and

bailed me out, or "sprung" me as I preferred to call it, I couldn't believe that there were no television cameras and delirious crowds with banners outside.

Just another squad car which screeched to a halt, scraping the kerb. About five drunks tumbling out.

James took me home.

He got the name of a solicitor from a friend and rang him.

He woke me in the morning, when I couldn't open my eyes because of the terrible sense of foreboding.

He wiped off my lipstick and told me it might be better for my case if I didn't look like a good-time girl.

He made me wear a long skirt and a high-necked blouse for the same reason.

He sat in the courtroom holding my hand as I waited for my turn to come.

He hummed little songs to me as I sat there white-faced and nauseous with the shock and the hangover.

I found the songs that he was humming very comforting.

Until I caught a few words of one.

Something about breaking rocks and being on a chain gang.

I turned and glared at him tearfully, ready to tell him to fuck off and go home if he found my predicament that amusing.

But I caught his eye.

And I just couldn't help it.

I started to laugh.

He was right.

The whole situation was so ridiculous that there was no point to *not* laughing at it.

The pair of us sniggered like schoolchildren.

The judge gave us a filthy look.

"That's another ten years onto your sentence," snorted James and the pair of us collapsed again.

I got off with a fifty pound fine, which James laughingly paid.

"You can pay it yourself the next time," he grinned at me.

I couldn't believe his attitude. If someone woke me at two in the morning to tell me that James had been arrested I would have been horrified. I certainly wouldn't have found the situation funny the way he had.

I would have seriously asked myself to think about what kind of man I had married.

I wouldn't have been indulgent and so completely supportive and forgiving the way James was.

In fact he wasn't even forgiving, because he never for a second acted as if I had done something wrong.

So now the next time I got arrested I wouldn't have anyone to hold my hand in the courtroom and make me laugh.

Not to mention having to pay the bloody fine myself.

Sometimes he was just so sweet. When I used to wake in the middle of the night to worry, he was wonderful.

"What's wrong, baby?" he used to ask.

"Nothing," I'd say, unable to put words on that horrible, nameless, free-floating anxiety.

"Can't you sleep?"

"No."

"Will I bore you to sleep?"

"Yes, please."

And I would eventually fall into a peaceful sleep, lulled by the sound of James's soothing voice explaining tax breaks for charities or the new VAT regulations set by the European Union.

I turned off the shower and dried myself.

I'd better ring him, I told myself.

I went back into my room and started to get dressed.

"Ring him," I ordered myself sternly.

"After I've fed Kate," I replied in a vague and wishy-washy fashion.

"Ring him!" I told myself again.

"Do you want the child to *starve*?" I asked, trying to sound outraged. "I'll ring him when I've fed her."

"No you won't. Ring him NOW!"

I was up to my old tricks again.

Procrastinating, avoiding responsibility, running away from unpleasant situations.

But I was so afraid.

I *knew* that I had to talk to James about money and the flat and all that. I wasn't denying that for a minute. But I felt that the moment that I actually spoke to him about these things they would become real.

And if they were real it meant that my marriage was over.

And I didn't want it to be.

"Oh God," I sighed.

I looked at Kate, lying in her cot, soft and plump and fragrant in her little pink babygro.

And I knew that I had to ring James.

I could be a yaller-bellied, lily-livered, cringing coward on my own account all I liked, but I owed it to this beautiful child of mine to sort out her future.

"Right," I said resignedly, looking at her. "You've twisted my arm. I'll ring him."

I went into Mum's room to use the phone there.

I started to dial the number of James's office in London and I began to feel dizzy.

Excited and frightened at the same time.

In a few moments I'd hear his voice.

And I couldn't wait.

I was warm and shaky with anticipation.

I'd be speaking to him, to my James, my best friend.

Except, of course, he wasn't anymore, was he?

But sometimes I forgot. Just for a second.

It was becoming very hard for me to breathe. My breath didn't seem to be able to go down all the way.

The phone connected and started to ring.

A thrill ran through me and I thought I might vomit.

The receptionist answered.

"Er, can I speak to Mr James Webster, please," I asked, my voice wobbling. My lips felt as if I'd been given an injection to numb them.

There were a couple of clicks on the line.

I'd be speaking to him in a moment.

I held my breath.

It wasn't as if the breathing that I had been doing had been particularly successful anyway.

Another click.

And the receptionist was back.

"I'm sorry, Mr Webster is away this week. Can anyone else help?"

The disappointment was so painful that I could hardly stammer out, "No, that's all right, thank you."

And I hung up the phone.

I stayed sitting on Mum's bed.

I didn't really know what to do now.

It had been such an ordeal to ring him. It was such a hard thing to do. And then, in spite of myself, I had been excited about talking to him. And he wasn't even there.

What a let-down.

I had gallons of adrenaline coursing through my body, making prickles of sweat break out on my forehead, making my hands wet and shaky, making me lightheaded, and I just didn't know what to do with it.

And then the thought just struck me, where *was* James?

Please don't tell me that he's gone on holiday.

On *holiday?*

How could he go on holiday when his marriage was breaking up? Had broken up, in fact.

Maybe he's on a course, I thought desperately.

I half-thought of ringing the receptionist back and asking her where James was.

But I stopped myself. I wasn't going to throw away the tiny bit of pride I had left.

Maybe he's sick, I thought. Maybe he has the flu'.

I probably would have welcomed the news that he had terminal cancer.

Anything, but don't let him have gone on holiday.

The thought of him having a life without me, the thought of him actually *enjoying* that life, was deeply unpleasant.

On the one hand of course I knew that he was having a life without me. I mean, all the evidence was there. He was living with another woman, he hadn't contacted me, not even to see how Kate was. But still, I suppose I hadn't stopped hoping that he might be pining for me and missing me terribly and that he would eventually come back.

But if he'd gone on holiday then that wasn't the case.

He mustn't have a care in the world, I thought, my imagination running riot. Probably off with his fancy woman in some exotic resort. Drinking Pina Coladas from Denise's shoe. His life resonating to the sound of champagne corks popping and fireworks exploding and surrounded by music and happy people, wearing party hats and decorated with streamers, dancing past him, whooping and doing the conga.

While I was freezing in this March weather, I was fully convinced that James was living it up in some very expensive Caribbean resort, where he had fourteen houseboys and a private swimming pool and the air was scented with frangipani blossoms.

I had no idea what frangipani blossoms were like. I simply knew that they regularly appeared in this type of scenario.

"Oh dear," I thought, swallowing. I certainly hadn't expected to feel like this.

Now what do I do?

Mum marched into the room with a huge bundle of freshly ironed clothes in her arms.

She stopped in surprise when she saw me.

"What's wrong with you?" she demanded, looking at my white miserable face.

"I rang James," I told her and burst into tears.

"Oh Lord," she said, putting the pile of clothes down on a chair and coming over to sit beside me.

"What did he say?" she asked.

"Nothing," I sobbed. "He wasn't there. I bet he's gone on holidays with that fat bitch. And I bet they flew first class. And I bet they have a Jacuzzi in their bathroom."

Mum put her arms around me.

And eventually I stopped crying.

"Do you want a hand putting the ironing away?" I asked Mum in a snivelly and tearful voice.

That made her look *really* worried. "Are you OK?" she said anxiously.

"Yes," I said. "I'm fine."

"Are you sure?" she said, still not convinced.

"Yes," I insisted, a bit annoyed.

I was fine.

I had better get used to feeling this upset, I decided.

Because it was going to happen a lot. At least

until I came to terms with the fact that it really was over with James.

All right, so I really did feel awful now.

Hurt and shocked.

But in a while those feelings wouldn't hurt so much. The pain would go away.

So I wasn't going to take to the bed for a week.

I was going to square my shoulders and get on with things.

And I'd ring him on Monday.

That'd be a really good time to talk to him.

He was bound to be feeling really miserable then anyway, what with being back at work and having the post-holiday blues and jet lag.

I was trying to cheer myself up by pretending that I would be glad to see him being miserable.

And if I didn't think too hard about it, it would work for a little while.

"Right then Mum," I said determinedly. "Let's put these clothes away."

I went purposefully over to the pile of freshly ironed clothes on the chair. Mum looked a little bit knocked for six as I started to quickly sort them out.

I picked up an armful and said to Mum, "I'll put these in Anna's drawer."

"But . . . " started Mum.

"No buts," I told her, soothingly.

"No Claire . . . " she said anxiously.

"Mum," I insisted, quite touched by her concern, but determined to pull myself together and be a dutiful daughter. "I'm fine now."

And I left her bedroom, making for Anna's.

Mum's door swung shut behind me. So her voice was muffled when she called out to me. "Claire! For God's sake. How am I going to explain to your father why his underpants are in Anna's drawer?"

I was on my knees in front of Anna's chest of drawers.

I paused in what I was doing.

I wasn't putting Dad's underpants in Anna's drawer, was I?

I was.

I realised that I had better move them. Because there was no way that Anna would realise that there was anything unusual when she changed her knickers and found herself wearing huge, baggy y-fronts.

Always assuming that she did in fact change her knickers.

Or wear knickers at all, now that I came to think of it.

I was sure I'd heard her going on about clothes – especially underclothes – being a form of fascism. Vague talk of air needing to circulate and skin needing to breathe and canalways needing to feel liberated and unrestricted just led me to suspect that knickers and the wearing thereof may not feature highly on Anna's list of priorities.

With a martyred sigh, I gathered up the bundle of underpants.

Chapter Thirteen

I was meeting Laura for a drink that evening.

I'd better give you a little bit of background here.

Laura, Judy and I were in college together. And we have been friends ever since.

Judy lived in London.

And Laura lived in Dublin.

I hadn't seen Laura since I fled from London, minus a husband and with a baby but I had spoken on the phone to her a few times.

I told her I was far too depressed to see her.

And because she was a good friend she didn't get all huffy with me but told me not to worry and that I would feel better eventually and that she'd see me then.

I told her that I would never feel better and that I would never see her again but that it had been lovely knowing her.

I had a feeling that she had rung Mum a few times over the past month, to make discreet enquiries about the state of my heart (still broken at the last check-up), my mental health (still very unstable) and my popularity (at an all-time low).

But she hadn't pestered me and for that I was very grateful.

But now I was feeling a good deal better so I rang her and suggested meeting in town for a drink.

Laura sounded delighted at this idea.

"We'll get plastered," she said enthusiastically over the phone.

I'm not sure whether this was a suggestion or a prediction.

Either way it was a foregone conclusion.

"I'd say we will all right," I agreed, if our encounters over the past ten years or so were anything to go by.

I was feeling quite alarmed.

I'd forgotten what an unbridled hedonist Laura was.

She could have shown those Roman Emperors a thing or two.

Mum said she was only too delighted to look after Kate.

After the dinner, (microwaved frozen shepherd's pie, not too bad actually), I went upstairs to get ready for my first social outing since my husband left me.

Quite an occasion.

A bit like losing my virginity or making my first Communion or getting married. Something that only happens once.

I hadn't a stitch to wear.

I began to feel very sorry and very foolish indeed at the martyrish way I had left all my lovely clothes behind in London. Behaving like a condemned man on his way to the gallows, crying dramatically, saying my life was over, and that I wouldn't be needing clothes where I was going.

I was only going to Dublin.

Not to the afterlife.

Honestly I was pathetic.

I should have known that sooner or later I would feel almost normal again.

Not wildly happy, or anything as wonderful as that, mind.

But able to cope.

In view of the fact that all my nice clothes were in a different city I was left with no option but to misappropriate some of Helen's things.

She would be annoyed.

There was no denying this.

But she was annoyed with me anyway for the alleged fancying of her boyfriend so what had I got to lose?

Various allusions to sheep, lambs and hangings.

I started to rifle frantically through Helen's hangers. Honestly, she had some really lovely clothes.

I felt the sap rising, the old juices start to flow.

I loved clothes.

I was like a man who was dying of thirst in the desert, who unexpectedly stumbles across a fridge full of ice-cold 7-up.

I had spent far too long in that nightdress.

I found a little wine-coloured pinafore type dress in her wardrobe. That'll do nicely, I thought, as I clambered feverishly into it.

I went back to my room and looked at myself in the mirror and for the second time in two days I was surprised and delighted with what I saw.

I looked tallish and slimmish and youngish.

Not a bit like a single parent.

Or a deserted wife.

Whatever they're supposed to look like.

With a pair of woolly tights and my boots I looked pleasingly girlish (ha!) and innocent (double ha!).

And, if the pinafore was a little bit too short for me, exposing an alarming amount of my thigh what with Helen being a good deal smaller than me, then so much the better.

Further allusions to clouds and linings that are silver.

And even more allusions, this time from my mother who came in to talk to me while I was getting ready, to lamb and some mutton that happened to be attired like the lamb.

More allusions from me pointing out the bone-breaking ability of sticks and stones and the fact that name-calling doesn't have quite the same devastating effects.

Another allusion from her regarding silk purses and sow's ears and the impossibility of converting one into the other.

I quickly tried to think of another proverb and couldn't.

"Fuck off," I told her.

I'd had enough of allusions for one evening. A little bit of plain speaking was called for.

Then I piled on the make-up. I was quite excited about going out. I'd forgotten what fun it was.

I usually loved going out.

I was normally a very sociable person.

When my husband hadn't just left me I was great fun to be around.

Never one to turn down an invitation.

We might as well enjoy ourselves while we can, I always say, because we'll be dead long enough.

There will be plenty of time for staying in and ironing our workclothes for the coming week in the next life.

I was usually one of the first to arrive at a party.

Invariably one of the last to leave.

A generous glob of foundation energetically larded onto my face took away the white pasty Winter pallor.

I subscribed to the quantity as well as quality school of make-up application.

And even though a tan is supposed to be an eighties status symbol and completely out of place in the natural and right-on nineties, I'm ashamed to say that I still wished I had one.

All right, all right, so excessive exposure to the sun gives us skin cancer and, worse again, gives us skin like Australians. But I thought a smooth brown face looked very healthy and attractive.

And what was the use of protecting ourselves from dying from skin cancer and obsessively avoiding the sun and going round looking like a cadaver when we could be knocked down by a bus tomorrow?

Anyway I didn't have a tan. I just wished I had one. I suppose that's nearly as bad.

And I was perfectly prepared to use make-up to

fake one. So you couldn't describe my made-up look as pale and interesting.

Interesting, maybe. But not pale.

Two stripes of blusher, one on each cheekbone.

Actually that looked a bit scary until I blended it.

I was sure I heard Mum muttering something that sounded like "Coco the Clown" and I turned around sharply but she was just inspecting her finger-nails with a completely impassive face.

I must have imagined it.

Some intense red lipstick, to make sure that, although I was wearing a girlish dress, you could never mistake me for anything other than a woman.

Woman.

I loved that word.

I was a woman.

I would have said it out loud but amazingly Mum hadn't stormed from the room when I used the "F" word and was still sitting on the bed while I put on my make-up and I felt that I had alarmed her enough over the past month.

But it was such an evocative word.

Woman.

So voluptuous. So sensuous.

Or was it sensual?

I always mix those two up.

Back to more mundane things.

Grey eyeliner and black mascara made my eyes look really blue.

And with my newly-washed shiny hair I was very pleased with the overall effect.

Of course Mum wasn't.

"Are you going to wear a skirt with that top?" she asked.

"Mum, you know perfectly well that this is a dress, not a top," I told her calmly.

Nothing she could say or do would stop me from feeling good about myself.

"It might well be a dress on Helen," she acknowledged. "But it's too short to be anything but a top on you."

I ignored her.

"And did you ask Helen could you borrow it?" she said, obviously hell-bent on destroying my good mood. "Because I'll get the flak from Helen. You won't care. You'll be in town with your rowdy friends knocking back the Malibu and Lucozade or whatever it is you drink. And I'll be here, being shouted at like a tinker's dog, by my youngest daughter. And it's not like any of us are in Helen's best books at the moment anyway."

"Oh shut up, Mum," I told her. "I'll leave a note for Helen explaining that I've borrowed it. And when I get my clothes from London she can borrow some of mine."

Silence from Mum.

"Is that OK?" I asked her.

"Yes," she smiled.

"And you look lovely," she added grudgingly.

Just before I left my bedroom to go downstairs, a glint from the dressing-table caught my eye. It was my wedding ring. I had forgotten to put it back on after my shower. It lay there winking up at me, obviously dead keen to get out of the house for a bit.

So I went over and picked it up. But I didn't put it on. My marriage is over, I thought and maybe I'll start to believe it if I don't wear my wedding ring anymore. I put the ring back down on the dressing table.

Of course it was furious – it just couldn't believe that I wasn't going to wear it. And then it was upset. But I didn't give in to it. I couldn't afford any sentiment. I decided to leave before the recriminations started. "Sorry," I said shortly, turning my back, switching off the light and walking from the room.

Dad was watching golf on the television when I went in to him to borrow his car keys.

I think I gave him a bit of a fright when I finally managed to wrench his attention away from the men in the Rupert the Bear trousers.

"You're very glamorous," he said, looking startled. "Where are you off to?"

"Into town to meet Laura," I told him.

"Well don't get the bloody car vandalised," he said alarmed.

Dad came from a small town in the west of Ireland and, although he had lived in Dublin for thirty-three years, he still didn't trust Dubliners. He thought that they were all petty criminals and thugs.

And he seemed to think that the centre of Dublin was like Beirut. Except that Beirut was far nicer.

"I won't get it vandalised, Dad," I told him. "I'll leave it in a car-park."

But that didn't calm him down either.

"Well make sure that you collect it by midnight,"

he said, getting very agitated. "Because all the car-parks close then. And if you don't get it, I'll have to walk to work in the morning."

I forbore from telling him, but only just, that he wouldn't have to walk anywhere in the morning if I got the car impounded. That there was actually nothing stopping him from borrowing Mum's car or using public transport.

"Don't worry Dad," I assured him. "Now give me the keys."

He reluctantly handed them over.

"And don't go changing the radio station. I don't want to turn it on in the morning and be deafened by pop music."

"If I change it, I'll change it back," I sighed.

"And if you adjust the seat forward make sure you move it back again. I don't want to get in in the morning and think I've put on loads of weight in the night."

"Don't worry Dad," I told him patiently, as I picked up my coat and bag, "See you later."

It is easier for a camel to pass through the eye of a needle than to borrow the car off Dad.

As I closed the sitting-room door behind me I heard him calling after me, "Where are you going without a skirt?" but I kept walking.

It was awful leaving Kate. It was the first time that I had gone out without her and it was a real wrench. In fact I nearly brought her with me but then I realised that she'd be spending enough time in noisy smoky pubs when she's older, so no call for her to start just yet.

"You *will* check on her every fifteen minutes," I said tearfully to Mum.

"Yes," she said.

"Every *fifteen* minutes," I emphasised.

"Yes," she said.

"You won't forget?" I said anxiously.

"No," she said, starting to sound a bit annoyed.

"But what if you're watching something on telly and you get distracted?" I suggested.

"I won't forget!" she said, sounding definitely annoyed. "I know how to look after a child, you know. I *have* managed to rear five of my own."

"I know," I told her, "it's just that Kate is special."

"Claire!" said Mum in exasperation, "will you just bloody well go!"

"Fine, fine," I said, quickly checking that the baby intercom was switched on, "I'm going,"

"Have a nice time," called Mum.

"I'll try," I said, bottom lip trembling.

The drive into town was nightmarish.

Did you know that if you listen hard enough *everything* sounds like a baby crying?

The wind in the trees, the rain on the roof of the car, the hum of the engine.

I was convinced that I could hear Kate crying for me, always faintly, nearly out of earshot.

It was unbearable.

I very nearly turned the car around and went back home.

If it wasn't for Common Sense making a guest appearance in my head, that's probably exactly what I would have done.

"You're being ridiculous," said Common Sense.

"You're obviously not a mother yourself," I retorted.

"No," admitted Common Sense, "I'm not. But you've got to realise that you can't be with her every moment for the rest of her life. What about when you go back to work and she has to go to a child-minder? Well, how are you going to cope then? Just think of this as good practice."

"You're right," I sighed, calming down for a moment. Then panic gripped me again. What if she died? What if she died that night?

Just then, like an oasis in the desert, I saw a phonebox. I swung the car over, much to the annoyance of the drivers behind me. Beeping their horns and shouting things at me, the heartless bastards.

"Mum," I said tremulously.

"Who's this?" she asked.

"It's *me*," I said, feeling as if I was going to burst into tears.

"*Claire?*" she said, sounding outraged. "What the hell do you want?"

"Has anything happened to Kate?" I asked, breathlessly.

"Claire! Stop this! Kate is absolutely fine."

"Really?" I asked, hardly daring to believe it.

"Really," she said, in a nicer voice. "Look, this does get easier, you know. The first time is the worst. Now go and enjoy yourself and I promise that I'll ring you if anything happens."

"Thanks Mum," I said, feeling a lot better.

I got back into the car and drove into town and parked the car (yes, in a car-park) and went down to the pub to meet Laura.

She was already there when I arrived.

It was wonderful to see her. I hadn't seen her in months.

I told her she looked lovely, because she did. She told me that I looked lovely. Although I'm not sure whether I did or not.

She said that she looked like an old hag.

I said that I looked like a dog.

I said that she didn't look like an old hag.

She said that I didn't look like a dog.

Pleasantries over, I went to get us some drinks.

There were several million people in the pub. Or at least that was how it felt. But Laura and I were lucky enough to get seats.

I suppose I must be getting old. There was a time when I would have cheerfully stood, pint in hand, in the midst of all these people, being swept along, like seaweed in the tide. Not minding that the person I was supposed to be talking to was now several yards away and that most of my pint was spilt on my wrist.

Laura wanted to know all about Kate. And I was only too happy to tell her.

When I was younger I promised myself that I would never turn into a baby-bore. You know, the kind of person who goes on and on about their baby and how she smiled at them for the first time today and how beautiful she is and all that, while all around them people are twitching and going into spasm with boredom. And I was a bit alarmed to find that that's exactly what I was doing. But I couldn't help it . It was different when it's your own baby.

The only thing I can say in my defence is that when you have one yourself you'll know what I mean.

Maybe Laura was bored out of her skull, but she did a very decent impression of being interested in Kate.

"I'm dying to see her," she said. Gamely, I thought.

"Why don't you come out at the weekend," I said. "And we'll spend an afternoon together and you can play with her."

And then Laura wanted to know what giving birth was like. So we discussed that in gory detail for a while.

Until Laura started to look a bit sweaty and faint.

And then of course, we moved onto the main item on the agenda. The real business of the evening. The main feature. The star act.

James.

James Webster, the Incredible Disappearing Husband.

Laura had all the details already.

From a variety of sources, my mother, Judy and a lot of other friends. So she didn't really need to know what had happened. She was more interested in how I was now and what I was planning to do.

"I don't know, Laura," I told her. "I don't know whether I'll go back to London or whether I'll stay here. I don't know what to do about my flat. I don't really know what to do about anything."

"You'll really have to talk to James," she told me.

"Oh don't I just know it," I said.

Slightly bitterly, I must admit.

So we discussed my responsibilities for a while. And we hazarded guesses as to what my future was going to be like.

Then I got a bit distressed talking about that, so I changed the subject and asked Laura who she was currently having sex with.

It was much more entertaining talking about that, let me tell you.

The lucky recipient of Laura's current sexual favours was a nineteen-year-old art student.

"Nineteen!" I shrieked, at a decibel that caused glasses to shatter in the hands of several startled drinkers in a pub about half a mile away. "Nineteen! Are you serious?"

"Yes," she laughed. "But it's a disaster really. He never has a penny so all we can afford to do is have sex."

"But couldn't you pay for the two of you to go out?" I asked.

"I could, I suppose," she said. "But he looks like such a tinker I'd be too ashamed to bring him anywhere."

"Is he always covered in paint?" I asked.

"He is," she said. "But it's not just that. He seems to have only one jumper. And no socks. And the less said about his jocks, the better."

"Ugh," I said. "'That sounds a bit awful."

"Ah no, it's not really," Laura assured me. "He's mad about me. He thinks I'm gorgeous. And my ego could do with it."

"So do you really just have sex?", I asked intrigued. "I mean don't you talk and that?"

"Not really," she said. "Honestly, we have nothing in common. He's from a different generation. He comes round. We have sex and a bit of a laugh. He tells me I'm the most beautiful woman he's ever met – I'm probably the *only* woman he's ever met – and he leaves in the morning – usually taking a pair of my sports socks with him – asks me for his bus fare and off he goes. It's great!"

Gosh, I thought, looking at Laura with frank admiration.

"You're such a nineties woman," I told her. "You're so cool."

"Not really," she said, "I'm just keeping the wolf from the door. Any port in a storm, that kind of thing."

"So is he your *boyfriend*?" I asked. "I mean, would you walk down Grafton Street holding his hand?"

"Lord no!" she said, looking horrified. "What if I met someone I knew? No, no, the little angel is purely a temporary measure. Keeping the bed warm until Mr Right gets here. Although I can't think what's taking him so long."

Although I was very happy to see Laura I was very aware that this was actually my first social outing as a single woman in over five years.

And it was my first social outing without my wedding ring. I felt very vulnerable and naked without it. It was only when I wasn't wearing it that I realised how secure I felt when I was wearing it. You know, it makes a statement, it says something like

233

"I'm not desperate for a man, because I already have one. No, really, I do. Just look at my wedding ring."

Laura had split up with her boyfriend, Frank, about a year or so before.

So, in spite of Laura's teenaged lover we were, to all intents and purposes, two single women sipping wine in a crowded city centre pub on a Thursday night in March.

I wondered if men could smell desperation from us.

I wondered if there was desperation to be smelt.

Was I giving Laura my undivided attention? Or was one part of my attention scanning the crowd for attractive men? Was I keeping tabs on how many men had given me admiring glances since I arrived?

None, actually, just for the record.

Not, of course, that I was counting or anything.

I laughed at something Laura told me.

But I couldn't be sure that I was really laughing.

Maybe I just wanted to show the men in the pub that I was perfectly happy and well-adjusted and not feeling like a quarter of a person without a man.

My God, but I was really starting to feel depressed. I felt as if I was wearing a neon sign over my head that said "Recently Dumped" in flashing pink and purple lights, and then "Worthless Without a Man" in orange and red lights.

All my confidence in myself had gone.

I had never realised that I would feel so stigmatised.

When James and I were happily married I would frequently meet girl-friends for drinks in pubs and not give it a second thought.

Why had it suddenly become such a problem?

Laura noticed that I had started to droop like a dying plant and made routine enquiries. I tearfully tried to tell her how I was feeling.

"Don't worry," she told me kindly. "When Frank left me for the twenty-year-old I felt so *ashamed*. Like it was all my fault that he had run off. And I felt that I was worth less than nothing without him. But that passes."

"Does it?" I asked her, my eyes brimming with tears.

"Honestly, it does," she promised me.

"I feel like such a reject," I tried to explain to her.

"I know, I know," she said. "And you feel like everyone else knows it."

"Exactly," I said, feeling thankful that I wasn't the only person who ever felt like this.

"All right," I said, drying my eyes. "Time for more drinks."

I fought my way through the happy crowds of people and finally got to the bar. I stood there, being jostled and having elbows stuck in my face and drinks spilt down my back as I tried to attract the barman's attention. Just as I was coming to the conclusion that I would have to lift up my dress and show him my boobs before he would notice me, someone put their hands on my waist and squeezed.

This was all I needed! Someone taking advantage of a single woman of a certain age!

Outraged, I turned round as quickly as I could in the confined space ready to apprehend someone for sexual harassment.

And came face to face, as it were, with someone's chest.

It was the beautiful Adam.

Adam, who might or might not be Helen's boyfriend.

The jury was still out.

"Hello," he smiled charmingly. "I saw you from the other side of the bar. Do you need a hand?"

"Oh hello," I said maintaining my composure, but feeling delighted to meet him. What a stroke of luck that Laura chose this pub, I thought.

"Am I damn glad to see you?" I said. "I haven't even placed my order yet. The barman hates me."

He laughed.

And I laughed. I had completely forgotten that we were supposed to be feeling awkward with each other after the little scene in my bedroom where he practically suggested that we make babies.

Adam said, "I'll order the drinks for you."

I gave him the money and told him to get two glasses of red wine and whatever he was having.

I took pride in remembering where I came from. I hadn't forgotten my roots. I too was once a penniless student. I remembered watching people practically lighting their cigarettes with fivers and wishing enviously that they would buy me a pint of Carlsberg, just one pint.

Adam squashed into the bar. My cheek was practically resting on his chest. I could faintly smell him. Soap. He smelt so fresh and clean.

I wryly told myself to get a grip on myself. I was starting to behave like Blanche Du Bois. Or the mad old alcoholic from *Sunset Boulevard*, whatever her name is. Or any of the myriad old hags that feature in any story about Beverly Hills, face-lifted to within an inch of their lives, consumed with lust for much younger men. Sad and pathetic. And I didn't want to be like that.

Naturally, in no time at all Adam had got the drinks. Barmen treat guys like him with respect. They have no time at all for women like me. Especially ones whose husbands have run off on them.

Like every other man in the universe the barman obviously knew I was a loser.

Adam handed me the two glasses of wine and then he said, "Here's your change."

"Oh, I've no free hands," I said, indicating the two glasses of wine.

"No problem," he said and slid his hand into a pocket on the side of the dress that I was wearing.

Just for a second his hand rested on my hipbone. I could feel the heat of it through the fabric of the dress.

I held my breath.

I think he did too.

Then he let go of the money and it jangled into my pocket.

What did you expect me to do? Slap him for taking liberties? I mean, the boy had to give me my change and I had no free hands. He did exactly the right thing.

Although I did think that people that attractive should carry permits. They should have to sit some kind of exam to prove that they can be trusted to behave responsibly out on the streets looking so gorgeous.

And it wasn't just that he was so handsome. Which he undeniably was. But he was so big and manly.

He made me feel like such a fragile little woman.

It was the large nightdress syndrome all over again.

He said, "Who are you here with?"

And I said, "My friend Laura."

He said, "Can I join you?"

I said, "Of course."

Why not, I thought. He's entertaining and sweet and Laura will enjoy him.

Although he might be a bit old for her.

He steered me through the packed pub. I must say people treated me with a lot more respect with him around.

I don't think I had more than one drop of alcohol spilt on me on my journey back from the bar as opposed to an entire brewery-full on the outward journey.

Very unfair, of course, but there we are.

We passed a crowd of people who seemed to know Adam.

"Adam, where are you going?" demanded one of the girls. Blonde. Pink pouty mouth. Very young. Very pretty.

"I've met an old friend," he told her. "I'm going to have a drink with her."

I quickly scanned the crowd to make sure that Helen wasn't there. Thankfully I couldn't see her.

However I did notice an older woman in amongst them, looking very anxious as Adam by-passed their little group. Could this be the poor lovesick Professor Staunton?

I was aware of several hostile looks. All from girls. It was almost funny.

Fuck them, I thought cheerfully.

If only they knew, they have nothing to fear from me.

My husband dumped me, I wanted to tell them, and he was only average good-looking. Not like Adam here. So what interest would an Adonis like Adam have in me?

And besides I still love my husband.

Faithless and all as he is.

I brought Adam over and introduced him to Laura.

She blushed.

So he did have this effect on every woman he met, I observed. And not just on the women in my family.

Somehow Adam found a spare seat.

He was that kind of guy.

"You're a terrible fibber," I smiled at him.

"Why?" he asked, opening his blue eyes very wide and looking all innocent and little boyish.

"Telling that poor girl that I'm an old friend," I told him.

"Well you are," he said. "You're old."

"As in 'older than me' kind of 'old'," he told me hastily as he noticed my eyes starting to narrow. "And I only know that because I asked Helen what age you were. I thought you were much younger."

I just looked at him.

I've got to hand it to him, I thought, he's redeemed himself.

"And," he continued, "even though we've only met once before I feel like you're a friend."

Yes, I thought, he's *definitely* redeemed himself.

It was at this stage that Laura later told me that she took off her knickers and lifted her skirt but that neither of us noticed. I don't believe her for a second.

But I do believe I understand the point she was making.

The evening took a definite upward swing from Adam's arrival.

I certainly felt a lot happier.

It shames me to admit it but I felt a lot more comfortable with a man around.

As though it validated me in some way.

Honestly, I did know how sad and pathetic this was. And I did intend to change my attitude.

But it was great to be around Adam.

Apart from anything else he was good conversationalist.

Laura asked Adam how he knew me and he said "I'm in college with Helen."

Laura gave me a look that said a lot. Something like, "Oh God no, a bloody student. We'll have to pretend to be interested in whatever boring subject he's studying."

But Adam spiked her guns.

He seems to have a habit of doing that.

"It's OK," he smiled at Laura. "You don't have to ask me what I'm studying."

"Oh," she said, a bit embarrassed. "In that case I won't."

There was a little bit of a pause.

"Well," said Laura, "I'm actually curious now."

"That wasn't my intention," laughed Adam. "But seeing as you've asked, I'm in first year doing English, Psychology and Anthropology."

"First year?" asked Laura, with a raise of her eyebrows, obviously alluding to his, what shall we say, less than boyish demeanour.

"Yes," said Adam. "I'm a mature student. Or so they tell me. I don't feel a bit mature. Only when I compare myself with my classmates, I suppose."

"Are they awful?" I asked, willing him to say yes.

"Not awful," he said. "Just young. I suppose somebody has to be. I mean, they're all seventeen or eighteen and they're all just out of school and they're only going to college to put off being responsible for another couple of years. Not because they have any great interest in learning. Or love of their subjects."

Laura and I had the grace to look extremely shamefaced as he said this. Laura and Judy and I had been prime examples of the lazy layabout, work-shy, spoilt, indulgent types he was describing.

"How awful for you," I murmured.

Laura and I smirked at each other.

"And how come you're going to college now?" I asked him.

"Well, I never wanted to go before. I never really knew what I wanted to do when I left school. So I did all the wrong things." he said intriguingly.

"And recently I've got my life back together. It was in a bit of a mess," he continued, even more intriguingly. "And now I'm ready for college. I really love it."

"Really?" I said, impressed by his maturity and his singlemindedness.

"Yes," he said.

Then he continued hesitantly, "I think I'm lucky to have waited until now. Because now I can really appreciate it. I think everyone should be made to go and work for a couple of years before deciding whether they want to study some more."

"Is that what you did?" I asked him. "Did you work?"

"Sort of," he said abruptly, obviously not wanting to say anymore.

Curiouser and curiouser.

So squeaky-clean Adam has A Past.

Well, that's how he was making it sound.

I bet he's just trying to be all mysterious and create a myth around himself, I thought uncharitably. He's probably worked in the Civil Service for the past six years. Probably in the least glamorous department, like the livestock licensing one, if there is such a thing.

Laura asked Adam the second question that one always asks students. (The first being, What are you studying?).

"What do you want to do when you get your degree?" she asked him.

I waited with bated breath.

Please God, oh please God, don't let him say he wants to be a writer or a journalist, I begged.

It would be just too much of a cliché.

I was starting to like and respect him and this would put the mockers on it entirely.

I put my hands together in prayer and sent my eyes Heavenwards.

"I'd like to do something with the Psychology," he said. (Phew! I thought) "I'm interested in the way people's minds work. I might like to be some kind of counsellor. Or I might like to get involved in advertising. And use the Psychology that way," he explained. "Anyway it's a long way away."

"And what about English?" I asked him nervously, "Don't you enjoy that?"

"Of course," he said, "It's my favourite. But I can't see myself getting a job out of it. Unless I want to try to become a writer or a journalist. And every second person wants to do that."

Thank God! I thought.

I'm glad that he likes it. I just couldn't bear to hear another person going on about how he wants to write a book.

So we chatted pleasantly. Laura went to the bar to get more drinks.

Adam turned to me and smiled.

"This is great," he said. "It's so nice to have a bit of intelligent conversation."

I glowed.

Adam moved a little bit closer to me.

So I may not have the body of a seventeen-year-old but I can still entertain a man, I thought smugly.

I felt like a mature strong woman, sure of herself and her place in the world. Confident, opinionated but amusing and entertaining. Witty and wise.

Rubbish, of course.

Not half an hour earlier I had been in tears because I was sure that everyone in the pub knew that I was a reject.

But it was all just a question of attitude.

Right then I felt good.

I felt good because Adam was making me feel good.

But did it matter who it was that made me feel good?

Wasn't it better than feeling bad?

"Adam, we're leaving now. Are you coming?"

The pretty blonde girl appeared at Adam's side.

"No Melissa, not yet. But I'll see you tomorrow. OK?" said Adam.

It was obviously far from OK. Melissa looked outraged.

"But . . . I thought . . . aren't you coming to the party?" she asked sounding as if she couldn't believe her ears.

"No, I don't think so," said Adam, a bit more firmly this time.

"Fine!" said Melissa, letting Adam know that it was far from fine. "Here's your bag," and she let a huge sports bag fall with a thud on the floor.

She cast venomous looks at both Laura and me.

Puzzled but venomous.

She really couldn't understand what Adam was doing with two old bags like us when he could have had his pick of all the nubile seventeen-year-olds in the place.

Quite frankly, neither could I.

Melissa flounced away and Adam sighed.

"I couldn't stand it," he explained wearily. "Another student party. Cans of warm Heineken. And not being able to get into the bathroom because someone's having sex in there. And you leave your jacket on the bed and someone pukes on it. And everyone playing musical snogs. I'm too old."

I suddenly felt genuinely sorry for him.

I thought he was being sincere when he told me he was enjoying a bit of intelligent conversation.

It couldn't be easy to be surrounded by giggly excitable eighteen-year-olds like Helen and Melissa when you're a lot more grown-up than that.

And it also couldn't be easy, I realised, to have so many young girls in love with you. Not if you were a kind person, like Adam seemed to be, and didn't want to hurt or upset them.

Sometimes, not that I'd know or anything, but being beautiful isn't all fun and games. You have to use your power wisely and responsibly.

For the next ten minutes or so a steady stream of young girls came over to say goodbye to Adam. Well, that was their pretext. Melissa had obviously reported back and they were really coming to see how hideous and old Laura and I were.

If the tables were turned I'd be one of the first over to criticise and ridicule the shoes, clothes, make-up and hair of the offending women.

As it happened Laura looked beautiful, red curls,

alabaster skin and nothing like her thirty years. I don't think I looked too awful either. But I'm sure that didn't stop anyone saying how ancient we looked. And what did it matter?

Someone stuck a can under my nose and rattled it a bit.

"Would you like to make a contribution to children in need?" asked a harassed looking man in a wet overcoat.

"Certainly," I said, rendered a little bit more generous than usual by the alcohol and shoved a pound into the can.

"Yourself?" he said, looking at Laura.

He hadn't even asked Adam to contribute. He obviously recognised a penniless student when he saw one.

"Oh, I make my contributions directly," she explained to the man.

"Do you?" I asked, puzzled. I hadn't known that Laura was involved in any children's charities.

"Well, I have sex with a child on a regular basis," she declared. "If that isn't contributing directly, I don't know what is."

The man looked horrified and moved onto the next table at high speed.

Adam roared with laughter.

"I've never met a paedophile before," he said to her.

"I'm only joking. I'm not really a child molester at all," she told Adam. "The child in question is nineteen."

We finished our drinks and put on our coats and got ready to leave.

The pub was starting to empty.

Everyone at the tables around us seemed in high spirits, except the barmen who were practically begging people to leave.

"I've worked thirteen nights in a row," I heard one barman telling a particularly rowdy table of revellers, "I'm knackered." In fairness, he did look exhausted, but I think he was wasting his time trying to appeal to their humanitarian side.

"You're bringing tears to my eyes," said a rather drunk young man with grave irony.

"Finish that pint, or I'm taking it," threatened another barman, at another nearby table, obviously well used to playing the role of a dapper Mine Host.

So the customer drank nearly a whole pint in one go, to the encouraging comments of his friends, "Good man," "waste not, want not," and various other shouts.

Even Laura called over "Swalley that down."

We passed the customer about five minutes later.

He was just outside the pub.

He was being assisted by a couple of his equally drunk friends and he was vomiting copiously.

When we got to the door of the pub, we found that the rain had started again.

"I'm only parked up the road," said Laura. "I'll run."

We hugged each other.

"I'll be out on Sunday to see Kate," she said. "Lovely meeting you, Adam." And off she ran into the wet night, almost colliding with the vomiting man.

"Sorry," she called to him, her voice floating back to us on the damp night air.

Adam and I stood at the door for a moment or two. I wasn't sure what to say to him and he said nothing at all.

"Can I give you a lift home?" I asked.

I felt a bit awkward about asking him.

As though I was the rich older woman who was desperate for love and sex and buying the penniless handsome young man.

"That would be really great," he said. "I think I've missed the last bus."

He flashed a smile at me.

I relaxed.

I was doing him a favour. Not trying to take advantage of him.

We walked briskly along the wet streets until we reached the car park.

And believe me, there was nothing even remotely romantic about the walk in the rain. Utter misery is what it was. My boots are suede. I'll have to spend the rest of my life standing with them over a steaming kettle to restore them to their former glory.

We got into the car. He threw his soaking bag on the back seat. He sat into the passenger seat and, I swear to God, he practically filled the whole front of the car.

Off we went.

He started fiddling with the radio station.

"Oh don't!" I told him. "Dad'll kill me."

I told him the conversation that I'd had with Dad before I left and he laughed heartily.

"You're a good driver," he said after a while.

Naturally as soon as he said that I got all flustered and stalled the car, and then nearly drove into a pole. He gave me directions to his flat in Rathmines and we drove along in the rain.

Neither of us spoke.

The only sound was of the swishing of the carwheels on the road and the squeaking of the windscreen wipers.

But it was a nice silence.

I pulled up outside his house and smiled goodbye at him. It really had been a lovely evening.

"Thanks for the lift," he said.

"You're welcome," I smiled.

"Er, em . . . would you like, I mean . . . can I offer you a cup of tea?" he asked awkwardly.

"When . . . like . . . now, do you mean?" I asked just as awkwardly.

"No, I was thinking of sometime around next December," he smiled at me.

My refusal was automatic.

It was in my mouth before I even knew it.

I had several excuses. It was late. I was soaked. This was my first night to leave Kate with someone else. Helen would machete me.

"Yes," I said, totally surprising myself. "Why not?"

I parked the car and in we went.

I was filled with trepidation. My fear was well-founded. I had been to enough students' flats to expect the worst.

All kinds of odd arrangements. You know, six or seven people sleeping in the front room, a couple of people living in the kitchen, having to go through a bedroom to get to the bathroom, having to go through the bathroom to get to the living-room.

Bedrooms divided by a tartan rug hanging from the ceiling, to give a pretence of privacy. Wardrobes in the hall. Chests of drawers in the kitchen. Saucepans and buckets in the bathroom. The fridge on the landing. The coffee table in the front room consisting of four blue milk crates and a slab of chipboard.

You know, that kind of thing.

A kitchen that looked like if it was struck by a bolt of lightning the process of evolution would begin all over again, curtains askew and crooked, broken blinds hanging from the windows, crushed cans of beer underfoot, the cistern being used to make home-brew.

Oh yes, believe me, I've paid my dues at the student flats of this world.

So I was greatly relieved when Adam opened the front door and let me into a flat that looked normal, in fact, I'd go so far as to say downright pleasant.

"Come into the kitchen," he said, taking off his wet jacket.

We went into the kitchen and Adam put on the kettle and a heater. Not one of those awful orange two-bar heaters that seem endemic to bedsit land but a normal gas heater, like one we had in the flat in London, in fact. The kettle was actually a kettle and not a tin can on a gas ring.

I was suspicious.

"The other people who live here," I asked him. "Are they students also?"

"No," he said, taking my coat off me and hanging it up near the heater. "They both work." Well that explained a lot.

"Are you soaked?" he asked nicely. "Would you like me to get you a jumper?"

"No, I'm fine," I said gamely. "My coat protected me from the worst of the precipitation."

He smiled.

"Well, I'll get you a towel to dry your hair," he said and left for a moment.

He was back almost immediately with a big blue towel in his hand and I'm glad to be able to put your mind at rest here and tell you that, no, he didn't dry my hair for me.

What do you think this is? A Mills and Boon story?

I'm sorry but if that's the type of scenario you're interested in then I suggest that you read a different book.

No, he gave me the towel and I gave my hair a few half-hearted scrubs. I didn't want to end up with it sticking up all over the place and drying at funny angles.

Quite frankly, I'd rather have caught pneumonia.

I took off my boots and put them in front of the heater. Adam gave me a cup of tea and we sat at the table in the pleasant warm kitchen. He even found a packet of biscuits.

"They're Jenny's," he explained. "I'll tell her in the morning that I had a special visitor last night. She'll understand."

He made it seem so easy to be charming. It never came across as smarmy or insincere.

"So how long is it since you've had Kate?" he asked, putting the sugar in front of me.

"Over a month now," I said.

"Look, I hope you don't mind," he said awkwardly. "But Helen has told me the situation with you and your husband."

"And?" I said, minding.

"Well, nothing really," he said hurriedly. "I mean, I know it's none of my business or anything but I'm sure it's not easy for you. I went through something a bit similar myself and I know how awful it is."

"Really?" I said intrigued.

"Well, yes," he said, "But I'm not trying to pry into your life or anything."

Never mind that, I was thinking, tell me!

You can pry into my life if I can pry into yours.

"And," he continued, "I know you've got lots of friends in Dublin but if you ever want to talk to me you can."

"You're not using me as some kind of experiment for your psychology course?" I asked suspiciously.

"Not at all," he laughed. "It's just that I liked you from the moment I met you. And I like you more after tonight. And I'd like it if we were friends."

"Why?" I asked, even more suspiciously.

Well, I was perfectly entitled to ask, wasn't I? I mean, I just didn't get it. I was just perfectly ordinary. Why had Adam decided that I was special and worth being friends with?

I wasn't putting myself down here. I had lots of good qualities, I knew that. I wasn't just being Queen of the Low Self Esteem. But lots of people have good qualities. There wasn't anything particularly *unusual* about me. Now Adam, on the other hand, must have met millions of women, funny, beautiful, clever, entertaining, rich, waif-like, cute, sexy, interesting women.

Why had he singled me out?

"Because you're nice," he said.

Nice! I ask you.

Who wanted to be picked by a beautiful man like Adam just because they were nice?

"And you're very funny. And clever. And interesting," he said.

That's more like it, I thought.

Any chance of sexy or beautiful?

I'd even have settled for attractive.

But nothing doing.

Sexy, beautiful or attractive were not on offer.

But what the hell. It was nice talking to him. I was enjoying myself.

I didn't fancy him.

Although I probably would have if circumstances had been different.

He didn't fancy me.

We were just two adults who happened to like each other's company.

I was a married woman.

On Monday I would be ringing James.

Adam was spoken for. If not by my sister Helen then by some other woman, I didn't doubt.

So no big deal.

"What are you doing tomorrow?" he asked.

"Well, I don't know," I told him. "I haven't really got into any routine since I came back from London. I suppose I just look after Kate."

"Well that's why I was asking you how long it is since you've had Kate. I was wondering if you'd like to come to the gym with me?"

"ME?!" I said in horror. "Why?"

"Not because I think you need to," he said anxiously. "But because I think you might like to."

Me, with my saggy, out-of-shape body go to the gym with this Adonis. Was he joking?

But on the other hand, my body would stay saggy and out-of-shape if I didn't do anything about it.

And I used to enjoy going to the gym before I had Kate.

Maybe this was the best suggestion I'd heard in a long time.

"Well . . . ," I said cautiously, "I'm very unfit."

"You've got to start somewhere," he said quickly.

"And who would mind Kate?"

"Wouldn't your Mum do it? It would only be for a couple of hours."

"Maybe," I said doubtfully. This was all moving a bit too fast for me.

Goddammit, I only went out to have a drink with Laura. Now I was signing up for some fitness programme with a person that I only met yesterday.

And yesterday evening, at that.

"Look, come tomorrow. I bet you'll enjoy it. What have you got to lose?" he said.

I thought about it.

What had I got to lose?

Apart from my life if Helen found out.

"OK, I'll come."

I arranged to meet him the following day in town at three o'clock though I could hardly believe I was doing it. I finished my tea. He saw me to my car.

He closed my car door for me and stood at the gate – in the rain, I might add – as I drove away.

I was starting to feel guilty before I even got to the end of the road.

Guilt at neglecting Kate.

Guilt at associating with my youngest sister's boyfriend, blameless and all as it was.

Guilt at the idea of wasting time in the gym when I should be talking to a solicitor and sorting out my finances and all that.

As soon as I got home I ran up the stairs to Kate. It was such a relief to see that she was alive and well. I felt so guilty that I was convinced that something terrible had to happen.

I held her so tightly I thought I would squeeze the life out of her.

"I missed you darling," I told her, as she struggled for breath. "On Monday I'm going to ring Daddy and I'll try and sort things out for us. Everything's going to be fine, I promise."

I had had such a lovely evening.

I simply couldn't understand why I felt so depressed.

Chapter Fourteen

I had planned to ring Mr Hasdell, the solicitor whose name Laura had given me, as soon as he got to his desk at nine o'clock the following morning.

But I just couldn't bring myself to do it.

I fed Kate.

I played with Kate.

I worried about what to wear to the gym.

I worried about what would happen if Helen found out that I was going to the gym with Adam.

I worried in case I was neglecting Kate.

I worried in case Mum refused to mind her on the grounds that it would make her an accomplice to me meeting Adam.

I worried about everything other than the important thing.

I knew that I had to ring my bank. I had practically no money.

But I was far more concerned about how my bum was going to look in the leotard and leggings that I had found in Rachel's room.

My child was growing up without a father but, instead of getting on the phone and ringing a family lawyer and trying to sort something out, I stood in front of a mirror holding my stomach in, checking

my profile and finally, as though the years had rolled
away and I was still fifteen, twisting my head round,
trying to see what my bum looked like in the mirror.

Mum was highly suspicious when I asked her
would she look after Kate for me in the afternoon.

"Again?" she asked.

"Yes, but only for a couple of hours," I muttered.

"Why?" she demanded. "What are you up to?"

"Nothing Mum. I just want to go to the gym and
start getting back into shape," I told her. I didn't want
to lie to her. But I wasn't too comfortable telling the
truth either.

"Oh, the gym," she said, sounding quite pleased.
"Well that's good. Just mind that you don't, you
know, pull any . . . you know . . . do yourself any
damage. It's not so long since you gave birth, don't
forget."

"Thanks Mum," I said amused at her delicacy.
"But I think my insides are in fine condition. Raring
to go, to be quite honest with you."

I shouldn't have said that.

It made her suspicious again.

I know that she had encouraged me to have a
fling with Adam but I felt so guilty about meeting
him that I didn't want anyone to know.

So off I drove into town, feeling sick with guilt
and the fear of being caught and the fear of
something happening to Kate.

About halfway there, I decided that I wasn't cut
out for this life of deceit and intrigue and child-
neglect and that I would turn around and go home.

But the traffic was so bad that, by the time I got

to turn the car, I was feeling guilty about just leaving Adam standing there. So I decided that I would go in, meet him, tell him that I couldn't meet him, if you follow me, and come straight back home again.

And then I couldn't find a parking space. I practically had to get a bus from where I had parked the car to where I had to meet Adam.

So I was dead late meeting him.

I was running along the road when I saw him standing outside the shop where we had arranged to meet. He was looking up and down the street with an anxious expression on his face, totally oblivious to all the admiring stares he was getting from passing women.

Every time I saw him I got a shock.

I'd forgotten how handsome he is.

This tall beautiful man with the long muscly legs is waiting for *me*, I thought, feeling a bit overwhelmed.

Why!?

"Claire!" he said, looking delighted to see me. "I thought you weren't coming."

"I'm not," I mumbled.

"So have you just sent a hologram of yourself along or what?" he asked smiling.

"No, I mean, Adam . . . look, I'm not sure if this is a good idea," I stuttered. "Like, you know . . . " I trailed off miserably.

"What isn't a good idea?" he asked gently, as he steered me out of the path of oncoming pedestrians.

"Meeting you and that . . . you know, I'm married and all that," I said, not meeting his eyes.

Then I looked up at him and I couldn't believe how hurt he looked.

"I know you're married," he said quietly, as he looked down into my eyes. "I wouldn't dare make any assumptions. I don't want to make any moves on you. I want to be your friend."

I was mortified. Absolutely mortified.

I nearly died with embarrassment.

Of course he wasn't coming on to me.

The nerve of me thinking that he was.

Why was I so cynical?

Or why was I so conceited?

What on earth made me say that to him?

All right, so I was feeling guilty about meeting him. But wasn't that my problem? Why should I attribute any improper motives to him just because I had some myself?

Or did I have some improper motives myself?

Oh God! I didn't know.

"Look, you'd better go home," said Adam.

He wasn't being cold and angry but it was as if he didn't want me to touch him or anything.

"No!" I said.

Jesus, would I ever make up my mind!

"No," I said, not quite so frantically. "I'm sorry. I shouldn't have said what I said. I was being silly and overreacting."

We were attracting all kinds of curious and interested looks from the shoppers as they passed in and out of the doorway.

"Great," I overheard one young woman saying gleefully to her companion. "There's nothing I love more than seeing other people arguing."

259

Her voice floated back to me from up the street, "It makes me feel like I'm not the only person in the world who's miserable."

Oh don't worry, I thought, you're not.

Adam stared at me and sighed in exasperation.

"What do you want?"

"Nothing," I said. "Can we forget that this happened and just go to the gym like we had planned."

"All right," he said. But not in a very friendly way.

"Ah be nice to her. Give her a kiss," called out a scruffy old man, who had several opened bottles of Guinness sticking out of his torn overcoat pocket and who had been watching the proceedings with great interest. "She's sorry. Aren't you love?"

"Come on," I mumbled to Adam.

I didn't want a crowd to start forming.

"Give her a dig," shouted the old man after us, who seemed to have suddenly turned a bit nasty. "It's the only language they understand!"

We hurried up the road, the old man's cries got a bit fainter.

"Jesus," I said in relief as we rounded a corner and we couldn't hear him anymore.

Adam smiled briefly but things still felt tense and uncomfortable.

We got to the gym and he tersely signed me in. I went off to the women's changing rooms and eventually sidled out, as self-conscious as a virgin bride in my leotard and leggings, hugging the wall for fear that anyone would catch a twenty-twenty, full-on, four-square view of my bum.

But I needn't have bothered.

He barely glanced at me.

"The bikes are over there," he said pointing. "And the free-weights are in this room here. The rest of the machines are over that way."

And he left me to get on with things.

"That's lovely," I thought resentfully. "I could be pulling muscles left, right and centre and he doesn't give a damn."

I stood for a moment waiting for him to come back and show me how to do things.

To be perfectly honest, I suppose that I had entertained all kinds of lovely thoughts, albeit guilty ones, about him bending over me as I lay flat on my back on the bench press, to adjust the weight or something. And for us to suddenly realise that we were close enough to kiss.

That kind of romantic tosh.

Adam ignored me completely, so I reluctantly decided that I might as well get a grip on my runaway imagination and do a bit of exercise.

I did my warm-ups and my stretches.

And before I knew it, I realised that I was enjoying myself.

"I'm not actually happy," I assured myself. "It's the artificial high that people get from exercise. Pheromones or something. No, it's endorphins, isn't it?"

Good God, I was turning into Helen.

I stole a glance at Adam.

(Whoops! That was very Romantic Novelish. People are always "stealing" glances in them.)

All right then, I stole nothing.

261

Not guilty of any kind of larceny.

Although I did know a bloke in a pub who would have taken a couple of boxes of glances off my hands for a decent price. No questions asked.

But I did look at Adam when he didn't know that I was.

He pushed and lifted vast quantities of weights.

He looked wonderful.

Very grim and serious-looking and handsome.

A man who took his body seriously.

And with good reason.

Although he was just wearing sweatpants and a T-shirt he was pretty spectacular looking.

Beautiful strong arms, with a glistening of sweat on them.

And a really lovely bum.

I'm sorry. I shouldn't have said that.

But he did.

After about an hour or so I decided that I had had enough.

"OK." He smiled. "Go and have a shower and I'll meet you in the café."

He was already sitting in the café when I emerged, having spent far too long doing my make-up.

His hair was all wet and shiny and he had what looked like about twenty cartons of milk in front of him.

"Finally," he said, when he saw me. "Well did you enjoy that?"

"It was great," I told him.

"Glad you came?" he asked, with a dead-pan expression.

"Yes," I said, looking him in the eye.

"Good," he said and started to laugh.

So did I.

Thank God! I was so relieved that he didn't seem to be annoyed with me anymore.

I got myself a cup of coffee and joined him.

We were the only two people in the cafe.

It was a Friday evening and I suppose most sensible people had better things to do.

Going to the pub and getting drunk, I'd be bound.

Suddenly things were very nice with Adam again. The tension was gone.

We didn't talk about anything unpleasant or sensible.

I didn't ask him if Helen was his girlfriend and he returned the favour by not asking me anything about James.

I didn't ask him about his lectures and he very decently reciprocated by not asking me about my job.

He asked me what my favourite animal was.

And I asked him what his earliest memory was.

We talked about going to discos when we were fifteen.

And we discussed what one ability we would choose if we could choose anything.

"I'd like to be able to fly," he said.

"Well, why don't you learn?" I asked him.

"No, I wish _I_ could fly," he said laughing. "You know, without a plane or anything. And what about you, what would you like?"

"Sometimes I wish I could see into the future," I told him, "Not everything and not years ahead or anything. Maybe a couple of hours ahead."

"That'd be great," said Adam. "Think of all the money you could win on the horses."

I laughed.

"Or I wish I could be invisible. That would be great fun. I bet you can find out much more about a person when they don't think that you're there."

"You're right," he said.

There was a little pause.

"I'd love to be able to travel through time," he said after a while.

"Oh that's a good one," I said excited. "Imagine going into the future. Or imagine going back to really exciting times, like ancient Egypt. Though knowing my luck I'd end up as some poor old gladiator."

"I'm not sure if there were any gladiators in ancient Egypt," he said. But in a nice way.

I suppose he's used to correcting Helen.

"Anyway," he continued, "I'm sure you'd be a princess. Maybe not Cleopatra. Your colouring is too fair," he said lightly touching my hair. "But you'd definitely be a princess."

"Er, would I?" I mumbled.

Witty and gracious, that's me.

Sparkling and Repartee are my middle names.

"Em, when would you like to travel back to?" I asked him, anxious for the conversation to return to a less intimate footing and for my breathing to return to normal.

"Well," he said, "sometimes I wish I could travel

back in my own life. You know, go back to a time when I was really happy. Or go back and change things. Fix things that I did wrong. Or do things that I should have done and didn't."

I was absolutely intrigued.

What had gone on in his life that sounded so traumatic?

But before I could probe I suddenly noticed the time.

It was ten past seven.

"Jesus!" I said, jumping up in alarm, all of a fluster. "Look at the time. I thought it was about five o'clock."

I picked up my bag and made for the door.

"I have to go. Thanks for bringing me. Bye."

"Wait," he said. "I'll walk you to your car."

"No, there's no need," I told him.

And off I ran.

I was in a total panic.

Where had the time gone?

How could I have neglected Kate like this?

God would punish me. Something was bound to have happened to her.

I couldn't believe that so much time had passed so quickly.

I drove home at high speed, the roads clear of rush-hour traffic because it was so late.

Mum was tightlipped and suspicious when I arrived.

"What kind of time do you call this?" she demanded.

"Sorry," I gasped. "I lost track of the time."

"I've fed Kate," she told me.

(Thank God! That must mean that she's still alive!)

"Thanks, Mum."

"Five times."

"Thanks, Mum."

"And I've changed her."

"Thanks, Mum."

"Three times."

"Thanks, Mum."

"I hope you're grateful."

"Oh, I am, Mum."

"She's not my child, you know."

"I know, Mum."

"My childrearing days are over."

"I know, Mum."

Then she was really suspicious.

Why was I being so nice?

Hurriedly, I raised my voice at her.

"She's your flesh and blood too, you know," I told her.

But it was a poor effort.

I just couldn't concentrate on getting annoyed by her. I'd think to myself, "My God, but she's being particularly irritating," but just as I was getting myself worked up into a nice bit of a lather of annoyance my thoughts would slide Adam-wards, and I'd suddenly feel happy.

Well happyish.

My head didn't know where it was. All manner of unusual behaviour going on.

A large battalion of my thoughts was marching determinedly on their way to Annoyance but they were distracted and took a wrong turning at Adam and they found, to their surprise, that they had ended up in the entirely different destination of Dreamy Contentment.

Which caused no end of confusion and consternation amongst them, I can tell you.

A lot of disgruntled thoughts, standing round in their donkey-jackets looking for their shop steward in the hope that he might throw a bit of light on the situation.

"Lads, what the hell are we doing here?" "Who's navigating?" "We're lost!" "This wasn't part of our job description," and "Demarcation!" and several other complaints.

I rushed upstairs to see Kate.

She was in her cot, fed, changed and asleep.

Not a bother on her.

The little angel.

She snuffled contentedly in her sleep, moving her fat pink little legs.

With a shock I realised how lucky I was.

This beautiful miniature human being was my child.

I gave birth to her.

She was my daughter.

For the first time, I realised, *really* realised that my marriage was not a failure.

James and I might not be together but we had created this wonderful little person.

This living miracle.

I was not becursed.

I was not benighted.

I was very, very lucky.

Chapter Fifteen

I spent Friday night watching television with Mum. I felt that I had done enough gallivanting over the past couple of days. And I was totally exhausted. Taking care of a young baby is a gruelling task. Although how would I know, I hear you asking.

All right, all right, I admit that I'd had a lot of help from my parents, but I still felt knackered.

How I was going to cope with returning to work was beyond me.

How do people do it?

It made me feel so inadequate.

Especially when I thought of women in, was it China? You know, when they're out digging up the fields with their bare hands and they say, "oh excuse me for a moment," as if they were going to the Ladies Room at a posh reception and they lift their skirt and out pops a new born baby, into a ploughed furrow or onto a bag of seeds or whatever.

"Aaah, that feels better," they might say.

And on they go, tilling and ploughing and uprooting mighty oaks with one hand, their newborn child attached to their breast.

And they're pregnant again by nightfall.

And the newborn child has been given a suit of clothes and set to work driving a tractor.

As I watched television with Mum, my thoughts kept straying to Adam. And in true adolescent fashion I would get a little tingle every time I thought of him.

I had had such a lovely time with him.

He was so nice.

So fresh and eager and interesting and interested.

It was because he was so uncynical, I thought, that I liked him so much.

He reminded me of what it was like to think positively.

The fact that he was so gorgeous made his undisguised admiration all the more pleasant.

There's almost nothing worse than undisguised admiration from absolute horrors.

I'd rather do without the undisguised admiration altogether.

But never mind the fact that Adam was gorgeous.

That wasn't why I liked being with him.

If I hadn't loved James, I might have been attracted to Adam.

That's not to say that I wasn't *un*attracted to him.

I mean, he was very attractive.

And I did have eyes in my head.

You know, I am only human.

Hypothetically speaking, it is possible to be in love with one man, in my case, James, and have a crush on another, in this case, Adam.

It wasn't as if a crush does any harm.

It didn't mean that I'm a fickle person.

It was good for me.

Because I didn't have to act on that crush.

269

And, even if, God forbid, I *did* act on it, well it wasn't the end of the world, now was it?

Yes, if Helen found out about it, it could well have been the end of the world.

But that was assuming that Adam was attracted to me.

But I thought he was.

Was that very conceited of me?

Maybe he used that trick with all the women.

You know, coming on all sincere and vulnerable and adoring, so the women would think he was the nicest man they ever met, that he was really different.

And before they knew it they'd be in Adam's bed with their knickers flung to one of the four corners of the room and Adam would be clambering off them, saying, "When I told you that I'd respect you in the morning, I lied."

And then he'd ring them exactly seventy-two hours later to say, "Oh, by the way, the condom burst. You did say you were ovulating, didn't you?"

Yes, I thought angrily, I bet he's a right bastard and just goes round taking advantage of poor widda women, like me. All right, so I'm not a widda woman, but I'm in a very vulnerable position.

How dare he! Making me feel beautiful and special. The barefaced cheek of him!

Well, if he thinks I'm going to have sex with him now, then I'm afraid that I've got some very bad news for him.

Adam, darling, I've changed my mind!

It took me a couple of seconds to realise that I had talked myself through an entire affair with Adam, from falling for him, to being dumped by him to being furious with him.

Whoops, I thought. It's that bad penny, Temporary Insanity, back again.

"What's wrong with you?" said Mum, tearing her attention away from Inspector Morse. "You're looking very cross."

"Nothing Mum," I told her, my head reeling slightly. "Just thinking."

"You can think too much," she told me.

For once I agreed with her.

But before she could expound on the evils of a University Education and the dangers of opening your mind, the phone rang.

"I'll answer it," I yelped and ran from the room, cutting her off mid-sentence.

"What's the use of being an intellectual?" she shouted after me. "I bet James Joyce couldn't change a plug."

"Hello," I said, as I picked up the phone.

"Helen?" asked a man's voice.

"No, Helen's not here," I said. "She's missing, presumed drunk."

The voice laughed.

"Adam?" I asked, wobbling slightly.

The shock of hearing his voice briefly destabilised me.

I could hardly believe that he had spent the afternoon with me and here he was ringing for Helen, my *sister*.

What kind of sicko was he, playing the two of us off against each other?

271

I *knew* it.

He *was* a bastard, just like all the others.

"Claire," he said. "Yes, it's me."

What do you want, I thought coldly, a bloody medal for being you.

"Yes?" I said icily. "Well, I'll tell Helen that you rang."

"No wait," he said. "I rang to talk to you."

"That's funny," I continued with great hauteur. "Because my name is Claire, not Helen."

"I know that," he continued in a reasonable tone. "But I thought it might be a bit off if I rang to speak to you and Helen answered and I didn't acknowledge her."

I paused.

"I mean," he continued gently, "Helen is my friend too. If it wasn't for Helen I would never have met you."

Still I said nothing.

"Are you annoyed?" he asked. "Have I done something wrong?"

Now I felt foolish.

Hysterical and female.

"No," I said, in much sweeter tones. "Of course I'm not annoyed."

"All right then," he said, "If you're sure."

"I'm sure."

"I hope you don't mind me ringing you," he said. "But you ran off in such a hurry today that I didn't get a chance to ask you if maybe . . . I mean . . . that's if you don't mind . . . if I could see you again. You know, if you've got time."

Relief and happiness rushed through me.

As they say, there's one born every minute.

"Yes," I told him breathlessly. "I'd love to."

"I had such a nice time," he said.

I glowed with happiness and pride.

"So did I," I told him.

"What are you doing tomorrow?" he asked.

Tomorrow, I thought.

Golly, but he didn't let the grass grow under his feet.

"I'm going into town to buy some clothes," I said.

This was news to me.

The first I had heard of it.

"So you can meet me for coffee if you like," I told him. "But I'll have to bring Kate."

"That's great," he said, sounding all excited. "Kate's beautiful. Please bring her."

"OK then," I said, a little taken aback at his enthusiasm.

Although, I mused, rather cunningly, I thought, if he likes Kate that much, maybe I could rope him in for some baby-sitting duties the next time I want to go out and get drunk with Laura.

But I must admit that the nicest thing about the night I went out and got drunk with Laura was the fact that Adam was there.

So we made an arrangement to meet in town the following day.

I went back into Mum.

"Who was that?" she asked, looking at my flushed, happy face.

I opened my mouth to tell her and I'm afraid to tell you that I stalled at the final hurdle.

I just couldn't tell her.
I really didn't know why.
Or maybe I did.
Maybe because it was no longer innocent.
Maybe it never was.

Chapter Sixteen

The following day brought it home to me good and proper, not that I had failed to notice already, how my life had been altered forever by my having given birth to Kate.

Especially one of the most important areas of my life.

I speak, of course, of the shopping area of my life.

My old shopping life, like the morning dew in the midday sun, gone forever.

No more running into a clothes shop, picking thirty or so garments up off the rails and then spending a leisurely six hours or more in the changing room admiring myself.

No sir!

You'd be amazed the difference having a child strapped to your front makes.

Ease of movement greatly hampered.

Not to mention the terrible fear I had that someone was going to bump into Kate and hurt her.

Or worse still, wake her.

It hadn't been too bad that day in the supermarket where civilised serene mothers glided through the roomy aisles. I trusted them not to jostle and bump Kate.

But this was Saturday afternoon, in clothes shops, for God's sake!

These girl-shoppers were surely mercenaries that had been given the afternoon off from causing bloodshed and mayhem in somewhere like the former Yugoslavia.

Vicious, I'm telling you.

Crazed.

I couldn't relax and just look for something to wear.

I was so afraid that Kate was going to get a blow on the head or a poke in her malleable little ribs from some demon of a shopper who was trying to reach a dress and would use any means to do so.

Anyway, I hardly knew what I was looking for as I had so completely lost my sense of self.

I stood at the door of one shop, a little bit dazed, swerving and ducking the passing shoppers as I wondered if I was a jeans and sweatshirt girl, or if I was an ankle-length skirt and cropped jumper kind of woman.

I mean, what was I now?

It was so long since I'd bought proper clothes.

Ones that weren't dungarees, I mean.

Or ones that didn't have expanding adjustable Velcro waists. Or acres and acres of fabric.

In fact, it was only a week since I started wearing normal knickers again.

Let me explain.

Maybe you don't know it but you don't return to normal living and, more importantly, normal clothes the moment you give birth.

No indeed!

It's a long time before certain bodily processes stop. I don't want to sound unnecessarily gory here but can I just say that I could have given Lady Macbeth a run for her money.

Don't talk to *me* about blood being everywhere, Missus!

And because of that I'd had to wear these funny mesh paper-type knickers.

They were horrible and they were huge.

Armpit huggers.

But I'm happy to announce that the previous week normal knickers had been restored. That's right, I repeat, normal knickers had been restored.

What about the rest of my clothes?

I was no longer a pregnant woman.

I was just a woman.

So what was I going to wear?

I had so little to define me now.

I wouldn't be going back to work for ages, so I didn't have to buy clothes for that.

So I didn't even have that to give me form.

I was just shopping for me.

Whoever she was.

I picked up a couple of little dresses from a rack and pushed through the hordes of people to get to the changing room, practically bent double over Kate to protect her.

A further shock awaited me at the changing room.

Where on earth was I going to put Kate?

She wasn't exactly like a gym bag that you just fling on the floor and don't care who stands on it.

A quick U-turn and back the way I came, easing my way through the throng, with my head lowered and thrust forward so that I looked a bit like a bull.

I bought a lot of things anyway, even though I hadn't tried them on. I *had* to buy something.

After all I had a reputation to uphold.

There was a time when my name was legendary amongst Women Who Shop.

A time when there was no such thing as choosing between the black pair and the green pair. No such thing as standing, agonising, my index finger pressed to my face, my brow furrowed in girlish consternation.

No siree, I bought the both of them.

And quite apart from upholding my reputation I hadn't a stitch to wear. And I had a man to impress.

I paid for everything with the credit card.

Or, I suppose I should say that James did.

I was quite amazed that alarm bells didn't go off when the assistant passed the bags over the counter to me and van loads of policemen and Alsatians didn't rush into the shop and drag me off.

Because I was sure that I had spent miles over the limit.

After my half-hearted, yet nonetheless prolific purchasing, I went off to meet Adam, who was, after all, my real reason for coming into town.

If I'm perfectly honest, the shopping was just a ruse.

A cunning ploy.

I fought my way up the street, arms protectively round Kate.

Wave after wave of shoppers came towards me.

Touch my child and I'll kill you, I thought fiercely, looking angrily at passers-by.

Who, in their innocence, looked very startled and afraid.

Apart from the anxiety about Kate getting hurt, I became aware of another funny feeling in my stomach.

Indigestion?

With a curious little shock I realised that the funny feeling was butterflies.

Butterflies that were dancing jigs in my intestines. They had obviously pushed back the tables and chairs in my stomach and were going for it in a big way. Linking arms and swinging each other round and high-kicking and whooping and changing partners and generally having a wild old time for themselves.

Oh dear, I thought, realisation dawning, so it's official.

I fancy Adam.

Or should I say I FANCY ADAM!!!!!

Should celestial trumpets have blown? Should I have suddenly seen the world with pink fuzzy edging? Should I have walked, or indeed run the rest of the way to meet him in slow motion? And be swung slowly into his arms, twirling round and round, both of us smiling like joyful idiots?

But no, being me, I had to go straight into worry-mode. I reluctantly dragged my feet the rest of the way to meet him, my head working at high speed.

Why did I have to fancy him?

What kind of person was I?

I was in love with James and it was only six weeks, well, nearly seven, actually, since we split up, so shouldn't I still have been faithful to him?

I felt so disloyal.

Although why the hell should I?

James was having his fun, so why shouldn't I?

But it wasn't that simple.

I was never any good at having sex with people without getting emotionally involved.

Although then again, who said anything about having sex?

Oh God!

I was so distraught.

I couldn't understand all the different ways I was feeling.

I was so confused.

I *did* fancy Adam. But I felt so guilty about it because that must make me a very shallow person, when I was supposed to be in love with James.

But was I in love with James?

I was afraid to think about that one. It was too huge to contemplate.

And then I felt angry with James. Why couldn't I flirt with Adam and have a bit of fun?

But then I felt guilty again because Adam was a person, a nice person and he deserved better than to be treated by me as some sort of ego-balm.

A bit like getting my hair done.

Or getting my legs waxed.

And then I felt angry again, because I didn't think of Adam that way. I got a real thrill from talking to him and being with him. Although I'd only known him a few days.

Which brought me neatly back to the question of how could I fancy someone that I'd only known a few days when I was still in love with James.

Oh, fuck it, I thought frantically.

I had to empty my head of these worrying thoughts. There was no way I could deal with them now. I was about to meet the man I fancied so I had to worry about entirely different things.

Like, did I look nice.

And, would he fancy me.

And how did I go about getting him into bed.

Important things.

I squared my shoulders and got ready for Adam.

I saw him standing outside the coffee-shop where I was to meet him.

My stomach gave a little lurch.

He looked so good.

"Hello," he grinned. "You're only fifteen minutes late. You're obviously getting the hang of this."

"Shut up," I smiled. "Sorry."

It was wonderful to be with him.

"Hello angel," he said looking in at Kate in her little pouch.

Although I preferred to think that he was just using this as an excuse to look at my tits.

Kate said nothing.

And in we went for coffee, fighting our way through the hordes of agitated and excited people.

It was Saturday afternoon and madness was abroad.

It was as though people were afflicted with some kind of lunacy.

Shopping syndrome, or something.

I'm sure there's a fancy medical name for it.

I suppose it must be something akin to the Mistral that descends every so often on villages in, is it Italy? All the men thump their wives and the dogs howl and the hens won't lay and the women shout and cry (well fair enough – their husbands are thumping them after all) and refuse to do any housework.

As though the entire village was afflicted with PMT and the Evening Primrose oil and B6 harvest was late that year.

The Mistral madness seems to be child's play compared to the carry-on this particular Saturday afternoon.

I once read somewhere that shopping has a huge affect on one's adrenaline levels.

Sending blood pressure levels soaring and causing one to hyperventilate and making one's eyes bulge and all kinds of other effects.

It made perfect sense to me – all that excitement!

Apparently this in turn affects one's blood sugar levels.

Which is why everyone needs strong sweet tea or coffee and a Club Milk (or whatever) after or indeed even during their shopping orgy.

A bit like a post-coital cigarette, I suppose.

As a result of excessive shopping Dublin was full of hyperventilating, bulgy-eyed, red-faced (that's from the high blood pressure) maniacs, with hundreds of shopping bags affixed around their persons, and wallets full of credit cards that were positively humming and zinging after all their activity.

So if it's a cup of coffee that you're after, as Adam, Kate and I were, don't hold your breath while you're waiting for a seat.

We stood in the middle of the crowded café as pitiful hollow-eyed souls roamed past carrying trays of coffee and doughnuts. They had obviously been there several weeks and still hadn't secured a chair for themselves.

But Adam, being Adam, found the only table that had been vacated in the last three weeks or so. That was one of the many advantages of having a tall man around.

And after he made sure that Kate and I were sitting comfortably, he went off to get coffee.

What a hero!

He was back in record time with a tray overflowing with buns.

"I didn't know what kind you liked," he explained. "So I got you one of each."

"Oh Adam," I said. "You shouldn't have! You're a penniless student."

I was so touched I could have cried.

He had probably just spent his entire Summer term grant on buns for me.

"And I'll never eat them all," I lied.

"Well, don't worry about it," he said smiling and looking really gorgeous. "I'm sure I'll eat whatever you don't."

Then he sat down and turned all his attention to me.

"How are you?" he asked. And he managed to make it sound as if he really was interested.

"Fine," I said, smiling shyly and feeling all silly and simpery and girlie.

What is it?

The moment you realise that you fancy someone you turn into a complete half-wit.

Well, at least I do.

"Will I hold Kate for a while for you?" he asked.

"If you like," I said, taking her out of the sling and tenderly passing her over to his gentle arms.

The lucky bitch!

What a pity that she can't talk yet, I thought regretfully. Otherwise I could debrief her fully on exactly what it felt like to be held in Adam's arms.

We sat there chatting idly while the tides of humanity, with their fluctuating blood-sugar levels, swirled and washed and ebbed and flowed around us. Adam, Kate and I were an oasis of calm in the chaos of Dublin.

As though the three of us were in our own little world.

We didn't really talk that much. We just sat in relaxed silence, drinking coffee, eating buns, my shopping strewn all around us.

Adam was busy playing with Kate, admiring her, and examining her tiny little fingers and touching her cute little face.

He had such a look of intense wonder, almost of

yearning on his face that I got slightly alarmed.

Never mind Laura, I thought, is Adam a child-molester!

"Do you reckon," he said thoughtfully, talking to me, but still looking at Kate, "that if people didn't know better, they'd think that I was Kate's Dad? You know, that we're just a typical nuclear family, as they say in my anthropology tutorials, out shopping on a Saturday afternoon."

He looked up and smiled at me.

And although I had been thinking almost exactly the same thing myself, I felt a little bit, I don't know, funny, yes funny and sad, about Adam saying that.

Disloyal, that's the way I felt.

I was glad that Adam seemed to be so fond of Kate.

But Adam wasn't Kate's father.

James was Kate's father.

And James wasn't here.

It was all so funny and mixed-up and strange and sad.

Why couldn't Adam be her father?

Or why couldn't her father care?

"Would you like to have children?" I asked Adam. "I don't mean now, but, you know, some day?"

He stopped what he was doing and sat very still for a minute. Then he turned and looked at me.

There was such an odd expression on his face.

He looked very sad. Lost almost.

But before he answered me we were interrupted by girls' voices.

"Hey look, it's Adam", "Great, where?", "Adam,

how are you?", "Oh hi, Adam, where were you last night?"

Three beautiful young women, obviously class-mates of Adam's, had arrived at the table and were clustering around him.

The way women did around Adam.

They were like beautiful exotic birds.

Very colourful and very noisy.

They oohed and aahed loudly at Kate and then lost interest in her completely when they discovered that she wasn't Adam's child.

Although why should she be, I wondered.

Adam introduced us all.

"Meet Kate," he said, picking up her little pink hand and waving it at the girls.

It looked so gorgeous, my little girl and this beautiful man, that I thought my heart would break.

Why can't James be here to do this, I wondered.

Even when I'm happy, the sadness is only a moment away.

"And this is Claire," he continued.

"Hi," I smiled gamely at the girls with their young translucent skin and their outrageous clothes, trying not to feel like an old hag.

"And these are . . . "

And he said three names that might have been Alethia, Koo and Freddie. Or could have been Alexia, Sooz and Charlie.

Or then again might have been Atlanta, Jools and Micki.

Odd names. Cool names.

And, I was prepared to take my oath, made-up names.

Names that sport a lot of 'K's when there should be 'C's and 'Z's where there should be 'S's.

Names that I was very sure did not appear on their birthcerts.

I knew their real names were something like Mairead, Dymphna and Mary. You know, nice ordinary names.

Sound names.

But at the risk of offending Maireads, Dymphnas and Marys, not very glamorous names.

These beautiful girls who had descended on Adam looked as if they needed glamorous names to match their glamorous appearances.

The three of them kind of looked the same.

They all had short hair.

And I do mean very short hair.

Sooz/Koo/Jools was nearly totally bald.

And Atlanta/Alexia/Alethia looked like a very unugly duckling, with her little cap of blonde fluffy hair.

She looked a bit like Kate, to be honest.

Which means that Adam, the suspected paedophile, is probably mad about her, I thought sourly.

I was feeling a bit jealous.

All four of them talked away about some party that had been on the previous evening.

I really wished that they would leave, so I could have Adam all to myself and Kate again.

I tried to be grown-up and adult about these three gorgeous young women clamouring for Adam's attention.

My face hurt from trying to look as if I was good fun too, that I didn't mind being ignored as they chattered and laughed charmingly and effortlessly.

It looked as if the three of them were settling in for a long stay.

My heart sank to my (new) boots as all three pulled over chairs and gathered around our tiny little table, each of them practically sitting on Adam's knee.

They hadn't even bought a cup of tea between them.

But, really I wasn't being judgmental.

I knew what it was like to be a poor student.

They'd got to save their money for beer and drugs.

Of course I understood.

But when Freddie/Charlie/Micki started to eat one of the buns, one of *my* buns I nearly burst into tears.

I wanted to stamp my foot and shout hysterically, like a child throwing a tantrum, "That's *my* bun. Adam bought it for *me*!"

I swallowed hard.

I was totally out of place here.

It was silly to think that someone like me could have any place in someone like Adam's life.

He was young and handsome and had a full and happy life.

And I felt tired and old and silly and foolish.

As Adam continued to talk animatedly to the girls, I stood up and put Kate's sling back on.

Then I leant over and took Kate rather brusquely from Adam's arms (Give me back my child!)

interrupting a lively conversation about someone called Olivia Burke who apparently had given Malcolm Travis a blow-job at the party last night, in full view of the guests.

Even through my self-pity and misery I was pleased to hear that Adam wasn't being in any way judgmental about Olivia Burke's behaviour. His censure was reserved for Malcolm because apparently Malcolm had a steady girl-friend, called Alison. And Olivia didn't know about her.

"That guy is so low," Adam said. "He's being disrespectful to the two women at once by behaving that way."

Right on, brother!

Kate started to cry when I took her from Adam's arms. I didn't blame her.

Adam turned and looked at me with a surprised look on his face.

"You're not going, are you?" he asked.

"Yes, I think so," I said, trying to sound casual. "Kate's tired and she'll need a change soon."

I turned to the gorgeous girls.

"Bye," I nodded. "Nice meeting you."

At least I could never be accused of being rude, I thought self-righteously.

"Bye," they chorused. "Bye bye Kate."

Then I felt ashamed.

They were nice girls. I was the one with the problem.

Jealous and insecure.

Childish and overly-sensitive and spoilt.

Off I struggled, loaded down with a baby, bags and huge quantities of feeling hard-done-by, trying to look dignified and unconcerned as I battled through the unyielding crowds.

I could feel Adam's eyes on me, but I refused to meet his look.

He caught up with me before I had gone two yards.

If I was to be perfectly honest – not always an easy thing to be – that was exactly what I wanted him to do.

"Claire," he said in surprised tones. "Where are you going?"

"Home," I mumbled.

I was hoping desperately that he hadn't realised how jealous I was.

"Look, I'm sorry," he said, looking into my eyes. "Were they really getting on your nerves?"

"No," I protested. "No, they were nice."

"You don't have to be polite," he said, looking at me with a concerned expression. "I know they must have seemed like silly little girls to a woman like you."

"No Adam, honestly, they were fine," I insisted.

I felt *really* awful.

I didn't enjoy being with Alexandria, Zoo and Gerri or whatever their bloody names were because I was *jealous* of them, not because I was terribly mature and disdainful.

Here was Adam attributing all kinds of noble motives to me.

Labelling me intelligent when I was, in reality, a

spoilt immature brat, who was demanding attention in the most childish fashion.

"Honestly, they're lovely girls," he said. "I just wanted to be with you and Kate but I didn't know how to stop them sitting down with us without seeming rude," he explained.

"It's really fine," I insisted.

"Look, I'd better go," I said as yet another person with a tray bumped into me and tisked at me for standing in the middle of an aisle.

"Are you sure?" he asked standing very close to me.

"I am," I promised him.

"Really?" he asked, his face moving nearer to mine.

"Really," I promised him.

But I didn't move.

I wanted to stay there, close to him.

Just for a moment.

I wanted him to kiss me.

But there was very little chance of that happening with several thousand people milling around us. Not to mention the fact that Kate would probably suffocate in her sling if Adam pulled me manfully into his arms.

"Will I walk you to your car?" he asked.

"No, really Adam, there's no need."

"I'll see you soon," he said gently.

"Yes," I gave him a little smile.

A nice smile.

A real one.

And he put his hands on my shoulders and pulled me to him (but with the utmost regard for Kate's comfort) and gave me the lightest little kiss on my forehead.

I closed my eyes, surrendering to the moment.

And I caught my breath because I could hardly believe that this was happening.

His mouth felt warm and firm.

He smelt of soap and warm smooth skin.

Through the din of voices that surrounded us in the café I heard someone say "Look, it's those two again."

A voice said "Which two?"

"You know, the two that were having the row outside Switzer's yesterday."

The voices belonged to the girls who had taken great comfort in witnessing the little exchange between Adam and me yesterday.

My God, was it really only yesterday?

They continued to loudly discuss us.

"Oh yes, them. Well it looks as if they've made it up."

"Ah shite!"

I opened my eyes and looked at Adam. We both started to laugh.

"All we need now is the Guinness man," he said.

"In that case I really am going," I told him.

I passed the girls on the way out.

"I'm sure she didn't have a baby yesterday," one of them said.

"Would you say it's his?" the other wanted to know.

I carried on.

My forehead didn't stop tingling until I was a hundred yards from home.

Yes, yes, I know.

A kiss on the forehead hardly qualifies as raunchy sex.

I couldn't name you even one Swedish film that was made about a kiss on the forehead.

But it was so yearning and so tender and in its own chaste way so erotic that it was lots better than raunchy sex.

Well, as good as, I suppose.

Chapter Seventeen

Laura came out on Sunday afternoon and we lounged around drinking tea, eating Jaffa Cakes (Michael's) and playing with Kate.

Playing with Kate involved for the most part, feeding her, winding her and changing her.

Laura wore a filthy paint-stained T-shirt, which I presumed belonged to her teenage lover.

She looked young and contented and happy.

And well she might.

She had had sex four times the previous night, stories of which she attempted to regale me with except we kept being interrupted by Mum or Dad.

"Any word from James?" she enquired, having given up on the idea of spending the afternoon talking dirty after Dad had left the room for about the twentieth time.

He came in, nodded at Laura and started lifting cushions off the couch and moving armchairs, muttering something about not having read the *Independent*, if Helen had taken it he'd kill her.

And how he was the one who paid for the papers so why was he always the one who didn't get to read them.

Then he was back about three minutes later to

see if the fire was lighting properly and had a big discussion, mostly with himself, about the merits of anthracite.

("There's great heat in it, even if it does cost more.")

Laura and I just sat there, curled up on the couch, Kate on Laura's lap, all of us, even Kate, looking bored as we waited for him to finish his tirade and leave.

He was no sooner gone than Mum arrived in, ostensibly to offer us tea, but really to see if I had spirited away the Jaffa Cakes.

She enquired after Laura's father.

"Geoff Prendergast is a lovely man," she told Laura. "I don't know where they got you from at all."

Then Mum left, taking the Jaffa Cakes with her.

"Any word from James?" Laura asked again, as the sitting-room door closed yet another time.

"He's away," I said shortly. "But I'll ring him tomorrow."

I didn't want to talk about James.

Not then anyway.

I was sick of it.

Hashing it and rehashing it and trying to make sense of it and worrying about what to do.

As they say in New York, Get over it and, if you can't get over it, Get over talking about it.

Sound advice.

Laura was in the house for a good hour before she broached the subject of Adam.

I'm amazed that it took her so long.

"So what's the story with yourself and young

Lochinvar?" she enquired ultra-casually, as she rubbed Kate's back with circular motions.

"Who?" I asked. Deliberately obtuse.

"The gorgeous Adam," she said in slight exasperation.

"What about him?" I asked.

"Well for one thing he's mad about you and for another thing he's absolutely beautiful looking. If he was five or six years younger I might even be interested myself."

"Laura, he's not mad about me," I protested.

Of course I only said this so that Laura would insist that Adam was indeed mad about me so that I could get that warm feeling of delight in my stomach again.

"He is mad about you," she told me. "And what's more, you know it."

"But so what?" I said. "Even if he is mad about me – and we have no proof that he is – what am I supposed to do about it?"

"Shag him," she said.

She hadn't an ounce of shame, that one.

"Laura! For God's sake I'm married," I yelled at her.

"Oh yes?" she said smugly. "So where's your husband?"

I was silent.

"Claire," she said kindly, after we sat saying nothing for five tense minutes. "All I'm saying is that he's a lovely man and he seems to really like you and you've had a rough time and even if things do eventually work out with James, maybe you should have a little bit of fun in the meantime."

"What is it around here?" I asked. "Everyone's encouraging me to have a relationship with Adam. Even my own mother!"

"Your mother told you to shag Adam?" screeched Laura in astonishment.

"Well, not exactly in those words, I suppose," I said. "But that's what she meant."

"So what's stopping you?" asked Laura in delight. "You've got your mother's blessing. What a brilliant omen."

I thought for a few moments.

"Yes," I sighed. "I suppose I should."

"What!" barked Laura. "Are you serious?"

"For God's sake," I raised my voice at her. "Isn't that just what you've been encouraging me to do?"

I *knew* this would happen. I just *knew* it.

People are always encouraging each other to do things that they know the other person won't do. And then get the shock of their lives when the person actually does it.

I'm culpable myself.

For years and years I encouraged Dad to get himself a pair of jeans.

"Honestly Dad, they'd be gorgeous on you," I often said.

And Dad would say "Ah go away, I'm far too old."

"No Dad, you're not."

The day that Dad actually turned up wearing a pair of board-stiff navy blue Wranglers, with a twelve inch turn-up on the hem, smiling shyly and proudly, the shock nearly killed me.

"Yes, I know," Laura said, seeming a little bit

distressed. "But it just seems so out of character for you. I mean you're always so loyal."

"Laura, I'm hardly being disloyal to James if I have sex with Adam, am I?" I asked her nicely.

I could see how shocked she was.

Although I had a veneer of good-time-girlness, I had pretty much always been Claire the Constant.

My veneer of debauchery was paper-thin, practically transparent, in fact.

I had played the "Got up, came home" game more times than I care to mention but my heart was never in it.

I always wanted to be boring and settled down with a man, but because that was considered to be the most insulting thing you can say about someone, that is that all she wants is to be settled down with a man, I'd done my level best to hide it.

Few people knew my shameful secret.

"Claire, do you fancy this Adam," she asked in concern.

I was amused to note that Adam had gone from being "the gorgeous Adam" to "this Adam" in a matter of minutes.

"Of course I fancy him," I told her, laughing at her horror. "He's delicious – or hadn't you noticed?"

"Handsome, I grant you," she said cautiously. "But what do you know about him?"

"I know that he's nice and he makes me feel clever and beautiful and desirable."

"Claire, don't forget that you're very vulnerable right now. You *are* on the rebound."

"No kidding?" I said. I thought I sounded very smart.

"Anyway," I asked with great curiosity. "What are you doing, encouraging me to have a fling with him and then when I say I will you go all judgmental on me?"

"Sorry Claire," she said humbly. "I really am. It's just that I thought it might be an ego boost for you to know that he fancied you. But I didn't think for a second that you'd actually do anything about it. You're such a one-man woman that this has come as a little bit of a shock."

"Laura, I'm a no-man woman at the moment," I reminded her.

"I know, but you love James so much that . . . I don't know . . . I just didn't think that you'd even consider anyone else."

"Things change, people change," I said. "I don't know how I feel about James anymore. All I really know is that being with Adam is lovely."

Laura suddenly pulled herself together.

"Well, if that's the case, you couldn't have picked a bigger hunk to have a fling with. He's so good-looking. And so nice. Smart too," she added as an afterthought.

This was good coming from Laura who is usually more concerned with the organ between his legs than the organ between his ears.

"And you'd better get into training," she grinned. "Didn't they give you exercises to do to tone yourself up. Pelvic floor exercises or whatever they're called. You don't want sex with Adam to be like throwing a sausage up O'Connell Street."

"Thank you Laura," I said dryly. "You make me sound like such a catch."

After Laura left I just couldn't settle to anything.

There was no one around.

Anna had done another of her disappearing acts.

Helen apparently was in Linda's.

Although I was glad about that.

I was feeling so guilty about Adam that I don't think I could have looked her in the eye.

I was pretty sure that Adam wasn't her boyfriend.

But it might be an idea to find out for sure.

But I felt that I couldn't cope with knowing that he was in fact her man because what would that tell me about him?

That he was some sort of weirdo who got great enjoyment wrecking homes and putting sister against sister and tearing families asunder.

If Adam was Helen's boyfriend and if she found out about me seeing him, by arrangement, not just once, but twice, then Nineteen Sixteen would seem like Christmas Morning compared with the mayhem and bloodletting that would surely follow.

And did I feel disloyal to Helen for seeing Adam?

Yes, of course I did.

But not disloyal enough.

If Adam was Helen's man then I would back off immediately and have nothing further to do with him.

That bit was easy.

But what if Adam wasn't Helen's man but Helen wanted him?

Well if Adam wanted her also, then, the same as before applied. I would back off immediately and have nothing further to do with him.

But what if Helen wanted Adam and Adam didn't want Helen and if, delicious thought, Adam wanted me, then what?

That was a tough one.

I did love Helen.

God knows why, but I did.

And I didn't want to do anything to upset her.

No, really, I didn't.

It wasn't just that I was afraid of her.

The best thing I could do was talk to Adam about all this.

Just ask him straight out what the story was between himself and Helen.

And if there was a story then move into a new phase of worry.

What it came down to was that if I didn't take a risk I'd never know.

I'd never thought i'd hear myself saying it, but life really was too short.

We should grab all our chances with both hands.

And that's what I was going to do with Adam.

That's right, you heard me correctly, the innuendo was there – I was going to grab him with both hands.

"My God Claire," Mum scowled at me as I changed the television channel yet again. "What's wrong with you? Can't you sit still? You're like someone with a feather in their knickers."

"Sorry, Mum."

Just then the phone rang.

"Jesus, Claire, my foot!" yelped Dad, like a dog with his tail caught in a door, as I raced to answer it and crushed several of his metatarsals in the process.

"Hello," I gasped into the phone.

"Hello, is your Daddy there?" slurred a voice on the other end.

"Dad," I called. "Daaad! Auntie Julia for you."

Dammit, I thought.

That meant Dad would be on the phone for hours.

Auntie Julia was impossible to get off the phone when she rang up drunk.

She usually rang to apologise for doing something like cheating at a game of rounders. A game of rounders that had taken place as recently as about forty-five years ago.

Why was I so bothered about the phone being free anyway, I wondered, nimbly sidestepping Dad as he grumpily hobbled past me on his way to the phone.

Had anybody said that they'd ring me?

Was I expecting any calls?

No and once again, no.

But a warm little glimmer of hope inside of me thought that maybe, just maybe, Adam would ring.

He hadn't said that he would.

But I felt that he might.

I sat down in the hall to eavesdrop unashamedly on Dad's conversation with Auntie Julia.

It usually made for interesting, if slightly bizarre, listening.

How long was this little chat going to take?

"Now Julia, listen to me," Dad said agitatedly.

Oh dear, I thought, it must have been a very important game of rounders for Dad to be getting so het-up.

"Dampen a tea-towel and throw it over it immediately!" he roared into the phone.

Oh Good, I thought, as I realised that Auntie Julia was only in the process of attempting to burn her house down and wasn't calling up for a long remorseful, apologetic, rambling, drunken conversation.

"No, under the tap, Julia, under the tap!" Dad yelled.

How on earth had she been proposing to dampen the tea-towel?

Best not to think about it.

"Now Julia, I'm going to hang up the phone here and you're to do the same," said Dad slowly and carefully, as if he was talking to a four-year-old child.

"And you're to dial 999 and ask for the fire brigade," he continued. "And then you're to call me back and tell me that you've done it and that they're on their way."

He slammed down the phone and leant against the wall.

"Christ," he said, looking exhausted.

"What's she done now?" asked Mum, who had appeared in the hall.

"Somehow she's set one of the rings on the cooker on fire and it's got out of control," sighed Dad. "God, will it ever end?"

The phone rang.

"That'll be her ringing back," said Dad, as Mum reached for the phone.

"Hello," said Mum.

Then her face changed.

"Yes, she's here. Who's calling please?"

"It's Adam, for you," she said, handing me the phone with an expressionless face.

"Oh," I said, taking the receiver from her, exhaling with relief.

This was what I had been waiting for all evening, without even realising it.

"Hello," I said, delighted, but trying to hide it in front of Mum and Dad.

"Claire," he said, in his lovely voice. "How are you?"

"Fine," I said, a bit awkwardly. Mum and Dad were still standing in the hall, both of them looking at me.

"Get lost," I hissed at them, waving my free arm.

"We've a bloody emergency on our hands," Dad barked. "Get off that phone!"

"In a minute," I told him.

"One minute," he said threateningly.

But then the pair of them left.

"Sorry about that," I told Adam, as Mum and Dad returned reluctantly to the sitting-room. "A minor family crisis."

"Is everyone OK?" he enquired anxiously.

"Fine," I said.

I was the one who felt anxious now.

Was he worried because he was concerned about Helen?

About his *girlfriend* Helen?

"Claire," he continued. "I hope you don't mind me ringing. I mean I don't want you to feel as if I'm plaguing you. Just tell me and I'll stop."

Plague me all you like, I thought.

"No Adam, of course I don't mind you ringing me. I like talking to you."

"Great," he said. I could hear the smile in his voice.

I sat on the floor and started to settle in for a comfortable hour or so of conversation.

And as I did so I heard the rattle of someone's key in the front door.

"Oh God," I said, as I heard Helen bellow. "I'm home. Feed me! Or I'll report you for neglect."

"What is it?" asked Adam.

"Helen's here," I said.

"Oh is she? Well say 'hello' from me."

"No, I won't," I blurted out.

"Why?" he asked, sounding shocked.

Helen passed me in the hall. She winked and gave me an enchanting smile.

"Hi Claire, your boots are lovely," she said and continued on.

Sometimes, in fact usually when I least expect it, she can be so sweet and so charming that I could kill her.

"Why?" asked Adam again.

Now's the time to get this thing sorted out once and for all, I decided.

If Adam is messing me and my little sister around, then this is my chance to put an end to it.

I was managing to get nicely worked-up.

The bloody cheek of him.

Just because he's really handsome he thinks he can waltz in here and ride roughshod over all of us, I thought, mixing my metaphors and quickly working myself up into a self-righteous fury.

"Look Adam," I said sharply as soon as I could hear Helen, Mum and Dad arguing in the living-room, and I knew that it was safe to speak. "I don't really know how to say this. In fact I don't even know what I should say."

"For God's sake, what?" he interjected forcefully.

Go on, you tell him, I encouraged myself.

You have every right to know.

But I was already starting to lose my nerve.

"Look, maybe it's none of my business but are you Helen's boyfriend?" I finally managed.

A silence followed.

Oh God, I thought. He *is* going out with Helen. And he was just being nice to me because I'm Helen's reject older sister. And now he knows that I fancy him.

Damn, damn, damn. I should have kept my fool mouth shut.

I've ruined everything because I have no patience.

"Claire," he eventually said, sounding stunned. "What on earth are you talking about?"

"You know," I said. I felt highly foolish, but even more relieved.

"No," he said, sounding a bit cold. "I don't know."

"Oh," I said, *really* embarrassed now.

"So you think I'm Helen's boyfriend?" he said stonily.

"Well, I thought you might be . . . " I said, mortified.

"And just what exactly did you think I was doing by asking if I could see you?" he continued, sounding almost contemptuous.

"Well?" he prompted as I remained silent.

"Either you think I'm extremely thick or extremely cynical," he said. "And I'm not sure which one I'm more offended by."

I still said nothing.

Mostly because I didn't know what to say.

I felt terrible.

Adam had been nothing but decent and respectful to me.

I had no proof that he was having anything at all to do with Helen.

I had hurt him by doubting his motives.

"Claire," he said sounding exhausted. "Claire, Claire, Claire, listen to me. I am not now, or have ever in the past been, your sister Helen's boyfriend. And I don't want to be either."

"She's a lovely girl," he added hastily. "But she's not for me."

"Look Adam," I stammered. "I'm really sorry, but I didn't know . . . "

"I'm sorry too," he said. "I keep forgetting what you've just been through. You've been badly hurt. Who could blame you for thinking that we're all a crowd of two-timing bastards?"

My hero, I thought, melting.

He'd taken the words right out of my mouth. He'd saved me the ordeal of telling him and taking a risk.

What a guy!

How was he so in tune with how I felt?

Maybe he's a transsexual, I thought in alarm. That's probably his big dark secret. That he was born a woman. Or that he's a woman trapped in a man's body – and what a man's body!

307

"Claire," he continued, dragging me away from
speculation about his sexuality. "I don't know what
kind of impression you've formed of me, but it's
obviously not the one I was hoping for."

"No . . . Adam . . . " I protested weakly. I had so
much to say and I didn't know where to start.

"Just give me a minute," he said. "Just listen to
me. Will you?"

He sounded so earnest and boyish how could I
resist?

"Of course," I said.

"I have lots of women friends but I don't do the
romance thing a lot. Hardly ever, in fact. Well, hardly
ever compared with the other people in my year in
college, but maybe they're just especially prolific."

"That's fine," I said, anxious for him to shut up
now.

You don't have to explain anything to me, I
wanted to tell him.

I had established that he wasn't Helen's boyfriend
and that was plenty to be going on with.

I felt mortified by my earlier histrionics and
accusations. I just wanted to forget the whole thing
now.

The poor guy!

He only knew me a few days and already we'd
had several mini-rows.

What on earth made him think that I was worth
the bother?

But before I got to think about this, Dad
reappeared in the hall with a face like thunder.

"Claire!" he yelled. "Off the phone, NOW!"

"You've got to go?" Adam asked.

"Yes," I said. "I'm sorry."

I didn't want to end the conversation until I knew that everything was all right. That Adam wasn't annoyed with me for thinking that he was some kind of home-wrecking Lothario.

I also wouldn't have minded some kind of indication that, apart from not wanting to do the romance thing, as he so delicately put it, with Helen, he might want to do the romance thing with me.

As Mum would say, I wanted jam on it.

"Oh, I nearly forgot why I actually rang you," he said.

"Why's that?" I asked.

Tell me that you really fancy me. Go on, go on, I urged him silently.

"There's a good film on at eleven o'clock. I'm sure you'd like it. You should watch it if you're not too tired."

"Oh," I said, the wind having been surgically removed from my sails good and proper, let me tell you. "Well thanks."

A bloody film!

In fairness!

"See you soon," he said.

No wait, I wanted to shout, don't go just yet. Talk to me for one more minute. Give me your number so that I can call you. Can I see you tomorrow? Never mind tomorrow, can I see you tonight?

"Claire," Dad rumbled threateningly from the living room.

"OK, bye," I said, hanging up.

Feeling, amongst other things, completely exhausted.

There was a disorderly surge from the living-room the moment the phone was hung up.

Dad and Helen scuffled at the door.

Dad wanted to get straight onto Auntie Julia to see if the inferno was under control.

While Helen had other plans for the phone.

"I have to ring Anthony," she shouted. "I need a lift to Belfast on Tuesday."

"Well, Julia's fire is more important," insisted Dad.

"Let her house burn down," said Helen, "That'd teach her. The alco."

Charitable to the end, that was Helen.

I walked away from the battle by the phone.

I went upstairs and moved Kate's cot into Mum's room and settled down to watch the recommended film on the little television there.

It was the least I could do after I had been so mean to Adam.

And I'll be able to discuss it with him the next time I see him, I thought.

If there is a next time.

Chapter Eighteen

Time had slowed to a standstill while I had been the Alcoholic Mother from Hell (and the Alcoholic Daughter from Hell and the Alcoholic Sister from Hell if I'm to be strictly accurate). But now that I had started living again it had started to trot briskly, and before I knew it, it had broken into a sprint.

The days had started to fly past the way they do in films when the director wants to convey time passing quickly, i.e. the pages of a calendar turning over very speedily in a high wind. And tearing off and blowing away. With brown leaves blowing with the pages to indicate Autumnal days and then a few flurries of snow to indicate Winter's arrival.

The weekend was over before I knew it.

Not of course that concepts like the difference between the weekend and the working week made a blind bit of difference to a layabout like me.

Every day was a holiday, etc.

But suddenly it was Monday morning.

James would be back from the Caribbean. Or Mustique. Or from a small, privately owned island just off the coast of Heaven. Or wherever he'd gone to, the faithless bastard.

So I was going to have to ring him.

But I felt quite calm about it. What must be done must be done.

Of course it was very easy for me to be calm about James when I was worried sick about Adam.

It was kind of difficult to be in a mess about the two of them at the one time.

Transference of affection, etc. and a big hand for Dr Freud.

But before I got to ring James I had another treat in store for me on Monday morning.

My six week, post-natal check-up with the doctor.

The fun just never seemed to stop in my life.

This was a kind of symbolic, watershed type of event.

It was a form of recognition that the birth had been a success. Sort of like the launch party they have after the release of a new film. Except at the party after the release of a new film, members of the cast and crew don't have to go round putting their feet in stirrups and have strange men examine their private parts.

Not unless they really want to, of course.

Kate also had an appointment at the Baby Clinic.

Off the pair of us went in the car.

I was proud of myself. Every day that I managed to get myself out of bed, functioning, was still a little bit of a miracle.

Living and all its attendant duties and responsibilities had begun to be a pleasure all over again.

Kate had been taken to the clinic a couple of times already.

It was old hat to her. But I wasn't really prepared for the cacophony of crying that greeted us on arrival. There seemed to be several thousand bawling babies with harassed and distraught mothers in the waiting-room.

In fact, some of the mothers were crying louder than their children.

"If only he'd stop crying," one women was saying tearfully, to no one in particular. "Just for five minutes."

"My God," I thought in horror. I suddenly realised how lucky I was.

Not only did Kate seem to be an abnormally placid baby, but I had Mum and Dad and, I suppose, Helen and Anna to share the burden of looking after her with.

Mum and Dad had taken her for her check-ups when I had been behaving like an anti-Christ.

My God, I can't tell you how ashamed I now felt.

How could I have neglected my beautiful child in such a terrible way?

It would never happen again.

No man would ever undermine me the way I let James undermine me.

I felt sick at the thought that, just because I was pining for a man, I didn't look after Kate the way I should have.

Kate had her check-up before me.

I carried her in her cot into the examination room.

The nurse was a glamorous red-haired young woman from Galway.

Why are nurses always good-looking and sexy?

I'm sure there's some old legend that explains it.

Long, long ago there was a tribe of women who were excessively beautiful.

The men were maddened by lust for them and they made all the other women feel inadequate and horrible.

All kinds of riots and outbreaks of violence occurred.

Homes broke up as previously happily married men fell in love with one of these babes.

Women from the non-good-looking tribes killed themselves because they could never compete with these sirens.

Something had to be done.

So God decreed that all the good-looking women had to become nurses and wear truly awful lace-up shoes and revolting A-line frocks that make their bums look huge, so that their attractiveness would be toned down considerably.

And to this very day good-looking women have to become nurses so that their beauty is diluted by the hideous uniforms.

Although how this little fable of mine squares with Supermodels and their revealing and flattering clothes, I'm at a loss to explain.

Anyway, never mind.

The nurse closed the door firmly behind us, but the noise of the roaring children in the waiting-room was still perfectly audible, interspersed now and again with wails of "Just five minutes, that's all I ask."

"Doesn't the noise drive you mad?" I asked her curiously.

"Not at all," she said. "I don't even hear it anymore."

She started to examine Kate.

Kate was so good. She didn't even cry.

I was very proud of her.

I felt like opening the door and saying, in school-marm fashion to all the children out there, "Look, this is how you're supposed to behave. Observe this model child in here and imitate."

I watched the nurse as she inspected Kate and her vital signs.

It would serve me right if there was something awful wrong with her, I thought, terror gripping me.

But no, everything was fine.

The guilty part of me was nearly disappointed.

"She's putting on weight just fine," said the nurse.

"Thank you," I beamed proudly.

"She's a perfectly healthy baby," smiled the nurse.

"Thank you," I said again.

I opened the door to leave and a fresh wave of screeching sent me reeling.

We fought our way back through the throng of red-faced and yelling children.

From what I could gather a bunch of them were getting their BCGs and this was contributing to the general upset.

I picked my way carefully through the deafening crowd, carrying Kate in her cot.

As I thankfully closed the door on the racket behind me, the last thing I heard was that poor woman wailing "Even three minutes. I'd settle for three."

Then we had to wait for a while until it was my turn to see the doctor.

I read a copy of *Woman's Own* that dated from sometime around the turn of the century (Crinolines are definitely *out* this Autumn). Kate had a little sleep.

She was such a good girl.

Eventually I was called and in we went.

The doctor was a nice old codger. Grey suit, grey hair, vague kindly manner.

"Hello, ah yes, Claire, yes Claire and baby er Catherine," he said reading from the notes on his desk. "Come in and sit down."

After a moment he looked up at the chair in front of him and when I wasn't there his glance darted anxiously around the room, wondering where I had gone.

I had placed Kate's cot on the floor and I was over at the examining couch with my knickers off and my feet in the stirrups with a speed that left his head spinning.

Old habits die hard.

The next time I'd have to go to the doctor, no matter what my complaint, from an earache to a sprained wrist, I'd be hard pressed to stop myself from whipping off my knickers and clambering up onto the couch.

The doctor did whatever it was he did, involving that old friend of mine, the lubricated glove.

I'm sorry if I'm being revolting.

Really, I have every sympathy with how you feel.

There was a time when I would have felt faint at even the thought of having a smear test.

Now, after being pregnant and giving birth I think

I could have a hysterectomy under just local anaesthetic and still be sitting up and cheerfully discussing last night's telly with the surgeon.

Hell, why bother with the anaesthetic?

But I forget that others haven't had the same hardening experiences that I've had.

"You've healed beautifully," he told me, making it sound like a great achievement.

"Thank you," I said, glowing, smiling up at him from between my legs

I felt as though I was five years old and had got all my sums right at school.

"Yes, no complications there at all," he continued. "Has all the bleeding stopped yet?"

(Sorry about this, I won't go on about it for long.)

"Yes, it stopped about a week ago," I told him.

"And the stitches have mended perfectly," he said, continuing to peer and poke.

"Thank you," I smiled again.

"Right, you can get down now," he told me.

"So is everything else all right?" he asked as I got dressed.

"Fine," I said. "Fine."

"Er, when can I have sex again?" I suddenly blurted out.

(Now *why* did I ask that?)

"Well, your six weeks are up, so anytime you like," he said genially. "You could start right now."

He threw back his head and guffawed loudly and then stopped abruptly as visions of the Medical Council hearings and motions to have him struck off swam before him.

There's a very fine line between an acceptable bedside manner and a lewd suggestion.

Perhaps Doctor Keating hadn't quite grasped the difference yet.

"Ahem," he said, calming himself down. "Yes, anytime you like."

"Will it hurt?" I asked anxiously.

"It may feel a little bit uncomfortable at first, but it shouldn't feel *painful* as such. Ask your husband to be particularly gentle with you."

"My *husband?*" I asked the doctor, in surprise.

I hadn't even been thinking of my husband.

"Yes, your husband," he said, sounding equally surprised. "You are a married woman, aren't you, Mrs, ah, Mrs Webster," he said consulting my notes.

"Yes, of course, I am," I said blushing. "But I was, er, you know, just making general enquiries. I wasn't actually planning on having intercourse with anyone."

I thought if I said the word "intercourse" instead of the word "sex" that it might help to neutralise this embarrassing and awkward atmosphere that seemed to have suddenly developed.

"Oh," he said baldly.

Silence and Dr Keating's bewilderment hung heavy in the air.

Time to leave, I thought.

Come on Kate.

Home we went.

"How did it go?" asked Mum as she answered the door to us.

"Fine," I said. "Fine. Kate's putting on weight nicely, the nurse says."

"And how are you?" she asked.

"Couldn't be better, apparently," I said. "I'm in tip-top condition. I've a vagina to be proud of."

Mum gave me a look of distaste.

"There's no need to be vulgar," she tisked at me.

"I wasn't being vulgar," I protested.

My God, if I was being vulgar she'd know all about it.

"Come and have a cup of tea with me before *Neighbours* comes on," said Mum.

"Er, did anyone ring for me while I was out?" I enquired of her, oh-so-casually, as I traipsed behind her into the kitchen.

"No."

"Oh."

"Why, who were you expecting to ring?" she asked, looking at me closely.

"No one," I said, setting Kate's cot down on the kitchen table.

"Well, why did you ask in that case?" she said in a tone of voice which reminded me that, however much she may act like one, my mother was no fool.

"And take the child off the table!" she said, whacking my arm with a tea-towel. "People have to eat off that."

"She's perfectly clean!" I protested, outraged.

How dare she.

I was always washing Kate.

She was totally sanitised.

You'd have had your work cut out to find even a bacterium on her.

My child was a germ-free zone.

So Adam hasn't rung me, I mused as I drank my tea.

I wondered if he was still annoyed with me.

Maybe he was never going to ring me again.

Not that I'd have blamed him.

Not with me behaving all neurotic and argumentative.

And I didn't have his number so I couldn't call him.

So that was probably the end of that.

The fling that never was.

The passionate affaire that was never consummated.

The soul-mates that were divided by circumstances.

The lovers who loved from afar.

Although then again it wasn't even lunch time yet.

Give the guy a chance.

But he didn't ring.

I hung around all afternoon feeling bored and dissatisfied.

I didn't want to do anything.

I couldn't be bothered reading.

And Kate was whinging and crying and I didn't feel very patient with her.

I half-heartedly watched the afternoon soaps with Mum, because I couldn't come up with a good reason for her why I shouldn't.

I think I would have preferred to sit through several third-rate Antipodean dramas, with the same actors reappearing in each successive programme, than get into another conversation with Mum on how my University education had given me notions above my station.

And she knew that something was wrong.

"You're very gloomy-looking," she said.

(Although her actual words were "Claire, you're like a tree over a blessed well.")

"Why the hell wouldn't I be?" I snapped back.

"Sorry," she said. "God knows it's not easy for you."

Well she was quite right, it was not.

But she was obviously referring to my situation with James. And not my lack of one, with Adam.

"No, I'm sorry," I told her, feeling rotten for biting her head off.

It was six o'clock and Dad's key was in the door before I realised with horror that I hadn't called James.

Dammit, dammit, dammit.

I really had meant to do it but because of all the things going on – the big event of going to the doctor and the major event of Adam not ringing – I had just totally forgotten.

I resolved to do it first thing in the morning.

The debacle that was dinner-time took my mind off things for a while.

Helen came home with Dad and was demanding McDonald's.

321

"No Helen," shouted Dad. "We only get McDonald's on bank holidays."

"Well that's stupid," she shouted back. "Other families, *normal* families get it on ordinary days."

Oh, but she could be very cruel.

So the upshot was that Helen got her way as usual and Dad drove off like a Grand Prix driver with a long and complicated order to McDonald's.

Helen roared after him, "No gherkins on the quarter-pounder!"

But he was already gone.

I shamelessly latched onto Helen for most of the evening, hoping that she might say something about Adam.

Of course, I could have taken the bull by the horns and just asked her for his number, seeing as she wasn't going out with him or anything.

But I still couldn't bring myself to do it.

I had established that he had no interest in her.

But I wasn't at all sure how Helen felt about him.

After dinner, which by the way, poor Dad had got all wrong – gherkins on Mum's apple pie, cheeseburgers instead of quarter-pounders with cheese (which of course gave rise to the accusation of 'cheapskate'), Coke instead of Diet Coke – Dad ordered Helen to go to her room and study.

Poor Dad.

He must have been doing some kind of assertiveness course.

Amazingly enough Helen went with only the most cursory of protests.

She called Dad a bastard and made references to the regime in the house being similar to the one in Nazi Germany.

But she actually went to her room.

That was nothing short of miraculous.

I gave her a few minutes, then I took Kate and we went up and knocked on her door.

There was a major scuffling. She seemed to be stuffing something down the side of the bed.

"Oh Jesus, Claire, don't do that! I thought you were Dad," she exclaimed, her eyes big and wide in her white face.

She retrieved a magazine called *True Crimes* or something similar from the gap between her bed and the wall.

"Do you *ever* do any study?" I asked her with curiosity.

"Noooooh," she said scornfully.

"What'll you do if you fail?" I asked her as I sat on the bed.

"Here, give me her," said Helen, taking Kate from my arms.

"I won't fail," she continued.

"How do you know?"

"I just know," she assured me.

Oh God, to have had her confidence.

"So how's college?" I asked her, willing her to talk about Adam.

"Fine," she said, looking surprised by my interest.

She said nothing at all about Adam.

And really, I couldn't, just couldn't ask.

Then I heard the phone ring.

The first time it had rung all day.

I was off that bed and down those stairs like greased lightning.

Thank God I didn't ask Helen for Adam's number, I congratulated myself in relief. I would have given the game away entirely and now there was no need!

"Hello," I said, trying to sound pleasant and unneurotic and apologetic all at the same time.

Sorry Adam, I'll never be mean to you again.

"Yes hello, can I speak to Jack Walsh?" said a voice.

My first thought was why on earth did Adam want to talk to Dad.

But then I realised that it wasn't Adam at all on the phone.

The bastard!

How dare he!

Getting me to practically break my neck coming down those stairs only for him not to be him at all.

"Yes, hold on Mr Brennan. I'll get him for you," I said.

And I trudged miserably back up the stairs.

A lot slower than I had come down.

I went back into Helen.

I was suitably humbled.

I still had every need of her.

She was playing with Kate and didn't see fit to comment on my death-defying flight down the stairs.

That was one of the great things about being with someone as selfish as Helen.

She so rarely took notice of anything that wasn't happening to her.

Just then Anna arrived in, all flowing hair and traipsy skirt and vague aspect.

I was delighted to see her.

We hadn't crossed paths since sometime the previous week.

She tramped across Helen's pink and fluffy bedroom in the boots that were breaking Mum's heart and sat down beside us on the bed.

Out of her bag (embroidered, covered in mirrors and beads) she took about a hundred bars of chocolate and proceeded to efficiently eat her way through them.

I've never seen anything quite like it.

I could only assume that it was drug-related in some way.

"Anna, have you the . . . er . . . the 'munchies'?" I asked, feeling like a right old fuddy-duddy.

I felt a bit self-conscious about using such a jargony word as "munchies."

"Um," she nodded, through a mouth that was crammed to capacity with raisin and biscuit Yorkie.

"Gerumph!" she gesticulated angrily as Helen started ripping papers off the bars and practically inhaling them whole.

"Get your own, Helen," she finally managed, as her mouth was momentarily empty.

"Just give me this Bounty and a bar of Mintcrisp and I won't take any more," said Helen.

Lying, of course.

Anna agreed.

Poor Anna.

I spent the rest of the evening thrown on Helen's

bed, eating chocolate, half-listening to the good-natured bickering between Helen and Anna, waiting for Adam to ring.

But, guess what, he didn't.

It doesn't matter, I told myself, he didn't say he would ring me.

He's bound to call tomorrow.

He'll definitely call in the next few days, I tried to comfort myself.

It's obvious that he really likes you.

But underneath all my bravado I knew he wouldn't ring me.

I don't know how I knew, I just did.

Obviously my ability to sense approaching disaster had improved slightly since James left me.

The bit of practice might have helped.

Chapter Nineteen

The next morning the house was like Grand Central Station.

Helen was going to Belfast for two days on a college trip and obviously believed that her preparations should not only be a last-minute affair but should also be a family event.

Instead of being woken by Kate grizzling, I woke to the sound of stealthy rustling at the foot of my bed.

Someone was in my room and up to no good.

I sat up sleepily.

"Who's that?" I yawned.

It was Helen.

I might have known.

She was making for the door with an armful of my new clothes.

"Oh Claire!" she said, jumping guiltily as she dropped one of my new boots on the floor. "I thought you were asleep."

"So I see," I said drily. "Now put them back."

"Bitch," muttered Helen, throwing a big pile of my clothes onto the floor. They had obviously been Belfast-bound.

I'm sorry lads, I told them. I'll take you another time.

I heard her go down to the kitchen and shortly afterwards there was the inevitable outbreak of raised voices.

What was it about her?

She shall have aggro wherever she goes.

Kate was awake in her cot, just lying there looking at the ceiling.

"Why didn't you cry, darling?" I teased her gently. "Why didn't you wake me and tell me that nasty Auntie Helen was stealing my clothes?"

I picked her up and took her into bed with me, holding her soft warm tiny little body in my arms.

We lay in bed for a while, drifting in and out of sleep, half-listening to the sounds of an argument in the kitchen. I really should get up, I thought. Maybe Helen will mention Adam before she leaves.

I just held Kate tighter. My precious beautiful child.

But then she started demanding to be fed so I got out of bed and quickly got dressed, tripping over the pile of clothes on the floor in the process. The two of us went downstairs.

Where a little dispute seemed to be in process.

Anna, Mum and Helen were sitting round the table surrounded by breakfast debris, pop-tarts and tea-pots and cereal packets and Club Milk wrappers all over the place.

Mum and Helen were arguing loudly.

Anna was smiling beatifically and doing something peculiar with a daisy and a paper clip.

"I know nothing about any green scarf and gloves," Mum told Helen hotly.

"But I left them on top of the fridge," Helen protested. "So what did you do with them."

"Well, if you hadn't left them on top of the fridge, if you'd put them in their proper place you'd know where to find them," Mum answered her.

"The top of the fridge *is* the proper place," Helen replied. "It's where I always leave my things."

"Morning," I said pleasantly.

They all completely ignored me.

For no obvious reason the back door was swinging open and blasts of Siberianesque morning air blew through the kitchen.

This was ridiculous.

I had a small child on the premises.

We would all catch our deaths.

I walked briskly over and, holding Kate with one hand, managed to shut the door and lock it securely with the other.

"You shouldn't have done that," said Anna darkly.

I looked at her in surprise.

I would have thought that it was far too early in the morning, even for Anna, to be all mystical and ethereal.

"Why?" I asked gently, fondly, prepared to humour her. "Is the Goddess of the Morn going to punish me for barring her entrance to our kitchen?"

"No," said Anna, looking at me as though I had gone stone mad.

Just then there was a muffled and frantic commotion outside the back door.

Someone or something was very annoyed to find the back door locked.

Lovely language for the Goddess of the Morn, let me tell you.

Anna sighed and clumped over and opened the door.

Dad stood on the step, almost totally obscured by the huge pile of washing which he held in his arms.

"Who locked the bloody door?" he roared through his armful of jeans and jumpers.

"I might have known you'd have something to do with it," he hissed at poor Anna, as she stood with her hand on the doorknob.

"No Dad, it was me," I told him hastily. Anna's bottom lip had started to quiver and she looked on the verge of tears.

"No, no, because we were *cold*," I explained, as Dad fixed me with a wounded look. "Not because I *wanted* to lock you out."

My God, what a crowd of neurotics!

I was so normal compared to the rest of my family.

"Right," declared Dad, throwing all the clothes onto the table, mindless of the half-eaten slices of toast and the bowls of abandoned cornflakes that were already on it. "Which of these clothes do you want?"

"Oh Helen, why are you so difficult," sighed Mum. "You have a roomful of clothes up there but the one thing you want has to be in the washing-machine or on the line."

Helen smiled like a little cat.

She loved to be told that she was difficult.

It made her feel powerful.

Which indeed she was.

Smirking, she selected a few garments from the mound on the table and handed them to Dad.

"What am I to do with them now?" he asked in surprise.

"But they have to be ironed," said Helen, sounding equally surprised.

"Ironed?" said Dad. "By me?"

"Are you going to send me to Belfast with wrinkled clothes?" asked Helen, outraged. "You know, I'm an ambassador for the Free State. I can't go up to Belfast looking like a knacker. They'll think all Catholics are dirty and scuzzy."

"Right, right, right," shouted Dad, putting his arms up to defend himself from her passionate appeal.

The poor man.

He never stood a chance.

Things settled down.

Toast started to be eaten, coffee started to be gulped, conversation – and I use the term oh-so-loosely – started to be made.

"Guess who I'm staying with in Belfast?" Helen asked in an innocent sing-song type of voice. She sounded far too casual and blasé.

I knew that tone.

I sensed trouble.

"Who?" asked Anna.

"A Protestant," said Helen in hushed and awed tones.

Mum continued sipping her tea.

"Mum didn't you hear me?" Helen said petulantly. "I said I was staying with a Protestant."

Mum looked up calmly.

"So?"

"But don't we hate all Protestants?"

"No Helen, we don't hate anyone," Mum told her, as if she was speaking to a four-year-old child.

"Not even Protestants?"

Helen was determined to have herself a row, one way or the other.

"No, not even Protestants."

"But what if I fall under their influence and go all funny and start doing flower arranging?"

Somewhere along the line Helen had picked up some kind of vague and fuzzy generalisation of what Protestants were like.

A funny mixture of Beelzebub and Miss Marple.

They had horns, of course, and cloven hoofs and breathed fire and made their own jam.

"Well, so what if you do," said Mum pleasantly.

"And what if I don't go to Mass anymore?" gasped Helen in assumed horrified tones.

"But you don't go anyway," said Anna, sounding bewildered.

A rather tense and nasty silence followed.

Luckily Kate, obviously sensing an awkward mood, smoothed things over by starting to cry like a banshee.

I felt that she had a great future ahead of her as an ambassador, or working for the United Nations.

There was a big rush to prepare her bottle, Anna and Helen practically tripped over themselves to help.

Dad busied himself by getting out the ironing

board and making a great production of the ironing, pressing the steam button on the iron until the kitchen resembled a sauna.

Mum sat as though she was made of stone.

But after a while even she became roused to activity. She started to clear the table and grimly threw some cold chewy toast into the bin.

Which was a pity because I kind of liked cold chewy toast. But I wasn't fool enough to cross my mother shortly after she had been notified of one of her daughters' non-attendance at Mass.

Even when the daughter in question wasn't me.

Things returned to normal.

Normal, being, of course, an entirely subjective concept.

One man's normality is another man's dysfunctional, anarchic, splintered, deeply unhealthy home environment.

Helen was never one to let any sort of a *faux pas* keep her down for long.

The inane prattle started again within moments.

"What'll it be like in Belfast. What if I get killed?" she mused. "I mean, anything could happen to me. I could get shot or blown up. This could be the last time you'll ever see me."

We all stared at her, struck dumb by emotion. Even Kate was silent.

Surely, *surely* we could never be that lucky.

"Or maybe I'll be kidnapped," she said dreamily. "I could be like Brian Keenan. And he has two ugly sisters too!" she said triumphantly, delighted to find a likeness between herself and a kidnap victim.

"Except I've got four ugly sisters," she said thoughtfully. "Well never mind."

"They're *not* ugly," said Mum, all indignant.

"Thanks Mum," I smirked at Helen.

"Yes, thanks Mum," said Anna.

"Not *you*," said Mum, annoyed. "I'm talking about Brian Keenan's sisters."

"Oh," I said subdued.

Helen was still talking about being kidnapped.

My heart twisted with pity for the imaginary kidnapper.

Anyone who kidnapped Helen would be convinced that they had been set up. That she was some kind of awesome secret weapon sent from the other side to destroy them from within.

Nothing frightened her.

She could be chained in some filthy basement with a lean young white-faced fanatic, all wiry muscles and burning eyes, laden with weaponry and she could start a conversation with him about where he bought his jumper.

Or about anything really.

"I suppose you'll have to torture me a bit," she would say offhandedly. "What'll you do? I suppose you could cut off my ear and send it in the post for the ransom money. I wouldn't mind that too much. I mean what do I need my ear for anyway. Because I hear with the inside of my ear. Not the outside bit. Although it would be a bit of a problem if I wanted to wear glasses. If I only had one ear they'd be all lop-sided. But I could always get contact lenses. Yes! I could make Dad buy me some of those coloured contact lenses. What about brown ones? Do you think I'd look nice with brown eyes?"

And the poor terrorist would be exhausted and horrified by her.

"Shut up bitch," he might say.

Although this being Northern Ireland, "Shot op botch," would be more like it.

And she might shut up for a moment or two before she'd be off again.

"These are lovely handcuffs. I have handcuffs too but they're only crappy old plastic ones. I suppose this must be one of the perks of the job, being allowed to borrow the good handcuffs. You know, to tie your girlfriend up and that. Although it must be a problem when you've got a prisoner. But I wouldn't mind. You could take them tonight and I promise I won't try to escape . . . "

And on and on until the terrorists cracked.

Grown men sobbing uncontrollably, "She's horrible, horrible! I'll do whatever you want, but just make her stop."

Helen would arrive back safely to her home, not only with the ransom money returned untouched, but with a whipround and a sympathy note for her family from the terrorists.

Anyway she eventually left. Some poor idiot called Anthony from her class had the dubious pleasure of her company on the three hour drive to Belfast.

Off she went, sitting in the front seat wearing a pious expression and clutching a bottle of holy water.

She didn't mention Adam before she left.

The cow.

Maybe he was going to Belfast also.

Maybe he was already there.

Maybe all the phone lines in Rathmines were down and that was why he hadn't rung me.

Maybe he had been knocked off his bike and was in hospital with a selection of injuries.

The important thing was that he hadn't rung me.

And he wasn't going to.

So now what was I going to do?

What I really found peculiar was the way I'd barely given James a thought over the last days.

My head had been full of Adam, Adam, Adam.

In the same way that the stewards on the Titanic were more concerned about the unemptied ashtrays on the bar than the enormous hole in the side of the ship which was letting in zillions of gallons of water, I too was worrying about the unimportant and ignoring the vital.

Sometimes it's easier that way.

Because although there was damn all I could do about the huge hole, it was still within my power to empty an ashtray.

A nice analogy.

But the practical consequences of me feeling that way were that I spent Tuesday mooning around the house.

Not *mooning* in the drunken-rugby-coach-party sense of the word.

Mooning in the feeling miserable and looking tragic sense of the word.

Did I ring James?

I'm sorry, but I didn't.

I was having a bad case of the Self-Pitys.

I was stricken by a particularly virulent form of the Poor-Mes.

No excuse, I realised.

God knows, I wasn't trying to justify myself.

But I was, I was . . . I was *depressed*, Goddammit.

Chapter Twenty

The next day I wasn't much better.

Jesus! Did you ever meet anyone as self-pitying as me?

It was ridiculous and it had got to stop.

So I dragged myself out of the bed and tended to Kate. Then I tended to myself.

Oh don't worry, we're not going to have a repeat performance of the getting drunk and not-washing-myself scenario.

Oh no, things weren't that bad.

I got through the day.

To be fair I didn't achieve anything outlandish.

I didn't find a cure for cancer.

I didn't invent non-ladder tights.

And I'm ashamed to tell you that I didn't even ring James.

I know, I know! I'm sorry. I know that I should have. I knew that I was ducking my responsibilities.

But I felt so empty and lonely.

Sad and alone and all the other emotions coming under the Genus "Loss," subspecies "Rejection."

Still, it was no excuse for letting the grass grow under my feet.

The grass in question being, of course, the grass that's always greener.

Especially when you no longer have it.

If you'll forgive the incoherent hotchpotch of adages and pithy sayings.

Anyway I *did* get up on Thursday.

Not only that, but I rang James.

And I wasn't even nervous.

And I had Adam to thank for that.

It's an ill wind, etc. etc.

Because I approached the ringing of James with the attitude of "Huh! Don't think that you're anything special. Because you're not. You're not the only man who can make me feel sad and lonely and rejected. Oh no! There's *millions* of others who can do exactly what you did. So there!"

Perhaps not an ideal attitude from a self-esteem point of view, but however.

I dialled the number in London and my hands didn't shake and my voice didn't quaver.

How interesting, I thought.

James no longer had the power to reduce me to a quaking wreck.

Well, at least dialling his office number no longer had the power to reduce me to a quaking wreck.

Let's not get carried away here.

In a confident and steady voice I asked the receptionist in his office in London if I could speak to him.

I felt as if London was a million miles away. As remote as another planet. You'd never have thought that I saw it every evening on the News. The receptionist sounded very far away, very foreign.

Mirroring the way I felt. My life with James had become very far away, very foreign.

Or maybe it was because the receptionist was Greek.

Either way, I was perfectly calm as I waited to speak to him.

I mean, what was the big deal?

What had I got to lose?

Nothing.

As someone once said – a miserable, sardonic, misanthropic someone – freedom's just another word for nothing left to lose.

Up until I heard that I thought freedom was being able to go swimming when you had your period.

How misinformed I was.

Of course you'd believe anything when you're about twelve.

Did you know that you can't have a baby if you do it standing up?

Honestly, it's true.

And did you know that you *can* have a baby if you suck the man's thing?'

But I knew that would never happen to me because I'd never do anything as disgusting as suck the man's thing.

And I didn't believe for one moment that anyone, anywhere, would do something so revolting and alien.

I hadn't heard the term "Unnatural Act" at the age of twelve but if I had I would have embraced it like a long-lost sister.

I could weep for the innocent child that I was, for the idealistic twelve-year-old that I once was.

But at the same time, I didn't know what I was missing.

Oh, sorry, sorry, you want to know how I got on with James.

Oh didn't I say?

He wasn't in.

At a meeting, or something.

And, no, I didn't leave my name.

And, yes, you're right if you suspect that I was a bit relieved at not having to talk to him.

But I was in an unimpeachable position.

I'd rung him, hadn't I?

I defy anyone to say that I hadn't.

Was it my fault that he was unavailable?

No, indeed it was not.

But it meant that I could stop feeling guilty for a couple of hours.

So spirits were high around Thursday lunchtime.

Happily, I picked Kate out of her cot and twirled her round.

What a beautiful picture we must make, I thought.

The beautiful child being lovingly held by her devoted mother.

Kate just looked frightened and started to cry, but never mind.

I meant well.

My heart was in the right place.

Even if Kate's centre of gravity wasn't.

"Come on darling," I said. "Let's put on our best babygro and go into town and see the people."

And so Kate and I went into town.

I couldn't, in all conscience buy any more clothes for me.

Not after the carry-on of me on Saturday.

But I *could* buy clothes for Kate.

Hah! Don't waste your time even trying to make me feel guilty about that one.

I'd a cast-iron alibi.

Every day I was finding out more good things about Kate. She continued to enhance every aspect of my life.

I bought her the tiniest, most beautiful denim pinafore.

Even the smallest one was too big for her, but she'd grow into it.

It was *gorgeous*.

And I got her the sweetest little babygro, light blue, patterned with dark blue polka dots and – get this – a matching little jacket with zip front and a hood.

So that she'd fit in if she ever met any cool street kids.

And the socks!

I could go on for hours about the socks I got her.

So tiny and fluffy and snuggly and warm and soft, to cover her tiny, tiny, tiny little pink feet.

Sometimes I got such a rush of love for her that I wanted to squeeze her so hard I actually feared for her safety.

Then we wandered around a bookshop for a while.

My adrenaline started pumping any time I was within about a hundred yards of a bookshop.

I loved books.

Nearly as much as I loved clothes. And that's saying something.

The feel of them and the smell of them. A bookshop was like an Aladdin's Cave for me. Entire worlds and lives can be found just behind that glossy cover. All you had to do was look.

So the entire world and life that I chose to enter belonged to someone called Samantha, who apparently "had it all." A palazzo in Florence, a penthouse in New York, a mews house next door to Buckingham Palace, more priceless jewels than you could shake a stick at, a publishing house or two, a Lear Jet, a ride of a boyfriend, some Count or Duke or something, and the absolutely essential dark secret and hidden tragic past.

My money was riding on her having been a lesbian prostitute before her luck changed.

No good her just being a prostitute. No shock value left in that.

You needed something a bit extra. Something with a hook.

Lesbianism hadn't been done to death yet. People still got a little bit hot under the collar about it.

And what was going to happen when people stopped raising eyebrows about lesbianism?

I dreaded to think.

People having sex with animals?

People having sex with corpses?

People having sex with advertising executives?

All pretty nasty and shocking prospects.

I could have bought an "improving book," I suppose.

Something by one of that Brontë crew. Or maybe even a bit of Joseph Conrad. He was always good for a laugh.

But I wanted something that wasn't very taxing.

So, just to be on the safe side, I bought complete rubbish.

After I came out of the bookshop, clutching my child and my gold-embossed bestseller, I just happened to be passing the café that I had gone to with Adam the previous Saturday and I just happened to have an hour or two to kill so I just happened to sit there and – guess what? – Adam just happened to walk in only an hour and a half after I arrived.

What a coincidence!

Too good to be true, huh?

What could that be put down to, if not divine intervention?

Explain that one, if you can.

I was not a very spiritual person but I knew when I was in the presence of God.

I'm not convincing you, am I?

Well, I suppose I had better come clean.

I had kind of, I suppose, nursed a little hope that maybe, just maybe that if I were to go into town that maybe, just maybe, I might run into Adam.

And that if he had been in that particular café on Saturday and several of his classmates had also been there that there was more than an outside chance that he might pass through it on Thursday afternoon.

Everyone knows that all students do, when they're not getting drunk and taking drugs, that is, is sit around café tables for several hours, with one cold cup of coffee between ten of them, and play with the sugar.

And maybe I lingered over my KitKat and pot of tea longer than was strictly necessary.

Some people might even have said that it looked as if I was waiting for him.

So I suppose that, when he finally walked in, I couldn't call it either a spiritual or a metaphysical event.

I could even be said to have engineered our meeting.

Although, dammit, that's not fair.

God helps those who help themselves.

And God can't drive a parked car.

If I had stayed at home in bed with the chocolate and the *Marie Claire* would I have met him?

The answer has got to be no.

I was sitting there, with half an eye on Samantha's takeover bid and the other eye on the door. Although I was hoping that he'd come in and even half-expecting him to appear, I wasn't prepared for how I felt when he actually did arrive.

He was so, he was so . . . so *gorgeous*.

So tall and strong-looking. But at the same time so boyishly cute.

"Easy, easy," I told myself. "Take deep breaths."

I resisted the urge to dump Kate on the table and run over and fling myself on him.

I reminded myself that I had used up my neuroses quota on him, and that it might be a good idea to behave like a normal well-balanced woman.

Hell, after a bit of practice I might even become one.

So I sat there, poised and perched, trying to exude calmness and well-balancedness and unneuroticness.

Finally he saw me.

I held my breath.

I waited for him to rear and neigh like a startled horse and then make for the door like the hounds of hell were after him.

I expected him to run like a hare through the café, knocking over tables and chairs, spilling pots of tea and cups of coffee over innocent by-standers, his hair standing on end, his eyes wide and staring and shout at anyone who'd care to listen, stabbing his finger wildly at me and Kate, "She's mad, that one, you know. Pure mental. Have nothing to do with her."

But he didn't do anything of the sort.

He smiled at me.

I have to admit that it was a bit of a wary smile.

But it was a smile.

"Claire!" he said and came over to the table.

"And Kate," he continued.

Correct on both counts.

Not much got past him.

He kissed Kate.

He didn't kiss me.

But I could live with it.

I was just so glad to see him, gladder still that he wanted to speak to me. I really wasn't that concerned with which one of us he kissed.

"Why don't you sit down and join us?" I said politely.

Poised. Polished. The hostess with the mostest, that was me.

Impeccably mannered. Emotions, if indeed I had any at all that is, firmly, strictly even, bound and strapped into place.

My chin was up, my upper lip was stiff, my expression was inscrutable.

Nothing was on display that might frighten him away.

"All right," he said.

Wary. Cautious. Watching me carefully. Maybe waiting for me to accuse him of having the hots for my mother.

"I'll just go and get a cup of coffee," he said.

"Fine," I said, giving a magnanimous smile, well-balancedness and relaxedness exuding (I hoped) from my every pore.

Off he went.

And I waited.

And waited.

Oh dear, I thought sadly, he must have done a runner. He mustn't want anything to do with me at all. I seemed to be developing quite a knack for this.

He was probably wedged in the tiny window in the Gents, struggling to get out amongst the smelly dustbins and cabbage leaves and empty brandy bottles that are found outside the back exits of restaurants and cafés.

I put my book in my bag – do you know I was so glad to see him that I totally forgot to hide the cover of the trashy novel? – and rearranged Kate in the sling.

At least I tried, I thought.

And I was glad.

I hadn't got what I wanted, but at least I'd taken responsibility for my life. I'd tried to fix something, I'd tried to make something happen.

I hadn't behaved like a passive victim, just letting life happen to me.

I had taken control.

It hadn't worked, but so what.

The important thing was to try.

And the next time I met a nice man I wouldn't go all slushy and school-girlie on him, thinking of him as a boyfriend and suspecting every other woman of coveting him.

I had just organised myself for the off when he jauntily arrived round the corner with a tray with coffee and buns on it.

The bastard!

I'd just been all grown up and mature and wise for absolutely bloody nothing.

I was feeling so *good* about myself, feeling saddened but enriched by the mistakes I had made and he had to come back and destroy it totally on me.

There went my rosy, introspective, pensive glow.

The selfish bastard!

I had a good mind to tell him to get lost and leave me alone. I had just come to terms, not even five minutes ago, with losing him so now what was I expected to do with him.

Enjoy his company?

Are you out of your mind?

"Sorry I was so long," he was saying. "The cashier had a fit and . . . hey! . . . where are you going?!"

He looked really surprised.

And then he looked upset.

"Sorry," I mumbled, feeling mortified.

If he ever had reason to think that I was hysterical and neurotic before now, this could only convince him that I was a complete tantrum-throwing little bitch.

"Why are you going?" he asked, sounding both angry and hurt. "I'm sorry I took so long. But I thought you'd wait."

"I thought you'd gone," I muttered.

"But why?" he asked in total exasperation. "Why would I leave?"

"I don't know," I said, feeling queasy with embarrassment.

Oh you've messed it up good and proper this time, I told myself.

"Look!" he said, and he banged his tray down on the table and sent coffee spattering everywhere.

I jumped with fright.

"Sit down," he said angrily. He put his hands on my shoulders and pushed me back down into my chair in no uncertain terms.

"Jesus!" I thought in shock. "Take it easy."

"Oh sorry Kate," he interjected apologetically. Her little face must have registered surprise at this abrupt change.

"Now!" he said, back in angry mode again. "What the hell is going on?"

"What do you mean?" I asked in a little voice.

He was obviously trying to keep a lot of anger in check and it was frightening.

"Why are you treating me like this?" he demanded angrily, his face very close to mine.

I couldn't believe that this was happening.

Where had nice pleasant understanding Adam gone?

Who was this furious man in his place?

"Like what?" I asked, mesmerised. I was scared of him but, like a rabbit caught in the headlights on an on-coming car, I couldn't tear myself away from the angry blue of his eyes.

"Like I'm some kind of low-life."

"I'm not," I protested in surprise.

I wasn't, was I?

"Yes, you bloody well are," he barked at me, his fingers digging into my shoulders. "You have, practically from the first time we met up."

"I met you, I really liked you, I wanted to see you, what's wrong with that?" he said furiously.

"Nothing," I whispered.

"So why do you behave as if I'm some kind of Casanova bastard type, why did you think I was messing with your little sister, why did you think I'd walk away and leave you sitting here, just tell me *why?*"

People from other tables were starting to glance interestedly at us, but Adam didn't notice and I didn't really think it would be terribly sensible to point them out to him, at least not while he's in his present mood.

"Don't you see how insulting it is?" he flung at me.

"No," I said, almost afraid to look at him.

"Well, it is!"

I didn't know what to say. I just sat there looking at him, his blue eyes boring into mine.

I suddenly became aware of just how close I was to him.

Our faces were inches apart.

I could see the individual hairs of his stubble, the lightly tanned skin stretched tightly over his beautiful cheekbones, the evenness of his white teeth, the sexiness of his mouth . . .

He suddenly went very still.

All the anger and violence seemed to lift from him.

We sat there like statues, his hands on my shoulders. We stared at each other.

I was so aware of him, his strength, his vulnerability.

There was tension between us, vibrating slightly in the stillness.

Then he pulled away from me. Exhausted and utterly, utterly weary, he sat with his arms hanging limply by his side.

"Adam," I ventured tentatively.

He didn't even look up at me.

He sat there with his head bent.

Giving me a view of his beautiful dark hair.

"Adam," I said again and gingerly touched his arm.

He stiffened slightly but he didn't pull away.

"It's not you, it's me," I said awkwardly.

There was a pause.

"What do you mean?" he asked.

Well, at least I thought that's what he'd said. It was kind of hard to hear him because his voice was all muffled because he was practically resting his head on his chest and talking into his jumper.

"Like it's my problem," I said. I found it very hard to say.

But I had to say it.

I owed it to him.

I had upset him and the least I could do was let him know what was going on in my head.

He said something else.

"Er, sorry Adam, but I didn't quite catch that." I told him apologetically.

He lifted his head and looked up at me.

He looked bad-tempered but beautiful.

"I said, what's your problem?" he repeated narkily.

Another thrill of fear ran through me.

I had to make this all right.

But it was very hard to talk to him when he was being so intimidating.

"It's because I'm insecure and suspicious," I said.

He said nothing.

Just sat there looking moodily at me.

"You haven't done anything wrong," I continued falteringly.

He gave a grim little nod at that.

Well, I thought it was a nod.

It looked very like a nod.

Even though it was a very little and very grim one.

Of course he might just have been readjusting his head's position on his neck.

But it was enough to encourage me to continue.

"I thought you'd left here because you didn't want to speak to me," I told him.

"I see," he said, without any noticeable emotion.

I felt like giving him a thump.

React, for God's sake!

Tell me I'm being ridiculous, tell me that you'd always want to see me.

He didn't.

Maybe he didn't appreciate being manipulated into complimenting me.

Fair enough.

Maybe it was time I stopped manipulating him.

Or anyone else for that matter.

But sometimes it was as instinctive as breathing.

Not that I was proud of it or anything, mind.

I tried to explain to him.

"I thought that you wouldn't want to speak to me after I'd been so unreasonable on the phone on Sunday night."

"You were unreasonable," he agreed.

"But I'm frightened," I said sadly.

"Of what?" he asked, not sounding quite as fierce.

"Of, of, of . . . everything really," I said. And to my horror my eyes filled up with tears.

I didn't do it on purpose, I *swear* I didn't.

I was as shocked by my unexpected ocular moistness as he was.

"Sorry," I sniffed. "I'm not doing this so that you'll be nice to me."

"Good," he said. "Because it won't work."

The heartless fucker, I thought briefly, but then banished the unworthy thought from my mind.

"I only respond to crying women if they're under the age of two," he continued, half-smiling, as he touched Kate's face.

"Oh," I said. I made a valiant attempt at a laugh, even though I was still crying.

"So what are you so frightened of that you have to be mean to me?" he asked. This time he almost sounded gentle.

"Oh the usual," I said, trying to pull myself together.

"Like what?" he persisted.

"Caring for people and then losing them, making a fool of myself, being hurt, scaring people away, being too forward, being too aloof . . . " I rattled off. "Do you want me to go on? I could do this for hours."

"No, that's all right," he said. "But we're all scared of those things."

"Are we?" I asked surprised.

"Of course," he assured me, "Why do you think you're so special? You haven't got a monopoly on feeling like that, you know. And anyway, how am I making you feel frightened?"

"Because I thought you were playing me off against Helen," I said.

"But I *told* you I wasn't," he said in exasperation. "And I *told* you that I could understand why you felt like that, even though I didn't like it."

"Anyway why are you so touchy about it?" I asked him, momentarily diverted from my own miseries. "I thought all men liked to be thought of as a bit of a lad."

"Well, I definitely don't," he said. He looked sad and thoughtful. I knew that he wasn't just thinking about me and Helen.

What had happened to him?

What kind of grief was he carrying?

I had to get to the bottom of this.

But first I had to sort out our current difficulties.

I ploughed valiantly on.

"And after I spoke to you on Sunday night, I felt that I had seemed hysterical and like I was overreacting and like I had scared you away and that you wouldn't ring me anymore," I blurted out and then watched him carefully from under my lashes to see how he reacted to this.

"Well . . . " he said slowly.

Oh speed it up for God's sake, I thought frantically, my nerves can't stand it.

"I wasn't going to ring you," he continued.

"Oh," I said.

So I had been right.

Ten out of ten for my instinct.

Minus several billion for my sense of well-being.

I felt as if I'd been kicked in the stomach by a horse.

Actually that's not true, because I'd never been kicked in the stomach by a horse.

Do you think that I'd be sitting here now talking to you if I'd been the lucky recipient of a kick in the stomach by a horse?

The answer has got to be no.

But I felt the way I felt when I was about ten and I fell off a wall and landed belly-flop fashion on my stomach, onto a lawn that had been baked hard by the Summer sun and was as hard as concrete. There was that horrible feeling of shock and nausea as all the breath of my body was abruptly forced out.

That was the way I felt now.

"Not because I didn't want to ring you," he continued, unaware of how much pain I was in. "But because I thought it would be best for you."

"How do you mean," I squeaked, feeling infinitely better.

"Because you've been through too much lately. I didn't want to upset you in any way or add to your troubles."

The angel!

"You weren't upsetting me," I told him.

"But I obviously was," he said.

"But you weren't doing it on purpose," I protested.

"I know," he said. "Which is why I lost my temper earlier – sorry about that, by the way – but just being in contact with you seemed to cause you to be annoyed or upset or whatever."

Relief washed over me in waves.

"I'm sorry I was difficult," I told him. "But . . . "

And here I took a deep breath.

I was taking a bit of a risk.

Putting my feelings on the line.

"I'd rather see you than not see you," I finally managed to tell him.

"Really?" he said, sounding hopeful and excited and boyish.

"Yes."

"Are you sure?"

"I'm sure."

"Do you trust me?"

"Oh Adam," I said half-laughing, half-crying. "I said I wanted to see you. No one mentioned anything about trust."

"OK," he said, laughing also (no sign of any tears). "But will you trust me when I say that I want to see you and not Helen?"

"Yes," I said solemnly. "I will."

"And if the cashier has a row with someone over their change and has a fit and runs off so that I have to wait hours to pay for my coffee you won't think that I've legged it out the back way?"

"No," I agreed. "I won't."

"So we're friends?" he asked oh-so-appealingly.

"Yes," I nodded in agreement. "We're friends."

Although my brain was saying to me, "excuse me, excuse me, *friends*, did you say *friends*? I don't think mere friends behave in the way you want to with Adam. Laura is your friend and you don't rip the clothes off her back anytime you see her and correct me if I'm wrong but isn't that precisely what you want to do with Adam?"

"Shut up," I muttered at it.

"Sorry?" said Adam looking at me in alarm, obviously thinking, "Oh God no, here she goes again."

"Nothing," i smiled at him. "Nothing at all."

"Well," he said. "Seeing as we've sorted out all this misunderstanding, when can I see you?"

"Oh I don't really know," I said, going all shy and girlie on him.

"Are you doing anything on Sunday night?" he asked.

"I don't think so," I said, pretending to consider. Although my social diary stretched ahead of me as empty and as formless as the Gobi desert.

"Well, can I cook you dinner?" he asked.

"Yes, that would be lovely," I said.

"Good," he said. "Jenny and Andy have gone away for the weekend so we'll have the place to ourselves."

"Oh," I said.

I was a woman of the world.

I knew very well that to go to a man's house, a man's house where all the other residents were absent, and submit to having a dinner cooked for oneself meant that it was more than pork chops and Black Forest Gateau that was being offered.

Great, I thought.

I couldn't believe my luck.

"Right Adam, that sounds lovely."

And so we agreed on a time for Sunday night. He walked Kate and me to the car and home we drove.

Chapter Twenty-One

The preparations for Sunday.

Ingredients:

One neglected, rejected, dejected twenty-nine year old woman, who had recently given birth

A generous helping of guilt

A pinch of anticipation

A packet of insecurity about the appearance of her body

A sprig of excitement (wild, if possible)

A spoonful of condensed deep despair

A minor stretch-marks panic

Two black hold-up lace-topped stockings

One interesting pair of black knickers

One black bra, of the miraculous rather than just the plain wondrous variety

One bottle of red wine

One dress

One pair of shoes

Decoration:

Whore-red lipstick

Several layers of dark mascara

Directions:

Put the stockings, knickers and bra to one side, for use later.

Take the woman.

Check her eyes and her skin to make sure that she hasn't gone past her sell-by-date.

Add the guilt, anticipation, insecurity, excitement, despair and panic.

Mix thoroughly.

Leave to stew for a couple of days.

In a medium-sized bathroom prepare the woman by shaving her legs, colouring her hair and painting her toenails.

About an hour before commencing, baste generously in expensive body lotion, turning frequently.

Add the stockings, the pair of interesting black knickers and the miraculous black bra. Have a couple of practice runs at looking seductive by letting her hair fall over her face and looking up through her eyelashes.

Check that she can still gasp and arch her back and say sentences like, "Oh baby, that was wonderful" and "Oh God, don't stop" while keeping a straight face.

Commandeer a sister, preferably Anna, to look after the aforementioned child.

Add a generous helping of whore-red lipstick, several layers of black mascara, a short, button-through, purple (it is, after all, the colour of passion) dress, sexy black shoes with suede ankle straps and one bottle of red wine.

Always take care not to start swigging from the bottle of red before arriving at your destination.

As an optional extra, condoms in the handbag are always a nice touch.

If it's not possible to procure them – for example they may be out of season – you will have to make do with large amounts of self-restraint. Not always ideal, but it does work.

Serve on a bed with a good-looking man.

I followed the instructions to the letter. I was lucky enough to be able to procure condoms – courtesy of Laura – what a woman!

I was feeling pretty good.

I didn't even get upset when I discovered that thanks to my hair-dye (it's hair-colour-*enhancer* darling, we don't need to dye our hair, we just *enhance* its natural lights and colour) all right then, thanks to my hair-colour-*enhancer* my ears and my hair were now colour-coordinated.

But I suppose if I had to have coloured ears, I could have done a lot worse than a rich, glossy, shiny chestnut colour.

None of your Ebony Shadow or Plum Sugar for my ears. No sir!

At about seven-thirty on Sunday evening, I prepared for the off.

About to go forth to sin and not a bother on me.

I kissed Kate goodnight.

As I was furtively making for the front door, my coat buttoned up practically to the eyebrows in case Mum should spot me looking so floozy-like, the phone rang.

"Claire, it's for you," shouted Helen.

Oh God!

But it was only Laura.

Ringing to wish me luck and wanting to know if I had practised putting on a condom with my teeth, as per her instructions.

"No, I didn't!" I told her.

I was dying to get off the phone out of the house because I was terrified of being caught.

"Why not?" she demanded. "You can't just arrive along and expect him to be happy with boring old sex. You have to be a bit inventive."

"But you only gave me two!" I said, all alarm. "I didn't want to waste them. And anyway what was I supposed to practise on?"

"Well, let's just hope that you perform adequately with the first one. Or else you won't get a chance to use the second one," she said darkly.

"Oh stop it Laura, I'm nervous enough!"

"Good," she laughed. "It's much better when you're nervous."

I promised to ring her the next day and tell her all the gory details.

"Or, if I get in early enough tonight, I'll ring you and tell you everything," I promised eagerly.

"If you get in early enough tonight to tell me everything, there won't be anything to tell," she told me.

"Oh," I said.

She had a point.

"Look, I'm going," I said in annoyance, and I hung up on her while she was in the middle of explaining some sort of complicated sexual activity that she said she had seen done in a show in

Bangkok. Whatever it was it could only be done by a woman who was a damn sight more supple than me.

I did know how to have sex, you know. I had given birth to a child. How did she think this actually came about?

While we're on the subject of sexual shenanigans I've got a confession to make.

Wait for it.

Here it comes.

I enjoy the missionary position.

There! I've said it.

I'm made to feel so *ashamed* of myself for feeling that way.

As if I'm terribly boring and repressed.

But I'm not. Honestly.

I'm not saying that it's the *only* position that I like.

But, really, I have no objection to it whatsoever.

Naturally, of course, this isn't the time to discuss favourite sexual positions.

But I'll just tell you very quickly that I think cunnilingus is the most boring thing God ever created. I'd rather spend a day filing than endure a five minute stint of it.

And when they're finished with their few minutes of slurping they act like you should be so *grateful* for it. Beaming up at you like they deserve a medal. And then act like they're entitled to a year's supply of no-questions-asked blow-jobs.

Of course, some women swear by it, but . . . sorry, sorry.

I finally left and drove over to his house.

Chapter Twenty-Two

I parked the car just outside his house and feeling a heady mixture of excitement and sordid shame walked up to the front door. Then I remembered that I had left the bottle of wine in the car and I quickly ran back to get it.

I was going nowhere without it.

Dutch courage.

Well, Chilean courage, but however.

Adam opened the door almost immediately.

If I didn't know any better I'd swear he had been hiding in the hall, lurking behind the curtain, waiting for me to arrive.

Well, actually, maybe he had been.

He was doing a good job of seeming to be as excited and affected by all of this as I was.

He looked a bit anxious.

Cold feet?

Change of heart?

Pre-game nerves?

But then he rallied strongly.

"Hello," he smiled. "You look lovely."

"Hello," I said. I smiled at him, in spite of my nerves.

How wonderful, I thought with a thrill.

I felt so dangerously decadent.

On an assignation with a beautiful man.

Have I ever fancied any man as much as I fancy Adam, I wondered.

Probably, I thought, sighing.

Just being realistic for a moment.

But right now it felt as if I'd never fancied anyone else, ever.

How long will it take for us to be in bed together, I wondered.

How long can I hold off if he doesn't make a move?

What if he doesn't make a move, I thought with horror.

Or what if it's a total disaster?

Maybe he'll think I'm completely hideous, with my post-childbirth body.

Maybe I'll think he's completely hideous because he doesn't look exactly like James.

Oh God!

I should have stayed at home. Watching *Coronation Street* doesn't throw up all these awful scenarios and dilemmas.

Before I could bolt for the door, stammering that it had all been a terrible mistake, he put his arm, (and what an arm!) round my shoulders and guided me towards the kitchen.

"Take off your coat," he said. "And have a drink."

"But . . . , oh all right. Make mine a pint of red wine," I said as I sat down at the kitchen table.

He laughed.

"Feeling nervous, darling?" he asked silkily, as he poured me a glass.

Jesus! I thought in alarm, don't ask me things silkily.

I was frightened enough. If he started behaving like some kind of arch-seducer, I was out of there.

All I needed now was for him to change his jeans and sweatshirt for a silk paisley dressing-gown and parade around with an onyx cigarette holder.

"I'm not nervous," I blurted out. "I'm fucking terrified."

"Of what?" he asked, with mock surprise. "My cooking isn't that bad."

Oh, so that's the way you want to play it, I thought.

Faux casual, is it?

Fine then.

I gave him a poised smile.

And flung my entire glass of wine down my throat before I realised what I had done.

"Relax," he said anxiously, coming over to sit beside me at the table and hold my hand. "I'm not going to bite."

Oh, aren't you, I thought, well then I'm definitely going home.

"We're just going to have something to eat and a little chat," he said kindly. "Nothing to worry about."

"All right then," I said, making a valiant effort to relax. "What are we having anyway?"

"Homemade Stilton and Muscat Grape Soup, Boeuf Bourguignonne, with Potatoes Dauphinois and my own recipe for Zabaglione for dessert."

"Really?" I asked astonished.

I hadn't put Adam down as a fancy cook.

More your spuds and chops type of fellow.

Quantity rather than quality.

"No," he grinned at me. "Are you joking? You're getting Spaghetti Bolognaese and you're lucky I was even able to manage that."

"I see," I laughed.

He was so nice.

No nonsense about him at all.

"And if you're very good . . . " – At this point he paused and gave me a meaningful look – "And I mean *very*, then you can have some Chocolate Mousse."

"Oh," I said, all excited, a combination of the meaningful look and the news of the Chocolate Mousse. "That's great. I love Chocolate Mousse."

"I know," he said. "Why do you think I got it?"

"And," he continued in a teasing tone. "If you're very, *very* good you can eat it off my stomach."

I burst out laughing.

He was such an angel.

I couldn't suppress a shiver of lust at the thought of his flat muscly stomach.

Although this was probably precisely the kind of reaction he was banking on.

I hurriedly poured myself another glass of wine, but this time I forced myself to sip it.

He served the dinner and it was obvious that this was not something he did on a regular basis. He seemed all out of place standing at the cooker. Rushing from the sink to the cooker and back to the sink again, while the pasta boiled over and the salad visibly wilted.

Although it did give me a beautiful view of his bum.

Cooking, unlike most other things, did not come naturally to him.

Which made it all the more touching that he had gone to such bother for me.

He looked so uncertain as he carefully carried the plates over to the table and reverently placed mine in front of me.

"Have some more wine," he said, pouring me another glass.

That made a change from him acting like the local branch of Alcoholics Anonymous not ten minutes earlier.

"Are you trying to get me drunk to take advantage of me?" I asked him, trying to sound annoyed.

"I'm trying to get you drunk so that you won't notice if the food tastes horrible," he laughed.

"I'm sure it's lovely," I assured him.

I'm sorry to relate that I couldn't eat more than a few mouthfuls. Not because it was horrible or anything.

Although it could have been.

I really couldn't tell you.

It's just that I was so nervous and the air was so fraught with tension and anticipation that I felt like saying to him, "Look Adam, darling, we both know why I'm here, so let's just cut to the chase."

He couldn't eat anything either.

But that might have been down to the food and not his nerves.

We sat facing each other at Adam's kitchen table, sliding spaghetti backwards and forwards on our plates, the salad totally untouched in its bowl, looking all mournful and abandoned.

Conversation was desultory.

Every now and again I'd look up at him and catch him watching me.

And the look on his face made me feel hot and awkward.

It put paid to any chances of me eating anything at all.

I was afraid that if I ate anything that my stomach would be all bulgy and sticky-outy.

And what kind of stomach was that to have on a first night with a man.

Or that I would swing a forkful of food mouthwards and the spaghetti would rebound onto my face with a whiplash-like effect and spatter me with red sauce.

The way I react to food when I'm around a man is a sure barometer of the way I feel about him.

If I can't eat it means that I'm mad about him.

When I can manage orange juice and some toast in the morning it's the End of the Beginning.

And by the time I get round to finishing the food left on his plate it's as good as over.

Either that or I marry him.

Well, that had been the pattern so far.

"Is that all you're going to eat?" he eventually asked, looking at the mound of food on my plate.

He looked disappointed and I felt awful.

"Adam," I said awkwardly. "I'm sorry. I'm sure

that it's lovely and everything but I just can't eat. I don't know why."

"I really am sorry," I looked at him appealingly.

"Never mind," he said, taking the plates away.

"Will you never cook for me again?" I asked sadly.

"Of course I will," he said. "And for God's sake please don't look so miserable."

"It's only because I'm nervous," I told him. "It's not because the food was horrible."

"Nervous?" He came over to my side of the table and sat down beside me. "You've nothing to be nervous about."

"Don't I?" I asked, looking him full in the eye.

I was quite shameless.

I'd be the first to admit it.

But, Goddamit, I'd wasted enough time this evening already.

"No," he murmured. "You've got nothing to be nervous about."

And, very gently, he put his arm around my shoulder and his hand on the back of my head.

I closed my eyes.

I can't believe I'm doing this, I thought wildly, but I'm not going to stop.

I inhaled the scent of his skin as his face came nearer.

I waited for his kiss.

And when it came it was beautiful. Sweet and gentle and firm.

The kind of kiss where the person doing it is very good at it but you don't feel like he became such a good kisser by practising on thousands of others.

He stopped kissing me and I looked up at him in alarm.

What was the meaning of this?

"Was that all right?" he asked quietly.

"All right?" I gasped. "It was better than all right."

He laughed slightly.

"No, I mean, is it all right to kiss you? You know I don't want to overstep any boundaries."

"It's all right," I told him.

"I know you've been hurt," he said.

"But you're my friend," I told him. "It's OK."

"I want to be more than your friend," he said.

"That's OK too," I told him.

"Really?" he said looking at me for confirmation.

"Honestly," I told him.

Oh Jesus! I hadn't left myself much room for manoeuvre here.

Not that I wanted to.

I'd started so I'd finish.

He kissed me again and it was just as nice as the first time.

He drew away from me and I pulled him back.

He looked at me almost wonderingly, and said "God, you're so beautiful."

"No, I'm not," I said, feeling a bit embarrassed.

"Oh you are," he said. "You really are."

"No," I said. "Helen's beautiful."

"Look," he said, smiling. "At the risk of going all Californian on you, you're a beautiful person."

"I am?"

"You are."

A little pause.

"*And* you're a babe."

"Thanks," I laughed. "What a pity that you're so hideous."

Then he laughed.

There was absolutely no vanity at all about the man.

Although perhaps when you're that handsome there's no need for it.

Everyone else has your vanity for you.

He kissed me again.

And, honestly, it was wonderful.

I felt so taken care of when I was with him and in his arms. But I also felt that I was taking care of him. That he needed me as much as I needed him.

"Do you realise that we know each other less than two weeks?" he asked me.

Oh no, I thought, does this mean that he won't go to bed with me yet? Is he going to impose some kind of time limit on it? That we can't have sex until we've known each other for three months, or something.

"Yes," I agreed cautiously. "Ten days actually."

"But it feels like much longer," he said. "Much, much longer."

Thank God!

"I'm so glad I met you," he continued. "You're so special."

"I'm not," I protested. "I'm very ordinary."

"You're special to me."

"But why?"

"Oh, I don't know," he said. He leant back in his chair and looked at me. "Because you're interesting and have opinions on things and you're very funny.

But mostly because you're so nice . . . Like, basically, you're a decent person."

"I'm not always," I told him. "I mean, you should have seen me a couple of weeks ago. I was like Myra Hindley with PMT."

He laughed.

And I got annoyed with myself.

Here I was, with a lovely man telling me lovely things about myself and I was trying to convince him that none of them were true.

It was usually the other way round. I would tell them lovely things about myself and they'd spend the rest of the time trying to convince me that none of it was true.

He leant over and kissed me again.

It was just blissful.

I just wanted to surrender to it.

To be with him, without any guilt or worry or awkwardness.

Being with him felt so *right*.

You're on the rebound, I sternly warned myself.

So what, I asked myself back, I mean, it's not as if I'm going to marry the guy. Can't I have some fun?

Well, yes, I suppose I could have some fun.

But at the same time, I can't be going round sleeping with any man who asks me to.

But, then again, this isn't just any man.

This is a nice, sweet man who cares for me, well, at least he *seems* to care for me, and I care for him.

With a little shock, I realised that I did, in fact, care for him.

I mean, I'm not saying I loved him or anything,

because that would be untrue. But there was something about him that touched me.

And I didn't want to hurt him.

But was I going to?

Did sleeping with him imply a commitment?

He did know that I was married.

He was fully aware of my feelings for James.

And maybe he didn't want a commitment.

Maybe he wanted to be with me because he knew that I was really with someone else and it would let him off the hook?

Oh Lord!

Traumaville!

Decision time.

I stood up and held him by the hand.

He looked at me questioningly.

"Are you OK," he asked. "Can I get you anything?"

"Yes," I murmured.

"What?" he asked.

"Laid."

But I only said it under my breath. I didn't want him to think I was *terribly* vulgar.

Because I wasn't really.

Not all the time, anyway.

I started moving towards the kitchen door, still holding his hand.

I felt so liberated and wanton.

"Where are we going?" he asked feigning innocence.

"Down the road for a drink," I told him.

I looked at him and disappointment was written all over his face.

"I'm joking, you thick," I smiled at him. "We're going upstairs."

So we walked up the stairs, me leading the way, still holding his hand.

With each step I took, I became more and more convinced that this was the right thing to do.

We got to the top of the stairs and he pulled me into his arms and kissed me.

It was gorgeous. He felt so big and strong. I could feel the smooth skin of his back through his sweatshirt. He turned me round and steered me towards a door.

"My room," he said. "Unless you brought me up here to give you a tour of the house."

"That can wait until later," I said, barely able to speak with excitement and nerves.

His room was nice.

It was so tidy that I knew, instantly, not that I had ever been in any real doubt, that he had meticulously planned to get me into bed.

Men's rooms are only ever tidy the first time you sleep with them. Once you've had sex with them the place goes right to hell.

It's as though the instant the relationship is consummated the man shouts, "Right lads, you can come out now!"

And out from under the bed appear armies of dirty underpants and sweaty socks and cups and plates and car magazines and hideous jumpers and filthy football kits and pint glasses and sexist calendars and Stephen King books and damp towels and jars of Wintergreen, all elbowing and clamouring and complaining loudly about the amount of time that they had to spend in hiding, and stretching and dusting themselves down and then draping themselves artistically on the bedroom carpet, delighted to be back where they belong.

"What took you so long?" a sock might shout cheerfully at the successful seducer. "Put up a bit of a fight, did she?"

"We thought we were stuck in there forever," a filthy pair of cricket trousers might goodnaturedly joke. "You must be losing your touch."

Adam eased my passage over the pristine floor to the bed by kissing me, so that I didn't have to march over and sit down on it, looking expectant and awkward.

No, he just kind of kissed me and sort of steered me across the room and, well, you know, we just arrived at the bed and as it was there, we thought it might be a good idea to lie on it, otherwise we would only have to go round it.

After a while he started to undo the buttons on my dress. And I put my hands under his sweatshirt onto the bare skin of his stomach and chest.

Very gently and very slowly, he unbuttoned my dress all the way down and started to take my clothes off.

It felt nice but weird. Weird but nice.

It had been a long, long time since I went to bed with someone for the first time, if you follow me.

It was funny that he wasn't James.

Not horrible, or unpleasant.

Just, as I say, a bit funny.

I felt a bit awkward about my body, and about Adam seeing it.

I wasn't exactly uninhibited at the best of times. I wasn't a great one for dancing round with no clothes on.

It was all right when I was with James. I had no problems with him. Eventually, that is. But even with him, I'd been very coy for ages.

Adam kept telling me that I was beautiful. He was so glad that I was there and stroking me and caressing me and holding me and kissing me. After a while I completely relaxed. Call me old-fashioned, if you want, but for me there is no bigger turn-on than being told that I'm beautiful, and being made to feel beautiful.

You can keep your fancy tongue work and elaborate hip-swerves. Five minutes of flattery works a whole lot better for me.

After a good deal more of kissing and getting to know each other, if that's what you'd like to call it, it became obvious that the evening was heading in a definite direction.

Adam pulled himself away from me.

"God!" he said. "You're a witch, you're driving me wild, you're gorgeous."

I sat up a little bit and looked down at him as his hands roamed over my stomach.

I was so thankful that I hadn't eaten anything.

He was lovely. Such a beautiful body. And such a gorgeous face.

And such a nice guy.

What had I done to deserve this?

My eyes travelled down his chest, admiring his taut stomach but I averted my gaze when my eyes moved down a little bit lower.

How do I describe the state of play below Adam's waist without being overly explicit or overly coy?

It's very difficult to discuss having sex without being so crude that I sound like a pornographic book or without being so discreet that I sound like a repressed, uptight Victorian novelist who suffers regularly from Vaginismus and still calls her husband Mr Clements after twenty-seven years of marriage.

How about if I just say that mighty oaks from little acorns grow?

Isn't that good? Discreet yet symbolic?

Offensive to no one but at the same time leaving you in no doubt whatsoever that Adam had a hard-on that could cut diamonds?

Whoops!

Vulgar, vulgar, vulgar!

Although while we're on the subject I might as well tell you that it was big enough to make me fear for the intactness of the light-fittings, if he made any sudden movements.

Which, naturally, I whole-heartedly hoped he would.

No, I'm only joking. It wasn't that big at all.

It was a medium size.

Neither alarmingly big or depressingly small.

Just right, really.

Of course there are some unscrupulous women who tell whatever man they're with that he has the biggest penis that they've ever seen.

You know, quite simply as a matter of course.

They shrink back against the mattress and stare round-eyed with mock horror at the man in question and squeal, "Oh my! You're not coming anywhere near me with that monster of a thing. What are you trying to do? Screw me or batter the door down?"

Sneaky tactics.

Because of course the man in question is delighted.

Believing himself to be in possession of a weapon-like member, he feels invincible and all man.

And gives them a seeing to that they won't forget in a hurry.

But you wouldn't catch me doing that.

No, sir!

Well, only very rarely.

And I also can't describe what was going on below Adam's waist because I can't think of a word that I feel comfortable with to describe his, well, you know, his . . .

Well, how can I tell you what I can't describe if I haven't got a word to describe it!

I mean, the correct word is, of course, penis.

But that sounds so clinical.

I don't think I'd like someone to say to me "Oh that's a beautiful vagina you've got there."

It's not exactly evocative or romantic, now is it?

Hardly the language of hearts and flowers.

And by the same token I think penis is far too reminiscent of biology lessons at school where a scarlet-faced relief teacher hurriedly and scantily explains the human reproductive system to a room full of sniggering adolescents.

It's not human enough a description.

But what else can I call it?

I know there are hundreds of words, but not one of them seems appropriate.

How about "knob"?

That one's currently very fashionable.

Weeeell, I don't know.

It sounds a bit functional to me.

Although then again, why shouldn't it?

Cock?

No, I don't like that one either.

For some reason I find it reminiscent of ageing rock stars with London accents and horrible stone-washed jeans and long grey hair.

And worse again are the situations where the man has christened his member with a name. I mean did you ever!

Sidelong smirk from man, followed by wheedling noises.

"I think George is waking up."

Meaningful and wheedley smile.

"I think George wants to come out and play."

Wheedley eye-contact and hopeful expression.

"George want to play hide and seek."

Glazed and sickly grin.

Ugh!

Well, George can just go right off and find someone else to play with.

That kind of carry-on is enough to make me want to embrace celibacy.

Well, in the absence of a moniker that I like I'm going to resort to the language of Mills and Boon and call it his Throbbing Manhood.

But Adam, thankfully, hadn't introduced me to his Throbbing Manhood by name.

Although I didn't know if I was ready to make friends with his Throbbing Manhood just yet.

I'd kind of got used to James's Throbbing Manhood. Not that it was an especially hard act (if you'll pardon the pun) to follow, but it suited me.

I had nothing *against* Adam's Throbbing Manhood (apart from my thigh, of course) but I felt nervous about becoming acquainted with it.

As if he sensed this, Adam caught me by the arm (No Adam, not my *arm* for God's sake. It hasn't got an erogenous atom in it) and said urgently, "We don't have to do anything Claire. We can just lie here if you want to."

Now, if I'd had a penny for every time I've been promised a "just lying there" scenario by a man, I'd be a very rich woman indeed. I couldn't count the number of times that I'd been promised this when I've had to spend the night with a man because I'd missed the last bus and didn't have money for a taxi.

"You can stay in my place. It's only round the corner," he'd say.

"I'll sleep on the couch," I'd say quickly.

"Well, you might as well stay in the bed with me. It's much more comfortable."

"Ah no, the couch is fine."

"Look, I'm not going to touch you. Is that what's worrying you?"

"Well, er, yes."

"No need to worry. I won't lay a finger on you."

And then those fateful words, *"We can just lie there."*

And of course not getting a wink of sleep because I had to spend the night doing some all-star wrestling with the man.

Or squashed with my face right up into the wall in a vain attempt to get away from the man, finding it damn near impossible to breathe because of the erect penis pressed into my back.

Being afraid that if I breathed out and thereby moved my lower spine, entirely involuntarily mind, about a tenth of a millimetre onto his hot member, this would be taken as a sign of encouragement and acquiescence.

And then, of course, if I didn't deliver the goods, as it were, there was the highly probable chance that the gentleman in question would badmouth me the length and breadth of Ireland, calling me a prick-tease and a frigid lesbian and all manner of other terrible and totally undeserved names.

Saying things like, "Oh she was coming onto me all night. She was fooling no one with that line about not having money for a taxi."

To this very day I think I still have a faint, penis-shaped indentation in my back.

But I believed Adam.

I knew that he meant it.

I trusted him.

I knew that if he said we could just lie there, that he meant it.

But was that what I wanted?

Quite frankly, no.

Yes, I was nervous.

But, dammit, I wanted to have sex with him.

If he went all respectful on me, I'd scream.

"I don't want to stop," I whispered to him.

I suppose there was no need for me to whisper.

I didn't want to overdo the nervous little-girl act.

All right, then, time to be proactive.

"Em," I said embarrassedly, "I left my bag downstairs."

"What do you need your bag for? Your make-up is perfect." He smiled at me.

"Not for my make-up, silly."

"What for then?"

But he was teasing.

"Claire, would you relax," he said in exasperation, rolling me over onto my back. "I presume you're referring to condoms?"

"Er, yes," I said, feeling a bit mortified.

"Well, no need to worry, I've some here."

"Oh."

I wasn't sure what else I could say.

His openness had taken the wind out of my sails nicely.

He was quite right, of course.

What was there to be embarrassed about?

All I had to worry about now was whether I'd be any good.

He kissed me again.

And things became a lot more serious.

That kiss certainly put a stop to any lighthearted banter.

I looked at him and his eyes were really dark, almost black, with desire.

"Claire," he whispered, (now *he's* at it). "I haven't, you know, been with someone in a long time."

Haven't you, I thought in surprise.

I would have thought that for someone as charming and handsome as Adam that every day of his life would be a Shagfest.

But, then again, he did seem to be very choosy. More than once I'd witnessed him fighting off gorgeous women.

And he's chosen me, I thought, my heart melting.

He could have just about anyone and he's chosen me.

There had to be a catch.

Any minute now, he'd offer to show me his knife collection or whip out a chainsaw and hack me to ribbons.

"It's OK," I whispered back to him. "It's ages since I've had sex either."

"Oh," he said.

Then he said in a louder voice, "why are we whispering?"

"I don't know," I giggled.

There then followed the condom ritual. You know, rustling round in a drawer for it, the crinkling of the wrapping paper being undone, saying, "is that the right way? Or does it go the other way?" Finally succeed in getting it on only to witness the erection disappear.

Except Adam's didn't.

Disappear, that is.

Thank God.

Now at this point I'm afraid that I'm going to have to become a little bit vague.

I'm sorry to disappoint you but I won't be giving you any detailed technical descriptions of my sexual encounters with Adam. (Yes, I hope you noted the plural "encounters").

Of course I *could* give you a description that would read more like a textbook belonging to a first year anatomy student.

And I *could* make the whole thing sound like a letter to the letters page in a pornographic magazine, all gasps and arching backs and outlandish gymnastics.

But that really wouldn't convey how lovely the whole thing was (well the whole three things, actually) and how *happy* I felt.

Could we just say that a good time was had by all.

Well, by all, of course, I mean all two of us.

I had no complaints.

He had no complaints.

Thoroughly enjoyable.

Great value for money all round.

We'd certainly go back again next year etc.

I would be just too embarrassed to tell you that he kissed me everywhere, and I mean *everywhere*. And that when he wasn't doing that, that he was covering me with delicious, shivery tiny little bites.

And there's no way that I can bring myself to tell you about the moment when he was eventually inside me. And how I was so afraid that it might hurt and how gentle he was with me. It didn't hurt and it was beautiful.

And if you think I'm going to relate how he frantically whispered things to me while he was on top of me, gorgeous things like how beautiful I was and how delicious my skin tasted and how turned on he was, then you've got another think coming.

You'll just have to use your own imagination to figure out that I wrapped my legs around his back to pull him deeper inside me and I thought I would die if he stopped and would die if he didn't.

And you really don't need me to tell you that when he, er . . . , when it was finished, that we were both panting and gasping and slippery with sweat that he looked down at me and grinned and gave a little laugh and said admiringly, "Jesus, you're some woman."

I'll have to resort to using a euphemism to describe the scenario.

How about, "One day my Prince will come."

Well, I'm happy to report that he already had.

And, so, for the record, had I.

And there's just one other thing.

Before I had Kate I had heard rumours, nothing more than vague unsubstantiated reports, that after having a child sex is usually, well, a lot better.

Because of the various commotions, upheavals and traumas in one's, er, birth-canal, including the dreaded stitches, certain changes have come about.

These changes resulting in, er, greater sensitivity and a greater awareness of one's erogenous zones, if you see what I mean.

And generally, all round, more exciting and enjoyable sex.

And I'm happy to be able to report that it was actually true.

Sex with Adam was different, very different from the way I remembered it with James.

Once I got over the initial uncomfortable feeling, it was really wonderful.

Actually better than I remembered it being with James.

So this is one side-effect of giving birth that doesn't get the good press that it deserves.

Although of course, there's a good chance that I'm talking a load of nonsense.

And that the alleged better sex had nothing to do with anything other than the fact that Adam had a larger TM than James.

I never bought into that 'size isn't everything' crap.

In the same way that you'll never catch a rich person saying 'money doesn't buy happiness', I think you'll find that the only people who say that size isn't everything are men with very small penises.

Later, when it was all over.

Over for the third time, that is, we just lay in bed chatting and laughing.

"D'you remember the day in the gym?" asked Adam.

"Mmmmmmm," I said, barely able to speak, I was so relaxed and contented.

"That was awful," he said.

"Why?" I asked.

"Because I fancied you so much."

"Really?" I asked, surprised and delighted.

"Yes, really."

"No, did you *really*?" I asked, like a true neurotic.

"Yes!" he insisted. "I couldn't even look at you in case I jumped you."

"But you were all serious and grim and just doing your weights," I reminded him. "You completely ignored me."

"Yes," he said dryly, "and I nearly pulled every muscle in my body. I couldn't concentrate on anything except you. You looked so cute in your gym-clothes."

"Oh," I said, thrilled, snuggling up closer to him.

At about half past one I said, "I'd better go home."

"Oh no," he said, wrapping his arms and legs tightly around me. "I won't let you. I'm going to keep you chained in here. You're going to be my sex slave."

"Adam," I said sighing. "You say the nicest things."

After a little while longer I said, reluctantly, "I'd really better go."

"If you really have to," he said.

"You know I do."

"Would you stay if it wasn't for Kate?"

"Yes."

He sat up in bed and watched me as I got dressed.

I looked up from doing up the buttons on my dress to find him smiling at me, but smiling in a sad kind of way.

"Is something wrong?" I asked.

"You're always running away from me," he said.

"Adam, I'm not," I said indignantly. "I *have* to go."

"Sorry," he said, giving me a real smile this time.

He hopped out of bed and said "I'll come down to the door with you."

"Not without any clothes, you won't," I said. "What if passers-by see?"

There was no doubt.

I was my mother's daughter.

He kissed me lingeringly at the front door.

And it was quite an achievement that I left at all.

"Stay," he murmured against my hair.

"I can't," I told him sternly, although I felt like going straight back up the stairs and getting back into bed with him.

"I'll call you tomorrow," he said.

"Bye."

Another kiss.

Further persuasion.

Stalwart resistance from me.

Reluctant letting go.

I finally made it to the car.

No mean achievement.

I drove home.

The streets were dark and empty.

I felt very happy.

I didn't even feel guilty about leaving Kate for so long.

Well, not *very* guilty.

Chapter Twenty-Three

I parked the car and I put my key in the front door. There was a light on in the front room. That's funny, I thought, everyone's usually fast asleep by this hour.

Please God, don't let it be Helen. Please don't let her have realised where I was and what I was up to.

I was sure that my recent activities were written all over my face.

Maybe it was Anna who was up.

Sacrificing a goat in the kitchen, or something like that.

You know, dancing round the garden wrapped in blood-soaked sheets, chanting at the moon, biting the heads off live bats, that kind of thing.

I walked into the hall. The front room door opened and Mum appeared, with Dad standing behind her. They were both in their night-clothes. Mum was wearing her pink quilted dressing-gown and had a few orange curlers stuck in the front of her hair.

They both looked white and shocked, as if something terrible had happened.

Which indeed it had, I suppose, if you want to regard my little indiscretion with Adam in that way.

"Claire!" said Mum. "Thank God you're home!"

"What?" I said, frightened. "What's happened?"

"Claire, come in and sit down," said Dad, taking charge.

My stomach lurched.

Something terrible *had* happened.

"Is it Kate?" I pleaded with Mum, clutching her arm. "Has something happened to her?"

A thousand horrible scenarios ran through my head.

She had had a cot death.

She had been kidnapped.

She had choked.

Helen had dropped her.

Anna had put a spell on her.

It was all my fault.

I had left her.

I had left her while I went off to have sex with Adam.

How could I?

"No, no," said Mum soothingly. "It's not Kate."

"Well who then?" I asked, the horrible scenarios starting all over again.

Had something happened to any of my sisters?

Had Margaret been killed by a gangster in Chicago?

Had Rachel disappeared in Prague?

Had Anna got a job?

Had Helen apologised for something?

"It's James," blurted out Mum.

"James," I said, dazedly, slowly sitting down on the couch. "Oh my God, James."

James.

I hadn't even thought of him when I was convinced that something awful had happened to someone that I loved.

While I'd been in bed with Adam, something had happened to my husband.

What kind of woman was I?

"What about James?" I asked them.

They both sat there, looking at me, with caring compassionate faces.

"Oh just tell me," I shouted. "Please tell me!"

I was prepared for the very worst.

James had had an accident or something while I had been writhing in the throes of passion with another man.

Of course, I realised that my life was over.

I had no other option but to embrace celibacy. Maybe I would enter a convent. It was the least I could do.

This was my punishment for sleeping with someone that I didn't love.

I never, ever wanted to see Adam again for as long as I lived.

It was all his fault.

If I hadn't gone to bed with him, James would have been all right.

"He's here," said Mum gently.

"Here!" I screeched. "What do you mean – here?"

I looked round the room frantically, as if I expected him to suddenly appear from behind a curtain or from under the couch, with a smooth smile, wearing a dinner jacket and smoking a cigar to say something like "My wife, I presume."

"Do you mean, he's on the premises?" I asked hysterically.

My head was spinning like a top.

Why now? I wondered.

Why had he picked now to reappear?

And what did he want?

"No," said Mum, sounding a bit annoyed. "Do you think we'd let him stay here after all that's happened? No, he rang. He's in Dublin all right, but he's staying in a hotel."

"Oh," I said. I thought I might faint.

"Does he want to see me?"

"Of course he does," said Dad. "But you don't have to if you don't want to."

"Jack," said Mum to him. "Of course she has to see him. How else are they going to sort anything out? She has the child to think of, you know."

"Mary, all I'm saying is that if she can't face it then we're not going to put her under pressure. We'll help her in every way that we can."

"Jack!" said Mum sharply. "She's a grown woman and . . ."

"But Mary . . . " interrupted Dad.

"Stop it!" I said loudly.

I knew that I had better nip this in the bud. This one could run and run, as they say. Steal an usherette's uniform, if you have to, etc.

They both looked at me in surprise. Almost as if they had forgotten that I was there.

"I want to see him," I said, a bit more quietly.

"You're right Mum, I *am* a grown woman. I'm the oniy person who can sort this out. And I do have

Kate to think of. She's the most important person in all of this."

"And thanks, Dad," I nodded at him. "It's nice to know that I can rely on you to round up a lynching mob, if I need one."

"A lynching mob?" he spluttered. "Well I don't know about that. But if you think you might need one, I could ask a couple of the chaps at the golf-club. See what they say."

"Oh Daddy," I told him wearily. "I'm kidding."

"He said that he'd ring in the morning," said Mum.

"What time?" I asked.

"Ten o'clock." said Mum.

"Right," I said.

If James said that he would ring at ten o'clock in the morning, James would ring at ten o clock in the morning.

Not at eighteen seconds past ten, you understand, or half a minute before ten.

But at ten.

He might have left me for another woman, but in some departments he was the most reliable man you could hope to meet.

"And what time is it now?" I asked.

"Twenty past three," said Dad.

"I suppose I'd better go to bed then," I said. "Big day tomorrow and all that."

Although I knew that I wouldn't sleep a wink.

"We'll all go to bed," said Mum. "Anyway, where were you until this hour?"

"Having sex with Adam," I told them.

Dad gave a loud bark of nervous laughter.

Mum looked stricken.

And well you might, I thought. You were the one who put the idea in my head in the first place.

"No, I'm being serious now," said Mum. "What were you up to?"

"I *am* being serious." I smiled. "Goodnight."

Mum looked appalled. She didn't know whether to believe me or not but she obviously suspected the worst. She stood there opening and closing her mouth like a goldfish as I shut the door behind me.

I don't think she even noticed Dad pulling at her dressing-gown and hissing at her, "Which one of them is Adam?"

Chapter Twenty-Four

I went to bed and I was right.

I didn't sleep a wink.

Why was James here?

Was this going to be a reconciliation attempt?

Or was it just to tidy up loose ends?

Could I bear it if he just wanted to tidy up the loose ends?

Did I want a reconciliation attempt?

Was he still with Denise?

A thought struck me -- Jesus, what if he had brought Denise with him?

I sat bolt upright in bed. Fury surged through me.

The rotten bastard, he wouldn't do that, would he?

I forced myself to calm down. I had no proof that he had done anything of the sort and there was no point getting angry over things that might not have happened.

I had to keep Kate in the forefront of my mind.

She was the most important person in all of this.

I wanted things to be civil with James so that he would be in Kate's life.

Even if he never wanted to see me again, I still wanted him to be there for her.

So I couldn't exactly go for him with a machete tomorrow when I saw him.

I couldn't really believe it.

I'd be seeing him tomorrow.

And what if the unthinkable happened and he wanted to try again with me?

Then what?

I didn't know.

And what about Adam?

The man whose bed I'd just left.

I can't think about that now, I thought.

My head was so crowded, it was standing room only. In fact a few hardy thoughts were standing outside my head, with their drinks, in the pouring rain, where at least there was a bit of space.

But there was no room at all for Adam.

Forget it, I told myself, you can't possibly think about it now. Wait till all this is over, one way or the other, and then think about him.

And then I started to wonder, Why.

You know, why had James left me. Why had James gone off with Denise when I had thought our relationship was so good. I hadn't tortured myself with these thoughts in a while.

But tomorrow I was going to at least try to get some answers to these questions.

If I could understand what had gone wrong, or what I had done wrong, maybe it wouldn't be so hard to live with.

I wished there was some kind of switch on my brain. That I could turn it off in the same way that I could turn off the television. Just click it off and immediately empty my mind of all these images and worrying thoughts. And simply leave a blank screen.

Or if I could just remove my head and put it on my bedside table and forget about it until morning. And then attach it on again when I needed it.

Morning finally rolled around and I was still no better off in the sleep department.

I jumped out of bed and was vaguely of a slight stiffness in my inner thighs. "Why's that?" I wondered. And then I remembered. "Oh, er, yes, that's right." I flushed a bit as I remembered what I had been up to the previous evening. "Adam. Sex. But I can't think about it now."

Honestly, damn James!

I was being denied the pleasure of lolling around in bed, dreamily recalling every detail of my Night of Lust with Adam.

Instead I had to get up and run around like a blue-arsed fly and Prepare For His Arrival. As though he was the Pope or a visiting head of state.

After I fed Kate her bottle, I bathed her and dressed her in her sweetest babygro. A fluffy pink one with little grey elephants all over it.

I covered her in talcum powder and held her close and inhaled her beautiful milky baby smell.

"You look gorgeous," I assured her. "Any man's fancy. And if he doesn't realise it then he's an even bigger fool than I already think he is."

I wanted her to look divine. I wanted her to look like the most beautiful baby on the planet. I wanted James to ache for her.

To hold her, to kiss her, to feed her, to smell her.

I wanted him to see just how much he had forsaken.

And I wanted to make him want us back.

The whole house seemed to be up at the crack of dawn. Anna and Helen knew that James had rung. Helen came into my room at about seven-thirty and ran over to Kate's cot and said "Oh good, you've made her look gorgeous. That'll show him. Let's just hope that she doesn't puke on him or do a poo in her nappy when he's holding her."

She picked up Kate and admired the babygro.

"Do you think we could put a pink ribbon in her hair, to match?" she asked.

"Helen, if she had more hair, I'd consider it," I told her.

But when Helen suggested that we put some make-up on her, I decided that that was going too far.

I'd save the make-up – and plenty of it – for me.

"Right, we have to make you look beautiful too," said Helen.

I wasn't too sure if I liked her tone.

It sounded a bit doubtful or defeatist, somehow.

Then Dad arrived.

"I'm off to work now," he said. "But remember what I said. You don't have to go back with him just for Kate's sake."

"Who says he's going to ask her to go back with him?" asked Helen loudly.

There was really no need for her to say that.

But she had a point.

Then Mum arrived into the room.

"How are you bearing up?" she asked kindly.

"Fine," I said.

"All right," she said. "You go off and have a shower. Helen and I will keep an eye on Kate."

"Oh all right." I was a little bit taken aback at all the organising and activity. It was nearly like the morning that I got married.

In came Anna.

I thought I might go downstairs and open the front door and start inviting strangers in off the street.

Anna smiled sweetly at me and held something out to me, "Claire, take this crystal and put it in a pocket or something. It'll bring you luck."

"She's going to need more than one of your crappy old crystals," said Helen bluntly.

"Stop that, Helen," said Mum sharply.

"What!" said Helen, outraged.

"Do you have to be so mean?" said Mum.

"I wasn't being mean," Helen defended herself hotly. "But if she looks nice and acts like she's fine he'll want her. You don't need a crystal to do that."

I looked at Helen almost in shock.

She might be one of the most irritating idiotic people I've ever met but when it comes to the psychology of men, I had to hand it to her, she was a master.

But I took the crystal anyway.

Because you never know.

I had to get away from my family for a little while. I couldn't think straight. I had to calm myself before I could talk to James.

I'd ring Laura, I decided. She'd tell me what to do.

"Laura," I said in a trembly voice, when she answered.

"Oh Claire," she burst out. "I was just about to ring you. Guess what!"

That's my line, I was thinking.

"What?" I asked.

"That little bastard Adrian has just dumped me."

Adrian, being, of course, her nineteen-year-old art student.

"What?" I said again.

"Yes," she said tearfully. "Can you believe it?"

"But I thought you didn't care about him," I said in surprise.

"So did I," she sobbed. "And wait until you hear! Guess why he dumped me."

"Why," I asked, wondering what was the reason. Had she finally run out of socks?

"Because he's met someone else," declared Laura. "And guess what age she is."

"Thirteen," I hazarded.

"No!", she shouted. "Thirty-bloody-seven!"

"Good God!" I said.

I was shocked.

"Yes," she said, barely able to speak because she was crying so much. "He says that I'm immature."

"The little pup."

"That he needs someone more centred."

"The *cheek* of him!"

"And I was just doing him a favour by going out with him. And he's just left me here," she sobbed. "Without a sock to my name. I'll have to go back to not knowing the names of anyone on *Top of The Pops*."

"Jesus, that's grim," I said shaking my head in a resigned way.

"Look," she said in a tragic way. "I have to go. I'll be late for work. I'll talk to you later."

And she hung up.

How about that? She probably thought I was ringing to spill the beans about my night of passion with Adam. Little did she know of the great drama that had occurred in the meantime.

I sat looking at the phone for a few seconds.

Who would I ring?

No one, I decided.

I'd try to deal with this on my own.

If I couldn't deal with my own life, I couldn't in all fairness expect anyone else to be able to.

I had a shower, washed my hair and went back into my room where some pointless argument seemed to be in process between Anna, Helen (of course) and Mum.

All three of them were shouting at the same time. Kate was lying in her cot being completely ignored.

"I did *not* make a face at you," Anna denied as emphatically as she could, which wasn't very much.

"You bloody well did," Helen said.

"It wasn't a face," Mum said, trying to pour oil on water that was very troubled indeed. "It was more of a look."

The babel of voices stopped abruptly as soon as I came into the room.

All three of them turned their faces expectantly towards me.

It seemed that they had decided to abandon their

internecine differences and unite with me against the common enemy, James.

They ran round, got me clothes and dressed me up.

"You have to look beautiful," said Anna.

"Yes," agreed Helen. "But you have to look as if you didn't try at all. Like you just flung on any old thing."

"But he's only ringing me at ten o'clock," I reminded them. "He didn't say anything about calling round."

"Yes," said Mum. "But he didn't come all the way to Dublin just to ring you. He could have done that from London."

Good point.

"Right girls," I said to Anna and Helen. "In that case make me beautiful."

"We said we'd loan you clothes and do your make-up," said Helen. "We never said that we could do miracles."

But she was smiling as she said it.

We finally agreed that I would wear the leggings and blue silk shirt that I had worn the day Adam came to tea.

Adam, I thought longingly, for a moment.

But then I pushed him firmly to the back of my mind.

Not now, I thought grimly.

"You look nice and skinny," said Helen, standing back and looking at me. "Now for your make-up."

Honestly, she was organising the whole thing like a military campaign.

Anna's eyes lit up at the mention of doing my make-up. She approached with a plastic bag that seemed to be full of crayons and pencils.

"Get away," Helen told her irritably, elbowing her aside. "*I'm* doing her make-up. You probably want to do face-painting and paint stars and suns and all that new-age crap on her."

Anna *did* look a little bit sheepish.

"No," Helen explained, a bit more kindly. "She has to look as if she's not wearing any make-up at all. Just naturally beautiful."

"Yes," I said all excited. "Make me look like that."

Why was Helen being so nice to me, I wondered.

Did she suspect that I was in competition with her for Adam? If I was back with James it would mean that she could have a clear shot at Adam.

Or maybe I was just being totally cynical.

I mean, she was my sister, after all.

And anyway, she probably didn't suspect a thing.

I must say, I did look beautiful by the time Helen was finished with me.

Fresh-faced, clear-skinned, bright-eyed, casually dressed.

"Smile," she ordered me.

I did.

They all nodded approvingly.

"Good," said Mum. "Do that a lot."

"What time is it now?" I asked.

"Nearly half past nine," said Mum.

"Half an hour to go," I said, feeling nauseous.

I sat on the bed.

Mum, Anna, Helen and Kate were already on it.

"Move over," I said. I was sitting on Anna's foot.

"Ouch," said Helen, as Anna moved and kind of elbowed her in the face.

We were all huddled on the bed, sort of lying on top of each other.

It was like a vigil.

They were going to stay there for me until he rang.

I felt as if we were a raft full of survivors from a shipwreck. All squashed and uncomfortable and crowded, but there was no suggestion that we leave each other.

"Right," said Mum. "We'll play a game."

"All right," we all said in unison.

Except for Kate, of course.

Mum had great games. Word games that we used to play to pass the time on long car journeys when we were young.

For some reason the game that we were actually playing when he rang was one thought up by (who else) Helen. Obviously done with more than a nod to my recent condition. It was one in which you have to think of all the different words to describe being pregnant.

I didn't think it was really what Mum had had in mind when she encouraged us to make up our own versions of the games that she had taught us.

"Up the pole," shouted Anna.

"On the bubble," screeched Helen.

"Expecting," muttered Mum, torn between disapproval and the desire to win.

"Your turn, Claire," said Anna.

"No," I said. "Shuusssh, is that the phone?"

The room fell silent.

It was.

"Will I answer it?" asked Mum.

"No. Thanks Mum, but I'll do it," I said.

And I left them.

Chapter Twenty-Five

"Hello," I said, for lack of anything better to say.

"Claire," said James's voice.

So, it was him.

We finally got to speak to each other.

"James," I replied.

And then I wasn't quite sure what to say.

I wasn't too genned-up on the etiquette of addressing runaway husbands. Especially since I was pretty sure that he wasn't in the process of trying to wheedle his way back into my affections.

We need a book. A book that tells us how to address returning runaway husbands.

You know, the type of book that tells us the correct knife to use to shell a scallop and the proper way to address, say, a bishop, for example (just for the record, "that's a lovely ring you're wearing, Your Grace", is usually regarded as polite enough for a first meeting.)

So this book would gently instruct us about the correct number of times the word "bastard" could be used in any one sentence, and when it is regarded as impolite not to use physical violence, etc.

For example, if your boyfriend/husband/fella has simply disappeared for a couple of days after a particularly important football match and has just returned to the family home looking green, unshaven and dishevelled, it would be appropriate to say

"Where the fuck have you been for the past three days, you drunken, selfish, louser?"

But as the person out there hadn't written the book yet I had to rely on my own instinct.

"How are you?" he asked.

As if you cared, I thought.

"Very well," I said politely.

A pause.

"Oh! . . . and how are you?" I asked hurriedly.

Honestly, where were my manners.

Is it any wonder that he'd left me?

"Well," he replied thoughtfully. "Yes, quite well."

Pompous fucker, I thought.

"Claire," he continued smoothly. "I'm in Dublin."

"I know," I said ungraciously. "My mother mentioned that you'd called last night."

"Yes, I don't doubt that she did," he said with faint irony.

You could never say that James was a fool.

A bastard, I grant you. But never a fool.

"Where are you staying?" I asked.

He named some city centre Bed and Breakfast. On a street that could only be described as On The Front Line. Not James's usual style at all. He was more likely to be found in a plush corporate type of place. All Bureau de Changes and little shops in the hotel lobby selling varnished blackthorn sticks and leprechauns in a tin. From James's address I deduced that he was not in Dublin on business. Because if he

"But certainly," I gave a little laugh. "What are you sounding so shocked about?"

Because when I've finished breaking every bone in your body, I'm going to cut off your penis and stick it in your mouth and I certainly can't do *that* over the phone either, now can I?, I thought.

"Well, er . . . nothing, nothing. That's . . . er . . . that's great," he said.

He still sounded surprised.

He obviously expected me to refuse to see him. That would account for the coaxing tone and the surprise at my calm agreement to meet him.

But, in all fairness, what would I gain from refusing to see him?

I wanted the answer to a couple of questions.

409

Like, why did you stop loving me?

And, how much money are you going to give me for Kate?

How else were we going to sort out our respective legal positions and our relationship to Kate if we didn't meet to talk about it?

Perhaps he expected to find that I'd gone to pieces totally.

But, well . . . hey! . . . I wasn't in pieces now, was I?

I wasn't better or anything like it, but, no matter what way I looked at it I couldn't deny that I'd greatly improved.

How odd!

When did that happen?

You know that bit at the end of a relationship when all your friends gather round and say lots of annoying things like "plenty more fish in the sea", and "he would never have made you happy". Well, when they get to the bit about "It'll mend with time", try to fight your initial instinct to blacken their eye.

Don't knock it, because it really does work.

I was living proof.

The only problem with time mending things is that it takes longer.

So, effective and all as it is, it's precious little use to those of us in a hurry.

I suppose the sex with Adam hadn't hurt my recovery either. But I had to drag my thoughts back to the present. James was talking again.

"Where should we meet?" he asked.

"Why don't you come out to the house here?" I suggested.

I didn't want this to be an away game. I wanted this meeting to be on my turf, if not on my terms.

"You can get a taxi. Or if you prefer you could take a bus and ask the conductor to let you off at the roundabout at the end of . . . "

"Claire!" he interrupted, laughing at how silly I was being. "I've been out to your house plenty of times. I *know* how to get there."

"Of course you do," I said smoothly.

I *knew* that.

But I couldn't resist the chance to treat him like a total stranger. To let him know that he no longer belonged.

"Will we say eleven-thirty?" I said with authority.

"Er, fine," he said.

"Lovely," I said acidly. "See you then."

And I hung up without waiting for his reply.

Chapter Twenty-Six

Now, I would be lying to both myself and you if I didn't admit that it would have given me a great deal of satisfaction if James had returned to me on his knees, a broken man. I would have been delighted if he had crawled up the driveway on all fours, sobbing and begging for me to take him back. I wanted him to be unshaven, filthy and wearing torn clothes. I wanted his hair to be all long and matted and for him to be deranged of aspect and obviously demented with grief and the terrible realisation that he had lost the only woman he had ever loved. And indeed could ever love.

So vivid was this mental image of mine that when eleven-thirty rolled around and he appeared at the gate, I was hugely disappointed to find that he was in fact walking fully upright.

Prehistoric man must have felt the same sense of disbelief when one of his fellows hopped down out of one of the trees and started to parade around on just two legs.

I stood at the window and watched him as he walked up the short drive. Mind you, I stood well back. I didn't think that it would enhance my dignity for him to see me with my nose pressed up against the window.

I had been wondering what he would look like. And now I would see.

That gave me a violent twist of pain.

He was no longer mine, so he would look different.

My subtle but definite mark on him would be gone.

He had been an extension of me so I had subliminally – subversively even sometimes I must admit – made him look a certain way.

Well, let's be fair, he was a reflection on me. I couldn't have had him going round looking like a gobshite.

Now all that power was gone.

And what did he look like?

Was he different?

Had Denise made him fat?

Was he badly dressed?

Had Denise kitted him out in the same little jackets and sweatpants which she dressed her three little boys in? All purples and turquoises. Very nasty.

Would he look like a cruel and heartless bastard, coming to take my home and my child away from me?

But he just looked so *normal*.

Walking along with his hands in his pockets. He could have been anyone going anywhere.

Although he looked different from the way that I'd remembered him.

Thinner, I thought.

And I was sure that something else was different too . . . what was it? . . . I wasn't sure . . . had he . . . had he *always* been that short?

And he wasn't dressed the way I'd expected him to be.

Every time I'd thought of seeing him, I'd imagined him dressed in his Grim Reaper suit that he wore that day at the hospital. Today he was wearing jeans, a blue shirt and some kind of jacket.

Very casual. Very laid-back.

Obviously not treating this occasion with the great weight that it deserved.

It felt wrong.

Incongruous.

Like a Hangman turning up to do a day's work wearing a Hawaiian shirt and a baseball cap on back-to-front, grinning from ear to ear as he told "knock, knock" jokes.

He rang the bell. I took a deep breath and walked to answer the door.

My heart was thumping.

I swung back the door and there he stood.

The same. He looked so heartbreakingly the same.

His hair was still dark brown, his face was still pale, his eyes were still green, his jaw was still lean.

He gave me a funny twisted half smile and, after an awkward pause, he said expressionlessly, "Claire, how are you?"

"Fine." I smiled slightly – politely – at him. "Why don't you come in?"

He came into the hall and I almost keeled over as a wave of nausea hit me.

It was one thing to banter calmly with him over the phone. But it was a hell of a lot harder to deal with him in the flesh.

However, unpleasant and all as it was, I had to behave like an adult.

The days of running crying to my bedroom were long gone.

And he wasn't looking too happy himself.

I knew he didn't love me anymore but he was only human. Well, I presumed he was only human. And couldn't help being affected by this momentous occasion.

But I knew James. He'd recover his aplomb in no time at all.

That was what I had to do.

I graciously said to him, "Will I take your jacket?" as though he was just someone who had come to try and sell me a central heating system.

"Yes, I suppose so," he said reluctantly and shrugged out of it, and warily handed it over to me, taking what seemed like excessive care to make sure that our hands didn't touch.

He looked longingly at the jacket, as though he was never going to see it again and wanted to memorise its every detail.

What was he afraid of?

I wasn't going to steal the bloody jacket.

It wasn't nice enough.

"I'll put this away," I said and for the first time our eyes met properly.

He did a quick scan of my face and said levelly, "You're looking well, Claire."

He said it with the enthusiasm an undertaker usually reserves for someone who, against all the odds, survives a terrible car crash. "Yes," he nodded, a tiny bit surprised. "You *are* looking well."

415

"Well, why wouldn't I?" I gave him a knowing little smile, conveying – at least I hoped I conveyed – dignity and irony in equal amounts.

Letting him know that although he no longer loved me, that although he had hurt and humiliated me, I was a reasonable human being and would get over it.

Almost making a joke of the whole sorry mess and practically inviting him, the perpetrator, to join in and laugh along with me.

I couldn't believe that I had managed that.

I felt pretty pleased with myself.

Because, although I did not feel calm and civilised, as God is my witness, I was going to do a damn good job at acting it.

However he didn't seem to find it as gently amusing as I managed to pretend I did.

He gave me a wintry look.

More undertakerish vibes.

The miserable fucker.

Since I was prepared to try and be nice and civil about all this, surely, *surely*, he could too. After all, what had he got to lose?

Maybe he had prepared a beautiful speech about how I would get over him, how he wasn't good enough for me, how we were never really suited, how I was better off without him. Maybe he was disappointed that he wasn't going to get to say it.

He'd probably stood in front of the mirror in his bedroom in The LiffeySide (Bord Failte approved, shower-ensuite, tea and coffee making facilities in all rooms, multi-channel TV, early morning drunken brawls in the street under your room on request) and practised flinging his arms around me in a beseeching manner while he told me in a voice choked with emotion that, although he still loved me, he was no longer *in love* with me.

We stood in the hall for a few seconds, James looking as if his entire family had just been wiped out in a machete attack. I didn't look much better. The tension was terrible.

"Come on into the dining-room," I told him, taking charge. Otherwise we could have stood there all day, white-faced, miserable and paralysed by nerves. "We won't be disturbed there and we can have the table in case we need to spread out documents or whatever."

He nodded grimly and walked down the hall in front of me.

The cheek of him! What was he looking so bloody uptight about?

Surely I was the one who should be afforded that right?

Kate was waiting in the dining-room.

She lay in her cot and looked beautiful.

I picked her up and stood holding her, her face against mine.

"This is Kate," I said simply.

He stared at the two of us, opening and closing his mouth.

He looked a bit like a goldfish. A pale, serious goldfish.

"She . . . she's got so big, she's grown so much," he finally managed.

"Babies do," I nodded at him sagely.

The sub-text being of course, "If you had stuck around, you bastard, you'd have been there for when she was doing that growing." But I didn't say it.

I didn't need to.

He knew it.

It was written all over his sheepish, shamed face.

"And she's called Kate?" he asked.

The surge of anger was so intense that I thought I would surely kill him.

He hadn't even found out her name.

There were plenty of people he could have asked.

"After Kate Bush?" he asked. Referring to a singer that, while I certainly liked her, I wouldn't have ever considered calling my first born child after.

"Yes," I managed bitterly. "After Kate Bush."

I wasn't going to bother giving him the real reason. What the hell did he care?

"Hey!" he said, the idea obviously just having occurred to him. "Can I hold her?" In different circumstances he could have been described as speaking with enthusiasm.

My anger and bitterness had obviously gone right over his neatly-combed head.

I *wanted* to shout at him, "Of course you can hold her, she's waited two months for you to hold her. You're her bloody FATHER!" But I managed not to.

I felt like a traitor, like a Third-World mother who is forced by economic circumstances to sell her child to the rich gringo. But I passed her from my arms to his.

And the look on his face.

It was as if he had suddenly become mentally retarded.

All smiles and shining eyes and reverential expression.

Of course he held her all wrong.

Crossways, instead of lengthways.

Horizontal, instead of vertical.

People who know nothing about babies hold them like that.

I know because I did it for the first day or so of Kate's life until one of the other mothers, who was sick of hearing Kate roaring, wearily set me right. ("Up, not across!")

But you wouldn't catch me being sympathetic to James for making the same mistake.

Kate started to cry.

Well, of course the poor child did!

Being held like a rolled up carpet by a strange man.

Wouldn't you cry?

James looked frightened.

"What's wrong with her?" he asked. "How do I make her stop?"

The reverential expression disappeared.

Replaced by naked fear.

I had known all that mister-nice-guy stuff was too good to be true.

"Here," he said, thrusting her at me. He looked at both of us with an expression of distaste.

There was obviously no room for crying women in James's world.

He hadn't always been like that, you know.

Well he'd married me. And I wasn't famous for blinking back the tears. Better out than in was always my motto.

But looking at him now, at his fastidious expression, I marvelled – and it wasn't for the first time, let's face it – at what a bastard he had become.

"Oh golly," I smiled acidly. "She doesn't seem to like you."

I laughed as if it was a joke and took her back from James's yielding arms.

He couldn't get rid of her fast enough. I cooed and shushed her. She stopped crying.

For a moment I felt bitter satisfaction that Kate had sided with me against him.

And then I felt sad and ashamed.

James was Kate's father.

I should do everything in my power to make them like each other.

I'd find another man to love.

But Kate had only the one father.

"Sorry," I smiled apologetically at him. "It's just that you're new to her. Give her a chance. She's scared."

"You're right. It'll probably just take a bit of time," he said, cheering up a bit.

"That's all," I reassured him. But at the same time thinking, horror-struck, when exactly does he propose spending this alleged "bit of time" with her?

If he had come to Dublin to try and take Kate back to London, then he had to die. It was really quite simple.

He hadn't done the doting father bit up until now, so what did he want?

"Coffee."

"What?" I asked him sharply.

"Is there any chance of a cup of coffee?" he asked.

He was looking at me as if I was a bit peculiar.

How many times had he asked me before I heard?

"Sure," I told him.

I put Kate back in her cot and went out into the kitchen to make him his coffee.

I should have offered before. But in all the excitement it never crossed my mind.

It was a bit of a relief to get into the kitchen.

I sighed long and deep and hard when I closed the door behind me.

My hands shook so much I could hardly fill the kettle.

Being with him was so hard.

Having to pretend that I was fine was exhausting.

And constantly keeping a lid on murderous anger was a demanding business.

But I had to do it.

I was going to salvage as much as I could for Kate out of this.

I brought the coffee back into the dining-room.

And, no, I didn't give him biscuits.

I'm sorry, but I just wasn't a big enough person.

He was leaning over the cot, attempting to talk to Kate.

He was having some kind of muttered, uptight discussion with her.

421

As if she was a business colleague and not a two-month-old baby.

He was not behaving the way nice, normal, warm people do in the presence of young babies. You know, as if they've left their brain out, overnight, in the rain.

All singsong noises and doting rhetorical questions.

Asking stupid things like "Who's the most beautiful girl in the whole world?" And the correct answer not, as you might expect, Cindy Crawford, but in fact Kate Webster.

Instead he sounded as if he was discussing tax reforms with her.

But he didn't seem to notice anything amiss.

I put the coffee down on the dining-room table and the moment the china touched the mahogany I realised that I had automatically made James's coffee the way that James liked it.

I was furious!

Couldn't I even *pretend* to have forgotten?

Couldn't I have given him a milk and two sugars instead of a black, no sugar and half cold water?

And then, when he gagged on it, nursing his burnt and over-sugared mouth, couldn't I have airily said something like "Oh sorry, I forgot, *you're* the one who doesn't like sugar?"

But no.

I'd missed a precious chance to let him know that he didn't matter at all to me anymore.

"Oh thanks Claire," he said, sipping from the mug. "You remembered the way I like it," and he smiled with satisfaction.

I could have happily gone to the kitchen and doused myself in petrol and set myself alight, so angry was I.

"You're welcome," I said from between gritted teeth.

There was a little silence.

Then James started to speak.

He seemed to have suddenly clicked into Relaxed Mode. The apparent nerves at the front door had evaporated.

I only wish mine had.

"You know, I can't believe that I'm actually here," he mused easily, leaning back in his chair, nursing the traitorous coffee between his cupped hands.

He sounded as if he had no trouble at all in believing it.

"I can't believe you let me in."

Well, actually you're not the only bloody one, I felt like telling him, but didn't.

"Why's that?" I asked with icy politeness.

"Oh," he said, shaking his head with a wry little smile, as though he couldn't quite credit his runaway imagination. "I thought that perhaps your mother and sisters might have done something really nasty when I arrived. You know, poured boiling oil down on top of me. Something like that."

And he sat there and, looking straight into my eyes, he smiled smugly, accepting the ease with which he had been readmitted to the Lion's Den as nothing less than his due, confident that, although I was from a mad family and a nation of savages, he was really quite safe.

I resisted the urge to lunge across the table at him and rip out his larynx with my teeth, hissing, "Boiling oil would be too good for you."

Instead I gave a cold little smile and said "Oh don't be ridiculous, James. We're perfectly civilised round here, no matter what you might like to think. Why would we hurt you? And after all" – tinkly little laugh. Like shards of ice banging off the side of a glass – "we need you to be in good health so that you can afford Kate's maintenance payments."

There was a resonant silence.

"What are you talking about, 'maintenance payments'?" he asked slowly, as though he had never before in his life heard of such a thing.

"James, you must know what maintenance payments are," I told him, faint with shock.

I just stared at him.

What the hell was going on?

He was a boring, swotty, accountant type person.

He and maintenance agreements should be best buddies.

In fact I was amazed that he didn't arrive with a huge itemised agreement for me to sign. You know, detailing all kinds of things, such as the cost of keeping Kate in shoes for the rest of her life, projected economies of scale, sinking funds, amortisation and suchlike.

After all this was the man who could, and probably frequently did, calculate a waitress's tip to within fourteen decimal places.

Not that he was mean, you understand.

But he was very, *very* organised.

Forever scribbling on the backs of envelopes or on napkins and coming up with immensely detailed calculations which, oddly enough, nearly always turn out to be correct.

In five minutes he could tell you to the nearest penny how much it would cost you to decorate your bathroom, taking everything into account, including paint, fittings, labour, biscuits for the workmen, workdays (your own, that is) lost from sleepless nights when the workmen disappeared for three weeks, leaving the bath in the landing etc. . . . Honestly, he thinks of everything!

"Maintenance payments," he said again thoughtfully. He didn't sound happy.

"Yes James," I said with steely resolve.

Although my stomach was lurching around like a Leitrim bricklayer on a ferry in rough seas. A Leitrim bricklayer who had drunk eighteen pints of duty-free lager.

If James was going to be difficult about money, I'd die.

No, let me take that back. I wouldn't.

I'd kill him.

"Right, right, I see," he said, sounding a bit stunned. "Yes, we obviously *do* have a lot to talk about."

"Yes, we certainly do," I confirmed, trying to sound jovial. "And you're here now so we're in the happy position of being able to do so."

I gave him a bright smile.

It was so reluctant that I think I damaged muscles in my face.

But I had to keep this as amiable and friendly as possible.

"So," I continued briskly, determined to sound as if I knew what I was talking about. "I know we're both unfamiliar with this sort of thing but don't you think we should try and sort out the basic issues ourselves and let the solicitors dot the 't's' and cross the 'i's'?" (I permitted myself a little smile at this. Which he completely ignored.) "Or would you prefer to do the whole lot, lock stock and barrel through our solicitors?"

"Aha!" he suddenly seemed to brighten up, He raised his indexfinger like Monsieur Poirot demonstrating the fatal flaw in the argument. "That would be fine if we had solicitors. But we haven't, have we?" He looked at me in a kindly but pitying sort of fashion as if I was a bit of a half-wit.

"But . . . well, actually I have," I told him.

"Have you?" he asked. "Have you indeed? Well, well, well." He sounded quite astonished. And not that pleased.

"Er . . . yes, of course I have," I said.

"My, my, weren't you the busy one?" he said a bit nastily. "You certainly didn't waste much time."

"James, what are you talking about? It's been two months," I protested.

And to think that I had felt guilty about all the procrastination and time-wasting.

I was confused.

Had I done something wrong?

Was there some sort of protocol? Some sort of time-limit that I had to observe before dealing with the wreckage of my broken marriage?

Like not being allowed to go dancing in a red dress until my husband had been dead for six years, or whatever it was that Scarlett O'Hara so scandalised the Atlanta community with.

"Yes," he said. "I suppose it has been two months."

He sighed.

For a moment the wild thought crossed my mind that he might be sad.

And then I realised that, yes, he probably was sad.

Wouldn't any man be sad when he suddenly realised that he now had two families to support?

And he probably envisaged solicitor's fees and estate agent's costs stretching as far as the eye can see into the future as we sorted out the severing of our marriage.

And of course keeping those three little brats of Denise's in pink nylon shell suits wouldn't come cheap either.

Although, by rights, it should.

So I put any sympathy that I might have entertained to one side and said, "James, did you bring the deeds to the flat with you?"

"Er, no," he said, looking a tiny bit bewildered.

"Why not?" I asked, slightly exasperated.

"I don't know," he said, looking at his shoes.

There was a perplexed pause.

"I suppose I just didn't think of it. I left London in such a hurry."

"Do you have *any* of our documents with you?" I asked, fighting the urge to thump him. "You know, bank statements, our pension details, that kind of thing?"

"No," he said shortly. His face had gone very pale. He must have been furious at being caught on the hop.

This kind of inefficiency was really very unlike him. He was acting totally out of character. Although he hadn't exactly been acting *in* character for quite a while. Maybe he was having a nervous breakdown? Or maybe he was so in love with fatso Denise that he'd turned into a bimbo.

His eyesight had obviously failed him when he ran off with her. What's to say that his brain hadn't gone the same way?

"Do we need all those documents?" he asked.

"Well, not straight away, I suppose," I said. "But, if we want to sort things out while you're here, it would be a lot handier to have them."

"I suppose I could get some of them faxed over," he said slowly. "If that's what you really want."

"Well, it's not exactly a question of what *I* want," I said, feeling a bit confused. "It's so that we can try and figure out who owns what."

"God, how sordid!" he said with great distaste, "You mean, things like 'I own that towel, you own that saucepan' kind of thing."

"Well, yes, I suppose I do," I said.

What was *wrong* with him? Hadn't he given this any thought whatsoever?

"James," I asked him as he sat on the chair looking totally shell-shocked. "What did you *think* was going to happen? That the divorce fairies would come along and magically sort it all out for us while we slept?"

He managed a pale little smile at that.

"You're right," he said wearily. "You're right, you're right, you're right!"

"I am," I reassured him. "And if it makes you feel any better, you can have all the saucepans."

"Thanks," he said quietly.

"And don't worry," I told him, all fake bonhomie and back-slapping jocularity. "One day I'm sure we'll look back and laugh at all of this."

Naturally enough, I was sure of nothing of the sort.

I was dimly aware that there was something deeply, *deeply* wrong with me having to comfort him, with me having to jolly him along and encourage him to be strong.

But it was all so weird anyway that, to be quite frank with you, I didn't know my arse from my elbow.

Not a mistake I'd normally make.

It wouldn't be usual to catch me putting haemorrhoid ointment on my elbow. Or soaking my arse in lemon juice for that matter. But, as I've already said, these were difficult times.

James suddenly got to his feet. He just stood there for a few moments looking lost. He was obviously planning how to get the mortgage documents and all that stuff sent over from London, I thought. He must be mortified that he's been so inefficient.

"I'd better go," he said.

"Right," I said. "Fine. Why don't you go back to

your hotel" (hotel! what a joke!) "and organise the deeds of the flat to be sent over? And then we can meet up later."

"Fine," he said, still being very quiet.

I couldn't wait for him to leave.

This was too much.

It was finally happening.

It really was really, really over.

We'd dealt with it like civilised human beings. Too civilised, in my opinion.

The whole thing had a dream-like quality.

It was horrible.

"I'll ring you this afternoon," he said.

He said goodbye to Kate and, although he looked as if he was explaining her pension entitlements to her, at least he made an effort to bond with her.

Finally I managed to get him to leave.

He looked as exhausted as I felt.

Chapter Twenty-Seven

I barely managed to close the door behind him before I started to cry.

As though they instinctively knew that he had left – hey, what am I talking about, because they had been lying on the floor in the bedroom above the dining-room with their ears pressed to a glass trying to hear everything that was being said – Anna, Helen and Mum magically emerged from the woodwork, wearing their Concerned Expressions.

I was distraught.

As though she sensed my grief, Kate started to bawl.

Or maybe it was just because she was hungry.

Either way it was a bit of a cacophony.

"The bastard," I managed to say between sobs, tears stung my face. "How can it be so easy for him? He's like a fucking machine, with no feelings at all."

"Wasn't he upset, even slightly?" asked Mum anxiously.

"The one thing, the *only* thing the fucker is worried about is how *sordid* it's going to be when we have to share out our possessions."

"But that's not so bad," said Helen soothingly. "Maybe then he'll just leave everything to you. And you'll get everything."

Nice try, Helen.

Not quite what I needed to hear though.

"So there was no mention of a reconciliation?" asked Mum, her face white, her eyes worried.

"None!" I burst out, prompting a fresh bout of wailing from Kate, who was being held by a miserable looking Anna.

"Reconciliation!" screeched Helen. "But you wouldn't take him back, would you? Not after the way he's treated you."

"But that's not the point," I sobbed. "At least I wanted the choice. I wanted the chance to tell him to fuck off and that I wouldn't touch him with a barge pole. And the bastard didn't even have the decency to do that."

The three of them nodded in sympathy.

"And he was so smug!" I burst out. "I remembered how he likes his bloody coffee!"

There was a sharp intake of breath from all three of them. They stood shaking their heads sadly at my foolishness. "That's bad," said Anna. "Now he'll know that you still care."

"But I *don't*," I protested violently. "I hate his guts, his uptight, unfaithful, accountant's guts!"

"And the bloody nerve of him!" I continued, tears pouring down my blotchy face.

"What?" asked the three, moving forward slightly to hear yet another of James's misdeeds.

"*He* was upset about the sharing out of our things and I, I, ME! was the one who ended up trying to make him feel better about it. Imagine it! *Me* comforting *him*. After all that's happened."

"Men," said Anna, shaking her head in weary disbelief. "Can't live with them, can't live with them."

"Can't live with them," continued Mum. "Can't shoot them."

There was a pause. Then Helen spoke.

"Says who?"

"So what's the outcome?" asked Mum.

"None yet," I said. "He's ringing this afternoon."

"What are you going to do until then?" Mum asked, her anxious glance straying inadvertently in the direction of the drinks cabinet, even though it had stood empty for many's the long year, but old habits die hard. It might have been more appropriate if her glance had strayed inadvertently out into the garden and under the oil tank, but never mind.

"Nothing," I said. "I'm so tired."

"Why don't you go to bed?" she said hastily. "It's been an ordeal for you. We'll take care of Kate."

Helen looked as if she was about to protest. She opened her mouth mutinously. But then she shut it again.

Nothing short of miraculous, I must say.

"OK," I said. I dragged myself up the stairs and got into bed still wearing the lovely clothes that I had been decked out in that morning. There was no trace of the smiling, well-made-up, attractive woman that I had been then. Only a red-faced, puffy-eyed, blotchy-skinned wreck.

Mid-afternoon, Mum woke me by gently shaking me by the shoulder, whispering "James is on the phone for you. Will you talk to him?"

"Yes," I said. I stumbled from the bed, clothes all

crumpled, half-blinded from sleep in my eyes, drooling like a lunatic.

"Hello," I mumbled.

"Claire," he said crisply, all authority and efficiency. "I've tried to get our deeds faxed over to me but there's no fax shop in this bloody city."

Instantly I felt guilty. He made me feel as if it was all my fault. As though I had personally gone round and shut every fax shop in Dublin, just to spite him.

"Oh sorry James," I stuttered. "If you'd mentioned it I would have suggested that they could have been faxed to Dad's office."

"Well, never mind," he sighed, sounding irritable and exasperated and conveying that, if he wanted something done, he was better off doing it himself and not involving me or any members of my immediate family. "Anyway it's too late now. They're being posted and should arrive in the morning."

You'll be lucky, I thought, thinking of the relaxed attitude of the Irish postal system, compared to the English one. But I said nothing. Doubtless when the time came and the documents didn't, I would somehow be made to feel that that was my fault also.

"But I do think that we should meet this evening anyway," he continued efficiently, ever the professional. Time is money, isn't that right James!

But in fairness he did have a point. We had to meet anyway. We had so much to speak about. It made sense.

I obviously wanted everything sorted out as quickly as possible so that I could get on with my new life.

I didn't have any other motive, did I?

I wasn't pathetic enough to think that, if he saw enough of me, he might realise that he still loved me?

Maybe I just enjoyed his company.

Maybe hell!

But I had to admit that I was fascinated by the fact that he no longer loved me.

You know, in the same sort of way that people always look at the blood on the road and the mangled vehicles being towed away after a carcrash. I know that it's horrible but at the same time I'm so drawn to it. I know that I'll be upset afterwards but I still can't stop myself.

Or maybe I just wanted the chance to beat the shit out of him. Who knows?

"Well, what should we do?" he asked. "I would come out to your house but I'm not sure I'm particularly welcome."

I could hardly believe my ears.

The *cheek* of him!

The unmitigated, undiluted cheek of him!

He had no right to feel welcome but, at the same time, I had treated him with the utmost good manners.

Which is more than the way he could be said to have treated me.

Hadn't I made him coffee?

Hadn't I not set the dogs on him?

Not that we had any dogs, but that wasn't the point.

Worse still, I could have set Helen on him.

Just what had he been expecting?

The roads from Dublin Airport to be lined with cheering natives, waving Union Jacks? Brass bands and red carpets? A national holiday to be declared? Me greeting him at my front door, wearing a sexy negligee, smiling and saying huskily "Welcome back darling?"

Frankly, I was baffled.

I wasn't sure what I should say.

Sorry sir, but we're fresh out of fatted calves.

He sounded as if he was sulking. As if he wanted me to say something like, "Oh don't be so silly, James. Of course you're welcome."

But James didn't sulk. He was far too grown up for that. And no man in his right mind could have expected me to welcome him back with open arms.

But what was I going to say?

"I'm sorry you feel that way, James," I managed to say humbly. "If my family or I have behaved in any kind of inhospitable fashion, then I can only offer my apologies."

Of course, I didn't mean a word of it.

If my family *had* offended him in any way, if, for example, Helen had attracted his attention when he left the house by making horrible faces or gestures at him from an upstairs window, or showing him her bottom – or something even worse – then I would personally offer rewards.

But I had to humour James.

Although I was gagging on my polite words, I always had Kate in the forefront of my mind.

Nothing would have given me greater pleasure than to tell James just how unwelcome he was, but that would be cutting off my nose to spite my face. I didn't want Kate to grow up without a father, so telling James that he wasn't *un*welcome (I'm afraid that that was as far as I was prepared to go) was the price I had to pay.

"Well, will I come over then?" he asked grudgingly.

What was *wrong* with him?

He was behaving like a manipulative child.

"Oh James," I said kindly. "I wouldn't want you to come over here if you're not feeling particularly welcome. We both want to be relaxed. Perhaps we should meet in town instead."

There was a long pause while James digested this.

"Fine," he said coldly. "We could go for dinner."

"That sounds nice," I said, thinking, that *does* sound nice.

"Well, I've got to eat something," he said ungraciously. "So you might as well come along."

"You always were a silver-tongued devil," I said, forcing a smile into my voice. But I felt suddenly so sad.

We arranged to meet at a city centre restaurant at seven-thirty.

And the preparations were, if anything, even more elaborate than the ones that morning.

I wanted, naturally, to look beautiful.

But I decided that I wanted to look sexy also.

James had always loved my legs and loved it when I wore high heels, even if they made me nearly as tall as he was.

So I wore my highest pair, with my shortest dress,

black, of course and the sheerest pair of tights I could find.

As luck would have it, hadn't I shaved my legs only the previous evening? When I was preparing to have sex with Adam, actually. But let's not talk about that right now.

I put on piles of make-up.

"More mascara," urged Helen from the sidelines. "More foundation."

The subtle approach had been, shall we say, less than successful this morning. So now we were going for overkill.

As I applied the stinging stuff that I put on my lips to keep my lipstick in place, it struck me how terrible this all was. So awful.

I used to apply my make-up with that kind of care when I was going out with James first. And now here I was dolling myself up, trying my damnedest to look beautiful for the Grand Finale of our relationship.

It was all such a waste.

Failed relationships can be described as so much wasted make-up.

Forget the laughs, forget the rows, forget the sex, forget the jealousy. But take off your hat and observe a moment's silence for the legions of unknown tubes of foundation, mascara, eye-liner, blusher and lipstick who died that it might all have been possible. But who died in vain.

I looked at myself in the mirror and, I had to admit it, I looked good. Tall and slim and nearly elegant. Not a watermelon in sight.

"Jesus," said Helen, shaking her head in undisguised admiration. "Look at you. And it's such a short time since you were a fat old bitch."

Praise indeed.

"Put your hair up," suggested Helen.

"I can't, it's too short," I protested.

"No, it's not," she said and came over to me and swept it up onto the top of my head.

Goddammit, she was right. It must have grown a bit while I completely neglected it over the previous two months.

"Oh," I said, delighted. "I haven't had long hair since I was sixteen."

Helen busied herself with slides and clips while I grinned like a lunatic at my reflection in the mirror. "James will be sickened," I said. "He'll be so sorry that he can't have a beautiful babe like me. I'll have him on his knees begging me to take him back as soon as I walk in the door."

My beautiful fantasy of a drooling and contrite James was interrupted by Helen saying loudly, "what have you done to your ears?"

"What's wrong with them?"

"They're kind of purple."

"Oh, that's just the dye. I suppose we'd better take my hair back down to cover them," I said sorrowfully. I had very quickly grown attached to this sophisticated look.

"No, no, we'll think of something," said Helen with a bit of a gleam in her eye. "Stay there." And off she went.

She arrived back with Anna, who whistled when

she saw me, and a couple of cloths and a bottle of turpentine.

"You do that ear," instructed Helen. "And I'll do this one."

I went to meet James with ears that were red, raw and almost bleeding, instead of a rich, glossy, chestnut colour.

But my hair remained up.

Chapter Twenty-Eight

I have to say that walking into that restaurant was one of the most gratifying experiences I'd ever had. James looked up from whatever he was reading and he literally, *literally* did a double take.

"Er, Claire," he said, all of a fluster, "erm, you're looking wonderful."

I smiled in what I hoped was a mysterious, enigmatic, sophisticated way.

"Thank you," I purred.

That'll teach you to leave me, you bastard, I thought as I swung into my seat, giving him an eyeful of my thighs in my sheer, shimmering tights and my short tight black dress.

He couldn't take his eyes off me.

It was wonderful.

I had got a few funny looks as I had walked from where I had parked the car to the restaurant. I suppose I was a bit overdressed for a bright Monday evening, in April, but who cared.

The waiter, a youth in an ill-fitting dinner suit, an alleged Italian, but with a Dublin accent, came rushing over and spent an unnecessary amount of time patting my napkin onto my crotch.

"Er, thank you," I said, when I felt that it had gone on far too long.

"You're welcome," he drawled, as Italian as bacon and cabbage. He winked at me over James's head.

Honestly!

And then I got really paranoid.

Maybe he thought I was a hooker.

Did I look like a prostitute?

I *knew* my dress was too short.

Oh what the hell, I decided.

James smiled at me. A beautiful, warm, admiring, approving smile. And for a moment I saw the man I married.

Then he noticed the young waiter bending down so he could get a better look at my legs under the table and the smile vanished, leaving me feeling bereft.

"Claire." He frowned like a Victorian patriarch. "Cover yourself. Look at the way the waiter is looking at you!"

I reddened.

I felt foolish and embarrassed now in my short dress, instead of sexy and sassy.

Fuck James for making me feel like this!

Behaving like a bloody Amish.

He hadn't always been like that, you know. I could remember a time when the shorter my dress was, the better he liked it.

Well, times, as they say, had changed.

I put my head down and spitefully looked for the most expensive thing on the menu.

"I suppose we should talk about money," I said after the waiter had gone away.

"It's all right," he said. "I'll pay. I'll put it on the card."

"No, James," I said, wondering if he was being deliberately obtuse. "I mean, we have to talk about *our* money. You know, yours and mine, our financial situation."

I spoke slowly and deliberately, as if I was talking to a child.

"Oh, I see." He nodded.

"So, do we have any?" I asked anxiously.

"Money? Of course we do," he said, annoyed. I'd hit him where it hurt. Casting nasturtiums on his ability to provide for his wife and family. Or should I say his wife and families.

"Why wouldn't we have any money?" he asked.

"Well, because of me not working and only getting the poxy maternity pay and with you paying the mortgage and then the rent on another flat and . . . "

"What do you mean, paying the rent on another flat?" he said, in loud and annoyed tones.

"You know, the flat that you and . . . and . . . Denise live in," I said. It nearly killed me to say her name.

"But I've moved back into our flat," he said, looking at me in a slightly baffled way. "Didn't you know?"

Several things occurred to me at once.

Could I fatally wound him with a fork?

Would a woman judge be more lenient?

What would prison food be like?

How would Kate turn out, if her mother murdered her father?

James's voice swam towards me through a haze of murderous rage.

"Claire," he was saying anxiously. "Are you feeling OK?"

I realised that I was gripping my butter knife so hard that my hand hurt. And, although I couldn't see my face, I knew it had gone bright red with fury.

"You mean to tell me," I finally managed to hiss at him, "that you've moved that woman into *my* home."

I thought that I would choke or vomit or do *something* anti-social.

"No, no, Claire," he said. Sounding hurried, anxious, afraid that – heaven forbid – I might cause a bit of a scene. "I've moved back into our flat. But Deni . . . er . . . she hasn't."

"Oh."

I was totally knocked for six. I didn't know what to say. Because I didn't know how I felt.

"I'm not . . . er . . . you know . . . with her anymore. I haven't been for some time."

"Oh."

In a way that was almost worse.

I still wanted to strangle him.

To think that he threw away our marriage, our relationship, for something that hadn't survived even two months of living together.

The *waste*. The sense of pointless loss was almost unbearable.

Then I burst out, "Why didn't anyone tell me?"

What had happened to the highly efficient bush telegraph system that I my friends and I operated?

James spoke to me soothingly.

"Maybe nobody knows yet. I haven't made much of a fuss about it. And I haven't seen much of anyone over the past month," he explained, obviously keen to keep me calm.

He *must* be having a nervous breakdown, I thought. He'd become a spooky, shadowy, Howard Hughes type reclusive figure.

"I've been away on a course," he continued.

"Oh."

All right, then he wasn't having a nervous breakdown. He *hadn't* become a spooky, shadowy, Howard Hughes type reclusive figure.

I might have known. James was far too practical to bother with nervous breakdowns. If they couldn't be justified in financial terms he wasn't interested.

At least that meant that he wasn't away on holidays with fatso Denise that time I rang him.

What a waste of all that angst and misery.

And then the curiosity started burning a hole in me.

What had happened with James and Denise?

I knew I shouldn't ask questions, but I just couldn't help myself.

"So did she kick you out?" I asked. I tried to say it lightly but it just sounded bitter. "Gone back to Mario or Sergio or whatever his name is."

"Actually, no, Claire," said James, looking at me carefully. "I left her."

"Gosh." Bitterness seeped out through my pores. "You're making quite a habit of it. Leaving women, that is," I added viciously, just in case he hadn't understood.

"Yes, Claire, I know what you meant." His tone of voice implied that somehow he felt he was *above* all this. But that he was a decent guy who was prepared to indulge me.

I carried on regardless. "And, anyway, I thought a gentleman would never say that he'd left a woman. I thought it was mannerly to say that she had left you, even if she hadn't."

Even I was amazed at how illogical I was being. I was aware of the edge of hysteria in my voice. But I was powerless to stop. I had no control over my runaway emotions.

"I'm not telling the whole world that I left her," he said tightly, "I'm telling you. You asked me, remember?"

"Well, why aren't you telling the whole world that you left her? I *want* you to tell the whole world that you left her," I said, a dangerous wobble in my voice. "Why should everyone know that you just dumped me – and Kate – and then think that she kicked you out? Why should she be spared the humiliation?"

"Fine, then Claire," he said, sighing loudly at my unreasonable and irrational demands. "If it makes you happy I *will* tell everyone what happened with Denise."

"Good," I said, my bottom lip trembling like jelly.

This was awful! Where had the recovered poised Claire gone? I had tried so hard to stay completely in control with James, not to let him see how much he had hurt me, how devastated I was. But all the pain was so close to the surface. I was on the verge of cracking.

It was all so *embarrassing*. I was very upset and he was in control. The contrast was mortifying.

"I'm going to the ladies," I said. Maybe I could get a grip of myself there.

"No, Claire, wait," said James as I made to stand up. He tried to grab my hand across the table.

I shook his hand away angrily. "Don't touch me," I said tearfully.

Next I'd be saying something like "You lost the right to touch me when you left me."

"You lost the right to touch me when you left me," I found myself saying.

I knew it, I just knew it! The person who had the job of writing my life's dialogue used to work on a very low-budget soap opera.

But I meant it.

I wanted to hurt him badly. I wanted him to feel the same loss that I had felt. To want someone so much that it aches. And to realise that you can't have them.

And most of all I wanted him to feel that it was his *fault*.

Who made it happen?

You did.

"Claire, please sit down," he said, letting go of my hand slowly. He was doing a good impression of looking pale and upset. For a moment I felt guilty. God, I couldn't win.

"Relax, James," I said coldly. "I'm not going to make a scene."

He had the grace to look ashamed.

"That's not what I'm worried about," he said.

"Oh really," I sneered at him.

"Yes, really," he said, sounding a bit more patient. "Look Claire, we've *got* to talk."

"There's nothing left to say," I responded automatically.

Whoops! There I went again. More bloody clichés! Honestly, I could have died. It was so embarrassing.

And I wouldn't mind but it wasn't even true. There was absolutely loads to say.

Whoa, whoa, steady, aisy, hold on, hold on, I told myself. "Isn't calm and civilised discussion the game-plan?" the reasonable part of my brain sweetly asked the argumentative bit. "Well, isn't it?"

"I suppose so," the argumentative part grudgingly conceded. Like a surly teenager.

"Can we at least try to be in control?" asked the reasonable part.

"I must stop," I told myself, taking a deep breath. "I will stop."

"Claire," he said, trying to sound gentle – as he pawed for my hand again. "I know I've treated you badly."

"Badly!" I exploded, before I could stop myself. "Ha! Badly! That's one way of putting it."

Well, so much for being reasonable and in control!

In spite of my pathetic efforts to keep a lid on my emotions the gloves were well and truly off now. All pretence of being calm and grown-up and civilised had gone by the board. Well, all pretence of me being calm and grown-up and civilised had. He still maintained a huge amount of equilibrium.

Equilibrium was one of the things he did best.

"Appallingly, then," he conceded.

He didn't sound very contrite. He sounded as if he was humouring me.

The unfeeling bastard! How could he be so self-contained? It wasn't human.

"How could you have been so irresponsible?" I burst out. I knew that would hurt him more than anything. He could take accusations of unkindness, cruelty, hardheartedness on the chin. But to call him irresponsible was a low blow.

"How could you just have abandoned us? I *needed* you."

I ended on a high impassioned note.

A silence followed.

He sat very still – ominously still – for a moment and some kind of emotion, although not one I was familiar with, flickered across his face.

When he spoke again it became clear that a change had come over him. Something had snapped. The patience well had run dry. He had gone to fetch a packet of tolerance and the cupboard was bare.

No more Mr Nice Guy. Not that he had been much in evidence anyway.

When he spoke it wasn't in his normal voice. But in a nasty singsong flippant tone. "Yip," he said with a long pause between each word. "You. Certainly. Did."

"Wha . . . at?" I asked, a bit taken aback.

I was still immersed in feelings of loss and abandonment but I managed to grasp that something had happened to James. And that this something was not to my advantage. It was immediately obvious that things weren't right when he agreed with me so readily. It was even more immediately obvious that things were very wrong indeed when he agreed with me so readily in such a peculiar tone of voice.

"Oh," he went on, still in the peculiar tone, "I'm just saying how right you are. That's what you want, isn't it? In fact, I'll say it again, will I? You *needed* me."

What had happened? Events had taken a sudden and unexpected turn. I felt as though I had wandered into someone else's discussion. Or as if James had, off his own bat, decided to change channels. I was still knee-deep in the old conversation, the one about James leaving me, and felt pretty wretched about it. But he had flicked over to a new conversation about something totally different. I struggled to catch up with him.

"James, what's going on here?" I asked in confusion.

"What do you mean?" he replied unpleasantly.

"I mean, why are you being so weird all of a sudden?" I said nervously.

"Weird," he said in a thoughtful, weighty tone and looked around the room as if he was appealing to an invisible audience. "She says I'm being weird."

This from the man who was chatting to people who weren't there.

"Well, you are," I said. In fact he was getting weirder by the second.

"All I said was that I needed you and . . . "

"I heard what you said," he interrupted angrily, the singsong flippant tone abruptly gone.

He leant across the table and fixed me with a furious face. "Here goes," I thought.

Relief mingled with my fear. At least now I'd know what the hell was up with him.

"You said that you needed me." He made some kind of narky, tisky sound and threw his eyes heavenward. "What an understatement!"

He paused – for impact? – and stared at me, his face hard and angry.

I didn't dare speak. I was enthralled. What was coming next?

"I *know* you needed me," he threw at me. "You needed me all the bloody time, for some bloody thing or other. How could I *not* know?"

I could only stare at him.

He didn't often get angry. So, on the special occasions when he did it was usually quite a treat. A bit spectacular. But not today. I didn't know where this anger of his came from but the message he seemed anxious to convey was that I was the one at fault.

That wasn't part of the script.

I was the one in the right. He was the bastard. That's the way it was.

"You needed me for *everything*," he almost shouted.

I think I should point out to you at this juncture that James never shouted. He'd never even almost shouted.

"You demanded constant attention," he went on. "And constant reinforcement. And you never gave a damn about me and how I felt and what I might need."

I stared openmouthed at him.

I couldn't believe what I was hearing.

Why was he attacking me?

He was the one who'd left me, right?

So if there was any accusing to be done, I was the correct person for the job.

"James . . . " I said faintly.

He ignored me and continued ranting and jabbing his finger at me.

"You were impossible. I was exhausted from you. I don't know how I stayed with you as long as I did. And I don't know how *anyone* could live with you."

Now lookit here! That was too much. Anger surged through me.

Talk about a kangaroo court.

I was being done a terrible injustice.

And I wasn't letting him get away with it.

I was *livid*.

"Oh, I see," I said, absolutely furious. "So now it's all my fault. I made you have an affair. I made you leave me. Well that's funny, because I don't actually recall holding a gun to your head. It must have slipped my mind."

It's true what they say. Sarcasm really is the lowest form of wit. But I couldn't help myself. He was criticising me. And I was burning, *scalded* with a sense of injustice.

"No, Claire," he said. He actually spoke through gritted teeth. Which I'd never seen anyone do before. I thought it was just a figure of speech. "Of course you didn't make me do anything."

"So then what are you saying?" I demanded.

I had a funny cold feeling in the pit of my stomach. I knew it was fear.

"I'm saying that living with you was a bit like living with a demanding child. You always wanted to go out. As though life was one big long party. And it was, for you. You were always laughing and enjoying yourself. So I had to be the grown up one. I had to worry about money and bills. You were so *selfish*. I had to be the one who reminded you at one in the morning, at a dinner party, that we both had to be at work the next day. And then I had to put up with you calling me a boring bastard."

I was dumbfounded at this torrent from James.

Apart from its unexpectedness, I felt that it was so unfair.

"James, that's the way it worked for us," I protested. "I was the funny one, you were the serious one. Everyone knew that. I was the light relief, the silly one who made you laugh and unwind. You were the strong one. That's the way we both wanted it. That's the way it was. And that's why it was so good."

"But it wasn't," he said. "I was so bloody tired of being strong."

"And I didn't ever call you a boring bastard," I exclaimed suddenly. I knew that something he had said there was wrong.

"It doesn't matter," he said irritably. "You made me feel like one."

"Yes, but you said that I . . . " I started to protest.

"Oh, for God's sake, Claire," he burst out angrily. "There you go again. Trying to score points. Can't you just let it be? Can't you, for once, just once, accept blame?"

"Yes, but . . . " I said weakly.

I wasn't even sure what I should accept blame for.

Never mind. I didn't have time to think about it. James drew another breath and was off again. And I had to give what he was saying all my attention.

"You just made messes." He sighed. "And I had to clean them up."

"That's not true!" I shouted.

"Well, believe me that's how it felt," he said unkindly. "You just don't want to admit that it's true. There was always a drama. Or a trauma. And I was always the one who had to deal with it."

I was silent. Totally dumbfounded.

"And you know, Claire," he continued solemnly. "You just don't magically wake up one morning and know how to be an adult. You don't know overnight how to pay bills. You work at it. You work at being responsible."

"I know how to pay bills," I protested. "I'm not a total moron, you know."

"So how come it was me who had to take care of that end of things?" he asked primly.

"James," my head whirled as I searched for ways to defend myself. "I did try to help."

I distinctly remembered a time when I had sat with James as he self-importantly flicked through cheque stubs and cash point receipts and tap-tap-tapped with a calculator. I offered to help him that day. And he told me with a suggestive twinkle in his eye that he would stick to what he was good at and that I should stick to what I was good at. And then, if I remember correctly, and I'm sure I do, we had sex on the desk. In fact the bank statements and the Access and Visa bills for July 1991 still bear certain rather interesting imprints. But I couldn't find the nerve to remind him of that.

"I really did offer to help," I protested again. "But you wouldn't let me. You said that you'd be much better at it because you had a head for figures."

"And you just accepted that?" he asked nastily, shaking his head slightly as if he could hardly believe how crass and stupid I'd been.

"Well . . . yes, I suppose," I said, feeling foolish.

He was right. I had let him worry about threatening letters and disconnection notices and all that. But I'd really thought he wanted to do it. Not, that there were ever any threatening letters or disconnection notices or the like. James was far too organised to allow that to happen. I thought he liked being in control. That it would be less haphazard if only one of us was involved. How wrong I was.

I wished I could turn the clock back. If only I'd paid more attention to things like the date we paid our mortgage.

"I'm sorry," I said awkwardly. "I thought you wanted to do it. I would have done it if I'd known you didn't want to."

"Why would I want to do it?" he asked nastily. "What person in their right mind would enjoy being entirely responsible for the bills of a household?"

"You're right, of course," I admitted.

"Well," said James, sounding a bit warmer. "I suppose it wasn't really your fault. You were always a bit thoughtless."

I swallowed back a retort. Now was not the time to antagonise him.

But I wasn't *thoughtless*. I know I wasn't.

James had other ideas however.

"If only you hadn't been thoughtless when it really mattered," he mused. "Because the problems in our marriage weren't just about you not pulling your weight. It was about the way you made me feel."

"What do you mean?" I asked. I braced myself for another round of accusations. Accusations that I didn't want to hear. But ones that I had to listen to if I wanted to make sense of why he left me.

"Well, it was always about you, wasn't it?" he said.

"How? In what way?" I asked bewildered.

"I'd come home from work, after having had a terrible day. And you wouldn't talk to me about it. You'd just go on about your day, telling me stories and expecting me to laugh at them."

"But I would ask," I protested. "And you always told me it was too boring to explain. I only told you funny stories because I knew you'd had a horrible day and I wanted to cheer you up."

"Don't try and justify yourself," he said forcefully. "It was so obvious that you never wanted to hear anything unpleasant. All you wanted were good times. You had no interest at all in hearing about anything unpleasant."

"James . . . " I said feebly.

What could I say?

His mind was so made up.

And I swear to you, this was all news to me. I had never suspected that he had felt this way. And I had no idea that I had behaved in such an insufferable way.

James wouldn't by any chance be interested in absolving himself of all guilt in this sorry fiasco, would he?

James wouldn't, by some freak chance, be manipulating me in any way?

I had to find out.

"James," I said in a little voice. "I'm sorry to ask this, but you wouldn't be trying to avoid the blame for leaving me? You know, by blaming me and making it all my fault."

"Oh for God's sake," snorted James. "That's exactly the kind of childish, selfish response I should have expected from you."

"Sorry," I whispered. "I shouldn't even have asked."

Another silence.

"Why didn't you tell me?" I burst out. "We were so close. It was so beautiful."

"We weren't so close and it wasn't so beautiful," he said bluntly.

"It was. We were," I protested.

He's taken enough away from me, I thought. He's not going to take my memories.

"Claire, if it was that beautiful, why did I leave you?" he asked quietly.

And, really, what could I say? He was so right.

But, hold on. He was off again. More accusations. His grievance was an unstoppable force.

"Claire, you were absolutely impossible. I had to keep so much from you. I had to carry so much worry on my own because I felt that you couldn't cope."

"Why didn't you try me?" I asked sadly.

He didn't even bother to answer.

"You were such a bloody handful. I'd come home from work, exhausted and you'd have decided on the spur of the moment to have a dinner party for eight people and I'd have to run around like a blue-arsed fly, buying beer and uncorking wine and whipping cream."

"James, that only happened once. And it was for six people, not eight. And it was for your friends who came down from Aberdeen. It was supposed to be a surprise for you. I was the one who whipped the cream."

"Look, I'm not going to get into specifics," he said testily. "Doubtless you can try and justify anything I say to you, but you were still in the wrong."

"I *can* try and justify anything I did because I feel that the things I did were right," I thought confusedly to myself. But I didn't say anything.

"I thought you liked me being spontaneous," I said timidly. "I thought you even encouraged it."

"Well, that's the way you would see it," he said sneeringly. "I suppose that's the way you want to see it," he said, a bit more kindly.

A smiling waiter approached our table with a lively gait. But froze in his tracks and then made a sharp right turn to another table when he noticed the glower that James gave him.

"So you thought you'd help me to grow up. You thought that if you left me that it might shock me into it," I said, realisation dawning gradually and unevenly. "What a pity you had to use such extreme measures."

"Oh, that wasn't why I left you," he said. "It wasn't done to make you grow up. Frankly, I didn't think that was possible. But I wanted to be with someone who cared about me. Someone who would take care of me. And Denise did."

I swallowed back the hurt.

"I *cared* for you. I *loved* you." I had to make him believe me.

"You never gave me the chance to help you. You never gave me the opportunity to be strong. I *am* strong now. I *could* have taken care of you."

He looked at me. He was wearing his fatherly, indulgent face.

"Maybe you could have," he said, quite kindly. "Maybe you could have."

"And now we'll never know," I thought out loud, my heart almost breaking with a sense of loss, missed opportunities, of being misunderstood.

There was a bit of an odd pause. Then he spoke.

"Er, ah, I suppose not," he said hurriedly.

So now what?

I felt sick, sad, sorry.

Sad for both of us.

Sad for James who had carried so much worry on his own.

Sad for me for being so misunderstood.

Or was it sad for me for being so misunderstanding?

Sad for Kate, the innocent victim.

"You must have thought I'd go to pieces completely without you," I asked him. I felt hot, angry with shame and mortification.

"Yes, I suppose I did," he admitted. "Well, you can hardly blame me, can you?"

"No," I said hanging my head.

"But I didn't, did I?" I said. Tears poured down my face. "I coped without you. And I'll manage fine in the future without you."

"I can see that," he nodded and looked with mild amusement at my wet, tear-streaked face. "Oh, you silly thing, come here." He kind of pulled me awkwardly across the table, pushing the flower vase and the salt and pepper holders aside, and patted my head onto his shoulder in a supposedly comforting manner.

I left my head there for a moment. I felt a bit uncomfortable and foolish. I sat up straight again. It would hardly do my cause any good if I continued to behave like a child needing comfort.

But that didn't seem to please him either.

"What's wrong?" he asked, sounding a bit annoyed.

"What do you mean?" I asked, wondering what I'd done now.

"Why are you pulling away from me? I may have left you for another woman, but do I have rabies or what?" He gave a small smirk at his little joke. Which I weakly tried to return.

"Er, no," I said, totally confused. What did he *want* from me? I couldn't please him whatever way I behaved.

I was exhausted.

Things were much more straightforward when he was a faithless, philandering bastard. I knew where I was then. I'd understood that situation. But he must be right. I must have enjoyed being irresponsible. Otherwise why couldn't I accept blame for my part in the marriage break-up?

But it was hard to accept that it was all my fault. He was the one who left me. He was the one who broke my heart.

Nothing that I had expected to happen had happened. I'd thought that he might ask if I would come back to him. Either that or for him to continue behaving like a total bastard. I certainly hadn't expected to end up apologising for causing this situation all by myself.

Things had been black and white. He had been the darkness and I was the light. He was the wrongdoer and I was the victim.

Now it was all mixed up.

I was the wrongdoer and he was the victim.

It didn't feel right.

That was hard for me, but I was prepared to give it a chance.

"Look James," I said swallowing back tears. "This is all a bit of a shock. I need to think about what you've said. I'm going now. I'll talk to you tomorrow."

And with that I hopped up and made for the door

leaving James, sitting at the table, mouthing silently like an agitated goldfish.

"Good on you, love," said one of the waiters to me as I swept past. "He's not your type, at all at all."

I drove home at high speed, jumping red lights and risking the life and limb of pedestrians and other motorists alike.

Chapter Twenty-Nine

I put my key in the door and, with a marvellous display of their psychic abilities, the kitchen door opened and Anna, Helen and Mum rushed out into the hall to greet me. Either that or they heard me parking the car.

"How did you get on?" asked Mum.

Obviously they were all at a very loose end at the moment. My real-life soap opera wouldn't have been afforded so much interest if they'd had anything better to do.

"What happened?" shouted Helen.

"Oh marvellous news," I yelled tearfully, as I started up the stairs to see Kate.

"Oh good." Mum beamed.

"Well, you know the way James left me and went off and lived with someone else and didn't even know Kate's name. Well, it's all OK now. Because it was my fault. I was asking for it. Apparently I was begging for it. Down on my knees gagging for it!"

I swung into my room, leaving three astonished faces at the bottom of the stairs, their mouths three ohs of surprise.

Kate started roaring when she saw me. And just for the hell of it, I decided to join in. I was not finding this blame-acceptance thing easy, as you may have gathered.

But I took my frustration with the situation out on Helen, Anna and Mum, when I should have voiced it to James. And that wasn't fair to the girls and Mum. A little voice reminded me that I had tried to tell James about it and he'd said it was further proof of my childishness. Well, he was probably right. He usually was.

What a pain in the arse, I thought rebelliously.

And now I had to stop being resentful and rebellious. I was no longer a twenty-nine-year-old adolescent. If I was going to be a sensitive, considerate, caring adult then I might as well start now.

I could begin by being responsive to Kate's needs.

"What can I get you, my darling?" I asked. I wondered if that would be *mature* enough for James. I must stop!

He was right, I was wrong.

I tried to calm the crying child in my arms.

"Clean nappy perchance? Or can I interest you in a bottle? And we have a wonderful selection of attention and affection? All are available. You only have to ask."

But no, I was even doing that wrong. According to James, people shouldn't even have to ask me for what they wanted. If I was really selfless I should know.

Just to be on the safe side I gave her the lot. I changed her nappy, fed her and told her she was more beautiful than Claudia Schiffer.

Mum, Anna and Helen materialised in the room. They crept in cautiously, wondering how mad I had gone.

"Oh, hi," I said when I saw the first tentative head appearing round the door. "Come in, come in. Sorry about that little display in the hall. I was upset. I had no right to take it out on you three."

"Oh, that's fine then," said Helen. The three of them marched in and took up residence on the bed while I tended to Kate and told them the story of my evening.

"So, in a funny way, knowing how difficult I was makes the fact that he left me a bit easier," I told them. "You know, at least it makes sense."

"Claire," said Mum slowly. "I'm sure that you couldn't have been as bad as he makes out."

"I know, I don't understand that either," I admitted. "But when I told him that, he said that was exactly the way he would have expected me to react."

There really wasn't anything anyone else could say.

James had me boxed in good and neatly.

That night was terrible. As bad as the early days when James had first left me. When the others finally left, having given up trying to reassure me that I couldn't be that bad, I couldn't sleep. I lay flat on my back, staring into the darkness. Questions buzzed round in my head.

This had all come as a terrible shock. I'd never known that I was so selfish and immature. No one else ever complained before. Granted, I was high-spirited. And maybe a bit noisy and lively. But I honestly thought I was considerate of other people's feelings.

The thought crossed my mind that maybe, just maybe, James was perhaps exaggerating how bad I had been. Was even making it up. I dismissed that idea again almost as quickly. That was just me trying to escape the blame. Why would James do something like that if it wasn't true? As he said himself – and his words kept going round and round in my head, "if I had been happy, why would I have left?"

I admit that I absolutely hated being wrong. I was really bad at graciously admitting that I was in error. I felt burning, raw, caught-out, mortified. I had been so smug. I thought that I had right on my side. It was very humbling to find that I hadn't.

Even when I was a little girl and didn't get all my spellings right at school, I found it very hard to bow my head and swallow and say, "you are right and I am wrong."

Well, practice makes perfect.

I finally slept.

Chapter Thirty

Dad woke me the following morning by thrusting a huge manila envelope under my nose. "Here," he said ill-temperedly. "Take this. I'm late for work."

"Thanks Dad," I said sleepily, dragging myself up in the bed, as I pushed my hair out of my eyes.

I looked at the letter. It had a London postmark. With a little cold thrill, I realised it was the deeds to the flat and all the other documents that James had asked to be send over.

I toyed with the idea of ringing the Vatican to report a miracle. Surely nothing had ever arrived from London to Dublin that quickly ever before?

I toyed with the idea of ringing James instead.

It might be better if I rang James.

Though I'd probably get a better reception at the Vatican.

I found the number of The LiffeySide in the phone book. Some woman answered. I asked to speak to James.

She told me to hold on a moment while she went to get him. While I was waiting I could hear noises in the background that sounded like machine-gun fire. Now, granted, it might only have been the washing-machine, but if you knew The LiffeySide and the street it was on, you'd be more inclined to put your money on it being machine-gun fire.

"Hello," said James. He sounded all officious and important.

"James, it's me," I told him.

"Claire," he said attempting to sound friendly. "I was just about to ring you."

"Were you?" I asked politely, wondering why that was. Had he just remembered some other awful way I used to treat him? Had he omitted some important criticism about my behaviour in public that he had meant to tell me last night?

Now, now, I warned myself. Be selfless and adult about this.

"Would you believe it?" he asked disbelievingly. "Not one paper shop in this city opens before nine o'clock. I've been trying to get the FT since I got up, not a chance."

"Well, well, would you credit that?" I said, feeling a surge of irritation. But I tried to hide it. I had to bear in mind that although the *Financial Times* wasn't important to me, it was important to another human being, namely James, so, as an altruistic, caring, empathetic person, I *should* care.

"Was that why were you just about to ring me?" I asked. "To tell me that?"

"No, no no. Why was it? Oh yes," he said, remembering. "I wanted to see if you were feeling all right after last night. I realise that I may have been a little bit . . . well . . . *hard* on you. I can see now that you had no idea that you were behaving so selfishly and thoughtlessly. My home truths may have come as a bit of a shock to you."

"Well, a bit," I admitted. The confusion started up again. I felt like a suspect being interrogated by two policemen, one nice one and one nasty one. Just when I'd got used to one of them being nasty to me, the other starts by being extra nice and making me want to cry and hug him. Except there was only one James. But the effect was the same. Now that he was being nice to me I wanted to, yes, you guessed it, cry and hug him.

"You weren't deliberately awful," he went on. "You just weren't aware."

"No," I sniffed. "I wasn't."

I was so *glad* that he was being nice to me at last. I could have cried with relief.

"Must try harder," he said with a little laugh. "Isn't that right?"

"Er, yes, I suppose so. Good news, James," I said, getting to the point of my phone call.

"What's that?" he asked. He sounded pleased and indulgent.

"The documents have arrived!" I said triumphantly. "I could hardly believe it. It must be a first for the Irish postal system."

"So?" he asked sharply.

Oh God, I thought, I've annoyed him again. I see what he means. I seem to do it without even realising it.

"So, it's good . . . " I said limply. "We needn't waste any more time. We can start sorting things out immediately."

"Oh." He sounded a bit dazed. A bit stupid.

"Oh," he said again. "Right. Fine."

"Why don't you come over here?" I suggested. "No boiling oil, I promise you."

I forced myself to laugh in a gently humouring way.

As though the very suggestion that he might suffer any kind of injury at my hands or at the hands of my family was ludicrous.

"Fine," he said shortly. "I'll be with you in an hour."

And he hung up! Just like that.

A brief thought flickered across my brain.

Was James schizophrenic?

Or if there was any history of madness in his family?

I was as sure as hell finding it difficult to keep up with all these mood changes.

Something had to be causing it.

Maybe I'd find out when he arrived. Meanwhile I was going to have a sneak preview of the deeds just to see if I actually had any rights at all.

Precisely one hour later, the doorbell rang. It was James.

He greeted me with a little smile and an enquiry after Kate's health.

"Well, why don't you ask her yourself?" I asked him.

"Oh, er, fine then," he said.

We went into the dining-room where Kate was. James hesitantly tickled her. I went to the kitchen to make coffee.

I reappeared with the coffee and turned to James with a smile. "Right then," I said pleasantly. "Will we start?"

I gestured to the documents which were spread out on the table.

We both sat down.

"I thought it would be best if we started with the deeds to the flat first," I said.

"OK," he said faintly.

"Now, if you look at this clause here," I said, pointing to one that referred to selling the flat before the mortgage was paid off, "you'll see that . . . "

I launched into explanations and suggestions, peppered with the odd bit of legalese. I was proud of myself. I sounded as if I knew exactly what I was talking about. Absently, I hoped that I was impressing him. Even though we had split up it was important to me that he started to think of me as a capable woman and not some spoilt, dizzy, bimbo.

After a while I noticed that he wasn't paying any attention to what I was saying.

He just sat back in his chair and looked at my face, not at the document that I was so painstakingly explaining to him.

I stopped mid disclaimer-clause and said, "James, what's wrong? Why aren't you paying attention?"

He ruffled my hair affectionately – which came as quite a surprise, let me tell you – and said with a little smile, "You can stop now, Claire. I'm convinced."

"Convinced about what?" I asked him.

What the hell was he talking about now?

"I'm convinced that you've changed. You don't have to keep up this act."

"What act?" I asked blankly.

"You know," he said smiling into my eyes. "This pretence that we're going to sell the flat and settle on a maintenance agreement for Kate. You can stop now."

I didn't say anything. What on earth could I say?

"It's not an act," I squeaked.

"Claire," he said, smiling indulgently. "Stop it! I must admit you really had me going at one stage. I nearly believed that you were serious. Did you really have to go through the charade of getting the deeds sent over? Wasn't that a bit over the top?"

"James," I said faintly.

He seemed to take this as some kind of capitulation. He put his arms around me and pulled me to him. I sat there with my head poised stiffly on his shoulder.

"Look, I know you've been very difficult. Bloody difficult," he said. I could hear the rueful smile in his voice. "But I can see that you're making an effort. I can see how hard you're trying to convince me that you're responsible and grown-up and considerate now."

"I am?" I asked.

"Yes," he said kindly. He pulled away from me and looked into my eyes. "You are."

"So, we can get rid of these for a start." He rustled the papers on the table and pushed them all into an untidy pile.

"Why?" I asked.

"Because we won't be selling the flat." He smiled.

He looked a bit more carefully at my white, shocked face.

"Oh God." He slapped his hand dramatically to his forehead. "You haven't realised, have you?"

"No," I said.

He grabbed me forcefully by the shoulders and put his face close to mine. "I love you," he said with a little laugh. "You little silly, hadn't you realised?"

"No," I said, feeling as if I might burst into tears.

Isn't it odd how relief can sometimes feel very much like dread?

How happiness can feel like disappointment?

"Why did you think I came to Dublin?" He shook me gently by the shoulders and gave me that same indulgent smile.

"I don't know," I faltered. "Maybe to tidy up loose ends."

"I suppose you thought I'd never forgive you for the way you behaved?"

Actually, no, I wasn't thinking anything of the sort, I thought.

"But I *have* forgiven you," he told me nicely. "I'm prepared to make a go of things in the future. I'm sure things will be very different because you've grown up so much."

I nodded mutely.

Why wasn't I happy?

He still loved me.

He had never stopped loving me.

I had driven him away.

But I was different now and things could be fixed.

Wasn't that what I wanted?

Well, wasn't it?

He looked at my silent, shocked face and chucked me under the chin.

"You're not still put out about that business with Denise, are you?" he asked, as if that was a totally ludicrous idea.

"Well, actually I am," I said in a little voice. I felt that I had no right to complain about anything now that he was being so nice to me.

"But it was nothing," he protested, laughingly. "It was just a reaction to the way you made me feel. I'm sure that you won't make that mistake again." He smiled as if it was funny.

But it wasn't.

"Er, right, James," I said. I felt as if my head was going to explode. I had to get away from him for a while.

"James," I said, faintly. "This has come as a terrible . . . "

"Surprise!" he interjected. "I know. I know."

"I need to be on my own to think about things a bit."

"What's there to think about?" he asked lightly.

"James," I said. "You hurt me an awful lot. Hurt me and humiliated me. I can't just bounce out of that feeling to please you."

"Oh dear," he sighed. "We're back to 'poor Claire' all over again. I thought you'd changed. What about the ways you hurt and humiliated me?"

"But I never meant to . . . "

"Well, I never set out to hurt you either," he replied. A slightly impatient tone in his voice. "It just happened."

"But you said you *loved* Denise," I said, remembering the bit that hurt most of all.

"I *thought* I loved her," he said carefully, as if he was explaining something to a very young child. "But it turned out that I didn't."

There was a pause.

Then he spoke.

"Fine, all right!" he said belligerently. "You want me to admit that I made a mistake. Fine, I'll do it. Just to show you how committed I am to making this marriage work."

He paused and said in a singsong voice, sounding like a little boy, the type of little boy that you'd like to kill, "'I Made a Mistake.' Will that do you?"

"Er, thank you," I said politely.

Would he please just *go*.

"Of course, if you're going to hang onto grudges and grievances then there's no point in my being here, is there?" he asked.

"If that's the case I'll just go straight to the airport and go back to London and I'll never refer to this again."

"No, don't do that." I felt panicky at the thought of him leaving me again.

I also felt panicky about the thought of him staying.

This was too much to cope with.

The fucker left me out of the blue.

He arrived back and told me it was all my fault that he left me.

But that he still loved me and wanted to try again.

Was that the behaviour of a logical person?

"Claire," he said, back to the gentle nice-guy James. "I can see how overwhelmed you are by all of this. It's perfectly understandable. You thought you were all alone. And now you find that you have your old happy life back. It must be hard to take on board all at once."

"That's right," I mumbled.

"So, I'll leave you by yourself for a couple of hours."

"Thanks," I sagged with relief.

"I'll see about plane tickets. What day would you like to fly back to London?"

"Oh, I don't know." Panic gripped me again. I didn't want to go back to London. At least I didn't want to go back with James.

"No time like the present, eh?" He winked. "How long will it take you to pack?"

"Oh James, I don't know," I said, feeling horrorstruck. "Ages, probably, what with all Kate's stuff and that."

"Oh yes, Kate," he said, as if he'd just remembered her. "I'd better book her on the plane too."

"Well, don't do anything just yet," I said. "Give me a little bit of time to sort things out."

"Well," he said frowning, "I'm missing work by being here. So I'd like to get back as soon as possible, now that we've got things sorted out."

"I'll talk to you later about it," I said, guiding him towards the front door.

"Well, don't take too long about it," he said, "after all . . . "

"Time is money, I know, I know," I wearily finished off the sentence for him.

I closed the door behind him and stood for a moment, leaning against the door, feeling quite weak.

"Is he gone?" hissed a voice.

It was Mum, sticking her head out of her bedroom and looking down at me in the hall.

"Yes," I said.

"What's wrong?" she asked, taking in my shocked appearance.

"Nothing," I said faintly.

"Good," she said.

"James told me he still loves me," I said blankly.

"What!" she screeched.

"I hope you told him where to stick it," shouted a voice from behind Mum.

"Claire, Claire," said Mum, running down the stairs, "come in. Sit down. Tell me all about it. This is great news."

She guided me to the kitchen.

"Where's Kate?" she asked.

"In the dining-room," I said, sitting down weakly at the kitchen table.

"I'll get her," said Mum and off she ran.

She was back in a moment, her face all eager and agog.

"So what did he say?" she demanded impatiently

"He said that he still loves me and wants me back," I said expressionlessly.

"Well, isn't that great?" exclaimed Mum.

"I suppose," I said doubtfully.

"And what was the situation with this Denise one?" she asked, looking at me carefully.

"Apparently, he never loved her," I said quietly. "He only turned to her when he felt that he wasn't getting any attention and care and love from me."

"And it's all over with her?" asked Mum.

"Yes," I said.

"Do you believe him?" she asked.

"Funnily enough I do," I said.

"Well, that's fine then," said Mum.

"Is it?" I asked.

Mum was silent for a few moments. She was thinking about something.

When she spoke it was in a funny solemn tone of voice.

"Claire," she said, "don't make the mistake of letting pride get in the way of forgiveness. You still love him. He still loves you. Don't throw it all away just because your feelings are hurt."

I remained silent. And she continued speaking. A misty faraway look in her eyes.

"Lots of marriages go through hiccups," she said. "And people get over them. They learn to forgive. And after a while they even learn to forget. And the marriage is usually stronger afterwards, if you work at it and stay together."

Oh no! I thought. I recognise this scenario. This is the one where the mother reveals to the daughter that the mother had an affair many years ago with someone like her husband's best friend. Or, more likely, that the daughter's father had an affair with someone. ("What? You mean Dad had an affair?") And the mother had been all set to leave him and take the children with her ("You were only a babe in

478

arms"). But the mother didn't leave. She forgave him. The father was distraught with contrition. And now their marriage was stronger than ever.

But if she had been about to tell me something like that she seemed to change her mind. The misty look cleared from her eyes.

She returned to the present.

"It'll take time for all the hurt to go away," she said. "You can't expect it to just disappear instantly. But, given time, it really will go."

"I don't know, Mum," I mumbled. "This feels all wrong."

"In what way?" she asked.

"I don't know . . . " I sighed. "There's no feeling of . . . of . . . of *triumph*. Of victory. And I still feel angry with him."

"It's fine to still feel angry with him," she said. "And you have plenty of right to feel angry with him. But talk it over with him. Maybe you could both go for marriage guidance counselling. But don't let the anger blind you to everything else. After all this is the father of your child we're talking about. If you can't swallow the anger on your behalf, think about Kate. Do it for her. Are you going to deprive your child of her father just because you're angry?"

She ended on a very impassioned note.

And before I could respond she was off again.

More impassioned invective.

"And as for wanting to feel triumph or victory at getting him back. That's so empty. So hollow. It really *is* childish to want to be a winner in this. There are no winners or losers in a situation like this. If you get your marriage back in working order then you will be a winner. You *will* be victorious!"

She should get a job writing speeches for revolutionaries. This was stirring stuff!

"All right," I said a bit doubtfully, "if you're sure."

"Oh I am," she said confidently. "Your marriage was very good for a while. Fair enough, you encountered problems. And they weren't dealt with very well. But you've probably both learnt from this."

"I suppose," I said.

"And it just goes to show that you can't have been as bad as he makes out if he wants you back," she grinned.

But I didn't find it funny.

I was still finding it hard to believe that I had been that difficult at all.

Who was it that said, "Be careful what you wish for. You might get it."

And some saint or other said, "There are more tears caused by answered prayers than unanswered ones."

I could see what they meant.

I had been so hurt. I had loved him so much. And I had wanted James and my marriage and my old life back. And now that I had it, I wasn't so sure what all the fuss was about in the first place.

Why?

I was being given my marriage back, but first of all I had to accept that I was immature and difficult and selfish. And that I had been a burden to James. And I was finding that very, very difficult. I mean, I knew it must be true. There was no other reason for him to have left me. But if I wasn't even sure what I was doing wrong, then how the hell could I possibly avoid repeating it?

I still felt great humiliation and hurt about him shagging that fat cow. But he wouldn't let me tell him. I felt as if I couldn't whinge about it because it made me look selfish and immature. I couldn't win.

I knew I loved him. But I couldn't really remember what it was that I loved about him. He seemed so . . . so . . . so *pompous*. Was he always like that? So sort of humourless and wintry.

And what was the future going to be like?

Would I be afraid to make flippant remarks and tell him funny stories?

Would I be afraid to lean on him and feel taken care of, the way I used to, in case he felt alone and uncared for?

Our roles had been reversed.

And I didn't know how we should behave towards each other.

Everything would have to be relearned. It was very frightening.

What was wrong with the way it had been?

Well, plenty, obviously, if you listened to James.

But I had liked it like that. And I wasn't sure that it could work any differently.

However, there was only one way to find out. And that was to go back with him and try again.

I'd got to do it, if only for Kate.

It was worth trying. Because it had been so good.

But right now it was terrible.

I still felt so raw and angry and humiliated. I

wanted to give him a thump every time he said how childish I was.

Fine then. Deep breath. Squaring of shoulders.

I would go back to London with him.

Kate was entitled to her daddy.

And I was going to get a chance to put things right.

Funny that. You want something so badly it hurts. And then you get it, but it needs so much restoration and renovation and knocking down of walls and rewiring of electricity and new plumbing put in that you think, fuck it, I don't want it any more. I'll settle for something a lot smaller, with no garden, but at least it's *finished*.

Mum was still sitting looking at me. Her expression was one of anxiety.

"It's OK Mum. I *am* going to go back to him. I will try again."

There really didn't seem to be anything else to say.

I stood up and sighed. "I'd better ring James and tell him that I'm coming back."

I went to the phone. I felt as if I was about to face a firing squad. I rang The LiffeySide.

"James," I said when he answered, "I've been thinking about what we talked about and I've made a decision."

"Which is?" he demanded brusquely.

"I'll come back. I'll try again."

"Good," he said. I could hear the faint smile in his voice. "Good. We'll try harder this time, eh? "

"And no more Denise?" I asked.

"No more anyone, if things work out," he said.

I didn't like the veiled threat in that.

"James," I said nervously, "you know, I'm not finding this easy. I still feel betrayed and hurt. And that won't go immediately."

"No," he agreed, in his ultra-reasonable tone. "Maybe not immediately. But you must work on getting rid of those feelings, mustn't you. There's no future in this if you can't forgive me."

"I know," I said, almost sorry that I had mentioned it.

Then I took a deep breath.

"You were wrong too, weren't you?"

"I've already admitted that," he said coldly. "Are we going to have to go through this every day for the rest of our lives?"

"Well, no . . . but . . . " I said.

"But nothing," he said. "It's in the past now. We have to forget it and look to the future."

That's a lot easier for you than it is for me, I thought. But I didn't say it. There was no point. It was getting me nowhere.

"Well, when should I book the tickets for going back to London?" he said, breaking my resentful silence.

"Oh James, I don't know. I'll need a couple of days to get everything sorted out," I said.

The thought of leaving was horrifying.

"Claire, I can't wait a couple of days more," he said irritably, "I've got a lot of work on at the moment."

"Well, aren't you lucky that I agreed to come back to you in just two days?" I asked bitterly. "What if I'd put up a fight and it had taken you a whole week to convince me?"

"Now, Claire," he said smoothly, "there's no good in thinking like that. I have convinced you. That's the main thing."

A pause.

"I *have* convinced you, haven't I?" he asked. And if I hadn't known better, I'd almost have said that he sounded uncertain.

"Yes, James," I said dully, "you've convinced me."

"It'll be fine," he said, "you'll see."

"Yes," I said, feeling far from sure, but I didn't have the energy or the inclination to disagree with him.

"James, you might as well go back to London straight away," I suggested. "I'll come early next week with Kate."

"Why will it take you a whole week?" He sounded annoyed.

"Well . . . I've got people to say goodbye to . . . and things . . . " I faltered.

"I'd prefer if you came sooner," he said sternly.

"No, James, really, I'm sorry, but . . . I need time to adjust," I said weakly.

"Just so long as you don't change your mind," he said, with what sounded like a forced guffaw.

"I won't," I said wearily, knowing that I couldn't. "I won't."

"Good!" he said. "Well then, I suppose I'll head back to London immediately. If I go to the airport now I'll be able to pick up a flight. I wonder if I can get a refund on tonight's accommodation?"

"What a pity I didn't make up my mind and tell you sooner," I said. "It's probably too late now to get your money back for tonight."

"Never mind," he said kindly, "it couldn't be helped."

What an asshole!

I was being totally sarcastic!

"I'll call you tonight when I get home," he promised.

"You do that," I said quietly.

"Give my love to Kate," he said.

"I will."

"And see you soon."

"Yes, see you soon."

Chapter Thirty-One

"So when are you leaving?" asked Mum.

"You're *leaving?*" screeched Helen.

"Yes," I mumbled, aware of how weak and pathetic I must look in her eyes.

"I think you're mental," she exclaimed.

"But Helen, you don't understand . . . " I struggled to explain to her. "It wasn't his fault. He had a really hard time with me. I was so demanding and childish. And he couldn't cope. So he looked elsewhere out of desperation."

"And you believe that?" she said, sneering in disgust. "You're mad. It's bad enough that he was shagging someone else but for him to blame it all on you, well, that's just totally *crazy.* Have you no self-respect?"

"Helen, it's more important than self-respect," I insisted, desperately trying to convince her. Maybe if I convinced her, I might even convince myself.

"He's the father of my child. And we were happy together. Very happy," – because we had been – "and if we work at it, we can be again."

"So how come you look so miserable?" she demanded. "Shouldn't you be happy? The man you love is taking you back. Even though he was unfaithful to you."

"Helen, that's enough," said Mum in a warning tone. "You can't understand. You've never been married. You've never had a child."

"Well, I certainly never want to, if it turns me into a total basket case like her," she stormed, looking at me with contempt.

"You're *mad*!"

And she thumped out of the room.

Silence followed.

"She has a point," Mum eventually said.

"What do you mean?" I asked listlessly.

"Well, you don't seem very, well . . . *happy* exactly. You're not having second thoughts, are you?"

"No," I sighed. "I'm not. I owe it to all of us to try again. But I feel it's all wrong. I feel manipulated. I feel kind of steaɪ rollered by him. As though he wasn't going to take no for an answer. I sort of feel as though I'm lucky to get him back. Yes, that's how he makes me feel. *Lucky*!"

"But, aren't you lucky to get a second chance? Not every woman does," said Mum.

"No, not that sort of lucky," I said, desperate to make her understand, to understand myself. "He makes me feel I'm lucky even though I don't deserve it. As though he's being nice to me even though he doesn't have to be. But because he's a good person. Out of the goodness of his heart. Or something. I don't really know. But it does feel wrong."

"But he is being nice to you," she said, seizing on the one important thing to her.

"Yes, but . . . "

"But what?"

"But . . . but . . . he's being nice to me, but like you'd be nice to a naughty child who was very bold, but that you've now decided to forgive. And although I'm lots of things, I'm not a naughty child."

"You're probably just paranoid," she said, trying to be helpful.

Thanks Mum!

"It can't have been easy for him, coming back, eating humble pie, admitting that he was wrong."

"But that's just it! He didn't eat humble pie. He barely admitted that he was wrong."

"Claire, your nose is probably out of joint. He didn't arrive back in floods of tears, with a whole shop's load of red roses, he didn't beg you to take him back," she suggested.

"It would have been nice," I admitted.

"But flowers count for nothing. And love does," she said.

"Yes," I agreed despondently.

"I feel like he has me trapped now," I burst out, finally, realising exactly how I felt. "I've got to be perfect all the time or else he'll leave me again. I can't say a word against him because it'll just prove that I'm only thinking of me. I feel I should be so grateful to be back with him that I can never dare complain about anything ever again. That he can misbehave any way he likes and I have to keep my mouth shut."

"Well, now, you don't have to put up with any more nonsense from him," blustered Mum. "Any suggestion of another woman and come back here immediately."

"Thanks Mum."

"But in the meantime, be glad you have another chance. And give it a go. Try your best. And I bet you'll be pleasantly surprised."

"I'll try," I promised.

After all, what had I left to lose?

"One other thing," she said a bit awkwardly.

"What's that?"

"I'm not sure that I should tell you."

"What! What aren't you sure that you shouldn't tell me? Tell me, for God's sake," I demanded.

"Well," she said looking sheepish, "that Adam rang for you."

Adam!

My heart gave a lurch. Or it might have been my stomach. Sure as anything *something* lurched.

"When?" I demanded, breathlessly. I felt excited, dizzy, happy.

You know, the way James should have been making me feel.

"A few times," she admitted, looking very sheepish indeed. "Yesterday morning. Yesterday afternoon when you were asleep. Last night when you were out."

"Why didn't you tell me?"

"I didn't think you needed any distractions while you were sorting things out with James," she said humbly.

"You should have let me be the judge of that," I said, annoyed.

A thought struck me.

"You didn't tell him where I was last night, did you?" I asked quickly.

"Yes," she said, sounding defensive, "I said you were out with your husband. Why shouldn't I? It was the truth, wasn't it?"

"Yes, but . . . " I trailed off.

What did it matter now? I was going back to London. I was going back to James. No more Adam.

But I had to see him. I had to say goodbye. I had to thank him for being so nice to me. For making me feel so beautiful and desirable and interesting and special.

"Did he leave a number?" I asked hopefully.

"Er, no," she said, looking away shamefacedly.

"Maybe he'll ring again," I said, a bit frantically.

"Maybe," she agreed, doubtfully.

What *had* she told him?

"And if he does, I want to talk to him, do you hear?" I told her.

"No need to bite my bloody head off," she muttered.

True to his word, James rang me later on Tuesday evening to say that he had arrived back safely. Had I set a date yet for my return?

"No, not yet," I said weakly, "but soon, I promise."

"Just make sure it is," he said with a suggestive leer in his voice. Which actually made a spasm of dread, fear, almost, run through me. The thought of sleeping with him, having sex with him again, was not a pleasant one.

As soon, as I – gratefully – hung up on James, the phone rang again.

It was Adam!

Beautiful, tall, kind, funny, sweet Adam.

"Hello Claire," he said, in his gorgeous voice.

"Hi Adam," I felt so happy to hear him. I felt all girlie and giggly and tingly and simpery.

"I hear congratulations are in order," he said in a cold, hard voice.

It was a bucket of cold water on my warm delight at hearing from him.

"Wh . . . what do you mean?" I asked. I was some hard-hearted bitch that seduced him, for the fun of it. Who had no real interest in him. Now that my husband was back I had no further use for him.

"Helen just told me that you're going back to London. Going back to James," he said accusingly.

"Well, that's right," I said apologetically. "I feel as though I must. You know, for Kate's sake."

"And what about for your sake?" he asked.

I wanted to burst into tears. I felt like telling him that I was thoroughly miserable at the thought of going back to that judgmental, sanctimonious pig.

As you can see, James was growing worse in my eyes with every second that passed. Adam was growing more desirable and attractive. I *ached* to be with him.

But I couldn't tell him that. I had to make a go of things with James. Wishing that I could be with someone else was not exactly productive.

"I'll be OK," I told him.

"It certainly looks that way," he said bitterly.

I felt too ashamed to say anything.

"And what about my sake?" he demanded. "What about me? Didn't Sunday night mean anything to you?"

"Of course it did," I faltered.

"Well, it can't have meant very much if less than two days later you're going back to another man," he said bluntly.

"Adam, it's not like that . . . " I tried desperately to explain. "I've got to . . . I've got to give it another chance."

"Why? He was horrible to you," Adam pointed out.

""Yes, but . . . you see, it wasn't really his fault."

Adam gave a bark of humourless laughter.

"So whose fault was it then? Don't tell me. No, please don't tell me. He said it was *your* fault," he said.

"Well, yes, but you see . . . "

"I just don't believe it," he interrupted angrily. "You're an intelligent woman – a *very* intelligent woman – and you let this idiot put you down."

"What did he tell you?" continued Adam, in full flight. "Let me see. He needed sex while you were pregnant but you couldn't oblige? Hmmm? Was that it?"

"No," I said in a little voice.

"Or that you were far too focused on the impending baby and he felt ignored and crowded out and had to go elsewhere for affection?"

"No, not that either," I told him, thankful that he hadn't come across the right reason yet.

"It's pretty obvious that you're not going to tell me exactly *why* it's your fault," he stormed, "but you can be damn sure that it's *not* your fault. Why are you letting him manipulate you like this?"

And well you might ask, I thought. Good point, why *was* I letting him manipulate me like this? Oh yes, I remember.

"Because it was so good once, that it's worth trying again," I told Adam. But it sounded insincere and feeble, even to me.

"And Adam," I continued tremulously, "I really had a lovely time with you. You made me feel beautiful and special and worthwhile again."

"Anytime," he said sarcastically.

"Oh, please don't be cross with me," I said sadly, "I'm really sorry. I really am. I've got no choice. I've got to do this."

"You do have a choice," he said.

"I don't," I replied. "Apart from anything else, what about Kate?"

"So you're going to go back to some awful relationship with a man who doesn't respect you or care for you, just because of Kate," he said.

"He does care about me," I protested.

"He has a funny way of showing it," said Adam.

"Look, is there any chance we can be friends?" I asked Adam, trying desperately to salvage something from all this unpleasantness.

"No."

"Why not?" I asked frantically.

"Because I can't believe I'm talking to the same woman that I was with on Sunday night. I thought that one was intelligent and had self-respect and knew what she wanted."

"I *am* intelligent. I *do* have self-respect," I said, almost in tears. I had to convince him. I didn't want to lose him. I knew that there could be no romance with Adam. Not now. But I still thought he was wonderful and I wanted so badly to be his friend.

"Anyway," he sighed. "I can't be friends with you. Because I want so much more from you. And I bet you couldn't be friends with me either. We're too attracted to each other."

"Well, if we can't be friends, then we can't be anything," I said. It was killing me, but I had to say it. I couldn't go back to James while I still carried a torch for Adam. I'd got to be hard. Because it would make things easier. A clean, honest break was less painful in the long run.

But I was hoping to call his bluff. Because I wasn't prepared for what he said next.

"Then we can't be anything," he said stiffly.

Panic swept over me.

At the tone of his voice. At the realisation that he was so disappointed in me. At the thought of never seeing him again.

"Can I have your phone number?" I blurted out.

I couldn't *bear* the idea of just ending things with him now. I was clinging on, hoping that he might be nice to me.

Hoping that if he said he was still my friend, it would prove I was doing the right thing.

"No," he said, in a voice that brooked no argument.

"Why not?" I asked, brooking an argument, anyway. Whatever that means.

"Because what would you need it for?" he asked.

"To ring you," I said.

"What would you want to ring me for?" he asked.

"To talk to you," I said, almost crying. "I don't want to lose you."

"Claire," he sighed, "don't be stupid. You've made your decision. You're going to London to live with another man. You can't have us both. There's no *point* in you ringing me to talk to me. We're not going to be friends. End of story."

"There's really nothing else I can say, is there?" I said sadly, realising that I wasn't going to get what I wanted. He was not going to give me his blessing.

Why on earth should he?

"No," he said.

"I've let you down, haven't I?" I asked.

"You've let yourself down," he said coldly.

"I've disappointed you, haven't I?" I said, unable to stop myself from rubbing salt into the wounds.

"Yes, you've . . . disappointed me," he said, after a little hesitation.

"Well, er . . . take care," I said, feeling foolish. Wanting to say so much. But being unable to say anything except platitudes.

"I will," he said.

"I'm sorry," I said, feeling wretched.

"Not as sorry as I am," he said.

And he hung up.

I stayed standing by the phone for a while. Feeling like my heart was breaking. And feeling terrible fear. Had I made a terrible mistake?

Was I standing at a turning point in my life? Was I really important to Adam?

But did it matter? Because I had decided on the direction I was going in.

But was it the right one?

How could I know?

My head was spinning. I felt frightened and out of control.

Two possible lives were being offered to me. The one with James. And maybe one with Adam.

Was I throwing the wrong one away? Had I misunderstood my destiny? Was the break-up with James meant to happen so that I could meet Adam and be a lot happier? Had I been given pain so that I would grow strong?

Had I misunderstood all the signs?

Had I got everything wrong?

But it was too late. I had made my decision. And I was going to go through with it. I'd send myself mad if I kept changing my mind.

My future was with James. Adam no longer existed in my life.

I was probably just a good lay for Adam. Well, I liked to think that I was a *good* one. But maybe it was just about sex.

But, then again, maybe it wasn't.

What should I do then?

I had to get over him. I would get over him.

Of course I would.

I had only known him about three weeks.

It's just that, well, you know . . . he had an effect on me. He touched me in an unexpected way. He made me feel like taking care of him. He made me feel special and wonderful in a way that James no longer did.

Hey! Maybe this was all just down to my

rampaging ego. James no longer made me feel good about myself. So I latched onto the next available man that did make me feel good.

But, in all honesty I really didn't think that was it.

Adam was special.

Adam and I were special.

Although not any more.

Adam despised me now. For my stupidity in buying James's crappy explanation. And for the speed with which I left his bed and went off with someone else. Even if that someone else was my husband.

It really hurt that Adam thought so little of me. Although I didn't blame him. I didn't have a lot of respect for myself either.

Chapter Thirty-Two

After the conversation with Adam on Tuesday, I worked hard on forgetting him. Everytime I thought of him, I blanked it out. I tried to think of nice things, like the buzz of London. And the comfort of getting back to my own flat. And how nice it would be to see all my friends again. And how interesting it would be to think about getting back to work. And how pleasant it would be to be back in a city where every second shop sells shoes.

And things would work out with James. I should be so happy. I had been granted everything that I absolutely *ached* after in the first month or so after he had left.

My life was going to be made all better. As though James's little indiscretion had never really happened. Hopefully I could just edit out these three months or so and carry on as planned. Kate was going to have her Daddy. I was going to have my husband. We would restart our old life. And, if I had to take care to be quieter and less giddy and more serious and solicitous of James's happiness and peace of mind, then that was a small price to pay.

I was sure that if I worked at it, it wouldn't be as awful as it sounded. I'd learn my new personality.

It'd be good for me. And the dread that I was feeling would pass.

And, of course, some of the sadness that I was feeling was the wrench of leaving my family. Bad and all as they were, I'd kind of grown used to them over the past while. Their anarchic version of family life seemed infinitely more desirable than the calm, ordered existence that lay ahead of me with James.

I'd miss them. I'd miss Mum, I'd miss Dad, I'd miss Anna.

Hell, I might even miss Helen.

But maybe not.

I was finding this difficult. I still got terrible surges of anger and feeling hard-done-by by James. It was hard to resist the urge to pick up the phone and tell him what a selfish bastard he was. That he had no right to make me feel as if everything that had happened was all my fault. That I wasn't a bad person. That I wasn't even a selfish person. Or an immature one. But then I envisaged how he would respond to my rage. He'd be all rational explanations and condemnations. And I would feel even worse. More frustrated. As if I'd let myself down even more.

The one thing that made me able to contain all this rage was the realisation that somewhere, somehow, entirely inadvertently mind, I had been wrong. The words that he said that night in the Italian restaurant kept echoing in my head, "If I'd been happy, why would I have left you?"

So I had no choice. I had to accept that it was my fault. He wouldn't have left me, he wouldn't have taken the terrible step of having an affair, of thinking that he was in love with someone else, if it hadn't been my fault.

James was not a womaniser. James was not a frivolous person. James thought long and hard – too bloody long and hard, if you asked me – about everything. He didn't do foolish and disruptive things just for the fun of it. He must have had no choice. He must have been at the end of his tether.

Things would be OK. Eventually things would get back to normal with James. It would just take a bit of time.

I was doing the right thing.

I finally decided that I would return to London the following Tuesday.

That would give me enough time to pack. But more importantly, to prepare myself to let go of my resentment against James, to be positive about my attitude to him.

On Friday afternoon, after two frantic days of packing clothes into a suitcase and then later finding them hanging in the back of Helen's wardrobe, removing them from the wardrobe, repacking them into the suitcase and then a few hours later, rediscovering them under Helen's bed, repacking them etc., I decided to ring James at work to tell him what time my flight was getting in on Tuesday. It was very odd. He had rung me at least once a day since Tuesday, making enquiries as to when I would be getting back. He seemed almost . . . *anxious* to see me. As though he was afraid that I wouldn't return. Of course, the nasty cynical part of me decided that he hadn't had either sex or his washing done since he moved out of the place with Denise and it was no wonder that he was awaiting my return with some anticipation.

But at the same time, it was unusual to feel wanted or needed by him. After the dismissive and patronising way he had treated me while he was in Dublin, when he had given me the impression that he was doing me a favour by taking me back.

Now, although he was doing a good job of hiding it, he seemed insecure and uncertain of me.

But he needn't have worried.

I was going back.

I might not want to. But I was coming back.

I rang and got his office. Some man answered and said "No, I'm afraid Mr Webster isn't in the office just now."

Now we all know what happens here. This is the part in the book when the disembodied voice continues and say, "No, Mr Webster has gone to the ante-natal clinic with his girlfriend Denise" or "No, Mr Webster has taken the afternoon off to go home and shag his girlfriend Denise silly" or something similar. And where I whisper, "Thank you. No, there's no message," and hang up with shaking hands and cancel the tickets back to London.

However, nothing of the sort happened. The disembodied voice asked, "Who's calling please?"

I had to think about that one for a minute.

Who *was* calling? Then I remembered.

"Oh, er, it's his wife," I said.

"Claire!" exclaimed the man, being ultra jovial. Probably to hide his awkwardness. "How are you? George here. Great to hear from you."

George was James's partner. And his friend as well. And, I suppose, in his macho, beer-drinking, laddish way, he was a friend of mine also.

George was a nice man. If you took certain characteristics of George as read then you would probably get on very well with him. For example, I wouldn't malign the man by saying that he played rugby. But there was no getting round the fact that he did watch it.

But he was kind. I liked him and his wife Aisling was a good laugh. We had all got drunk together on many an occasion.

"Hello George," I said, feeling a bit embarrassed.

This was the first time that I had spoken to him since the break-up and I found that I didn't know what to say. Should I refer to it or not?

Should I pretend that nothing at all had happened? That everything was fine.

Or maybe I should just brazen it out. Deal with it head-on, as it were, by trying to turn it into some kind of joke, with rueful, self-deprecating remarks? Perhaps say "Hi, this is Claire. But you can call me Denise if it's easier to remember."

I realised that I was going to find myself in this kind of situation very often for the first couple of weeks after I returned to London.

God, it was going to be humiliating.

But George rescued me by launching straight into it.

"So, you're coming back to him," laughed George. "Well, thank God for that. We might get a decent day's work out of him now."

"Oh," I said politely.

"Yes," continued George, with great joviality and bonhomie. Which made me suspect that he had had a long and liquid lunch. – Well, let's be fair. It was Friday, after all. "How can I put it, Claire? Let's just say that it hasn't been easy. I mean, you know what he's like. Finds it hard to talk about his feelings – well, don't we all, I suppose – and too proud for his own good. But a blind man can see how much he loves you. And it's been obvious just from looking at him that he's been devastated without you. Devastated! What! Don't talk to me about it! All I can say is it's a blessing that you took him back. We'd have had to sack him otherwise." Big bellow of Three Pints At Lunchtime laughter from George.

What on earth was George saying?

He wasn't . . . he couldn't be . . . surely he wasn't *laughing* at me, was he?

Hot angry ashamed tears filled my eyes.

Had I become a public laughing-stock?

Was everyone having a good laugh at my expense?

Yes, yes, OK, to be honest, I admit that in different circumstances I'd have been the first one to laugh like a drain at a deserted wife welcoming her errant husband back into the fold with such grateful haste. And I would be a fool if I thought that people wouldn't privately snigger at how pathetic I was being by taking James back so blithely.

But I couldn't believe that George was being so openly mocking. I was well aware that James hadn't been devastated without me. And George was aware that I was aware. Well, he *must* have been. I knew that they were both men, but surely to God they must occasionally have discussed something other than football and cars.

But George was usually so nice. I didn't understand why he was joking about what happened between James and me. Why was he being so cruel?

I felt so hurt. But I couldn't cry. I had to stand up for myself. Nip this in the bud. Because if I didn't everyone would think they had the right to make fun of me.

"Really?" I said, with thick sarcasm to George.

Trying to convey in one word that, although James may have treated me with a total lack of respect, it didn't make me some kind of public target. James could treat me badly – well he couldn't, but you know what I mean – but it didn't give anyone else the right to make fun of me.

The nerve of George! And to think that I had always liked him.

But George didn't respond to my "really?"

Well, he certainly didn't seem to take any offence.

Because he continued good-naturedly, "I'm no expert on relationships, but I'm so glad that the two of you have sorted this whole sorry mess out. All I can say to you is fair play for forgiving him. It must have been awful for you. But I suppose when you saw the state of him – a bit like the living dead, wasn't he? – you realised just how sorry he was."

My head felt as if it was growing tighter with confusion.

What was going on?

Was George making fun of me?

I wasn't so sure that he was. He *sounded* sincere.

But if he wasn't mocking me, then what the hell was he talking about?

What did he mean "living dead"? – Were we talking about the same James? The same sanctimonious, judgmental James who came to see me in Dublin?

But before I could gather together my confused thoughts, George was off again.

He was in the mood to talk. Friday afternoon boredom and three pints at lunch-time had obviously loosened his tongue.

"Now, Claire," he said, mock stern. "I hope you were a sensible girl and didn't forgive him straight away. I hope you held out for at least a couple of serious pieces of jewellery and a holiday in the Maldives."

"Are you joking?" I thought in bewilderment. "I was lucky that he took me back at all. I nearly had to promise *him* the jewellery and the holiday."

"Er . . . " I said.

But George kept talking.

"He loves you so much and he thought he had no hope at all, do you know? He thought that you wouldn't have anything further to do with him. And, in a way, who could blame you?"

"George!" I interjected forcefully. I had to establish just what was going on! "What are you talking about?"

"About James," he said in surprise.

"You're saying that he was *sorry* that he and I split up," I asked.

505

"Well, 'sorry' is one way of putting it," said George with a little laugh. "'Destroyed' would be a better word in my opinion."

"But how do you know?" I asked faintly, wondering where George was getting his information from. Because it was obvious that he had been sorely misled.

"James told me," he said. "We do talk now and again, you know. It's not just women who have the monopoly on frank and open discussions!"

"Yes, but . . . I mean, are you *sure*?"

"Of course I am," said George indignantly. "He was tortured by the thought of being without you. Tortured! He kept saying to me, 'George, I love her so much. How can I get her back?' and I just said to him, 'James, tell her the truth. Tell her you're sorry'. He had me driven round the bend!"

"Is that right?" I stammered.

That was all I could manage to say. My head was spinning. This was nothing like what had actually happened.

So what was going on?

"And Claire," said George, in a sympathetic tone. "I know it must have been very hard for you. But I'm sure it was very hard for James also. Because you know how he hates to be wrong. Let's face it, he very rarely is. So for him to admit that he'd made a terrible mistake, and then to apologise for it, must have been damn near impossible for him. Although, having said that, I'm sure you feel that if you hear the word 'sorry' ever again, you'll puke. You must be *sick* hearing it!"

Another bellow of laughter from George.

By now I was sure that George wasn't making fun of me. That this wasn't some kind of elaborate and cruel trick. George sounded very serious. But I couldn't understand why his version of events was so different from the one James had presented to me.

I wasn't sick of hearing the word "sorry". I would have dearly loved to hear the word "sorry". But I didn't think I would have recognised "sorry" – certainly not from mes's lips – if it jumped up and bit me.

But I had to pay attention because George was off again.

"The weird thing was that James always thought that you'd be the one to have an affair and not him,"

"Why's that?" I asked. Although I kind of knew what he meant. I was always perceived as the rowdy one and James as the Goody-Two-Shoes.

"Because you've always been the party animal," said George. "The lively, charismatic one. And James never thought he was good enough for you," continued George. "Never! Always afraid that he was too serious and boring for you. Us accountants don't have an easy time with the women, you know. They think we're not exciting enough, would you believe?"

"I never knew that James thought he was too serious and boring for me," I said faintly.

"Come on now," said George disbelievingly. "Wouldn't you agree that of the two of you, you're usually the life and soul of things."

"Yes," I tentatively agreed, desperate to keep George talking.

"And James!" laughed George. "Well, you couldn't find a better bloke but at the same time he wouldn't exactly be surrounded by people and keeping them all in stitches, now would he?"

"No, I suppose not," I said. "But if I was to quieten down a bit, then maybe he wouldn't feel so boring."

"But what would be the point of that?" exclaimed George. "Then you wouldn't be you."

"I *know*," I thought frantically. "But that's what James wants me to do."

"Well, maybe James didn't enjoy living with someone as noisy and lively as me," I suggested to George. "Maybe I got on his nerves."

What I was doing was unforgivable. I was now blatantly fishing for information from George. I was encouraging him to shop his mate.

"Don't be so silly," laughed George. "Of course you didn't get on his nerves. He *did* find it difficult sometimes. But that was only his ego and his insecurity playing up. It can't always be easy living with someone who's a lot more popular than oneself."

"Oh," I said faintly. "I see."

And, do you know something? I think I did. I think I had started to understand.

Should I tell George that?

But I had to think about everything I had just heard. I couldn't listen to anymore or my head would burst.

I started to ease my way out of the conversation with George.

"How come you're such an expert on relationships all of a sudden?" I asked him teasingly. "You've gone all sensitive and new-mannish on me."

"Oh, er," he said, sounding both embarrassed and pleased. "Aisling bought me a book about it."

"I see," I laughed. "Well, thanks a lot George, you've been a great help."

"Good," he said. "I'm glad. Everything will work out, you'll see."

"Oh no, I won't," I thought.

"James was threatened" (self-conscious usage of relationship jargon from George) "by your vitality. Instead of realising that your liveliness complemented" (more self-consciousness) "his calmness," said George, who sounded like he was quoting from a psychology text-book.

"But you can grow from this crisis and," – slightly embarrassed pause, – "redefine the parameters of your relationship."

"Wow, George," I said, desperate to get him off the phone. I wasn't sure how much longer I could sustain this conversation. "You certainly have got in touch with your emotions."

"Yes," he said, shyly. "I'm even exploring my feminine side."

This would be hilarious if I wasn't feeling so confused and frightened.

"George," I said, "it's a pleasure to talk to such a sensitive man. You have a great understanding of the dynamics of James and me. It's not every man who would be so in touch."

"Thank you, Claire," he said proudly. I could

almost hear him beaming. "I feel as though I've learnt an awful lot. And I'm no longer afraid to cry."

"Good, good," I said heartily, terrified that he might offer to give me a demonstration there and then.

How could I get him off the phone without sounding as if I wasn't interested in his emotional growth, I thought desperately.

I found myself asking him another question.

"And do you care for and nurture your inner child?" I asked in a gentle voice.

"Er, what?" he asked, confused.

I had lost him. Aisling hadn't given him the sequel yet. "I haven't any children, Claire. You know that."

"I know," I said kindly. No point in pushing him too far and undoing all the good work that Aisling had done.

"George . . . " I interrupted, abruptly cutting short his lyrical descriptions of how it had all worked out for James because James had followed his advice and how happy James and I were going to be and . . .

"George," I repeated a bit louder. I managed to get his attention.

"So, George, let me see if I've got this right," I said to him. "James loves me. James always loved me. James felt insecure and afraid that he might be too boring for me. Have I got that right?"

"But, you know all this," said George sounding confused.

"Just checking," I said lightly.

George was still prattling on. Maybe I was imagining things but could he have been talking about something called the male period?

But I could barely listen to him. I had far more important things to worry about.

Namely, why had James told George that he loved me frantically and was afraid of losing me and why had he told me that I was damn near impossible to live with but he would take me back as almost an act of charity?

Even a blind man could see that there was a slight discrepancy between the two stories.

He was either lying to George or lying to me.

And some little tickle of instinct somewhere told me that he had been lying to me.

I had to talk to him. I had to find out.

"George," I said, interrupting him again, "I need to speak to James. Will you ask him to call me? It's important."

"Yes," he said, "will do. He should be back in about half an hour."

"Thanks," I said, "bye now."

And I hung up.

I sat trying to make sense of what George had inadvertently told me. So James had always loved me. And James felt threatened by me being, well . . . *me*, I suppose, for want of a better description.

Is that why he needed to have an affair with another woman? And why did he have to tell me that it was all my fault? And why did he have to tell me that I'd have to change totally if our marriage was to have a future?

I wasn't sure what the hell was going on. But I did know one thing. Something was.

Chapter Thirty-Three

Just to make sure I rang Judy.

"Claire!" she answered, sounding delighted. "Are you back?"

"No, Judy, not yet," I said, miserably.

Before she could say anything I went on talking.

"Look Judy," I blurted out, "I need to talk to you about something."

"Talk away," she said. "Are you OK? You sound a bit agitated."

"I am, Judy," I said. "I'm agitated and confused and I don't know what's going on."

"What do you mean?" she asked gently.

"Well, you know that James and I have made it up," I started.

"Yes," she said.

"Well, did you know that it was my fault that James had the affair?"

"What on earth are you talking about?" she said, sounding horrified.

"He told me that it was all my fault. That I was immature and selfish and demanding and inconsiderate and that he'd only take me back if I changed radically."

"He's talking about *him* taking *you* back?" said Judy in disbelief. "Claire, Claire, slow down a minute. There's something very wrong here."

Well, if Judy thought there was something wrong then I wasn't imagining it.

But I wasn't sure whether to be relieved or not.

"Now Claire, can we start again please?" she asked. "James said that he was forced to have an affair because you were so difficult to live with. Have I got that right?"

"Yes," I said, feeling distressed. I admit that it sounded very spurious the way that Judy said it. James made it sound a lot more *reasonable*, somehow.

"And now he's saying that *he'll* take *you* back if you change?" she continued. "What way does he want you to change?"

"Oh, you know," I mumbled. "He wants me to be less of a party-giver. And less of a party-goer. Quieter. More considerate."

"Oh, I see," she said hotly. "He wants you to be a boring fucker like him, is that right? Or else he wants you where he can keep his kill-joy little eye on you. What a shit!"

She paused. And then another thought struck her.

"And what kind of idiot are you? You mean to tell me that you *believed* this crap! Can't you see that it's the oldest trick in the book?"

"In what way?" I asked. Not wanting to hear.

"He has an affair. He realises what a huge mistake he's made. He wants you back because he really loves you – any fool can see that – but he's afraid that you'll tell him to take a hike. So he makes out that it was all your fault so you feel guilty and then you feel grateful because, even though you were an awful person, he still wants you."

"And anyway," she said, drawing breath and launching into another furious speech, "I happen to know for a fact that he's lying."

"Oh?" I said. It was about all I could manage.

"Yes," she said. "Michael told me."

Michael being Judy's boyfriend. Michael being James's friend.

"About a month ago Michael went out with James for a couple of pints, well, more like a couple of dozen pints, but anyway, and James got plastered and wouldn't stop talking about you. Michael says that James is bonkers about you. That he always was. And that he was always much more in love with you than you were with him. And always thought that he was going to lose you. And he couldn't handle it. So with the pressure of the baby and all that he decided to throw in the towel. And legged it with Denise, who, let's face it, couldn't believe her luck to land a catch like James."

"I see," I said evenly. "That's interesting because George told me something very similar today."

"I can't *believe* you needed to hear this from George or me. Didn't you know that James was crazy about you? And totally insecure about you?"

Judy was obviously disgusted with me.

"And he's being so manipulative," she fumed. "Taking advantage of the situation just so he can get you under his thumb. Telling you it's your fault that he left you, and that if you're not the way he wants you to be, he'll leave you again. Typical!"

"Judy," I said. "I need you to be calm for a moment. This is very important."

"Oh, er, right," she said, sounding slightly embarrassed. "Look, when I said that he was a boring fucker I didn't mean . . . "

"It's OK Judy," I said kindly. "I know you did, but it doesn't matter."

"You know how it is," she went on. "The heat of the moment and all that."

"*Judy,*" I said. "For Christ's sake! Forget it! I need to get this straight in my head."

"Sorry, sorry," she said. "Go ahead."

"James had an affair, but he said it was my fault. Right?" I asked Judy.

"So you say," she agreed.

"He should have apologised to me, but wouldn't. Right?"

"Er, right," said Judy.

"He has convinced everyone that he loves me. Except me. Right?"

"Right."

"He has hurt me, humiliated me, confused me, compromised me, lied to me, undermined me, made me apologise for being me. Right?"

"Right."

"And he won't apologise to me or comfort me. Right?"

"Right."

"I don't need a man like that. Right?"

"Right! But . . . er . . . Claire, what are you going to do?"

"Kill the fucker."

"No, Claire, go easy now," stuttered Judy.

"Oh relax Judy," I sighed. "I'm not going to kill him. But I'm going to hurt him real bad."

"That's OK then," she said, with relief. "He's not worth going to prison for."

"Thanks for your plain-talking advice," I said. "You're right. He *is* a boring fucker, isn't he?"

"Completely," she said, with passion.

"I'll talk to you soon," I said. "Good luck. Bye."

So now what?

I supposed I'd better wait for James to ring me.

But I was no longer confused. James had made me very, very angry.

And I thought it was only fair that I should let him know.

In person.

James rang back a short time later. He seemed delighted that I had called him.

I could barely bring myself to be civil to him. My anger kept threatening to boil over.

"Claire, lovely to hear from you," he said.

"What are you doing tonight, James?" I asked brusquely.

"Er, well nothing," he said. I like to think that he was a little bit shocked by my abrupt tone.

"Good," I said. "Be in around eight o'clock. I need to talk to you."

"Er, what about?" he asked, sounding a little bit anxious.

"You'll see," I said smoothly.

"No, no, tell me now," he said, sounding quite a bit anxious.

"No, James, wait until tonight," I said pleasantly, but very, very firmly.

He was silent.

"Eight o'clock tonight then, James," I concluded pleasantly.

"OK," he muttered.

I hung up the phone.

Still thinking about what I had recently found out.

You know, I had *known* that I wasn't as bad as James had made me out to be. And really, that wasn't just because I didn't want to believe that I was a bad person. Although I *didn't* want to believe that I was a bad person but . . . anyway, you know what I mean. I had had a feeling that James had been lying to me, or at least exaggerating greatly when he told me what a horrible, childish, selfish, inconsiderate bitch I had been throughout our marriage.

But I couldn't see what reason he had to lie to me about it.

And I had a feeling that he had tried to cut me down to size – well, at least to a size that suited him – by telling me that I had been such a person.

He hadn't liked my confidence. He had been frightened by it. So, in a nasty cynical way, he decided to completely undermine me so that I'd be dependent on him.

What a bastard.

You know, I think I'd hated him less when I found he had been having sex with Denise. This was a worse kind of betrayal.

"Mum," I called down the stairs.

"What?" she shouted from the kitchen.

"I need you."

"What for?"

"I need you to mind Kate tonight. And I need you to drive me to the airport."

"What on earth are you talking about?"

"I'm going to London. I need you to mind Kate," I said reasonably.

"Is it Tuesday already?" she asked in confusion.

"No Mum, today is Friday. But I'm still going to London."

"And will you be going again on Tuesday?" she asked, looking a little bewildered.

"Maybe," I said. I couldn't answer her. I didn't know myself whether I would or not.

"What's this all about?" she asked suspiciously.

"I've got some things to sort out with James," I said.

"I thought you had sorted things out with James," she said, reasonably enough, I suppose.

"So did I," I said sadly. "But other, what will I call it?, *evidence* has come to light in the last hour or so, so I have to go and see him."

"When will you be back?" she asked.

"Soon," I promised. "Please Mum, this is important. I need your help."

"Oh all right then," she said, sounding a bit nicer. "Take as long as you need."

"It won't be more than a day or so," I said.

"Fine then."

"I'll need to borrow money."

"Don't push your luck."

"Please?"

"How much do you need?"

"Not much. I'll put the flight on the card. But I'll need money for incidentals. You know, tube fares, knuckle-dusters, etc."

"So long as I get it back by next week, I can give you fifty."

"Fifty is plenty," I said.

Well, I hoped it would be. I had no idea where I would be sleeping tonight. But something told me it wouldn't be in my double bed in London with James.

Never mind. I had an ex-boyfriend or two who had never really got over me. So I would at least have a roof over my head.

As well as an erection in my back.

I dressed to kill.

I thought it would be appropriate.

But not as you might have expected, in battle fatigues, a hard hat with a net with leaves in it and a couple of rounds of ammo slung across my chest. Oh no, I wore a sexy, short, black skirt with a black jacket and sheer stockings and high, high heels. I would have worn a little black pillbox hat with a veil if I'd had one. But luckily I hadn't.

I wanted to look like a killer bitch from Hell. But in retrospect I suppose the hat would have been overdoing it.

I would just have looked like one of those glamorous widows who look beautiful at the graveside but the whole town hate because they suspect her of killing her husband and inheriting the money that he had intended to leave to the townfolk to build a new hospital.

Mum looked a little bit taken aback at my dramatic appearance as I came down the stairs but took a look at my determined, angry face and thought better of commenting on it.

"Are we ready?" I asked.

"Yes," said Mum. "I've just got to find the car keys."

I sighed. This could take *days*.

While Mum was running in and out of rooms and emptying handbags onto the kitchen table and feeling around in coat pockets and muttering to herself like the white rabbit (it *was* the white rabbit, wasn't it?) in *Alice in Wonderland*, the front door opened and Helen arrived in with her usual pomp and ceremony.

"Guess what?" she yelled.

"What?" I answered. Surly. Uninterested.

"Adam has a girlfriend!"

The blood drained from my face and my heart nearly stopped beating. What was she talking about? Had someone found out about me and Adam?

"And wait until you hear!" continued Helen, sounding delighted. "He has a baby!"

I stared at her. Was she serious?

"What kind of baby?" I managed to ask.

"A *baby* baby, a girl baby," said Helen scornfully. "What did you expect? A giraffe baby? God, sometimes I worry about you!"

My head was spinning. What did this mean? When had all this happened? Why hadn't Adam told me?

"But is it a new baby, or what?" I asked. I didn't even try to keep the desolation from my voice, but

Helen, with her customary sensitivity, didn't seem to notice.

"No," said Helen. "I don't think so. She doesn't look like Kate. She has hair and she doesn't look like an old man."

"Kate doesn't look like an old man!" I said hotly.

"Yes, she does," laughed Helen. "She's bald and fat and hasn't any teeth."

"Shut up!" I said viciously. "She'll hear you. Babies can understand these things, you know. She's beautiful."

"Keep your knickers on," said Helen mildly. "I don't know what you're so narky about."

I said nothing.

This was all a terrible shock.

"It was hilarious," continued Helen. "Adam brought the girl and the baby into college and half my class are talking about killing themselves. And he can forget about passing any of Professor Staunton's exams. The look she gave him! I swear to God, she *hates* him."

"So, er, hadn't you met this girl before now?" I asked, trying to make sense of this. Had he been going out with her while he was leading me on? Well, he must have been. You don't just go out and buy a baby with hair in a supermarket. These things take time.

"No, we hadn't," said Helen. "Apparently they had some big row ages and ages ago and he hadn't seen her or the baby for a long time. But now they're all reunited."

Helen began singing at the top of her voice. Some

awful song about being reunited and it feeling so good. She waltzed up the stairs, still singing.

"Wait!" I wanted to shout after her. "I'm not finished. There's loads more that I want to ask you."

But she went into the bathroom and slammed the door shut behind her. I could still hear her singing, but it was a bit fainter now.

I stood in the hall, feeling desolate.

And very foolish.

It's so true what they say. There's no fool like an old fool.

"I can't think about it now," I told myself. "I must forget it. I'll think about it some other time when everything is different. When I'm happy and sorted out. But not now."

I forced myself to stop thinking about it. I went to the room in my brain where all my thoughts about Adam lived and disconnected the electricity and boarded up all the doors and windows, so nothing could get in or out.

Obviously it was very unsightly. There would bound to be complaints from the neighbouring thoughts. But I had no choice. I was trying to sort out my marriage, one way or the other, and I could do without any distractions.

Mum eventually found the keys to the car. Kate, Mum and I piled in and we drove to the airport. We didn't speak. I could tell that Mum was itching to ask me what was going on. But thankfully she kept her mouth shut.

It was miraculous, but I really did stop thinking about Adam. I was so upset and angry about James that I suppose there just wasn't any room in my head left to worry about anything else. My worry arena was packed to capacity with thousands and thousands of thoughts worrying about James. And there wasn't even standing room left for any thoughts that might have hoped to get in and worry about Adam.

Unfair, perhaps. But it was on a first come, first served basis.

Leaving Kate was awful, but I had to do it. It wouldn't have been right to bring her. I believe it has a terrible effect on children if they happen to witness their mother murdering their father.

I kissed Kate goodbye in the departure hall. "See you soon, darling," I said.

I hugged Mum.

"Can I ask you just one thing?" she said anxiously, inspecting my face for any imminent explosions of rage.

"Go on," I said, trying to sound nice.

"Has James gone back to that Denise woman?" she asked.

"Not that I know of." I smiled bitter reassurance at her.

"Thank God," she said, breathing out with relief.

Oh dear. Poor Mum. If only she knew. Denise wasn't a problem. But there *was* a problem. A problem that was much bigger than Denise. And, hey, that was really saying something.

Honestly, wouldn't you think that by now I might have begun to forgive and forget? Wasn't it time that I stopped being nasty about Denise?

It's just that it was so easy.

I turned on my sexy high heels and tried to march purposefully across the departure lounge. It wasn't easy to be purposeful when I kept colliding with all kinds of easygoing people who stood around chatting, surrounded by suitcases and bags, resting their elbows on their trolleys, as if they had all the time in the world. As if this wasn't an airport at all and nobody had a flight to catch. Certainly not one departing in the next decade or so.

I tried briskly to book a flight to London.

But it wasn't possible.

The pleasant, laid-back Aer Lingus rep would only allow me to book it in a relaxed, easygoing fashion.

In between a discussion on the Russian presidency (isn't the drink a scourge?) and a chat about the weather (let's hope the dry spell lasts) I just happened to get myself a stand-by booking on a flight leaving shortly for London.

There were no problems at all. Which I thought was an awful waste because it wasn't often that I was in a filthy mood and able to stand up for myself and insist on my rights and cause trouble and all that and today would have been just ideal to do it.

I was all fired up for a good row.

But everybody was so decent and accommodating and it all went beautifully.

Damn it.

It was ten minutes past five.

The flight was uneventful.

It would have been great if the important-looking businessman beside me had tried to talk to me, or even better, tried to flirt with me, just so that I could take full advantage of my bad mood.

Honestly, I was so childish. I was just *itching* for a chance to say something mean. I thought I might like to experiment with a Joan Collins type voice. You know, all posh and scary, my words sounding like pieces of ice dropping into a glass. And say something like, "I really wouldn't bother trying to talk to me. I'm in a very bad mood, and I'm not sure how long I can be polite to you for."

But apart from giving me a vague "sorry" as he fumbled round my haunch for his seatbelt, he totally ignored me. He just opened up his impressive-looking leather briefcase and in no time at all had his nose buried in a Catherine Cookson novel. I'm sure you know it. It's the one about the illegitimate girl with the wine-coloured birthmark, whose cousin fancies her, who gets scourged with a riding crop by her stepmother, raped when she is thirteen by the Lord from the Big Hall and, while escaping from him, gets her foot caught in a rabbit trap and has to have it amputated and the wound cauterised by a red hot poker, while her screams echo throughout the slag heaps.

Or is that all of them?

Anyway the man was far more interested in Catherine Cookson than he was in me and that made me a bit fidgety. I was dying to exercise my bad mood. Limber up, as it were, for the real nastiness that I'd be involved in later. But nothing doing.

And then I felt ashamed of myself and tried to strike up a conversation with him, smiling above and beyond the call of duty at him when he passed me my food tray, gently offering to open his little container of milk for him when he ran into difficulties, giving him my mint to bring home to his little girl, even though he ate his own – that kind of thing.

He turned out to be a lovely man. We discussed the book he was reading. I recommended a couple of other writers to him. And, by the time we landed at Heathrow, we were on first name terms. We shook each other by the hand, said that it had been a pleasure to meet each other and warmly wished each other a safe onward journey.

Then I was on my own again. On my own with my thoughts and fears and anger.

Apart from the ninety billion other people in Heathrow I was completely alone in London.

Now if this was a film instead of a book, you'd be shown shots of red buses and black cabs passing the houses of Parliament and Big Ben, and policemen with funny hats directing traffic outside Buckingham Palace and smiling girls in very short skirts standing underneath a "Welcome to Carnaby Street" sign.

But as this is a book, you'll just have to use your imagination.

Heathrow was, well . . . Heathrow was, well . . . it was busy. That's one way of putting it.

It was totally crazy.

I couldn't believe that there were so many people. It was like a Renaissance painting of the Day of Judgement come to life.

Or like the opening ceremony at the Olympics.

People of all nationalities, with all manner of exotic outfits, rushed past me, speaking every language under the sun.

Why was everyone in such a *hurry?*

And the noise was deafening. Announcements over the tannoy. Small boys lost. Grown men lost. Expensive luggage lost. Patience lost. Tempers lost. Marbles lost. You name it and there was a good chance that it was lost.

I had forgotten that London was like this. There was a time when I would operate at this kind of speed with the greatest of ease. But I was now on Dublin tempo so I had slowed down and kicked back and chilled out. I stood in the arrivals hall, terrified, looking like a hick from the sticks, feeling overwhelmed by the number of people, feebly apologising as people bumped into me and tisked loudly at me.

Then I pulled myself together. This was only *London*, after all.

I mean, I could have been somewhere really scary.

Like Limerick, for example. Sorry, no, only joking.

And everywhere I looked, *everywhere*, were small clusters of businessmen. Standing round in their nasty suits, either waiting for their bags or waiting for a flight, their briefcases that were probably full of porn mags by their feet.

They were all drinking beer, out-firmhandshaking each other, determinedly exuding "nice-guyness" and bonhomie, having competitions to see who could laugh the most uproariously and who could make the most disparaging remark about their wives or the most vulgar remark about any of the women at the conference that they had just been to or were just about to go to. "I wouldn't throw her out of the bed for farting" and "Nah, her tits are too small" and "Everyone's had her, even the lads in the post room" drifted over to me from the various groups.

I wonder what the collective noun for a group of businessmen is? Surely there's got to be one.

A conference of businessmen? A briefcase of businessmen? A meeting of businessmen? A polyester of businessmen? A pinstripe of businessmen?

It's no good. None of those words really convey the *nastiness* of the little groups. How about an insincerity of businessmen? A disloyalty of businessmen? An infidelity of businessmen?

I caught a man from one of the groups leering over at me. I looked away hastily. He turned back to the four or five men that he was with and said something. There was a big burst of laughter and they all started bending and stretching and craning their necks to get a good look at me.

The bastards! I wanted to kill them!

And they were all so unattractive and nondescript. How dare they be so arrogant about me? Or any woman for that matter. They should be grateful if any woman would touch them with a stick. Fuck them! I thought furiously.

Time to leave.

I had no bags to collect. I wasn't planning on staying long enough to need them. So at least I was spared the carousel hell.

I took a deep breath, squared my shoulders, set my jaw firmly and started to push through the arrivals hall. I was heading in the direction of the tube station, determinedly making my way through all the other human beings, like an Amazon explorer hacking his way through dense undergrowth.

I finally got to the station. Japan was obviously holding its national census there. After waiting for what seemed like several years while the sons of Nippon figured out how to operate the ticket machines – I thought they were all supposed to be technological wizards? – I bought myself a tube ticket and boarded a train for central London. Funds didn't run to a taxi. The train was full and every nation on earth had a representative on it.

I don't need to go to an Emergency Council meeting of the United Nations. I've already been there.

The tube journey was so crowded and uncomfortable and unpleasant that in a way it was a God-send. Even if I hadn't already been feeling totally homicidal before I got on the train, there was a good chance that I would be when I got off.

A fellow passenger was kind enough to take my mind off my forthcoming antler-locking with James by pressing his erection against me every time the train turned a corner.

And at about ten minutes to eight I arrived at my station.

Chapter Thirty-Four

When I came out of the tube and onto the road where I lived, my stomach gave a sudden lurch. Everything was so achingly familiar, the newsagents, the launderette, the off-licence, the Indian takeaway.

In one way I felt that I'd been away for light years, but in another I felt that I'd never left. I started to walk towards my flat, my heart pounding, my knees feeling peculiar and kind of trembly.

I was surprised. A bit shocked.

I hadn't expected to be so affected by being back in my old neighbourhood. When I came round the corner and saw my flat, the home that I had shared with James, my forehead started to prickle with sweat.

I walked slowly, reluctantly.

Now that I had arrived I didn't really know what to do.

I just wished that I wasn't there. That I didn't have to be there.

"Do I have to have this confrontation?" I asked myself wildly. "Maybe I'm wrong. Maybe James really does love me as I am. Maybe I should just turn round and go back home and pretend that everything is fine."

I stood at the entrance door to the block of flats and leant my burning face against the cool glass.

I wasn't so angry now. I wasn't angry at all. I felt afraid and so, so sad.

A taxi came round the corner. It had its light on. Hope surged through me. I could hail it and just get out of here, I thought. I don't have to go through with this.

Let this cup pass from my lips.

Speaking of cups, I thought, my mind wandering. I really must remember to pick up some of my bras while I'm here. Now that my tits have – regrettably – returned to their normal size, all the bras that I have in Ireland are too big for me.

This momentary lapse of concentration was fatal and I watched the taxi drive past me.

I wasn't leaving, it seemed. Not just yet, in any case.

I was going to see James and find out what was going on.

– Remind me again why I'm here – oh yes, I remember. Because James has lied to me. Lied about the fundamentals of how he feels about me, about the essence of our relationship.

I started to feel angry again. That was good. The whole thing wasn't quite so nightmarish when I felt angry.

I took a deep, shaky breath.

Should I ring the doorbell and give James a slight warning that I had arrived? Or should I just march on in like I own the place? When everyone knows that I only own half the place. But then I thought, dammit no, it's my home. I'm going to let myself bloody well in.

My hand was shaking as I fumbled round in my bag for my bunch of keys. It took me ages to get the key in the lock.

The familiar, evocative smell of the entrance hall hit me in the pit of my stomach. It smelt like home. I tried hard to ignore it – this was no time for sentimentality.

The lift delivered me to the second floor. I reluctantly walked down the corridor to my front door. When I heard the noise of the television coming from my flat my heart sank even further. It meant that James was home. Now there really was no getting out of it.

I let myself in and, with an attempt at nonchalance, strolled into the front room.

James nearly died of shock when he saw me.

In a perverse way I would have been glad if I had caught him up to no good. Maybe in the throes of SM bondage with a fourteen-year-old-girl. Or even better, a fourteen-year-old boy. Or better still, a fourteen-year-old sheep. Or best of all, watching *Every Second Counts* (now that *is* heinous and unforgivable).

It would have meant that I wouldn't have had to confront him. I could have walked away from him, knowing that he was a terrible person. No room for any doubt. All neatly tied up. No loose ends.

But, contrary bastard that he was, he couldn't have looked more wholesome and innocent if he had been rehearsing all day. He was reading the paper and had *Coronation Street* on in the background. Even the mug beside him contained Coke and not alcohol. Clean as a Goddam whistle.

"Cl . . . Claire, what are you doing here?" he gasped, leaping up from the couch. He looked as if he had seen a ghost.

In fairness, it must have been a terrible shock. As far as he knew I was hundreds of miles away in another city.

But at the same time, under ordinary circumstances, he should have been a *bit* glad to see me. Surprised delighted, instead of Shocked horrified.

If he really loved me and didn't have a guilty conscience and had nothing to be afraid of, or to feel ashamed about, wouldn't he have been just over the moon to see me?

He looked nervous. You know, edgy, watchful. Wondering why I had come. He *knew* something was wrong.

And with a jolt I realised that I hadn't been imagining things. Something was badly amiss. I had only to look at James's face to know.

I can't be sad now, I told myself. I can let myself be heartbroken and go to pieces later, but for the moment I have to stay strong.

"Gr . . . great to see you Claire," he said, sounding horrified. He seemed a bit hysterical.

I looked into his white, anxious face and I felt such a surge of anger that I wanted to bite him.

But I *wanted* to feel angry. I wanted anger to course through me.

Anger is good, I told myself. Anger keeps the pain away. Anger empowers me.

I looked round the front room. I smiled graciously at him, even though I was shaking.

"The place looks nice," I told him pleasantly. I was surprised that my voice wasn't trembling. "I see you've moved your books and records and stuff back. And . . ."

I pushed past him and marched into the bedroom and flung open the wardrobe, " . . . I see you've moved all your clothes back also. *Very* cosy."

"Claire, what are you doing here?" he managed to ask.

"Aren't you glad to see me?" I asked, all coquettish and simpery.

"Yes!" he exclaimed, "Of course, it's just . . . I mean I wasn't expecting you . . . you know . . . I thought you were going to ring."

"I know exactly what you thought, James," I said fixing him with a judgmental stare.

I must say, in spite of the feeling of impending doom, I was starting to enjoy this.

There was a little silence.

"Is something wrong, Claire?" he asked cautiously.

He looked frightened. From the moment James had watched me walk into the flat, he knew that I hadn't come on a mission of love. He was acting far too guilty and scared.

Maybe he had already spoken to George and knew that I knew about his duplicity?

Maybe he had been expecting some kind of showdown?

But at least he wanted to discuss whatever was wrong.

That had got to count for something, didn't it?

Maybe it was all going to be fine.

Or was I just too pathetic for words?

"Claire," he said again, a bit more urgently, "is something wrong?"

"Yes, James," I said sweetly. "Something is wrong."

"What is it?" he asked, watching me warily.

"I had a very interesting conversation with George today," I said idly.

"Did you?" asked James, trying to appear unflustered. But a spasm of something – fear maybe? Or could it be annoyance? – passed over his face.

"Hmmm," I said inspecting my fingernails, "yes, I did actually."

There was a pause. James stood watching me, the way a mouse watches a cat.

"Yes," I continued in a very casual tone, "and he gave me a very different version of events concerning you and me."

"Oh," said James and swallowed heavily.

"Apparently you've always loved me," I said. "And apparently the only problem you've had with me was that you were afraid that I'd leave you."

James was silent and sullen.

"Is that right, James?" I asked sharply.

"You wouldn't want to take any notice of George," he said, recovering his aplomb somewhat.

"I know that, James," I replied smoothly, "so that's why I rang Judy. And, guess what, she told me exactly the same thing."

More silence.

"James." I sighed. "It's about time you started to tell me what's going on."

"I have," he muttered.

"No, you haven't," I corrected him loudly. "You had an affair with another woman, you left me the day I gave birth to your child, then you decided that you wanted me back. But, instead of telling me that, you had to manufacture a whole pack of lies, and malign me and call me selfish and childish and inconsiderate and stupid." (Voice going up several decibels here). "And instead of apologising for the lousy way you treated me, you made out that it was all my fault." (Voice continuing to rise). "And you decided that you'd browbeat me into being something other than what I am. Some meek little woman who wouldn't answer you back. And wouldn't overshadow you. And wouldn't make you feel insecure!"

"It wasn't like that," he protested feebly.

"It was *exactly* like that," I shouted. "I just can't believe that I was fool enough to believe your ridiculous story!"

"Claire, you've got to listen to me," he said, sounding bad-tempered and irritated.

"Oh, no, I do not," I corrected him angrily. "Why do I have to listen to you? Are you going to try and tell me a whole lot more lies?"

"Well, are you?" I shouted when he didn't answer.

I sat and looked at him, willing him to speak, willing him to make everything all right.

"Convince me," I begged silently. "I want to be

wrong. *Tell* me I'm wrong. Please explain it to me. I'll even settle for an apology. Just an apology will do."

He slowly sat down on the couch with his face in his hands. And, even though I was expecting some kind of reaction, it still gave me a little jump to realise that he was crying.

Jesus! What was I to say to him?

I hate to see a grown man cry.

Actually, that's not true at all.

Usually, there's nothing I enjoy more than seeing a grown man cry.

Especially if I'm the one that made him cry.

That feeling of power! You just can't beat it.

If he was crying it must mean that he was really sorry that he'd been so horrible to me and that everything was going to be fine.

He was going to apologise.

He was going to admit that he was completely in the wrong.

My heart started to soften.

But then he looked up at me and I couldn't believe the expression on his face. He looked so angry! "That's just typical of you," he shouted.

"What?" I asked faintly.

"You're so bloody selfish," he yelled, all traces of the tearful man magically vanished.

"Why?" I asked baffled.

"Everything was fine!" he shouted, "Everything was all sorted out and we were going to start again and you were going to try and be mature and a bit more considerate. But you just couldn't let it lie, could you?"

"But what was I supposed to do?" I asked meekly. "George tells me one thing and you tell me something completely different. George's story is a lot more believable than yours. Especially when Judy confirmed it."

I was trying very, very hard to be reasonable. I could see how angry James was and it was frightening but, at the same time, I was trying to stand my ground. Please God, I prayed, give me the strength to stand up to him. Don't let me end up taking the blame for everything again. You know, just for once, it would be nice not to be a wimp.

"Well, of course you'd believe George and Judy," he said nastily. "Of course you want to believe nice things about yourself. You just couldn't take the truth from me, could you?"

"James," I said, struggling to stay calm, "I just want to get to the bottom of things. I just want to know why you told George that you really loved me and that you were afraid that you'd lose me, and why you told me that you could barely tolerate me. It just doesn't add up!"

"I told you the truth," he said sulkily.

"So what was it you told George?" I asked.

"George got it wrong," he said shortly.

"And did Judy get it wrong also?" I asked coldly.

"I suppose," he said offhandedly.

"And Aisling and Brian and Matthew got it wrong too?"

"They must have," he said carelessly.

"Look, James," I said earnestly, "be reasonable. They can't *all* be wrong, can they?"

"They can," he said abruptly, "they are."

"James, please, you're a logical man," I said, starting to feel desperate. "Can't you see that *someone* isn't telling the truth? And didn't you think that sooner or later the different stories would get back to me? Don't you know that my friends and I discuss everything?"

He said nothing. He sat on the couch with his arms folded and looked at me defiantly.

Jesus! It was like pulling teeth.

Right! I'd try again. No matter what happened I would stay calm. I would try not to kill him. I would try not to be angry. I would try not to hurt him, the way that I wanted to. I would swallow my pride one more time. I would make it clear that I would forgive him for the affair. This was not easy, let me tell you.

Especially when, at the same time, I was trying to stand my ground and not be completely bullied by him.

I was trying to bear in mind that there was a fine line between being understanding and being a doormat, between standing up for oneself and being a crazed axe-woman.

"James," I said, miraculously managing to sound calm, "we really have to try and sort this out. If I ask you questions, will you just answer me 'yes' or 'no'?"

"What kind of questions?" he asked, suspiciously.

"Well, like did you lie to me when you told me that it was my fault that you left me?"

"You mean that you want to sit here and interrogate me?" he said, outraged. "You must be

539

joking! Who the hell do you think you are? You're trying to make me out to be some kind of criminal!"

"James," I said. I was on the verge of tears of frustration, "I'm not! Really, I'm not. I'm just trying to get you to talk to me, to tell me what you really feel, what's really going on. I want you to be honest with me. Otherwise we won't have a future."

"I see," he said nastily, "so you want me to say something like, 'you're a wonderful person Claire and I don't know why I had an affair because you're so great'. Is that what you want to hear?"

"Yes," I thought.

"No . . . " I said weakly, "It's just . . . ."

"You want me to take all the blame, is that it?" he said, raising his voice. "You want me to be the bad guy, the 'man you and all your friends love to hate', is that it? After all I've done for you? Is that what you want?!" he ended on a shout, his face close to mine.

"But you are the bad guy," I said, bewildered. "You were the one who had the affair, not me."

"Oh Jesus!" he shouted, *really* shouted, this time. "You'll never stop harping on about that, will you? Trying to make me feel guilty about it. Well, I don't feel guilty, right? I've been so good to you always. Everyone knows that. I am not the bad person here. You are!"

Silence followed. The room reverberated with it.

I sat very still. Feeling shell-shocked.

James exhaled hard, angrily, and started pacing the room. He didn't look at me.

I realised that I was shaking.

Am I a bad person? I asked myself.

Am I really?

A little voice in my head told me not to be ridiculous. This had gone far enough. I had to hold onto what I knew to be the truth. James was the one who had an affair. Not me. I didn't force James to have an affair. He chose to do it. James told me that I was almost impossible to love, but he told everyone else that he loved me very much.

James wanted me to take the blame for *his* affair.

As I sat there trembling, my head swimming, something became very clear to me. Something that I hadn't seen before now. James did not want to admit, would not admit, that he was in the wrong. He could not accept that he had had an affair. Well, obviously, he knew he had one – I'd say the memory of Denise wasn't that easy to erase – but he didn't want it to be his fault.

A little time passed. Tension hung heavy in the air.

From James's reaction I realised that he was not going to admit, not in a million years, that he had lied to me and told the truth to George.

And I happened to believe George. I was sure he wasn't making anything up – quite apart from anything else he was too stupid! And I was sure that James didn't think for one moment that what he said to George would get back to me. He thought he was perfectly safe in telling George that he loved me very much while telling me that it was hard for him to love someone as difficult and selfish as me. I knew James hated to feel insecure about anything. He hated to be vulnerable, even about his work, not to

541

have total control. And he wanted to feel secure around me.

I still intended to get to the bottom of the great George/Claire contradictory stories controversy but this time I decided to try a different approach. On the one hand I felt like telling James to fuck off, that he was an irresponsible, immature, emotional cripple and that a child could see that he was trying to manipulate me. But on the other hand, it was obvious that he was afraid. Or confused.

Maybe he needed someone to voice his fears, because he was too frightened to do it himself, and then I could try and put his mind at rest.

This was worth one more try.

"James," I said, gently, "There's no shame in loving me, you know. It's not a sign of weakness to love someone and sometimes feel insecure. It's human. There's nothing wrong with it. And, if you told George that you loved me very much, there's no need to lie to me about it. I'm not going to use it as a weapon against you. And when you came to Dublin there was no need to pretend that you barely loved me. No one's going to condemn you for loving your wife, for God's sake. And as for the affair, you made a mistake." (This was extremely hard to say, believe me, but I said it.) "No one is perfect," I continued. "We all make mistakes. You can be honest with me, you know. You don't have to play games to protect yourself. We can work all this out and have a proper marriage."

I finished speaking. I was exhausted.

There was a pause. I hardly dared to breathe.

James sat silently, looking at the floor. Everything hinged on this.

"Claire," he finally said.

"Yes," I said, tense, terrified.

"I don't know what kind of psycho-babble crap you're talking but it makes no sense to me," he said.

So that was it.

I had lost.

"I can't see what the problem is," he continued. "I never said I didn't love you. I just said that you'd have to change for us to go on living together. I said that you'd have to grow up. I said that you were so inconsiderate . . . "

"I know what you said, James," I interrupted. I decided to stop him before he delivered the entire speech again. He sounded as if he was reading from a script. Or as if he was a robot programmed to say these things – press a button and he was off.

As for me, I'd had enough.

No more humiliation for me, thanks very much. No more swallowing my anger. Honestly, I couldn't manage another mouthful. But it was delicious. Did you make it yourself?

I had done my best. It wasn't good enough. But I was damn well not doing any more. Quite simply, it wasn't worth it.

"Fine," I said.

"Fine?" he said quizzically.

"Yes, fine," I agreed.

"That's good," he said, sounding paternal and smug, "but is it really? I don't want you bringing this up every couple of months or so and throwing it in my face."

"I won't," I said shortly.

I started to gather up my bag and newspaper with a lot more rustling and fuss than was necessary. I got to my feet and started to put on my jacket.

"What are you doing?" asked James, confusion written on his face.

I affected a startled and innocent face. "What do you think I'm doing?"

"I'm not sure," he said.

"I'd better tell you then, hadn't I?" I said smoothly.

"Er . . . well, yes," said James. It gave me a cold thrill to hear him sounding a bit anxious.

"I'm leaving," I said.

"*Leaving?*" he hooted. "What the hell are you leaving for? We've just sorted everything out."

Then he started to laugh in relief. "Oh God, sorry," he said, "for a minute there . . . " He shook his head at his own silliness. "But of course, you've got to go back. You've got to get your things and bring back Kate. But I must admit that I was kind of hoping that you'd stay the night and we might get . . . er . . . reacquainted. Never mind. We can wait a few more days. So what time on Tuesday should I expect you?"

"Oh James," I said with a mock-sympathetic little laugh, "you haven't realised, have you?"

"Realised what?" he asked carefully.

"I won't be here on Tuesday. Or any other day for that matter," I explained nicely.

"For God's sake, what is it now?" he bellowed. "We've just sorted it all out and now you . . ."

"No, James," I cut in icily. "We've sorted nothing

out. Nothing at all. *You* may have sorted something out – your image of yourself as a nice guy is good and intact – but I've sorted nothing out."

"But what have we been talking about for the past hour?" he asked belligerently.

"Exactly," I said.

"What?" he barked, looking at me as if I'd gone a bit mad.

"I said 'exactly'. Just what the hell *have* we been talking about?" I asked him. "Because for all the good it's done me, I might as well have been talking to the wall."

"Oh, we're back to you again, are we?" asked James nastily. "It's all you care about, you and your feelings and . . . "

That was it!

"Shut up!" I commanded, my voice coming out much louder than I had expected.

James was so shocked that he actually did shut up.

"I'm not listening to any more of your crap about what a terrible person I am," I shouted. "*I* didn't fuck someone else. *You* did. And you're so immature and selfish that you just can't own up to it and take the blame."

"*I'm* immature and selfish?" said James in astonishment. "*Me?*" he said, dramatically pointing in disbelief to his chest. "Me!? I think you're slightly confused here."

"No, I'm bloody well not," I shouted. "I know I'm not perfect. But at least I can admit it."

"So why won't you own up to being selfish and

inconsiderate in our marriage?" he asked, with an air of triumph.

"Because it's not true!" I said. "I *knew* it wasn't true, but I loved you and wanted to please you so I convinced myself that it had to be true. I thought if I could fix myself that I could fix our marriage. But there was nothing wrong with me. You were just manipulating me."

"How dare you?" he said, his face red with rage. "After all I've done for you. I've been a perfect husband!"

"James," I said with icy calm. "There is no doubt that you have been very good to me over the years. I think if you look back you'll find that it was mutual. We loved each other, it was part of the deal. But you seem to have started to believe your own publicity. Having an affair with another woman is not being good to me. You cannot justify it." There was a pause. For once James didn't have an indignant answer ready. "But," I continued, "you're not the first person to behave badly, to step out of line. It's not the end of the bloody world. We could have got over it. But you're too interested in looking squeaky clean and whiter than white. That's the choice that you've made."

I started towards the door.

"I can't understand why you're leaving," he said.

"I know," I said.

"Tell me why," he said.

"No."

"Why the hell not?" he demanded.

"Because I've tried. And I've tried. Why should you listen now when you haven't any of the other

times. I'm not wasting any more time. I'm not trying
any more."

"I love you," he said quietly.

The bastard.

He sounded as if he really meant it.

I bit my lip. This was not the time to weaken.

"No you don't," I said firmly.

"I do," he protested loudly.

"No, you don't," I told him. "If you had loved me
you wouldn't have had an affair."

"But . . . " he interrupted.

"And," I continued loudly, before he started his
speech again, "if you loved me, you wouldn't have
wanted me to change into some wimpy woman who
was afraid of you. If you loved me you wouldn't
have tried to manipulate me or to control me. And,
most of all, if you loved me, you wouldn't be afraid
to admit that you're in the wrong. If you loved me
you could rise above yourself and your ego and
apologise to me."

"But I do love you," he said, trying to hold my
hand, "you've got to believe me!"

"I don't believe you," I told him, shrugging his
hand away with disgust. "I don't know who or what
it is that you love, but it certainly isn't me."

"It is!"

"No James, it isn't," I replied, ultra-calmly. "You
just want some kind of moron that you can control.
Why don't you go back to Denise?"

"I don't want Denise. I want you," he said.

"Well, that's a pity," I said evenly, "because you
can't have me."

The shock was a bit much for him. He looked like he'd been kicked in the stomach. You know – a bit like the way I had looked the day he told me he was leaving me.

Not that I desired anything as crass as vengeance, you understand.

"And do you know what the worst thing of all is?" I asked him.

"What?" he said, whitefaced.

"The fact that you made me doubt myself. I was prepared to try and change the way I am, change *who* I am, just for you. You made me abandon all my integrity. You tried to destroy who I am. And I let you!"

"It was for your good," he said, but without conviction.

I narrowed my eyes at him.

"Choose your next words very carefully, you asshole. They may be your last," I told him.

He went even whiter, if that was possible, and kept his mouth firmly closed.

"I'm never going to let myself be bullied ever again," I said with determination. I like to think that I had some of the grit of Scarlett O'Hara when she gave the "As God is my witness, I'll never be cold or hungry again" speech. "I'll always be true to what I know I am," I continued. I'm going to be me, whether it's good or bad. And if any man, even Ashley, tries to change me, I'll get rid of them so fast they'll be dizzy."

James totally missed the *Gone with the Wind* reference. No imagination.

"I never tried to bully you," he said, all indignant.

"James," I said, starting to feel weary, "this discussion is closed."

"Well, never mind the past," he said, sounding anxious and hasty. "But how about, hey . . . how about if I promise that I won't bully you in the future?"

He sounded as if he had just hit on the most innovative and novel idea. Archimedes hopping out of the bath in his pelt would have seemed restrained and reserved in comparison.

I looked at him with scornful pity. "Of course you're not going to bully me in future," I said, "because you won't get the chance."

"You don't mean it," he said. "You'll change your mind."

"I won't," I said with a tinkly little laugh.

"You will," he continued to insist. "You'll never last without me."

Wrong thing to say, I'm afraid.

"Where are you going?" he asked, outraged, when he saw me picking up my bag.

"Home," I said simply. If I left now I'd catch the last plane back to Dublin.

"You can't go," he said, standing up.

"Watch me," I said. And did another one of those swivels that my heels were so handy for.

"What about the flat? What about Kate?" he asked.

Well, it was nice to know where his priorities were, the flat being higher up on his list than Kate.

"I'll be in touch," I promised, with a pleasing echo

of the words he had uttered to me that awful day in the hospital.

I walked towards the front door.

"You'll be back," he said following me out to the hall. "You'll never last without me."

"So you keep saying," I said.

"But don't hold your breath," were my last words before I pulled the door out behind me.

I managed to get all the way to the tube station before I started to cry.

Chapter Thirty-Five

I can't really remember much about the tube journey out to Heathrow.

The whole thing passed in a daze.

I knew I had done the right thing. At least, I thought I had done the right thing. It was just that this was real life and no decision was clearly signposted. It's not like you take the right turning and you get everlasting happiness and you take the wrong one and your life's a disaster. In real life it's often well nigh impossible to tell which decision is the one you should make because what you stand to gain and what you stand to lose is sometimes – often – neck and neck.

How could I really know if I'd done the right thing? I wanted someone to come up to me with a gold cup or a medal and shake me on the hand and clap me on the back and congratulate me on making the right decision.

I wanted my life to be like a computer game. Make the wrong decision and I lose a life. Make the right one and I gain points. I just wanted to know. I just wanted to be sure.

I kept listing the reasons why there could be no future for me and James. James wanted me to be someone that I wasn't. James wasn't happy with me the way I was. And I wouldn't be happy if I changed so that James was happy. And I wasn't happy with James's saint complex. If I took him back James would be happy because then James would think that I condoned everything he did. The way he already condoned everything he did himself. It would probably mean that the first argument that I had with James in our new improved marriage, everything would split wide open all over again. James was pompous and sanctimonious and James thought that I was flighty and immature. I was sure it was for the best that the marriage really was over now. It was just that there was always room for a little bit of doubt.

You know, I wondered if I had been nicer, if I had been stronger, more gentle, more forceful, more patient, sweeter, kinder, nastier, crueller, if I had laid down the law more, if I had kept my mouth shut more, would I have saved my marriage?

I was torturing myself with these thoughts.

Because, at the end of the day, I was the one who made the decision. I was the one who said that the marriage could no longer work. I knew, I knew that James hadn't given me much of an option, much of a choice, but I was still the one who pulled the trigger, as it were.

I felt so *guilty.*

And then I told myself not to be so silly. What James was offering me wasn't worth the paper it wasn't written on. It was only a sham of a relationship and it would have been entirely on his terms and it wouldn't have lasted a week. And if it had lasted, it would have been at the expense of my happiness. It would have just been a pyhrric victory.

Round and round went my thoughts, as I rocked gently on the tube, my head chasing its own tail.

God! I hated this business of being grown-up. I hated having to make decisions where I didn't know what was behind the door. I wanted a world where goodies and baddies were clearly labelled. Where ominous music starts playing the minute the baddy comes on screen, so you can't possibly mistake him.

Where someone asks you to choose between playing with the beautiful princess in the fragrant garden and being eaten by the hideous monster in the foul-smelling pit. Not exactly a difficult one, now is it? Not something that you would agonise over, or that would take the night's sleep off you?

Being a victim isn't very nice, but Goddammit, it takes a lot of the confusion out of things. At least you know you're in the *right*.

And I suppose I was disappointed. Very disappointed. I had loved James once. I didn't know whether I did anymore. Or if I did, it wasn't in the same way. But a reconciliation would have been nicer than no reconciliation, if you know what I mean. A reconciliation that worked, that is. Not some kind of useless compromise.

And I was sad. And then I felt angry. And then I felt guilty. And then I felt sad again. It was a bloody nightmare!

One thing stopped me from going totally round the bend. I realised that there was nothing stopping me from going back to James. Right then, that *minute*, I could get off the train and cross the platform and go straight back to the flat and tell him that I had been wrong and that we should try again.

But I didn't.

And thick and all as I was, confused, bewildered, mixed-up, distraught, that told me something.

If I'd really loved him, really wanted to be with him, I would have gone back.

So I knew I was doing the right thing. I thought.

And off I'd go again.

Heathrow had calmed down a lot. Much quieter. Like the first day of the January sales. It was lovely.

I got on a practically empty flight back to Dublin.

I had a whole row of seats to myself so I was able to sniff and cry in discreet comfort should the urge take me.

The air hostesses were intrigued.

I kept catching little huddles of them looking at me worriedly.

They probably thought that I'd just had an abortion.

When I got to Dublin it was raining. The runway was slick and shiny in the dark. And the arrivals hall was deserted. I walked past the silent carousels, my sexy high heels echoing on the tile floors.

I hadn't told anyone that I was coming back, so there was no one to meet me.

There didn't seem to be anyone there to meet anyone.

I spotted a lone porter. He was busy telling some

bewildered man that to miss one flight was unfortunate but to miss two was careless.

I click-clacked past all the shuttered shops, the bureaux de change that stood in darkness, the deserted car rental stands. I finally got as far as the rain-soaked entrance.

There was a single taxi waiting outside in the wet night. The driver was reading a newspaper.

He looked as though he'd been there for several days.

He drove me home in unexpected silence. The only sounds were the swish of the windscreen wipers and the noise of the rain drumming on the roof of the car.

We drove through the sleeping suburbs and he eventually deposited me outside my home. It was all in darkness. I civilly thanked him for the journey. He civilly thanked me for the sum of money I handed over. We said goodbye.

It was ten minutes past one.

I let myself in quietly. I didn't want to wake anyone.

Not out of consideration for them, I'm afraid. But because I didn't want to answer any of the inevitable questions.

I was longing to see Kate but she wasn't in my room.

Mum must have thought that I wouldn't be home and moved the cot into her and Dad's room.

But I ached to hold her. I missed her so much.

I tiptoed into Mum's room to take Kate, hoping desperately that I wouldn't wake Mum.

I rustled the child successfully. And then fell into bed, exhausted. Asleep with Kate in my arms.

Chapter Thirty-Six

When I awoke the next morning, I felt a tiny bit better. Not healed or cured or anything of the sort, but more prepared to wait. To wait for things to get better, to wait for the pain to go.

I had made the decision not to be with James and, being "Instant Gratification Girl", I wanted to feel wonderful immediately. I had wanted the fruits of my decision to fall into my impatient lap right now.

I wanted it to be "Out with the old and in with the new!" To throw off the trappings of my previous incarnation, to have not a jot of feeling left for James, not an iota of doubt, not a crumb of indecision. I wanted an immediate, miraculous transformation. I wanted the Relationship Fairy to touch me with her magic wand, to sprinkle me with her sparkling recovery dust, and for me to instantly forget everything I ever felt for James, to forget that he even existed.

I wanted to leave my grief under my pillow and for it to be gone in the morning. I wouldn't even have cared if there wasn't any money left in its place.

But there was no magic cure, there was no Relationship Fairy. I'd realised that a long time ago.

I had to get through this on my own. I realised that I had to be patient. Time would let me know if I had made the right decision.

I still didn't know if I had done the right thing by leaving James. But to stay with him would definitely have been the wrong thing.

Get your head round that one, if you can.

And if you get the hang of it, would you mind explaining it to me?

James rang at eight o'clock the next morning. I declined to speak to him. And at eight forty. Ditto. And at ten past nine. And ditto once again. Then came an unexpected lull until almost eleven, when there were three calls in quick succession. Ditto, ditto and ditto. Twelve fifteen there was another one. Ditto. Five to one, five past one and twenty past one, all saw calls. Ditto, etc. Calls remained steady for most of the afternoon, coming every half hour or so. Then a final flurry came around six o clock. Ditto re above.

Mum very decently fielded the calls all day. I have to say it, when the chips are down, that woman is worth her weight in Mars Bars.

Dad came home from work at twenty past six and at twenty to seven burst into the room where I was sitting with Kate and all the documents relating to the flat and roared at me, "Claire, for God's sake will you go and talk to him!"

"I've nothing to say," I said sweetly.

"I don't care," he bellowed, "this has gone too far. And he says he's going to call all night until you come and talk to him."

"Leave the phone off the hook," I suggested, turning my attention back to the deeds of the flat.

"Claire, we can't do that," he said in exasperation. "Helen keeps hanging the bloody thing back up."

"Yes, why should my social life suffer just because you married a lunatic," came Helen's muffled voice from somewhere outside the door.

"Please, Claire," pleaded Dad.

"Oh, all right then," I sighed, putting down the pen I had been using to make notes with.

"James," I said into the phone, "what do you want?"

"Claire," he said, sounding cross, "have you come to your senses yet?"

"I wasn't aware that I had taken leave of them," I said politely. He ignored this.

"I've been ringing all day and your mother says you don't want to talk to me," he said, sounding all narky and put-out.

"That's right," I agreed pleasantly.

"But we've got to talk," he said.

"No, we don't," I said.

"Claire, I love you," he said earnestly. "We have to sort this out."

"James," I said coldly. "There will be no sorting out. We've sorted as much as we can. And now we're at the end of the line. You think you're right. I think you're wrong. And I'm not wasting any more time or energy trying to convince either of us to change our minds. Now, I wish you well and I hope we can keep this civilised, especially for Kate's sake, but there really is nothing further to discuss."

"What's happened to you, Claire?" asked James, sounding shocked. "You were never like this before. You've changed so much. You've got so hard."

"Oh, didn't I tell you?" I said casually. "My husband had an affair. It kind of made an impact on me."

Very unkind, I know. But I couldn't resist it.

"Very funny, Claire," he said.

"Actually no, James," I corrected him, "it wasn't funny at all."

"Look," he said, starting to sound annoyed, "this is getting us nowhere."

"That's fine by me," I said, "because nowhere is precisely where we're going."

"Very witty, Claire. Very droll," he said nastily.

"Thank you," I replied, with excessive sweetness.

"Now listen," he said, suddenly sounding all official and even more pompous than usual. I could almost hear papers rustling in the background. "I've an . . . er . . . proposition to put to you."

"Oh?" I asked.

"Yes," he said. "Claire, I do love you and I don't want us to split up so if it makes you feel better I'm prepared to er . . . make . . . er . . . a concession to you."

"What's that?" I asked. I was hardly interested. I barely cared.

I realised, with a shock, that there was nothing, absolutely nothing that he could say now to make things better.

I didn't love him anymore.

I didn't know why or when I stopped.

But I had.

James continued to speak and I tried to concentrate on what he was saying.

"I'm prepared to forget all about you having to change when you come back to live with me," he was saying. "You obviously feel very strongly about having to try harder at being mature and considerate and all the other . . . er . . . things we discussed. So if it means that you'll abandon this idea that we're splitting up, I can put up with you being the way that you were in the past. I suppose you weren't that bad," he said grudgingly.

Anger surged through me. I forgot for a moment that I no longer cared. I mean, the sheer *gall* of the man! The bloody cheek of him. I could hardly believe my ears.

I said as much.

"Are you glad?" he asked cautiously.

"Glad! Glad?" I screeched. "Of course I'm not bloody well glad. This makes it all even worse."

"But why?" he whined. "I'm saying here that I forgive you and that everything will be fine."

I nearly exploded. I had so many things to say to him.

"Forgive me?" I said in disbelief. "*You* forgive *me*. No, no, no, no, *no* James, you have it all wrong. If there's any forgiving to be done round here, it's me forgiving you. Except that I'm not."

"Just a minute . . . " James blustered.

"And this is supposedly the reason you had the affair with that fat cow. Me being immature and selfish. But you're prepared to overlook it now, at the drop of a hat. Yet it was important enough for you to be unfaithful to me. Make up your mind, James! Either it's important or it's not."

"It is important," he said.

"Well, then you can't overlook it," I said furiously. "If you want me to be a certain way and it's important, then what kind of relationship will we have if I can't be that way?"

"All right then," he said, sounding a bit desperate, "it's not important."

"Well, if it's not important then why did you have an affair because of it?" I said triumphantly.

"Can't we just forget it?" he said. I could hear panic in his voice.

"No, James, we can't. You might be able to, but it's not so easy for me."

"Claire," he pleaded, "I'll do whatever you want."

"I suppose you would," I said sadly, "I suppose you would."

I didn't want to bicker and argue and fight with him any more. I couldn't be bothered.

"James, I'm going now," I said.

"Will you think about what I said?" he asked.

"I will," I agreed. "But don't hold out any hope."

"I know you, Claire," he said, "you'll change your mind. Everything is going to be fine."

"Goodbye, James."

In fairness, I *did* think about what James had said. I owed it to Kate.

The arguments in favour of and against reuniting with James went over and back in my head like a tennis ball.

561

But the one thing I couldn't ignore, the one thing I couldn't argue my way out of, the one thing that I couldn't convince myself was otherwise, was the fact that I no longer cared about James.

I mean, I cared about him. I didn't want anything too terrible to happen to him. But I didn't love him the way I used to. I wished I knew what had caused this to happen. But it could have been so many things. He had had an affair – much as he'd like me to overlook it. That must have done a lot to destroy my trust in him. And me getting the blame for it, well, I wasn't too happy about that. Or it could be the fact that he wasn't man enough to own up to what he had done and just apologise. That went a long way in destroying any respect I might have had for him. Even now he wouldn't admit he was in the wrong. Even though he was scaling down his requirements of me, he was still making it sound as if he was doing me a favour.

He'd betrayed me. And then compounded it by treating me like an idiot.

Or maybe I'd just gone off short men.

I just knew one thing, if it was dead, it was dead. No one can resurrect love once it has breathed its last.

I rang James two days later and told him that there would be no reconciliation.

"You're letting your pride get in the way," he said. As though he'd been briefed.

"I'm not," I said wearily.

"You want to punish me," he suggested.

"I don't," I lied. (*Of course* it was nice to have the boot on the other foot.)

"I can wait," he promised.

"Please don't," I replied.

"I love you," he whispered.

"Goodbye," I said.

James continued to ring, maybe twice or three times a day. Checking up on me, wondering if I'd changed my mind yet, if I had, as he put it, come to my senses.

I was nice to him on the phone. It was no skin off my nose. He said he missed me. I suppose he did.

I found the phone calls a bit irritating. It was hard to believe that only three months ago I would have killed to have got a call from him. Now, it was more likely that I would kill if the calls *didn't* stop.

Then I stopped being irritated, and all I felt was sad.

Life is a very peculiar creature.

Chapter Thirty-Seven

I couldn't have said that I was happy. But I wasn't miserable. Or devastated the way I had been when James first left me.

I suppose I was calm. I had accepted that my life would never be the same again and would never be the way I had planned it. The things I had hoped for were never going to happen. I was not going to have four children with James. James and I would not grow old together. Even though I had always promised that my marriage would be the one that survived, the one that didn't break up, I could now accept, without too much heartache, that it *had* broken up.

Of course, I felt sad. Sad for the idealistic me, the one who had got married with such high, high, expectations. Even sad for James.

I really did feel older – and how! – and wiser.

I suppose I had learnt – the long, hard way – a bit of humility.

I really had control over so little. Either in my life. Or in any other people's.

And if I heard someone say "everything happens for a reason," or "when God closes one door, he opens another," it was no longer too difficult to stop myself from punching them in the face. Not difficult at all, in fact.

I didn't feel that my life was totally over.

Irredeemably altered, maybe. But not totally over.

My marriage had broken up, but I had a beautiful child. I had a wonderful family, very good friends and a job to go back to. Who knew, one day, I might even meet a nice man who wouldn't mind taking Kate on as well as me. Or if I waited long enough maybe Kate would meet a nice man who wouldn't mind taking me on as well as her. But in the meantime I had decided that I was just going to get on with my life and if Mr Perfect arrived along, I'd manage to make room for him somewhere.

I did all the boring legal things that I should have done ages ago. Well, maybe I shouldn't have done them ages ago. Maybe I wasn't ready then. Maybe now was the right time.

Either way it didn't make a blind bit of difference. The fact is they *weren't* done then and they were being done now.

I wanted custody of Kate. James said that he wouldn't fight it if he was given plenty of access to her. I was delighted because I wanted Kate to know her father. And I knew I was very lucky that James was being so reasonable. He could have been deliberately nasty and uncooperative and, in fairness to him, he wasn't.

James and I came to an agreement about the flat. We decided to sell it. He was going to live in it until it was sold.

That was pretty dreadful, actually. When he

received the documents from my solicitor he took it quite badly. I suppose he finally realised that it was over.

"You're really not coming back, are you?" he said sadly.

And even though I had instigated the whole thing, even though it was what I really wanted, I felt so sad also.

I had a pang of intense regret. If only things hadn't turned out this way. If only things had never gone wrong.

But they had.

Tearful eleventh-hour reunions are the stuff of Mills and Boon. They rarely happen in real life.

And, if they do, they usually occur when either one or both parties have drink taken.

No one showed any interest in buying the flat for ages and ages. In a way I was glad, because the thought of anyone else living in what I still considered to be *my* home was too awful to contemplate. But on the other hand it was a real worry because money was so tight. I like to hold James responsible. He probably nabbed any prospective buyers and bored them to death with talk of tax-relief on mortgages and suchlike. They probably fell asleep before they'd even seen the bedroom. But I shouldn't be so unkind. He meant well.

I spoke to my boss and told her that I'd be back in the saddle by early August. Now if I hadn't been feeling pretty miserable before now, the reminder that I had to go back to work was nearly enough to tip me back over the edge.

Maybe I was in the wrong job, maybe I didn't have a true vocation, maybe I was just bone lazy. Well, whatever it was I wasn't one of those lucky people (although I just think they're weird) who get great joy from their job. At best I thought of it as a means to an end, at worst a hell on earth. And I couldn't wait until I retired. Only thirty-one years to go. Unless I got lucky in the meantime and died.

No, honestly, that was just a joke.

So, in five weeks' time, it was back to the office for me. Back to administering seven hours a day, five days a week, forty-eight weeks of the year.

Jesus!

Why couldn't I have been born rich?

Sorry, sorry, I know I shouldn't complain. I was lucky to have a job. It was just that I wished that I could have someone to take care of me and Kate. I was just fantasising. Even if I had stayed with James I would still have had to return to work. It was simply that having to go back to work reminded me of how alone I really was now. How much responsibility I had. It was no longer just me that I was working for. A child was dependent on me.

I knew that James would provide for Kate – oh yes I knew. Believe me, I knew it. And I had an expensive solicitor to prove it! Not that James was stingy or mean in any way. Credit where it's due, etc., etc. But the days when I could spend my entire month's salary on lipstick, magazines and alcohol had gone. Long gone.

Being grown-up is not all you're led to believe it is. Not even slightly. It was too late now but I wished I'd read the small print.

I wanted my money back. But I'd used the damn thing now so I couldn't even exchange it.

I found somewhere for Kate and me to live in London.

Well, actually Judy did.

It would have been impossible for me to find somewhere in London while I was still in Dublin. Not unless I was willing to pay the National Debt in agency fees.

Some friend of a friend of a friend of Judy's was going to work in Norway in July and needed his flat looked after for nine months. I could afford the rent and the area wasn't too awful. Judy had seen the flat and assured me that it had a roof, a floor and the full complement of walls. Then Judy lied through her teeth and told the friend of a friend of a friend that I was neat and clean and quiet and solvent. I'm not sure if she even mentioned Kate at all.

Andrew – that was his name – rang me to put his mind at rest that I wasn't some kind of maniac who would douse his precious flat with petrol and set it alight before he'd even reached Terminal Two.

On the phone I was at my most prim and proper. I emphasised that I felt that cleanliness should be joined at the hip with Godliness and that I was in favour of bringing back the death sentence for burglars and litter-bugs.

"Well, perhaps a public flogging would be adequate. It might thrash some respect back into them," he suggested.

"Hmmmm," I said non-committally, because I wasn't certain whether he was joking or not.

Andrew sent me a contract and I sent him all kinds of references and bank details and, most importantly, some money. (Borrowed from Dad – would I ever grow up?)

Over the next ten days or so we had detailed phone conversations about what I was to do with his post. And which of his plants needed to be told jokes to. I had to tape *Brookside* and post it to him every week.

He gave me all kinds of useful advice.

He warned me that the woman downstairs was mad. "That's fine," I said unguardedly, "I'll probably like her."

"And don't go to the first Chinese," he warned. "They got caught with an Alsatian in their freezer. The one further up is far better."

"Thanks," I said.

"Use up anything that's left in the cupboards or the drinks cabinet," he offered.

"Thanks," I said enthusiastically.

"And if anything goes wrong," said his disembodied voice, "then don't hesitate to ring me. I'll leave you a number that you can contact me at."

"Thanks," I said again.

"I'm sure you'll be happy here," he promised, "it's a lovely airy flat."

"Right," I said, swallowing, "thanks." I was trying not to think of my own lovely flat which I had decorated and designed and made beautiful over the years. Some day I will have another one, I promised myself. When the time is right.

I felt even worse when I realised that "lovely, airy

569

flat" is usually what estate agents say when they mean the windows are broken.

Oh dear.

"I'll be in London briefly in October," he said, "I hope we can meet up then."

"That would be lovely," I said.

Nice guy, I thought, as I hung up the phone.

For a Neo-Nazi.

I wondered what he looked like.

Chapter Thirty-Eight

Men.

Ah, yes, men. I suppose the issue was bound to rear its ugly head sooner or later.

Now look, I want to make one thing clear. I didn't fancy this Andrew guy. It's just that he sounded nice (apart from the public flogging sentiment). And I was officially a single woman again and there were some thought patterns that I just slipped back into. I couldn't help it! It was obviously genetic. Or hormonal.

Anyway I was only curious. It didn't hurt to wonder about these things. I wasn't planning on acting on it.

And it didn't mean that I was going to jump into bed with the first man who gave me the glad eye.

I mean, if I was that desperate for a man, wouldn't I have stayed with James?

Although I realise that after the way I behaved with Adam there's a good chance that you won't believe me.

OK, fine, you don't have to believe me but Adam was an exception.

Adam was special.

So you heard that Adam had a girlfriend and a

baby. Well, what do you think of that? Pretty sensational, eh?

I suppose it made sense. There was always a hint that there was more to him than met the eye. But I was kind of expecting his Terrible Secret to be something like a drug habit, or a minor prison sentence, or something with a little bit of notoriety, even glamour, to it. I certainly wasn't prepared for the news that Adam was a Family Man.

It was a shock. I'd go so far as to say that it was an unpleasant shock. But, when Helen broke the news to me, I wasn't able to give it my full attention and indignation. I was a bit distracted what with being on my way out to catch a plane to London to end my marriage and all that. No, it was definitely not good news but I was too preoccupied to look it in the face and think about how I actually felt.

And I tried not to think about it in the following weeks.

Well, I had an awful lot of things to sort out and I couldn't afford to waste time day-dreaming. And Adam and I, such as it was, had been over even before I found out about his baby, so there was nothing to be gained by thinking about him. Adam was the past.

Anyway to be perfectly frank I didn't like thinking about Adam. It didn't make me happy. It was painful. If he accidentally strayed into my head, he didn't last five seconds, a bit like an overboard sailor in the icy waters of the Antarctic. Alarms would go off and a couple of burly security guards would be sent to chuck him out double fast.

If he even crossed my mind, I was lucky enough to have some kind of incredibly complicated, tedious legal document to immerse myself in.

And Helen was around a lot. She was studying for her exams and causing no end of disruption, complaining bitterly and asking questions and talking about having to have sex with all her lecturers if she hoped to pass. So she took my mind off Adam. She took my mind off everything except slow-motion fantasies of brutal murders.

But it was June and the weather had suddenly got so beautiful and hot. And sometimes when I was alone with Kate in the back garden, half asleep, the sun on my face, feeling so relaxed, when maybe I should have been thinking of James, instead my mind would accidentally drift Adam-wards and I would remember how sweet he had been and how lovely he had made me feel.

And at times like that, when my guard was down, I allowed myself to miss him, to feel sad that he wasn't there. But only for a moment. I didn't like to miss him. I didn't really like to think about him at all.

Let's face it, I didn't like what Helen had told me. It was not news that gladdened my heart. Or any other one of my internal organs. It's not that I felt he had two-timed me. I was hardly in any position to object, what with me being married. And, from what I'd managed to piece together from Helen's garbled narrative, I was fairly sure he was estranged from his girlfriend while he had his little fling with me.

If it's even worthy of being called a fling.

If I hadn't found it so unpleasant I'd probably call it the one-night-stand that it so obviously was.

I think I felt a bit, oh I don't know, *set-up*, I suppose. Fool that I was, I had been flattered by all the attention that Adam had paid me. It had been wonderful to feel so desired and admired. Especially after what had happened with James.

And now I felt that he only wanted me because of Kate. Not that he wanted Kate, or anything sick like that. But he wanted me because I was a mother. I probably reminded him of his girlfriend. I didn't know what the set-up with Adam and his girlfriend was but, if she had run off with the child, it must have been really hard for him and maybe I was some sort of replacement.

I felt, I felt . . . a bit mortified, I suppose. I had been thrilled that Adam had chosen me. But it wasn't really me that he had chosen at all. It was my circumstances.

I was hurt.

And I felt foolish for thinking that someone as gorgeous as him could seriously be interested in someone as ordinary as me. What could I have been thinking of?

The only thing I could say in my defence was that I wasn't myself. I'd been through a lot and my sanity was an infrequent caller.

But while we're on the subject of Adam I should admit that I was angry with him.

Not very. But a bit. I was pissed-off with him for playing with my feelings. For making me feel special when I wasn't. And then for giving me that sanctimonious speech about going back to James. He had no business doing that if he didn't care about me. People have to *earn* the right to make me feel guilty. It was something that I really should try not to give away as easily as I used to.

But as time passed and I spent more time dozing in the sunny garden, my feelings began to change. I started to see the other side of the coin. In fact I started to feel downright metaphysical about it. Not something I was normally prone to.

It might have been the excess of sun.

Maybe Adam was sent to me for a reason, I thought. Adam made me feel so good about myself, Adam restored my confidence so much that it probably gave me the strength to stand up to James. Maybe Adam's judgmental speech was even instrumental in helping me to make the right decision about James.

It would have been nice to think that Kate and I helped Adam to deal with the pain of being separated from his child and his girlfriend. Maybe we'd helped him to realise how important they were to him, depending on whether he had left them or whether they had left him.

It was so lovely to feel the bitterness leave me. I began to feel happy that I had met Adam. I felt that Adam and I had met for a short time for a special reason. It *had* to be shortlived. And I liked to think that both of us benefited from it.

This might well be a load of mystical, superstitious nonsense. But I wasn't normally the kind of person who sees signs and portents and reasons and explanations in events. On the contrary. As I said earlier, I was always making fun of people who claimed that everything happens for a reason. Of course I wasn't as unkind as Helen, but at the same time I was far from indulgent. Oh, existentialism, thy name is Claire.

My usual approach would have been to say something like "Adam and I had sex because we both fancied a shag. Nothing else to it." But I just couldn't be cynical, hard and all as I tried.

Very worrying, of course, but what was I to do?

But it meant that lying out in the back garden was a lot more pleasant now. Every time I thought of Adam I didn't feel as if a knife had been twisted in my gut. Some kind of peace stole over me. I didn't need to feel let down, or lied to, or humiliated or foolish. It had been a pleasure to know him for the short time that I had. Perhaps it was better that way.

You know what it's like. Sometimes, you meet a wonderful person, but it's only for a brief instant. Maybe on holidays, or on a train or maybe even in a bus queue. And they touch your life for a moment, but in a special way. And instead of mourning because they can't be with you for longer, or because you don't get the chance to know them better, isn't it better to be glad that you met them at all?

There was a very discernible feeling that a chapter had ended in my life. I started preparing myself, both emotionally and sartorially, for the return to London.

I began to pack clothes. I gathered enthusiastically and spread my net widely, visiting all wardrobes in the house, especially Helen's, and leaving no drawer unopened, no hanger unexamined.

Although I continued to bicker with everyone in the family, I knew that leaving them would be awful. It would be especially hard leaving my mother. Not just because she was so handy to have around Kate. No really, I mean it, I knew I was going to miss her terribly. It would be like leaving home all over again. Worse, in fact, because when I'd first left home seven years ago, I was delighted to be going, couldn't leave fast enough in my haste to capitalise on my imminent freedom.

It was different now. I was seven years older and wearier. I knew that there was no novelty in ironing my own clothes, paying my own bills.

But I had to go back to London.

After all my job was there. And I hadn't noticed anyone in Dublin breaking down my front door to offer me a job. Although I hadn't applied for any jobs, to be fair.

But more importantly, Kate's father was in London. I wanted her to see lots of him, to know that she had a father who loved her (well, I was sure he would when he got to know her better), and to grow up with a man in her life. Because if she was looking to me to provide her with a live-in father figure, I wasn't sure that I would be able to oblige. Maybe I would meet another man some day, but I didn't feel very hopeful.

And now that I thought of it that threw up another entirely new set of worries. What if Kate didn't like the new man? What if she got all jealous and threw tantrums and ran away from home? Oh God!

Well, I wasn't going to worry about that yet. It was jumping the gun slightly when I'd already got my hands full worrying about never meeting a man again.

I didn't mean it really. I wasn't *agonising* about never having a man again.

Just mildly concerned.

I decided that I'd go back to London on the fifteenth of July. I could move into my new flat and give myself and Kate a couple of weeks to settle in and find a child-minder, before I went back to work.

Then, in time-honoured fashion, I discovered an entire new set of worries. How would I take care of Kate when I was all on my own? I'd become very dependent on having my mother around to suggest reasons why Kate wouldn't stop crying, or eating, or puking or whatever.

"You can always ring me," promised Mum.

"Thanks," I said tearfully.

"And I'm sure you'll be fine," she said.

"Really?" I asked, pathetically. Even though I was nearly thirty I could still behave like a child when I was round my mother.

"Oh yes," she said. "No one knows how strong they are until they have to be."

"I suppose you're right," I admitted.

"I am," she said firmly. "How about you? You haven't managed too badly in spite of all you've been through."

"I suppose," I said doubtfully.

"Really," she said. "Remember, if it doesn't kill you, it makes you stronger."

"Am I stronger?" I asked faintly, in my most childish voice.

"Jesus," she said, "when you put on that voice, I do actually wonder."

"Oh," I said, annoyed. I wanted her to be nice to me and tell me that I was wonderful and could cope with anything.

"Claire," she said, "there's no point asking me if you're stronger. You're the one who knows that."

"Well, I am then," I said belligerently.

"Good," she smiled, "and remember. You said it. Not me."

The Wednesday before I was due to go back, Anna, Kate and I were out in the garden. The weather was still beautiful. Anna was, er, how can I put it, between jobs, so the pair of us had spent the last week lounging round the garden, dressed in an assortment of bikini tops and cut-off shorts, trying to get a tan.

I was winning.

I tanned easily, and Anna didn't. But then again, Anna was tiny and dainty and looked lovely in a bikini and I felt like a huge heifer beside her. I wasn't fat anymore. But she was so petite and delicate that she made me feel huge by comparison. I *liked* being tall. I just didn't like feeling like an East German Olympic athlete.

So if I was winning in the tanning war, it was really only right and just.

When the genes were distributed she got the cute little body. I got the smooth, golden skin.

She got thin legs. I didn't.

I got breasts. She didn't.

Fair is fair.

Our attention was drawn to the kitchen window. Mum had lifted the curtain and was gesturing and knocking.

"What does she want," said Anna sleepily.

"I think she's saying 'hello,'" I said, slowly raising my head from the lounger to look at her.

"Hello," we both said languidly, and waved our arms limply. Mum continued to knock. The gestures that she made seemed to be a lot more frantic and vulgar.

"You go," I said to Anna.

"I can't," she said, "you go."

"I'm too sleepy," I said, "you'll have to go."

"No, you go," she said, closing her eyes.

Mum came marching round into the garden.

"Claire, phone!" she roared. "And the next time I knock on the window you're to come in. I don't do it for the good of my health, you know."

"Sorry Mum."

"Keep an eye on Kate," I told Anna, as I ran into the house.

"Mmmmm," she mumbled.

"And put some more sun-block on her," I shouted over my shoulder.

I stumbled into the kitchen, almost blinded by coming into the dim house after the blazing sunlight of the garden.

I picked up the phone. "Hello," I said.

"Claire," said James.

"Oh hello James," I said, wondering what the hell he wanted. If he hadn't rung me to tell me that he'd sold our flat, I didn't want to talk to him.

"How are you, Claire?" he asked politely.

"Fine," I said shortly, wishing he'd get on with it.

"Claire," he said, with great weight, "I have something to tell you."

"Well, go ahead," I cordially invited.

"Claire, I hope you don't mind, but I've met someone else."

"Oh," I said. "Well, what do you want me to say? Congratulations?"

"No," he said. "There's no need for that. But I thought I had better tell you seeing as you made such a fuss the last time."

With monumental self-control I didn't hang up the phone.

"Thank you James," I managed. "That's very thoughtful of you. Now, if you'll excuse me, I must go."

"But don't you want to know all about her?" he said quickly.

"No," I said.

"Don't you mind?" he asked anxiously.

"No," I laughed.

"She's lots younger than you," he said nastily. "She's only twenty-two."

"That's nice," I said mildly.

"Her name's Rita," he said.

"Nice name," I commented.

581

"She's an actuary," he said, sounding a bit desperate.

"How lovely," I exclaimed. "You must have so much in common!"

"What the hell is wrong with you?" he shouted.

"I don't know what you're talking about," I protested.

"Why are you acting as if you don't give a damn?" he thundered. "I've just told you I've got a new girlfriend!"

"I suppose I must be acting like I don't give a damn, because I actually don't give a damn," was the only thing I could come up with.

"Oh, and James," I continued.

"Yes?" he said hopefully.

"Kate is fine," I said. "I'm sure it's just an oversight that you forgot to ask. Now I'm going. Great news! I'm delighted for you. Long may it last and all that. Goodbye." I slammed the phone down.

How pathetic can you get? What did he expect me to do? Burst into tears and beg him to take me back? Hadn't he learnt anything?

I went back out to the garden. Anna had come to and was sitting up playing with Kate. She was so beautiful. Kate, that is. Although Anna was lovely too, no doubt about it. But, Kate, she was more lovely. She had started to develop a little personality all of her own. When you spoke to her she made gurgly noises and laughed sometimes and made eye-contact. It was almost like having a conversation with her.

Although she wasn't doing too much laughing at

that moment. Her fat, little face was bright pink and shiny under her yellow sun-hat and she looked as if she didn't want to do any more sun-bathing. "I'm hot and bored," her look said. "And I've had quite enough of talking to this flake."

"Who was it?" asked Anna.

"James," I spat, barely able to say his name.

"What's up with him?" asked Anna.

"He has a new girlfriend," I said curtly.

"Do you mind?" she asked anxiously.

"Of *course* I don't mind," I said, outraged.

"So why are you acting so cross?" asked Anna.

"Because he disturbed my sunbathing – made me get up off the lounger and *walk* – just to tell me that. I can't believe it! I really can't. What an asshole."

Never mind James. I was worried about Kate.

"You don't think she's burning, do you?" I asked Anna anxiously. "Maybe I should have used a higher factor."

"Maybe," agreed Anna doubtfully, "but I don't think they *make* a higher one."

It was true. I had smothered Kate with a sun-block that had the highest protection factor known to man. Was I being an overprotective mother? I couldn't help myself. I worried about her. I mean, after all, she was a baby and her skin was very delicate. I didn't want to take any chances.

"I think I'll bring her inside," I said, "just to be on the safe side."

"Relax," advised Anna.

"No, I'd better take her in," I said. "She might burn."

"Oh don't go," pleaded Anna. "I'll have no one to talk to."

Just then we heard voices in the kitchen. It sounded as if a small commotion had broken out.

"Helen's home," I said to Anna, "you can play with her."

"Oh no," groaned Anna. "She'll be talking about killing herself if she fails and could she stomach having sex with Professor Macauley and asking me all these stupid questions about Ancient Greece."

"I mean, what do I know about Ancient Greece?" she asked, sounding wronged and hard-done-by. "Just because I worked in a bar for six weeks in Santorini she thinks I should know about Zeus and all that crowd."

She sighed and began to gather her things. "I think I'll come in with you."

But before she could make her escape, Helen burst into the garden. She was wearing a little denim skirt and a T-shirt. Her hair was wound up on top of her head and as usual she looked beautiful.

She stopped when she saw us and stared long and hard.

"Look at them," she said bitterly. "Just look at them, the lucky bitches."

"Hi Helen," said Anna, warily.

"Lazy cows, just lying around doing nothing while I have to work my arse off studying," she continued resentfully.

I shaded my eyes with my hand to look at Helen, at her furious little face. And it was only then that I realised that Helen was not alone.

She had brought a guest.

A male guest.

A tall, handsome male guest.

A gorgeous, blue-eyed, dark-haired, square-jawed, tall, handsome, male guest, who was wearing faded jeans and a white T-shirt.

One who'd got a tan since I last saw him.

I hadn't thought that he could get any better-looking, but it would appear that I was wrong.

The bastard!

"Hi Adam," I said, wanting to burst into tears.

"Hi Claire," he said politely.

I held my breath and waited for him to go back into the house. Then I realised, with horror, that he wasn't going.

"Oh shit," I thought frantically, "he's coming over."

Helen and Adam made their way over to the little oasis of sun-loungers, Diet Coke, suntan lotion, women's magazines and crisps that Anna, Kate and I had created. Adam stood for a moment, and loomed over Anna and I, prostrate on the loungers. He didn't seem too relaxed. His usual, easy charm was missing. He looked awkward, a bit unfriendly.

My heart pounded. I felt at such a terrible disadvantage. Jesus, why couldn't Helen have given me some warning that she was bringing the beautiful Adam here. I could have put on some make-up and a nice bikini. Because when I said earlier that I was lying round the garden wearing cut-off shorts and little tops, I wasn't for a moment implying that I looked like one of those sexy babes from *Baywatch*.

God no! The shorts were ancient and made from really nasty brushed denim and were cut in a really weird way. They were totally unflattering and made my bum look really wide. And the lycra had gone in my bikini top so it was all droopy and stretched.

It's the Mills and Boon versus real life syndrome all over again. Whenever they're caught unawares by their man they just happen to have got out of the shower and are covered in fragrant body lotion, their hair is in damp little tendrils which escapes from their towel and they look absolutely beautiful in a totally innocent and natural way.

Enough to make you puke.

But in real life you can put money on looking at your very, very worst when the man you like/love/fancy arrives unexpectedly. Well, that's always been *my* experience. You might be a bit luckier.

I wish he wouldn't just stand there looking down at me, I thought nervously.

"Adam, you're blocking out the sun," I said, trying to make it sound like a joke. "Why don't you sit down." He sat down. It was quite amazing how a man so big and tall could make sitting down look so graceful. Sorry, I shouldn't have noticed that. I certainly shouldn't have remarked on it.

He smiled over at Anna.

"Hello," he said.

"Hi Adam," she simpered.

"How are you?" He sounded as if he was really interested.

"Never mind her! What about me?" I nearly shouted.

"I'm fine," said Anna, smiling back shyly.

"Jesus," muttered Helen, giving Anna a "you're so pathetic" look.

Adam and Anna continued to murmur to each other.

Then Helen turned her attention to me.

"Get off that," she ordered, trying to push me off the lounger. "I've just done an exam. I need to lie down."

"That's fine," I said, getting up. "I was just going anyway."

It was important for me to let her know that she hadn't forced me into relinquishing my sun-lounger. That I was doing it of my own accord.

Power games.

I was so childish.

"Yes," said Anna hastily, her face like a tomato. "I'm going too."

"Why, where are you going?" demanded Helen.

"Inside," I said.

"Oh great," she said. She was really pissed-off. "I've just done an awful exam and I've got to learn the entire Anthropology course this evening and you won't even stay for five minutes to have a chat and help me unwind."

"But Kate's too hot," I said.

"Go on then," she said gloomily. "Go."

She looked at Adam. "We'll start in ten minutes, OK?"

"OK," he agreed.

"What'll we do first?" she asked.

"What do you want to do?" he replied.

Correct answer. He obviously had a good idea of how to treat Helen.

"I suppose we could do Dysfunctional Families," said Helen. "Seeing as you know so much about that."

She laughed nastily.

"Helen," said Anna, in a shocked voice.

"What?!" said Helen, all belligerent. "It's only a joke. Anyway, he *does*. Don't you?" she demanded of Adam.

"I suppose I do," he said politely.

That was enough. I was going. I picked up Kate and walked across the lawn (lawn! What a joke!) with her. The couple of yards felt like miles and miles. All I could think about was Adam's eyes homing in on my highly unattractive arse in the awful shorts.

I finally reached the safety of the kitchen.

I realised that I had left my magazine in the garden. Well, it could stay there! You wouldn't catch me going anywhere near Adam of my own volition.

Oh dear!

I was very upset. Because, over the past few weeks, I had begun to suspect that maybe Adam hadn't been that attractive at all. That, in my recently-deserted state, my judgement had been impaired. Perhaps I had been so grateful for the attention from him, that I had managed to convince myself that he was gorgeous.

But no. It wasn't true. The bastard was gorgeous. I hadn't imagined it. I hadn't been deluded.

And he looked even nicer with a tan. And his arms were so big and muscly in that T-shirt.

Jesus! It was too much to bear what with me being celibate for nigh on five months, not counting that one night with Adam.

Actually, it was a lot longer than that, because James wouldn't touch me with a stick in the last four or five months of my pregnancy.

Anyway, what was Adam's problem? Why was he all cold and unfriendly to me? Surely that was a bit unnecessary? Was he afraid that I was going to attempt to jump on his bones? That I wouldn't be able to restrain myself? Did he feel that he had to keep me at bay?

Well, he needn't worry, I thought. He was safe. I wouldn't attempt to come between him and his girlfriend. I wasn't as stupid as I used to be. I recognised a no-win situation when I was looking it in the face.

"Isn't it weird," I thought, as I carried Kate upstairs. "The last time I saw Adam I had just got out of his bed. We had been as intimate as two human beings could possibly be. And now we're acting like polite strangers."

Chapter Thirty-Nine

Kate was a lot happier inside. All smiles and gurgles and kicks when I put her into her cot. I held her hot little feet and cycled her legs – she loved that. Well, at least I hoped she loved it because I enjoyed it immensely – when I heard the knock on my bedroom door.

What was going on? *No one* knocked in our house.

The door opened and Adam loomed into the room. Everything instantly looked much smaller, like a doll's house.

"Oh Lord," I thought, going into shock and abruptly abandoning Kate's little legs. "What does he want?"

Maybe he wasn't able to believe how awful my shorts were and was coming for a second look.

"Claire," he said, sheepishly, "can I talk to you for a moment?"

He stood there, so big, so beautiful, an anxious look on his handsome face.

I looked at him and something happened inside me (no! not that!), something wonderful.

My heart lifted and a surge of *gladness* rushed through me, so strong it nearly knocked me over. I was suddenly filled with hope and gladness and happiness. That elation when you thought all was lost, and then you realised that everything was going to be fine.

You know the one I'm talking about. The one that only happens once or twice in a lifetime.

"Yes," I said, "of course."

He came over and shook Kate's foot and then sat down beside me on the bed. The mattress nearly hit the floor, but never mind that.

"Claire," he said, looking at me beseechingly with his blue, blue eyes, "I'd like to explain about my girlfriend and my baby."

"Oh yes?" I asked, trying to sound brisk and businesslike. As if he wasn't having a very unsettling effect on me.

His bigness and nearness was a bit overwhelming. As I said before, the first thing I had ever noticed about him was his manliness. And now it was as if he had doused the bed with testosterone. Or as if he'd walked round the room with one of those incense disperser things that the priests wave around at Benediction, except, instead of incense, his dispenser thing was filled with Essence of Man.

I couldn't *help* it if I thought about having sex with him. I was only human. If you prick me do I not bleed? If you stick a gorgeous man under my nose, do I not want to rip the clothes off him?

I mean, *I* don't make the rules.

It was imperative that I got myself under control. Adam was not here to offer me his body. He was here, well at least I hoped he was here, so we could untangle whatever was happening in our lives when we met each other. Then maybe we could be friends.

I realised that I'd really, really like to be friends with him. He was so interesting and entertaining and sweet. He was a lovely person to be around. Special, you know. Whoever this girlfriend of his was, she was one lucky woman.

"Claire," he said, "thank you for giving me this chance to explain."

"Oh God," I said, "get a grip. Stop sounding so humble."

"It's just . . . I don't know," he faltered. "It must have been a bit of a, a . . . *surprise* when Helen told you about me having a child."

"Yes, it was a . . . surprise," I said with a little smile.

"OK, OK," he said. He ran his hand though his lovely, silky hair. "Maybe surprise is the wrong word."

"Maybe," I agreed. But in a nice way.

"I should have told you," he said.

"Why?" I asked. "It's not as if we were going out with each other or anything."

He stared at me. He looked sad.

"Well, even if we weren't going out with each other, I still felt that I should have told you," he said.

"But I was afraid that I'd frighten you off," he continued.

"That was hardly likely considering my circumstances," I replied.

"But I thought you'd wonder what kind of guy I was that I wasn't allowed to see my own child. I wanted to tell you. I nearly did loads of times but I always lost my nerve at the last minute."

"And why are you telling me now?" I asked.

"Because it's all fixed," he said.

"Well, wasn't it a stroke of luck that Helen invited you here today and that I just happened in?" I asked a bit tartly.

"Claire," he said anxiously. "If you hadn't been here today I would have rung you. I thought you'd gone back to London ages ago. Otherwise I would have been in touch sooner."

"No, *honestly*," he assured me when he saw the sceptical look that I gave him.

"All right," I conceded. "I believe you."

"So tell me all about it," I suggested, forcing myself to speak gently. Trying to keep the urgent curiosity out of my voice.

I always enjoy a good human interest story, even if I happen to be peripherally involved.

A series of peculiar, gurgly type noises came from Kate's cot. Oh please don't cry darling, I hoped desperately. Not right now. I *really* want to hear this. It's important to Mummy.

And would you believe it? She quietened down again. She obviously inherited something good from her father.

But sshush now, ladies and gentlemen, Adam was going to explain all.

"I had gone out with Hannah for . . . " he began.

"Who's Hannah?" I interrupted.

It's always good to sort out who all the main characters are before the story begins.

"The mother of my child," he explained.

"Fine," I said, "go on."

"I had gone out with her for a long time, about two years," he said.

"Yes," I nodded.

"And it ended," he said.

"Oh," I said, "that sounds a bit abrupt."

"No, no, it wasn't," he said. "What I mean is neither of us ran off with someone else or anything like that. It had just run its course."

"Yes." I nodded.

"So we split up," he said.

"Yes," I said. "I'm with you so far."

"But I was still really fond of her," he said. "I missed her. But every time we saw each other it was awful. She'd cry and ask why hadn't it worked and could we try again and that kind of thing."

"Yes," I said. This was all very familiar.

"And we always ended up going to bed together," he said.

He looked a bit embarrassed when he said this. I didn't know why. I mean, *everyone* does that when they split up with someone they once loved and still do in a way, don't they?

It's the rule.

You split up, you say you'll still be friends, you meet up a week later for your first "friendly" drink, you get drunk, you say how weird it is not being able to touch each other even in an affectionate way, you kiss each other, you stop and say, "No we mustn't", you kiss again, you stop and say "This is ridiculous", you kiss again, you say "Maybe just this once. It's only because I miss you so much". You get the bus back to his place, you practically have sex in someone's garden when you get off the bus, you get to his house, everything is so familiar and you cry because you know you don't belong there anymore. You have sex, you cry again, you go to sleep, you have horrible dreams where one minute you're back together and the next you've split up again and you wake up the next morning wishing you were dead.

Everyone knows that rule. It's one of the first principles governing the end of a love affair. Adam must be very naive if he thought it's only ever happened to him.

"Anyway, Hannah got pregnant," he said.

"Oh dear," I said sympathetically.

He looked at me a bit sharply. He thought that I was being sarcastic. I wasn't, honestly.

"We talked about it and we considered everything. She wanted to get married. I didn't want to, because I thought it was a stupid thing to do. I didn't see the point in getting married to give the child a stable home, if its parents didn't love each other any more."

"Mmmmm," I said non-commitally. I mean, technically he was right. But as one woman to another, my heart went out to the misfortunate Hannah.

"I suppose you think I'm a total bastard," he said, looking a bit wretched.

"No, not really," I said. "I agree with you that getting married achieves nothing in that situation."

"You *do* think I'm a bastard," he said, "I can tell."

"I *don't*," I said exasperated. "Get on with it, would you."

There was far too much developing of the characters and not enough action in this story for my liking.

"We thought about her having the baby and putting it up for adoption but Hannah didn't want to do that. Then we talked about her having an abortion."

I flashed a quick look at Kate. I couldn't help it. I just felt so incredibly lucky that I hadn't had to consider an abortion when I found out that I was pregnant.

"Anyway, an abortion seemed like some sort of solution," he said wearily. "But neither of us wanted to do that."

"I'm sure you didn't," I murmured, trying to sound like I believed him.

But I wondered to myself "Is this guy for *real*?"

I'd always suspected that most men thought that abortion was almost a Sacrament, a gift generously bestowed on them by Heaven to make their lives uncomplicated and pleasant. To deal with nasty little nuisances, like children, which look like interfering with their life of gay bachelorhood.

Of course there's always the crowd who get all sanctimonious and self-righteous and say that abortion is murder. You'll find that the men who are quite happy to say this are the ones whose girlfriends aren't pregnant. But the minute their woman has an "accident" and is with child, it's usually a very different story. Quick as a flash, the SPUC stickers have disappeared from the back window of the car to be replaced by "My body, my choice" or even more likely "Her body, my choice".

They're often the very first to tentatively suggest that maybe now is not the right time to have a baby, and that there's nothing to an abortion, really. That it's easier than having a tooth out. And that in most cases you don't even have to stay overnight. And there's no need to feel guilty because, at this stage, it's not even a child, just a few cells. And that they'll come with her and collect her afterwards. And maybe in a few weeks they'll go away for a weekend to help her get over it. And then, before the woman knows what's happening to her, she's lying on an operating table in an expensive "nursing home", wearing a paper frock that opens all the way up the back, with a needle stuck in her arm, counting down from ten.

Sorry, sorry! I got a little bit distracted there.

As you may have noticed this is something I feel very strongly about, but maybe now isn't the time to go into it. Suffice it to say that Adam had me convinced that he wasn't one of those men.

But just one more thing and then I'll shut up. Show me a man who's pregnant, penniless and partnerless and *then* invite him to stand on the soapbox and tell me that he still thinks abortion is completely wrong. Hah! I'd put money on him being a gibbering blur on his way to the Sealink office.

Anyway, back to Adam the feminist.

He was still explaining, all anxious and earnest, staring at me with a beseeching look in his beautiful eyes.

D'you know, he had the most gorgeous eyelashes? Really thick and long and . . . sorry.

Ahem.

"I said that if she had the baby, I'd do whatever I could to help," he said. "I promised I'd support her financially and that I was happy for the baby to live with me. Or with her. Or we could share. Whatever Hannah wanted. I wanted her to have the baby but I knew that at the end of the day the decision was hers. I couldn't decide for her and I didn't want to put pressure on her to have the child because I knew she was scared. She was only twenty-two."

"Oh dear," I said, "that's very sad."

"It was," he said miserably. "It was really awful."

"And then what happened?" I asked.

"Her parents got involved. And when they found out that we'd discussed her having an abortion, they went mad. Fair enough, I suppose. And they took her away, from my supposedly evil influence, to their house in Sligo."

"Jesus," I said, imagining Hannah being locked up in a tower, in the middle of nowhere, like the princess with the long golden hair. "How awful. It's barbaric! Like something out of the dark ages."

"No," he said quickly, eager to put me right, "it wasn't that bad. They meant well. They only wanted the best for the baby. After all it was their grandchild and they wanted to make sure that Hannah didn't have an abortion. But then they wouldn't let me talk to Hannah any time that I rang up. And they said that, when the baby was born, I was to leave them alone."

"Are you serious?" I said, outraged. "I've never heard anything like that. Well, I suppose I have. But only about uncivilised, mad people. And then what happened? Didn't this Hannah have any mind of her own? Didn't she tell these parents of hers where to get off? I mean, she was a grown woman!"

"Well," he said awkwardly, "then Hannah didn't want to see me either. I went to Sligo and she spoke to me and told me that she didn't want anything further to do with me and she didn't want me interfering when the baby was born."

"But why?" I cried.

"I don't really know," he said unhappily. "I think she felt very bitter that I wouldn't marry her. And she was angry with me for getting her pregnant. Her parents had convinced her that I must be the son of Satan to have thought about an abortion."

"I see," I said, "so what happened next?"

"I got legal advice to see what I could do. And, do you know what? I've got almost *no* rights at all. Practically none. But, even if I could have insisted on my right to see my child, I didn't want it to be a vicious legal battle. I really couldn't believe that Hannah would do that to me. It was terrible."

He was silent for a few moments.

Kate was being suspiciously quiet, I thought in alarm. But she *looked* fine.

"The worst time of all was when the baby was born," Adam went on. "I didn't even know if it *had* been born or not. I didn't know if it was healthy. I didn't know whether it was a boy or a girl. Then I rang her house and her father told me that it was a girl and she was fine. And that Hannah was fine too. But he said she didn't want to speak to me."

"Isn't that awful?" I breathed.

"Yes, it was. And for a whole year I heard nothing," he said. "It was a nightmare. I was totally powerless."

My attention was distracted from Adam's sorry plight by the sound of feet pounding up the stairs. Then Helen burst into the room. She stared from me to Adam and back again. "What's going on here?" she asked in astonishment.

I went totally dumb. I couldn't speak. I didn't know what the hell to say to her.

Adam, in time-honoured fashion, came to the rescue.

"Helen," he said gently, "would you mind giving me a few moments with Claire."

"Yes!" she said truculently. "I would mind."

A pause while she wrestled with her curiosity. Then she demanded, "Why?"

"I'll explain later," he said, with a kindly look.

She stood at the door for a while, suspicion and jealousy written all over her exquisite little face.

"Five minutes," she said, throwing me a poisonous look and she flounced from the room.

"Oh God," I said, "you'd better go."

"No," he said, "she's already pissed off with me. I might as well stay and finish what I'm telling you."

"On your head be it, in that case," I said nervously, marvelling at his courage.

"Fine," he said, unbothered. "Well, as I said, I didn't hear from her for a whole year – I was just starting to come to terms with it. And then about a month ago she turned up out of the blue. I couldn't believe it! And she brought Molly with her."

"Who's Molly?" I interrupted, "is that your baby?"

"Yes," he said. "Isn't it a terrible name for a baby?"

"I like it," I said huffily. I suppose I'm a bit defensive because my baby's name isn't the most glamorous one you could imagine either.

"Maybe," said Adam, "but you'd have to see her. She's gorgeous. She should be called something beautiful. Like Mirabelle or . . . "

"Isn't that a restaurant?" I interrupted. I didn't like the direction this conversation was taking. Especially with Kate within earshot. I didn't want her to get a complex. God knows, the cards were stacked against her enough as it was. I was afraid that in thirty years time when she was a drug-addict and an alcoholic and bulimic and addicted to shop-lifting, that I'd get the blame. That she'd say that it was all my fault for not calling her something pretty and girlie.

"Look, don't worry about your child's name," I said. "Keep going with the story."

"OK," he said. "Well, anyway, we made it up, I suppose. She said she was sorry that she hadn't involved me from the beginning with Molly. But she wanted to know was it too late to start now?"

"And?" I asked.

"Well, at first I really wanted to tell her to fuck off," he said.

Jesus! I nearly gasped. I could hardly believe that Adam was acting so *normal.*

Hold the front page. Shocking new headlines – "Adam holds grudge!"

"But then I realised that I'd be cutting off my nose to spite my face," he continued.

How disappointing, I thought. For a moment there I thought he was going to act immature and childish. Well, never mind. There's always another time.

"So we've come to a civilised agreement about Molly's custody. Hannah and I are friends again – well, at least we're working on it," he said.

"Oh!" I said, startled. "Oh."

What did "friends" mean, I wondered. Did it mean that they had sex at every available opportunity or did it really mean just "friends"?

Only one way to find out. I took a deep breath.

"Er, so does that mean that you and Hannah aren't, you know, going out with each other?" I asked, trying to sound very casual.

"No," he laughed, giving me a "Haven't you been paying attention to *anything* I've been saying" look.

("Thank God!")

"No," he said. "I thought that was obvious. That's the whole point. That's why this is all so great. I can be involved in my child's life without having to be romantically involved with her mother."

"But at the same time I can be friends with Hannah because I respect and admire her," he added hastily, always anxious to be right-on and decent.

"Are you really happy about seeing your child?" I asked gently.

He nodded and looked as if he might cry.

Oh please don't, I thought frantically. I think I'm sick of all this new man business. *Stop* being in touch with your bloody emotions. Keep away from your feminine side! If I catch you near it I'll slap you.

A little voice in my head prompted, "Ask him!"

"Fuck off," I muttered back to it.

"Go *on*," it said again, "ask him. What have you got to lose?"

"*No,*" I said, feeling very uncomfortable. "Leave me alone."

"You're dying to know," reminded the voice. "In fact, you deserve to know."

"Just shut up," I said through gritted teeth. "I'm not going to ask him anything!"

"Well, if you won't," said the voice, "then I will."

And to my horror I found myself opening my mouth and a voice came out and asked Adam, "So was that why you liked being around me? You know, because of Kate? Because I had a baby?"

I was mortified!

I couldn't believe that I had found the nerve to ask it.

You couldn't take my subconscious *anywhere*.

"No!" said Adam. Well, he didn't so much say it as shout it. "No, no, no. I was so afraid you'd think that. That you'd go all Freudian on me and think that I liked being with you just because I was looking for some sort of replacement for my lost child and girlfriend."

"Well, you can hardly blame me, can you?" I asked. But not in a nasty aggressive way.

"But why would I need some kind of bait to want to be with you?" he asked. "You're wonderful!"

I said nothing. Just sat there, feeling half embarrassed, half delighted.

"Seriously," he went on. "You've got to believe me. What kind of self-esteem have you got? You're amazing. Don't tell me you didn't know that?"

"Well, didn't you?" he asked again, when I didn't answer.

"No," I muttered.

"Look at me," he said. He put his hand gently on my cheek and turned my face up to his. "Please listen to me. You're so beautiful. And kind and clever and funny and lovely and a laugh. *They're* some of the reasons that I like being with you so much. The fact that you had a child was neither here nor there."

"Really?" I asked. Blushing like a beacon and going all girlie and shy.

"Really," he laughed. "I would have liked you even if you hadn't had a baby."

He smiled.

He looked beautiful.

Oh God! I was melting.

"Honestly," he said.

"I believe you," I said.

I smiled too. I couldn't help myself.

We sat on the bed smirking at each other like morons.

After a while he spoke again.

"So you took my advice in the end," he said, gently teasing.

"About what?" I asked. "Oh, you mean about James. Well, I didn't go back to him after all, but it wasn't because of anything *you* said."

"Fine, fine," he laughed. "I'm just glad you changed your mind. It doesn't really matter who changed it for you. You deserve a lot better than someone like him."

"Can I ask you something?" I said.

"Of course," he replied.

"What does Hannah look like?"

He gave me a knowing look and laughed slightly before he spoke. "She's got long curly blonde hair. She's about the same size as Helen or Anna. She's got brown eyes."

"Oh," I said.

"Happy now?" he asked.

"What are you talking about?"

"That she looks nothing like you? That I wasn't trying to replace her with you?"

You had to hand it to him. You couldn't say he wasn't perceptive. I was satisfied that this Hannah was nothing like me. But now I was all jealous because she sounded tiny and beautiful.

Jesus! Was I ever satisfied?

I started to laugh. I was being ridiculous. "Yes Adam, I'm happy that you weren't trying to replace her with me. But, right now, you'd better get back to Helen," I said.

I stood up.

Then he stood up, instantly making me feel tiny.

There we stood, not really knowing what to say. I just knew that I didn't want to say goodbye.

"You're a very special woman," he said. And he pulled me to him and tightened his arms around me.

And fool that I was, I let him.

Big mistake. Huge, colossal, *enormous* mistake.

I hadn't been too bad until we made physical

contact. But the minute I was in his arms all hell broke loose on the emotions front. Longing and yearning and lust (yes, even more!) and loss and a warm fuzzy feeling. Being in his arms reminded me of how he had made me feel. I thought I had forgotten how wonderful it was to be with him. But it all came rushing back.

My head was buried against his chest. I could feel his heart beating through the thin material of the T-shirt. The same beautiful hint of soap and warm male skin that I remembered.

I wanted to stay there forever, safe, pressed up against his beautiful hard body, his arms holding me tenderly.

I pulled away from him.

"You're not so bad yourself," I replied. For the life of me I couldn't understand why I had tears in my eyes.

"Be happy," he said.

"You too," I replied.

I wriggled out of his arms.

"Well, goodbye," I sniffed.

"Why 'goodbye'?" he asked, smiling.

"Because I'm going back to London on Sunday, so I probably won't ever see you again," I said. I felt as if I was going to burst into tears. And wondered what the hell he was smiling at. Who gave him the right to look so smug and happy? Had he no sense of occasion? This was no laughing matter! On the contrary.

I couldn't believe how wretched I felt. This was so painful.

I wished he would just *go!*

"Won't you ever go out again?" he asked. "Can't you get a babysitter?"

"Oh course I will," I said sadly. "But I still won't be able to see you. Not unless you jet over to London now and then for an evening out. And I can't see you doing that."

"No," he said thoughtfully. "You're right. There would ·be no point jetting over to London for an evening out when I'm already there."

For a moment I thought I'd misheard him. But I looked at him, at his smiling face and knew that I hadn't.

Hope rushed through me, such a feeling of something wonderful that I thought I might burst from it.

"What are you talking about?" I asked, barely able to breathe.

I had to sit down.

"Er, I'm, er, moving to London," he said quietly. He sat down beside me on the bed. He was trying to look very serious but a smile kept breaking through.

"Are you?" I squeaked. "But why?"

And then a thought struck me.

"Hey, don't tell me. You've nowhere to stay and you were wondering, just wondering if you could sleep on my floor. Just for a couple of nights, a year max. Is that right?" I said bitterly.

He burst out laughing.

"Claire, you're so funny!" he said.

"Why?" I asked annoyed. "What are you laughing at?"

"You!" he said, still in hysterics. "I've *got*
somewhere to stay. I'm not stupid enough to be nice
to you just so I can ask you if I can stay with you. Do
you think I have a death wish? I know you'd kill me."

"Good," I said slightly mollified. At least he had a
little bit of respect.

"Is that why you think I came up here to talk to you?"
he asked, a lot more seriously. "Maybe I'm the stupid
one here, but I thought I'd made it clear how much I
like you and care for you. Don't you believe me?"

"Well, you can't blame me for being suspicious," I
said sulkily.

"No," he sighed. "We'll just have to work on
convincing you how wonderful you are and that I
have no ulterior motives for wanting to be around
you. I don't want you for your child. I don't want
you for your flat. I just want you for you."

"Do you want me?" I whispered, suddenly feeling
very alive and sexy. So powerful, so aware that I was
a woman and that he was a man and that
unavoidable physical attraction pulsed between us.
His eyes darkened, the blue almost turned to black
and he looked and sounded very serious.

"I want you very much," he said.

The room suddenly went quiet and still. Even
Kate wasn't making a sound. You could have cut the
sexual tension with a knife.

I broke the mood before one or both of us
combusted spontaneously.

"Let me get this straight," I said, trying to
businesslike. "You're coming to London. What for?
Why?"

"I've got a job,' he said, as if it was the most reasonable explanation in the world.

"But, what about college?" I asked bewildered. "Are you giving it all up?"

"No," he said, "but it's going to be different. I'll study at night."

"Why?" I asked, still not really understanding. "Why are you doing this?"

"Because I've got to work now that I've got a child to support. And there aren't any jobs in Dublin. And my Dad was able to get me into some merchant bank in London. And I'll still be able to do my degree. It'll just take longer."

"But what about your baby?" I wailed. "You've just got to know her and now you'll have to leave her again. That's awful!"

It was his turn to look bewildered.

"But Molly's coming with me," he said, sounding a bit baffled. "I'm taking Molly to London."

"Jesus," I said in hushed tones. "Don't tell me that you're abducting her? I've heard of fathers doing that."

"No!" he said, exasperated. "Hannah *wants* me to take her. Hannah wants to go round the world, she's had enough of being responsible for a while. I suppose it's no coincidence that she was suddenly overcome with remorse about not letting me see Molly when she suddenly realised that she needed a babysitter for a year."

"Golly," I said. "It hardly sounds ideal. What about poor Molly? And why didn't Hannah's parents insist on minding her?"

"Oh, Hannah had a major falling-out with them

when she decided that she was going off on holiday for a year," explained Adam. "And Molly will be fine, I hope. I'll get her into therapy as soon as she's able to talk."

"I'm only joking," he said, when he saw my horrified face. "I know it's not the perfect upbringing for a child. To be uprooted from her home and for her mother to run away for a year and to be landed on a father who doesn't even know her. But all I can do is my best."

"And what about when Hannah comes back and wants to take Molly back to Ireland?" I said, racked with worry.

"Oh Claire," he said gently, taking my hand in his. "Would you relax. Who knows what's going to happen in a year's time? I'll worry about that when I come to it. Can't we just live in the now for a little while?"

I said nothing.

I was thinking.

He was right, I decided.

When happiness makes a guest appearance in one's life, it's important to make the most of it. It may not stay around for long and when it *has* gone wouldn't it be terrible to think that all the time one could have been happy was wasted worrying about when that happiness would be taken away?

"So, if I could get to the main point of my visit," he continued, suddenly very brisk. "May I ask you something?"

"Of course," I smiled.

"If I'm being too forward, please stop me," he

said, all self-deprecating charm. "But do you think it would be possible for us to meet each other some time in London? Perhaps we could share a babysitter? And, of course any time you need a babysitter, I'll be only too happy to oblige."

"Thank you Adam," I said politely. "I would love to see you in London. And of course, if you too should need a babysitter, please don't hesitate to ask."

"Seriously," he said, his voice dropped several octaves. "This is very important to me. Will we really be able to see each other in London?"

"Of *course*," I said, laughing. "I'd love to see you."

I looked up and caught his eye. When I saw the look on his face – admiration, like, almost certainly lust. In fact there might even have been love – the smile froze on my face.

"Oh Claire," he breathed, as he bent to kiss me. "I've missed you."

It was at this point that Kate decided that she'd had enough of being ignored and started up like a police siren.

At the same time Helen burst through the door and stopped abruptly when she saw us. She took in the pair of us sitting on the bed. Adam holding my hand, my head raised for Adam's kiss and she said slowly, "I don't fucking believe it."

I braced myself for the onslaught.

Retribution would be both swift and terrible.

I looked at my feet and I was horrified to hear her crying.

Helen? Crying? Surely some mistake. It was unheard of!

I looked up at her, filled with remorse and compassion. I was almost in tears myself.

And then I realised that she wasn't crying.

The bitch was laughing!

She laughed and laughed. "You and Adam," she said, shaking her head, tears of laughter pouring down her face. "The *shame* of it."

"Why?" I demanded, all annoyed, compassion and remorse quickly forgotten. "What's wrong with me?"

"Nothing," she laughed. "Nothing. But you're so old and . . ." She stopped, unable to speak, she found it all so funny. "The look on your face! You looked terrified. And I thought he fancied me!" she exclaimed and she was off again. It was all so hilarious that she couldn't even stand straight. She leant up against the wall and then doubled over.

I sat and stared coldly at her while Kate roared like a banshee.

Adam looked slightly bemused.

If there was something funny, then I certainly couldn't see it.

I picked up Kate before she burst a blood vessel and nodded to Adam. "Talk to Helen," I suggested.

Adam unfolded himself and left the room after Helen.

I rocked Kate in my arms and tried to soothe her. She was a lovely child, but, I swear to God, sometimes her timing was so off.

I could hear Helen laughing all the way down the stairs.

And a while later she arrived back in.

"You fucking bitch," she said cheerfully, sitting

down on the bed beside me. "You had us all fooled. Pretending to be totally heartbroken about James and all the time you had the hots for Adam."

"No, Helen . . . " I protested weakly. "It wasn't like that."

She ignored me. She had more important things on her mind.

"What's he like?" she said, drawing conspiratorially nearer to me and dropping her voice several decibels. "Has he got a big one?"

"What kind of a question is that?" I asked, pretending to be horrified.

"I won't tell anyone," she lied.

"Helen!" I said, my head swimming slightly. I think I would have preferred it if she had been furious with me.

Now I'd have to put up with her being my best friend so that she could find out what Adam was like in bed so that she could tell everyone.

"Where is he anyway?" I asked her.

"In the kitchen sucking up to Mum. But never mind that," she said enthusiastically. "I think he loves you."

"Oh Helen, go away," I said, starting to feel exhausted.

"No, really, I do," she promised.

"Really?" I asked tentatively. I was such a sucker. I shouldn't have listened to anything she said. At my age I really should have had more sense.

"Yes," she said, sounding unusually serious.

"Why?" I asked.

"Because he had a huge hard-on when he was

talking about you just now." She screamed with laughter. "I really got you going there, didn't I?"

"Oh, go away, would you," I said.

I'd had enough for one day.

"Sorry," sniggered Helen. "No, I am, I promise. I do think he loves you. I really do. And let's face it, if anyone's an expert on men being in love, it's me."

She had a point.

"Do you love him?" she demanded.

"I don't know," I said awkwardly. "I don't really know him well enough to say. But I like him a lot. Will that do?"

"It'll have to," she said thoughtfully. "I hope you do love each other. I hope you'll be very happy together."

"Gosh, thank you Helen," I said, really touched. Tears sprang to my eyes. I was overwhelmed by her good wishes.

"Yes," she said vaguely. "I've a bet on with that cow Melissa Saint that she won't get off with him before the end of the Summer. I was actually starting to get a bit worried but this is brilliant. A God-send. She hasn't a hope now because you'll keep him well out of her way."

"That's the easiest hundred quid I ever earned," she said, rubbing her hands together gleefully.

"Yes," she continued, sounding very pleased. "I must say this has all worked out very well. Very well indeed."

LUCY
SULLIVAN
IS GETTING
MARRIED
MARIAN
KEYES

Acknowledgements

Thanks are due to the following people who helped me when I was writing this book.

To Kate Cruise O'Brien, my editor, for being mean to me and returning my first three chapters and telling me that I was a better writer than I thought I was and to begin again. Then for her endless enthusiasm and praise once I trusted her and took risks. And for her patience when I didn't trust myself and felt that I wasn't a real writer and the whole thing had been a horrible mistake. I really am grateful.

Thanks to everyone at Poolbeg who worked so hard on this. Thanks to Nicole Hodson and Lucy Keogh who read the manuscript as I wrote it and gave me lots of encouragement and let me know I was on the right track. Thanks to Paula Campbell for enjoying the Russian restaurant scene so much. I want to say a special thank you to Brenda Dermody for her hard work and extreme patience with the you-know-what. (All of them.)

Thanks to Louise Voss and Jenny Boland, who read the book chapter by chapter as it was written and insisted (sometimes quite forcibly) that I wrote the next one. I might never have finished it otherwise. Words can't express how much I appreciated the enthusiasm and encouragement.

Thanks to Belinda Flaherty who read the finished product and gave me her comments, suggestions and stamp of approval, before I sent it off.

Thanks to Jill Richter and Ann Brolan for reading the beginning and for encouraging me to keep going.

Thanks to Paula Whitlam for the "stamp".

Thanks to Geoff Simmonds for the truncheons.

Thanks to Eileen Prendergast for all the advice given and hard work done. Especial thanks for letting me steal her video shop story.

Thanks to my darling Tony for everything. For putting up with me working on our honeymoon and for not complaining when I paid more attention to my laptop than to his. For being brave enough to give me constructive criticism, I'm sorry about the black eye. For the outrageously extravagant praise, for laughing out loud at the funny bits, for always doing the washing-up so that I could get on with writing. For the constant and patient reassurance, for making me write "excitement" out a thousand times, for the advice on everything from character development to grammar. Especial thanks for the chocolate and soleros.

I really could not have written this book without him.

For Liam

Chapter One

When Meredia reminded me that the four of us from the office were due to visit a fortune-teller the following Monday, my stomach lurched slightly with shock.

"You've forgotten," accused Meredia, her fat face aquiver.

I had.

She slapped her hand down on her desk and warned, "Don't even *think* of trying to tell me that you're not coming."

"Balls," I whispered, because that was just what I had been about to do.

Not because I had any objections to having my fortune told. On the contrary – it was usually a bit of a laugh. Especially when they got to the bit where they told me that the man of my dreams was just around the next corner, that part was always *hilarious*.

Sometimes even *I* laughed.

But I was skint. Although I had just been paid, my bank account was a post-holocaust, corpse-strewn wasteland because the day I'd been paid I'd spent a fortune on aromatherapy oils that had promised to rejuvenate and energise and uplift me.

And bankrupt me, except it didn't say that on the

1

packaging. But I think the idea was that I'd be so rejuvenated and energised and uplifted that I wouldn't care.

So when Meredia reminded me that I'd committed myself to paying some woman thirty pounds so that she could tell me that I would travel over water and that I was quite psychic myself, I realised that I'd be going without lunch for two weeks.

"I'm not sure that I can afford it," I said nervously.

"You can't back out now!" thundered Meredia. "Mrs Nolan is giving us a discount. The rest of us will have to pay more if you don't come."

"Who's this Mrs Nolan?" Megan asked suspiciously, looking up from her computer where she had been playing Solitaire. She was supposed to be running a check on debtors older than a month.

"The tarot-reader," said Meredia.

"What kind of name is Mrs Nolan?" demanded Megan.

"She's Irish," protested Meredia.

"No!" Megan tossed her shiny, blonde hair in annoyance. "I mean, what kind of name is 'Mrs Nolan' for a *psychic*? She should be called Madam Zora or something like that. She can't be called 'Mrs Nolan'. How can we believe a word that she says?"

"Well, that's her name." Meredia sounded hurt.

"And why didn't she change it?" said Megan. "There's nothing to it, so I'm told. Isn't that right, so-called Meredia?"

A pregnant pause.

"Or should I say 'Coral'?" Megan continued with triumph.

"No, you shouldn't," said Meredia. "My name is Meredia."

"Sure," said Megan, with great sarcasm.

"It is!" said Meredia hotly.

"So let's see your birth cert," challenged Megan.

Megan and Meredia didn't see eye to eye on most things and especially on Meredia's name. Megan was a no-nonsense Australian with a low bullshit threshold. Since she had arrived three months ago as a temp she had insisted that Meredia wasn't Meredia's real name. She was probably right. Although I was very fond of Meredia, I had to agree that her name had a certain makeshift, ramshackle, cobbled-together-out-of-old-egg-cartons feel to it.

But unlike Megan I couldn't really see a problem with that.

"So it's definitely not 'Coral'?" Megan took a little notebook out of her holdall and drew a line through something.

"No," said Meredia stiffly.

"Right," said Megan. "That's all the 'C's done. Time for the 'D's. Daphne? Deirdre? Dolores? Denise? Diana? Dinah?"

"Shut up!" said Meredia. She looked on the verge of tears.

"Stop it." Hetty put a gentle hand on Megan's arm, because that's the kind of thing that Hetty did. Although Hetty was posh, she was also a good kind person, who poured oil on troubled waters. Which meant, of course, that she wasn't much fun, but no one was perfect.

Immediately upon meeting her, you could tell that

Hetty was posh. Not just because she looked like a horse, but because she had horrible clothes. Even though she was only about thirty-five she wore awful tweed skirts and flowery frocks that looked like family heirlooms. She *never* bought new clothes, which was a shame because one of the chief ways that office workers bonded was by displaying the spoils of the post-payday *Principles* run.

"I wish that Aussie bitch would leave," Meredia muttered to Hetty.

"It probably won't be long now," soothed Hetty.

Then she said a posh thing. She said, "Buck up."

"When are you going to leave?" Meredia demanded of Megan.

"As soon as I've got the readies, fat girl," Megan replied.

Megan was doing her grand tour of Europe and had temporarily run out of money. But as soon as she had enough money to go, she was going, she constantly reminded us, to Scandinavia, or Greece, or the Pyrenees, or the West of Ireland.

Until then Hetty and I had to break up the vicious rows that broke out regularly.

I was sure that a lot of the animosity was because Megan was tall and tanned and gorgeous. While Meredia was short and fat and not gorgeous. Meredia was jealous of Megan's beauty, while Megan despised Meredia's excess weight. When Meredia couldn't buy clothes to fit her, instead of making sympathetic noises like the rest of us did, Megan barked, "Stop whinging, lardbucket, and go on a bloody diet!"

But Meredia never did. And in the meantime she

was condemned to cause cars to swerve whenever she walked down the road. Because instead of trying to disguise her size with vertical stripes and dark colours, she seemed to dress to enhance it. She went for the layered look, layers and layers and layers of fabric. Really, *lots*. Acres of fabric, yards and yards of velvet, draped and pinned and knotted and tied, anchored with broaches, attached with scarves, pinned and arranged along her sizeable girth.

And the more colours the better. Crimson and vermilion and sunburst orange and flame red and magenta.

And that was just her hair. She had a social worker's fondness for henna.

"It's either me or her," muttered Meredia, as she glared balefully at Megan.

But it was just bravado. Meredia had worked in our office for a very long time – to hear her tell it, since the dawn of time; in reality, about eight years – and she had never managed to secure another job. Nor had she been promoted. This she bitterly blamed on a sizeist management. (Although there seemed to be no bar to any number of tubby men on the fast track to success, reaching all kinds of exalted positions within the ranks of the company.)

Anyway, wimp that I was, I gave in to Meredia without much of a fight. I even managed to convince myself that having no money would be a good thing – being forced to go without lunch for two weeks would be a shot in the arm for the diet that I perpetually seemed to be on.

And Meredia reminded me of something I'd overlooked.

"You've just split up with Steven," she said. "You were due a visit to a fortune-teller *anyway*."

Although I didn't like to admit it, she was probably right. Now that I had discovered that Steven wasn't the man of my dreams, it was only a matter of time before I made some sort of psychic enquiries to find out exactly *who* was. That was the kind of thing that my friends and I did, even though it was all just a bit of a laugh and no one *believed* the fortune-tellers. At least none of us would *admit* to believing them.

Poor Steven. What a disappointment he'd turned out to be.

Especially as it had started with such promise. I had thought he was gorgeous – his only average good looks were upgraded, in my eyes, to Adonis class, by blond curly hair, black leather trousers and a motorbike. He seemed wild and dangerous and carefree – well, he would, wouldn't he? What were motorbikes and black leather trousers if not the uniform of a wild, dangerous and carefree man?

Of course, I thought I hadn't a hope with him, that someone as beautiful as him would have his pick of the girls and that he certainly wouldn't have any interest in someone as ordinary as me.

Because I really *was* ordinary. I certainly looked ordinary. I had ordinary brown curly hair, and I spent so much money on anti-frizz hair products that it would probably have cut down on administration if I'd had my salary paid directly into the chemist near work. I had ordinary brown eyes and, as a punishment for having Irish parents, I had about eight million ordinary freckles – one for every single Irish person who died in the potato famine as my father used to say when he was a bit drunk and in maudlin mood about "the old country."

But despite all my ordinariness, Steven asked me out and acted as if he liked me.

At first I could barely understand why such a sexy man like Steven wanted to be with me.

And, naturally, I didn't believe a word that came out of his mouth. When he said that I was the only girl in his life, I assumed that he was lying, when he told me I was lovely I looked for the angle on it, walked all around it, inspecting it, to see what he wanted from me.

I didn't really mind, I just assumed that those were the kind of terms you went out with a man like Steven on.

It took a while for me to realise that he was sincere and that he *wasn't* saying it to all the girls.

So I tentatively decided that I was delighted, but what I really was was confused. I had been so sure that he had a whole secret other life, one that I was supposed to know nothing about – middle-of-the-night dashes on the Harley to have sex on the beach with unknown women and that sort of thing. He looked that type.

I had expected a short-lived, passionate, roller-coaster of an affair, where my nerves would be stretched to twanging point waiting for his call, then my whole body would be flooded with ecstasy when he *did* ring.

But he always rang me when he said that he would. And he always said that I looked gorgeous no matter what I wore. But instead of being happy, I felt uncomfortable.

What I saw was actually what I got, and I felt strangely short-changed by life.

He started liking me too much.

One morning I woke up and he was propped on his elbow, staring down at me. "You're beautiful," he murmured, and it felt so *wrong*.

When we had sex he said "Lucy, Lucy, oh God, Lucy," millions of times, all feverishly and passionately and I tried to join in and be all feverish and passionate also, but I just felt silly.

And the more he seemed to like me, the more I went off him, until in the end I could barely breathe around him.

I was suffocating from his adulation, smothering in his admiration. I wasn't *that* attractive, I couldn't help thinking, and if he thought that I was, it meant there was something wrong with him.

"Why do you like me?" I asked him, over and over.

"Because you're beautiful," or "Because you're sexy," or "Because you're all woman," were the nauseating replies that he gave me.

"No, I'm not," I would reply desperately. "How can you say that I am?"

"Anyone would think you were trying to put me off you." He smiled tenderly.

The tenderness was probably what drove me over the edge. His tender smiles, his tender gazes, his tender kisses, his tender caresses, so much *tenderness*, it was a nightmare.

And he was so touchy-feely! Mr Tactile – I couldn't bear it.

Everywhere we went he held my hand, proudly displaying me as "his woman". When we were driving he planted his hand on my thigh, when we were watching television he almost lay on top of me. He was always at me, stroking my arm or rubbing my hair or caressing my back, until I could bear it no more and had to push him away.

Velcro man, that's what I called him in the end.

And eventually to his face.

As time went on, I wanted to tear my skin off every time he touched me, and the thought of having sex with him made me feel sick.

One day he said he'd love a huge garden and a houseful of kids and that was it!

I finished with him, forthwith.

And I couldn't understand how I had once found him so attractive, because by then I couldn't think of a more repulsive man on the face of the earth. He still had the blond hair and the leather trousers and the motorbike, but I was no longer fooled by them.

I despised him for liking me so much. I wondered how he could settle for so little.

None of my friends could understand why I finished with him. "But he was lovely" was their cry. "But he was so good to you" was another one. "But he was such a catch," they protested. To which I replied, "No, he wasn't. A catch isn't supposed to be that easy."

He had disappointed me.

I had expected disrespect and instead got devotion, I had expected infidelity and instead got commitment, I had expected upheaval and instead got predictability and (most disappointing of all) I had expected a wolf and had been fobbed off with a sheep.

It's upsetting when the nice bloke you really like turns out to be a complete, lying, two-timing bastard. But it's nearly as bad when the bloke that you thought was an unreliable heartbreaker turns out to be uncomplicated and nice.

I spent a couple of days wondering why I liked the blokes who weren't nice to me? Why couldn't I like the ones who were?

Would I despise every man who ever treated me well? Was I fated only to want men that didn't want me?

I woke up in the middle of the night wondering about my sense of self-worth – why was I comfortable only when I was being ill-treated?

Then I realised that the "Treat 'em mean, keep 'em keen" maxim had been around for hundreds of years. And I relaxed – after all, I didn't make the rules.

So what if my ideal man was a selfish, dependable, unfaithful, loyal, treacherous, loving flirt who thought the world of me, never rang when he said he would, made me feel like the most special woman in the universe and tried to get off with all my friends? Was it my fault that I wanted a Schrödinger's cat of a boyfriend, a man who was several directly conflicting things simultaneously?

Chapter Two

There seemed to be a direct link between how difficult it was to get to a fortune-teller's house and how good their reputation was. The more inaccessible and off-putting the venue, the higher the quality of the predictions, was the widely held view.

Which meant that Mrs Nolan must have been brilliant because she lived in some awful, faraway suburb on the outskirts of London. So obscure and distant that we had to go in Hetty's car.

"Why can't we get the bus?" asked Megan when Hetty announced that we'd all have to contribute to the cost of the petrol.

"The buses won't go out there anymore," said Meredia vaguely.

"Why not?" demanded Megan.

"Just because," said Meredia.

"Why?" I was intrigued.

"There was an . . . incident," muttered Meredia, and that's all she would say on the subject.

On Monday at five on the dot, Megan, Hetty, Meredia and I assembled on the front steps of our place of work. Hetty went and got her car from where it was parked, several miles away, because that was parking in central London for you, and in we got.

"Let us depart this accursed place," one of us suggested. I can't remember which one of us it was because we always said that every day at going-home time. Although I suppose it mightn't have been Hetty.

The journey was a nightmare. We spent hours either stuck in traffic or travelling through anonymous suburbs, then we went onto a motorway. After driving for ages more, we turned off a slip road and finally turned into a council estate.

And what a council estate!

I and my two brothers ("Christopher Patrick Sullivan" and "Peter Joseph Mary Plunkett Sullivan" as they had been christened by my rabidly Catholic mother) had been brought up in a council house, so I was allowed to criticise council estates and their inhumanity without being called a bleeding-heart liberal. But the estate I was brought up on was nothing like as apocalyptic-looking as the one where Mrs Nolan lived.

Two huge grey blocks loomed like watch towers over what seemed like hundreds of miserable little grey box houses. A couple of stray dogs roamed aimlessly, half-heartedly looking for someone to bite.

There was no greenery, no plants, no trees, no grass.

In the distance there was a small concrete row of shops. It was nearly all boarded up except for a chip-shop and a bookies office and an off-licence. It was probably just my over-active imagination but through the evening gloom I could have *sworn* I saw four horsemen loitering outside the chip-shop. So far, so good. Mrs Nolan was obviously better than I had already realised.

"My God," said Megan her face twisted in disgust. "What a dump!"

"Yes, isn't it?" Meredia smiled with pride.

In the middle of all the greyness was a small patch of ground that some urban planner had obviously anticipated would be a little oasis of abundant greenness where laughing families would play in the sunshine. But it looked like it had been a long time since any grass had grown there.

Through the twilight gloom we could see a group of about fifteen children gathered on it. They were clustered round something that looked suspiciously like a burnt-out car.

Even though it was a bitterly cold March evening, none of them were wearing coats (not even their shell suit jackets) and, as soon as they saw us, they paused from whatever criminal activity they were up to and ran towards us, whooping loudly.

"Good God!" cried Hetty. "Lock your doors!"

All four locks snapped shut as the children swarmed round the car, staring at us with their old and knowing eyes.

What made them look even more scary was that they were smeared with black stuff, which was probably only oil or charred metal from the burnt car, but it looked like war paint.

They were mouthing something at us.

"What are they saying?" asked Hetty in terror.

"I think they're asking us if we've come to see Mrs Nolan," I said doubtfully.

13

I opened the window a fraction of an inch and through the babel of childish voices established that that was indeed what they were asking us.

"Phew! The natives are friendly," smiled Hetty, making a great show of wiping the sweat from her forehead and breathing deeply with relief.

"Talk to them, Lucy."

Nervously, I opened the window a bit more.

"Er . . . we've come to see Mrs Nolan," I said.

A cacophony of shrill voices answered us.

"That's her house."

"She lives over there."

"That's the one."

"You can leave your car here."

"That's her house."

"Over there."

"I'll show you."

"No, I'll show you."

"No, *I'm* showing them."

"No, *I'm* showing them."

"But I saw them first."

"But you got the last lot."

"Fuck you, Cherise Tiller."

"No, fuck *you*, Claudine Hall."

A vicious ruck broke out between four or five of the little girls while we sat in the car and waited for them to stop.

"Let's get out." Megan sounded a bit bored. It took more than a crowd of semi-savage children to frighten her. She opened the door and stepped over a couple of children wrestling on the pavement.

Then Hetty and I got out.

As soon as Hetty put foot outside the car a wiry,

skinny, little girl with the face of a thirty-five-year-old card sharp began tugging at her coat. "Hey, me and my mate'll guard your car," she promised.

Her mate, who was even more skinny and little and looked like an unfriendly monkey, nodded silently.

"Thank you," said Hetty, her face a picture of horror, trying to shake the little girl off.

"We'll make sure that nothing happens to it," said the wizened little girl, a bit more threateningly, still holding onto Hetty's coat tightly.

"Give them some money," suggested Megan in exasperation. "That's what she's really saying."

"Excuse *me*!" said Hetty, outraged. "I will not. That's blackmail."

"Do you want the wheels to be on your car when you get back or don't you?" Megan demanded.

The little girl and her monkey patiently watched the exchange with folded arms. Now that a sensible streetwise woman like Megan was on the case they knew that the outcome would be to their liking.

"Here," I said, giving the thirty-five-year-old little girl a pound.

She accepted it with a grim nod.

"*Now* can we please go and have our fortunes told?" asked Megan impatiently.

Meredia, the big fat wimp, had cowered in the car during the entire exchange with the Children from Hell. She waited for them to drift away before levering herself out.

But the minute they saw her emerging from the car they returned at high speed. It wasn't often that they got a sixteen-stone woman dressed head to toe in crimson crushed velvet, with matching hair, round their way. But when they did they knew how to make the most of it, recognising a free evening's entertainment, making mock and pouring scorn.

The screeches of laughter that emerged from those parodies of children were blood curdling.

The comments ranged from "Fuck me! Look at that fat cow," to "Fuck me! She's wearing her mum's curtains!" to "Fuck me! Isn't it horrible?" to "Fuck me! Where are the Greenpeace boats?"

Poor Meredia, her face as crimson as the rest of her, lumbered the short distance to Mrs Nolan's front door like the Pied Piper of Hamlin, swarms of horrible brats running and dancing after her, laughing and shouting insults. A carnival atmosphere prevailed, as though the circus had come to town while Hetty, Megan and I jostled protectively around Meredia, making half-hearted attempts to shoo the children away.

Then we saw Mrs Nolan's house. You couldn't miss it.

It had stone cladding, double-glazing and a little glass porch stuck onto its front. All its windows had scalloped, lacy, net curtains and elaborately looped Austrian blinds. The windowsills were crammed to capacity with ornaments, china horses and glass dogs and brass jugs and little furry things on little wooden rocking chairs. Evident signs of prosperity that set it apart from all the other houses around it. Mrs Nolan was obviously a bit of a superstar among tarot-readers.

"Ring the bell," Hetty told Meredia.

"No, you do it," said Meredia.

"But you've been here before," said Hetty.

"*I'll* do it," I sighed, reached over and pressed the button.

When the first couple of verses of *Greensleeves* began chiming in the hall, Megan and I both started to snigger.

Meredia turned and glared.

"Shut up," she hissed. "Have some respect. This woman is the best. She's the master."

"She's coming. Oh my God. She's coming," whispered Hetty in hoarse excitement as a shadowy shape moved behind the frosted glass of the porch.

Hetty didn't get out much.

"Jesus, Hetty, you need to git a loife!" said Megan disdainfully.

The door opened and instead of an exotic, dusky, psychic-looking woman, a young man with a bad-tempered face stood there.

A small child with a dirty face peeped out from between his legs.

"Yes?" he said, looking us over. His eyes widened with mild shock as he clocked Meredia in all her crimsonness.

None of us spoke. We had come over all middle class and shy. Even me, and I was working class.

Hetty gently nudged Meredia and Meredia elbowed Megan and Megan elbowed me.

"Say something," hissed Hetty.

"No, you do," muttered Meredia.

"Well?" enquired the narky-looking man again, none too civilly.

"Is Mrs Nolan here?" I asked.

He eyed me suspiciously, then decided that I could be trusted.

"She's busy," he muttered.

"Doing what?" demanded Megan impatiently.

"She's having her tea," he said.

"Well, can we come in and wait?" I asked.

"She's expecting us," volunteered Meredia.

"We've come a long way," explained Hetty.

"We were led by a star from the East," sniggered Megan from the back.

All three of us turned and frowned at her.

"Sorry," she muttered.

The young man looked mortally offended at the disrespect shown to his mother or granny or whatever Mrs Nolan was to him and began to close the door.

"No, please don't," pleaded Hetty. "She's sorry."

"I am," called Megan cheerfully, not sounding a bit of it.

"All right then," he said grudgingly and let us into a tiny hall.

There was barely space for the four of us.

"Wait here," he ordered and went into another room. It must have been the kitchen judging by the smoke and the clinking of teacups and the smell of fried eggs that emerged when he opened the door and disappeared when he shut it again.

There was hardly an inch of wall space in the hall that wasn't covered with pictures or barometers or tapestries or horseshoes. Meredia moved slightly and knocked a photograph of a very large family off the wall. She bent down to pick it up and her bum sent about ten other pictures tumbling to the floor.

For ages, we loitered in the hall, totally ignored, while sounds of talk and laughter came from behind the closed door.

"I'm *starving*," said Megan.

"Me too," I agreed. "I wonder what they're having."

"This is stupid," said Megan. "Let's go."

"Please wait," said Meredia. "She's wonderful. She really is."

Eventually Mrs Nolan finished her tea and came to walk amongst us. I couldn't help feeling disappointed when I saw her – she looked so ordinary. There wasn't a red head scarf or a gold hoop earring in sight.

She had glasses and a short perm and was wearing a beige jumper and track-suit bottoms and, worst of all, *slippers*. And she was *minute*! I wasn't very tall myself but she barely came up to my waist.

"Right girls," she said, brisk and businesslike, in a Dublin accent. "Who's first?"

Meredia went first. Then Hetty. Then me. Megan wanted to wait until last to see if the rest of us thought it was worth the money.

Chapter Three

When it was my turn I went into what was obviously the family "good room". I barely got past the door because the room was so crammed with furniture and stuff. An embroidered fireguard stood next to a huge mahogany sideboard which groaned under the weight of yet more ornaments. There were footstools and nests of tables everywhere you looked and a three-piece suite in brown velvet which still had the plastic covers on it.

Mrs Nolan was sitting on one of the plastic covered chairs and she gestured to me to sit on the one opposite her.

As I fought through the furniture to get to the seat, I began to feel nervous and excited. Because although Mrs Nolan looked like she would be more at home on her knees scrubbing Hetty's kitchen floor, she had obviously earned her wonderful reputation as a fortune-teller, *somehow*. What would she tell me? I wondered. What was in store for me? "Sit down, me dear," she said.

I sat, my bum balanced on the edge of the plastic-covered chair.

She looked at me. Shrewdly? Wisely?

She spoke. Prophetically? Portentiously?

"You have come a long way, me dear," she said.

I gave a little jump. I hadn't been expecting that we'd start immediately. And for her to be so accurate! Yes, indeed I *had* come a long way from my childhood in the council estate in Uxbridge. "Yes," I agreed tentatively, quite shaken by her perception.

"Was the traffic bad, me dear?"

"*What?* The *what?* Er . . . oh . . . the traffic? No, not really," I managed to reply.

Oh I see. She had only been making conversation. The reading hadn't started yet. How disappointing. Well, never mind. "Yes, me dear," she sighed. "If they ever finish that bloody bypass it'll be a miracle. At the moment the tailbacks would take the night's sleep off of you."

"Er, yes," I nodded.

Discussing traffic and tailbacks just didn't seem appropriate, somehow.

But then it was straight down to business.

"Ball or cards?" she shot at me.

"S . . . sorry?" I asked politely.

"Ball or cards? Crystal ball or tarot cards?"

"Oh! Well, let's see. What's the difference?"

"A fiver."

"No, I meant . . . never mind. The cards please." "Right," said Mrs Nolan and with that she started shuffling the deck with the finesse of a river-boat poker player.

"Shuffle them, me dear," she said, handing me the cards. "And whatever you do, don't drop them on the floor."

21

It must be bad luck to drop them on the floor, I thought knowingly.

"Me back is banjaxed," she explained. "The doctor said no bending."

"Now, ask yourself a question, me dear," she advised. "A question that the cards will answer for you, me dear. Don't tell it to me, me dear. I don't need to know it" – a little pause, meaningful eye contact – "me dear."

I could have chosen one of several questions. Like, would there be an end to world hunger? Would they find a cure for AIDS? Would there be peace on earth? Will they manage to mend the hole in the ozone layer? But interestingly enough the question that I decided that I wanted the answer to was the "will I ever meet a nice man?" one. Funny that.

"Have you decided on the question, me dear?" she asked, taking the deck back from me.

I nodded. She started flinging cards on the table at high speed. I didn't know what any of the pictures meant, but I thought that they didn't look very promising. There seemed to be a lot of them with swords, and surely that couldn't be good? "Your question concerns a man, me dear?" she said.

But even *I* wasn't impressed with that.

I mean, I was a young woman. I had few concerns in my life. Well, actually, I had plenty. But the *average* young woman would only seek guidance from a fortune-teller for two reasons – her career and her love life. And if she was having problems with her career, she would probably do something constructive about it herself.

Like sleep with her boss.

So that just left the love life option. "Yes," I answered wearily. "It concerns a man."

"You have been unlucky in love, me dear," she said sympathetically.

Once again, I refused to be impressed.

Yes, I had been unlucky in love. But show me a woman who hasn't.

"There is a fair-haired man in your past, me dear," she said.

I suppose she meant Steven. But I mean, who *hadn't* got a fair-haired man in their past? "He was not the one for you, me dear," she continued.

"Thanks," I said, a bit annoyed, because I'd already worked that out myself.

"But waste no tears on him, me dear," she advised.

"Don't worry."

"For there is another man, me dear," she said, giving me a big smile.

"Really?" I asked, delighted, leaning closer to her, the plastic covers squeaking against my thighs. "Now you're talking."

"Yes," she said, studying the cards. "I see a marriage."

"Do you really?" I demanded. "Whose? Mine?"

"Yes, me dear," she said. "Yours."

"Really?" I said. "When?"

"Before the leaves have fallen on the ground for the second time, me dear."

"Sorry?"

"Before the four seasons have rolled a time and half a time again," she said.

23

"Sorry, I'm still not sure what you mean," I apologised.

"In about a year," she snapped, sounding a bit annoyed.

I was slightly disappointed. In about a year, it would still be winter, and I'd always seen myself getting married in the spring. On the rare occasions that I could see myself getting married at all, that was. "You couldn't make it a bit longer than a year, could you?" I asked.

"Me dear," she said sharply. "I do not ordain these things. I am simply the messenger."

"Sorry," I muttered.

"Well," she said, in a nicer tone, "let's say up to eighteen months just to be on the safe side."

"Thanks," I said, thinking that was very decent of her. So I was getting married, I thought. Momentous stuff. Especially when I would just have settled for a boyfriend.

"I wonder who he is?"

"You must be careful, me dear," she warned me. "At first you may not recognise him for who he truly is."

"I'll meet him at a fancy dress?"

"No," she said ominously. "At first he may not be who he appears to be."

"Oh, you mean he's going to lie to me," I said understanding. "Well, fair enough then. Why should this one be any different?"

I laughed.

Mrs Nolan looked annoyed.

"No, me dear," she said irritably. "I mean that you

must take care not to wear cupid's blinkers. You may have to seek this man out and look at him with clear and fearless eyes. He may not have money, but you must not humble him. He may not have looks, but you must not humble him."

Oh great, I thought. I might have known! A deformed pauper.

"I see," I said. "So he's going to be poor and ugly."

"*No*, me dear," said Mrs Nolan, in exasperation and dropping her mystical language. "I just mean that he mightn't be your usual type."

"I *see*!" I said.

If only she'd said that to begin with. Clear and fearless eyes, indeed! "So," I continued, "when Jason, the seventeen-year-old with all the spots and those awful baggy clothes, meets me at the photocopier and asks me out to take some drugs, I shouldn't laugh in his face and tell him that I'll see him ice-skating in hell."

"That's the idea, me dear," said Mrs Nolan, sounding pleased. "For the flower of love may flourish in the most unexpected of places and you must be ready to pluck it."

"I understand," I nodded.

. All the same, I'd want to be pretty desperate before Jason would be in with any kind of chance. But there was no need to tell Mrs Nolan that.

Anyway, if she was worth her salt, she already knew. She started pointing briskly at cards and barking out staccato sentences, thus indicating that the audience was nearing its end. "You will have three children, two girls and a boy, me dear," and "You will never have money, but you will have happiness, me dear," and "You have an enemy at work, me dear. She is jealous of your success." I had to laugh – slightly bitterly – at that one. She would have laughed too if she knew how menial and awful my job was.

Then she paused.

She looked at the cards, then she looked at me. Something like concern was on her face.

"There has been a cloud over you, me dear," she said slowly. "A darkness, a sadness."

Suddenly, to my horror, I had a lump in my throat. A dark cloud was exactly how I described the bouts of depression that I sometimes got. Not the usual "I wish I owned that suede skirt" type of depression – although I suffered from *that* kind of depression too. But since I had been seventeen, I had had bouts of actual clinical depression.

I nodded, almost unable to speak.

"Yes," I whispered.

"For many years you have carried this," she said quietly, looking at me with great sympathy and understanding.

"Yes," I whispered again, feeling my eyes fill with tears.

"You have carried it almost entirely alone," she said gently.

"Yes," I nodded, feeling a tear make it's way slowly down my cheek. Oh my God! It was awful! I thought that we had come for a laugh. But instead this woman, who was almost a complete stranger, had seen through to the essence of me, had touched me in a place where few human beings had ever been.

"Sorry," I sniffed, wiping my face with my hand.

"Don't worry, me dear," she said, handing me a tissue from a box that was obviously there for that sort of thing. "It's always happening."

She waited for a few moments while I recovered my composure and then she began to speak again.

"OK, me dear?"

"Yes." Sniff. "Thanks."

"This can get better, me dear. But you must not hide from people who wish to help you. How can they help you if you won't let them?"

"I don't really know what you mean," I mumbled.

"Maybe you don't, me dear," she agreed kindly. "But I hope that you will learn."

"Thanks," I sniffed. "You've been very nice. And thanks, you know, for the bloke and me getting married and all that. It was nice to hear."

"Not at all, me dear," she said pleasantly. "Now that'll be thirty pounds, please."

I paid her and launched myself out of the crackling plastic.

"Good luck, me dear," she said. "And will you send the next young lady in?"

"Who's next?" I wondered. "Oh it's Megan, isn't it?"

"Megan!" exclaimed Mrs Nolan. "Isn't that a lovely name? She must be Welsh."

"Australian, actually," I smiled. "Thanks again. Bye now."

"Bye, me dear," she nodded, smiling. I went back

out into the tiny hall, where the other three fell on me with urgent questions. "Well?" and "What did she say?" and "Was it worth the money?" (this last one from Megan).

"Yes," I told Megan. "You should go."

"I'll only go if you all promise not to tell anything until I'm back out and we're all together," said Megan sulkily. "I don't want to miss anything."

"Well, OK," I sighed.

"Selfish cow," muttered Meredia.

"Careful, fat girl," hissed Megan.

Chapter Four

When Megan emerged smiling about twenty minutes later, it was time to go back out into the cold night to see what Satan's children had done to the car.

"It will be all right, won't it?" asked poor Hetty anxiously, as she broke into a run.

"I sincerely hope so," I answered, walking briskly after her. I really *did* sincerely hope so. The chances of getting home any other way were apparently very slim indeed.

"We should never have come," she said miserably.

"Yes, we should have," said Megan gregariously. "I've had a great time."

"So've I," came Meredia's voice, as she lumbered along about fifty yards behind the rest of us.

Unbelievably, the car was fine.

As soon as we rounded the corner the little girl who was supposed to be guarding the car appeared as if from nowhere. I don't know what kind of threatening look she gave Hetty but it was enough to make her immediately grope round in her bag, looking for another couple of pounds to give to the girl.

We couldn't see any of the other children, but we could hear whooping noises and shrieks and the sound of smashing glass coming from somewhere nearby.

As we drove out of the estate we passed a crowd of them. They were doing something to a camper van. Completely destroying it, I think.

"Don't they have to be in bed at any time?" asked Hetty anxiously, appalled by her first brush with a ghetto. "I mean, where are their parents? What are they doing? Surely *something* can be done?"

The children were delighted to see us. As our car approached them they began laughing and shouting and pointing and cackling. Obviously they were still greatly interested in Meredia. Three or four of the boys gave chase to us and managed to run alongside us, laughing and making revolting faces at us, for quite a distance before we managed to shake them.

As soon as it became obvious that we had made good our escape from the little brats, we relaxed. It was time for the post-mortem on what Mrs Nolan had said and the four of us were a bit excitable. We all wanted to know what the others had been "given" – like little girls at a lucky dip, comparing prizes. "What did you get? Show me your present! Look at mine!"

The noise in the car was deafening, with Meredia and Megan competing to tell their stories.

"She knew that I was Australian," burst in Megan excitedly. "And she says that I'm going to have some sort of split in my life, but that good will come of it and I'll cope with it marvellously, the way I do with everything." She said the last piece a bit smugly.

"So maybe it's time to go travelling again," she

continued. "Either way it looks as if I won't have to be looking at your lot of ugly mugs for much longer."

"She said I'd come into money," said Meredia happily.

"Good," said Hetty, sounding oddly bitter. "Then you can give me back that twenty-pound note you owe me."

I noticed that Hetty was quieter than usual. She wasn't joining in with the general hilarity and excitement but was just driving the car and staring straight ahead.

Was her *Telegraph*-reading body still in shock from such close contact with working-class children? Or was it something else?

"What did she say to you, Hetty?" I asked, a bit concerned. "Did she tell you something bad was going to happen?"

"Yes," said Hetty, in a little voice. She even sounded a small bit tearful!

"What was it? What did she say?" we all blurted out at once, drawing our faces nearer to hers, eager to hear predictions of terrible things – accidents, illness, death, bankruptcy, mortgage companies foreclosing, boilers bursting – whatever.

"She said that very soon I'm going to meet the love of my life," said Hetty tearfully.

A silence fell in the car. Oh dear! That was bad. Very bad.

Very bad indeed.

Poor Hetty!

It's unsettling to be told you're going to meet the love of your life when you're already married with two children.

31

"She says I'm going to be completely smitten with him," sniffed Hetty. "It's going to be awful. There's never been a divorce in our family. And what about Marcus and Montague?" (Or it might have been "Troilus and Tristan" or "Cecil and Sebastian".) "They're finding boarding school difficult enough without the embarrassment of their mother being a bolter."

"Oh dear," I said sympathetically. "But it's only a bit of fun. It probably won't happen."

But that just made her tears flow faster. "But *why* shouldn't I meet the love of my life? I *want* to meet him."

Megan, Meredia and I exchanged shocked looks. Good Lord! It was most irregular. Was the normally sane and calm – I'd even go so far as to say boring – Hetty having some kind of nervous fit?

"Why can't *I* have some fun? Why do *I* have to be stuck with boring old Dick?" she demanded.

She thumped the steering wheel everytime she said "I" and the car lurched alarmingly into the other lane. All around us cars were beeping their horns, but Hetty didn't seem to notice.

I was amazed. I had worked with Hetty for two years and, while we were never soul mates, I thought I knew her quite well.

There was a nonplussed silence in the car while Meredia, Megan and I swallowed and tried and failed to think of comforting things to say.

It was Hetty who rescued the situation. She didn't have a fourteenth cousin, three times removed, as a lady-in-waiting to the Queen for nothing. She hadn't gone to a hugely expensive finishing school without learning to smooth over awkward social situations. "Sorry," she said, suddenly seeming to become Hetty again, the veneer of polite, posh, calm, reserve firmly clipped back in place. "Sorry, girls," she said again. "You must forgive me."

She cleared her throat and squared her shoulders, indicating that there was nothing further to say on the subject. Dick and his boringness were not to be topics for discussion.

Such a pity. I had always wanted to know. Because to be honest, Dick did seem *extremely* boring. But, then again, and I mean this in the nicest possible way, so did Hetty.

"So then, Lucy," she said crisply, deflecting the last few remaining crumbs of interest away from her. "What did Mrs Nolan predict for you?"

"Me?" I said. "Oh yes. She says I'm getting married."

Another silence fell in the car.

Another stunned one.

The disbelief of Megan, Meredia and Hetty was so tangible it was like a fifth person in the car. If it wasn't careful it would end up having to contribute to the cost of the petrol.

"Really?" asked Hetty, somehow managing to get sixteen syllables from the one word.

"You!" shouted Megan. "She said that *you* are getting married."

"Yes," I said defensively. "What's so wrong with that?"

"Nothing really," said Meredia kindly. "It's just

that, you know, you haven't been exactly lucky with men."

"Not through any fault of your own," said Hetty hurriedly, tactfully.

Hetty was good on tact.

"Well, that's what she said," I said sulkily.

They didn't really know what to say and conversation remained subdued until eventually we reached civilisation again. I was the first to be dropped off because I lived in Ladbroke Grove. The last thing I heard as I got out of the car was Meredia telling anyone who cared to listen that Mrs Nolan had said that she would travel over water and that she was very psychic herself.

Chapter Five

I shared a flat with two other girls, Karen and Charlotte. Karen was twenty-eight, I was twenty-six and Charlotte was twenty-three. We were a bad example to each other and spent a lot of time drinking bottles of wine and not very much cleaning the bathroom.

When I let myself in, Karen and Charlotte were asleep. We usually went to bed early on a Monday night to recover from the excesses of the preceding weekend.

There was a note on the kitchen table from Karen saying that Daniel had phoned me.

Daniel was my friend and, while he was the closest thing that I had to a steady man in my life, I wouldn't have become romantically involved with him if the future of the human race depended on it. So that will give some idea of just how male-free my life was.

My life was the Reduced-Male variety, the Male Lite life.

Daniel was wonderful, really. Boyfriends came and boyfriends went (and believe me, they went), but I could always rely on Daniel to be the boyfriend figure in my life, to annoy me with sexist comments and say that he preferred the shorter, tighter skirt.

And he wasn't unattractive, or so I was told. All my friends said he was lovely. Even Dennis, my gay friend, said that he wouldn't kick Daniel out of the bed for eating crisps. And whenever Karen answered the phone to him she made faces like she was having an orgasm. Sometimes Daniel came to our flat and, after he'd gone, Karen and Charlotte would lie on the bit of the couch where he'd been sitting and roll around and make noises like they were in ecstasy.

I couldn't see what all the fuss was about. Because Daniel was a friend of my brother Chris, I'd known him for years and years and years. I just knew him too well to fancy him. Or for him to fancy me, for that matter.

There might have been a time, once, several thousand light years in the past, when Daniel and I smiled shyly across a Duran Duran record and contemplated snogging each other. But then again, there might not have been, I couldn't actually *remember* ever feeling like that about him, I just assumed that I had because, in the free-for-all of emotions that was my adolescence, I fancied just about everyone.

It was really for the best that Daniel and I didn't fancy each other because, if we *did* get off with each other, Chris would have to go to all the bother of beating Daniel up for violating his sister's honour and I didn't want to put anyone to any trouble.

Karen and Charlotte – quite mistakenly – envied me my relationship with Daniel.

They would shake their heads in wonder and say, "You lucky bitch, how can you be so relaxed around him? How are you able to be funny and make him laugh? I can never think of a thing to say."

But it was easy because I didn't fancy him. When I *did* fancy someone I panicked and knocked things over and opened conversations by saying things like, "Do you ever wonder what it's like to be a radiator?"

I looked at the note that Karen had left for me – there was even a little stain on it that she had marked "dribble" – and wondered if I should ring Daniel. I decided not to, he might be in bed.

Accompanied, if you follow me.

Damn Daniel and his active sex-life. I wanted to talk to him.

What Mrs Nolan had said had given me food for thought. *Not* what she had said about me getting married – there was no way that I was fool enough to actually take that seriously. But what she had said about me being under a dark cloud had reminded me of my bouts of Depression and how awful they'd been. I *could* have woken Karen and Charlotte, but I decided against it. Apart from the fact that they could turn nasty if roused from their slumber for any reason other than an impromptu party, they didn't know about my Depression.

Of course, they knew that sometimes I said I was depressed, and then they said "But why?" and I would tell them about an unfaithful boyfriend or a bad day at work or not fitting into last summer's skirt and they were more than sympathetic.

But they didn't know that I sometimes got

depressed with a capital "D". Daniel was one of the few people outside my family who actually knew.

That's because I felt ashamed of it. People either thought that Depression was a mental illness and that consequently I was a total nutter who had to be spoken to very slowly and was better avoided. Or more often they thought that there was no such thing as Depression, other than a vague, neurotic concept. That it was just an updated version of "suffering from her nerves" which everyone knows translates as "she feels sorry for herself for no good reason." That I was merely indulging myself, wallowing in teenage angst that was way past its use-by date. And that all I had to do was to "pull myself together" and "snap out of it" and "take up sport."

I could understand that attitude, because *everyone* got depressed sometimes. It was part of being alive, part of the deal, sunny days and earaches.

People got depressed about money (about not having enough of it, I mean, not about the fact that money wasn't doing too well at school or had lost a lot of weight recently). Unpleasant things happened to people – relationships fell apart, jobs were lost, televisions broke down two days after the guarantee ran out and so on and so on – and people felt miserable about them.

I *knew* all that, but the depression that I suffered from wasn't just an occasional bout of the blues or a dose of Holly Golightly's mean reds – although I got them also, and fairly regularly at that. So did a lot of people, especially if they had just had a week of heavy drinking and very little sleep, but the blues and the mean reds were mere child's play compared to the savage black killer demons that descended on me from time to time to play crucifixion with my head.

Mine was no ordinary depression, oh *no*, mine was the super, de luxe, top-of-the-range, no-expense-spared version.

Not that any of it was immediately obvious on first meeting me. I wasn't miserable *all* of the time, in fact a lot of the time I was bright and personable and entertaining. And even when I felt dreadful I tried very hard to act as though I didn't. It was only when things got so desperate that I couldn't conceal it any longer that I took to my bed for anything from a couple of days to a week and waited for it to pass. Which it invariably did, sooner or later.

The worst bout of depression that I ever had was actually my first one.

I was seventeen and it was the summer that I had left school, and for no reason – apart from all the obvious ones – I got the idea into my head that the world was a very sad, lonely, unfair, cruel, heart-breaking kind of a place.

I got depressed about things that were happening to people in far-flung corners of the world, people that I didn't even know and wasn't ever likely to know, considering that the main reason that I felt depressed about them was that they were dying of hunger or of a plague or from their house falling in on top of them during an earthquake.

I cried at every piece of news that I heard or saw – car crashes, famines, wars, programmes about AIDS victims, stories of mothers dying and leaving young children, reports on battered wives, interviews with men who had been laid off in their thousands from coalmines and knew that even though they were only forty they would never work again, newspaper articles about families of six who had to feed themselves on fifty pounds a week, pictures of neglected donkeys. Even the funny bit at the end of the news, where a dog cycles a bike or says "sausages" pierced me with pain, because I knew it was only a matter of time before the dog would die.

I found a child's blue and white mitten on the pavement near my house one day and the grief that it triggered was almost unbearable. The thought of a tiny chilled hand, or of the other mitten, all alone without its mate was so poignant that I cried wet, hot, choking tears every time I saw it.

After a while I wouldn't leave the house. And shortly after that I wouldn't get out of bed.

It was horrendous. I felt as though I was personally in touch with every ounce of grief in the world, that I had an Internet of sorrow in my head, that every atom of sadness that had ever existed was being channelled through me, before being packaged up and transported on to outlying areas, like I was a kind of centralised misery depot.

My mother took charge. With the efficiency of a despot being threatened with a *coup d'etat,* she imposed a total news blackout. I was banned from watching television, and luckily this coincided with one of those times when we had fallen behind in some of our payments – probably our rates – and the baliffs had impounded various items of our furniture, including the television, so I couldn't have watched it *anyway*.

And every evening when my brothers came home, my mother frisked them at the front door to relieve them of any copies of newspapers that they may have had secreted about their person, before they could gain admittance to the house.

Not that her media clampdown made any difference. I had the admirable skill of being able to locate a tragedy – however small – in absolutely anything and managed to cry at the description of little bulbs dying in a February frost that was in the gardening magazine that was my only permitted reading material.

Eventually Dr Thornton was sent for, but not before a day or so was spent tidying and cleaning frantically in honour of his arrival. And he diagnosed depression and – surprise, surprise – prescribed antidepressants for me, which I didn't want to take.

"What good will they do?" I sobbed at him. "Will the antidepressants give those men in Yorkshire back their jobs? Will the antidepressants find the pair to this . . . to this . . . " (by now I was gasping and incoherent with crying) ". . . to this MITTEN!?" I wailed.

"Oh, would you ever shut up about that bloody mitten," tisked my mother briskly. "She has my heart scalded with that self-same mitten. Yes, doctor, she'd be delighted to start on the tablets."

My mother was like a lot of people who hadn't been allowed to finish their schooling in that she believed that anyone who had been to university, especially doctors, were almost Pope-like in their infallibility, and that taking prescribed narcotics was a mystic and sacred kind of a thing.

("I am not worthy to receive them but only say the word and I shall be healed.")

Also she was Irish and had a huge inferiority complex and thought that everything English people suggested had to be right. (Dr Thornton was English.)

"Leave it to me," my mother grimly assured Dr Thornton. "I'll see that she takes them."

And she did.

And after a while I felt better. Not happy or anything like that. I still felt that we were all doomed and that the future was a vast wasteland of bleak greyness, but that it mightn't hurt if I got up for half an hour to watch *Eastenders*.

After four months Dr Thornton said it was time for me to stop taking the antidepressants and we all held our breath, waiting to see if I could fly on my own or if I would dive-bomb back to that salty, single-mittened hell.

But by then I had started at secretarial college and I had faith, however fragile, in the future.

My world opened up at college, I learnt many strange and wondrous things – I was amazed to hear that the quick brown fox jumps over the lazy dog, that "i" comes before "e", except and *only* except after "c", that if I began a letter with "Dear Sir" and ended it with "Yours sincerely" that the world would come crashing to an immediate end.

I mastered the demanding art of sitting with a wire-bound notebook on my lap and covering the page with squiggles and dots, I strove hard to be the perfect secretary, quickly working up to four Bacardis and diet cokes on a night out with the girls, and my knowledge of the stock of Miss Selfridges was, at all times, encyclopaedic.

It never occurred to me that perhaps I could have done something else with my life – for a long time I thought it was such an honour to get the chance to train as a secretary that I didn't realise how much it bored me. And even if I *had* realised how much it bored me, I wouldn't have been able to wriggle out of it because my mother – a very determined woman – was adamant that that was what I would do. She actually cried with joy the day I got my certificate to say that I could move my fingers quickly enough to type forty-seven words a minute.

In a fairer world, *she* would have been the one to enrol in the typing and shorthand course, and not me, but that's not the way it happened.

I was the only girl from my class at school who went to secretarial college. Apart from Gita Pradesh, who went to Physical Education college, everyone else either got pregnant, got married, got a job stacking shelves in Safeway, or a combination of the three.

I was quite good at school, or at least I was too afraid of the nuns and my mother to be a complete failure.

But I was too afraid of some of the other girls in my class to be a complete success either – there was a gang of "cool" girls, who smoked and wore eyeliner and had very developed chests for their age and were rumoured to have sex with their boyfriends. I badly wanted to be one of them but I hadn't a hope because I sometimes passed my exams.

Once, I got sixty-three per cent in a biology exam and I was lucky to escape with my life, which wasn't really fair because the exam was on the reproductive system, and they probably knew a lot more about it than I did, and would have all got high marks if they had only turned up.

But every time there was an exam they brought faked sick notes from their mothers.

Their mothers were even more scary than they were and if the nuns cast doubts on the authenticity of the sick notes and administered punishment accordingly, the mothers – and sometimes even the dads – came to the school and caused uproar, threatening to thump the nuns, accusing the nuns of calling their daughters liars, and shouting wildly of "reporting" them.

Once, when Maureen Quirke brought three sick notes in the one month, each of them asking for her to be excused because she had her period, Sister Fidelma slapped her and said "Do you take me for a fool, girl?", and within hours Mrs Quirke arrived at the school like an avenging angel. (As Maureen said later, the funniest part of all was that she was actually pregnant at the time, although she didn't know it when she wrote the notes.) Mrs Quirke shouted at Sister Fidelma, "No one lays a finger on any of my children. No one! Except me and Mr Quirke! Now get yourself a man, you dried-out old mickey-dodger, and leave my Maureen alone."

Then she marched imperiously out the gate, dragging Maureen with her, and thumped Maureen all of the way home. I knew that for a fact because when I got home from school at lunch-time my father fell on me eagerly, and said, "I saw that Quirke child passing up the road earlier with her mother, and the mother thumping forty shades of shite out of her. Tell us, what happened at all?"

So when I stopped taking antidepressants and went to secretarial college, my depression didn't return in all it's savagery, but it hadn't entirely gone away either. And because I was terrified of being depressed again and didn't want to take pills, I dedicated my life to finding out the best ways of keeping it at bay, *au naturel*.

I wanted to banish depression entirely from my life, but had to be content with just stemming it by constantly reinforcing my emotional sandbags.

So along with swimming and reading, fighting depression became a hobby. In fact, strictly speaking, swimming wasn't really a hobby in its own right, it was more accurate to say that it came under the heading of Fighting Depression, sub-heading Exercise, category Gentle.

I read everything on the subject of depression that I could lay my hands on, and nothing raised my spirits like a good, juicy, story of a famous person who suffered agonies from it.

Accounts of people who spent months on end in

bed, not eating, not speaking, just staring at the ceiling, tears trickling down the sides of their faces, wishing they had the energy to kill themselves, thrilled me.

I was in very exalted company.

Churchill called his depression his "black dog", but, at eighteen, that confused me because I loved dogs. However, that was before the media had invented pit bull terriers. Once that happened, I understood exactly what Winston had been getting at.

And everytime I went to a bookshop, I pretended that I was just aimlessly browsing but, before I knew it, I had bypassed the new releases, the fiction, crime, science fiction, cookery, home decoration and horror sections, kept going through the biography section (pausing only briefly to see if any depressed person had recently published their life story) and somehow, as if by magic, always ended up at the self-help section, where I would spend hours reading through books that I hoped might fix me, that might have the magic solution, that would take away, or even just ease, the corrosive gnawing that was nearly always with me.

Of course a lot of self-help books were so full of mad rubbish that they could reduce the most happy, well-balanced person to despair. There were books which even someone as dippy as a native San Franciscan would have had trouble keeping a straight face reading. Titles such as *Agoraphobia? Don't leave home without it* or *Kleptomania – a guide to helping yourself* were not beyond the realms of possibility.

Nevertheless, I usually parted with money for a

little volume that encouraged me to perhaps "feel the fear and do it anyway" or maybe to "heal my life" or it mightn't be a bad idea to "rediscover" my "child within" or asked me to consider "why I need you to love me before I can like myself".

What I really needed was a self-help book to help me stop buying self-help books, because they didn't help.

As my dad would have said, they were feck all use.

They just made me feel guilty. It wasn't enough just to read the books. For them to work, I had to *do things* – like stand in front of a mirror and tell myself a hundred times a day that I was beautiful – that was called affirmation. Or spend half an hour every morning imagining myself being showered in love and affection – that was called visualisation. Or writing lists of all the good things in my life – that was called writing lists of all the good things in my life.

I usually read the book and did what it suggested for about two days and then got tired, or bored, or caught by my brothers as I spoke seductively to my reflection. (I never forgot The Great Scorning that followed *that.*)

And then I would feel depressed *and* guilty. So I would say that the hypothesis of the book must be fundamentally faulty because it hadn't made me feel any better and then I could abandon the whole project with a clear conscience.

I tried lots of other things also – Oil of Evening Primrose, vitamin B_6, excessive exercise, subliminal self-help tapes that you play when you're asleep, yoga, pilates, a flotation tank, aromatherapy massage, shiatsu, reflexology, a yeast-free diet, a gluten-free diet, a sugar-free diet, a food-free diet, vegetarianism, a "lots of meat" diet (I don't know if there's a name for it), an ioniser, an assertiveness course, a positive-thinking course, dream therapy, past-life regression, praying, meditating and sun-light therapy (a holiday in Crete, to be precise). For a while I ate nothing but dairy products, then for a while I gave up dairy products completely (I'd misread the article the first time), then I felt that if I had to go another day without a bar of chocolate I was killing myself anyway.

And while none of my measures turned out to be the Final Solution, at least they all worked for a while and I never again got as depressed as I had the first time.

But Mrs Nolan had said something about help being available if I only asked for it. I wished now I'd brought a tape recorder into the room with me because I couldn't remember exactly what she'd said.

What did she mean?

The only thing I could think of was that maybe she meant that I should go for professional help, and see some kind of therapist or counsellor or psycho something or other. The problem was that about a year ago I *had* seen a therapist kind of a woman for a while, about eight weeks or so, and that had been a complete waste of time.

Chapter Six

Her name was Alison and I used to go to see her once a week where we sat in a bare, tranquil little room and tried to figure out what was wrong with me.

Although we had discovered all kinds of interesting things – like the fact that I still held a grudge against Adrienne Cawley for giving me a game that the box said was "suitable for 2-5-year-olds" at my sixth birthday party – I didn't seem to have learnt anything more than what I had already managed to figure out for myself on many a sleepless night.

Naturally, the first thing that Alison and I did was the psychotherapy witch hunt called "Cherchez La Famille", where we tried to hold my family responsible for everything that was wrong with my damaged psyche.

But there was nothing funny about my family, unless normal was funny.

I had a perfectly normal relationship with my two brothers Chris and Peter – that is, I spent my childhood hating their guts and they reciprocated in traditional fraternal fashion by making my life a misery. They made me go to the shop for them when I didn't want to, they hogged the telly, broke my toys, scribbled on my homework, told me that I was adopted and that my real parents were in prison for robbing a bank. Then they told me they were joking about that and that my real mother was actually a witch. And when Mum and Dad went out to the pub they told me that they had really run away and were never coming back and that I'd be sent to an orphanage and be beaten and fed burnt porridge and cold tea. The usual sibling playfulness.

I told all of this to Alison and when I got to the bit about Mum and Dad going to the pub she seized on it joyfully.

"Tell me about your parents' drinking," she said, settling back in her chair, making herself comfortable for the great pouring forth of revelations that she expected to follow.

"I can't really tell you anything," I said. "My mother doesn't drink."

Alison looked disappointed.

"And your father?" she asked, hopefully, realising that all was not lost.

"Well, *he* drinks," I said.

She was delighted!

"Yes?" she said, in her extra-gentle voice. "Do you want to talk about it?"

"Well, yes," I said, confused. "Except there's nothing really to talk about. When I say he drinks, I don't mean that he has a problem."

"Mmmmmm," she nodded gently, knowingly. "And what do you mean by 'having a problem'?"

"I don't know," I said. "I suppose I mean being an alcoholic. And he isn't."

She said nothing.

"He's not," I laughed. "Sorry, Alison, I'd love to be able to tell you that my father was drunk throughout my childhood and we never had any money and that he hit us and shouted at us and tried to have sex with me and told my mum that he wished he'd never married her."

Alison didn't join in with my laughter and I felt slightly silly.

"*Did* your father tell your mother that he wished he'd never married her?" she asked quietly and with dignity.

"No!" I said, embarrassed.

"No?" asked Alison.

"Well, hardly ever," I admitted. "And it was only when he was drunk. And that was hardly ever either."

"And *did* you feel that your family never had enough money?" she asked.

"We were never short of money," I said stiffly.

"Good," said Alison.

"Well, that's not really true," I felt forced to admit. "We were always short of money, but it wasn't because of Dad's drinking, it was just because we . . . didn't have much money."

"Why didn't you have much money?" asked Alison.

"Because my dad couldn't get a job," I explained eagerly. "You see, he didn't have any qualifications because he had to leave school when he was fourteen because his father died and he had to look after his mother."

"I see," she said.

In fact, Dad used to say an awful lot more on the subject of his unemployment but I felt strangely reluctant to tell Alison.

One of the clearest memories of my childhood was Dad sitting at our kitchen table, passionately explaining the faults in the system. He used to tell me that in the English workplace the Irishman will always get "the shitty end of the stick" and that Seamus O'Hanlaoin and Michael O'Herlihy and all the rest of them were nothing but a crowd of crawlers and "arse-lickers" because they sucked up to their English bosses, but that you should hear what they said behind their backs. And that although Seamus O'Hanlaoin and Michael O'Herlihy and all the rest of them might have jobs, at least he, Jamsie Sullivan, had integrity.

That must have been very important to him, because he said it a lot.

He said it an awful lot the time that Saidbh O'Herlihy and Siobhán O'Hanlaoin were going with the school to Scotland and I wasn't.

I didn't want to tell Alison because I was afraid that I might offend her, in case she took my father's condemnation of his English would-be bosses personally.

I started to tell Alison about all the jobs my father went for and didn't get, when she cut into my memories.

"We're going to have to leave it there for this week." She stood up.

"Oh, is the hour up already?" I asked, shaken by how abruptly the session had ended.

"Yes," said Alison.

A wave of guilty fear overwhelmed me. I hoped that I hadn't sounded disloyal about Dad.

"Look, I don't want you to think that my dad wasn't a nice man or anything," I said desperately. "He's lovely and I really love him."

Alison gave me her Mona Lisa smile, giving nothing away and said, "See you next week, Lucy."

"Honestly, he's great," I insisted.

"Yes, Lucy," she smiled, not showing her teeth. "See you next week."

And the next week was worse. Somehow Alison got it out of me about not going on the school trip to Scotland.

"Didn't you mind?" she asked.

"No," I said.

"Didn't you feel angry with your father?" she asked.

"No," I said again.

"But why not?" She had sounded quite despairing at that point – the first time I'd ever seen her show any emotion.

"Because I just didn't," I said simply.

"How did your father react when it became clear that you couldn't go?" she asked. "Can you remember?"

"Of course I can remember," I said in surprise. "He told me that his conscience was clear."

In fact, "My conscience is clear," was something Dad often said. And, "I can sleep easy in my bed at night," was another. And he was right. Very often he would sleep easy even before he got to his bed. That

usually happened on the nights when he had a drop
·taken.

Somehow I ended up telling all of this to Alison
also.

"Tell me about the nights when he . . . er . . . had
a drop taken," she asked.

"Oh, you make it sound so bad," I complained. "It
wasn't bad at all, it was nice. He just kind of sang
and cried a bit."

Alison looked at me without saying anything and
to fill the silence I blurted, "But it wasn't sad when
he cried because I knew that in a funny way he was
glad to be sad, if you know what I mean?"

Alison obviously didn't.

"We'll talk about it next week," she said. "Our
hour is up."

But we didn't talk about it next week because I
never went back to Alison.

I had felt manipulated by her into being mean
about Dad and the guilt was awful. Besides, I was
the one who was depressed so I couldn't understand
why two whole sessions had been devoted to my
father and how much he did or didn't drink.

In the same way that dieting makes you fat, I felt
that analysis gives you problems. So I sincerely
hoped that Mrs Nolan hadn't been suggesting that I
go and see another Alison because I really didn't
want to.

Chapter Seven

We would have all forgotten about Mrs Nolan, the whole experience would have been consigned to some dark and dusty room somewhere in the attic of our memories, if a couple of things hadn't occurred.

The first thing that happened was that Meredia's prediction came true. Well, sort of . . .

The day after we had had our fortunes told, Meredia arrived into work waving something above her tie-dyed head in a triumphant fashion.

"Look," she commanded. "Look, look, look."

Hetty, Megan and I hopped up from our desks and went over to Meredia's to have a look. The thing that she had been waving above her head was a cheque.

"She said I'd come into money and I *have*," shouted Meredia excitedly as she attempted to do an ill-advised little dance, knocking nine or ten files off her desk and sending shudders throughout the entire building.

"Show me, show me," I begged, trying to grab it off her. But, for such a large woman, she was surprisingly deft.

"Do you know how long I've waited for this

money?" she demanded, looking from one of us to the other. "Have you *any* idea how long?"

Mutely, the three of us shook our heads. Meredia certainly knew how to create a captive audience.

"Well, I've waited *months*!" she bellowed, throwing her head back. "Literally *months*!"

"Wonderful," I said. "Isn't that amazing?"

"Who's it from?" asked Hetty.

"How much is it for?" asked Megan, asking the only truly important question.

"It's a refund from my bookclub," sang Meredia joyfully. "And you simply cannot *imagine* the number of letters I've had to write to get it. I was on the verge of going to Swindon in person to complain."

Megan, Hetty and I exchanged puzzled looks.

"Your . . . *book*club?" I asked slowly. "A refund from your bookclub?"

"Yes," said Meredia, sighing dramatically. "It's been the most awful palaver. I said I didn't want the book of the month and they sent it anyway and . . . "

"So how much did you get?" interrupted Megan abruptly.

"Seven fifty," said Meredia.

"Is that seven hundred and fifty or seven pounds fifty?" I asked, fearing the worst.

"Seven *pounds* fifty," said Meredia, sounding annoyed. "What do you mean, seven hundred and fifty? The book of the month would need to be made of solid gold for me to spend that much on it. Honestly, Lucy, sometimes I wonder about you!"

"I see," said Megan, very matter-of-factly. "You got

a cheque for seven pounds fifty – a *quarter* of the cost of the reading from Mrs Nolan – and you're saying that her prediction that you would come into money has come true? Have I got that right?"

"Yes," said Meredia, all indignant. "She didn't say how *much* money I'd come into. She just said that I would."

"And I did," she added defensively.

"What's wrong?" she shouted, as we all drifted back to our desks, disappointment on our faces. "Your expectations are too high. That's your trouble."

"For a moment there I thought the predictions were going to come true. But it doesn't look like I'll be meeting the love of my life," said Hetty sadly.

"And I won't be having my big split," said Megan. "Unless it's a banana split."

"And I won't be getting married," I said.

"Not a hope," agreed Megan.

"None," said Hetty, sighing heavily.

Our conversation was cut short by the arrival of our boss, Ivor Simmonds. Or "Poison Ivor" as we sometimes called him. Or "that mean bastard" as we othertimes called him.

"Ladies," he nodded at us, the expression on his face indicating that he thought we were anything but.

"Good morning, Mr Simmonds," said Hetty with a polite smile.

"Mumble, mumble," said the rest of us.

That's because we hated him.

For no particular reason. Not for his complete absense of a sense of humour – as Megan said, he must have had all charisma surgically removed at

57

birth – or his shortness, or his receding wispy ginger hair, or his hideous gingery beard, or his salesman's tinted spectacles, or his plump red lips that always seemed to be wet, or, worst of all, for his round, low-slung, womanly bottom, or for his nasty, cheap, shiny suit that covered – just about – the aforementioned bottom, or the visible panty line you could see through the shiny seat of the suit.

Of course all these factors *helped*. But mostly we just hated him because he was our boss. Because it was the *rule*.

His disgustingness did come in handy on several occasions. Once, when Megan was feeling really nauseous after a night on the Fosters and Peach Schnapps, it was a great help.

"If only I could puke," she complained. "Then I'd be fine."

"Imagine having sex with Ivor," I suggested, anxious to help.

"Yes," said Meredia gleefully. "Imagine having to snog him, that mouth, that beard. Ugh!"

"Christ," muttered Megan, heaving slightly. "I think it's working."

"And I bet he's a real slurper," said Meredia, her face twisting in delighted horror.

"And think about what he'd look like just in his underpants," I suggested. "Think hard. I bet he doesn't wear normal ones. No nice boxers or anything."

"No, he doesn't," said Hetty, who didn't usually join in.

We all swivelled round.

"How do *you* know?" we asked in unison.

"Because . . . er . . . you can see . . . you know . . . the line." Hetty blushed delicately.

"Fair enough," we conceded.

"I bet he wears knickers," I said gleefully. "Women's knickers. Big, pink, interlock ones that come up to his armpits, that his wife has to buy for him in an old ladies' shop because he can't get any normal ones to fit him."

"And imagine what his willy looks like," suggested Meredia.

"Yes," I said, feeling my stomach begin to turn. "I bet it's tiny and skinny and that he has ginger pubic hair and . . . "

That was enough to do it. Megan bolted from the office and returned, beaming, about two minutes later.

"Wow," she grinned. "Projectile! Anyone got any toothpaste?"

"Honestly, Megan," said Hetty coldly. "You're just too much sometimes."

Megan, Meredia and I exchanged raised eyebrow looks, wondering what had annoyed the normally pleasant and polite Hetty.

By a happy coincidence Mr Simmonds seemed to hate us as much as we hated him.

He glared at us, went into his office and slammed the door.

Meredia, Megan and I made desultory attempts to switch on our computers. Hetty didn't, because hers was already on.

Hetty did most of the work in the office.

There was a very scary period when Megan first arrived and she had worked really, really hard. Not only did she start work on time, but she actually *started work if she came in early*. She didn't unfold a newspaper and look at her watch and say, "Three more minutes. Those bastards aren't getting a second more out of me than they're owed," like the rest of us did.

Meredia and I took her aside and explained that not only was she putting our jobs in jeopardy, but that she could even end up working herself out of a job. ("And *then* how would you get to Greece?") So she slowed down, even managed to make a few mistakes. We all got on a lot better after that.

"Get Hetty to do it," was the office motto. Only Hetty didn't know about it.

I couldn't ever really figure out why Hetty had a job. She certainly didn't need the money. But Meredia and I decided that the boards of all the charities in London must have been oversubscribed when Hetty decided that she was bored and needed amusing, so she lowered her sights and came to work for us instead.

Which wasn't *unlike* working for a charity.

Indeed, Meredia and I often joked that working for Wholesale Metals and Plastics was exactly the *same* as working for a charity, so pitifully small were our stipends.

The day progressed. We went about our work. Sort of.

No further mention was made of Mrs Nolan, loves

of lives, big splits, coming into money or of me getting married.

Later that day my mother rang and I braced myself for news of a disaster, because she never called me just for a chat, to shoot the breeze, to aimlessly while away a few minutes of my employer's time. She only rang to breathlessly report catastrophes – deaths were her favourite, but most things would do. A chance of redundancies at my brothers' place of work, a lump on my uncle's thyroid, a fire in a barn in Monaghan or an unmarried cousin falling pregnant (a particular favourite, up there with deaths in the works of a combine harvester).

"D'you know Maisie Patterson?" she demanded excitedly.

"Yes," I said, thinking "Maisie *who*?" but knowing better than to say so because we could have been there all day while I got the Maisie Patterson family tree. ("She was one of the Finertans before she married . . . but, of *course* you know the Finertans, don't you remember when you were small I took you over to their house, a fine big house with a green gate, just behind the Nealons, but you *know* the Nealons, don't you remember Bridie Nealon, the day she gave you two Marietta biscuits, sure you know what a Marietta biscuit is, don't you remember squeezing the butter out through the holes . . .")

"Well . . . " said my mother, building up some suspense. Maisie Patterson had obviously gone to meet her maker, but it wasn't enough just to say it like that.

"Yes," I said patiently.

"They buried her yesterday!" she finally exclaimed.

"Why did they do that?" I asked mildly. "Had she annoyed them? When are they letting her out?"

"Oh, you're very smart," my mother said bitterly, annoyed that her news hadn't sent me gasping and reeling. "You're to send them a Mass Card."

"How did it happen?" I asked, hoping to cheer her up. "Did she catch her head in the combine harvester? Drown in the grain silo? Or was she savaged by a hen?"

"Not at all," she said, annoyed. "Don't be ridiculous, sure, hasn't she been living in Chicago this long time?"

"Oh, er . . . yes."

"No, t'was terribly sad," she said, dropping her voice a couple of decibels as a mark of respect and for the next fifteen minutes she gave me Maisie Patterson's medical history. The mysterious headaches that she got, the glasses she was prescribed to correct the headaches, the CAT scan she was given when the glasses didn't work, the X-rays, the medication, the spells in hospital being prodded and poked by bewildered specialists, the eventual all-clear and, finally, the red Toyota that knocked her down, ran her over, ruptured her spleen and sent her somersaulting into the next world.

Chapter Eight

On Thursday morning the day started badly and got worse.

When I woke up feeling totally miserable, I wasn't to know that Megan's "prediction" was due to come "true" that day.

If I *had* known I might have found it easier to get up.

As it was, it was touch and go whether I'd manage to break free from my bed's loving, warm embrace.

I always found it hard to get up in the mornings – one of the legacies of my teenage bout of depression, at least that's what I liked to say.

It was probably just laziness, but calling it depression made me feel a lot less guilty.

I could barely drag myself into the bathroom and once I was there I had my work cut out to force myself to have a shower.

My bedroom was freezing and I couldn't find clean knickers and I hadn't ironed anything so I had to wear the same clothes that I had worn to work the day before and that I'd just thrown on the floor the previous night and I couldn't find any clean knickers in Karen's or Charlotte's rooms either so I had to go to work wearing my bikini bottoms.

And when I got to the tube station all the nice papers were sold out and I'd just missed a train. And while I was waiting I thought I'd try and buy a packet of chocolate buttons from the machine on the platform and for once the bloody thing worked and then I ate the buttons in two seconds and immediately felt really guilty and then I started to worry that maybe I had an eating disorder if I was internalising chocolate first thing in the morning.

I was miserable.

It was cold and wet and there seemed so little to look forward to and I wanted to be at home in my warm bed, watching Richard and Judy, eating crisps and biscuits, weighty piles of glossy magazines beside me.

Megan looked up from her newspaper when I dragged myself in, twenty minutes late.

"Didn't you get undressed last night?" she asked cheerfully.

"What do you mean?" I asked wearily.

"I mean did you sleep in your clothes?" she said.

"Oh shut up," I said. On days like that one, Megan's Australian plain speaking was just too much for me.

"And anyway," I said, "if you think I look bad on the outside, you'd want to see what I've got on as knickers."

Even if Megan had only had five minutes sleep, she still got up in time to iron her clothes. And if she didn't have any clean knickers, she gave herself enough time to stop somewhere on the way to work and buy a pair. Not that Megan ever didn't have clean knickers because she always did her washing long before her knickers drawer was empty.

But that was Australians for you. Organised. Hardworking. Capable.

The day proceeded along normal lines. Every now and then I would fantasise about a Lockerbie-style disaster where a plane would fall from the sky and land on my office. Preferably on my desk, just to be on the safe side. Then I wouldn't have to come to work for ages. I might be dead, of course, but so what? I still wouldn't have to come to work.

The door to Mr Simmond's office would open regularly and he'd stomp out, bottom wobbling, and throw something on my desk or Meredia's desk or Megan's desk and shout, "there's forty-eight mistakes in that. You're getting better," or "which one of you has bought shares in Tippex?" or something equally unkind.

He was never mean to Hetty, because he was afraid of her. Her poshness reminded him that he was a middle-class boy made average and that he wore suits of man-made fibres.

At about ten to two, when I was slumped over my desk reading some article about how coffee is actually good for you again, and Meredia was snoring gently at her desk, a large bar of chocolate by her hand, a small drama burst into the office, and lo and behold Megan's prediction proceeded to come true.

Kind of . . .

Megan lurched in, her face as white as a ghost, blood pouring from her mouth.

"Megan!" I shouted in alarm, jumping up from my desk. "What *happened* to you?"

"Eh? What?" said Meredia, jerking awake, all confused, the merest hint of a dribble exiting her mouth by the left side.

"It's nothing," said Megan, but she looked a bit wobbly and sat on my desk. Blood was pouring down her chin and onto her shirt.

"I've got to ring an ambulance," said Megan.

"Jesus, no you don't," I said panicking, giving her a handful of tissues, which were soaked red in an instant. "I'll do it. You'd better lie down. Meredia, get up off your fat arse and help her to lie down!"

"No, it's not for me, you fool," said Megan irritably, shaking Meredia off her. "It's for the bloke who fell off his bike and landed on me."

"Oh my God!" I exclaimed. "Is he badly hurt?"

"No," said Megan shortly, "But he bloody well will be by the time I've finished with him. He'll need a body-bag, not an ambulance."

Before I could do it, she had picked up the phone and, through a mouthful of blood, called the emergency services and asked for an ambulance.

"Where is he?" asked Meredia.

"Out front, lying on the road, holding up the traffic," said Megan.

She was in a *very* bad mood.

"Is someone looking after him?" asked Meredia, an acquisitive gleam appearing in her eyes.

"Loads of people," barked Megan. "You Brits love a good accident, don't you?"

"Well, I'd better check on him anyway," said Meredia, lumbering towards the door. "He may be in shock so I'll cover him with my shawl."

"No need," complained Megan, blood bubbling as she spoke. "Someone's already put a coat over him."

But Meredia was gone. She had heard opportunity knocking. Although she had a pretty (if extremely fat) face, she had little success with men. The only men who actively pursued her were the peculiar ones who had a definite "thing" for highly obese women. And as Meredia said, with dignity, "Who wants a man who just wants you for your body?"

But the alternative was nearly as bad, I thought. She liked meeting men when they were vulnerable, either emotionally or physically, taking care of them, making herself indispensable, giving them all the support a weak person might need.

The only fly in the ointment was that the moment they were well enough to move, that's exactly what they did. Headed for the hills and away from Meredia's loving embrace as fast as their recently healed legs could carry them.

"Well, I'd better clean up this mess," said Megan, wiping her mouth on her sleeve.

"Don't be ridiculous," I said. "You're going to need stitches."

"No, I'm not," said Megan scornfully. "This is nothing. Have you ever seen what a combine harvester can do to a man's arm . . . ?"

"Oh stop being so . . . so . . . *Australian*!" I exclaimed. "You need stitches. You need to go to hospital. I'll come with you."

If she thought I was going to miss the chance to have an afternoon off work, then she had another think coming.

"No, you bloody well won't come with me," she said tartly. "What do you think I am? Some kind of kid?"

Just then the office door opened and in came Hetty back from lunch. She looked suitably appalled at the showing of *Apocalypse Now* that was taking place on Megan's face.

Two seconds later, Mr Simmonds arrived, also back from lunch. A separate lunch from Hetty's lunch, he seemed peculiarly keen to emphasise. Apparently they had just bumped into each other at the front door, not that anyone cared.

He too looked appalled. He was obviously upset about Megan's blood being spilt, but I think he was more upset about *where* Megan's blood was being spilt. On the desks and files and phones and letters and documents of his precious little empire.

He said that of course Megan must go to the hospital, and that of course I must go with her and when Meredia returned to say that the ambulance had arrived he said that she could go too. He said that Hetty had better stay behind because he wanted someone to hold the fort.

As I joyfully turned off my computer and got my coat, it suddenly struck me that whatever it was Mr Simmonds wanted Hetty to hold, it certainly wasn't his fort.

Chapter Nine

When we got to the ambulance, there was no room for Meredia. I felt so bad for her. But, with all the equipment, the two paramedics, the injured cyclist, Megan and I, there simply wasn't room for a woman the size of an elephant.

But undeterred, she said she'd get a taxi and see us there.

As we drove away from the kerb, I felt a bit like a pop star – it must have been the tinted windows and the small crowd of onlookers staring after us.

They were reluctant to leave, wringing the last few drops of excitement from the accident before they started to drift back to their lives, disappointed that the drama was over, and even more disappointed that someone hadn't died.

"He looked OK, didn't he?" said one bystander to another.

"Yes," came the bitter reply.

We spent four hours sitting on hard chairs in a crowded, manic, overworked casualty department. People with injuries far worse than Megan's or Shane's (the cyclist – by now we were all fairly intimate) sat waiting also, stoically holding in their laps whatever limbs they had severed and managed to retrieve. Trolleys with dying people on them were rushed past us at a rate of knots. No one seemed able to tell us what was happening or when Megan or Shane would be seen. The coffee machine wasn't working. The sweet shop was closed. The place was freezing.

"Just think." I closed my eyes in bliss. "We could be in work now."

"Yes," sighed Megan, bits of dried blood flaking away from her face as she spoke. "What a stroke of luck, eh?"

"God." I smiled. "I was so *miserable* earlier. I wish I'd known what a treat I had in store for me."

"I hope I'll be seen soon," said Shane looking anxious and confused. "Because they're waiting for those documents in WC1. They said they were urgent. Has anyone seen my radio?"

Shane was a bike messenger and had been en route to a delivery when he veered off his path and landed on Megan.

He kept kind of dozing off to sleep and then jerking awake and going on about his delivery in WC1. Megan and I exchanged long-suffering looks when he launched into it for about the tenth time, while Meredia smiled at him like he was a sweet little child and it gradually dawned on us that maybe he wasn't a moron and that perhaps he was concussed.

Apart from these regular bursts from Shane, conversation was desultory.

"Well, look on the bright side." I smiled at Megan, referring to her mutilated mouth. "You got the big split that you were promised. But I bet you weren't expecting it to be a split lip."

At that, Meredia jerked up straight like she'd been shot in the back and grabbed my wrist, digging her nails into me.

"My God," she hissed, staring straight ahead, a peculiar light in her eyes. Mad, actually, that was the word I needed. A *mad* light in her eyes.

"She's right!" she said, still talking in the hissy voice, still staring into the middle distance. "My God, she's right!"

"I've got a name," I said, annoyed at her histrionics. And my wrist hurt.

"Hey, you're right," said Megan, starting to laugh. "Ouch!" she complained, as her laughter started her face bleeding again.

"What a blast," she went on, laughing in earnest, blood pouring in Niagraesque fashion down the side of her face. "Yeah, I got my big split, all right. Just like she said. I can't see what good has come out of it, though."

"Maybe all will become clear with time," said Meredia, in a mysterious voice and giving Shane pseudo-covert looks and winking meaningfully at Megan and then jerking her head in Shane's direction again.

"If you know what I mean . . . " continued Meredia, with heavy emphasis.

"Yeah, maybe," laughed Megan lightheartedly.

I wasn't sure if Meredia had Shane in mind for herself or Megan, but past experience told me that Meredia wanted him for her own. That situation had her hallmark stamped all over it.

Although, by rights, he really should have been Megan's. Didn't she break his fall? And she handled the whole trauma so bravely that she deserved a treat.

"So now it's just you and Hetty, Lucy," said Megan. "Soon it'll be your turn for your fortune to come true."

"Do the words 'cold day' and 'in hell' mean anything to you?" I asked, laughing.

"Oooh, you doubting Thomas," admonished Meredia. "But you have to admit that it *is* peculiar."

"No, I don't," I said. "Don't be so silly! You can adjust any facts to fit into any predictions if you try hard enough."

"Such cynicism in one so young," said Meredia, shaking her head sadly.

"Has anyone seen my radio?" croaked Shane, coming to again. "I've got to talk to my controller."

"Shush, lovie, it's fine," said Meredia comfortingly, as she forced his head down onto her shoulder.

He mumbled some kind of protest, but it didn't do him any good.

"Just you wait," Meredia said threateningly to me, talking over Shane's confused head. "You'll see. It'll all come true. And then you'll be sorry."

I smiled longsufferingly at Megan, expecting her to smile longsufferingly back but to my great alarm, she didn't. She was too busy nodding agreement with Meredia.

Golly, I thought, my stomach tightening with shock, could her brain have been affected by the accident? I mean, Megan was possibly the most cynical person that I'd ever met, including myself – and I prided myself on having the highest standards of cynicism. I had my days when I was sure I could out-cynic some of the best cynics currently operating on the circuit.

Megan, like me, was so cynical that she didn't even fancy Daniel. "He doesn't fool me with his nice manners and his good looks," she had said after she first met him.

So what had happened to her?

Surely she didn't think that the predictions for herself and Meredia had come true? And worse again, surely she didn't think that because of that, that the predictions for Hetty and I would come true?

Eventually, when the nurses had run out of heart-attack victims and other nearly dead people to deal with, they stitched up Megan's face and said that Shane wasn't concussed, that he was just diligent.

We were all finally allowed to leave.

"Where do you live?" Meredia asked Shane, as we stood in the hospital carpark.

"Greenwich," he said warily.

That was in south London. *Very* south London.

"What a stroke of luck," said Meredia quickly. "We can get a taxi home together."

"But . . . " I started to protest, about to remind Meredia that she lived in Stoke Newington – which was north-east London – nowhere *near* Greenwich.

But Meredia fixed me with a murderous glare and my protests died away.

"But I've got to get my bike," said Shane backing

away in fear. "And I really have to deliver these documents."

"Don't be so silly," said Meredia, all faux-cheerful. "You can do that tomorrow. Come on now. Night, girls, see you both at work in the morning."

"If I'm able to walk," she muttered in an aside – one that was loud enough for Shane to hear and flinch at.

"Know what I mean, eh?" she leered, gesturing in the direction of her crotch. And with a final meaningful wink off she went, dragging the terrified Shane along by the arm.

He looked back pleadingly at Megan and I, his face one big cry for help, but there was nothing we could do for him.

An innocent lamb to the slaughter.

Chapter Ten

The following day all hell broke loose, when Megan and Meredia notified everyone in the whole world that I was getting married. They didn't actually tell everyone in the whole world, they just told Caroline, the receptionist at work. But that was as good as – better probably than, actually – telling everyone in the whole world.

Meredia and Megan had decided, notwithstanding my lack of boyfriend, that Mrs Nolan's predictions for me would come true, just as her predictions for them had.

Of course they apologised later and said they hadn't meant to do any harm and that they had really only been joking, etc., etc., but by then the damage was done and the idea had been planted in my mind and I had got to thinking that maybe a boyfriend would be a nice thing, a soul mate, someone to feel safe with, someone to be intimate with.

It opened up old longings. I began to *want* something from my life, which was always a mistake.

But all that was still ahead of me when my alarm went off, and I thought I felt miserable *then*.

The only good thing about it was that it was Friday.

When I woke up I was as badly organised as I had been the previous day. I still hadn't washed my clothes, so I still hadn't any clean knickers, so I had to wear Steven's boxers that he had left behind when I forced him to leave my flat rather suddenly about three weeks before. I had washed them, with the vague intention of returning them to him, so at least they were clean.

At the station, the chocolate machine was a bastard, it worked for me – again! Machinery hated me. It gave me a bar of fruit and nut and I didn't have the willpower not to eat it. I was becoming more and more convinced that I had an eating disorder. Buttons only had 170 calories, while a bar of fruit and nut had 267. Or was it 269? Anyway, it was *more*. I was getting worse, not better. The following day I'd probably try to get one of those huge family-size bars out of the machine, I thought, and a week later, I'd be on a two-kilo box of Roses before breakfast.

I finally got to work and I was very, very late indeed, even by my standards.

As I rushed past reception I was almost knocked to the ground by Mr Simmonds going at high speed in the direction of the Gents, his bum scurrying along about three yards behind the rest of him, trying hard to keep up. He looked flustered and agitated and he was a small bit red about the eyes. In fact, if I had thought the man was capable of human emotion, I would have sworn that he was crying. Something had obviously upset him.

My spirits rose.

I smiled brightly at Caroline, the receptionist, because it was more than my life was worth not to. She took offence easily and withheld my personal calls if she felt that I had slighted her. She smiled brightly back. As I raced past I thought I heard her call something after me – in fact it sounded oddly like "Congratulations" – but I was too eager to find out what disaster had befallen Mr Simmonds to stop.

I breezed into the office, no longer so worried about being late. Mr Simmonds obviously had bigger fish to fry.

Megan's bruises had come up beautifully and a white bandage covered the lower right-hand corner of her face.

I stopped in my tracks when I noticed that Megan and Meredia weren't rowing. Indeed, they compounded my confusion by talking civilly to each other.

How peculiar, I thought! Some kind of cease-fire must be in process. The pair of them were huddled around the biscuits – always a great bonding area, the office biscuits – and were whispering furtively.

It was unlikely that they were discussing Megan's injuries or Meredia's sex-life. It would take a bigger event than either of those to bring Megan and Meredia together.

This had to mean that something was definitely up.

Great! My spirits rose even further. I loved a bit of excitement. Maybe Mr Simmonds had been sacked. Or his wife had left him. Something good like that, I hoped.

I gave a quick glance round the office. Where was the diligent Hetty?

"Lucy!" declared Meredia dramatically. The way she often did. "Thank God you're here. There's something you *have* to know."

"What?" I demanded, a thrill of anticipation running though me.

"Is it you? Did you get lucky with Shane?"

A brief shadow passed over Meredia's face. "We'll talk about that later," she said. "No, it's something to do with here."

"Really?" I gasped in excitement. "I thought something must be up. I just passed Poison Ivor in the hall and he was . . . "

"Lucy, I think you'd better sit down," Megan interrupted.

"What is it?" I demanded, absolutely *dying* to know.

"Something has happened," said Meredia, in a dramatic whisper, keen to create an atmosphere. "Something that you should know."

"Well, if I should know it, why won't you bloody well tell me," I demanded.

"It's Hetty," said Megan solemnly, talking out of the uninjured side of her mouth.

"Hetty?" I hooted incredulously. "But what's Hetty got to do with Poison Ivor? Or me? Oh God – she's not having an affair with him, is she?"

"No, no, no," said Meredia, shuddering. "No, it's a *good* thing. But she won't be in for a couple of days because something has happened to her."

"Well, would you mind telling me just what that

something is," I said querulously. "Or do I have to sit here all day while you string this out?"

"Jesus! Have a bit of patience," said Meredia, not pleased.

"Tell her," said Megan of the gangsteresque mouth.

"Tell me what?" I said, the way I was expected to.

"Hetty," started Meredia. And then she paused. Building suspense. Christ, she was annoying.

"Hetty," she said again. Another pause.

I bit back the urge to scream.

"Hetty has met the love of her life," Meredia finally intoned.

A silence followed. You could've heard a tab of acid drop.

"Really?" I managed to ask, my voice hoarse.

"You heard me," said Meredia with a smug smile. I looked at Megan. Hoping for a bit of sanity and normality. But she just nodded at me and she had the same smug smile.

"She's met the love of her life and she's left Dick and she's moving in with Roger immediately.

"And Poison Ivor's heart is broken," guffawed Megan, slapping her slim, golden thigh.

"Don't be ridiculous," I said absently. "He hasn't got a heart."

More chortling from Megan and Meredia but I couldn't bring myself to join in.

"He must have the hots for Hetty big-time," said Megan. "Yuk, poor Hetty, how awful. Imagine! He must have been going round with a constant hard-on."

"Shut up, Megan!" I begged. "Or I'll throw up."

"Me too," said Meredia.

"So, have I got this right?" I asked weakly. "Roger is the other bloke?"

"Yes," smiled Megan.

"But Hetty doesn't do this sort of thing," I said.

I was upset and confused. I mean, Hetty really *didn't* do that sort of thing. Well, at least, she certainly didn't used to. It felt all wrong. Hetty was steady and steadfast and stable and stalwart and all those other words beginning with "st". She just didn't go round meeting the love of her life and leaving her husband and that kind of thing. She just *didn't*.

I would have felt as upset and disoriented if the earth changed direction and the sun rose in the west instead of the east or if I dropped a slice of toast on the floor and it landed with the buttered side facing up.

Hetty's leaving of Dick contradicted everything that I believed to be true, the very foundations of my universe were shaken.

"Aren't you happy for her?" asked Meredia.

"Who is he?" I blurted out. "Who's this love of her life?"

"Wait till you hear," said Meredia with relish.

"Yes, get this," interrupted Megan, also with relish.

"The love of her life is none other than Dick's brother," said Meredia with a flourish.

"Dick's brother?" I whispered. Things were getting more bizarre by the second. "So what happened?

She's known the guy for all these years and she suddenly decides that she loves him."

"No, no, no," said Meredia, smiling at me as though I was a naughty child. "It's so romantic. She'd never met him before until three days ago and they just clapped eyes on each other and *'voilà!'*, a *coup de foudre, l'amour, je t'adore*, er . . . um . . . *la plume de ma tante* . . . " she trailed off, having run out of French phrases to describe Hetty falling in love.

"How come she'd never met him before?" I asked. "She's been married for years."

A thought struck me.

"Oh no," I said in alarm. "Oh no. Don't let it be so."

"What?" gasped Megan and Meredia in unison.

"Please don't tell me that this is Dick's younger brother and he's been out in foreign parts – maybe Kenya or Burma or somewhere – for the past twenty years or so, like something out of *Last Days of the Raj* and that he's come back and he's all tanned and has blonde floppy hair and he's lounging round in a white linen suit, and sitting in a rattan chair and drinking gin and looking at Hetty with lazy, come-to-bed eyes. I mean, I just couldn't *bear* it! It would be too much of a cliché."

"Honestly, Lucy," scolded Meredia, "you have such an over-active imagination. No, it's nothing like that."

"He hasn't given her an ivory bracelet?" I asked.

"Well, if he did she didn't mention it," said Meredia doubtfully.

"Phew." I breathed a sigh of relief. "Good."

"It's Dick's *older* brother," said Megan.

"Good," I said again. "Already this is going against the stereotype."

"And she had never met him before because there had been some kind of family row," continued Meredia. "Dick and Roger hadn't spoken for years. But they're the best of friends now . . . Although maybe not, now that Hetty has . . . "

I stared at the pair of them, at their happy, excited faces.

"What's wrong with you, you miserable cow?" demanded Megan.

"I don't know," I said. "It doesn't feel right."

"Yes it does," sang Meredia. "The fortune-teller told her that she'd meet the love of her life. And now she has!"

"But it's all wrong," I said desperately. "There's something wrong with Hetty and Dick. I mean, that was obvious when she got upset on the drive home from Mrs Nolan's."

Meredia and Megan sat silently and sullenly.

"But instead of doing something about it, she believes some cock-a-mamie story from a charlatan of a fortune-teller . . . "

"She *wasn't* a charlatan," interrupted Meredia angrily. "I didn't see her changing colour."

"That's a chameleon, not a charlatan," I said in exasperation. "Anyway, she's told that she'll meet the love of her life, so she latches onto the first man she meets, one who hasn't even got the decency to have a linen suit or a rattan chair, and without giving any thought to the consequences, she ups and runs off with him!"

"In fact," I added, "I think she was having some kind of flirtation or something going with Poison Ivor – that's how miserable she was."

I paused in case either of them needed to vomit.

They both looked pale and sweaty and I waited a short while before I continued.

"We weren't wrong to get our tarot cards read, but we weren't supposed to take it seriously. It was only a bit of fun. Not some kind of solution to real problems."

They were both silent.

"Can't you see?" I begged them, but they avoided my eyes and looked at their shoes. "This isn't the right thing for Hetty."

"But how do you know?" demanded Meredia. "Why don't you have any faith? Why don't you believe Mrs Nolan?"

"Because Hetty has real problems with her marriage," I said. "And they're not going to be fixed because she wants to believe she's met the love of her life. That's just escapism."

"You're just scared," Megan suddenly blurted out, lopsided but passionate. She sounded angry and her face was flushed and emotional.

With the bruises and the bandage it was exactly like a scene out of *Sons and Daughters* or *Home and Away*.

"Of what?" I asked in surprise.

"You're just afraid to admit that the predictions have come true for me and Meredia and Hetty, because you'll have to admit that your prediction will come true also."

"Megan," I said in desperation. "What's wrong? I rely on you to be the sane one around here. The voice of reason."

Meredia bristled angrily and visibly expanded, which was quite something as I had thought she was already at bursting point.

"Look, Megan," I continued. "You don't really believe all this rubbish about predictions. Tell me you don't."

"The facts speak for themselves," she said haughtily.

"Yeah," sneered Meredia, much braver once she knew she had Megan on her side. She even tried to curl her lip. "Yeah. The facts do speak for themselves. So you'd better face it! You're getting married!"

"I can't listen to any more of this nonsense," I said calmly. "I don't want to fall out with either of you about this, but as far as I'm concerned the subject is closed."

The pair of them exchanged a look, a funny one – worried? guilty maybe? – which I chose to ignore.

I sat down at my desk, switched on my computer, fought back the urge to hang myself that passed fleetingly, but intensely, though me and started my day.

After a little while I noticed that the two of them still weren't doing any work – not that there was anything unusual about that, especially considering that Mr Simmonds hadn't yet returned – but instead of making personal calls to Australia or flicking through *Marie Claire* or eating their lunch (which Meredia did most days around ten-thirty) they just sat and looked at me in an odd way.

I stopped typing and looked up.

"What's wrong?" I asked in exasperation. "Why are you both being so weird?"

"Tell her," muttered Meredia to Megan.

"Oh no," said Megan with a grim little laugh. "Oh no, not me. It was your idea so you get to tell her."

"You little bitch!" exclaimed Meredia. "It was not my idea. It was *our* idea."

"Fuck you!" cried Megan. "You're the one who started all . . . "

My phone rang interrupting the exchange. I managed to answer it without taking my eyes off the pair of them going for each other hammer and tongs. I hated to miss a good row, and you could depend on Meredia and Megan to have some humdingers. It was amusing to see how short-lived their entente cordiale had been.

"Hello," I said.

"Lucy!" said a voice.

Oh dear. It was my flatmate Karen. She sounded cross. I must have forgotten to leave a cheque for the gas or the phone or something.

"Karen, hi!" I said quickly, trying to cover my nervousness. "Look, I'm sorry I forgot to leave the cheque for the phone. Or is it the gas? I got home late last night and . . . "

"Lucy, is it true?" she interrupted.

"Of course it's true," I asked indignantly. "It was well after midnight when I got in and . . . "

"No, no, no," she said impatiently. "I mean about you getting married?"

The room tilted slightly.

"Excuse me?" I said faintly. "Who on earth told you that?"

"The woman on the switch," said Karen. "And I must say that it's a bit much having to find out from her. When were you going to tell Charlotte and I? I thought we were your best friends. And now we'll have to put an ad in for a new person and we all get along so well and what if we get someone horrible who doesn't drink and who doesn't know any good-looking men and it won't be the same without you and . . . "

Her voice continued plaintively.

Megan and Meredia had gone suspiciously quiet. They were both sitting very, very still, guilt and fear written on their fool faces.

The guilt on their faces? Karen talking about me getting married? Megan and Meredia's insistence that Hetty's prediction had come "true"? Mrs Nolan foretelling that I would be getting married.

The guilt on their faces.

Chapter Eleven

The penny finally dropped.

It was so outrageous I could hardly believe it.

Was it really possible that, because they thought that Mrs Nolan's predictions for Meredia, Megan and Hetty had come true, her predictions for me were also bound to come true? Could it really be that this pair of idiots had gone round telling people that I was getting married, as if it was a *fact* and not the prediction of a tarot-reader?

Rage surged through me. And bewilderment. How could they be so stupid?

I realised that I was no one to talk. My life had been a series of one stupid thing after another, interspersed with some really ridiculous things and one or two downright insane things. But I was pretty sure that I'd never have done anything as daft as that!

I narrowed my eyes at them. Meredia shrunk back in her chair, the very picture of craven fear. (Of course, when I say "Meredia shrunk" I mean it entirely metaphorically.) Megan set her mouth, well one side of it anyway, in a stubborn and brazen fashion, she wasn't so easy to scare.

Karen continued to talk at high speed.

" . . . I suppose we could get a bloke but what if he fancied one of us and . . . "

"Karen," I said, trying to get a word in edgeways.

" . . . and he'd piss all over the bathroom, you know what men are like . . . "

"Karen," I said again, a bit louder.

" . . . of course *he* might have good-looking friends, in fact he might even be good-looking himself, but we wouldn't be able to go round with no clothes on although if he was good-looking maybe we'd want to and . . . "

"Karen!" I shouted.

She shut up.

"Karen," I said with relief, glad to have arrested the unstoppable train of her stream of consciousness. "I can't really talk right now but I'll call you back as soon as I can."

"It's Steven, I suppose," she interrupted. "I'm glad, he's lovely. I don't know why you had to go and dump him, unless you *wanted* him to ask you to marry him, all along. Smart move, Lucy, I wouldn't have expected that from you . . . "

I hung up. I had to. I didn't know what else to do.

I stared hard at Meredia and then at Megan and then back to Meredia. And then quickly flicked another glare at Megan just to let her know that I was still on her case.

After a few seconds I spoke.

"That was Karen," I said, in a daze. "And she seems to be under the impression that I'm getting married."

"Sorry," muttered Meridia.

"Yeah, sorry," muttered Megan.

"Sorry for what?" I said unkindly. "Perhaps you'd care to tell me just what exactly is going on?"

I mean, I had a fairly good idea of what was going on. But I wanted to know the full facts and I also wanted to put the pair of them through the very awkward experience of having to explain. To have to say, out loud, in words, in front of people, the exact nature of their stupidity. The door opened and Catherine from the director's office breezed in and flung something in the in-tray. "Lucy," she called. "Great news! I'll be down later to hear all the details."

And breezed out again.

"What the fu . . . " I began.

The phone rang.

It was my other flatmate Charlotte.

"Lucy," she said breathily. "Karen's just told me! And I want to tell you that I'm really happy for you. I know Karen says that you're a stupid bitch for not telling us, but I'm sure you had your reasons."

"Charl . . . " I tried to say. But, as with Karen, there was no getting a word in edgeways with her.

"And, Lucy, I'm so glad things have finally worked out for you," she chattered on. "To be quite honest, I never thought that they would. I know I always disagreed with you when you went on about how you were going to end up as an old lady in a bedsit, with a one-bar heater and forty cats, but I was beginning to be afraid that that was what really was going to happen . . . "

89

"Charlotte," I interrupted her angrily – one-bar heater, indeed! – "I've got to go."

And I slammed down the phone.

Which rang again immediately.

This time it was Daniel.

"Lucy," he croaked, "tell me it's not true. Don't marry him! No one could love you as much as I do."

I waited grimly for him to shut up.

"Lucy," he said after a while. "Are you there?"

"Yes," I said shortly. "Who told you?"

"Chris," he said, sounding surprised.

"Chris?" I yelled. "Chris, my brother?!!"

"Er, yes," said poor Daniel. "Is this supposed to be a secret or something?"

"Daniel," I tried to explain. "Look, I can't go into this, right now. But I'll call you as soon as I can, OK?"

"OK," he agreed. "And I was only joking earlier. I really am very hap . . . "

I hung up.

The phone rang again.

And I let it ring.

"One of you two better answer it," I said grimly.

Meredia picked up the phone.

"Hello," she said nervously.

"No," she said, looking fearfully at me. "She can't come to the phone right now."

A pause.

"Yes, I'll tell her," she said, and hung up.

"Who was it?" I asked, feeling like I was dreaming.

"Er, the boys in the storeroom. They want to take you out for a drink to celebrate."

"Just how bad is this?" I asked, my head swimming with horror. "Have you e-mailed everyone in the entire organisation? Or just several hundred of my closest friends? I mean, how does my *brother* know?"

"Your brother?" asked Megan, alarm flitting across her face.

Meredia swallowed. "Lucy," she said nervously. "We haven't e-mailed anyone. Honestly."

"No," chimed in Megan, laughing slightly in what I can only hope for her sake was relief. "We've told hardly anyone. Just Caroline. And Blandina and . . . "

"Blandina!" I interjected sharply. "You've told *Blandina*. If you've told Blandina we don't need bloody e-mail. The whole world must already know. They probably know on Mars. In fact I bet my mother knows."

Blandina was the PR person, and gossip was her currency, the air that she breathed.

My phone rang again.

"One of you better answer that," I said threateningly. "If it's anyone else ringing to congratulate me on my impending nuptials I may not be responsible for my actions."

Megan picked up the phone.

"Hello," she said, a nervous quaver in her voice.

"It's for you," she said, handing the phone over to me, almost throwing it as if it was red-hot.

"Megan," I hissed, gesturing to her to cover the mouthpiece. "I don't want to talk to anyone. I'm not taking this call."

"I think you'd better," she said miserably. "It's your mother."

91

Chapter Twelve

I stared pleadingly at Megan, then at the phone, then at Megan again.

This did not bode well. Surely it was too soon for someone else to have died? And she definitely wasn't just calling for a chat – my mother and I had never had the, "Oh go on, buy it, I won't tell Daddy, no one would believe you've got a grown-up daughter, it looks better on you that it does on me, can I have a squirt of your perfume, you've a better figure now than the day you got married, now let's go for several G and Ts because you're my best friend," type of relationship. So it meant that my mother must somehow have got wind of the whole me-getting-married fiasco and I was very reluctant to talk to her.

To be honest, I was quite afraid of her.

"Tell her I'm not here," I hissed desperately at Megan.

Immediately there was an eruption from the receiver, which sounded like two parrots fighting but which was my mother yelling that she had heard that, so I took the phone.

"Who's dead?" I said, playing for time.

"You are," she roared, with an uncharacteristic flash of wit.

"Ha, ha," I said nervously.

"Lucy Carmel Sullivan," she sounded furious. "Christopher Patrick just telephoned me and he tells me that you're getting married. Married!"

"Mum . . . "

"What a lovely state of affairs that your own mother has to find out such a thing from common gossip!"

"Mum . . . "

"Of course I had to let on that I knew all about it. But I knew this day would come, Lucy. I always knew it. Since you were a child you've been flighty and feckless. We couldn't depend on you to do anything – except to get it wrong. There's only one reason that a young woman gets married in such a hurry and that's if she's stupid enough to get herself into trouble. Although you're bloody lucky that you've got the lad to say he'll stand by you, although what kind of a useless eejit he is, God only knows . . . "

I didn't know what to say, because it was kind of funny – there was a long-standing joke in my family that everything I ever did, my mother found fault with it. I had so much experience of her disapproval and disappointment that it no longer really bothered me.

And years ago, I'd given up hoping that she'd approve of my boyfriends, that she'd admire my flat, that she'd be in awe of my job and that she'd like my friends.

"You're just like your father," she said bitterly.

Poor Mum – nothing I ever did was good enough for her.

When I finished secretarial college, I got a job with the London office of a multi-national company and on my first day my mother rang me, not to congratulate me and wish me well, but to tell me that the company's shares had dropped ten points on the FTSE index.

"Mum, listen to me, you fool," I interrupted loudly. "I'm not getting married."

"I see. So you're going to shame me by presenting me with an illegitimate grandchild," she exclaimed, still sounding furious. "And where do you get off calling me names . . . "

(About ten years previously she'd visited her sister Frances in Boston and had come back with her vocabulary awash with Americanisms which sounded really odd against the backdrop of her Monaghan accent.)

"Mum, I'm not pregnant and I'm not getting married," I said briskly.

There was a confused pause.

"It's a joke." I tried to sound a bit friendlier.

"Oh, it's a bloody joke, right enough," she snorted, back in her stride. "The day you come home to me and tell me that you've got some decent lad to marry you, that'll be a right joke. Oh, I'll laugh that day. I'll laugh till I cry that day."

To my surprise, I suddenly felt very angry. Out of the blue I wanted to shout at her that I wouldn't ever come home and tell *her* that I was getting married, that I wouldn't even invite her to the wedding.

Of course, the funniest thing of all was that, in the unlikely event of me ever winding up with a respectable man, one who had a job and a fixed abode and no ex-wives or criminal records, I wouldn't be able to stop myself from parading him in front of my mother and smugly inviting her to try and find some fault with him.

Because even though I often felt as if I hated her, there was still a part of me that wanted her to pat me on the head and say, "Good girl, Lucy."

"Is Dad there?" I asked her.

"Of course your beloved father is here," she said bitterly. "Where else would he be? Out at work?"

"Can I talk to him please?"

If I could talk to Dad for a few moments, I would feel a bit better. At least I could console myself that I wasn't a complete failure, that one of my parents loved me. Dad was always good at cheering me up and making fun of Mum.

"I doubt it," she said harshly.

"Why?"

"Think about it, Lucy," she said wearily. "He got his giro yesterday so what kind of condition do you expect him to be in?"

"I see," I said. "He's asleep."

"Asleep!" she barked mirthlessly. "The man is *comatose*. And has been, off and on, for twenty-four hours. The kitchen is like a bloody bottle bank!"

I said nothing, my teetotal mother thought that anyone who had an occasional drink was automatically an alcoholic. To hear her tell it, Dad could outdrink Oliver Reed.

"So you're not getting married?" she said.

"No."

"So you've created all that fuss for nothing."

"But . . . "

"Well, I'm going now," she said before I was able to think of something scathing to say. "I can't stand around here all day chatting. It's well for them that can."

Fury surged through me. *She* had rung *me*, after all, but before I could shout at her she was off again.

"Did I tell you that I'm working in the dry-cleaners now," she said, changing, without warning, to a much more conciliatory tone. "Three afternoons a week."

"Oh."

"As well as doing the service washes on Sunday and Wednesday."

"Oh."

"They closed down the mini-mart, you see," she went on.

"Oh."

I was too annoyed to bother talking to her.

"So I was delighted to get the few hours at the dry-cleaners," she went on. "The couple of bob comes in handy."

"Oh."

"So between doing the cleaning at the hospital and the flowers for St Dominics and organising a retreat with Father Colm, I've been keeping busy."

I *hated* when she did this. This was almost worse than when she was being bitter and horrible. How was I supposed to suddenly switch into a civilised conversation with her after the things she had just said to me?

"And are you keeping all right yourself?" she asked awkwardly.

"All the better for not seeing you," I felt like saying but managed not to.

"Fine," I said vaguely.

"We haven't seen you in ages," she said in a tone that was meant to be jolly and slightly teasing.

"I suppose."

"Why don't you come over some night next week?"

"I'll see," I said, starting to feel panicky. I couldn't think of anything more awful than spending an evening in my mother's company.

"Thursday," she said firmly. "Your dad will have run out of money by then so there's a good chance he'll be sober."

"Maybe."

"Thursday," she said, with finality. "And now I'd better go."

She was trying to sound good-humoured and friendly, but her inexperience showed. "All them . . . *yuppies* or whatever it is they're called, from the new townhouses, will be queueing up for their lovely Armada suits and their expensive silk shirts and whathaveyou. Do you know some of them even get their ties dry-cleaned? I ask you! Their *ties*. What next! Oh it's well for them that has the money to squander . . . "

"Well, you'd better go then," I said, with a sick heart.

"God Bless. See you on Thu . . . "

I slammed down the phone.

"And it's *Armani*!" I shouted at it.

I stared tearfully at Megan and Meredia who had been sitting silent and shamefaced throughout the lengthy conversation.

"Now look at what you've done, you stupid cows," I said, surprised by the hot, angry tears that spilt down my face.

"Sorry," whispered Meredia.

"Yeah, Lucy, sorry," muttered Megan. "It was Elaine's idea."

"Fuck off, bitch," hissed Meredia. "My name is Meredia and it was your idea."

I ignored them both.

They tiptoed round, shocked and frightened at how angry I was. I very rarely got angry. At least that was what they thought. In fact, I often got angry, I just very rarely showed it. I was much too afraid of people not liking me to court confrontation and that had both pluses and minuses. The minus being that I would probably have burnt a hole all the way through my stomach lining by the time I was thirty, but the plus being that on the rare occasions when I did give vent to my anger it commanded some respect.

I wanted to put my head down on my desk and sleep. But instead I got a twenty-pound note out of my purse and put it in an envelope and addressed it to my father. If Mum was no longer working in the mini-mart, money must be even tighter than usual.

The news that I wasn't getting married spread through the company at least as fast as the original news that I *was*. There was a constant flow of people to my office on the most unlikely of pretexts. It was a nightmare. Groups of people fell silent, then sniggered, as I walked past them in the corridors. Apparently someone in Personnel had started a collection for me and a nasty scuffle had broken out when attempts were made to return the donations because the sums being reclaimed were a lot more than the sums that were originally contributed and although it wasn't my fault I still felt somehow that it was.

The awful day seemed to last forever but it finally came to an end.

It was Friday evening and on a Friday evening it was traditional for me to go for "just the one" with the people from work.

But not that Friday.

I was going straight home.

I didn't want to be with anyone.

I was taking my embarrassment and my humiliation and other people's pity at my single status home. I'd had enough of being a talking point and a laughing stock for one day.

Luckily, on a Friday evening Karen and Charlotte also traditionally went for "just the one" with their respective workmates.

As "just the one" usually entailed a good seven hours of solid drinking, ending up in the early hours of Saturday morning in an anonymous, tourist-trap nightclub in a basement somewhere near Oxford Circus, dancing with young men in cheap suits wearing their ties knotted around their heads, there was a good chance that I would have the flat to myself.

Marian Keyes

I was glad about that.

Whenever I had a tussle with life and came out the loser – and I usually did come out the loser – I would hibernate.

I hid myself away from people. I didn't want to talk to anyone. I tried to limit human contact to ringing for a pizza and paying the delivery man. And I preferred it if the delivery man kept his crash-helmet on because it cut down on eye contact.

It passed after a while.

After a couple of days I'd have regained the energy I needed to go out into the world and deal with other human beings. I'd have managed to reassemble my protective armour so that I wasn't a whinging, miserable, pain in the neck. So that I was able to laugh at my misfortunes and actively encourage others to do so also, just to show what a good sport I was.

Chapter Thirteen

When I got off the bus it had started raining and it was bitterly cold. Although I was mute with misery and desperate for the shelter of home, I stopped at the row of shops beside the bus stop to buy supplies for my couple of days of isolation.

First I visited the newsagents and bought four bars of chocolate and a glossy magazine which I managed to procure without one word being exchanged between myself and the shopkeeper. (That was one of the many benefits of living in Central London.)

Then I went next door to the off-licence and guiltily bought a bottle of white wine. I felt uncomfortably sure that the man knew I intended to drink the entire bottle on my own, but I don't know why I was so worried because he probably wouldn't have turned a hair even if I was knifed in the queue, just so long as he got paid. But it was hard to shake my inherited small-town mentality.

Next I stopped at the chip-shop and, apart from a rudimentary discussion involving salt and vinegar, I was able to avoid any real human contact *and* buy a bag of chips.

Then I went into the video shop, hoping that I

could very quickly pick up something light and diverting, with the minimum of conversation.

But it was not to be.

"Lucy!" called Adrian, the video shop man, sounding all excited and delighted to see me.

I could have kicked myself for coming in! I had forgotten that Adrian would want to talk to me, that his customers were his social life.

"Hi, Adrian." I smiled demurely, hoping to calm him down.

"Great to see you," he shouted.

I wished he wouldn't. I was sure that the other people were looking at me.

I tried to make myself smaller inside my inconspicuous brown coat.

I quickly – a lot more quickly than I had originally intended – found what I wanted and took it to the desk.

Adrian smiled broadly.

If I wasn't so curmudgeonly I would have had to admit that he really was sweet. Just a bit too enthusiastic.

"So where've you been?" he asked loudly. "I haven't seen you for, oh . . . *days*!"

The other customers paused from perusing the racks and looked at me waiting for my answer. Well, at least, that was how it felt to me, but I *was* self-conscious to the point of paranoia.

I burned with embarrassment.

"So you went and got yourself a life?" asked Adrian.

"I did," I murmured. (Shut up Adrian, *please*.)

"And what happened?" he asked.

"It fell through," I smiled wistfully.

He guffawed. "You're a laugh, do you know that?"

I gave a tight smile.

I was sure that I could feel all the other customers craning their necks, looking at me and thinking "Her? – *that* insignificant little thing. Are you sure? She doesn't *look* like a laugh."

"Well, it's good to see you again," announced Adrian. "And what are you going to view this evening?"

"Oh no!" he said. His broad smile vanished in disgust and he almost threw my choice of video back at me. "Not *Four Weddings and a Funeral*."

"Yes, *Four Weddings and a Funeral*," I insisted, sliding it back across the counter at him.

"But, Lucy," he pleaded, sliding it firmly back to me, "it's sentimental crap. I know, I know! What about *Cinema Paradiso*?"

"I've seen it," I told him. "And on your recommendation. That was the night you wouldn't let me take out *Sleepless in Seattle*."

"Aha!" he said triumphantly. "But what about *Cinema Paradiso, The Director's Cut*?"

"Seen it."

"Jean de Florette?" he asked hopefully.

"Seen it," I said.

"Babette's Feast?"

"Seen it."

"Cyrano de Bergerac?"

"Which version?"

"Any of them."

"Seen them all."

"La Dolce Vita?"

"Seen it."

"Something by Fassbinder?"

"No, Adrian," I said, fighting back despair, but trying to sound firm. "You never let me take out anything I want. I've seen every cult and foreign film that you stock in here. Please, *please,* just this once, let me watch something light-hearted."

"That's in English," I added hastily, before he attempted to find me something light-hearted in Swedish.

He sighed.

"Well, OK," he said sadly. *"Four Weddings and a Funeral* it is. What have you got for your tea?"

"Oh," I said, thrown slightly by the abrupt change in subject.

"Give me up your bag," he said.

I reluctantly put my carrier bags up on the counter.

This was a ritual that Adrian and I usually went through. A long time ago he had confessed to me that his job made him feel very isolated. That he never had his meals at the same time as anyone else. And that it made him feel as though he still belonged to the real world if he kept in contact with the nine-to-fivers and what they did with their evenings and, more specifically, what they ate.

Normally I had a lot of sympathy for him, but that evening I wanted to get out of the outside world and be alone with my chocolate and my wine so that I could revel in the complete absence of any other human beings.

Also I was ashamed of the high-sugar, high-saturated-fat, low-protein, low-fibre purchases.

"I see," he said, poking through my carrier bags. "Chocolate, chips, wine – the chocolate will melt if you leave it next to the chips, you know – are you feeling a bit depressed?"

"I suppose," I said, trying to smile, trying to be polite. While every atom in me ached to be at home, with the door locked behind me.

"Poor you," he said kindly.

Again I tried to smile, but I wasn't able. For a moment I thought I might tell him about the whole me-getting-married fiasco, but I couldn't find the energy.

Adrian was sweet. Really sweet.

And cute, I realised vaguely.

And I kind of thought that he fancied me.

Maybe I should consider him, I thought half-heartedly.

Maybe that's what Mrs Nolan meant when she told me that at first I may not recognise my future husband, or whatever it was exactly that she said.

With a little burst of irritation, I realised that even *I* had started to believe Mrs Nolan, that I was just as bad as Megan and Meredia.

Angrily, I told myself to get a grip, that I wasn't marrying anyone and *certainly* not Adrian.

It would never work.

To begin with, there were financial considerations. I wasn't sure what kind of money Adrian was earning, but it couldn't have been much – it certainly couldn't have been much more than the pittance I earned. I certainly wasn't mercenary, but face it, I thought – how could we possibly keep a family on our combined incomes? And what about our children? Adrian seemed to work twenty hours a day, seven days a week, so they'd never even get to see their dad.

In fact, I'd probably never get to see him long enough for him to actually impregnate me.

Oh well.

Adrian had keyed in my account number, which he knew by heart and was telling me that I owed a fine for something that had been taken out ten days previously and hadn't yet been returned.

"Really?" I asked, turning pale at the thought of the amount I owed and the fear that I might never actually get out of that shop.

"Yes," he said, looking concerned. "That's not like you, Lucy."

He was right. I never did anything risky. I was far too afraid of annoying someone or of being told off.

"Oh God," I said in alarm. "I don't even *remember* taking out something in the last fortnight. What is it?"

"The Sound of Music."

"Oh," I said, worried. "That wasn't me. That must have been Charlotte using my card."

My heart sank. That meant that I was going to have to tell Charlotte off for impersonating an officer. And I'd have to get money from her for the fine. Extracting teeth would be easier.

"But why *The Sound of Music*?" asked Adrian.

"It's her favourite film."

"Really? Is there something wrong with her?"

"No," I said defensively. "She's very sweet."

"Ah, come on," scoffed Adrian. "She must be thick."

"She's not," I insisted. "She's just young." And maybe just a *bit* thick, I thought, but there was no need to tell Adrian.

"If she's over the age of eight, she's out of the 'just young' category," he snorted. "How old is she?"

"Twenty-three," I muttered.

"Old enough to know better," he said.

"I bet she has a pink duvet cover and Mr Blobby slippers," he added, his lip curled in disgust. "And she loves children and animals and gets up early on Sunday mornings to watch *Little House on the Prairie*."

If he only knew how close he was.

"You can tell an awful lot about a person by the video they choose," he explained. "Anyway, why is it charged to *your* card?"

"Because you closed her account. Remember?"

"She's not the blonde girl who took *Planes, Trains and Automobiles* to Spain?" said Adrian, his voice rising in alarm. He looked appalled at the realisation that he'd lent out one of his precious videos to the awful girl who had taken one of his babies across Europe and then refused to pay her fine on her return. That somehow the trade sanctions that he'd imposed against Charlotte had been breached.

"Yes."

"I can't think how I didn't recognise her," he said, looking upset.

"Don't worry, don't worry," I said soothingly,

willing him to calm down and let me go home. "I'll get it back. And I'll pay the fine."

I would have agreed to pay *anything* so that I could leave.

"No," he said. "Just get it back."

The way tearful mothers of missing children do on television appeals.

"Just get it back," he repeated. "That's all I ask."

I left. I was exhausted. So much for not wanting to talk to anyone.

But I wouldn't speak to anyone else that evening, I decided.

I *couldn't* speak to anyone else that evening.

I was taking a vow of silence.

Although it felt more like a vow of silence was taking me.

Chapter Fourteen

The flat was in a terrible mess. The kitchen was in a shambles, with dirty dishes and pans piled higgledy-piggledy in the sink. The bin needed to be taken out, the radiators were covered with drying clothes, two pizza boxes were flung on the living-room floor, perfuming the air with onion and pepperoni, and there was a funny smell coming from the fridge when I opened it to put in my bottle of wine.

Although the state of the place made me more depressed than I already was, I couldn't summon the strength to do anything more than put the pizza boxes in a bin-liner.

But at least I was home.

As I foraged gingerly around in the kitchen for a cleanish plate to put my chips on, the phone rang. And before I had realised what I was doing I had answered it.

"Lucy?" said a man's voice.

At least, for a moment, I *thought* it was a man. But then I realised that it was just Daniel.

"Hello," I said, trying to sound polite but cursing myself for answering the phone. He was obviously ringing to gloat over the fortune-teller marriage nonsense.

"Hello, Lucy," he said in a friendly, concerned tone. "How are you?"

I had been right. He was *definitely* ringing to gloat.

"What do you want?" I said coldly.

"I rang to see how you are," he said, doing a passable imitation of a surprised voice. "And thank you for the warm welcome."

"You're ringing to laugh at me," I said huffily.

"I'm *not*," he said. "Honestly!"

"Daniel," I sighed. "Of course you are. Whenever something bad happens to me you ring to rub it in. The same way as whenever something bad happens to you, I laugh myself hoarse. It's the *rule*."

"It's not actually," he said mildly. "I can't deny that you seem to get great enjoyment whenever I come a cropper, but it's not true to say that I laugh at any of your misfortunes."

A pause.

"Let's face it," he said kindly. "I'd spend my entire life laughing if that was the case."

"Goodbye, Daniel," I said coldly, pulling the phone towards me.

"Wait, Lucy!" he shouted. "It was a *joke*."

"Good Lord," he muttered. "You're so much nicer when you have your sense of humour plugged in."

I said nothing because I wasn't sure whether or not to believe that he had been joking. I was very sensitive about the seemingly disproportionate amount of disasters that befell me. I was terrified of being ridiculed and, even more so, of being pitied.

The silence continued.

What a waste of a phone bill, I thought sadly.

Then I tried to pull myself together. Life was bad enough, I thought. There was no need whatsoever for me to go into a total slump about the tragedy of unspoken words on a telephone connection.

To pass the time I flicked through my magazine. I found an article on colonic irrigation. Ugh, I thought, that looks disgusting. It must be good.

Then I ate two rolos. One on its own wasn't enough.

"I hear you're not getting married," Daniel finally said, after the silence had stretched taut.

"No, Daniel, I'm not getting married," I agreed. "I hope I've made your weekend. Now I want to go. Goodbye."

"Lucy, *please*," he begged.

"Daniel," I interrupted wearily, "I'm really not in the mood for this."

I didn't even want to talk to someone, let alone bicker with them.

"I'm sorry," he said apologetically.

"Are you?" I asked suspiciously.

"I am," he said. "Really."

"Fine," I said. "But I really want to go now."

"You're still pissed off with me," he said. "I can tell."

"No, Daniel, I'm not," I said wearily. "But I just want to be left alone."

"Oh no," he said. "Does this mean that you're going to disappear until next weekend with a box of biscuits?"

"Maybe." I laughed slightly. "See you in a week."

"I'll call over every so often to turn you," he said. "I don't want you getting bedsores again."

"Thanks."

"No, look, Lucy," he said. "Why don't you come out with me tomorrow night?"

"Tomorrow night?" I asked. "*Saturday* night?"

"Yes."

"But Daniel, even if I wanted to go out tomorrow night – and I don't – I certainly wouldn't go out with you," I explained.

"Oh."

"No offence," I said nicely. "But *Saturday* night. That's the night for going to parties and trying to meet men, not for going out with old friends. That's what God invented Monday nights for."

An alarming thought suddenly struck me.

"Where are you?" I demanded suspiciously.

"Er, at home," he said, sounding shamefaced.

"On a Friday night?" I asked in astonishment. "And you want to go out with me on a Saturday night? What's wrong?"

Then I knew. And my spirits lifted perceptibly.

"She's dumped you, hasn't she?" I said, coaxingly. "That woman Ruth has come to her senses. Although I have to admit that up until now I didn't actually think she *had* any senses to come to."

I always made unkind remarks about Daniel's girlfriends. I thought that any woman stupid enough to become involved with someone so obviously flirtatious and commitment-shy as Daniel deserved to have disparaging things said about them.

"Now aren't you glad that I rang?" he said nicely.

"Aren't you glad that you didn't just pawn me off on the answering machine?"

"Thanks, Daniel," I said, feeling slightly better. "You're very thoughtful. A trouble shared is a trouble doubled. So what happened?"

"Oh," he said vaguely. "Just one of those things. I'll tell you all about it when I see you tomorrow night."

"Daniel," I said gently, "you're not seeing me tomorrow night."

"But Lucy," he said reasonably. "I've booked a table at a restaurant."

"But Daniel," I said, equally as reasonably, "you shouldn't have done that without consulting me. You know how unpredictable my moods are. And at the moment I'm no fun at all."

"Well, you see," he explained, "I had it booked ages ago and I was supposed to go with Ruth, but with me and her no longer being an item . . . "

"Oh, I see," I said understanding. "You don't specifically want *me* to go with you. You just need *someone*. Well, that should be no trouble at all to organise considering how women love you. Although, quite frankly, it's beyond me why . . . "

"No, Lucy," he interrupted. "I do specifically want you to come with me."

"Sorry, Daniel," I said sadly. "But I'm just too depressed."

"Hasn't the news that my girlfriend has left me cheered you up?" he asked.

"Yes, of course," I said, starting to feel guilty. "But I just couldn't face going out."

113

Then he played his trump card.

"It's my birthday," he said hollowly.

"Not until Tuesday," I said quickly.

I had forgotten that it was his birthday, but, quick as a flash, I had my excuse in place. I'd had a lot of practice in getting out of things I didn't want to do and it showed.

"But I really want to go to this particular restaurant," he said wheedlingly. "And it's so hard to get a table."

"Oh, Daniel," I said, starting to feel despairing, "why are you doing this to me?"

"You're not the only one who feels miserable, you know," he said quietly. "You haven't got a monopoly on it."

"Oh, I'm sorry, Daniel." I felt both guilty and resentful. "Are you heartbroken?"

"Well, you know how it is," he said, still sounding all quiet and defeated.

"And have I ever abandoned you when you've been upset?" he asked, sealing my fate.

"That's blackmail," I said heavily. "But I'll come with you."

"Good," he said gleefully.

"Are you very miserable?" I asked. I was always interested in other people's despair. I would compare and contrast it with my own just to make me feel like I wasn't such an oddity.

"Yes," he said sorrowfully. "Wouldn't you be? Not knowing where your next shag was coming from?"

"Daniel!" I said outraged. "You bastard! I might have know that you were only pretending to be upset. You haven't got a sincere emotional bone in your body!"

"A joke, Lucy, a joke," he said mildly. "That's just *my* particular way of dealing with unpleasant things."

"I never know when you're joking and when you're being serious," I sighed.

"Neither do I," he agreed. "Now let me tell you about this wonderful restaurant that I'm taking you to."

"You're not *taking* me to it." I felt uncomfortable. "When you say it like that it sounds like we're going on a date – which we're not. You mean this restaurant that you've press-ganged me into going to."

"Sorry," he said. "This restaurant that I've press-ganged you into going to."

"Good," I said. "That's better."

"It's called The Kremlin," he said.

"The *Kremlin*?" I said sounding alarmed. "Does that mean that it's Russian?"

"Well, obviously," he said, anxiety in his voice. "Is that a problem?"

"Yes!" I said. "Won't it mean that we'll have to queue for hours and hours and hours for our food? In sub-zero temperatures? And that although there'll be loads of delicious food on the menu, the only thing that they'll be serving is raw turnip?"

"No, no, honestly," he protested. "It won't be anything like that. It's *pre*-Bolshevik and it's meant to be wonderful. Caviar and flavoured vodka and very plush. You'll love it."

"I'd better," I said grimly. "And I still don't

understand why you're insisting that I come. What about Karen or Charlotte? They both fancy you. You'd have much more fun with either of them. Or *both* of them now that I think of it. Wouldn't you like a little flirtation with your borscht? A threesome with your blinis?"

"No thanks," he said firmly. "I'm a bit battle-scarred. I'm off women for a while."

"You?" I hooted. "I don't believe it! Womanising comes as naturally to you as breathing."

"You have such a low opinion of me," he said, sounding amused. "But, honestly, I'd much rather be with someone who didn't fancy me."

"Well, I mightn't be much good for most things, but at least I can oblige you in that respect," I said, in an almost jolly tone.

I seemed to have cheered up a little.

"Great!" he said.

There was a small pause.

Then he spoke.

"Lucy," he said awkwardly, "can I ask you something?"

"Of course."

"Well, it's not really important, or anything," he said. "I'm just slightly curious, but, er, *why* don't you fancy me?"

"Daniel!" I said in disgust. "You're pathetic."

"I just want to know what I'm doing wrong . . . " he protested.

I hung up.

I had just managed to get my lukewarm chips onto a plate when the phone rang again, but this time I was smarter. This time I switched on the answering machine.

I didn't care who it was, I wasn't speaking to them.

"Er, ah, hello. This is Mrs Connie Sullivan ringing for her daughter Lucy Sullivan."

It was my mother.

How many Lucys did she think lived in my flat, I thought in irritation. But at the same time joy at my narrow escape ran through me! I was so relieved that I hadn't picked up the phone. So what did the old bag want?

Whatever it was, she wasn't too comfortable sharing it with the answering machine.

"Lucy, love, er, um, eh, it's, um, Mammy."

She sounded a bit humble. Whenever she called herself "Mammy" it was a sign that she was trying to be friendly. She was probably ringing to grudgingly apologise for being so nasty to me earlier that day. That was her usual pattern.

"Lucy, love, I, er, think I might have been a bit hard on you on the phone today. If I was it's only because I want the best for you."

I listened with curled lip and disdainful expression.

"But I had to ring you. It was on my conscience," she went on. "I got a bit of a shock, you see, when I thought you might be . . . *in trouble* . . . " She whispered "in trouble", doubtless as a precaution against anyone else inadvertently listening to her message and hearing such a filthy notion being uttered.

"But, I'll see you on Thursday and don't forget that Wednesday is a Holy Day of Obligation and the start of Lent . . . "

I threw my eyes heavenward, even though there was no one there to see me do it, and walked back to the kitchen to get some more salt. It would have killed me to admit it, but, you know, I felt a bit better now that my mother had rung, now that she had kind of apologised . . .

I ate my chips, I ate my chocolate, I watched my video and I went to bed early. I didn't drink the bottle of wine, but maybe I should have because I slept badly.

All night there seemed to be people in and out of the flat. The bell being rung, doors opening and closing, the smell of toast being made, "How do you solve a problem like Maria" coming from the front room, stifled giggles coming from the kitchen, bangs and thumps of falling furniture from someone's bedroom, more giggles, not so stifled this time, rattling in the cutlery drawer while someone was probably searching for a corkscrew, male voices laughing.

That was one of the downsides of having an early night on a Friday in a flat where the two other occupants went out and got drunk. Very often I would be in the thick of the giggling and banging and thumping so I wouldn't mind anyone else doing so either.

But it was a lot harder to put up with when I was sober and miserable and wanted oblivion. I *could* have got out of bed and marched down the hall in my pyjamas, my hair all askew, my face bare of make-up and begged Karen and Charlotte and whatever guests they had to keep the noise down, but it wouldn't have done me any good. Either they would have drunkenly ridiculed me and my pyjamas and my hair or else I would have been forced to drink half a bottle of vodka in a "If you can't beat them, join them" exercise.

Sometimes I wished I lived on my own.

I had been thinking that a lot lately.

I eventually got to sleep and then, what seemed like a little while later, I woke up again.

I didn't know what time it was but it was still pitch dark. The house was quiet and my room was cold – the heating mustn't have come on yet. Outside I could hear that it was raining and the wind rattled my bedroom's shaky Victorian windows. The curtains moved slightly from a stray draught. A car passed, its wheels hissing on the wet road.

A pang of something unpleasant shot through me – emptiness? loneliness? abandonment? – if it wasn't one of them, it was at least a member of their extended family.

"I'm never going out again," I thought. "Not while the world is the way it is. Bad weather and people laughing at me. I want none of it."

After a while I couldn't help noticing that, even though it was five-thirty on a Saturday morning, I was awake.

That was always happening to me – from Monday morning to Friday morning I couldn't open my eyes,

119

even with the help of the alarm clock and the threat of losing my job if I was late one more morning. Getting out of bed was almost impossible, as though the sheets were made of Velcro.

But come Saturday morning, when I didn't have to get up, I woke of my own accord and couldn't persuade myself, under any circumstances, to turn over and shut my eyes and snuggle under the covers and go back to sleep.

The only exception to this pattern occurred on the occasional Saturdays when I had to go to work. Then I found it as hard to wake up as I had done on the previous five mornings.

If my mother knew she would probably have held it up as evidence of my – at least according to her – contrariness.

"I know," I thought, "I'll eat something."

I got out of bed – the room was freezing – and ran down the hall to the kitchen and to my dismay there was a person already there.

"But I don't care who it is," I thought belligerently. "I'm not talking to them."

It was a young man who I had never seen before. He was dressed only in red boxer shorts and he was energetically gulping tap water from a mug. He had a spotty back.

That was not the first Saturday morning I had bumped into a man in our kitchen whom I was sure I had never seen before. The only difference that particular Saturday morning was that I hadn't brought him home myself.

Something about him – it might have been the

way he was drinking the water like he was dying of thirst or it might just have been his spotty back – made me feel like being nice to him.

"There's coke in the fridge," I told him, hospitably.

He jumped and turned around. He had a spotty face also.

"Oh, er, hello," he said, his hands going automatically to his groin in protective fashion. (Was that spotty too, I wondered idly.)

"Sorry," he stuttered. "I hope I didn't frighten you. I came home with . . . er . . . your flatmate last night."

"Oh," I said. "Which one?"

Who had had the attentions of this spotty person forced upon them the previous evening? Karen or Charlotte?

"Er, this is rather embarrassing," he said sheepishly. "But I can't actually remember her name. I had quite a bit to drink."

"Well, describe her," I said nicely.

"Blonde hair."

"That's no use," I told him. "They both have blond hair."

"Er, big, um," he said, sketching something expansive with his hands.

"Oh, you mean big tits." I suddenly understood. "Well, once again, it could be either of them."

"I think she had a funny accent," he said.

"Scottish?"

"No."

"Yorkshire?"

"Yes!"

"That's Charlotte."

I got my bag of twiglets and went back to bed.

A few minutes later the spotty boy walked into my room.

"Oh," he said, looking confused and flustered, his hand going to his crotch again. "But where's . . . ? I thought . . . "

"Next door," I said sleepily.

Chapter Fifteen

When I woke again, it was almost midday. Someone was in the bathroom and steam was billowing out from under the door so that I could hardly see down the hall. I found Karen lying under her duvet on the couch in the front room. She was coughing and smoking, there was an overflowing ashtray on the floor beside her and she looked like a panda because she hadn't taken off her previous night's make-up.

"Morning." She smiled, looking a bit pale and wan. "What did you get up to last night?"

"Nothing," I said absently. "Why is the flat like a sauna? Who's in the bathroom? Why are they taking so long?"

"It's Charlotte. She's purging herself with the scalding water and the brillo pads, scrubbing herself till she bleeds, atoning for her sin."

I felt a powerful rush of sympathy.

"Oh no, poor Charlotte. So she slept with spotty back?"

"When did you see him?" asked Karen, attempting to sit up in her excitement and then thinking better of it.

"I bumped into him in the kitchen about five-thirty this morning."

"Awful, wasn't he? But Charlotte was wearing her beer goggles, well, her tequila goggles, actually, so she thought he was gorgeous."

"Judgement impaired?"

"Very much so."

"Was she being all raunchy and dancing seductively round the place?"

"Yes."

"Oh no."

Charlotte was a lively but well-brought up, respectable girl from a small town outside Bradford. She had only been living in London for about a year and was still going through the painful process of trying to find out who she really was. Was she still the sprightly, cheeky, but very decent, apple-cheeked girl from Yorkshire who said things like, "Eee, there I was, stood with whippet"? Or was she the blonde, busty temptress that she turned into when she drank too much? It's an odd thing, but when she was behaving like a temptress her hair really did seem to turn a couple of shades lighter and her bust really did seem to increase at least one cup size.

She found it very, very hard to marry these two different aspects of self. When she acted like the blonde, busty temptress she spent the following days bitterly berating herself. Guilt, self-loathing, self-hatred, fear of retribution, disgust with herself and her behaviour were her constant companions.

She took far too many very hot baths during those times.

It was unfortunate that Charlotte was blonde and busty because she was also a bit thick, and it confirmed too many prejudices. People like Charlotte gave blonde girls a bad name. But I was very fond of her and she was a lovely person and an amiable flatmate.

"But never mind her. Tell me about *you*," said Karen gleefully. "Tell me the whole mad story of you and the getting married bit and all."

"No."

"Why not?"

"I don't want to talk about it."

"You always say that, Lucy."

"Sorry."

"Please."

"No."

"Please!"

"Well all right, but you're not to laugh at me and you're not to feel sorry for me."

Then I told Karen everything about going to see Mrs Nolan and her predictions and about Meredia coming into seven pounds fifty and Megan getting a split lip and Hetty running off with Dick's brother and Meredia and Megan telling everyone that I was getting married.

Karen listened awestruck.

"My God," she breathed. "How awful. And how embarrassing."

"Indeed."

"Are you upset?"

"A bit," I admitted reluctantly.

"You should kill Meredia. You shouldn't let her away with this. And I can't believe that Megan got involved. She always seemed so *normal*."

"I know."

"It must have been some kind of mass hysteria," suggested Karen.

"What other kind of hysteria could you have around a big lump like Meredia, if not mass hysteria," I said.

Karen laughed and then convulsed with consumptive coughs.

Charlotte shuffled into the room, wearing a heavy, shapeless polo-necked purple knitted dress that came almost to her ankles. It was her version of a hairshirt.

"Oh Lucy," she wailed, bursting into tears and rushing towards me. (She pronounced it, "Loose-eh".)

I wrapped my arms around her as best I could, bearing in mind that she was eight inches taller than me.

"I'm so ashamed," she sobbed. "I hate myself. I wish I was dead."

"Shush, shush," I said with the ease of practice. "You'll feel better soon. Don't forget that you were drinking a lot last night and that alcohol is a depressant. You're bound to feel depressed today."

"Really," she said, looking at me hopefully.

"Honest."

"Oh Lucy, you're so good. You always know the right things to say when I'm miserable."

And of course I did. I'd had so much first-hand practice myself that it would have been churlish not to share what I had learnt the hard way.

"I'm never going to drink again," she promised.

I said nothing.

"Ever!"

I inspected my nails.

"At least I'm never going to drink Tequila again," she said vehemently.

I gazed out of the window.

"I'm going to stick to wine."

I stared at the television (though it wasn't on).

"And every second drink will be a mineral water."

I straightened a cushion.

"And I'm not going to have more than four glasses of wine in an evening."

I looked at my nails again.

"Well, six, maybe."

Another gaze out of the window.

"Depending on the size of the glass."

The television again.

"And I won't have more than fourteen units a week."

And on and on she went until she had finally persuaded herself that a bottle of tequila a night was fine. I'd heard it many times before.

"Lucy, I was terrible," she confided. "I took off my blouse and I danced around in my bra."

"Just your bra?" I asked solemnly.

"Yes."

"No knickers?"

"Of *course* I had my knickers on. And my skirt."

"Well, that wasn't so bad then, was it?"

"No, I suppose not. Oh Lucy, cheer me up. Tell me a story. Tell me . . . let me see, tell me . . . *tell me* about the time that your boyfriend chucked you because he'd fallen for another bloke."

My heart sank.

But I could only blame myself. I had carefully cultivated a reputation for myself as a bit of a comic raconteur – at least among my close friends – with my own life tragedies in the starring roles. A long time ago it had dawned on me that one way I could avoid being a tragic and pitiful figure was to be a witty and amusing figure instead. Especially if I was being witty and amusing about my tragic and pitiful aspects.

That way no one could laugh at me, because I'd already beaten them to it.

But right then I just couldn't manage it.

"Oh no, Charlotte, I can't . . . "

"Oh go on!"

"No."

"Please! Just tell me about when he made you cut your hair short and he *still* chucked you."

"Oh . . . oh . . . damn you! All right then."

Who knows, I thought, it might cheer me up.

So, as amusingly as I could, I regaled Charlotte with the story of one of my many humiliating losses in love. Just to make her feel that no matter how much of a disaster her life was, it could never be as bad as mine.

"There's a party on tonight," said Karen. "Are you coming?"

"I can't."

"Can't or won't?" asked Karen shrewdly. As she was Scottish, she was good at asking things shrewdly.

"Can't."

"Why not?"

"I got strong-armed into saying that I'd go out for dinner with Daniel."

"Dinner with Daniel. Lucky *you*," breathed Charlotte, her face aglow.

"But why did he ask *you*?" shrieked Karen in disgust.

"Karen!" said Charlotte.

"Oh, you know what I mean, Lucy," said Karen impatiently.

"I do."

Karen didn't mince words but, in fairness, she was absolutely right – I couldn't understand either why Daniel had wanted to take me.

"He's split up with whatshername," I said, and immediately there was uproar. Karen sat bolt upright on the couch, like a corpse risen from the dead.

"Are you serious?" she asked, an odd, manic look on her face.

"Absolutely."

"Wow," breathed Charlotte, with a beatific smile. "Isn't this wonderful?"

"So he's a free man?" asked Karen.

"He is indeed," I said solemnly. "Repaid his debt to society and all that."

"Not for long, if I've anything to do with it," said Karen, her voice full of steely determination, her head full of images of herself and Daniel walking hand-in-hand into posh restaurants, herself and Daniel smiling at each other radiantly on their wedding day, herself and Daniel tenderly tickling their first-born child.

"Where's he taking you?" asked Karen, when she

had returned to the present and the general fuss had died down a bit.

"Some Russian place."

"Not The Kremlin?" asked Karen, sounding shocked.

"Yes."

"You lucky, lucky, lucky, lucky, *lucky* cow."

The pair of them stared at me, naked jealousy on their faces.

"Don't look at me like that," I said fearfully. "I don't even want to go."

"How can you say that?" asked Charlotte. "A good-looking . . . "

"Rich," interjected Karen.

"A good-looking, rich man like Daniel wants to take you to some posh restaurant and you don't even want to go?"

"But he's not good-looking and rich . . . " I protested lamely.

"He is!" they chorused.

"Well, maybe he is. But, but . . . but it's no good to me," I said weakly. "*I* don't think he's good-looking. He's just a friend. And I think it's a total waste to have to go out with a friend on a Saturday night. Especially when I'd rather not go out at all."

"You're weird," muttered Karen.

I didn't deny it. She was preaching to the converted.

"What are you going to wear?" asked Charlotte.

"Don't know."

"But you've *got* to know! You're not just going to the pub for a pint."

Daniel arrived at about eight and I wasn't ready. But I would still have been in my pyjamas if Charlotte and Karen hadn't bullied and cajoled me into having a bath and putting on my glamorous gold dress.

Not that I thanked them for it. I just accused them of dressing up and going out with Daniel vicariously.

They gave me lots of advice on what to wear and what way to do my make-up and my hair, and they started every sentence with, "Now, if *I* was going out with Daniel . . . " and, "If Daniel had asked *me* . . . "

"Wear these, wear these," said Charlotte in excitement, pulling some silky, lacy stockings out of my underwear drawer.

"*No,*" I said, taking them from her and putting them back.

"But they're lovely."

"I know."

"So why won't you wear them?"

"What for? It's only Daniel."

"You're so ungrateful."

"I'm *not*. What's the point in wearing them? It's a waste – who's going to see them?"

"Jesus," said Karen, pulling out a bra, "I didn't know they made bras this small."

"Show me," demanded Charlotte, pulling it from her and then dissolving into convulsions. "My God! It's like a doll's bra, a little Sindy bra. My nipple would just about fit into it."

"You must have tiny nipples," laughed Karen, elbowing Charlotte. "I didn't know they made triple A cups."

131

I stomped around the bedroom, my face red with shame, waiting for them to finish making fun of me.

Just as the doorbell rang, Karen raced into my room and sprayed me energetically with her perfume.

"Thanks," I said, my eyes watering, waiting for the clouds to disperse.

"No, silly," she said. "It's so that you'll smell like me. You're paving the way for me with Daniel."

"Oh."

Charlotte and Karen fought over who was going to answer the door to him and Karen won because she had lived in the flat longer.

"Come in," she said brightly and exuberantly, flinging wide the door for him. Karen was always bright and exuberant when Daniel was around and the door was probably not the only thing she would have liked to be flinging wide for him.

Daniel looked just like Daniel, but no doubt at some later date, I'd have to listen to Karen and Charlotte boring on about how lovely he was.

It was funny that women liked him so much because there was nothing really remarkable about him.

It wasn't as if he had piercing blue eyes and blue-black hair and a sexy, sulky mouth and a jaw-bone the size of a handbag. Nothing of the sort.

He had grey eyes, which weren't a bit piercing – grey eyes were boring, I thought.

And his hair was that non-colour – brown. As indeed was mine, except that he had been touched by the Good-Hair Fairy so his hair was straight and shiny. While mine was springy and curly and after I'd been caught in the rain, I looked like I'd had a home perm.

He smiled at Karen. He smiled a lot. And everyone that ever found Daniel attractive kept going on about what a nice smile he had and I couldn't see why. It was only a row of little lumps of enamel.

OK, so he seemed to have a full set and they looked like they were real. And none were missing, or black, or green and mossy, or at right angles to his face, but so what?

The secret of his success, I reckoned, was that he looked like a nice bloke, like a decent, friendly man, one with old-fashioned values, who'd treat you like a lady.

Which was so far from the truth that it was funny. But by the time his women found that out, it was far, far too late.

"Hello, Karen," said Daniel, doing the smile thing again. "How are you?"

"Wonderful!" she declared. "Just great!"

And immediately she launched straight into open, unashamed flirting. She gave him lots of level looks and knowing smiles. And with supreme self-confidence she possessively brushed imaginary fluff from his dark winter coat.

"Hello, Daniel." Charlotte sidled slowly out of her bedroom. She also flirted unashamedly with him, but she played the sweet shy smiles and fleeting eye contact card. All rosy cheeks and delicate blushes and clear-eyed, clear-skinned, milk-drinking wholesomeness.

Daniel stood in our little hall, and smiled and looked very tall.

He resisted Karen's attempts to steer him into the front room. "Thanks, but no," he said. "I've a taxi waiting outside."

He looked at me rather meaningfully as he said that and then he looked at his watch.

"You're early," I accused. I rushed up and down the hall trying to find my high shoes.

"Actually, I'm exactly on time," he said mildly.

"Well, you should have known better," I called from the bathroom.

"You look nice," he said, grabbing me as I hurried past again and attempting to kiss me. Charlotte looked woebegone.

"Ugh," I said, wiping my face. "Get off, you'll ruin my make-up."

I found my high heels in the kitchen, in the gap between the fridge and the washing machine. I put them on and stood beside Daniel. He was still far too tall.

"You look beautiful, Lucy," said Charlotte wistfully. "I love that golden dress on you. You look like a princess."

"Yes," agreed Karen, smiling straight into Daniel's eyes and holding his gaze for far longer than was necessary – not that he seemed to mind, the womaniser.

"Don't they make a lovely pair?" asked Charlotte, smiling from me to Daniel and back again.

"No we don't," I grumbled, shifting from high-heel to high-heel in embarrassment. "We're ridiculous.

He's far too tall and I'm far too short. People are going to think the circus is in town."

Charlotte made shocked and effusive denial of this, but Karen didn't contradict me.

Karen was very competitive.

She couldn't help it.

She was one of those people who never put herself down, was never self-deprecating, never made rueful little jokes at her own expense. Whereas I, on the other hand, rarely did anything else. I really think she actually *couldn't*.

She was perfectly nice most of the time but if things went wrong you crossed her at your peril – especially when she was drunk, when she could be quite terrifying. She had a big thing about respect. In fact, she was nearly obsessed about it if you asked me.

About two months previously her boyfriend Mark had timidly suggested that they might be getting a bit too serious, and she barely let him finish the sentence before she ordered him to get out of the flat and never to come back. She hardly even gave the poor lad time to dress himself. (In fact, she still had his underpants which she waved in triumph out the window after him as he slunk off home.) Then she bought a three-litre case of wine and insisted that I stay in with her while she drank her way through it.

It was a terrible night – she sat there, looking like thunder, saying nothing, just occasionally muttering "bastaird" while I nervously sipped wine by her side, murmuring what I hoped were comforting platitudes. Then out of the blue, she turned nasty.

She turned to me and grabbed the front of my dress and slurred, "Eff ah doan' respec' mahsell, then who's goan tay?"

"Eh?" she asked me again, her Scottish accent pronounced, her eyes half-closed and her face too close to mine. "Ansairrr me!"

"Indeed," I agreed nervously. "Who's, er, goan tay?"

But she apologised the following day and hadn't behaved the same way since. Apart from being competitive, she was a great flatmate. She was good fun, had lovely clothes that she would loan without too much begging, she could be extremely vulgar and she always paid her rent on time. Of course, I was aware that if our interests ever clashed I should be prepared to either back out gracefully or start enjoying hospital food. But our interests hadn't ever clashed yet – and they were hardly likely to start clashing over Daniel.

She was making the most of her close proximity to Daniel.

"There's a party on tonight," she told him, addressing him and him alone. "Perhaps you'd like to come along afterwards."

"That sounds good," he agreed, smiling at her. "I'd better take down the address."

"It's all right," I said, quite touched by the air of romance in the hall. "I have it."

"You're sure?" Karen asked anxiously.

"I'm sure. Now let's go. Let's get this over and done with."

"Please come to the party," called Karen. "Even if Lucy doesn't want to."

Especially if Lucy doesn't want to was what she really meant, I thought with a laugh.

We left, Daniel bestowing his game-show-host smile on Karen and Charlotte, me bestowing an amused look on Daniel.

"What?!" he demanded as we went down the stairs. "What've I done?"

"You're outrageous!" I laughed. "Have you ever met a woman that you *didn't* flirt with?"

"But I wasn't flirting," he protested. "I was just being normal. I was only being polite."

I gave him a "You don't fool me" look.

"You look beautiful, Lucy," he said.

"You're such a bullshit merchant," I replied. "In fact, you should be forced to wear a warning. To protect women from you."

"I don't know what I've done wrong," he complained.

"Do you know what it should say?" I ignored him.

"What should it say, Lucy?"

"Beware of the bull."

He opened the front door for me and the cold air, the outside world, hit me like a slap. "Oh God," I thought bleakly. "How am I ever going to get through tonight?"

Chapter Sixteen

We arrived at the restaurant and the saddest-looking man I have ever seen confirmed our booking.

"Dmitri will take your cloaks," he said heavily, in a thick Russian accent.

He paused, as if he could barely summon the energy to continue speaking. "And then," he sighed, "Dmitri will see you to your table."

He half-heartedly clicked his fingers and about ten minutes later Dmitri arrived, a short, lumpy man in a badly fitting dinner suit. He looked on the verge of tears.

"The Vatson party?" he murmured, like a mourner at a funeral.

"Er, sorry?" said Daniel.

I nudged him. "He means us. *You're* Mr Vatson."

"Am I? Oh right, yes."

"This vay please," Dmitri whispered hoarsely.

First he led us to a little counter where we gave our coats to a very beautiful but very bored-looking young woman. She was all angular bone structure and porcelain skin and raven hair and longsuffering ennui. Even Daniel's hundred-watt grin didn't get a flicker of response from her.

"Dyke," he muttered.

Then we followed Dmitri through the restaurant, in what he obviously thought was stately fashion, but which was in fact just very, very slowly, so that I kept bumping into him. Then I stood on the back of his shoe and he stopped and turned round and gave me a look that was more in sorrow than in anger.

Even though I had made much of not wanting to be there, I had to admit that the place was beautiful. There were glittering chandeliers and lots of red velvet and huge gilt-framed mirrors and big palm plants. The place hummed and clinked and tinkled with the sound of young, good-looking people laughing and drinking Ribena-flavoured vodka and spilling caviar down their fronts and onto their laps.

I was very, very grateful that I'd let myself be bullied into wearing the gold dress. I may not have felt like I belonged, but at least I looked like I did.

Daniel put his arm lightly around my waist.

"Get off," I muttered, squirming away from him. "What do you think you're doing? Stop treating me like I'm one of your women."

"Sorry, sorry," he said earnestly. "Second nature. For a moment I forgot it was you and went straight into restaurant mode."

I gave a little laugh and immediately Dmitri's head whipped round to glare at me.

"Er, sorry . . . " I muttered, feeling somehow ashamed, as if I had been disrespectful or blasphemed or something.

"Your table," said Dmitri, with a feeble flourish, indicating acres of snow-white, starched linen and

Marian Keyes

hundreds of glinting, winking crystal glasses and
several miles of dazzling cutlery.

We might only be getting raw turnip to eat but
The Kremlin provided very nice surroundings to eat
said raw turnip in.

"This is very nice." I smiled at Daniel.

Then Dmitri and I did a little dance where we
both tried to pull my chair out and then we both
pulled away from it and then we both lunged for it
again.

"Er, can we order a drink please?" asked Daniel,
when we were both finally installed on opposite
sides of the vast round table.

Dmitri sighed, his sigh indicating that he had
known that a request such as this was probably
going to be made, that the request was entirely
unreasonable, but that he was a good, hardworking
man and he would do his best to oblige.

"I'll fetch Gregor, your vine vaiter," he said and
plodded away.

"But . . . " said Daniel to his retreating back.

"Oh God," he said, "I only want to order us some
vodka, now we'll have to go through the whole vine
palaver."

Gregor arrived promptly and, smiling sadly,
produced a very long list of drinks, which included
every flavour of vodka under the sun.

I liked the look of it very much indeed. I nearly
felt glad that I had come.

"Mmmm," I said, getting excited, "what about
strawberry flavour? Or mango? Or, no, no, wait . . .
what about blackcurrant?"

"Whatever you want," called Daniel from the far side of the table. "You choose for me."

"Well, in that case," I said, "why don't we try the lemon flavour to start with and then maybe try a different one in a while."

When I had been younger I had been dazzled by cocktail lists, wanting to try everything, wanting to work my way through the menu in alphabetical order, never having the same thing twice, but I had been far too frightened of getting drunk to actually do it. And I suppose what I was suggesting to do with the flavoured vodkas was just the grown-up version of that. I was still frightened of getting drunk, but that evening somehow I felt I could live with it.

"Lemon it is," said Daniel.

As soon as Gregor had left, Daniel hissed across at me, "Come over here. You're too far away."

"No," I said nervously. "Dmitri said I was to sit here."

"So what? You're not in school."

"But I don't want to annoy him . . . "

"Lucy! Don't be such a wimp. Come over here."

"No!"

"Right, I'll come over to you then."

He stood up and moved his chair several feet around the table, and sat down almost on my lap.

The two glamorous young-professional couples at the next table looked appalled and I threw them a kind of rueful, poor-me, look-at-this-maniac-I'm-with, I'm-very-refined-and-I'd-never-do-that-kind-of-thing-myself look, but Daniel just looked delighted.

"There!" he smiled. "That's much better. Now I

can see you." Then he started moving his knives and forks and glasses and napkin over to near mine.

"Daniel, please," I said desperately, "people are looking."

"Where?" he asked, looking around. "Oh yes, I see."

"Now will you behave?" I thundered with righteous indignation. But I had lost him because he'd made eye contact with the better looking of the two women at the next table and was up to his usual tricks. He looked at the woman and she blushed and looked away. Then he looked away and she looked discreetly at him again. Then he looked at her and caught her looking at him and gave her a smile. Then she smiled back at him and I gave him a thump on his arm.

"Look, you stupid bastard, I didn't even want to come out with you tonight!"

"Sorry, Lucy, sorry, sorry, sorry."

"Just cut it out, OK? I'm not going to spend my evening with you talking over my shoulder."

"Fair enough, sorry."

"You were the one who wanted me to come here with you, so you'd better have the bloody manners to talk to me. If you wanted to flirt with someone then why did you invite me?"

"Sorry Lucy, you're right Lucy, forgive me Lucy."

He *sounded* humble but he certainly didn't look it.

"And you can knock off that naughty little boy smile," I continued. "Because it cuts no ice with me."

"Sorry."

Gregor arrived with two hefty glasses filled with a bright yellow liquid. It looked as if it had come straight from Chernobyl, but I thought it might seem ungracious if I said so.

"Christ," said Daniel doubtfully, holding his glass up to the light. "It's rather radioactive looking."

"Shut up," I said. "Happy birthday."

We clinked glasses and threw the vodka back.

I immediately felt a tingling, Ready Brek, warm kind of glow start to radiate out from my stomach.

"Oh God." I giggled.

"What?"

"It's *definitely* radioactive."

"Nice, though."

"Oh very."

"More?"

"Oh, yes, I think so."

"Where's Gregor?"

"Here he is."

Gregor was making his way towards us and Daniel flagged him down.

"We'll have two more of those Gregor, thanks," said Daniel.

Gregor looked pleased. If it was possible for someone to look totally heartbroken and pleased simultaneously. "Pink ones please," I called.

"Strawberry?" said Gregor.

"Is it pink?"

"Yes."

"Strawberry then."

"And I suppose we'd better think about having something to eat."

"Fine," I said, picking up my menu. The pink ones came and they were so nice that we decided to have two more.

As I said, "They're only small. There can't be much harm in them."

The two new drinks came – blackcurrant this time – and we drank them.

"They don't last long, do they?"

"More?" enquired Daniel.

"More."

"Food?"

"I suppose we'd better. Ah, here's Dmitri now. Anytime you like with the raw turnip, Dmitri," I said jovially. With a shock I realised that I was enjoying myself.

"I've something to tell you, Lucy," said Daniel, suddenly going all serious on me.

"Well, go on then," I said. "For a moment there I thought I was cheering up but I think it's best if we put a stop to that."

"Sorry, I shouldn't have said anything. Forget it."

"I can't forget it, you idiot. You'll *have* to tell me now."

"Oh all right, but you're not going to like it."

"Tell me."

"It's about Ruth."

"*Tell* me!"

"I ended it with her. Not her with me."

Was that it, I thought, slightly dazed. And then I remembered about my mission to keep Daniel in his place.

"You bastard! How could you?"

"But I was *bored*, Lucy. I was so bloody bored. It was a nightmare."

"But she had big tits."

"So what?"

"So it was a case of 'thanks for the mammaries', was it?" I said, dissolving into fits of laughter. It was one of those rare occasions where I thought I was being very funny.

"Exactly," said Daniel, laughing also.

"And now you're Ruthless," I said, still finding myself hilarious.

"I am."

"You're very callous."

"Oh, Lucy, I'm not. I tried to be nice to her."

"Did you make her cry?"

"No."

"You're still a bastard."

Daniel looked slightly upset, a bit tearful. The vodka was making us both a bit emotional.

"I'm sorry I told you now," he said, sulkily. "I knew you wouldn't like it."

"Maybe not, but I'll have to put up with it."

I gave him a little smile. Suddenly I didn't seem to care that much about Ruth. None of it seemed to really matter somehow.

"That's very philosophical of you, Lucy."

"I know, I feel very philosophical."

"That's funny, so do I."

"What do you think it is? Maybe it's the vodka?"

"It's got to be."

"I feel kind of funny, Daniel, sort of sad like I always do, but happy too. Happy in a sad way."

"I know," he said eagerly. "That's exactly how I feel. Except I think I feel happy like I always do but sad in a happy way."

"This must be how Russians feel all the time." I giggled. I felt very light-headed and knew that I was talking rubbish, but it didn't matter. It didn't sound like rubbish, it seemed very important and true. "Do you think they drink so much vodka because they're philosophical and miserable, or are they philosophical and miserable because they drink so much vodka?"

"That's a tough one, Lucy."

"Why don't I ever meet the right woman, Lucy?" asked Daniel, seriously.

"I don't know, Daniel. Why don't I ever meet the right man?"

"I don't know, Lucy. Will I always be lonely?"

"Yes, Daniel. Will I always be lonely?"

"Yes, Lucy."

There was a little pause while we both smiled sadly at each other, united in our bittersweet melancholy. Thoroughly enjoying it, actually. At some stage food arrived. It might have been then.

"But, Dan, you see, it doesn't matter, because at least we're being *essentially* human. We're in touch with the pain of being alive. Will we get another drink?"

"What colour?"

"Blue."

Daniel leaned back in his chair, trying to grab a waiter. "The lady wants two more of these," he called, waggling a glass around. "Well, she doesn't want two for herself . . . or maybe she does, actually. Do you, Lucy?"

"The same again, sir?" asked Gregor. At least I think it was Gregor. I gave him a melancholy smile and he gave me an identical one back.

"The exact same as this," said Daniel. "Except two of them. No, make it four. And . . . oh yes," he called after him, "they have to be blue."

"Now, where were we?" said Daniel, smiling sweetly.

I was so glad I had come, I felt so *fond* of him.

"We were talking about existential pain, weren't we?" said Daniel.

"Yes," I said. "Indeed we were. Would I look nice with my hair the way that girl has hers?"

"Where?" he asked, turning round. "Oh yes, lovely. You'd look even *nicer* than her."

"Good." I giggled.

"What's it all about, Lucy?"

"What's what all about?"

"All of it, you know, any of it? Life, things, death, hair?"

"How do I know, Dan. Why do you think I'm so bloody miserable all the time?"

"It's good, though, isn't it?"

"What is?"

"Being miserable."

"Yes." I giggled. Again. I couldn't stop. He was right. We were both miserable, but we were soaring, almost ecstatic, in our misery.

"Tell me about you getting married."

"No."

"Please."

"No."

"Don't you want to talk about it?"

"No."

"That's what you always say about everything."

"What?"

"That you don't want to talk about it."

"Well, I *don't* want to talk about it."

"Did Connie go berserk?"

"Totally. She accused me of being pregnant."

"Poor Connie."

"Poor Connie, my eye!"

"You're very hard on her."

"No, I'm not."

"She's a good woman, you know, who only wants the best for you."

"Ha! That's easy for you to say because she's always nice to you."

"I'm very fond of her."

"I'm not."

"That's a terrible thing to say about your mother."

"I don't care."

"You can be very stubborn, Lucy."

"Oh Daniel." I laughed. "Stop it, for God's sake. Has my mother paid you to tell me nice things about her?"

"No, I genuinely like her."

"Well, seeing as you like her that much, you can come with me on Thursday to see her."

"Fine."

"What do you mean, 'fine'?"

"I mean, 'fine'."

"Don't you mind?"

"No, of course I don't mind."

"Oh. I mind."

A little pause.

"Can we stop talking about her now, please?" I asked. "It's making me feel depressed."

"But we were miserable anyway."

"I know, but it was a different kind of miserable. A nice miserable. I liked it."

"OK. Will we talk about the fact that we're all going to die anyway and that none of this matters?"

"Oh yes, please. Thanks, Dan, you're an angel."

"But first," declared Daniel. "More drinks. What colour haven't we tried?"

"Green?"

"Kiwi fruit?"

"Perfect."

More drinks came and I know we both ate lots, but afterwards I was at a complete loss to actually say what I'd had. I believe I liked it though. Daniel said that I kept saying that it was delicious. And we had a wonderful conversation. I can't really remember much of it now, but I know that it had something to do with everything being pointless and meaningless and that we were all doomed and at the time it made perfect sense to me. I was completely at peace with myself and the universe and with Daniel. I can vaguely remember Daniel thumping the table and saying fervently, "I couldn't agree more" and stopping one of the waiters (Gregor? Dmitri?) and shouting, "Listen to this woman, she speaks the truth, she doesn't speak with forked tongue."

It was a wonderful evening and I probably would still be there shouting "Lilac! Have you any lilac ones?" if Daniel and I hadn't noticed at some stage that we were the only customers left and that a row of short, bulky, dinner-jacketed waiters were lined up behind the bar staring at us.

"Lucy," he hissed, "I think it's time we left."

"No! I like it here."

"Really, Lucy, Gregor and the rest of them have to get home."

I felt very guilty then.

"Of course they do. Of course they do. And it'll take them *hours* to get back to Moscow on the night-bus, the poor things. And I bet they're all on early starts tomorrow."

Daniel shouted for the bill – the reverential behaviour we had assumed on our arrival had long disappeared.

The bill came – very promptly – and Daniel looked at it.

"That national debt of Bolivia?" I enquired.

"More like Brazil," he said. "But what does it matter?"

"Exactly," I agreed. "Anyway, you're loaded."

"Actually, I'm not. It's all relative. Just because you get paid a pittance you think anyone who earns above a pittance is loaded."

"Oh."

"All it means is the more you earn the more you can owe."

"Dan, that's wonderful! That's such a profound economic truth – in the midst of life we are in debt. No wonder you have such a good job."

"No, Lucy," said Daniel sounding hoarse with excitement. "*That's* wonderful, what you just said, it's so true – in the midst of life we are *indeed* in debt. You must write that down. In fact we should write down everything we've talked about tonight."

My head was spinning slightly with how wise both Daniel and I were. I told him how wise and wonderful I thought he was.

"Thanks, Daniel," I said. "This has been fabulous."

"I'm glad you enjoyed it."

"It's been great. So much makes sense now."

"Like what?"

"Well it's no wonder I never felt like I belonged anywhere, because I'm obviously Russian."

"How do you figure that?"

"Because I'm miserable but I'm happy. And I feel like I belong here."

"You might just be drunk."

"Don't be silly. I've been drunk before and I've never felt like this. Do you think I'll get a job in Russia?"

"Probably, but I don't want you to go."

"You can come and visit me. You'll probably have to anyway, when you run out of girls to go out with here."

"Smart thinking, Lucy. Will we go to this party Karen told us about?"

"Yes! I'd forgotten about that."

Chapter Seventeen

"Did you give them a big tip?" I hissed at Daniel as we finally left The Kremlin, waved off by the assembled staff.

"Yes."

"Good. They were nice."

I laughed all the way up the stairs out of The Kremlin and I laughed even more when we got out into the cold night air.

"What a laugh. That was great fun," I said, leaning against Daniel.

"Good," he said. "Now behave, or we'll never get a taxi."

"Sorry, Dan, I think I'm a bit drunk, but I feel so *happy*."

"Good, but please shut up for a minute."

A taxi stopped. It had a cross-looking man driving it.

"Smile," I sniggered. Luckily he didn't hear me.

In I clambered, Daniel pulling the door behind us.

"Where to?" asked the man.

"Anywhere you like," I said dreamily.

"Eh?"

"Wherever you want," I said. "What does it matter? Because in a hundred years time you won't be here, I won't be here and your cab *certainly* won't be here!"

"Stop it, Lucy." Daniel elbowed me, trying not to laugh. "Leave the poor man alone. Wimbledon, please."

"We'd better stop at an off-licence and get some booze for the party," I said.

"What'll we get?"

"Vodka? It's my new favourite drink now."

"Fine."

"No, I've changed my mind."

"Why?"

"Because I'm drunk enough."

"So what? Aren't you enjoying yourself?"

"Yes, but I think I'd better stop."

"Don't."

"No, I must. We'll get something else, something not so strong."

"Lager?"

"I don't mind."

"Or will I get a bottle of wine?"

"Whatever you like."

"How about Guinness?"

"It's up to you."

"Lucy, for God's sake. Stop being so meek and tell me what you want! Why are you always so self-effacing and . . ."

"I'm not being meek and self-effacing," I laughed. "I really don't mind. You know I'm not much of a drinker."

The taxi driver gave an outraged snort. I don't think he believed me.

153

We could hear the music as soon as the taxi turned into the street.

"Sounds like a good party," said Daniel.

"Yes," I agreed. "I wonder if the police will come – the true mark of a great party!"

"Oh no. The neighbours are bound to call the local copshop so we'd better get in there and start enjoying ourselves fast before the whole thing is closed down."

"Don't worry," I said soothingly. "Many copshops are called but few parties are closen."

Daniel laughed.

A bit too much, I thought.

The vodka was obviously still doing its rounds.

Then there was a little scuffle while both Daniel and I tried to pay the taxi driver.

"I'll get it."

"No, *I'll* get it."

"But you paid for dinner."

"But you didn't want to come."

"All the same, fair's fair."

"Why can't you ever relax and let someone be nice to you? You're so . . . "

"Oi! Sor' yourselves aht! I ain't go' all noi'." The taxi driver was quick to interrupt Daniel's pocket psychoanalysis of me before it got into full flight.

"Pay him," I muttered. "Quick, before he gets out the hammer from under his seat."

Daniel paid the man who grumpily accepted Daniel's no doubt lavish tip.

"You take too much lip from that bint," was his parting comment. "I 'ate a lippy woman." And the taxi roared away.

I stood shivering, staring balefully at the back of the disappearing taxi.

"The cheek of him! I'm *not* lippy."

"Lucy, relax."

"Oh, all right."

"Actually though, he had a point. You *are* quite lippy sometimes."

"Oh shut up."

I tried to be annoyed with Daniel, but I couldn't help laughing.

That was unusual behaviour for me, but, all in all, it had been an unusual night.

We rang at the door of the house where the party was on, but no one came.

"Maybe they can't hear the bell," I said, as we stood shivering in the misty night air, our cans of Guinness under our arms, listening to the sounds of music and laughter behind the heavy wooden door. "Maybe the music is too loud."

And still nothing happened and we remained where we were, shivering and expectant.

"At least let me give you half of it," I said.

Daniel looked at me like I'd gone mad.

"*What* are you talking about?"

"The taxi. At least let me give half."

"Lucy! Sometimes I could happily thump you! You drive me . . . "

"Shush! Someone's coming."

The door opened and a young man in a yellow shirt stared at us.

"Can I help you?" he asked politely.

It was then that it dawned on me that I had no idea of who was having the party.

155

"Er," said Daniel.

"Um, John invited us," I muttered.

"Oh right!" said yellow shirt, grinning, suddenly a lot friendlier. "So you're John's friends. Mad bastard, isn't he?"

"Er, yes," I agreed brightly, throwing my eyes to heaven. "Mad!"

That was obviously the correct thing to say because the door swung wide and we were admitted over the threshold to partake of the festivities and merriment within. I noticed, with a sinking heart, that there were an awful lot of girls there. About a thousand to every man, which seemed to be par for the course for London parties, and they were all eyeing Daniel with interest.

"Who's this John?" hissed Daniel as we pushed into the oestrogen-sodden hall.

"Didn't you hear? He's a mad bastard."

"Yes, but who *is* he?"

"No idea," I whispered furtively, making sure we were out of yellow shirt's earshot, "but I thought there was a good chance that someone called John either lived here or was a friend of the people who live here. Law of averages and all that."

"Gosh, you're a marvel," said Daniel admiringly.

"No, I'm not," I said. "You've just gone out with too many stupid women."

"You're right, you know," he said thoughtfully. "Why do I always pick thick ones?"

"Because they're the only ones who'll have anything to do with you," I said kindly.

He threw me a bitter look. "You're very mean to me."

"No, I'm not," I said reasonably, "It's for your own good. It hurts me more than it hurts you."

"Really?!"

"No."

"Oh."

"Now, no sulking. It'll ruin your manly jawline and you'll scare the girls away."

Our fledgling row was interrupted by a bright, vivacious, Scottish voice shouting, "Great, you're here!"

Gimlet-eyed Karen made her way towards us, through the crowds of people standing round in the hall with cans of beer in their hands. She must have been watching the front door all evening, I thought uncharitably, and then immediately felt guilty. It wasn't a criminal offence to find Daniel attractive, it was just a terribly unfortunate lapse of taste and judgement. Karen looked lovely – very much Daniel's type – all blonde and vivacious and glamorous. If she played her cards right and toned down her sharp intelligence I was sure she was in with a very good chance of being Daniel's next girlfriend. She, very gaily, told us how delighted she was to see us and threw questions at us with the speed of raindrops hitting the ground in a thunderstorm. How was the restaurant? Was the food lovely? Were there any famous people there?

For a few moments I was foolish enough to think that it was a real conversation and that I was part of it. Until I noticed that Karen received my would-be hilarious stories of Gregor and Dmitri with stony silence and that every time Daniel opened his mouth she collapsed with squeals of laughter. And whenever I caught her eye she gave me very energetic, meaningful frowns – her eyebrows ricocheted from her hairline to her cheekbones and back again – and then I noticed that she was mouthing something at me. I squinted, following the shape of her mouth, trying to make out what it was. She did it again. What was it? . . . What could it be? . . . First letter? Sounds like? Two syllables?

"Fuck *off*!"

She leant over and hissed it into my ear while Daniel was momentarily distracted taking off his coat. "For Goad's sake, fuck oaf!"

"Oh, er, righto."

My conversational seed was falling on barren ground and I was definitely excess baggage. It was time for me to go. As it was, I knew that I was probably for it the following day. Karen would read me the riot act. ("For Goad's sake, why did ye no' jest fuck oaf? Oanestly! I cannae believe how daft ye air.")

I knew when I wasn't wanted. In fact, I was usually exceptionally good at it, very often knowing it even before the other person did. I was uncharacteristically thick-skinned that evening.

My face reddened with embarrassment – I hated feeling like I'd done something wrong – and murmuring "I'll, er, be over here," discreetly shifted away from the pair of them and stood by myself in the hall.

Neither of them objected. I felt the faintest flicker of disappointment that Daniel hadn't tried to stop me, or at least asked me what I was doing but I knew that if the situations were reversed and *I* was on the pull that I wouldn't appreciate him being around.

But then I felt a bit mortified – I was on my own and I couldn't see anyone that I knew and I was still wearing my coat and I was sure that everyone was looking at me and thinking that I had no friends. The earlier euphoria had worn off and my usual acute self-consciousness had returned. Suddenly I felt very, very sober.

I had spent most of my life feeling that life was a party to which I hadn't been invited. Now I really was at a party to which I hadn't been invited and it was almost reassuring to discover that the feelings I'd had for most of my life – isolation, awkwardness, paranoia – were indeed the correct emotions to have had.

In the confined space I managed to inch off my coat. I fixed a bright smile on my face, hoping to convey to the noisy, happy people around me that they weren't the only ones who were having a good time. That I too was happy and that I had a fulfilled life and loads of friends and that I was only on my own because I had decided to be, but that I could be in the middle of a huge crowd of people any time I liked. Not that it mattered because no one paid the slightest bit of attention to me. From the way one girl bumped into me and stood on my toe while she was excitedly running to answer the door and the way another girl tipped her glass of wine on me when she tried to look at her watch, I felt like no one could even see me.

It wasn't so much my wet dress that upset me, it was the way she tisked at me like it was all my fault, because then I felt like it really *was* all my fault, that I shouldn't have been standing there in the first place.

I seemed to spend my whole life oscillating between feeling horribly conspicuous and then feeling totally invisible.

Then, through a parting in the crowd, I spotted Charlotte and my heart lifted. I gave her a big smile and called to her that I was on my way over. But she gave me an infinitesimal, but nevertheless quite definite shake of the head. She seemed to be talking to a young man.

After what seemed like ages of grinning like the village idiot I thought of something I could do – I could put the beer in the fridge! I was delighted to have a purpose. A use. A function. In my own tiny way I mattered!

Thrilled with myself and my new-found worth I fought my way through the crowds of people in the hall and the even bigger crowds in the kitchen and put four cans of Guinness in the fridge. Then I tucked the other two under my arm and attempted to fight my way back out again, making for the big front room where all the fun seemed to be happening.

And it was then that I met him.

Chapter Eighteen

In the months that followed I replayed that scene in my head so often that I remembered absolutely everything about it, down to the smallest details.

I was just on my way out of the kitchen when I heard a man's voice saying admiringly, "Behold – a vision in gold! A goddess. A veritable goddess."

Naturally I kept pushing and shoving to leave the room because, although I was wearing a gold dress, I was also wearing my well-tailored inferiority complex so I didn't, for a second, think that I was the one being called a goddess.

"And not just any kind of goddess," the voice continued. "But my favourite kind of goddess, a Guinness goddess."

The bit about the Guinness broke through my humility barrier so I turned around and there, wedged in beside an upright freezer, leaning against the wall, was a young man. Not that there was anything unusual about that because it was, after all, a party, and the place was full of people, even a couple of men, leaning against household appliances.

The young man – and it was hard to say just how young he was – was very cute with longish black curly hair and bright green, slightly bloodshot eyes, and he was smiling straight at me, as though he knew me, which suited me just fine.

"Hello." He nodded in a civil and friendly fashion.

Our eyes met and I had the oddest sensation. I felt as though I knew him too. I stared at him and, although I knew I was being rude, I couldn't stop. Hot confusion swept over me and at the same time I was totally intrigued because, although I was certain that I had never met him, that I had never before in my life seen him, somehow I knew him. I don't know what it was but there was *something* about him, something very familiar.

"What's kept you?" he said cheerfully. "I've been waiting for you."

"You have?" I swallowed nervously.

My head raced. What was happening, I wondered? Who was he? What was this instant recognition that had flashed between us?

"Oh aye," he said. "I wished for a beautiful woman with a can of Guinness and here you are."

"Oh."

A pause where he lounged against the wall, the picture of relaxation, happy and good-looking, if a little bit bleary-eyed. He didn't seem to find anything unusual about the conversation.

"Have you been waiting long?" I asked. In an odd way it felt like a very normal thing to ask, as though I was making conversation with a stranger at a bus stop.

"The best part of 900 years." He sighed.

"Er, 900 years?" I asked, raising an eyebrow. "But they hadn't invented cans of Guinness 900 years ago."

"Exactly!" he said. "My point exactly! God knows, but wasn't I the sorry one. I've had to wait for them to come up with the technology and it's been so boring. If I'd only wished for a jug of mead or a pitcher of ale I could have saved both of us a whole lot of trouble."

"And you've been here all this time?" I asked.

"Most of the time," he said. "Sometimes I've been over there," – he pointed to a spot on the floor about a foot away from where he was standing – "but mostly I've been here."

I smiled – I was totally captivated by him and his story-telling.

He was *exactly* the kind of man I liked, not dull or staid, but imaginative and inventive and so *cute*.

"I've been waiting for you so long that it's hard to believe you're finally here. Are you real?" he asked. "Or just a figment of my Guinness-starved imagination?"

"Oh, I'm perfectly real," I assured him. Although I wasn't at all sure myself. And I wasn't sure whether *he* was real either.

"I want you to be real and you're *telling* me that you're real, but I might be imagining it all, even the bit where you're telling me that you're real. It's all very confusing – you can see my problem?"

"Indeed," I said solemnly. I was *enchanted*.

"Can I have my can of Guinness?" he asked.

"Well, I don't know," I said anxiously, forgetting for a moment that I was enchanted.

"Nine hundred years," he reminded me gently.

"Yes, I know," I said. "I see your point perfectly,

but they're Daniel's. I mean, he paid for them and I was just about to give him one, but . . . oh never mind. Have one."

"Donal may have paid for them, but destiny says they're mine," he told me in a confidential tone, and somehow I believed him.

"Really?" I asked, my voice wobbling, torn between a desire to just surrender to whatever supernatural forces were operating around this man and I, and the fear of being accused of not standing my round and making free with other people's Guinness.

"Donal would have wanted it this way," he went on, gently removing something from under my arm.

"Daniel," I said absently, casting a glance down the hall. I could see Daniel's head and Karen's head close together and I didn't think Daniel looked as if he cared about a can of Guinness, one way or the other.

"Maybe you're right," I agreed.

"There's only one problem," said the man.

"What's that?"

"Well, if you're imaginary, then, by definition, your Guinness will also be imaginary and imaginary Guinness isn't half as nice as the real stuff."

He had such a beautiful accent, so gentle and so lyrical, it sounded familiar, yet I couldn't quite place it.

He opened the can and poured the contents down his throat. He drank the whole lot in one go as I stood looking at him. I have to say I was impressed. I'd seen very few men able to do that. In fact the only one I'd ever seen do it was my dad.

I was delighted – completely captivated by this man-child, whoever he was.

"Hmmm," he said thoughtfully, looking at the empty can and then looking at me. "Hard to tell. It *could* have been real and then again it might have been imaginary."

"Here," I said, pushing the other can at him. "It's real, I promise."

"Somehow I trust you." And he took the second can and repeated the performance.

"Do you know," he said thoughtfully, wiping his mouth on the back of his hand, "I think you might be right. And if the Guinness is real then that means that you're real too."

"I think I am," I said sorrowfully. "Even though a lot of the time, I'm not sure."

"I suppose you sometimes feel invisible?" he asked.

My heart leapt. Nobody, *nobody,* had ever asked me that before and that was *exactly* how I felt for huge chunks of my life. Had he read my mind? I was mesmerised. So much recognition! Somebody understood me. A total stranger had just looked straight into my soul and seen the essence of me. I felt light-headed with exhilaration and joy and hope.

"Yes," I said faintly. "I sometimes feel invisible."

"I know," he said.

"How?"

"Because so do I."

"Oh."

There was a pause and the two of us just stood looking at each other for a little while, smiling slightly.

"What's your name?" he asked suddenly. "Or will I just call you the Guinness Goddess? Or, if you like, I could shorten it to GG. But then I might mistake you for a horse and try to back you and let's face it, you don't look anything like a horse and although you have nice legs . . . " (At this point he paused and leant over sideways so that his head was level with my knees.) "Yes, very nice legs," he continued, straightening up, "I'm not sure if you could run fast enough to win the Grand National. Though you might come in the first three, so I suppose I could do an each way bet on you. We'll see. We'll see. Anyway, what's your name?"

"Lucy."

"Lucy, is it?" he said thoughtfully, looking at me with his green, green, slightly bloodshot eyes. "A fine name for a fine woman."

Although I was certain that it was the case, I had to ask him anyway – "You're not . . . by any chance . . . *Irish*, are you?"

"Sure, bejibbers and bejabbers and what else would I be, only Oirish?" he said, in a stage Irish accent, and did a little dance. "All the way from County Donegal."

"I'm Irish too," I said excitedly.

"You don't sound it," he said doubtfully.

"No, I am," I protested. "At least both my parents are. My surname is Sullivan."

"That's Irish all right," he admitted. "Are you of the species Paddius, variety Plasticus?"

"Sorry?"

"Are you a plastic paddy?"

"I was born here," I admitted. "But I *feel* Irish."

"Well, that's good enough for me," he said cheerfully. "And my name's Gus. But my friends call me Augustus for short."

"Oh." I was charmed. It got better and better.

"I'm very pleased to meet you, Lucy Sullivan," he said, taking my hand in his.

"And I'm very pleased to meet you, Gus."

"No, please!" he said, holding up his hand in protest, "Augustus, I insist."

"Well, if it's all the same to you, I'd rather call you Gus. Augustus is a bit of a mouthful."

"Am I?" he said, sounding surprised. "A mouthful? And you've only just met me!"

"Er, you know what I mean . . ." I said, wondering if perhaps we were slightly at cross-purposes.

"No woman has ever said that about me before," he said, looking at me thoughtfully. "You're a most unusual woman, Lucy Sullivan. A most *perceptive* woman, if I may say so. And if you will insist on formality, then Gus it is."

"Thank you."

"It shows that you were well brought up."

"It does?"

"Oh yes! You've a lovely manner, very gentle and polite. I suppose you can play the piano?"

"Er, no, I can't." I wondered what had sparked the abrupt change of subject. I wanted to tell him that I could play the piano because I was desperate to please him, but at the same time too afraid to tell a barefaced lie, in case he suggested that we play a duet there and then.

"It'd be the fiddle then?"

"Er, no."

"The tin whistle?"

"No."

"In that case it must the accordion?"

"No," I said, wishing he would stop. What was all this about musical instruments?

"You don't look like you've got the wrists to be a bodhrán player, but you must be one all the same."

"No, I don't play the bodhrán."

What was he talking about?

"Well, Lucy Sullivan, you have me well and truly bet. I give up. So tell me, what *is* your instrument?"

"What instrument?"

"The one that you play?"

"But I don't play an instrument!"

"What! But if you don't play, then you're surely a poet?"

"No," I said shortly, and started thinking about how I could escape. It was too weird, even for me, and I had a very high weirdness threshold.

Flann O'Brien characters were all very well in Flann O'Brien books, but they were a different matter when you had to make small talk with them at parties.

But, as if he had read my mind, he put his hand on my arm and suddenly became a lot more normal.

"Sorry, Lucy Sullivan," he said, humbly. "I'm sorry. I've scared you, haven't I?"

"A bit," I admitted.

"I'm sorry," he said again.

"That's OK," I smiled, relief filling me. I had no

objection to people being quirky, slightly eccentric even, but when they started to display psychotic tendencies, I knew when to throw in the towel.

"It's just that I had a great feed of class A drugs earlier this evening," he continued, "and I'm not quite myself."

"Oh," I said faintly, not sure what to think now. So he took drugs? Did I have a problem with that? Well, not really, I supposed, so long as he wasn't mainlining heroin because we were short of teaspoons in the flat as it was.

"What drugs do you take?" I asked tentatively, trying not to sound condemnatory.

"What have you got?" He laughed. Then he stopped abruptly, "I'm doing it again, aren't I? I'm scaring you?"

"Weeell, you know . . . "

"Don't worry, Lucy Sullivan. I'm partial to the odd mild hallucinogenic or mood-relaxant, nothing more. And in small quantities. And not very often. Hardly ever, really. Apart from pints. I have to admit to a fondness for a great feed of pints early and often."

"Oh that's all right," I said. I had no problem with men who drank.

But, I wondered, if he was currently under the influence of some narcotic, did that mean that normally he didn't tell stories and dream up things and was just as dull as everyone else? I desperately hoped not. It would be unbearably disappointing for this gorgeous, charming, unusual man to disappear along with the last traces of drugs from his bloodstream.

"Are you normally like this?" I asked cautiously. "You know, er, imagining things and telling stories and all that? Or is it just the drugs?"

He stared at me, his shiny curls falling into his eyes.

Why can't I get *my* hair to shine like that, I wondered absently, I wonder what conditioner he uses.

"This is an important question, isn't it, Lucy Sullivan?" he asked, still staring at me. "A lot depends on it."

"I suppose," I mumbled.

"But I've got to be honest with you, you know," he said sternly. "I can't just tell you what you want to hear, now can I?"

I wasn't at all sure whether I agreed with that. In an unpredictable and unpleasant world it was both unusual and very pleasant to hear what I wanted to hear.

"I suppose." I sighed.

"You won't like what I'm going to tell you, but I'm morally bound to tell you anyway."

"Fine," I said sadly.

"I have no choice." He touched my face gently.

"I know."

"Oh!" He shouted suddenly and theatrically threw wide his arms. He attracted worried looks from all around the kitchen – people as far away as the back door turned to look. "'O, what a tangled web we weave, when first we practice to deceive!' Wouldn't you agree, Lucy Sullivan?"

"Yes." I laughed. I couldn't help it, he was just so mad and funny.

"*Can* you weave, Lucy? No? Not much call for it these days. A dying art, a dying art. I'm no good at it myself – two left feet, that's me. Now, to tell you the God's honest truth, Lucy Sullivan . . . "

"I wish you would."

"Here goes! I'm even worse when I'm a drug-free zone. There! I've said it! I suppose you'll be getting up and leaving me now?"

"Actually no."

"But don't you think I'm a lunatic and an embarrassment and a holy show?"

"Yes."

"You mean to tell me that lunatics and embarrassments and holy shows are your particular bag, Lucy Sullivan?"

I had never really thought of it that way before but now that he had mentioned it . . .

"Yes," I said.

Chapter Nineteen

He took me by the hand and led me through the hall and I let myself be led. Where was he taking me, I wondered in excitement. I pushed past Daniel and he raised his eyebrows questioningly, then waggled his finger admonishingly, but I ignored him. He was a fine one to talk.

"Sit here, Lucy Sullivan." Gus pointed at the bottom stair. "We can have a nice, quiet chat."

That seemed to be very unlikely in view of the fact that there was more traffic up and down the stairs than there was up and down Oxford Street. I wasn't quite sure what was going on upstairs – the usual, I suppose, drug-taking, sex with your best friend's boyfriend on your best friend's coat and the like.

"Now, I'm sorry I scared you back there, Lucy, but I just assumed that you had to be some kind of creative person," Gus said when I was installed on the foot of the stairs.

"I'm a musician myself and music is something I feel very passionately about," he went on. "And I sometimes forget that not everyone else feels the same way."

"That's fine," I said, delighted. Not only was he

not mad, but he was a musician, and my favourite men had always been musicians or writers or anything that involved the creative process and behaving like a tortured artist. I had never fallen in love with a man who had a proper job and I hoped I never would. I couldn't imagine anything duller than a man with a regular income, a man who was sensible with money, a man who knew how to live within his means. I found financial insecurity a great aphrodisiac. My mother and I disagreed rather violently on that point, but the difference was that she didn't have a romantic bone in her body while I would be hard-pressed to find a portion of my skeleton that wasn't. The radius, the ulna, the patella, the femur, the pelvic girdle (especially that!), the sternum, the humerus, the scapula – both of them in fact – sundry vertebrae, a wide selection of ribs, a whole plethora of metatarsals, nearly as many again metacarpals, the couple of tiny ones in my inner ear – you name it, they were romantic.

"So you're a musician?" I asked with interest. Maybe that was why I felt I knew him – maybe I'd seen him or heard of him or seen a picture of him somewhere.

"I am."

"Are you a famous musician?"

"Famous?"

"Yes, are you a household name?"

"Lucy Sullivan, I'm not a household name, not even in my own household."

"Oh."

"I've disappointed you now, haven't I? We've only

just met and already we're at a crisis. We'll have to go for counselling, Lucy. You stay here and I'll go and find a phone book and look up the number for Relate."

"No you won't." I laughed. "I'm not disappointed. I just felt like I knew you, but I didn't know from where, and I thought that if you were famous that that might be how."

"You mean we don't know each other?" he asked, sounding shocked.

"I don't think so," I said, amused.

"We *must*," he insisted. "At least in a previous existence, if not in this one."

"That's all very well," I said thoughtfully. "But, even if we knew each other in a previous existence, who's to say we liked each other then? I've always had a problem with that – just because people recognise each other from another life doesn't mean they have to *like* each other, does it?"

"You're absolutely right," said Gus, gripping my hand tight. "I've always thought that too but you're the first person I've met who's ever agreed with me."

"I mean, imagine if I had been your boss in another life – well you wouldn't be too pleased to meet me again, would you?"

"No! Oh Christ, wouldn't it be awful? Dying and travelling through space and time and getting born again and meeting the same terrible bloody people that you met the last time round. Remember me from Ancient Egypt? Good, because you made a terrible job of that pyramid, so go back and do it again."

174

"Exactly. Or what about, remember me? I was the lion that ate you when you were a Christian in Rome? Remember me now? Good, let's get married."

Gus laughed delightedly. "You're wonderful. All the same, the two of us must have got on in whatever life we met in before now. I have a good feeling about you – you probably explained Pythagaros's theorem when Pythagaros had run out of patience with me – he was a very short-tempered man, that fella – or lent me money at the turn of the century or *something* nice. Now is there any more of that Guinness?"

I sent Gus to the fridge and I sat on the stairs and waited. I was thrilled, delighted, bursting with happiness. What a lovely man. I was so glad I had come to the party – my blood ran cold at the thought that I could so easily not have come and then I'd never have met him. And maybe Mrs Nolan had been right after all. Gus could be The One, the man I'd been waiting for.

Speaking of waiting, where the hell was he?

How long did it take to go to the fridge and steal the rest of Daniel's Guinness?

Hadn't he been gone ages? While I'd been sitting on the step with a dreamy, half-wit's grin on my face, had he started chatting to some other young woman and forgotten all about me?

I started to get nervous.

How long could I wait before I started to look for him, I wondered? What could be considered a decent interval?

And wasn't it a little *early* in the relationship – even for me – for him to start giving me the runaround?

My state of dreamy, happy introspection abruptly dispersed. I should have known that it was too good to be true. I became aware of the noise and the jostling of the other people around me – I had totally forgotten about them all while I'd been talking to Gus – and I wondered if they were all laughing at me? Had they seen Gus do this to thousands of women? Could they sense my fear?

But, no, here he was, looking a bit dishevelled.

"Lucy Sullivan," he declared, sounding anxious and distracted. "I'm sorry I was gone for so long but I've been involved in a terrible fracas."

"Oh God," I laughed. "What happened?"

"When I got to the fridge, some man was trying to help himself to your friend Donal's Guinness. 'Unhand them', I shouted. 'I won't,' says he. 'You will,' says I. 'They're mine,' says he. 'They're not,' says I. A tussle ensued, Lucy, where I sustained minor injuries, but the Guinness is safe now."

"Is it?" I said, in surprise, because Gus had a bottle of red wine in his hand and there was no sign of Guinness anywhere.

"Yes, Lucy, I made the ultimate sacrifice and it's safe now. No one else will try to steal it."

"What've you done?"

"Done? But, I drank it, of course, Lucy. What else could I do?"

"Err . . . "

I looked over my shoulder nervously and, sure enough, through the bars of the banisters I could see

Daniel making his way through the hall, his face like thunder.

"Lucy," he shouted. "Some little bastard has stolen . . . "

He paused when he saw Gus.

"You!" he yelled.

Oh dear. Daniel and Gus had obviously met.

"Daniel, Gus. Gus, Daniel," I said weakly.

"That's him," said Gus, in great annoyance. "That's the light-fingered character who was stealing your friend's Guinness."

"I might have known," said Daniel, shaking his head in resignation, ignoring Gus's accusatory finger. "I just might have bloody well known. How do you pick them, Lucy? Just tell me how."

"Oh go away, you sanctimonious pig," I said, annoyed and embarrassed.

"Do you know this person?" Gus demanded of me. "I don't think he's the type of person you should be friends with. You should have seen the way he . . . "

"I'm going," said Daniel, "and I'm taking Karen's bottle of wine with me." And he whipped the bottle of wine out of Gus's hand and disappeared back into the throng.

"Did you see that?" shouted Gus. "He's done it again!"

I tried not to laugh, but I couldn't help myself – I obviously wasn't as sober as I had thought.

"Stop it," I said, pulling Gus by the arm. "Sit down and behave."

"Oh, sit down and behave is it?"

"Yes."

"I see!"

There was a short pause while he looked down at me, a fierce frown on his handsome little face.

"Well, if you say so, Lucy Sullivan."

"I say so."

He meekly sat down beside me on the stairs, wearing an a over-docile expression. We sat in silence for a few moments.

"Ah well," he said, "it was worth a try."

Chapter Twenty

Suddenly I had run out of things to say. I sat squashed up against him on the step, racking my brain for something to say.

"Well!" I said, too cheerfully and trying to hide my sudden shyness. What happens now, I wondered. Should we say it had been nice meeting each other and easily slip away from each other, like ships leaving their mooring bays. I didn't want that.

I decided to ask him a question – most people seemed to like talking about themselves.

"What age are you?"

"As old as the hills and as young as the morn, Lucy Sullivan."

"Would you mind being a bit more specific?"

"Twenty-four."

"Fine."

"Well, 924, actually."

"Are you indeed?"

"And what age have you Lucy Sullivan?"

"Twenty-six."

"Hmmm, I see. You realise that I'm old enough to be your father?"

"If you're 924, you're old enough to be my grandfather."

"Older, I'd say."

"But you look really well for your age."

"Clean living, Lucy Sullivan, that's what I put it down to. That and the deal I did with the devil."

"What was that?" I was *loving* this, I was having such a good time.

"I didn't age for any of the 900 years that I was waiting for you but, if I ever put foot inside an office to do a proper job, I'll age instantly and die."

"That's funny," I said, "because that's exactly what happens to me every time I go to work, but I didn't have to wait 900 years for it to happen."

"You don't work in an office, do you?" he asked in horror. "Oh my poor wee Lucy, this can't be right. You shouldn't have to work at all, you should spend your time lying on a silken bed in your golden dress, eating sweetmeats, surrounded by your admirers and your subjects."

"I couldn't agree more," I said warmly, "except for the bit about the sweetmeats. Would you mind if I had chocolate instead?"

"Not at all," he said expansively. "Chocolate it is. And speaking of a silken bed, would it be terribly forward of me if I asked if I could accompany you home tonight?"

I opened my mouth, feeling light-headed with alarm.

"Forgive me, Lucy Sullivan," he said, gripping my arm, his face a picture of stricken shock. "I can't believe I said that. Please, please, banish it from your mind, try to forget that I ever said it, that such a crass suggestion ever passed from my lips. May I be struck down! A bolt of lightning is too good for me, though."

"It's OK," I said nicely, reassured by his mortification. If he was that embarrassed, then surely he didn't make a habit of inviting himself home with women he'd just met?

"No, it's not OK," he said in alarm. "How could I have said something like that to a woman like you? I'm just going to walk away from you now and I want you to forget that you ever met me, it's the least I can do. Goodbye, Lucy Sullivan."

"No, don't go," I said, seized by alarm. I wasn't sure that I wanted to sleep with him, but I certainly didn't want him to go.

"You want me to stay, Lucy Sullivan?" he asked, an anxious look on his face.

"Yes!"

"Well, if you're really sure . . . hold on here while I get my coat."

"But . . . "

Oh God! I had wanted him to stay as in stay talking to me at the party, but he seemed to think that I had invited him to stay with me in the silken bed with the sweetmeats and I was too afraid to upset him by explaining the misunderstanding to him, so it looked as if I had an overnight guest.

He was back, a lot more promptly than the last time, trailing scarves and a coat and a jumper under his arm.

"I'm ready, Lucy Sullivan."

I bet you are, I thought, swallowing with nerves.

"There's only one thing, Lucy."

What now?

"I'm not sure I have quite enough money to pay my full share of the taxi fare. Ladbroke Grove is a long way away, isn't it?"

"Well, how much money do you have?"

He pulled a handful of change out of his pocket. "Let me see, four pounds . . . five pounds . . . no, sorry, they're pesetas. Five pesetas, a dime, a miraculous medal and seven, eight, nine, *eleven* pence!"

"Come on." I laughed. After all, what had I expected? I couldn't wish for a penniless musician and then complain when he didn't have any money.

"I'll see you right, Lucy, just as soon as I get my big break."

Chapter Twenty-One

A long time later we arrived at Ladbroke Grove. Gus and I held hands in the taxi but we hadn't kissed yet. It was only a matter of time and I felt very nervous about it. An excited sort of nervous.

Gus insisted on chatting to the taxi driver, asking him all kinds of annoying questions – who was the most famous person he'd ever had in his cab, who was the least famous person he'd ever had in his cab, that kind of thing – and only stopped when the taxi driver screeched to a halt somewhere around Fulham and, in a volley of short, brusque, Anglo-Saxon words, conveyed to us that if Gus didn't shut up we could both get out and make our own travel arrangements for the rest of the way.

I was ill-aspected in my house of taxi-drivers that evening.

"My seals are lipped," shouted Gus and we spent the rest of the journey whispering and nudging each other and giggling like schoolchildren, speculating on why the taxi-driver was so bad-tempered.

I paid for the taxi and Gus absolutely insisted that I take his handful of foreign change.

"But I don't want it," I said.

"Take it, Lucy," he insisted.

"I've got my pride, you know," he added with more than a hint of irony.

"Well, OK." I smiled, happy to humour him. "But I don't want your miraculous medal, I've got thousands of my own, thanks all the same."

"I bet your mother gave them to you."

"But of course."

"Yes, Irish mothers are like a bottomless pit of miraculous medals. They always have one hidden *somewhere*. And do you find that she's always forcing things on you?"

"How d'you mean?"

Gus prodded me in my side with his finger, as I tried to open the front door, "Will you have a cup of tea? Ah, you will. Give her a whole pot, it'll warm her up."

He thumped up the stairs calling after me, "Will you have a slice of bread, go on, you'll have the entire loaf. Have a four stone sack of potatoes, have an eight course banquet, go on, sure, you need fattening up. There isn't a pick on you. I know you've just had your dinner, but another can't hurt."

I couldn't help laughing even though I was worried that the other residents of the building would complain about being woken at two in the morning by a drunken Irishman insisting that they would like a haunch of beef.

"Go on," he shouted. "We'll even cook it for you."

"Shush," I said, giggling.

"Sorry," he stage whispered. "But will you?" he said, pulling on my coat-sleeve.

"Will I what?"

"Will you eat an entire pig?"

"No!"

"But we'll only be throwing it out if you don't eat it. And we killed it specially."

"Stop it."

"Well, you'll at least have a drop of holy water and a miraculous medal, won't you?"

"OK, just to please you."

We got into the flat and I suggested tea, but Gus wasn't interested in tea.

"I'm really tired, Lucy," he said. "Will we go to bed?"

Oh God! I knew what that meant.

There was so much to worry about, not least the question of contraception and Gus didn't strike me as being in any kind of condition to care about such matters. Or even for them to occur to him. Perhaps he was a more responsible citizen when he wasn't drunk – although I wouldn't have counted on it – so it looked as though it was down to me to be the sensible, careful party. Not that I minded – I preferred men who erred on the side of wildness rather than caution.

"How about it, Lucy?" He smiled at me.

"Sure!" – trying to sound bright, breezy, unconcerned, like a woman in control. Then I thought that perhaps I had sounded too eager and while I didn't want him to realise that I was a bag of nerves, neither did I want him to think that I was desperate to go to bed with him.

"Er, come on," I muttered, hoping my tone was striking a neutral middle ground.

I realised that I hadn't been entirely sensible. I had invited a complete stranger, a complete *male* stranger, a very strange stranger, into my empty flat. If I ended up raped and robbed and murdered, then I would only have myself to blame. Although Gus wasn't acting like he had rape and pillage on his mind. He was too busy dancing round my bedroom opening drawers, reading my credit card bills and admiring my fixtures and fittings.

"A real fireplace!" he shouted. "Lucy Sullivan, you realise what this means?"

"What does it mean?"

"It means that we must pull up our chairs and sit in the flickering firelight and tell stories."

"Yes, but you see, we don't actually use the fireplace, because the chimney needs to be . . . "

But I'd lost him because he opened my wardrobe and was flicking through the hangers.

"Aha! A rough-hewn cloak," he said, pulling out an old coat of mine, a long velvet one with a hood. "What do you think?"

He tried it on (and, in fairness, that was all he seemed to be interested in trying on), pulled up the hood and stood in front of the mirror swishing it around.

"Beautiful," I laughed. "It's you."

He looked a bit like an elf, but quite a sexy elf.

"You're laughing at me, Lucy Sullivan."

"I'm not."

And I wasn't because I thought he was gorgeous. I was delighted with his enthusiasm, the way he found everything interesting, his unusual way of looking at things. There's no other word for it – I was enchanted.

I was also very relieved that he was playing dressing-up instead of trying to get me into bed. I did find him attractive – very attractive – but it seemed a little bit soon to be hopping into bed with him. But I had, after all, said that he could come home with me and I felt that in that case etiquette dictated that I couldn't really *not* go to bed with him.

In theory, I knew that it was my right not to go to bed with anyone I didn't want to and to change my mind at any stage in the proceedings, but the reality was that I would be far too embarrassed to say no.

I suppose I felt that after he had come all this way it would be inhospitable to send him away empty-handed. It went back to my childhood, where generosity to our visitors mattered above all else, where it didn't matter if we had to do without our dinners so long as the guests were fed.

I also felt that Gus and I were somehow meant to be together and *that* was very seductive. Not only would it be unforgivably rude to refuse to sleep with him, but it would be actively flying in the face of fate, calling the wrath of the gods to be delivered down on top of me. It was a great relief to think that, actually, because it took all the "Will I, won't I?" out of it. I had no choice. I *had* to sleep with him. No agonising, everything was nice and simple.

All the same, I was still nervous.

I suppose the gods can't think of everything.

I sat on my bed and fiddled with my earrings, while Gus roamed around the room, picking things up, putting them down, and making all kinds of comments.

"Nice books, Lucy. Apart from all this Californian stuff," he muttered, reading the back of *Who Gets the Car in the Dysfunctional Family of the Nineties*. I was glad to see that, while Gus was slightly eccentric, he wasn't totally neurotic.

I put my earrings back on so that I could take them off again. I had always found that wearing jewellery was a good idea in a seduction-type situation because, while it gave me the appearance of taking things off and made me seem as if I was a good sport and game for anything, in actuality the other person was down to his undergarments long before I ever was, giving me the chance to back out or change my mind without exposing, among other things, my own hand.

I learnt that trick the summer I was fifteen and Ann Garrett and Fiona Hart and I used to play strip-poker with some of the boys from our road. Ann and Fiona both had bosoms and in a summer that was awash with sexual undertones and overtones – none of them emanating to or from me, I have to say – they were keen to be forced into a situation where they had to display themselves. I had no bosoms, and even though I was delighted to feel that I had friends, I would rather have died than sit in the field behind the shops on a balmy summer evening in my vest and knickers with Derek Wheatley and Gordon Wheatley and Joe Newey and Paul Stapleton.

So I solved the problem by wearing as much jewellery and accessories as I could lay my hands on. My ears weren't pierced – I didn't get that done until I was twenty-three – so I had to wear clip-on earrings which stopped the circulation and turned my earlobes into two throbbing red balls of agony but it was a small price to pay. (Although it was always a relief to lose the first couple of hands of poker.) And I smuggled out and wore my mother's cameo ring that she kept wrapped in tissue paper in a box in the bottom of her wardrobe and only wore herself on her wedding anniversary and her birthday. It was far too big for me and I lived in terror of losing it. And with three pink plastic bracelets that I got in a lucky bag and my Confirmation cross and chain, I made sure that I never had to take off more than my socks and sandals. But just to be on the safe side I wore three pairs of socks.

Curiously enough, Ann and Fiona never wore *any* jewellery.

And they seemed to have no hang of the game either, throwing away aces and kings like they were going out of fashion and in what seemed like no time at all, they were down to their bra and knickers, giggling and saying how embarrassed they were and sitting up straight with their stomachs in and their shoulders back and their chests thrust out. While I remained fully clothed, with just a neat little pile of pink bracelets and earrings on the grass beside me.

It was odd. I hardly ever won at anything but I somehow nearly always managed to win at strip-poker. But the oddest thing of all was that none of the other players acted very impressed. It took me several years to realise that they hadn't been, as I so smugly thought, sore losers.

I was a very naïve teenager.

I went on taking my earrings on and off while Gus familiarised himself with the contents of my bedroom.

"I'll just have a little lie-down, Lucy, if that's OK."

"Fine."

"Do you mind if I take my boots off?"

"Er, no, not at all." I had been expecting him to take off a lot more than his boots. If he just took off his boots I'd be getting away lightly. I hadn't expected to get much change out of a full suit of clothes.

He lay down on the bed beside me.

"This is nice," he said, holding my hand.

"Mmmm," I murmured. It *was* nice.

"D'you know something, Lucy Sull . . . ?"

"What?"

He said nothing.

"What?" I said again, turning to look at him.

But he was asleep. Stretched out on my bed, still in his jeans and shirt. He looked so *sweet,* his eyelashes black and spiky, throwing shadows onto his face, faint stubble on his jaw and chin, his mouth smiling slightly.

I stared down at him.

That's what I want, I thought. He's the one.

Chapter Twenty-Two

I tugged the duvet from under him and covered him with it, which made me feel very caring and tender. I pushed back a lock of hair from his forehead just to enhance the feeling. Was it all right to leave him to sleep fully-clothed, I wondered. Well, it would have to be because I wasn't going to undress him. I certainly had no intention of rummaging around in his undergarments and taking covert looks and sneak previews.

Then feeling a bit, well, *at a loose end,* I suppose, I got ready for bed. I put on my pyjamas – I was pretty sure that Gus wasn't a sexy negligée type of man, which was good because I didn't have a sexy negligée. Gus was probably more likely to be frightened by a sexy negligée than turned on by it. Although, then again, you never know . . .

And I brushed my teeth. Of *course* I brushed my teeth. I brushed them so much my gums were raw. I knew that brushing my teeth was the single most important thing I had to do when sharing my bed with an unfamiliar man. Magazines and past experience could not stress just how important it was. It was a bit sad to think that a man who liked you enough to have sex with you in the night would make a break for the door if your breath was less than fragrant the following morning, but that, unfortunately, was the way things were. Being sad about it wouldn't change it.

And instead of removing my make-up, I put on lots more. I wanted to look lovely in the morning when Gus woke up and I figured that my extra make-up would compensate for his sobriety, even it out, if you like. Then I climbed into bed beside him. He looked so cute asleep.

I lay staring into the darkness, thinking about everything that had happened that evening and, call it excitement or anticipation, or disappointment, or even relief, but I couldn't sleep.

After a while I heard the front door and then I heard Karen and Charlotte and someone with a man's voice talking and tea being made and murmured conversation and muffled laughs. It was a lot more peaceful than the previous night – no *Sound of Music*, no falling furniture, no raucous screeches of laughter.

After ages more of lying in the dark I decided to get up again and see what was going on without. I was feeling a bit left out of things. But that was nothing new. I inched out of bed carefully, not wanting to disturb Gus, and tiptoed out my room and, as I backed out into the hall, quietly closing my bedroom door, I bumped into something big and dark that wasn't usually positioned just outside my room.

I jumped a mile!

"Jesus!" I exclaimed.

"Lucy," said a man's voice. The thing put its hands on my shoulders.

"Daniel!" I spluttered, as I turned round. "What the hell are *you* doing? You scared the life out of me, you idiot!"

Instead of being apologetic, Daniel found this hilarious. He collapsed into convulsions.

"Hello, Lucy," he wheezed, barely able to speak he was laughing so much. "What a lovely welcome you always give me. I thought you'd be halfway to Moscow by now."

"What were you doing lurking in the dark outside my door?" I demanded.

Daniel leant against the wall, still laughing. "The look on your face," he said, wiping tears from his eyes. "I wish you could have seen it."

I was shaken and annoyed and I didn't think anything was funny, so I gave Daniel a thump.

"Ouch," he said, still laughing, holding his arm where I'd hit him, "you're dangerous."

Before I could thump him again, Karen arrived into the hall and suddenly it all became clear. She gave me a meaningful wink and said, "*I* invited Daniel back. Nothing to do with you, don't worry."

Hats off to Karen. I was impressed. Very impressed. It seemed as if she had made definite progress on her Daniel project.

"I was just about to leave actually," said Daniel. "But seeing as you're up I think I'll stay a bit longer."

We trooped into the front room, me feeling a bit awkward about Daniel catching me in my blue winceyette pyjamas, where Charlotte was stretched out on the sofa, looking blissfully happy. The room bore signs of recent tea-drinking.

"Lucy," said Charlotte in delight. "Wonderful! You're up. Come over here and sit beside me." She sat up and patted the place beside her on the sofa and I snuggled up next to her, modestly pulling my legs under me. I had chipped nail varnish on my toes and a blister on my instep and I didn't want Daniel to see.

"Any tea left?" I asked.

"Loads," said Charlotte.

"I'll get you a cup," said Daniel, making for the kitchen. He was back in a moment and poured tea into a mug and added milk and two spoons of sugar and stirred it and handed it to me.

"Thanks, you have your uses sometimes."

He stood beside the sofa, looming over me.

"Oh, take off your coat," I said in exasperation. "You look like an undertaker."

"I *like* this coat."

"And sit down. You're blocking out the light."

"Sorry."

Daniel sat on the armchair nearest me and then Karen sat on the floor leaning her head on the armrest of his chair. Her eyes were shining and she looked all dreamy and romantic. I was, in all honesty, shocked.

She was behaving so out of character. Karen always played damn near impossible to get. She tied men into knots of uncertainty, turned many a well-balanced bloke into Insecurity in a Suit. She was always a bit, I suppose, *hard* and now she looked soft and pretty and sweet.

Well, well, well.

"I met a bloke," Charlotte announced.

"So did I," I said gleefully.

So did Karen, but perhaps it wasn't quite the right time then for her to talk about it.

"We know," said Charlotte. "Karen's been listening at your door, trying to see if you were at it with him."

"You blabbermouthed *cow* . . . ." said Karen in a fury.

"Oh shush," I said. "Don't row. I want to hear all about Charlotte's bloke."

"No, I want to hear all about yours," said Charlotte.

"No, you first."

"No, you."

Karen affected a bored, grown-up face, but she only did that for Daniel's benefit, to make him think that she didn't do silly, girly things like indulge in gossip. But that was all right – we had all done the same when the bloke we were mad about was present. No one was more culpable than I was. It was just a ploy and as soon as she was sure that he was interested, she could be herself again.

"Please, Lucy, you go first," intervened Daniel.

Karen looked surprised and then she said, "Yes, come on Lucy. Stop being so bloody coy."

"OK," I said, delighted.

"Great." Charlotte hugged her knees in excitement.

"Where do you want me to start?" I asked, grinning from ear to ear.

"Look at her," said Karen drily. "She's like the cat that got the cream."

"What's his name?" said Charlotte.

"Gus."

"Gus!" Karen was horrified. "What an awful name. Gus the Gorilla. Gussie Goose."

"And what's he like?" asked Charlotte, ignoring Karen's noises of disgust.

"He's lovely," I began, my description gathering steam. And then I noticed that Daniel was looking at me rather oddly. He sat forward in his chair, with his hands on his knees and was staring, looking sort of puzzled, sort of sad. "What are you looking at me like that for?" I said indignantly.

"Like what?!"

But it was Karen who shouted it, not Daniel.

"Thank you, Karen," said Daniel politely to her, "but I think I can manage to cobble together a couple of words."

She shrugged and haughtily tossed her blonde hair. Apart from the slight pinkness in her cheeks no one would have known that she was embarrassed. I envied her her poise and aplomb.

Daniel turned back to me. "Where were we?" he said. "Oh yes. Like what?!"

I began to laugh.

"I don't know," I giggled. "Funny. Like you knew something about me that I didn't."

"Lucy," he said gravely. "I would never be foolish enough to presume that I knew something that you didn't. I value my life."

"Good," I smiled. "Now can I tell you about my bloke?"

"Yes," hissed Charlotte. "Get on with it, would you."

"Weeell," I said, "he's twenty-four and he's Irish and he's brilliant. Really funny and a bit, you know, off the wall. He's not like anyone I've ever met before and . . . "

"Really?" said Daniel, sounding surprised. "But what about that Anthony bloke that you had a thing with?"

"Gus is nothing like Anthony."

"But . . . "

"Anthony was mad."

"But . . . "

"Gus isn't," I said firmly.

"Well, what about that other drunken Irishman you went out with?" suggested Daniel.

"Who?" I said, starting to feel slightly annoyed.

"Whatshisname," said Daniel. "Matthew? Malcolm?"

"Malachy," murmured Karen helpfully. The traitor.

"That's right. Malachy."

"Gus is nothing like Malachy either," I exclaimed. "Malachy was always drunk."

Daniel said nothing. He just raised an eyebrow and gave me a meaningful look.

"OK!" I burst out. "I'm sorry about your Guinness. But I'll replace it, don't worry. Anyway, since when did you get so mean and stingy?"

"But I'm not . . . "

"Why are you being so nasty?"

"But . . . "

"Aren't you happy for me?"

"Yes, but . . . "

"Look, if you can't say something nice, don't say anything at all!"

"Sorry."

He sounded so contrite that I felt guilty. I leant over to him and rubbed his knee, apologetically, awkwardly. I was Irish – I wasn't equipped to deal with hot weather or spontaneous affection.

"I'm sorry too," I muttered.

"Maybe you're getting married after all," suggested Charlotte. "This Gus could be the man your fortune-teller told you about."

"Maybe," I agreed quietly. I was embarrassed to admit that that was what I had thought too.

"You know," said Charlotte, looking a bit shamefaced. "For a little while I thought that Daniel might be your mystery man, your husband-to-be."

I burst out laughing.

"Him! I wouldn't touch him with a pole – you never know *where* he's been."

Daniel looked all affronted and Karen looked absolutely *furious.*

Hastily I backtracked and winked affectionately at Daniel.

"Only joking, Daniel. You know what I mean, but if it's any consolation, my mother would be delighted. You're her ideal son-in-law."

"I know," he sighed. "But you're right, it would never work. I'm too ordinary for you, isn't that right, Lucy?"

"How d'you mean?"

"Well I have a job and I don't turn up to meet you blind drunk and I pay for you when we go out and I'm not a tortured artist."

"Shut up, you bastard," I laughed. "You make all

my boyfriends sound like drunken, free-loading layabouts."

"Do I indeed?"

"Yes. And you'd better watch it because they're not."

"Sorry."

"That's OK."

"All the same," he said. "I don't think Connie's going to be too thrilled when she meets Gus."

"She won't meet him," I said.

"She'll have to if you're going to marry him," he reminded me.

"Daniel, please shut up!" I begged. "This is supposed to be a happy occasion."

"Sorry, Lucy," he murmured.

I caught his eye. He didn't look very sorry. Before I could complain he said, "Come on, Charlotte, tell us about your bloke."

Charlotte was only too happy to oblige. Apparently he was called Simon, tall, blond, good-looking, twenty-nine, in advertising, had a flash car, at the party had been all over her like a rash and was ringing her the following day to take her out for lunch. "And I just know he'll ring," she said, her eyes shining. "I have such a good feeling about this."

"Great!" I said, delighted. "It seems like we all got lucky this evening."

Then I left and slipped back into bed beside Gus.

Chapter Twenty-Three

Gus was still asleep and still looked gorgeous. But what Daniel had said had upset me slightly. It was true – my mother wouldn't like Gus. In fact, my mother would hate Gus. The good had gone out of the evening slightly. I marvelled at my mother's unerring ability to tarnish all the happy things she touched.

She always had, as far back as I could remember.

When I was a little girl and Dad came home in a good mood because he'd just got a job, or won money at the races or whatever, she always managed to defuse any celebrations. Dad would come into the kitchen, all smiles, his coat pocket filled with sweets for us and a bottle in a brown paper bag under his arm. And instead of smiling and saying, "What's happened, Jamsie? What are we celebrating?" she ruined it all by making a face and saying something awful like "Oh Jamsie, not after the last time" or, "Oh Jamsie, you promised."

And even at six or eight or whatever age I was, I felt terrible. Appalled at her ingratitude. Anxious to let him know that I thought she was behaving dreadfully, that I was on his side. And not just

200

because sweets were a rare event. I wholeheartedly agreed with Dad when he said, "Lucy, your mother is a right oul' misery guts."

Because there was no one else to do it, I felt that it was my job to provide an up-beat mood.

So when Dad sat down and poured himself a glass, I sat at the table with him, to keep him company, to show solidarity, so that he wasn't celebrating whatever he was celebrating alone.

It was nice to watch him. There was a rhythm to his drinking that I found comforting.

My mother indicated her disapproval by banging and clattering and washing and wiping. Intermittently Dad tried to get her to cheer up. "Eat your Crunchie, Connie," he said.

If the phrase, "Lighten up," had been invented, he probably would have made good use of it.

And after a while he usually got out the record-player and sang along to "Four Green Fields" and "I wish I was in Carrickfergus" and other Irish songs. He played them over and over again and occasionally between songs he said, "Eat the feckin' Crunchie!"

And after a while more he usually began to cry. But he kept singing, his voice hoarse with tears. Or it might have been the brandy.

I knew that his heart was breaking because he wasn't in Carrickfergus – I often felt so sad for him that I cried also. But my mother would just say "Jesus! Sure that eejit doesn't even know where Carrickfergus is, never mind wishing he was there."

I couldn't understand why she had to be so miserable. Or so cruel.

And he'd say to her, in a kind of slurred voice, "It's a state of mind, my dear. It's a state of mind."

I wasn't really sure what he meant by that.

But when he slurred at her, "But how would you know, because you don't have a mind," I *did* know what he meant by that. I'd catch his eye and we'd both snigger conspiratorially.

Those evenings always followed the same pattern. The uneaten Crunchie, the rhythmic drinking, the banging and clattering, the singing and crying. Then, when the bottle was nearly all gone my mother usually said something like, "Here goes. Get ready for the performance."

And Dad would get to his feet. Sometimes he wouldn't be able to walk too straight. Most times, actually.

"I'm going home to Ireland," my mother would say in a bored voice.

"I'm going home to Ireland," my dad would shout in the slurred voice.

"If I leave now I can catch the mail-boat train," my mother said, still in the bored voice, as she leant against the sink.

"If I leave now I can catch the mail-train boat," my dad would shout. Sometimes his eyes would go crossed, like the way they go if you're trying to see the end of your nose.

"I was a fool ever to have left," Mum would say idly, inspecting her fingernails. I couldn't understand her complete lack of emotion.

"I was a bloody eejit ever to have left," Dad would shout.

"Oh, it's a 'bloody eejit' this time, is it?" Mum might say. "I liked 'fool' myself, but a bit of variety is nice."

Poor Dad would stand there, swaying slightly, hunched over and looking a bit like a bull, staring at Mum but not quite seeing her. Probably seeing the end of his nose, actually.

"I'm going to pack a bag," Mum would say, like a stage prompter.

"I'm going to bag a pack," Dad would say lurching towards the kitchen door.

Even though it happened lots of times and he never got further than the front door, every time I thought he was really leaving.

"Dad, please don't go," I beseeched him.

"I won't stay in a house with that oul' guzzery mits of a woman who won't even eat the Crunchie I bought her," he usually said.

"Eat the Crunchie," I begged Mum, as I tried to block Dad from leaving the room.

"Don't stand in me way, Lucy, or I won't be brespon . . . I mean I won't be rospensible . . . I mean, ah fuck it!" and he'd fall out into the hall.

Then we'd hear the sound of the hall table falling over and Mum would mutter, "If that louser has broken my . . . "

"Mum, stop him," I'd beg frantically.

"He won't get further than the gate," she'd say bitterly. "More's the bloody pity."

And although I never believed her, she was right. He very rarely did.

Once he made it up the road as far as the

O'Hanlaoins, clutching a plastic bag that contained four slices of bread and the rest of the bottle of brandy under his armpit. His sustenance for the journey home to Monaghan. He stood outside the O'Hanlaoins for a while and shouted things. Something about the O'Hanlaoins being dishonest and how Seamus had to leave Ireland to avoid a prison sentence. "Ye were run outta the place," my dad shouted.

Mum and Chris had to go and get him and bring him back. He came quietly. Mum led him by the hand past the censorious stares of all our neighbours who were standing, arms folded, looking over their small gates, silently watching the spectacle. When we got as far as our house Mum turned back and shouted at them, "You can go back in now. The circus is over."

I was surprised to see that she was crying.

I thought it was with shame. Shame for the way she'd treated him, for ruining his good mood, for not eating the Crunchie he'd bought for her, for urging him to try and leave. Shame that she richly deserved.

Chapter Twenty-Four

I awoke to find Gus leaning over me, anxiously looking down into my face.

"Lucy Sullivan?" he asked.

"That's me," I said sleepily.

"Oh thank God for that!"

"For what?"

"I thought I might have dreamt you."

"That's so sweet."

"I'm glad you think so, Lucy," he said ruefully. "But I'm afraid it's not really. With my track record, I very often wake up and wish that I *had* dreamt the previous evening. It makes a change for me to hope that it wasn't a dream."

"Oh."

I was confused, but I *thought* it sounded like a compliment.

"Thank you for letting me avail of your lying down facilities, Lucy," he said. "You're a wee angel."

I sat up in alarm. That sounded valedictory. Was he leaving?

But no, he didn't seem to be wearing a shirt, so he wasn't going just yet. I snuggled back into bed and he lay down beside me. Though the duvet was between us, it felt wonderful.

"My pleasure." I smiled.

"Now, Lucy, I'd better ask you how many days I've been here?"

"Less than one, actually."

"Is that all?" he said, sounding disappointed. "That was very restrained of me. I must be getting old. Although it's early days yet. Still plenty of time."

Fine with me, I thought. Stay as long as you like.

"And now can I avail myself of your bathroom facilities, Lucy?"

"Down the hall, you'll see it."

"But I'd better cover my shame, Lucy."

I eagerly hoisted myself up onto my elbow – all the better to get a good look at his shame before he covered it – and saw that at some stage during the night Gus had removed his clothing and was now only wearing his boxer shorts. And what a lovely body he had. Beautiful smooth skin and strong arms, and a tiny waist and a flat stomach. I couldn't get a proper look at his legs because he was nearly lying on top of me, but if they were anything like the rest of him, they were bound to be delicious.

"Wear my dressing-gown, it's on the back of the door."

"But what if I meet one of your flatmates?" he asked in mock fear.

"What about it?" I giggled.

"I'll be shy. And they'll, you know . . . *think* things about me."

He hung his head and went all coy and simpery.

"What kind of things?" I laughed.

"They'll wonder where I slept and my reputation will be ruined."

"Go on, I'll defend your honour if anyone says anything."

His voice and his accent were so beautiful, I could have listened to him forever.

"Great dressing-gown!" said Gus. It was a white towelling one with a hood and he put it on and put up the hood and shadow boxed round my bed.

"Are you in the Ku-Klux Klan, Lucy Sullivan?" he asked, looking at himself in the mirror. "Have you any burning crosses hidden under the bed?"

"No."

"Well, if you ever decide to join, you won't have to buy the uniform, just throw on your dressing-gown, up with the hood and Bob's your uncle!"

I lay back against my pillow and smiled at him. I was happy.

"Right," he said. "I'll be off."

Gus opened the bedroom door and immediately slammed it shut again.

I jumped.

"What's wrong?"

"That man!" said Gus, sounding horrified.

"What man?"

"The tall one, who stole your friend's beer and my bottle of wine. He's right outside this door!"

So Daniel had stayed the night – how funny.

"No, no, listen to me," I wheezed.

"He *is* Lucy, I swear he is," insisted Gus. "Unless I'm having the visions again."

"You're not having any visions," I said.

"Well, then we have to get him out of here! You won't have a stick of furniture left in the place otherwise – honestly! I've met his type before. Thorough professionals . . . "

"No, Gus, please listen to me," I said, trying to be serious. "He won't steal our furniture – he's my friend."

"Really? Do you mean it? Well, I know it's none of my business and I know we've just met and I've no right to comment, but, a common criminal – I wouldn't have expected it, that's all . . . and I can't see what you think is so funny. You won't think it's funny when you see your couch on sale at Camden Market and you have to sleep on the floor. *I* certainly don't think it's a laughing matter . . . "

"Please shut up and listen to me, Gus," I managed to splutter. "Daniel, that's the tall man, outside the door. He didn't steal anyone's beer."

"But, I saw him . . . "

"It was his beer, though."

"No, it was Donal's beer."

"But he is Donal and his name is Daniel."

A pause while Gus digested this fact.

"Oh God," he groaned.

He lurched over and threw himself on my bed, his face in his hands.

"Oh God, oh God, oh God," he moaned.

"It's OK," I said gently.

"Oh God, oh God, oh God."

Gus looked up at me from between his fingers.

"Oh God," he said, his face stricken.

"It's fine."

"It's not."

"It is."

"No, it isn't. I accused him of stealing his own beer and then I drank it all. And then I took his girlfriend's bottle of wine . . . "

"She's not his girlfriend . . . " I said irrelevantly. "Although maybe she is now . . . "

"The scary blonde one?"

"Er, yes." Karen *could* be described that way.

"Believe me," insisted Gus. "She's his girlfriend, all right, at least if *she* has anything to do with it."

"I suppose you're right," I admitted.

How interesting, I thought. So Gus could be perceptive and clued-in? How much of his flighty, madcap carry-on was an act? Or was he both perceptive and flighty? Could it all be part of the same man? And had I the energy for it?

"I'm not usually obnoxious like that, Lucy, honestly I'm not," he insisted. "It was the drugs. It must have been."

"OK," I said, feeling almost disappointed.

"I must apologise to him," said Gus, jumping up off the bed.

"No," I said. "Come back here. It's too early in the morning for apologies. Later."

Gus lurked by the door for a while, looking stressed and anxious, then he opened it a crack. "He's gone," he said with relief. "It's safe for me to go and hose myself down." And off he went.

While he was gone I lay in bed feeling very pleased with myself. I had to admit that I was relieved that he was slightly ashamed of himself for running off with Daniel's Guinness. It showed that he was a decent person.

And a smart one too – he'd got the measure of Karen fairly quickly.

He looked even nicer than I remembered – smiley and attractive and not half as bloodshot round the eyes.

What would happen, I wondered, when he came back from the bathroom? Would he get dressed and leave, awkwardly omitting to say anything about ringing me? Somehow I thought not. I certainly *hoped* not.

There wasn't that awful sordid feeling that often goes with waking up on a Sunday morning, either with a complete stranger in your bed, or in a complete stranger's bed.

At least Gus had woken me up. He hadn't inched carefully out of the bed and silently dressed in the dark and bolted out of the flat, his underpants in his pocket, his watch forgotten on my bedside table.

I hadn't woken to the sound of the front door slamming behind him. And, with my history of relationships, that counted as a flying start.

Being with Gus felt natural and right. I wasn't even nervous. Well hardly even.

He was back from the bathroom, with a pink towel round his waist, his hair wet and shiny, all clean and fragrant.

Suspiciously fragrant, actually.

I had been right about his legs.

He wasn't very tall, but he was all man.

A shiver ran through me. I was looking forward to . . . er . . . getting to know him better.

"You're looking at a man who has been exfoliated to within an inch of his life, Lucy." He grinned, looking very pleased with himself.

"Exfoliated, defoliated, cleansed, conditioned, emolliated, moisturised, massaged, anointed! What! You name it, I've had it done to me in the last ten minutes. Can you remember the days when all we were expected to do was wash ourselves, Lucy? But not anymore. We must keep up with the times, mustn't we, Lucy Sullivan?"

"Yes," I giggled. He was so funny.

"Can't let the grass grow under our feet, can we Lucy Sullivan?"

"No."

"You'd be hard pressed to find a cleaner man in the whole of London."

"I bet."

"Wonderful bathroom facilities, Lucy. You must pride yourself on them."

"Er, yes, I suppose . . . "

The state of my bathroom wasn't something that exactly occupied my thoughts much.

"Lucy, I hope it's OK, but I used some of Elizabeth's stuff."

"Who's Elizabeth?"

"Well, there's little enough point in asking me, you should know, you live here. Isn't she your flatmate?"

"No, there's only me and Karen and Charlotte."

"Well, she has a nerve in that case, because the bathroom is full of her things."

"What on earth are you talking about?"

"Elizabeth, what was her surname? Began with 'G'. Ardent, that's what it was, I think. Elizabeth Ardent – I remember now because I was thinking it was a good name for a romantic novel writer – anyway she's got a load of bottles and tubes in the bathroom with her name on them."

"Oh God," I started to laugh.

Gus had used Karen's very expensive jars of Elizabeth Arden shower gel and body lotion. Or Elizabeth Hard-on as Charlotte and I called them. That was because we were jealous and coveted them, but we were afraid to touch them.

In fact even Karen didn't use them – they were really just exhibition pieces that she kept for show, to impress the likes of Daniel, not that he noticed things like that, what with him being a man. Up to now I'd even suspected that there was only coloured water in the bottles.

Heads would roll over this.

"Oh no," said Gus nervously. "I've done it again, haven't I? I've committed another *faux pas* – surely I'm well over my quota already? – I shouldn't have used that stuff, should I?"

"Don't worry," I said. There really was no point worrying now – it was done – if Karen kicked up a fuss . . . no . . . *when* Karen kicked up a fuss, I'd offer to replace them.

"But, Gus, I think it would be better if you didn't use Karen's things again."

"Who's Karen? Oh aye, I get you – Karen owns Elizabeth's things? Poor Karen, getting hand-me-down bottles and tubes with someone else's name on them. A bit like me really, all my school books – even my copies – had someone else's name on them because I have so many older brothers . . . Anyway, I'll use your things in the bathroom the next time."

"Good," I smiled, delighted at the suggestion that there would be a next time.

"But which are yours?" he asked. "The only other things I could see had 'Boots' written on them and surely you're not going to try and tell me they're yours because no one in their right mind could call you a boot."

"Thank you, Gus," I said, bewitched, *mesmerised*, by the rollercoaster journey his conversation was taking me on. "But actually the 'Boots' things are mine."

"Well, I just hope you realise that they could get you under the Trade Descriptions Act." He grinned.

"A beautiful woman like you," he added casually.

I felt blood rush to my face. The compliments sounded extra sexy in Gus's Donegal accent.

"Thanks," I stammered.

"Lucy," he said. He came over and sat beside me on my bed and held my hand. His hand was smooth and warm. Mine looked tiny beside it.

I liked to feel tiny beside men. A couple of the men that I had gone out with were really skinny and nothing demoralised me more than going to bed with a man who had a smaller bum and thinner thighs than me.

"I really am sorry," said Gus earnestly, making circles on the back of my hand with his thumb, sending little shivers of delight through me. I could barely concentrate on what he was saying.

"You're very nice and I really like you," he went on awkwardly. "And I've got an awful lot of things wrong already and we've only just met. Sometimes I joke at the wrong time and when something is important to me I get it even more wrong. Sorry."

My heart dissolved. I hadn't been cross with him anyway, but after his little speech I felt so tender, so . . . so, *cherishing* towards him.

"And about the stuff in the bathroom, perhaps if I spoke to Elizabeth and explained . . . ?"

"Karen!" I insisted. "She's Karen! Not Elizabeth."

I trailed off when I saw the twinkle in his eye.

"I'm joking, Lucy," he said. "I know she's called Karen and that there's no Elizabeth living here."

"Oh," I said, a bit embarrassed.

"You must think I'm a right half-wit," he said. "But it's very kind of you to humour me, all the same."

"I just thought . . . you know . . . " I limply tried to explain.

"It's OK," he said.

We gave each other a knowing little smile, this would be our little joke.

Already we had shared secrets, in-jokes, verbal shorthand!

"It's fine," I said. "Everything's fine."

"If you say so. And now, Lucy, we'll go for a walk."

He had made me laugh with a lot of the things he had said, but that suggestion made me laugh most of all.

"What's so funny, Lucy?"

"Me? A walk? On a Sunday?"

"Aye."

"No."

"Why not?"

"Because it's freezing outside."

"But we'll wear warm clothes. And we'll walk briskly."

"But, Gus, I never leave the house on any Sunday from October to April, except to go to the Cash'n'Curry in the evening."

"Then it's about time you started. What's this Cash'n'Curry place?"

"It's the Indian restaurant round the corner."

"Great name."

"Well, it's not really called Cash'n'Curry, it's called something like The Star of Lahore or The Jewel of Bombay."

"And you go there every Sunday night?"

"Every Sunday night without fail, and we always have exactly the same thing."

"OK, well we might go there later, Lucy, but right now we'll go to Holland Park, it's only down the road from here."

"Er, is it?"

"Aye. How long have you lived here, Lucy Sullivan?"

"A couple of years." I mumbled it and tried to make "years" sound like "weeks".

"And in all that time you've never been to the park? That's a disgrace, Lucy."

"I'm not really an outdoor creature, Gus."

215

"I am."

"Will they have a telly there?"

"Aye."

"Really?"

"No. But I'll entertain you, don't worry."

"OK."

I was really very pleased. Delighted, in fact. He wanted to spend the day with me.

"Can I wear this jumper?"

"Yes, in fact you can have it, I hate it."

Gus was rummaging around in my cupboards and had unearthed a revolting dark blue Aran jumper that my mother had knitted for me.

I had never worn it precisely *because* she had knitted it for me. And she had got the tension all wrong so the neckline was like a car-tyre – which was surprising because tension was something she was normally very good at. I looked like a fourteen-stone tortoise when I wore it.

"Wow, thanks, Lucy Sullivan."

Chapter Twenty-Five

I went to have a shower and when I got back my room was empty – Gus was gone and I felt slightly panicky. I was afraid that he might have left the flat completely but I was more afraid that he hadn't. He had an admirable capacity to create havoc and, despite his touching apology earlier, I wasn't yet convinced that it was safe to let him roam my flat without a minder.

Visions of finding him lying in bed with Daniel and Karen, blithely chatting, while they put a reluctant and ill-tempered halt to their sexual activities, appeared before me.

But it was fine.

Gus was in the kitchen, sitting at the table with Daniel and Karen. They were all drinking tea and the papers were spread out. To my intense relief, everyone was getting on nicely and having a nice civilised Sunday morning chat, stolen Guinness and misappropriated Elizabeth Arden toiletries notwithstanding. Gus and Daniel seemed to have resolved their differences regarding Gus's unauthorised drinking of Daniel's Guinness. Gus and Karen appeared to be the best of friends.

"Lucy," smiled Gus when I appeared in the

kitchen doorway, "come in and sit down and partake of some nourishment."

"Oh," I said faintly, a bit taken aback by all the camaraderie. I was a little bit, well, not *annoyed* exactly, but a bit put out, I suppose because all these people, who only knew each other because of me, were getting along fine without me.

"I explained to Karen about me using her Elizabeth Ardent things," sang Gus, his face a picture of innocence. "And she says it's OK."

"It's fine," said Karen, smiling at Gus, smiling at Daniel, smiling at me.

Gosh! I'm sure Karen wouldn't have been quite so reasonable if Charlotte or I had used said Elizabeth Arden toiletries.

She obviously liked Gus.

Or maybe Daniel had surpassed himself between the sheets the previous night. No doubt I'd find out later. She would tell everything, in the minutest possible detail, when the menfolk were gone.

I spent *hours* getting ready. It was the hardest thing in the world to look as if I was dressed sensibly and to look pretty and feminine and skinny at the same time. It was far harder to do that than getting ready for dinner with Daniel the previous evening had been. The trick with dressing for a visit to the great outdoors was to look as if I didn't care how I looked, as though I'd just grabbed anything that came to hand and slung it on me. I wore my jeans – I couldn't really see any way round it, even though I hated the way they made my thighs stick out.

I hated my thighs more than life itself and I would have given anything to have skinny ones. I even used to pray for them. Well, I had once. It was one Christmas day at Mass (my mother insisted that we still went to Mass *en famille* and I had learnt to go along with it. Any complaints meant no Viennetta later.) When the priest said that we should pray for our own special intentions, I prayed for thinner thighs. Afterwards my mother asked me what my "special intention" was and when I told her she was furious and told me that that was a completely unworthy and inappropriate thing to pray for. So I shamefacedly slunk back into the church, piously bowed my head and prayed for thinner thighs for her, Dad, Chris, Pete, Granny Sullivan, the poor people in Africa and anyone else who might like them.

But God didn't reward my altruism by granting me slimmer thighs and I found that the only way to make them look small was to surround them with big things. So I put on my heavy, clumpy boots. But then I had to cancel out the trucker image that they conjured up by wearing a girly, pink angora jumper. And a big checked blue and black jacket, to make me look fragile and tiny.

I spent another hour or so trying to make it seem as if I had just loosely bundled my hair up on top of my head. It took forever to arrange my curls so that they looked as if they had just fallen down around my face at random.

Then a heavy application of make-up to achieve the Unmade-up Look, or Bare-faced chic, if you prefer. All pink cheeks and clear white skin and bright eyes and fresh lips.

I found Gus in the front room, obviously firmly bonded with Karen, Charlotte and Daniel. They looked as if they'd known each other all their lives and my heart lifted. I wanted my flatmates and friends to like him. And I wanted him to like my flatmates and friends.

Although not too much obviously.

There's only one thing worse than your boyfriend and flatmates not liking each other and that's when they like each other a bit too much. It can lead to all sorts of terrible complications and confusion over the sleeping arrangements.

Charlotte's Simon had rung and Charlotte, all made-up and perfumed, was excitedly preparing for the off.

"Condoms," she said feverishly, sitting down and rummaging through her bag. "Condoms, condoms, have I got condoms?"

"But you're only meeting him for lunch," I said.

"Lucy, don't be ridiculous," she said scornfully. " . . . Oh good . . . damn, there's only one – what flavour is it? Pina Colada – but it'll just have to do."

"You look lovely, Lucy," said Daniel admiringly.

"Aye, you do. Beautiful." Gus turned round to have a good look at me.

"Yes, you do," echoed Charlotte.

"Thanks."

"Are we right?" Gus got up.

"We are," I said.

"Very nice meeting you all," said Gus to the general assembly, all rancour from the previous evening seemingly long forgotten. "And good luck with the . . . er . . . um . . . " he nodded to Charlotte.

"Thanks." She smiled nervously.

"Have fun." Daniel winked at me.

"And you." I winked back.

Chapter Twenty-Six

At least it wasn't raining. It was cold, but the sky was blue and clear and the air was still.

"Have you gloves, Lucy?"

"Yes."

"Well, give them to me."

"Oh." *Selfish bastard*.

"Och, no, not for me!" he laughed. "Look, one for your right hand and one for my left hand and then we'll hold hands with our two middle ones. See?"

"I *see*."

That was great because it took care of the awkward matter of hand-holding. A matter which wasn't a problem at all on the previous alcohol lubricated evening, but which could have become a bit of an issue in the cold sober light of day.

On we marched, swinging hands, the cold air reddening our faces.

We lolled on a bench and held hands and watched the squirrels running and jumping about.

Even though I felt a little bit shy, I couldn't take my eyes off Gus. He was gorgeous, his hair so black and shiny, his jaw covered in stubble (he obviously hadn't found Karen's epilator), and his eyes bright green in the cold, winter light.

It was wonderful to be with him.

"This is lovely." I sighed. "I'm so glad you forced me to come."

"I'm glad you're glad, wee Lucy Sullivan."

"And the squirrels are so sweet," I said. "I love watching them running about, jumping, gambolling."

Gus quickly sat up and stared at me.

"Are you serious?" he demanded, looking very alarmed.

What *now*, I wondered, feeling anxious. Was he about to go off on another mad flight of fancy?

He was, apparently.

"Well," he spluttered. "I have to say that the barbarians are well and truly at the gates when the dumb beasts of the fields have to entertain themselves by illicit betting . . . but that's London for you, I suppose. Next they'll be smoking crack!"

Oh my God, I thought, he's *bonkers*. But I couldn't take it seriously, I was laughing so much that I could barely speak.

"Not gambling, *gambolling*," I said.

"I heard you the first time, Lucy Sullivan," he said.

"And what is it, Lucy?" he demanded. "The dogs? The horses? Bingo? Eyes down and two fat ladies for the little squirrels! Cards? Blackjack? Roulette? *Rien ne va plus! Rien ne va plus,* is bloody right. There's no innocence anymore, Lucy! None. There's nothing unspoilt. To think that the little squirrels are gambling, it breaks my heart – you wouldn't get that in Donegal. What was wrong with gathering nuts? No thrill left in it, I suppose . . . The influence of television."

He stared at me, realisation dawning.

"Oh," he said, shamefaced. "Oh. Oh no. You meant the gambolling type of gambling. Not the gambling type of gambling."

"Yes."

"Oh. Oh. Well, sorry about that. A misunderstanding. You must think I'm fit to be locked up. The bouncy room for Gus."

"No. I think you're hilarious."

"That's very decent of you, Lucy" he said. "Most people just say that I'm mad."

"Why's that?" I asked, amused.

"Search me," he said, his pixie face a picture of assumed innocence.

I'd be delighted to, I thought.

"Anyway," he continued, "if they think *I'm* mad, they should meet the rest of my family."

Oh oh! I sensed an unpleasant revelation hovering on the horizon. But I squared my shoulders and met it head on.

"Er, and what are they like, Gus?"

He gave me a sidelong grin and said, "Och, well now, insane isn't a word I care to bandy about, Lucy, but . . ."

I tried to hide my alarm, but it must have shown on my face because he burst out laughing.

"Poor wee Lucy. Would you look at the worried little face!"

I tried to smile gamely.

"But settle yourself, Lucy, I'm only having you on. They're not actually insane . . ."

I breathed a sigh of relief.

" . . . *as such* . . ." he continued. "But very, very emotional, I suppose is the best way of describing it."

"How do you mean?"

I might as well deal with it there and then, I decided.

"I'm kind of afraid to tell you, Lucy, in case I convince you that I'm stone mad. When you hear the kind of background I come from, you'll probably run away screaming."

"Don't be silly," I said reassuringly.

But I had a little knot in my stomach. Please God, don't make this too awful. I like him too much.

"Are you sure you want to hear this, Lucy?"

"I'm sure. Nothing can be that bad. Have you parents?"

"Oh aye. The full complement. A matching pair. A complete set."

"You already mentioned that you had lots of brothers . . . ?"

"Five of them."

"That's a lot."

"Not really, not in the area I come from. I was always ashamed that my number of brothers didn't run to double figures."

"Older or younger?"

"Older. They're all older than me."

"So you're the baby."

"I am, although I'm the only one of the lads who doesn't still live at home."

"Five grown men all living at home – that must create a lot of problems."

"Jesus! You don't know the half of it. But they

225

have to, really, because they work on the farm and in the pub."

"You own a pub?"

"We do."

"You must be loaded."

"Well, we're not."

"But I always thought owing a pub meant you could almost print your own money."

"Not our pub. It's my brothers, you see. Fond of the drop."

"Ah, I see, they drink the profits."

"No they don't," he laughed. "There aren't any profits to drink, because they drink the drink."

"Oh Gus."

"And we hardly ever have any stock because they drink it all and we owe money to every brewery in Ireland so almost none of them will deliver to us anymore. Our name is a hissing and a byword among the distillers of Ireland."

"But don't you have customers, couldn't you make a profit from them?"

"Not really, because we're in such a remote area. Our only customers are my brothers and my da. And the local constabulary of course – and *they* only come after closing hours any night looking for a lock-in. And they can't be charged the full price, in fact they can't be charged any price, because they'd close us down for breaking the licensing laws, if we tried to."

"You're joking."

"I'm not."

My head was racing, trying to come up with

money-spinners, profit-making schemes for Gus's family's pub. Karaoke evenings? Quiz nights? Special promotions? Food at lunch-time? And I said as much to him.

"No Lucy." He shook his head and looked amused and sad at the same time. "They're not great organisers. Something would go wrong because they're forever getting drunk and fighting each other."

"Are you serious?"

"I am! Most nights in our house are conducted in a state of high drama. I'd come home of an evening and the brothers would be in the kitchen and a couple of them would be covered with blood and another would have his hand wrapped up in a shirt after putting his fist through a window and they'd be calling each other names and then they'd start crying and telling each other that they loved each other like a brother. I hate it."

"And what would they row about?" I asked, intrigued, *fascinated*.

"Oh anything at all. They're not picky. A dirty look, an inflection in a voice, anything!"

"Really?"

"Yes. I was home at Christmas and the first night I was back we all had a huge feed of drink. And it was great crack for a while, until things went wrong, the way they usually do. At about midnight PJ thought Paudi was looking funny at him so PJ hit Paudi, then Mikey shouted at PJ to leave Paudi alone and John Joe hit Mikey for shouting at PJ, then PJ hit John Joe for hitting Mikey and Stevie started crying because of brother being set against brother. And then PJ started crying because he was sorry for upsetting Stevie, then Stevie hit PJ for starting it all, then Paudi hit Stevie for hitting PJ because he had wanted to hit PJ . . . And then my da came in and he tried to hit all of them. "

Gus paused for breath. "It was terrible. It's the boredom, I'm sure of it. But the whole thing is fuelled by alcohol. They calmed down a bit a few years ago when we got Sky Sports, but then the Da wouldn't pay the bill for it, so the ructions started up again."

I was spellbound. I could have listened forever to Gus's beautiful, lyrical accent, telling the story of his fascinatingly dysfunctional family.

"And where do you fit into it all? Who do you hit?"

"No one. I don't fit into it at all, at least I try my very best not to."

"The whole thing sounds hilarious," I said. "Like something out of a play."

"Really?" said Gus, sounding shocked, annoyed even. "Maybe I've told it wrong because it wasn't funny at all."

Immediately I felt ashamed.

"Sorry, Gus," I muttered. "I forgot for a moment that this is your life we're talking about. It's just that you tell it so well . . . But I'm sure it was terrible really."

"Well, it was you know, Lucy," he said, indignantly. "It left terrible scars, it made me do awful things."

"Like what?"

"I used to walk the hills for hours and talk to the rabbits and write poetry. Of course it was only because I wanted to get away from the family and because I didn't know any better."

"But what's wrong with walking the hills and talking to the rabbits and writing poetry?" I thought it sounded wild and romantic and Irish.

"Plenty, Lucy, as I'm sure you'd agree if you ever read any of my poetry."

I laughed, but only a little bit, I didn't want him to think I was making fun of him.

"And rabbits make very poor conversationalists," he said. "Carrots and sex, that's all they talk about."

"Is that right?"

"So as soon as I got away from there, I knocked the poetry and the tortured soul image on the head."

"Well, there's nothing wrong with being a tortured soul . . ." I protested, desperate to cling on to the image of Gus as a poetic figure.

"Oh, there *is*, Lucy. It's embarrassing and boring."

"Oh, is it? I quite like tortured souls . . ."

"No, Lucy, you mustn't," he said firmly. "I insist."

"So what are your parents like?" I asked, changing the subject.

"My father is the worst of the lot of them. A terrible man when he has drink taken. Which is most of the time."

"And what about your mother?"

"She doesn't really do anything. Well, I mean she does *plenty* – all the cooking and washing and stuff, but she doesn't try to keep them in line. I suppose

229

she's too afraid. She prays a lot. And cries – we're a great family for crying, a very lachrymose crowd. She prays for my brothers and father to give up the drink and become Pioneers."

"And do you have any sisters?"

"Two, but they escaped when they were very young. Eleanor got married when she was nineteen to a man who was old enough to be her grandfather, Francis Cassidy from Letterkenny."

Gus seemed to cheer up at the memory. "He only came up to the farm once and that was to ask the da for her hand, and maybe I shouldn't tell you this because you'll think that we're a right crowd of savages, but the lot of us ran him out of the place. We tried to set the dogs on poor oul Francis, but the dogs refused to bite him. Afraid they might catch something, probably."

Gus peered at me closely. "Should I bow my head in shame, Lucy?"

"No," I said. "It's funny."

"I know it wasn't very hospitable, Lucy, but we had little to amuse us and Francis Cassidy was awful, far worse than any of us. He was the most miserable-looking old stick you ever clapped eyes on and he must have had the evil eye because the hens didn't lay for four days afterwards and the cows had no milk."

"And what about your other sister?"

"Eileen? She just disappeared. None of the local boyos came looking for her hand – I suppose Francis Cassidy warned them off. We only noticed she was gone when the breakfast wasn't on the table one morning. It was summer and we were making the hay and had to get up at the crack of dawn and Eileen was supposed to make the food before we all went off to the fields."

"And where had she gone?"

"I don't know, Dublin, I think."

"And wasn't anyone worried about her?" I asked, appalled. "Didn't anyone try to go after her or to find her?"

"They were worried all right. They were worried that they'd have to make their own breakfasts from then on."

"But that's terrible," I said, feeling upset. The story of Eileen had upset me far more than the story of Francis Cassidy and the dogs. "Really, really terrible."

"Lucy," said Gus, squeezing my hand. "*I* wasn't worried about having to make my own breakfast. *I* wanted to go after her, but my da said he'd kill me."

"Fair enough," I said, feeling a bit better.

"I missed her, she was lovely, she used to talk to me. But I was glad for her that she was gone."

"Why?"

"She was too bright just to be a skivvy and the oul' fella was talking about making a match and marrying her off to one of two ancient laddoes who lived in the next farm along, so that he could get his hands on their land, you see."

"That's barbaric," I said in horror.

"Some people might call it good economics," said Gus.

"But I wouldn't be one of them," he added hastily, when I gave him a glare.

"And what became of poor Eileen?" I asked, feeling as though my heart would break from the sadness of it all. "Did you ever hear from her again?"

"I *think* she went to Dublin, but she never wrote to me, so I don't know for sure."

"It's so sad," I breathed.

Then a thought struck me and I looked at him sharply. "You're not making any of this up, by any chance, are you? This isn't one of your inventions like the squirrels gambling and my flatmate Elizbeth Ardent?"

"No." he protested. "Of course it's not. Honestly, Lucy, I wouldn't joke or make things up about something important. Although I wish the story of my family *was* a fairytale. I suppose it sounds very peculiar to a sophisticated city girl like yourself."

Oddly enough it didn't.

"But, you see, we were very isolated," Gus went on. "The farm was remote and we didn't meet that many other people so I didn't know any better. I had nothing to compare my family to. For years I thought that the fights and the crying and the shouting and everything were perfectly normal and that everyone lived like us. It was a big relief, I can tell you, to find out that my suspicions were correct and that they were really as mad as I had thought they were."

"So that's the story of my origins, Lucy."

"Well, thank you for telling me."

"Have I scared you away?"

"No."

"Why not?"

"I don't know."

"Your family must be mad too."

"They're not, sorry to disappoint you."

"Then why are you so tolerant about my crowd?"

"Because you're you, not your family."

"If only it was that simple, Lucy Sullivan."

"But it can be, Gus . . . Gus *what*?"

"Gus Lavan."

"Pleased to meet you, Gus Lavan," I said, shaking hands with him.

Lucy Lavan, I was thinking. *Lucy Lavan?* Yes, I liked it. Or how about it being double-barrelled. *Lucy Sullivan Lavan?* That had a lovely ring too.

"And I'm very pleased to meet you, Lucy Sullivan," he said solemnly, clasping my hand. "Although I've already said that, haven't I?"

"Yes, you said it last night."

"But it doesn't make it any less true, Lucy. Will we go for a pint, Lucy?"

"Er, yes, if you want. Have you walked enough?"

"I've walked enough to work up a thirst, ergo I've walked enough."

"Fine."

"What time is it, Lucy?"

"I don't know."

"Haven't you got a watch?"

"No."

"Neither have I. It's a sign."

"Of what?" I asked warmly. That Gus and I were soul mates? That Gus and I were ideally matched?

"That we'll always be late."

"Oh. Um, what are you doing?"

Gus had leant back almost horizontally on the

bench and was staring at the sky, sucking his teeth and muttering things like "a hundred and eighty degrees" and "seven hours ahead in New York" and "or maybe that's Chicago".

"I'm looking at the sky, Lucy."

"Why?"

"To find out the time, of course."

"Of course."

A pause.

"Any conclusions?"

"Yes, I think so." He nodded his head thoughtfully. "I think so."

There was another pause.

"Lucy, I've made up my mind that it's almost definitely – of course there's always room for human error here, you understand – but I'm prepared to say that it's almost definitely daytime. Eight-seven per cent certain. Or maybe eighty-four."

"I'd say you're right."

"I'd be interested to hear your views on the matter, Lucy."

"I'd say it's about two o'clock."

"Oh God." He jumped up from the bench. "That late, is it? Well come on then, we'll just have to do our best."

"What are you talking about?" I giggled, as he dragged me after him through the park.

"Closing time, Lucy Sullivan, closing time. A dirty word. Two dirty words, actually. Filthy, heinous words," he said, almost spitting them out. "Filthy! The pubs close at three o'clock today and they don't open again until seven – am I right?"

"Yes." I tried to keep up with him, "unless they've made any changes to the licensing laws this morning."

"Do you think they might have?" asked Gus, stopping abruptly.

"No."

"Well, then, come on," he said, almost running. "We've only got an hour."

Chapter Twenty-Seven

We stopped at the first pub we came to when we got out of the park. It wasn't too awful, which was just as well because I sensed that Gus would have made me go in even if the roof had caved in and the walls were falling down.

He put his hand on my arm at the door.

"Lucy, I'm sorry about this but I'm afraid that you'll have to finance this mission. I get my giro on Tuesday so I'll make it up to you then."

"Oh . . . oh . . . fine."

My heart sank, but I caught it before it hit the ground. After all it wasn't Gus's fault that I met him on a weekend when he was broke.

"What would you like to drink?" I asked him.

"I'll have a pint."

"Of what?"

"Guinness, of course . . ."

"Of course."

" . . . and a small one," he added.

"A small one?"

"Jameson, no ice."

"Er, right you are."

"But make it a big one," he suggested.

"Sorry?"

"A big small one."

"What . . . ?

"A big Jameson. A *large* one."

"Oh, OK."

"I hope you don't mind Lucy, but I don't see any point in doing things by half," he said apologetically.

"It's fine," I said faintly.

"And whatever you're having," he added.

"Um, thanks."

If I had been Karen, I would have said my "um, thanks" sarcastically, but seeing as I was only me I just said "um, thanks" like I really meant "um, thanks".

"There's a table just over here, Lucy. I'll guard it while you get the drinks."

I stood at the bar and I felt sad for just a moment. Then I forced myself to stop. I was being silly. He'd have money on Tuesday.

"And maybe some crisps," said Gus's voice in my ear.

"What flavour?"

"Salt and vinegar . . ."

"OK."

" . . . and if they have any beef and mustard . . ."

"Consider it done."

"Good woman." I got myself a modest diet coke.

Gus had finished his pint and his large small one before I finished my drink. In fact he nearly had them finished by the time I sat down.

"We'll have another," announced Gus.

"I suppose we will."

"You stay where you are," he said kindly. "Just give me the money and I'll get them."

"Oh, OK," I said, fishing in my pocket for my purse which I had just replaced and pulled out a fiver.

"Five of your earth pounds?" he said doubtfully. "Are you sure that'll be enough, Lucy?"

"Yes," I said firmly.

"Don't you want one for yourself?"

"Yes!"

While he was gone I drank the rest of my drink quickly. I decided that if he didn't give me back my change without me having to ask I would . . . I would . . . I don't know . . .

"Here's your change, Lucy."

I looked up from where I had been staring gloomily into my empty glass. Gus was looking at me anxiously, a few pennies in his open palm.

"Thanks." I smiled and took all thirteen pence or whatever it was. I suddenly felt better.

After all, it was the principle as much as the money.

"Lucy," Gus said earnestly. "Thank you, for the drinks and all that . . . it's very good of you. I get my giro on Tuesday and I'll take you out that night and I'll see you right. I promise. Er . . . thanks."

"You're welcome," I smiled, feeling a lot, lot better. He had redeemed himself, perhaps he had sensed how disappointed I had begun to feel.

He was good at that – redeeming himself, that is. At pulling himself back from where he hovered on the brink of my disapproval, just at the last minute.

It wasn't that I minded spending money on him – or anyone for that matter – especially when it was for something as important as lunch-time drinks for them, but I minded very much feeling as if they thought I was an idiot, a soft touch.

He had several more drinks which I happily paid for ("I'll see you right on Tuesday, Lucy"). A short hour later, we were several drinks down.

"Fair play to us, we've done marvellous things in the short time slot we had available to us, Lucy." Gus surveyed the table full of empty glasses as three o'clock approached and the barman invited us to leave.

"Isn't it truly amazing what you can achieve when you set your mind to it?" He waved his remaining half-empty pint glass around to emphasise his point. "All it takes is a bit of effort."

"Although I'm disappointed in you, Lucy." He affectionately touched my face. "I'm sorry to have to tell you. But two diet cokes and a gin and tonic? Are you sure you're Irish?"

"Yes," I said.

"Well, you'll just have to pull your weight more the next time, you can't just leave it all to me, you know."

"Gus," I giggled. "I've a bit of bad news for you."

"What is it?"

"I don't really drink all that much. And I never drink during the day . . . Usually," I added hastily as he looked accusingly at my gin glass.

"Really? But I thought . . . Didn't you say? . . . But you don't mind *other* people drinking lots, though, do you?" he asked hopefully.

"Not at all," I assured him. "Not at all."

"That's fine then." He sighed with relief. "Christ, you had me worried there for a moment. Would you say the bar really *is* closed?"

"Yes."

"Maybe I'll just go up and make sure," he suggested mischievously.

"Gus! It's closed!"

"But there's a barman there. They *must* still be serving."

"He's washing glasses."

"I'll just go and check."

"Gus!"

But he had hopped out of his seat and was up at the counter having a conversation with the barman that involved Gus in a lot of energetic gesticulation. Then to my horror I heard slightly raised voices, which stopped abruptly when Gus slammed his hand down on the wooden counter with great finality. He made his way back over to me.

"They're closed," he murmured, subdued. He picked up his pint and wouldn't meet my eye.

I was aware that the few remaining customers were watching us with amused interest. I was slightly embarrassed but it was funny.

"I don't know what was up with him at all, but that barman fella was a very unreasonable character," Gus muttered. "Unreasonable and unpleasant. There was no need for what he said to me. And whatever happened to 'the customer is always right'?"

I laughed and Gus glared at me.

"*Et tu,* Lucy?" he demanded.

I laughed again. I couldn't help it – it must have been the gin.

"We won't come here again, Lucy. Oh no! I don't come to a pub to be insulted, so I don't, Lucy. Indeed I do not!"

His good-looking, mobile face was grim with annoyance.

"I've plenty of other places I can go to be insulted," he added gloomily.

"What did he say to you?" I asked, trying to stop my mouth from twitching.

"Lucy, I wouldn't repeat it and certainly not in your presence," he said earnestly. "I would neither soil my own mouth nor pollute the fragrant air round your delicate ears by repeating what that son of a hoor, that . . . that . . . *lousy* bastard, that mean-spirited, bureaucratic, anal-retentive fucker, called me."

"Fair enough," I said, somehow keeping a straight face.

"I've too much respect for you, Lucy."

"I appreciate that."

"You're a lady, Lucy. And there are certain rules, certain personal restraints, that I apply when I'm in the presence of a lady."

"Thanks, Gus."

"And now," he said, standing up, and draining his glass, "our work here is done."

"What would you like to do now?" I asked.

"Well, it *is* Sunday afternoon and we're after having had a couple of drinks and it's cold and we have just met the previous evening, therefore it is written that we go back to your flat and snuggle on the couch and watch a black and white film." Gus smiled meaningfully at me and slipped his arm around my pink angora waist. He pulled me slightly towards him and I felt light-headed with . . . well, it must have been lust, I suppose. It was lovely to be held by him. Even though he wasn't very tall, he was strong and manly.

"That sounds wonderful." A thrill ran through me. Although I was afraid that there mightn't be a black and white film on and that Daniel and Karen might be having sex on the living-room floor. We could always call into Adrian and get a video if there wasn't anything suitable on the telly, but I wasn't quite so sure how to deal with the Daniel and Karen problem.

And what if Adrian got upset when he saw me with a bloke? How would I cope? It was a sorry state of affairs but such was life, where every silver lining had a cloud and every piece of happiness had its price in someone else's pain.

Chapter Twenty-Eight

That night, after Gus had gone home my happiness was almost uncontainable. I was itching to talk about Gus, to go into minute detail of what I was wearing when I met him, what he said to me, what he looked like, and all that.

But my usual confidantes were unavailable – Karen and Charlotte were out and Daniel was with Karen and I was too cross with Megan or Meredia, so I rang Dennis. And amazingly, he was in.

"I thought you'd be out," I said.

"Is that why you rang?"

"Don't be so touchy."

"What do you want?"

"Dennis," I breathed dramatically. "I met a man."

He gasped. "Do tell." Sometimes he talked like that, even though he was from Cork.

"Come over, it's more exciting if I tell you in person."

"I'm on my way."

I had to rush around and put on make-up and comb my hair because Dennis always scrutinised my appearance, telling me whether I had lost or gained weight, what my ideal weight should be, whether he liked or hated my hair and so on. He was worse than my mother, but at least he had an excuse – he was a gay man, he couldn't help himself.

He arrived in about ten minutes. Every time I saw him, he had cut his hair shorter and shorter and all he had now was a little cap of blond fuzz. Which, with his long skinny neck, made him look like a duckling.

"That was quick," I said as I opened the door. "Did you get a taxi?"

"Taxi, schmaxi! The journey I've had – stop! I'll tell you later, I want to hear your hot news."

Dennis sometimes overdid his flamboyant homosexual act but I was too grateful to have someone to talk to, to tell him to stop. I braced myself for him to say something vulgar. He always did. And he didn't disappoint me.

"Christ," he declared, rubbing his backside. "My ring is on fire!"

I ignored it because I didn't want to talk about him. I wanted to talk about Gus.

Then he inspected my appearance and I passed, with a couple of recommendations. He demanded tea and complained about the pattern on the mug. "A cat, a CAT! – Really, Lucy, I don't know how you can live like this."

There were only about four things in Dennis's flat, but they were really beautiful and expensive.

"You're my para-girlfriend squad," I told him as we sat down.

"What's that?"

"In an emergency, when I need to girltalk and there's no girls available, you rush to my side," I explained. "I have visions of you pulling on a uniform and sliding down a pole."

He blushed so red his face was darker than his bleached hair.

"Do you mind?" he said haughtily. "My private life is my own affair."

"Assume gossiping positions," I said so we both sat on the sofa, facing each other.

I told him about going to the fortune-teller. "You should have told me," he grumbled. "I would have liked to come."

"Sorry." I quickly moved on to the awful rumour at work that I was getting married.

"Honestly, Dennis, I was *miserable*. Apart from the humiliation and all that, it made me feel so lonely. Like I really would never get married."

"I really will never get married," said Dennis. "I won't be *permitted* to." He sort of spat when he said "permitted".

"Sorry, that was very insensitive of me," I said hurriedly. I didn't want Dennis to start going on and on about gay men being discriminated against and how they should be allowed to get married just like "breeders", as he insisted on calling heterosexuals.

"It made me feel old and left on the shelf, empty and pathetic. You know?"

"Ooooh, I do, my dear." He pursed his lips.

"Dennis, *please* don't go all poofy on me."

"What do you mean?"

"Don't call me 'my dear'," I begged. "It's so affected. You're Irish and don't ever forget it."

"Fuck off with yourself, so."

245

"That's more like it, now where was I? Oh, yes, I can't believe that so much changed in twenty-four hours."

"It's always darkest just before the dawn," said Dennis sagely. "So you met this man on Saturday night?"

"Yes."

"He *must* be the one that was predicted for you," said Dennis, telling me exactly what I wanted to hear.

"I think he might be," I said shamefacedly. "I know I shouldn't believe it, and please don't tell anyone that I do, but wouldn't it be nice to think so?"

"Can I be your bridesmaid?"

"Of course."

"Except I can't POSSIBLY wear pink, it makes me look like DEATH!"

"Fine, fine, have whatever colour you like." I wasn't interested in anything except keeping the discussion centred directly on Gus. "Oh Dennis, he's exactly what I want, he's so me. If I'd gone to God and described my perfect man, and God had been in a good mood, he would have given me Gus."

"Really? That good?"

"Yes. Dennis, I'm a bit ashamed to think this way, but he's too good for it just to be random. The fortune-teller must have been for real. I feel like it was meant to happen."

"This is fabulous," said Dennis, all excited.

"And I feel different about my whole life, my past," I said, waxing philosophical. "All those awful people that I went out with in the past were for a reason. You know the way I always seemed to lurch and drift from one awful relationship to the next?"

"Yes, only too well."

"Well, sorry about that, but it won't happen again. But, you see Dennis, all the time I had been moving one step closer to Gus. All those wasted years when I felt as if I was wandering in the wilderness, I had actually been on the right path."

"Do you think it's the same for me?" he asked hopefully.

"I'm *sure* of it."

"I have been led safely through the Minefield of Wrong Men," I went on, getting carried away, "sustaining mere flesh wounds, and I've reached the clearing on the other side and there, waiting for me, was Gus."

"Oh, Dennis, if only I had *known* that there would be an end to my loneliness."

"If only we both had known," said Dennis, no doubt thinking of all the nights spent listening to me going on and on.

"I should have had faith."

"You should have listened to *me*."

"We just have no idea what is out there for us, what life is leading us to," I said, getting misty-eyed. "I used to think that I was master of my own destiny, captain of my own ship. In fact, Dennis, I suspected that that was why my life was such a shambles – because I had had a hand in it . . ."

"Right, that's enough of that," said Dennis impatiently. "Knock off the philosophy, I see what you're getting at, but tell me about *him*. I want exact measurements!"

"Oh, Dennis, he's great, really great, everything about him feels right. I feel that this is a good one."

"Details," he said impatiently. "Has he muscles?"

"Well, sort of . . ."

"That means he hasn't."

"No, Dennis, really, he is quite muscly."

"Is he tall?"

"No."

"What do you mean 'no'?"

"I mean he's not tall."

"You mean he's short."

"OK, Dennis, he's short. But so am I," I added hurriedly.

"Lucy, you always had rotten taste in men."

"That's rich," I said. "Coming from the man who fancies Michael Flatley."

Dennis hung his head in shame.

"The man who has watched the *Riverdance* video a hundred times," I taunted.

One night when he was drunk, Dennis had told me that.

He regretted it bitterly.

"It's a big world," he said humbly. "There's room for all kinds of taste."

"*Exactly,*" I said. "So Gus might be short . . ."

"He *is* short."

" . . . but he's really good-looking and he has a lovely body and . . ."

"Does he work out?" asked Dennis hopefully.

"Somehow I'd say he doesn't." I was sorry to disappoint Dennis, but I couldn't lie to him. Anyway he'd notice when he met Gus.

"Does that mean that he drinks a lot?"

"It means he's a party animal."

"I see. He drinks a lot."

"Oh, Dennis, stop being so negative." I rolled my eyes in exasperation. "Wait until you meet him – you'll love him, honestly! He's wonderful, so funny and charming and intelligent and nice, and I swear to God, *really* sexy. And he mightn't be your type, but I think he's perfect!"

"So what's the catch?"

"What do you mean?"

"Well, there's always a catch, isn't there?"

"Get lost," I said, "I know I haven't exactly been lucky but . . ."

"I don't just mean with *your* men," he sighed. "With *every* man. Nobody knows that more than me."

"Dennis," I said. "I don't think there is a catch."

"Trust me," he said. "There's a catch. Is he rich?"

"No."

"Is he actively poor?"

"Well, he's on the dole . . ."

"Oh, Lucy, not again! Why do you always pick these paupers that have horrible clothes?"

"Because I'm not shallow like you. You're far too concerned with boys' clothes and the way they cut their hair and the watch they have."

"Maybe I am," he said huffily. "But you're not concerned enough!"

"Anyway," I said. "I don't pick them, it just happens."

"I bet if you lived in California, you wouldn't get away with saying that. But never mind – so how come he's on the dole?"

"It's not what you think," I explained eagerly. "It's

not as if he's a layabout or work-shy or any of the things my mother would call him. He's a musician and work is hard to come by."

"A musician – again?"

"Yes, but this one's different, and I have the utmost respect for anyone willing to endure financial hardship for the sake of his art."

"I know."

"And I'd happily give up my own nine-to-five drudgery except that I'm not talented at anything."

"But don't you mind being with someone who never has any money? And don't give me that line about love will conquer all, and that other things are more important. Let's be practical here."

"I don't mind at all. It's just that I'm not sure I have enough money to keep both of us in the manner to which Gus seems to be accustomed." I felt awkward about admitting this.

"What manner is that? Does he take cocaine?"

"No." Then I thought about it. "Well, maybe he does, actually."

"You'll have to get an evening job, in fact, you'll have to go on the *game* if that's the manner to which he's accustomed."

"Shut up, I'm trying to tell you, earlier this evening, Gus and I went for a pizza, at Pizza My Mind . . ."

"But it's Sunday – why didn't you go to the Cash'n'Curry?"

"Because Daniel and Karen went there and they were looking deeply in love and I didn't want to disturb them."

"Daniel and KAREN?!" shrieked Dennis, blanching. "Karen and DANIEL?"

"Er, yes." I had forgotten that Dennis had a crush on Daniel. "Karen, from here? Karen McHaggis, or whatever her tartany, Caledonian name is." Dennis didn't like Karen. He'd like her even less now.

"Yes, that Karen."

"With Daniel, *my* Daniel?"

"If that's Daniel Watson you're talking about, then yes, *your* Daniel."

"Oh dear, that's upset me now." He looked very shaky. "I need a drink."

"There's a bottle of something over there."

"Where?"

"Over there, on the bookcase."

"You're such peasants, keeping your booze on your bookcase."

"Well, what can we do? We haven't any books, we have to keep something on it."

He rummaged around on the shelves, "I can't see it."

"I'm sure it was there earlier."

"It's not here now."

"Maybe Karen and Daniel drank it. Sorry, sorry!" I said hurriedly, as he winced again.

"You can take it from me, it won't last." His voice had a slight tremor. "He's gay, you know."

"But you say that about every man in the whole universe."

"Daniel really is. Sooner or later, he'll see the light. And when he does, *I'll* be there."

"Fine, fine, whatever you say." I didn't want to upset him, but really! Every gay man I knew insisted that every straight man they knew was really a closet gay.

Chapter Twenty-Nine

Dennis sat down again and placed his hand on his chest and breathed deeply for ages while I wriggled with impatience. Finally he said, "It's all right now, I'm over it."

"OK." I launched back into the story. "So at Pizza My Mind, Gus hadn't any money – well, obviously he hadn't, because he didn't have any last night or earlier today and even though he's a talented man, I don't think that alchemy is one of his particular gifts . . ."

"So you had to pay for the two of you."

"Yes, which is fine because it's extremely reasonable . . .

"And the waiter has a lovely bum . . ." Dennis was a gay man twenty-four hours a day, he never let up.

"Quite. But Gus drank about ten bottles of peroni and . . ."

"Ten bottles of peroni!"

"Relax," I said. "I've no problem with that in principle, especially because peroni is weak, but it has to be paid for."

"You don't feel like he's taking advantage of you, do you?" said Dennis, looking levelly at me.

The thought *had* crossed my mind earlier in the day while we were in the pub, and that upset me because I lived in fear of being thought an idiot, taken for a fool.

But I absolutely hated arguments about money. It reminded me of my childhood. Memories of my mother shouting at Dad, her face red and distorted. I would never behave like that.

"No, really, Dennis, because then he said some really lovely things in the restaurant."

"Ten peronis worth of loveliness?"

"Easily."

"Let's hear it."

"He took my hand," I said slowly, trying to build up effect, "and said, very seriously, 'I really appreciate this, Lucy'."

"And then he said, 'I hate not having money, Lucy,' and get this Dennis, *especially when I meet someone like you.*' What do you think of that, eh?"

"What did he mean?"

"He said that I was lovely, and should be taken to beautiful places and have beautiful things given to me."

"Except that you won't be getting them from him." Dennis could be very blunt.

"Shut up," I said. "He said that he'd love to wine and dine me and buy me flowers and chocolates and fur coats and fitted kitchens and electric carving knives and one of those small little Hoover things that does the couch and everything my heart desires."

"And what does your heart desire?" asked Dennis.

"It desires Gus."

"I don't think that's your heart we're talking about."

"You're so vulgar, do you ever think of anything but sex?"

"No. Then what did he say?"

"He said that the little Hoover things were great for getting fluff out of your coat pockets."

"He sounds like a sugar bowl short of a Fornasetti dinner service to me," snorted Dennis. "Carving knives and Hoovers and fur coats, honestly!"

But he didn't know the half of it and I felt reluctant to tell him. I didn't want negative comments, I wanted great rejoicing, to match my mood.

Because the conversation with Gus had got a little bit tangled after that.

"Do you like flowers?" he had asked.

And I had said, "Yes, Gus, they're lovely, but my life isn't incomplete without them."

Then he said, "And chocolate?"

"Yes, I like chocolate an awful lot, but I don't go short of it."

"Oh! Don't you?" Concern crossed his face, and he suddenly seemed to go into a deep slump.

"Well, what did I expect?" he said mournfully. "A beautiful woman like you. How could I have been so stupid to think that I might be the only man in your life?"

"Oh pride comes before a fall!" he said dramatically, while I stared at him, wondering what was going on *now*.

"I was warned, Lucy, I can't say I wasn't. Several

times, by well-meaning people. Watch that pride, Gus, they said. But would I listen? Oh no, oh no! I had to march on in there and think that a goddess like you would have time for the likes of me. When you must have enslaved suitors eating their hearts out just for a kind look from you."

"Gus, please stop. What are you talking about? No, it's OK," I said to the waiter who had come running when he heard Gus's outburst. "No, really, everything is fine, thanks."

"You might as well get me another one of these, while you're at it," said Gus waving a peroni bottle at the waiter. (That must have been his ninth.) "I'm talking about you, of course, Miss Lucy Goddess Sullivan – it *is* Miss, I presume . . . ?"

"Yes."

" . . . And the suitors that bring you the chocolate."

"Gus, I don't have suitors bringing me chocolate."

"But didn't you say . . . ?"

"I said that I don't go short of it. And I don't. But I buy it myself."

"Oh," he said slowly. "You buy it yourself. I see . . ."

"Good." I laughed. "I'm glad you see."

"An independent woman, Lucy. That's what you are. You don't want to be under an obligation to them, and you'd be right. To thine own self be true, as our friend Billy Shakespeare was forever telling me."

"Er, who don't I want to be under an obligation to?"

"The suitors."

255

"Gus, there aren't *any* suitors."

"No suitors?"

"No. Well not just at the moment." I didn't want him to think I was a total loser.

"Why not!!?"

"I don't know."

"But you're beautiful."

"Thank you."

"I never heard before that the English were a short-sighted race, but they must be. It's the only explanation I can come up with."

"Thank you."

"Stop saying 'thank you'. I mean it."

There was a pleased little pause where we sat smiling at each other, Gus's eyes slightly glazed over, probably from the excess of peronis.

There was no need to tell any of that to Dennis. I decided to pass over it and tell him the next good thing.

When Gus said, "Er, Lucy, can I ask you something?"

And I answered, "Of course."

"I couldn't help overhearing that you're currently without a suitor . . ."

"Yes."

" . . . So would I be right in thinking that there's a vacancy?"

"Yes, I suppose that's one way of putting it."

"I know that this is going to sound outrageously forward of me, but is there any chance at all that you might consider me for the position?"

And I looked at the red and white checked

tablecloth, too shy to meet his eyes and murmured "Yes".

Dennis was disappointed in me.

"Oh, Lucy." He sighed. "Haven't you listened to anything I've told you – you're not supposed to submit so easily. Make them work for it."

"No, Dennis," I explained firmly. "You've got to understand that I was afraid to play games with him – he was liable to get the wrong end of the stick even when I was being totally straightforward. Introducing manipulation and feminine wiles – saying 'no' when I meant 'maybe', saying 'maybe' when I meant 'yes' – could be the undoing of us."

"OK, if you insist. So what happened then?"

"He said, 'I'm also unattached romantically, are you finishing that pizza?'"

"The silver-tongued devil," muttered Dennis, clearly unimpressed.

"I was thrilled," I said.

"Isn't it going a bit far to be thrilled?" asked Dennis. "I mean, it was paid for, so someone might as well eat it but, really, Lucy, thrilled?"

I let it pass.

"And what's he like in the scratcher?" asked Dennis.

"I don't actually know."

"You wouldn't let him?"

"He didn't try."

"But you were together for nearly twenty-four hours. Aren't you worried?"

"No." I wasn't. Granted his restraint was unusual. But not unheard of.

257

"He's probably gay," said Dennis.

"He's not gay."

"But you don't seem upset that he didn't jump you?" said Dennis, sounding confused.

"That's because I'm not upset," I said. "I like men to take things *slowly*, men who want to get to know me before they sleep with me."

That really was true, it wasn't just bravado for Dennis's benefit – I was horrified by men who were up-front (as it were) about their need for sex, big grown-up men with huge sexual appetites. Men with come-to-bed eyes, men with big thighs and hairy chests and huge unshaven jaws, men who got erections six times an hour, men who smelt of sweat and salt and sex. Men who entered rooms by saying bodily, "Here's my hard-on, the rest of me will be along in about five minutes".

Pelvo-centric men put the fear of God in me.

Probably because I thought that they'd be very demanding and critical of my performance. These men could pick and choose from any woman they wanted so they'd be used to the best. If I clambered into their bed with no chest, no long legs, no tan, they'd be bitterly disappointed.

"What's the meaning of this?" they'd demand when I removed my clothes. "You're not like the one I shagged this afternoon. You're not a woman. Where are the tits?"

I hoped that, if a man got to know me before we went to bed together, I would have a better chance of him being nice and not laughing at me. That he would be more prepared to overlook my obvious physical shortcomings because I had a nice personality.

That's not to say that I *hadn't*, once or twice, slept with men I had just recently met. There were times when I felt that I had no choice. Times when I had liked a man and was afraid that, if I repulsed his sexual advances, he would run away and have nothing further to do with me. If Gus had insisted on sexual relations I probably would have complied. But I was a lot happier that he hadn't.

"You and your Catholic guilt," said Dennis, shaking his head sadly. I had to stop him before he launched an attack on the Catholic Church and the nuns and the Christian Brothers and how they damaged the psyche of every young boy or girl that came into contact with them, taking away their capacity for guilt-free sensuous pleasure. We could have been there all night.

"No, Dennis, it's not Catholic guilt that stops me from being promiscuous."

I suspected that if I had big bouncy breasts and long, slender, cellulite-free golden thighs I could have overlooked my Catholic guilt. I would probably have been a lot more likely to confidently hop into bed with total strangers. Maybe sex would have been an activity that I could just enjoy, instead of it mostly being an exercise in damage limitation, trying to act like I was enjoying myself while at the same time managing to hide a bum that was too big, a chest that was too small, thighs that were too . . . etc., etc.

"Well, if you're sure." Dennis still sounded a bit doubtful.

"Really, Dennis, I'm very sure."

"OK."

"So, all in all, to wrap up, to summarise, what do

you make of the whole thing?" I asked gleefully. "Doesn't he sound lovely?"

"Well, I don't think that it would be what I want . . ."

I mouthed "Michael Flatley" at him.

" . . . but," he said hurriedly. "He does sound cute. And if you will insist on choosing men that haven't any money, I hope you know what you're doing. I wouldn't recommend it but I seem to be talking to the wall."

"And isn't it amazing what the fortune-teller said?" I urged, steering him back onto the track of positive comment.

"I have to admit that the timing is spot-on," he agreed. "It must be a sign. I would normally advise caution, but this does seem to be written in the stars."

That was exactly what I wanted to be told.

"Apart from the money, is he nice to you?" asked Dennis.

"Very nice."

"OK. I'll have to see him before I can fully endorse him, but at the moment, you have my provisional blessing."

"Thank you."

"Right then, It's twelve-thirty, I'm off out."

"Are you going to take poppers and wear a check shirt and dance to The Pet Shop Boys?"

"God, Lucy." He was disgusted. "That's outrageous stereotyping."

"But are you?"

"Yes."

"Well, have a lovely time. I'm going to bed."

I went to sleep happy.

Chapter Thirty

Of course it was a different story the following morning when I woke up and realised that I was expected to get out of bed and go to work.

I felt like hiding, but then again it was Monday and it was hard to change the habit of a lifetime. Meeting a new bloke, even someone as lovely as Gus, couldn't transform me overnight into someone who bounded out of bed before the alarm went off, singing "I'm glad I didn't die in the night".

I pawed around until I found the snooze button, negotiating another five minutes of guilt-ridden dozing for myself. I would have given anything not to have had to get up. *Anything*.

Someone was in the bathroom, which was nice. There was no point in me getting up until it was free. A short reprieve.

Time for me to lie in bed, half asleep, idly contemplating the various suicide options available to me, because, naturally, they seemed a lot more inviting than getting the tube to work.

I had toyed with the idea of suicide several times – most weekday mornings actually – and a long time ago I had realised how *badly* the modern flat is equipped for the killing of oneself. Not a lemonade

261

bottle of paraquat, not a noose, not a farm implement anywhere.

But I shouldn't have been so negative – they do say where there's a will there's a way. But then again, if I hadn't been so negative, I wouldn't have wanted to kill myself and the whole discussion would be moot anyway.

I ran through the list of possibilities available to me.

I could have taken an overdose of paracetamol. But I was fairly sure that that didn't work, at least not for me, because a couple of times when I had a very bad hangover I had taken about twelve tablets and I didn't even feel sleepy, never mind dying.

The idea of being smothered with a pillow didn't seem to be too awful. Quite a nice, peaceful way to go, with the added advantage of not having to leave your bed to do it. But it was a little bit like synchronised swimming – rather pointless if you tried to do it on your own.

Just then I heard someone coming out of the bathroom and I stiffened with horror but, quick as a flash, someone else went in. I breathed out with relief – no need to get up just yet. Although I was living on borrowed time and I knew it.

But for the moment I could stay horizontal and contemplate doing myself in although I knew that I didn't really want to kill myself at all – the taking of one's own life is unnatural.

It is also an awful lot of trouble.

It was ironic, really – you want to die because you can't be bothered to go on living – but then you're expected to get all energetic and move furniture and stand on chairs and hoist ropes and do complicated knots and attach things to other things and kick stools from under you and mess around with hot baths and razor blades and extension leads and electrical appliances and weedkiller. Suicide was a complicated, demanding business, often involving visits to hardware shops.

And if you've managed to drag yourself from the bed and go down the road to the garden centre or the chemist, by then the worst is over and you might as well go to work.

No, I didn't want to kill myself. But it was a long way from not wanting to kill myself to actually *wanting* to get up. I may have won the battle, but there was, as yet, no sign of me winning the war.

Karen burst into the room. She looked chic and efficient and her make-up was perfect. The effect was a bit scary at that hour of the morning. Karen always looked *groomed* and her hair never went frizzy, not even when it rained. Some people are like that. But I wasn't one of them.

"Lucy, Lucy, Lucy, wake up," she ordered. "I want to talk about Daniel, has he ever been in love, I mean *really* in love?"

"Er . . ."

"Come on, you've known him for years."

"Well . . ."

"He hasn't really, has he?"

"But . . ."

"And wouldn't you say it's about time that he was?" she demanded.

"Yes," I said. It was easier to agree.

"Me too."

Karen slumped onto my bed. "Move over. I'm wrecked."

We lay in silence for a short time. We could hear Charlotte, in the bathroom, singing *Somewhere over the Rainbow*.

"That Simon bloke must have a big one," commented Karen.

I agreed.

"Oh, Lucy," she sighed dramatically. "I don't want to go to work."

"Me, either."

Then we played the Gas Explosion game.

"Wouldn't it be great if there was a gas explosion?" said Karen.

"Yes! Not a bad one but . . ."

"Well, bad enough to keep us at home . . ."

"But not bad enough to hurt anyone . . ."

"Exactly, but the house would collapse and we'd be stuck here for days with just the telly and the magazines and we'd have to eat all the stuff in the freezer and . . ."

Although the stuff in the freezer was nothing but a beautiful fantasy. We never had anything in it except a huge bag of peas that had been there when Karen moved into the flat four years before. Sometimes we bought big tubs of ice cream with the intention of having modest little amounts every so often and making it last for months, but they usually didn't even last the evening.

Sometimes, for variety, we played the Earthquake

game instead. We wished for an earthquake that had our flat at its epicentre. But we were always careful not to wish death or destruction on anyone other than ourselves. In fact, all we wished destruction on was the way out of our flat. Magazines, televisions, beds, sofas and food were miraculously saved.

Sometimes we used to wish for a broken leg or two, lured by the idea of several weeks solid, uninterrupted lying down. But the previous winter Charlotte had broken her little toe at her flamenco dancing class (at least that was the official story, the truth was that she had broken it jumping over a coffee table while under the considerable influence of alcohol) and she said the agony was beyond description. So we no longer wished for broken limbs, but sometimes we wished for a burst appendix.

"OK," said Karen with determination. "I'm going to work."

"The bastards," she added.

She left and Charlotte arrived.

"Lucy, I've brought you a cup of coffee."

"Oh, er, thanks," I said grumpily, dragging myself upright.

In her work clothes and without any make-up, Charlotte looked about twelve. Only her enormous chest gave it away.

"Hurry up," she said, "and we'll walk to the tube together. I need to talk to you."

"About what?" I asked warily, wondering if it might be about the pros and cons of the morning-after pill.

"You see," she said, looking miserable, "I slept with Simon yesterday and do you think I'm awful to sleep with two people in the one weekend?"

"Nooooo . . ." I said soothingly.

"I am, I know I am, but I didn't *mean* to, Lucy," she said anxiously. "Well I meant to when I did it, but I didn't ever decide to sleep with two people. How was I to know on Friday night that I'd meet Simon on Saturday night?"

"Exactly," I fervently agreed.

"It's awful, Lucy, I keep breaking my own rules," said poor Charlotte, intent on chastising herself. "I always said that I'd never, ever sleep with someone on the first night – not that I *did* sleep with Simon on the first night, because I waited until the following afternoon – and it was evening really. After six."

"That's fine then," I said.

"And it *was* lovely," she added.

"Good," I said encouragingly.

"But what about the other bloke, the Friday night one – God, I can't even remember his name – isn't that awful, Lucy? Imagine! I let someone see my bum and I can't even remember his name. Derek, I think it was Derek," she said, her face screwed up in concentration. "You saw him – did he look like a Derek to you?"

"Charlotte, please, stop being so hard on yourself. If you can't remember his name, you can't remember it. And does it really matter?"

"No, of course it doesn't really," she said, agitatedly. "Of course it doesn't. Or it might have been Geoff. Or Alex. Oh God! Come on, are you getting up?"

"Yes."

"Do you want me to iron something for you?"

"Yes, *please*."

"What?"

"Anything."

Charlotte left to get the iron and I dragged myself up to sit on the edge of my bed. Charlotte called to me from the kitchen, something about having read somewhere about an operation you can have in Japan where you can get your hymen sewn back up and thereby have your virginity restored to you, and did I think she could have it done.

Poor Charlotte. Poor all of us.

It was very nice and we were very grateful to get the beautifully wrapped (albeit reluctantly given) gift of sexual liberation, but who was the out-of-touch, aged great-aunt that gave us the hand-crocheted coordinating packages of guilt?

She wouldn't be getting a thank you card.

It was like being given a present of a beautiful, short, tight, sexy, shiny, red dress on the condition that you wear flat brown brogues and no make-up with it.

Giving with one hand and taking away with the other.

Work wasn't too awful. I certainly felt a lot better than when I had left on Friday.

Megan and Meredia were very contrite and sweet. They weren't speaking to each other, but that was nothing unusual. Except from time to time when Megan said casually to Meredia, "Would you like a biscuit, Eleanor?" or "Pass me the stapler, Fiona," and Meredia would hiss in reply, "My name is Meredia."

They were very nice to me. True, I was still getting the occasional amused look from some of the other employees but I no longer felt so raw and vulnerable and embarrassed. I could see things differently – I realised that everyone must think that Megan and Meredia were the daft ones, not me. After all they had started the stupid story.

And, of course, there had been one major change in my life since Friday. I had met Gus. Every time I thought of him I felt as though I'd been wrapped in a protective armour, that no one could now think of me as a sad pathetic loser because, well . . . I *wasn't*, was I?

It was kind of ironic that on Friday everyone had thought that I was getting married when I didn't even have a boyfriend and now, on Monday, when I had met someone very special, no one would dare to bring up the subject of marriage in my presence.

I was bursting to tell Meredia and Megan about Gus, but it was too soon to forgive them, so I had to keep my mouth shut until the correct annoyance time-span had been observed.

Another reason that I no longer felt the centre of attention at work was because I really wasn't – I was yesterday's news.

The story had broken about Hetty and the big crush that Poison Ivor had on her. Apparently he had gone out on Friday night and got plastered and told the entire company, from the managing director to the porters and everyone in between, that he was in love with Hetty and that he was distraught that she had left her husband, although strictly speaking he wasn't distraught that she had left her husband, he was only distraught that she hadn't left her husband for him.

As for Hetty, there was no word from her.

"Is Hetty coming in today, or is she still unwell?" I asked Ivor, all innocence. Hetty wasn't well – at least that was the pretence that we seemed to have decided to observe.

"I don't know," he said, his eyes watering. "But seeing as you're so concerned you can take over her work until she gets back," he hissed at me.

The bastard!

"Certainly, Mr Simmonds."

In your dreams, pal.

"What's happening with Hetty?" I asked Meredia and Megan when Ivor had gone into his own office and shut the door, doubtless to put his head down on his desk and sob like a child. "Have either of you heard from her?"

"Yes, yes, I have," said Meredia, eager for a chance to rebond with me. "I called round to her yesterday . . ."

"You *vulture*!" I exclaimed.

"Look, do you want to hear or don't you?" she asked sourly.

I wanted to hear.

" . . . and she doesn't seem at all happy."

"At all happy," repeated Meredia, heavily and gloomily, *thrilled* with the drama of it all.

The phone rang, interrupting her. She grabbed it and listened impatiently for a few moments, then she barked, "Yes, I see, but unfortunately our systems are down at present and I'm unable to check your account, but let me take down your number and I'll call you back. Um," she nodded, writing nothing down. "Yes, got that. I'll call you back as soon as I can." She slammed down the phone. "Christ! Bloody customers!"

"*Are* our systems down?" I asked.

"How should I know?" said Meredia, sounding surprised. "I haven't turned anything on yet. I wouldn't have thought so, though. Now, where was I? Oh yes, Hetty . . ."

We did that kind of thing a lot in the office. Sometimes we said our systems were down, sometimes we answered the phone and said that we were only the cleaner, sometimes we pretended that the line was very bad and that we couldn't hear the customers, sometimes we hung up and pretended that we'd been cut off, sometimes we pretended that we couldn't speak English very well ("I am not spigging Engrish"). Customers got very annoyed with us and often demanded to speak to our managers and when that happened we put them on "hold" for a few minutes and then we came back on the line, all unctuous and soothing, reassuring the furious customer that the offending employee was in the process of cleaning out her desk.

Meredia told me at length how miserable Hetty was, how thin and gaunt she looked.

"But she always looks thin and gaunt," I protested.

"No," she said, annoyed. "You can tell that she's suffering a great deal, that she's involved in a very traumatic . . . traumatic . . . er, trauma."

"I can't really see what she's miserable about," commented Megan. "She's got two men, instead of just one, willing to poke her. Two heads – and not just heads – are better than one, I always say."

"Oh, God, honestly!" spluttered Meredia in disgust. "How like you to reduce everything to . . . to . . . *base* animal lusts."

"There's a lot to be said for it, Gretel," said Megan vaguely, a secret little smile playing about her luscious, ripe mouth.

She murmured something else before gliding from the room. I think it might have been "threesome".

"My name is Meredia," Meredia roared after her.

"Stupid bitch," she muttered. "Now, where was I. Oh yes."

She cleared her throat.

"She's torn between two lovers." Meredia was passionate. "On the one hand there's Dick, dependable, reliable Dick, the father of her children. And on the other hand there's Roger, exciting, unpredictable, passionate . . ."

On and on she went until eventually it was lunchtime. Which of course was the time when I stopped work and left the office and went round the shops for an hour.

The fact that I hadn't actually started work yet wasn't of any real importance.

I went out to get Daniel a card and a birthday present, which was always a bit of an ordeal.

I never knew what to get him.

What do you buy for the man who has everything? I wondered. I could get him a book, I thought – but he already had one.

271

I must remember to tell him that, he'd enjoy it.

I always ended up getting him something awful and unimaginative like socks or a tie or hankies.

And it was made worse by the fact that he always got me something lovely and thoughtful. For my last birthday he gave a voucher for a day at the Sanctuary, which was total and absolute bliss. A guilt-free day, lying around by a pool, being massaged and pampered.

Anyhow, I got him a tie. I hadn't got him one of those for a couple of years, so I thought I might get away with it.

But I got him a nice card, a nice, funny, affectionate card and signed it "love, Lucy" and hoped that Karen wouldn't see it and accuse me of trying to get off with her bloke.

The wrapping paper cost nearly as much as the tie. It must have been made out of spun gold.

I did the wrapping of the tie in the office but I had to go back out to the post office to post the parcel. I *could* have put it through the office post but I would have liked Daniel's present to reach him sometime this century and the two Neanderthals that worked in the post room couldn't necessarily guarantee that. It's not that they weren't nice – they were very nice, in fact, their congratulations on my bogus marriage had been sincere and effusive – but they didn't seem too bright, somehow. Ready, willing, but not overly able, would be the best way to describe them.

Eventually five o'clock rolled around and, like a bullet departing the barrel of a gun, I left for home.

Chapter Thirty-One

I loved Monday evenings. I was still at that stage in my life when I thought that weekdays were for recovering from the weekend. I couldn't understand the rest of the world who seemed to be under the impression that it was the other way round.

Monday night was usually the only night in the week when Karen, Charlotte and I were all at home in the flat, worn out from the rigours of the preceding weekend.

On Tuesday night Charlotte had her flamenco dancing class. (Or her flamingo dancing, as she thought it was. No one had the heart to correct her.) A couple of us were often to be found missing in action on Wednesday night. And very often on Thursday night all of us would be out, in a warm-up session for the full-blown socialising that the weekend entailed, when we'd all be out, all of the time. (My depression, permitting, of course.)

Monday night was the night when we went to the supermarket and bought enough apples and grapes and low-fat yoghurts to last us the week. It was the night that we ate steamed vegetables and said that we really must cut out the pizzas, that we would never drink again, at least not until the following Saturday night.

(By Tuesday we were back on the supernoodles and wine, by Wednesday the ice cream and chocolate biscuits and a couple of pints at the local, by Thursday the drinking session after work and the Chinese takeaways and there was never any restraint to speak of between Friday and Sunday. Until Monday rolled around and we bought apples and grapes and low-fat yoghurts again.)

Charlotte was already in when I got home, taking things out of a Tesco bag and throwing out vast tracts, *acres,* of very-past-their-use-by-date, uneaten, low-fat yoghurts that were dancing jigs with each other in the fridge.

I put my Waitrose bag down next to her Tesco bag, so that they could chat to each other.

"Show me, show me, what did you get? Anything nice?" asked Charlotte.

"Apples . . ."

"Oh. Me too."

" . . . and grapes . . ."

"Me too."

" . . . and low-fat yoghurts . . ."

"Me too."

"So, no, sorry, nothing nice."

"Oh dear, but it's just as well because I'm going to eat sensibly from now on."

"Me too."

"And the less temptation the better."

"Exactly."

"Karen's gone up to the corner-shop. Let's hope she doesn't buy anything nice there."

"Mr Papadopoulos's?"

"Yes."

"She won't."

"Why not?"

"Because there isn't anything nice there to buy."

"I suppose you're right," said Charlotte. "Everything there looks a bit . . . well, dirty, doesn't it? Even nice things like the chocolate looks dodgy, like it's been there since before the war."

"Yes," I agreed. "We're very lucky, really. Can you imagine what we'd look like if we lived near a nice shop, that sold nice things."

"Huge," agreed Charlotte. "We'd be enormous."

"In fact, if you think about it," I said, "it's really one of the amenities of the flat. It should've been in the ad – 'three-bedroomed flat, fully furnished, zone two, close to tubes and buses, miles from a shop that sells undodgy chocolate'."

"Absolutely!" said Charlotte.

"Oh, here's Karen now."

Karen marched in with a face like thunder and banged her shopping down on the kitchen table. She was clearly annoyed.

"What's up Karen?" I asked.

"Look, who the hell put some pesetas in the kitty? I'm so embarrassed. Mr Papadopoulos thinks I tried to swizz him and you know what everyone says about Scottish people and money!"

"What do they say?" asked Charlotte. "Oh yes, that you're really mean. Well, you can see their poi . . ."

She stopped when she saw the expression on Karen's face.

"*Who* put them there?" she demanded. She could be very scary.

I toyed with the idea of lying and blaming, say,

Spotty Back, poor discarded Spotty Back, who had phoned on Sunday evening to speak to Charlotte, only to be told that there was no one of that name living here.

I thought about denying all knowledge.

"Er . . ."

And then thought better of it.

Karen would find out eventually. Karen would break me down. My guilty conscience would eat away at me until I confessed.

"Sorry, Karen, it was probably my fault . . . I didn't put them into the kitty *as such*, but it's my fault that they're in the house at all."

"But you haven't even been to Spain."

"I know, but Gus gave them to me and I didn't want to take them and I must have left them on the table and someone else must have put them in thinking that they were real money . . ."

"Oh well, if it was Gus, that's OK."

"Really?" chorused Charlotte and I, in surprise. Karen was rarely so compassionate and merciful.

"Yes, he's a sweetie. So cute. Mad as a brush, of course, but in such a cute way."

" . . . Elizabeth Ardent . . ." she chuckled to herself. "He makes me laugh."

Charlotte and I exchanged alarmed looks.

"But, don't you want to thump him?" I asked anxiously. "And make him go round to Mr Papadopoulos and explain that you're not a dishonest Scottish skinflint and . . ."

"No, no, no," she said, waving her hand dismissively.

I was touched by the change in Karen, she seemed so much less aggressive, so much *nicer.*

"No," she continued. "You'll do. You can go. You can go up to Mr Papadopoulos and apologise."

"Er . . ."

"But you needn't go straight away. Wait until you've had your dinner, but don't forget he closes at eight."

I stared at her, unable to figure out if she was serious or not. I had to be sure because I didn't want to go to all the trouble of feeling nervous, just to find out that I hadn't needed to.

"You are joking, aren't you?" I asked hopefully.

There was a tense little pause and then she said, "OK, I'm joking – I'd better be nice to you, what with you being Daniel's friend and all."

She gave me a charming, disarming, I'm-so-brazen-but-you-can't-help-liking-me-for-it grin, and I grinned weakly back.

I was all for plain speaking. Well, actually that's a complete lie, I thought it was one of the most overrated things I had ever heard of. But Karen behaved as if plain speaking was a great virtue, the kindest act she could do for you. Whereas I felt there were some things that didn't need to be said or shouldn't be said. And that sometimes people used "I'm just being honest" as an opportunity to be malicious. That they opened the nastiness floodgates, were viciously cruel, completely trashed a life and then absolved themselves with an innocent face and a plaintive, "But I was only being honest."

But I had no right to complain about these people

– Karen may have been too fond of confrontation, but I was phobically frightened of it.

"Just make sure you keep telling him what a fabulous person I am," she said. "And tell him that millions of blokes are in love with me."

"Er, right," I agreed.

"I'm steaming some broccoli," said Charlotte, turning the conversation to matters domestic. "Would either of you like some?"

"Well, I'm steaming some carrots," I said, "so would either of you like some of them?"

We hammered out a tripartite agreement concerning the equable sharing out of our steamed vegetable assets.

"Oh, Lucy," said Karen casually. Too casually. I braced myself. "Daniel rang."

"Oh, er, good . . . did he?"

Was that non-committal enough for her?

"For *me*," she said triumphantly. "He rang to talk to me."

"Great."

"Not you. Me."

"Great, Karen," I laughed. "So you two must be an item, then?"

"Certainly looks that way," she said smugly.

"Good for you."

"You'd better believe it."

We had our steamed vegetables, we watched the soaps and a harrowing documentary about natural childbirth that had us all squirming in our seats. Women with contorted faces, covered in sweat, panting and gasping and groaning.

And that was only me, Charlotte and Karen.

"Jesus," said Charlotte, staring at the screen transfixed, her face rigid with shock. "I'm never having a baby."

"Me neither," I agreed fervently, suddenly aware of all the advantages of *not* having a boyfriend.

"But you can have an epidural," said Karen. "And then you wouldn't feel anything."

"But it doesn't always work," I reminded her.

"Really? How would you know?" she demanded.

"She's right," said Charlotte. "My sister-in-law said that it didn't work for her and that she was in absolute *agony* and that they could hear her screams three streets away."

A good story, well told, but I wasn't sure whether to believe her because Charlotte was from Yorkshire where they seemed to thrive on stories of terrible pain.

Karen didn't look terribly convinced by Charlotte's bloodthirsty tale. The sheer force of Karen's will would ensure that her epidural would work, it wouldn't dare not to.

"What about gas and air?" I asked. "Isn't that supposed to help with the pain?"

"Gas and air!" snorted Charlotte scathingly. "Gas and air! As good as putting a sticking plaster on an amputated hand!"

"Oh dear," I said faintly. "Oh dear. Can we watch something else?"

At about nine-forty the short-term fix of the steamed vegetables wore off and real hunger kicked in.

Who would crack first?

The tension built and built until finally Charlotte

said casually, "Does anyone feel like coming for a walk?"

Karen and I breathed surreptitious sighs of gratitude.

"What kind of walk?" I asked carefully.

I wasn't signing up for anything that didn't involve food, but Charlotte didn't let me down.

"A walk to the chip-shop," she said shamefacedly.

"Charlotte!" chorused Karen and I in outrage. "For shame. What about all our good intentions?"

"But I'm hungry," she said in a little voice.

"Eat a carrot," said Karen.

"I'd rather eat nothing than eat a carrot," admitted Charlotte.

I knew how she felt. I'd have preferred to eat a piece of the mantelpiece than eat a carrot.

"Well," I sighed. "If you're really starving, I'll come with you." I was delighted. I was dying for chips.

"And," sighed Karen, as if it was a real hardship, "just to make you feel better you may as well buy me a bag of chips too."

"You mustn't if it's just to make me feel less guilty," said Charlotte sweetly. "Just because I've no willpower doesn't mean you have to break your diet."

"It's no bother," protested Karen.

"No honestly," insisted Charlotte. "There's really no need for you to have any. I can live with my guilt."

"Just shut up and buy me chips!" shouted Karen.

"Large or small?"

"Large! With curry sauce and a saveloy!"

Chapter Thirty-Two

Gus was taking me out on Tuesday after work. He had said so on Sunday night.

But spirits had been very high on Sunday night, particularly in Gus's blood to alcohol ratio, the ten minute walk from the pizza place to my flat took over half an hour because he was so skittish and playful and I was little bit concerned that he might have got the arrangements confused for Tuesday night.

I was afraid he might get the place wrong or the time wrong or even the day wrong.

Trying to finalise the details with Gus turned into a bit of a confused nightmare.

Because when he walked me home on Sunday night, he politely shook my hand and said, "Lucy, I'll see you tomorrow."

"No, Gus," I corrected gently. "You won't see me tomorrow. Tomorrow's Monday. You're meeting me on Tuesday."

"No, Lucy," he corrected back, just as gently. "When I go home tonight I'll make some, er . . . certain pharmaceutical arrangements and when I wake up it'll be Tuesday. So to all intents and purposes, Lucy Sullivan, I'll see you tomorrow. At least I'll see you on *my* tomorrow."

"Oh, I see," I said doubtfully. "Where will I meet you?"

"I'll collect you from work, Lucy. I'll rescue you from the administration mines, from down Credit Control pit."

"Good."

"Remind me again," he said, holding my upper arms and pulling me to him, "it's 54 Cavendish Crescent and you're liberated at five-thirty?"

He gave me a sweet, slightly unfocused grin.

"No, Gus, it's not Cavendish Crescent, it's Newcastle Square, and it's number 6," I told him.

In fact I had told him several times and even written it down on a post-it for him, but it had been a long day and he had had an awful lot to drink.

"Oh really?" asked Gus. "I wonder why I thought it was Cavendish Crescent? What goes on there, would you say?"

"No idea, Gus," I said briskly. I was *not* going to indulge in conjecture about what went on in 54 Cavendish Crescent, if indeed such a place existed – I was busy, hanging on by my fingertips to control the conversation, trying to ensure that Gus knew where, when and how to meet me.

"Where's the piece of paper I gave you with the address on it?" I asked, aware that I sounded like a mother or a schoolteacher, but if it had to be done, then it had to be done.

"I don't know," he said, letting go of my arms and feeling around in his pockets and patting his jacket. "Oh no, Lucy, I think I've lost it."

I wrote it out for him again.

"Try and remember," I smiled nervously, handing him the piece of paper. "It's 6 Newcastle Square, at five o'clock."

"*Five* o'clock? I thought you said five-thirty."

"No, Gus, five o'clock."

"Sorry, Lucy, I can never remember anything. I'd forget my own name – in fact I often do. Many's the conversation I've had where I've had to say to the other person, 'Sorry, I didn't catch my name'. I've a head like a . . . like a, you know, one of those round things, lots of holes in it?"

"Sieve." Anxiety made me abrupt.

"Oh Lucy, don't be cross." He laughed softly. "It was only a wee joke."

"OK."

"I think I've got it right finally," he promised, giving me a slow smile that made my stomach flip. "It's five o'clock at 56 Newcastle Crescent . . ."

" . . . No, Gus . . ."

" . . . no, no, no, sorry, Cavendish Square . . ."

It wasn't his fault, I thought, trying to calm myself. In a way it was very sweet. And anyone would be confused and mixed up if they had drunk as much as Gus had.

" . . . no, no, no, don't be cross with me Lucy, 56 Newcastle Square, at five o'clock."

"Six."

Confusion passed over his harassed face.

"You just said five o'clock!" he complained. "But it's no problem, Lucy, isn't it a woman's prerogative to change her mind, so change it if you must."

"No, Gus, I haven't changed my mind. I meant five o'clock, at number six."

"OK, I have it now, I think," he smiled. "Five o'clock at number six. Five o'clock at number six. Five o'clock at number six."

"I'll see you then, Gus."

"Not six o'clock at number five?" he asked.

"No!" I said in alarm, "Oh I see, you're only joking . . ."

He raised a hand in farewell to me and said, parrot-like, "Five o'clock at number six, five o'clock at number six, sorry, Lucy, but I can't stop to say goodbye to you because I'll forget five o'clock at number six, five o'clock at number six, but I'll see you then, five o'clo . . ."

And off he went up the road still saying " . . . at number six, five o'clock at number six . . ."

I stood in the gateway, staring up the dark road after him. I was disappointed that he hadn't tried to kiss me. Never mind, I told myself. It was far more important that he remembered where he was supposed to be meeting me on Tuesday. Assuming he made it to the correct building on the right day at the appointed time, there would be plenty of time for kissing then.

" . . . five o'clock at number six, five o'clock at number six . . ." floated back to me on the cold night air, as he marched in time to his mantra.

I shivered, partly from the cold, partly from delight and went inside.

So the anxiety I felt on Tuesday morning was as much fear that he wouldn't turn up at all as pleasurable anticipation.

I was sure he liked me and that he wouldn't deliberately stand me up, but I wasn't at all convinced that he hadn't been too drunk on Sunday night to forget the arrangement entirely.

Nevertheless, I put on a very nice pair of knickers, because it was always better to be prepared. I tried on my green little thing that looked like a jacket with a nipped-in waist but was really a very short flared dress and then I pulled on my boots. I admired myself in the mirror. Not bad, at all, I thought. Very principal boyish.

Then a little thrill of panic ran through me – what if he didn't turn up? Oh, why couldn't I have got his phone number from him, I thought in anguish. I should have asked for it, but I was afraid if I did that I'd seem too keen.

And I knew I would arouse the suspicions of everyone at work that I was going out on a date that night by wearing something to the office where you could see my bum if I lifted my arms. They were like that at work – you couldn't even comb your hair without a rumour starting that you fancied someone, you couldn't get your fringe trimmed without everyone concluding that you had some new bloke.

There were 300 employees spread across five floors of office space and they all had a keen interest in the affairs of their co-workers. It said a lot about how interesting they found their workloads.

It was like working in a goldfish bowl. Nothing happened that didn't cause some comment. Even speculation about the fillings of people's sandwiches could take up the best part of an afternoon. ("She never used to eat egg sandwiches, it was always ham. And she's had egg twice this week. I'd say she's pregnant.")

Caroline, the receptionist, was the source of most of the gossip. She had a gimlet eye, she missed *nothing* and, if there was nothing to miss, she just made it up. She was always stopping people and saying things like "Ooh, that Jackie from accounts is looking a bit peaky today. Romantic trouble, eh?" And before you knew it the entire building would be buzzing with the rumour that Jackie was getting divorced. And all because she had got up too late that morning to apply her foundation before coming to work.

So I could hardly bear to think of the utter humiliation of spending the day avoiding doing my office chores half-naked and then no man turning up at five o'clock to account for it.

I *could* have brought my going-out clothes into the office in a separate bag and changed after work, but that would probably have created even more of a scandal. ("Did you see that Lucy Sullivan? Coming in with an overnight bag? On a Tuesday? She's on a promise, no doubt about it.")

As it was, there was utter mayhem in the office when I unwrapped myself from my horrible brown winter coat and revealed myself in all my short-skirted glory.

"Jeez," declared Megan, "you're looking a bit breezy today!"

"Who is he?" demanded Meredia.

"Er . . ." I blushed. I tried to pretend that I didn't

know what they were talking about, but it was no good. I was a hopeless liar.

"I, er, met a bloke at the weekend."

Meredia and Megan threw each other triumphant looks. Smug, "I knew this was going to happen" kind of looks.

"Well, we can see that," said Meredia scornfully. "And you're meeting him this evening . . ."

"Yes." Well, I certainly *hoped* that I would be.

"So tell us about him."

I hesitated for a moment. I was still supposed to be cross with the two of them, but the desire to talk about Gus was overwhelming.

"OK." I smiled, giving in. I pulled up a chair to Megan's desk, settling in for a long one and off I went with Gus's resume. "Well his name is Gus and he's twenty-fo . . ."

Megan and Meredia listened intently and oohed and aahed appreciatively and squirmed with delight when they heard of the nice things Gus had said to me.

" . . . And he said he'd like to give you one of those little Hoover things for the couch?" asked Meredia impressed.

"Yes, isn't that so sweet?"

"Christ," muttered Megan, throwing her eyes to heaven. "Never mind that. What kind of knob has he? Short and fat? Long and skinny? Or my own personal favourite, long and fat?"

"Er, um . . . it was nice," I said vaguely.

Before I was forced to admit that I hadn't actually seen it yet, Poison Ivor marched in and caught us sitting round doing nothing. He shouted a bit and we all slunk shamefacedly back to our desks.

"Miss Sullivan," he barked, "you appear to have forgotten the bottom half of your suit this morning."

Heartbreak was turning him mean and ugly. Not that he hadn't been mean and ugly before Hetty ran off with her brother-in-law.

"It's a dress, actually," I said brazenly, Gus-induced happiness making me bold.

"Not the kind of dress that I'm familiar with," he shouted. "Not the kind of dress that I want in this office. Wear something decent tomorrow." And he slammed into his office and banged the door.

"Prick," I muttered.

Chapter Thirty-Three

At about twenty to five, I departed the office to go to the Ladies to apply my make-up in anticipation of Gus's estimated time of arrival of seventeen hundred hours.

I was almost sick with anxiety. Almost as soon as I had finished telling Meredia and Megan about Gus, I regretted ever opening my mouth. I was so, so sorry that I had spilt the Gus beans, if only I had kept my runaway mouth shut, but I hadn't been able to help myself.

I had been dying to boast about him, but now I was sure I had jinxed the whole thing. By talking about him I had tempted fate and he wasn't going to arrive.

I'll never see him again, I thought.

But I'll put my make-up on just in case.

On the way to the Ladies I saw a couple of the porters out by the front desk tussling with someone. Winos and down-and-outs were always trying to come into the building out of the cold, and the porters had the unpleasant task of having to eject them. The saddest thing of all was that I often *envied* the down-and-outs. If I had had a choice between sitting in my office and sitting on some cardboard in a freezing doorway, I think I'd have chosen the freezing doorway option.

The porters were supposed to police the building, only admitting people who were expected and who signed in and got a visitor's pass. But the poor porters weren't proper security guards and weren't great at defending themselves and occasionally, when they tried to throw someone out, it could turn nasty, usually if the trespasser was drunk.

That was always good fun and, if Caroline was in a good mood with us she would ring our office and we would all rush up to have a ring-side view.

I craned my neck to get a good look. A foreign body was frogmarched to the door but he was putting up a good fight, struggling hard, and I smiled as I saw him kick Harry. I always sympathised with the underdog.

I turned away, thinking vaguely that there was something very *familiar* about the intruder who was being ejected when I suddenly heard my name being called. "There she is, Lucy Sullivan, Lucy, Lucy, Lucy!"

"Lucy, Lucy," called the voice frantically. "Tell them who I am."

I slowly turned around, with a horrible feeling of impending doom.

It was Gus. The struggling, flailing, kicking person in the arms of Harry and Winston was Gus.

He twisted around and turned wild eyes upon me. "Lucy," he beseeched, "save me."

Harry and Winston paused, poised on the brink of flinging Gus bodily into the street. "Do you know this man?" asked Winston disbelievingly.

"Yes, I do," I said calmly. "Perhaps you could tell me what's going on here."

I was trying to speak with quiet authority, trying not to show that I was *dying* with embarrassment and it seemed to work.

"We found him on the fourth floor and he didn't have a pass and . . ."

The fourth floor, I thought in shock

"I was looking for you, Lucy," declared Gus passionately. "I had every right to be there."

"No you bloody well did not, sunshine," said Harry threateningly. You could tell he was itching to pull Gus along by the ear, to treat him like an urchin chimney-sweep from a Dickens's novel. "Up on the fourth floor, 'e was, no less. Acting like he owned the bloomin' place, sitting in Mr Balfour's chair, 'e was. I've worked here man and boy for thirty-eight years and it's the first time . . ."

The fourth floor was where the high-ranking managerial staff had their quarters and it was treated with as much reverence as if it was heaven. The fourth floor was Wholesale Metals and Plastics version of the Oval Office.

I had never been there myself because I was far too insignificant, but Meredia had been hauled up there once for some offence or other and from what she said it was a cosseted wonderland of thick, beautiful carpets, thick, beautiful secretaries, mahogany panelling, works of art, leather chaises-longues, globes that opened out to be drinks cabinets and lots of fat, bald men taking Zantac.

Horrified though I was I had to marvel at Gus's

daring, but Harry and Winston seemed to be badly shaken by his profane, irreverent behaviour.

I decided I had better take charge.

"Thanks, guys," I said to the two porters, trying to make light of things. "But it's all right. I'll take care of this."

"But he still 'asn't got a pass," said Harry stubbornly. "You know the rules, love. No pass, no entry."

Harry was a nice man but he liked to do things by the book.

"OK," I sighed. "Gus, would you mind waiting over here by the front door for a little while and at five o'clock I'll come and get you."

"Where?"

"Just here," I said, gritting my teeth and steering him to the row of seats by the entrance.

"And I'll be all right here, will I, Lucy?" he asked anxiously. "They won't come and rough-house me again, will they?"

"Just sit there, Gus."

I went to the Ladies, burning with anger. I was furious. Furious with Gus for making a spectacle of me at work and even more furious that he had made the spectacle of me before I had put on my make-up.

"Fuckit!" I hissed, almost in tears I was so angry. I kicked the bin, my unmade-up face puce. "Fuckit, fuckit, fuckit!"

I could have died.

Caroline had witnessed the whole thing, so the entire building would know in five minutes. It was only a few days since I had last been a laughing stock in my workplace and I wasn't sure if I was ready for it to happen again. And worse than that Gus had seen me without my make-up.

I had known Gus was a little bit eccentric and I had liked it, but I wasn't at all happy about the scene I had just witnessed. My faith in Gus was shaken and it felt horrible. Could I be wrong about Gus? Was this relationship going to be another disaster? Was Gus more trouble than he was worth? Should I just get out now?

But I didn't want to feel that way about Gus.

Please God, don't let me become disillusioned with him. I couldn't bear it. I liked him so much and I had so much hope for us.

But a little voice whispered to me that I could leave him sitting at the front door and do a runner out the back way. And the notion momentarily filled me with huge relief until I realised that he'd probably wait all night and then come back again the next morning and wait for all eternity until I eventually showed up.

What should I do? I wondered.

I decided to brazen things out.

I would go up to the front door and be nice to him and act like he had done nothing wrong.

By the time I applied my fourth and final coat of mascara I had calmed down considerably.

There is obviously something very soothing about putting on lipstick and foundation and eyeliner.

Teething troubles, that's all Gus and I were having. First night nerves.

I reminded myself of Saturday night and the joy I

had felt at meeting him. I reminded myself of the lovely day we had had on Sunday, how we had so much in common, how he was everything I had ever wanted, how he made me laugh, how he seemed to understand me.

How could I possibly have considered abandoning him? I wondered.

Especially when, against all the odds, he had managed to arrive at the right time (roughly), on the right day in the right place. I started to feel compassionate and forgiving. Poor Gus, I thought. It wasn't his fault. He was like a child in his innocence – how was he to know about the rules and regulations of Wholesale Metals and Plastics?

The whole thing had probably been awful for him too. He must have had a terrible shock. Harry and Winston were big, burly men. Gus was probably terrified.

When I finally collected Gus not only was I a lot calmer but a change seemed to have come over him also. He seemed much more normal, more sensible, more grown-up, more in control.

He stood up as he saw me approaching.

I was aware of the shortness of my skirt and the interested glances I got from the other employees who were milling around in the hallway, pushing and shoving, trying to get out.

Gus's eyes briefly flickered appreciatively over me before he assumed a funereal expression, white, grim, anxious.

"Lucy," he said quietly, gently. "So you came back? I was afraid that you might escape out the back way."

"It did occur to me," I admitted.

"I can't say I blame you," he said, looking tense and miserable.

Then he cleared his throat and launched into a speech of apology, which he had obviously rehearsed while I was in the Ladies furiously applying layer after layer of make-up.

"Lucy, I can only apologise from the bottom of my heart," he said rapidly. "I had no intention of doing anything wrong and I hope you can find it in your heart to forgive me and . . .

On and on he went, saying that even if I forgave him, that he wasn't sure he could ever forgive himself etc., etc.

I waited for him to stop, for his apology to run its course. His self-denigration became more and more outrageous, his demeanour more and more abject, his expression just slightly too sheepish and humble. Suddenly the entire episode struck me as hilarious.

What the hell did it matter? I wondered, unable to stop a smile spreading across my face as I realised how *silly* the whole thing was.

"Here!" said Gus, suddenly pausing in his overblown prostration. "What's so funny?"

"Nothing." I laughed. "Just, you, you know, and the look on your face, like you were going off to be executed and Harry and Winston and the way they were acting like you were some sort of dangerous criminal and . . ."

"Well, it wasn't very funny for me, Lucy," said Gus huffily. "It was like *Midnight Express*. I thought I'd be thrown in the slammer and I feared for my bodily integrity."

"But Harry and Winston wouldn't hurt a fly," I reassured him.

"What Harry and Winston do with insects is no concern of mine," said Gus, all indignation. "Their private lives are their own affair, but, Lucy, I was sure they were going to kill me."

"But they didn't kill you, did they?" I asked nicely.

"No, I suppose not."

He suddenly relaxed.

"You're right." He grinned. "Jesus, I thought you were never going to speak to me again. I'm so embarrassed . . ."

"*You're* embarrassed . . ." I snorted.

Then I laughed and he laughed and I realised that this would be one of those little incidents that we would tell to our grandchildren. ("Grandad, Grandad, tell us about the day you got thrown out of Grandma's offices . . .") That this was history in the making.

"I hope I haven't got you into loads of trouble," said Gus anxiously. "There's no danger that you'll lose your job?"

"No," I said. "No danger."

"Are you sure?"

"I'm certain."

"How can you be so sure?"

"Because nothing nice ever happens to me."

We both laughed a bit at that.

"Come on." He smiled and put his arm around my waist and steered me down the steps. "Let me take you somewhere nice and spend lots of money on you."

Chapter Thirty-Four

It was a wonderful evening.

First he took me to a pub and bought me a drink. He even paid for it.

Then, when he was back from the bar and sitting next to me, he fished around in his bag and presented me with a small bunch of squashed flowers. But, squashed and all as they were, they looked as if they'd been bought in a shop and not nicked from someone's garden, so I was delighted.

"Thank you, Gus," I said. "They're beautiful."

Because they were in a kind of dishevelled way.

"But you shouldn't have," I protested. "There was no need."

"Of course I should have, Lucy," he insisted. "What else could I do? A wonderful woman like you?"

He smiled at me and he looked so handsome my heart flipped over. Happiness rushed through me and everything suddenly seemed right.

I was so *glad* that I hadn't given him the slip and escaped out the back way.

"And that's not all," continued Gus, putting his hand back into his bag and, like Santa Claus, pulling out a parcel wrapped in paper that had pictures of babies and nappies and storks on it.

"Oh God, sorry about the paper, Lucy," he said, looking at it in disappointment. "I didn't notice in the shop that it's wedding paper."

"Er . . . well, don't worry," I reassured him, tearing off the offending paper.

It was a box of chocolates.

"Thank you," I said, delighted, *thrilled* that he had gone to such trouble for me.

"And there's more," he announced, starting the fishing process again, his arm in his bag up to his shoulder. He reminded me of someone out of *It Shouldn't Happen to a Vet,* doing something to a cow.

If it's the small Hoover thing for the couch, I'll die laughing, I decided, absolutely charmed by Gus's thoughtful parade of presents, which he had based on our conversation in the pizza place on Sunday night.

He must like me, I thought. He must *really* like me to go to so much trouble. I was soaring with happiness.

Eventually he pulled out a small package, also wrapped in the stork paper.

It was about the size of a box of matches so it couldn't have been the small Hoover thing for the couch.

What a pity. Meredia would have been impressed, but never mind. So what was it, if it wasn't the small Hoover thing for the couch?

"I couldn't afford the entire coat in one go," he said, as if that was some kind of explanation. "So instead I'm buying it in instalments for you."

"Open it." He laughed, when I stared at him in confusion.

So I opened it and it was a little fur key-ring.

How sweet! Gus had remembered about the fur coat.

"May the furs be with you," he said. "I think it's mint."

"Or maybe you mean mink," I said nicely.

"Oh, maybe I do," he said. "Or it could be stable. But, Lucy, you're not to worry, I know how some people get upset about fur and the killing of animals and all that – I don't myself because I'm a country lad, but I know that others do – but no animals came a cropper to make this little key-ring for you."

"I see."

That would mean that it wasn't mink. Or mint. Or even stable. But it didn't matter. At least I would be safe from the animal rights activists and their buckets of red paint.

"Thank you very much, Gus," I said, slightly overwhelmed. "Thank you for all the lovely things you've given me."

"You're welcome, Lucy," he said.

Then he gave me a knowing wink. "And that mightn't be all you're getting – you mustn't forget that the night is still young," he grinned.

"Er, yes," I muttered, blushing.

Perhaps tonight would be the night, I thought, nervous excitement fluttering about in the pit of my stomach.

"And, tell me," I giggled, keen to change the subject, "what on earth were you doing sitting in Mr Balfour's chair?"

"Sitting in it, like the man said," said Gus. "Not desecrating a sacred shrine."

"But Mr Balfour is our managing director," I tried to explain.

"But so what?" said Gus. "It was only a chair, and Mr Balfour – whoever he is – is only a man. I really can't see what all the fuss was about. Isn't it well for them that that's all they have to worry themselves with?"

Gus was absolutely right, I thought. What a really great attitude he had.

"Send them two lads to Bosnia for a couple of weeks and we'll see how concerned they'll be about Mr Balfour's chair when they get back," he added. "And send Mr Balfour too while you're at it. Now, drink up your drink there, Lucy, till I take you somewhere and feed you."

"Oh, Gus, I can't let you spend all your giro on me," I wailed. "I couldn't. The guilt would kill me."

"Lucy, hush yourself, you're going to eat your dinner and I'm going to pay for it and let that be the end of it."

"No, Gus, I can't, really I can't. You've bought me all these presents and a drink, let me pay for the dinner, please."

"No, Lucy, I won't hear of it."

"I insist, Gus, I absolutely insist."

"Insist away, Lucy," said Gus. "But it won't do you any good."

"Shut up Gus," I said. "I'm paying and that's that."

"But Lucy . . ."

"No," I said. "I won't hear another word about it."

300

"Well, if you're sure," he said reluctantly.

"I'm sure," I said, firmly. "Where would you like to go?"

"Anywhere, really, Lucy. I'm easy to please. So long as it's food, I'm happy to eat it . . ."

"Good," I said, delighted, my head racing with the possibilities available to us. There was this brilliant Malaysian place down by . . .

" . . . especially pizzas, Lucy," continued Gus. "I'm fond of pizzas."

"Oh," I said, reeling my imagination back from south-east Asia. ("Come back, come back, there's been a change of plan.")

"OK, Gus, then a pizza it is."

It was one of those perfect nights. We fell over ourselves in our attempts to talk to each other, we had so much to tell each other about ourselves. Neither of us could get our words out quickly enough to keep pace with our enthusiasm and excitement.

Every second sentence was one of us saying, "*Exactly*, that's *exactly* what I think," and "I don't believe it – do you feel like that about it, too?" and "I couldn't agree more with you, I really couldn't."

Gus told me about his music, about all the instruments he could play, about the type of things he liked to write.

It was all wonderful. I know that we had talked a lot on Saturday night and we had spent all day Sunday together, but this was different. This was our first date.

We stayed in the restaurant for hours and hours and talked and held hands across the garlic bread.

We talked about ourselves as children, we talked about ourselves now, and I felt that no matter what I said to Gus, no matter what I told him about myself, that he would understand. Understand like no one else ever had, or could.

I allowed myself to daydream a little about what it would be like to be married to Gus. It wouldn't be the most conventional of marriages, but so what? The days of the little woman staying at home and doing the housework in a little cottage with roses round the door, while the man went out and toiled from dawn to dusk, were long gone.

Gus and I would be each other's best friends. I would encourage him in his music and I would work and support both of us and then, when he was discovered and was famous, he'd tell Oprah and Richard and Judy that he couldn't have done it without me and that he owed all his success to me.

Our house would be full of music and laughter and great conversation and everyone would envy us and say what a wonderful marriage we had. And, even when we were really rich, we would still take pleasure in the simple things in life and would each be the other's favourite person. Loads of interesting and talented people would drop round without being invited and I'd be able to throw together wonderful dinners for them, out of leftovers, while discussing the early films of Jim Jarmusch in a thought-provoking and incisive way.

Gus would be totally supportive of me and I wouldn't feel so . . . so *lacking* when I was married to him. I would feel whole and normal, as if I belonged just like everyone else.

Gus would never be tempted by the glamorous groupies that he might meet on tour because none of them would give him the same feeling of total love and security and belonging that he'd get from me. After the dinner Gus said, "Are you in a hurry to get home, Lucy, or would you like to go somewhere else?"

"I'm in no hurry," I said. I wasn't. I was, by then, *certain* that our relationship would be consummated later on that evening and, while I was delighted, I was also petrified; I wanted it, yet I was afraid of it.

Any delay of the moment of truth was something I rejected, yet welcomed.

"OK," said Gus, "I'd like to take you someplace."

"Where?"

"It's a surprise."

"Great."

"We'll have to get a bus, Lucy, do you mind?"

"Not at all."

We got the number 24 and Gus paid my fare. The proprietorialness of the gesture delighted me. It was such a sweet, teenagery thing to do.

When the bus reached the delights of Camden Town, Gus and I got off.

Gus held my hand and led me through the carpet of empty Special Brew cans and past the people, lying on cardboard, asleep in doorways, the young men and women sitting on the filthy street asking for any spare change. I was appalled – because I worked in central London, I knew about the homelessness problem in the city, but there were so *many* homeless people here that I felt as if I had stumbled into another world, a medieval world where people were forced to live in dirt and die from hunger.

Some of the people were drunk, but lots more of them weren't. Not that that was a yardstick.

"Stop, Gus!" I said, as I got my purse out of my bag.

The awful dilemma – should I give all my change to one person so that he could do something decent with it, like get something to eat or drink, or should I try and share it out amongst as many people as possible so that lots of people got 20p? But what can you do with 20p? I anguished, it wouldn't even buy a bar of chocolate.

I stood on the street, people passing and bumping into me, as I tried to make up my mind.

"What do you think I should do, Gus?" I beseeched.

"Actually, I think you should toughen up, Lucy," he said. "Learn to close your eyes to it. Even if you gave away every penny you have, it wouldn't make any difference."

He was right – every penny I had didn't exactly amount to very much, but that didn't matter.

"I can't close my eyes to it," I said. "At least let me give away my loose change."

"Well, give it all to one person then," said Gus.

"Do you think that's the right thing to do?"

"If you try to visit every down-and-out in Camden, sharing your money between them, the pub I'm taking you to will be closed by the time you finish, so, yes, I think that giving it all to one person is the right thing to do " he said good-humouredly.

"Gus! How can you be so heartless?" I exclaimed.

"Because I have to be, Lucy, we all have to be," he said.

"OK, who will I give it to then?"

"Anyone you like."

"Anyone?"_

"Well maybe not just anyone, it might be better if you gave it to someone who is actually skint and homeless – don't go accosting people in the wine bars or the restaurants, trying to get them to take your money."

"But I want to give it to the person who deserves it the most," I explained. "How will I know who that is?"

"You won't, Lucy."

"Oh."

"You're meant to be committing a selfless act of charity, Lucy. Not making a moral judgement."

"But, I'm not . . ."

"Aye, you are. You want to feel that you're getting value for your money by giving it to the person whom you think deserves it the most," he said. "Would you feel bad if your money went to a drunken, thieving, wife-beater?"

"Well, yes . . .

"Then you've got it all wrong, Lucy," said Gus. "The giving should be the important bit, not the receiving, or rather the receivee."

"Oh," I said faintly. Maybe he was right. I was humbled.

"Right," I said, making up my mind. "I'll give it to that bloke sitting down over there."

"Oh, no don't, Lucy," said Gus, pulling me back by my arm. "Not him. He's a right bastard."

I stared at Gus in annoyance for a moment and then the pair of us exploded with laughter.

"Are you joking?" I finally asked.

"No, Lucy," he laughed apologetically. "I'm not. Give your money to anyone in the whole of Camden, except him. Him and his brothers are a right crowd of shysters. *And* he's not even homeless – he has a council flat in Kentish Town."

"How do you know all this?" I asked, intrigued, but not certain whether to believe him.

"I just do," said Gus darkly.

"Well, what about that man over there?" indicating another poor unfortunate, sitting in a doorway.

"Work away."

"He's not a bastard?" I asked.

"Not that I know of."

"What about his brothers?"

"I've heard nothing but good things about them."

After I unloaded my pathetic handful of coins, I turned round and bumped into an older man who was lurching along the street.

"Oh hello, good evening to you," he said to me, in a very friendly way, as if we knew each other. He had an Irish accent.

"Hello." I smiled back.

"Do you know him?" asked Gus.

"No," I said doubtfully. "At least, I don't think so, but he said 'hello' so it was only polite to say 'hello' back."

Gus led me across the road and down a side street and into a brightly lit, warm, noisy pub.

It was completely packed with people, laughing and talking and drinking. Gus seemed to know absolutely everyone there. In a corner were three musicians, a man with a bodhrán, a woman with a tin whistle and someone of indeterminate sex playing a fiddle.

I recognised the tune – it was one of my dad's favourites. All around me were the sounds of Irish accents.

I felt as if I had come home.

"Sit here," said Gus, guiding me through the throngs of red-faced, happy people and indicating a barrel. "I'll be as quick as I can getting the drinks."

He was gone for ages, while I sat perched uncomfortably on the barrel, the rim of it gouging a furrow in my bum.

What time was it? I wondered. I was sure it was well past eleven, yet the barmen were still serving.

A thought suddenly struck me – could this be an illegal lock-in – the type my dad often waxed lyrical about?

Perhaps it was, I thought in excitement.

I didn't have a watch and neither did the woman beside me and neither did her friends, but one of them knew someone on the far side of the pub who had and she insisted on fighting her way through the throng to locate the person and ascertain the time for me.

She was back a while later.

"Twenty to twelve," she said, returning to her pint.

"Thanks," I said, a thrill of excitement running through me. So I had been right – this *was* a lock-in.

307

How wonderful.

Daring, decadent, dangerous.

Maybe it was wrong of Gus to bring me here and put me in danger of being arrested, but I didn't care.

I felt as if I was walking on the wild side, as if I was truly living.

Gus finally came back with the drinks.

"Sorry I was so long, Lucy," he apologised. "I ran into a crowd of Cavan men and . . ."

"Fine, fine," I interrupted, clambering down from the barrel. I was too eager to discuss our breaking of the law to be bothered with his apologies.

"Gus, aren't you worried about the police?" I breathed, my eyes round with delighted horror.

"No," he said. "I think they're well able to look after themselves."

"No," I giggled, "I mean, aren't you worried that they might arrest us?"

He felt around his jacket pockets, then sighed with relief and said, "No, Lucy, not at this particular moment, I'm not."

He wasn't taking me seriously and I was annoyed.

"No, Gus," I protested. "Aren't you afraid that they might raid here and beat us all up and arrest everyone?"

"But why would they do that?" asked Gus, puzzled. "Haven't they got plenty of people out on the street to arrest when they feel the need for a punch-bag? Weren't they given the Vagrancy Act specially for that reason?"

"But, Gus," I said in exasperation, "what if they hear the music? What if they realise that we're all in here drinking when it's way past eleven?"

"But we're not doing anything wrong," said Gus. "Although that's never stopped them in the past," he added.

"But we *are*," I insisted. "This is a lock-in. Closing time is eleven o'clock. We're breaking the law."

"No we're not." He laughed.

"Yes, we are."

"Lucy, Lucy, listen to me! This pub has a special licence until twelve. No one's doing anything wrong – apart from that gobshite of a barman who couldn't pull a pint to save his life!"

"Oh."

I was terribly disappointed.

"You mean this is all legal and above board?" I asked, subdued.

"Yes, Lucy, of course it is." He laughed. "You don't think I'd bring you somewhere where you might get into trouble, do you?"

"Well, er, you know . . . I just thought . . ."

At the end of the evening Gus came home with me. There was no question about it, no awkwardness, it seemed like the most natural thing in the world. Nothing was said, it just happened.

When we finally escaped from the pub and all the people Gus knew, we both just assumed that we would get a taxi back to Ladbroke Grove. And so we did.

Gus didn't suggest that we go back to his house and it never occurred to me to suggest it either.

I didn't think there was anything odd about that. Maybe I should have.

Chapter Thirty-Five

On Thursday there were two blots on my otherwise pristine landscape of happiness.

The news broke that Hetty had officially handed in her notice. And it made me sad. Not just because she was the only one of us who ever really did any work, but because I would miss her.

I hated change and I wondered with trepidation what we would get in her place.

Secondly, I had agreed to visit my mother on Thursday when I finished work.

I was at that phase of the relationship with Gus when my every waking thought was of him. I was delightfully happy nearly all of the time (except for the hours between seven-thirty and ten o'clock and even they had improved, especially if Gus was with me then, but more of that later). If I wasn't actually *with* Gus, I wanted to talk about him, to anyone, to everyone. To describe how gorgeous he looked, to tell how smooth his skin was or how sexy he smelt or how green his eyes were or how silky his hair was or how beautiful his accent was or how fascinating his conversation was, or how nice his teeth were for someone who'd been brought up on a remote farm, or how his bum was the size of a stamp. Or to recount, in great detail, stories of the nice things that he'd said and what he'd given to me.

I was buzzing with happiness and adrenaline and it never occurred to me that I might be the most boring person in the world.

I was delirious with happiness and loved everyone and felt that everyone else was as happy for me as I was.

Of course they weren't and they consoled themselves by saying to each other, "It'll never last," and "If I hear once more about how he opened her bra and took it off with his teeth, I'll scream."

Not, of course, that Gus did remove my bra with his teeth. Although we did indeed consummate our relationship on Tuesday night, *Nine and a half Weeks* it wasn't. Which was fine with me – being blindfolded and fed pickled onions wasn't my idea of pleasant sex. Because I had such an inferiority complex and wasn't very sexually confident, I liked straightforward carry-on in bed. Men who expected lots of different positions scared the lust out of me.

Even without the different positions I was still a bag of nerves when Gus and I got back to my flat. Luckily, I was a very drunk bag of nerves and that removed most of the potential awkwardness. In fact we were both roaring laughing, and fell into the bedroom straight away.

Gus pulled off his clothes at high speed and then jumped onto the bed with me.

I fully intended not to look at his erect penis – I thought I was far too shy. But, as though against my will, my eyes kept being drawn to it. And drawn to it. And drawn to it. I couldn't stop, I was mesmerised by it.

Very attractive it was too, for a six inch lump of throbbing, veiny purpleness. It never ceased to amaze me how something so intrinsically, well . . . weird looking, I suppose, could be so erotic.

Then it was my turn to disrobe.

"What's going on here?" Gus plucked at my clothes in mock alarm. "You're still dressed. Come on, get them off, quick, quick."

It was great fun, it reminded me of when I was a little girl being undressed by my mother.

"Legs out straight," he ordered, as he stood at the foot of the bed and held the toes of my tights and pulled. When I heard the sound of them ripping, all I could do was laugh and laugh.

"Arms up," he barked, as he tugged off my top. "Jesus! Where's your face gone?"

"In here." I muffled through my top. "You've to do the neck hole as well as the arm ones."

"Thank God for that – I thought I'd decapitated you with my passion."

I was undressed in record time, but, for once, I wasn't shy and embarrassed and ashamed of my body. There was no chance to be modest and coy because Gus was so matter-of-fact about it all.

"You're not a medical student, are you?" I asked suspiciously.

"No."

Of course he wasn't. I'd forgotten that medical students were the very ones to snigger uncontrollably every time they heard the word "bottom".

Gus didn't bother much with foreplay. Unless him asking me, "Are you on the jack and jill?" counted. He was really frenzied and keen to get stuck in straight away – an interestingly apt phrase. Of course, I was delighted with his enthusiasm, it showed that he really fancied me.

"You're not to come in three seconds," I admonished. And when he did come in three seconds, the pair of us fell about the bed laughing.

Then Gus practically fell asleep on top of me. But I wasn't disappointed or annoyed. I didn't scream at him and demand that he get it up again immediately and service me until I had had ten orgasms – as was my right as a nineties woman. I was relieved that he wasn't very sexually sophisticated, because it meant that there was nothing for me to live up to. For me, sex was more about warmth and affection than orgasms. And he was good at the warmth and affection bit.

With Gus, I had bypassed all that gentle, getting-to-know-you nonsense and gone straight for the falling-in-love jugular.

So I bitterly resented having to go and see my mother, and waste time that could have been better spent if not with Gus, at least telling people about him.

The only thing that made it remotely bearable was the fact that Daniel was coming with me. I couldn't talk about Gus while I was actually with my mother, but on the train journey both there and back I could bend Daniel's ear.

After work on Thursday I met Daniel and we caught the tube to the far reaches of the Piccadilly Line.

"I can think of far nicer things to do this evening than going hundreds of miles to see my mother," I muttered, as we stood swaying on a packed train, the air thick with the smell of damp overcoats, the floor awash with briefcases and Tesco bags. "Like mining salt in Siberia. Or licking the M6 clean."

"Don't forget your dad," reminded Daniel. "You're going to see your dad also. Doesn't that make you happy?"

"Well, yes, but I can't talk to him properly when she's around. And I hate leaving him, I feel so guilty."

"Oh, Lucy, you make life so difficult for yourself," sighed Daniel. "It doesn't have to be that bad, you know."

"I know," I smiled, "but maybe I enjoy it."

I didn't want Daniel to start counselling me, because I knew it wouldn't do any good, but he was the type of person who, once they got the bit between their teeth, wouldn't give up easily. And many a friendship has come aground on the rocks of misguided help.

"Maybe you do actually enjoy it," he admitted, looking a bit surprised at the discovery.

"Good." I smiled. "I'm glad we agree. Now I don't have to put up with you worrying about me."

When we came out of the tube it was dark and cold and there was a fifteen-minute walk to my house.

Daniel insisted on carrying my bag.

"My God, Lucy, this weighs a ton. What's in here?"

"A bottle of whiskey."

"Who's that for then?"

"Not for you anyway." I giggled.

"I might have known. You never give me anything except abuse."

"That's not true! Didn't I give you a lovely tie for your birthday?"

"Yes, you did, thank you. At least it was one step up from last year."

"What did I give you then?"

"Socks."

"Oh yes."

"You always get me 'Dad' presents."

"What do you mean?"

"You know – ties, socks, hankies – they're the type of thing everyone gives to their dad."

"I don't."

"Don't you? What do you give him?"

"Money, mostly. And sometimes a bottle of nice brandy."

"Oh."

"Anyway, this year I was going to get you something different. This year I was going to get you a book . . ."

"But I have one already, yes, I know, I know, Lucy," he interrupted briskly.

"Oh," I laughed. "Have I said that to you before?"

"You could say that, Lucy. Once or twice, maybe."

"Whoops, how embarrassing. Sorry."

"Sorry for what? Sorry for repeating your crappy joke for the hundredth time? Or sorry for calling me an uncultured philistine?"

"Palestine," I said vaguely.

"Filipino," he countered.

"Sorry for repeating my crappy joke – hey, it's not crappy anyway – for the hundredth time. I'm certainly not sorry for implying that you're not very bright. Look at the women you go out with!"

"Lucy!" he barked. I looked at him in alarm – he sounded like he was really annoyed. Then he laughed, shaking his head in disbelief.

"Lucy Sullivan, I let you away with so much, I really don't know why I haven't killed you before now."

"Actually, neither do I," I said thoughtfully. "I am very unkind to you. And the thing is I don't really mean it. I don't really think you're thick at all. I *do* think you have awful taste in women and I *do* think you treat them very badly, but apart from that you're quite all right really."

"Jesus, praise indeed," grinned Daniel. "Can I have that in writing?"

"No."

We marched on in silence, past rows and rows of boxy little suburban houses. It was freezing.

Daniel spoke after a while.

"So who's it for then?"

"Who's what for?"

"The whiskey. Who's it for?"

"Dad, of course. Who else?"

"Is he still on the sauce?"

"Daniel! Don't say it like that."

"Like what?"

"You're making it sound like he's a down-and-out or a wino or something awful."

"But it's just that Chris said he'd given up."

"Who, Dad?" I said scornfully. "Given up drinking? Don't be ridiculous. What would he want to do that for?"

"I don't know," said Daniel, ultra-mildly. "That's just what Chris told me. He must have got it wrong."

We trudged on in silence.

"So what did you get your mum?"

"Mum?" I asked in surprise. "Nothing."

"That's a bit mean."

"No, it's not. I never get her anything."

"Why not?"

"Because she works. She has money. Dad doesn't work, Dad doesn't have any money."

"So you wouldn't ever think of bringing her a little present?"

I stopped walking and stood in front of Daniel, forcing him to stop also.

"Look, you big crawler," I said angrily. "I get her presents on her birthday, at Christmas and on Mother's Day and that's enough for her. *You* might get *your* mother presents every time you see her, but I don't. Stop trying to make me feel like a bad daughter!"

"I only meant . . . oh never mind." He looked so woebegone that I couldn't stay angry with him.

"OK," I said, touching his arm, "if it makes you feel any better, I'll get her a cake when we get to the shops."

"Don't bother."

"Daniel! Why are you so sulky?"

"I'm not."

"Yes, you are. You said 'don't bother'."

"Yes," he laughed, sounding exasperated. "I said don't bother, because I've got a cake for her."

I tried to look disgusted.

"Daniel Watson, you are *such* a crawler."

"No, I'm not. It's good manners. Your mum is giving me my dinner, I'm just being polite."

"You might call it politeness. I call it crawlerness."

"OK, Lucy." He laughed. "Call it what you want."

We rounded the corner and I saw my house and my heart sank. I hated my house. I hated coming out here.

I thought of something.

"Daniel," I said urgently.

"What?"

"Mention Gus to my mother and you die."

"As if I would." He looked hurt.

"Good, I'm glad we understand each other."

"You don't think she'll be pleased then?" asked Daniel archly.

"Shut up."

Chapter Thirty-Six

I saw a curtain twitching in the front room. Mum had the front door open before we even had a chance to ring the bell.

For a moment I felt a little bit sad.

Hadn't she anything better to do? I wondered.

"Welcome, you're welcome!" she said gaily, all hospitality and bonhomie. "Come in out of the cold night. How are you, Daniel? Aren't you very good to come all this way to visit us? Are you perished?" she asked, grabbing Daniel's hands. "No, you're not too bad. Take off the coats and come on in, I've just made a pot."

"I didn't know you'd taken up pottery." Daniel smiled at Mum all twinkley and knowing.

"Stop!" She laughed with a girlish tinkle and rolled her eyes at him. "You're a terrible man."

I stuck my fingers down my throat and made gagging noises.

"Stop it," muttered Daniel.

"Why are you being mean to me?" I said in surprise. "You never usually are."

"Because sometimes you're childish and horrible."

That annoyed and upset me, so as we took off our coats in the tiny hall and left them on the bottom of the banisters, I mimicked "childish and horrible" about fifty times in a stupid voice.

Daniel looked at me with raised eyebrows but I knew he was trying not to laugh.

"If you say to me 'that's very mature behaviour', I'll thump you," I warned him.

"That's very mature behaviour."

So we had a little skirmish. I tried to hit him but he grabbed my wrists and held them tightly. And then he laughed at me while I pushed and twisted against him, trying to get free. But I couldn't budge, not even an inch, while he looked totally unconcerned and grinned down at me.

I was disturbed by his macho carry-on. In fact, if it had been anyone other than Daniel, it would have been quite erotic.

"You big bully." I knew that would upset him. I was right, he let go immediately. And then, perversely, I felt disappointed.

We went into the warm kitchen where Mum was messing around with biscuits and sugar and pints of milk.

Dad was in an armchair, snoring quietly, his hair white and wispy and sticking up from his head. I patted it down tenderly. His glasses were all askew and with a painful twist I realised that he was starting to look old. Not middle-aged or even elderly, but like a little old man.

"You'll be grand now when you have a nice warm cup inside you," Mum said. "Did you get a new skirt, Lucy?"

"No."

"Where's it from?"

"It's not new."

"I heard you the first time. Where's it from?"

"You won't know it."

"Try me – I'm not the old fuddy-duddy she thinks I am," she said, laughing girlishly at Daniel, shoving platefuls of biscuits across the table at him.

"Kookai," I said between gritted teeth.

"What kind of name for a shop is that, at all?" she asked, pretending to laugh.

"I told you you wouldn't know it."

"I don't. And I don't want to know it. What's it made of?" She grabbed the fabric.

"How do I know?" I said, annoyed, trying to pull my skirt back from her claw. "I buy things because I like them, not because of what they're made from."

"I'd say it's only synthetic," she said, rubbing it. "Look! Look at the way it balls!"

"Stop it."

"And the finish on it – a child could do that hem better. What did you say you paid for it?"

"I didn't."

"Well, how much did you pay for it?"

I wanted to say that I wasn't going to tell her, but I knew how childish that would sound.

"I can't remember."

"I'd say you can remember, all right. But you're too ashamed to tell me. Way over the odds, I bet. Much more than it's worth."

I said nothing.

"You were always hopeless with money, Lucy."

Still I said nothing.

"You know the old saying. A fool and their money are soon parted."

The three of us sat in silence, me sullenly refusing to drink my tea, because she had made it.

She always brought out the worst in me.

Daniel broke the tension by going out into the hall and coming back with the cake he had bought for her.

Naturally she was delighted and was all over him like a skin disease.

"Aren't you very good? There was no need for you to do that. Although it's a sorry state of affairs that my own flesh and blood brings me nothing."

"Oh, it's from the two of us, not just me," said Daniel quickly.

"Arselicker," I mouthed across the table at him.

"Oh," said Mum. "Well, thanks, Lucy. Except you know I've given up chocolate for Lent."

"But cake isn't chocolate," I said weakly.

"Chocolate cake is chocolate," she said.

"You could freeze it to have after Lent is over," I suggested.

"It'd never keep."

"It would."

"Anyway that would be contrary to the whole spirit of Lent."

"All right then! *Don't* eat it. Daniel and I will."

The offending cake sat in the middle of the table, it had suddenly become something frightening, like a bomb. If I hadn't known better I would have sworn that it was almost pulsating. I knew that it would never be eaten.

"What have you given up for Lent, Lucy?"

"Nothing!"

"I have enough misery in my life," I added cryptically, hoping that she would realise that I was talking about visiting her, "I don't need to give up anything."

And to my surprise she didn't retaliate. She looked at me, almost . . . *tenderly* . . . for a moment.

"I've made your favourite," she said.

"My favourite what?"

"Your favourite dinner!"

"Have you?"

I wasn't even aware that I had a favourite dinner. It would be interesting to see what crap she dished up.

But just to be mean I said, "Oh great, Mum. I didn't know you could cook Thai."

Mum made a kind of a "let's humour her" face at Daniel. "What's she talking about? Cooking ties? You were always a bit peculiar, Lucy, but just to please you we'll get a few of your father's old ties from upstairs."

"He won't be needing them," she added bitterly. "He hasn't worn a tie since his wedding day."

"Feck off," slurred a voice from the corner. "Didn't I wear a tie to Mattie Burke's funeral?"

Dad had opened his eyes and was looking confusedly round the room.

"Dad!" I said, delighted, "you're awake."

"Oh the dead arose and appeared to many," called Mum sarcastically as Dad struggled to sit up straight.

323

"They did not!" said Dad. "That wasn't Mattie Burke, that was Laurence Molloy. Did I ever tell you about that, Lucy? A great couple of days when Laurence Molloy pretended to be dead so we could have a right good oul' wake for ourselves. Except Laurence wasn't too happy when it dawned on him that he had to lie there, stretched out on some hard plank of wood, getting nothing to drink, save the fumes from our breath, so up he jumps out of the coffin and grabs a bottle out of someone's hand. 'Gimme that' he says . . ."

"Shut up, Jamsie," barked my mother. "We have a visitor and I'm sure he doesn't want to hear stories about your misspent youth."

"I wasn't telling him stories about my misspent youth," grumbled Dad. "Laurence Molloy's wake was only a couple of years ago . . . oh hello, son," he said, spotting Daniel, "I remember you. You used to come round to play with Christopher Patrick. A big, long, lanky article you were then, stand up till I see if you've got any shorter!"

Daniel stood up awkwardly, amid much scraping of chairs.

"Longer, if anything!" declared Dad, "and I wouldn't have thought it was possible."

Daniel gratefully sat down again.

"Lucy," said Dad turning his attention to me, "my darling girl, my little sweetheart, I didn't know you were coming."

"Why didn't you tell me she was coming?" he demanded of my mother.

"I did tell you."

"You did not tell me."

"I did tell you."

"You most certainly did not tell me!"

"I di . . . oh what's the use. I might as well be talking to the wall."

"Lucy," said Dad, "I'll go up and smarten myself up a bit and I'll be back before you know it, in two shakes of a lamb's rattle."

He shuffled out of the room and I smiled affectionately after him.

"He's looking great," I said.

"Is he?" said Mum coldly.

An awkward little pause followed.

"More tea?" Mum asked Daniel, following the great Irish tradition of filling any conversational gaps by pressing nourishment on people.

"Thanks."

"Another biscuit?"

"No thanks."

"A little piece of the cake?"

"No, really, I'd better not. I must leave room for my dinner."

"Go on, sure, you're a growing lad."

"No, honestly."

"Are you certain now?"

"Mum, leave him!" I laughed, remembering what Gus had said about Irish mothers. "So what *have* you made for our dinner?"

"Fish fingers, beans and chips."

"Er, nice one, Mum."

True, it had been my favourite dinner well over half a lifetime ago, until I moved up to London and became acquainted with such exotica as Tandoori supernoodles and Peking duck flavoured crisps.

"Great," grinned Daniel. "I love fish fingers, beans and chips."

He sounded as though he really meant it.

"You'd say that no matter what you were being given, wouldn't you, Dan?" I said. "Even if Mum said 'Oh Daniel, I thought we'd serve up your testicles in a white wine sauce' you'd say 'mmmmh, lovely, Mrs Sullivan, that sounds delicious'. Wouldn't you?"

I giggled at his horrified expression.

"Lucy," he winced, "you really must be more careful about saying that kind of thing."

"Sorry," I laughed. "I forgot I was talking about your most prized possessions. Where would Daniel Watson be without his genitalia? Your life would be over, wouldn't it?"

"No, Lucy, that's not why. Any man would find that suggestion upsetting, not just me."

My mother had finally found her voice.

"Lucy – Carmel – Sullivan!" she gasped, apoplectic with horror. "*What* on *earth* are you talking about?"

"Nothing, Mrs Sullivan," said Daniel hastily. "Nothing at all. Nothing, honestly."

"Nothing, Daniel? Well that's not what Karen says." I winked at him, while Daniel began a frenzied conversation with Mum. How was she? Was she working? What was it like in the dry-cleaners?

Mum's head jerked from me to Daniel and back again. She was torn between delight at being the centre of Daniel's attention and the suspicion that she was letting me get away with something totally heinous and unforgivable.

But her vanity won. Soon she was regaling Daniel with stories of the spoilt rich bastards whom she had to serve in the dry-cleaners, how they wanted everything done yesterday, how they never said thanks, how they parked their cars, "big flashy BMXs or BLTs or whatever they are," so that they blocked the traffic, how critical they were, "In fact only today one of them arrived in – a right young pup – and threw – yes! *threw* – a shirt at me and shoved it in my face and said 'what the hell have you done to this?' Well, Daniel, first and foremost there was no need to swear at me and I said as much to him and I looked at the shirt and there wasn't a speck on it . . ." and so on and so on.

Daniel had the patience of a saint. I was so glad he had come with me. I simply couldn't have borne it on my own.

" . . . and I said 'it's as white as snow' and he said 'exactly, it was blue when I brought it in' . . ."

On and on droned my mother. On and on smiled and nodded Daniel sympathetically. It was wonderful, I barely needed to be there, just the occasional nod or "mmm" was all my mother required from me. All her attention was focused on Daniel.

Finally, the dry-cleaning saga came to an end.

" . . . So he says to me 'see you in court' and I says to him 'see you in court yourself' and he says 'you'll be hearing from my solicitor' and I says 'well, I hope he can shout good and loud because I'm nearly deaf in one ear' . . ."

"And how are you, Daniel?" asked Mum finally.

"Fine, Mrs Sullivan, thanks."

"He's better than fine, aren't you, Daniel? Tell Mum about your new girlfriend."

I was delighted. I *knew* that that would upset her. She still held out hopes that I might somehow get Daniel to fall for me.

"Stop, Lucy," muttered Daniel, looking embarrassed.

"Oh, don't be shy, Daniel." I knew I was being annoying but I was enjoying it tremendously.

"Anyone we know?" asked Mum, hopefully.

"Yes," I said happily.

"Oh?" She was trying, rather badly, to hide her excitement.

"Yes, it's my flatmate Karen."

"Karen?"

"Yes."

"The Scottish one?"

"Yes. And they're mad about each other. Isn't it great?"

"Well, isn't it?" I asked again, when she didn't answer.

"I always thought she was a bit brassy . . ." said Mum and then clapped her hand over her mouth in pretend horror. "Oh, Daniel, can you believe I just said that? I'm so sorry. Sacred Heart of Jesus, how could I be so tactless? Would you ever please forget I said anything, Daniel – it was a long time ago when I saw her. I'm sure she's not half so common looking now."

"Consider it forgotten," said Daniel, smiling

slightly. He was so *good*. He should have just thumped the old cow and there wasn't a jury in the land that would have convicted him.

"Bad and all as Lucy is," my mother said, in a pretend vague fashion, as if she was just talking to herself, "at least she was never common looking. You'd never catch her going out with her bosom on display."

"That's because I haven't *got* a bosom to have on display. If I had you can be bloody sure that I'd display it."

"Language, Lucy," she said, hitting me on the arm.

"Language?" I spluttered. "You think *that's* language. I could show you language . . ."

I stopped and inwardly cursed Daniel for being there. I couldn't row with her properly while we had a visitor. Not that Daniel counted as a visitor, as such, but all the same.

"Excuse me a moment," I said and left the room. I got the bottle of whiskey from my bag in the hall and went upstairs. I wanted to get Dad on his own.

Chapter Thirty-Seven

He was in his bedroom, sitting on the bed, putting on his shoes.

"Lucy," he said. "I was just on my way back down to you."

"Let's just stay here a minute," I said, hugging him.

"Grand," he said. "We'll have a little chat all on our own."

I gave him the bottle of whiskey and he hugged me again. "You're very, very good to me, Lucy," he said.

"How are you, Dad?" I asked, tears in my eyes.

"Grand, Lucy, grand. Why the tears?"

"I hate to think of you stuck here, all on your own, with . . . with *her*," I said, nodding towards downstairs.

"But I'm fine, Lucy, so I am," he protested, laughing. "She's not the worst. We jog along together all right."

"I know you're only saying that so I won't worry about you," I sniffed, "but thanks."

"Oh, Lucy, Lucy, Lucy," he said, squeezing my hand, "you mustn't take it all so seriously. Try and enjoy yourself, because we'll be dead long enough."

"Oh no," I wailed and then I *really* started to cry. "Don't talk about dying. I don't want you to die. Promise me you won't die!"

"Er . . . well . . . if it makes you happy, I won't die, Lucy."

"And if you have to die, promise me that we can die at the same time."

"I promise."

"Oh Dad, isn't it awful?"

"What, love?"

"Everything. Being alive, loving people, being afraid that they'll die."

"Is it?"

"Yes, of course it is."

"Where did you ever get such terrible notions from, Lucy?"

"But . . . but . . . from *you*, Dad."

Dad hugged me awkwardly and said that I must have misheard him, that surely he never said anything of the sort and that I was young and had a life to live and that I should try and enjoy it.

"But why, Dad?" I asked, "you never tried to enjoy your life and it hasn't done you any harm."

"Lucy," he sighed, "it was different for me. It *is* different for me – I'm an old man now. You're a young woman. Young, beautiful, educated – never forget the benefits of an education, Lucy," he insisted fiercely.

"I won't."

"Promise me."

"I promise."

"You have all these things going for you so you should be happy."

"How can I be?" I pleaded. "And how can you expect me to be? We're the same, Dad, you and I. We can't help seeing the futility, the waste, the darkness when everyone else walks in the light."

"What is it, Lucy?" Dad searched my face for some sort of clue. "Is it a fella, is it? Some youngster is after leading you up the garden path? Is that what it is?"

"No, Dad," I laughed even though I was still crying.

"It's not that lanky article beyont in the kitchen, is it?"

"Wha . . . oh Daniel? No."

"He didn't, er, you know . . . take liberties with you, Lucy, did he? Because if he did, so help me God, as long as there's breath in my body, I'll get your two brothers to knock him into the middle of next week. A kick in the arse and a map of the world, that's what that fella needs and that's what that fella will get. He's a bigger fool than he looks if he thinks he can interfere with the daughter of Jamsie Sullivan and live to tell the tale . . ."

"Dad," I wailed. "Daniel hasn't done anything."

"I've seen the way he looks at you," Dad said darkly.

"He doesn't look at me *any* way. You're imagining things."

"Am I? Sure maybe I am. It wouldn't be the first time, I suppose."

"Dad, this isn't about a fella *at all*."

"But then why are you so lonesome?"

"Because I just am, Dad. The same way as you are."

"But I'm fine, Lucy, honest to God so I am. Never bebther."

"Thanks, Dad," I sighed leaning against him. "I know you're only saying it to make me feel better, but I appreciate it all the same."

"But . . . ," he said, looking a bit bewildered. He looked like he was searching for something to say, but couldn't think of anything.

"Come on," he said eventually, "till we go down for our chips."

Down we went.

The evening was rather grim what with my mother and I at loggerheads and Dad staring suspiciously at Daniel, convinced that he had improper motives concerning me.

Our spirits lifted slightly when dinner was banged down in front of us.

"A rhapsody in orange," declared Dad, looking at his plate. "That's what it is. Orange fish fingers, orange beans and orange chips and, to wash it all down, a glass of the finest Irish malt, which as luck would have it, also happens to be orange!"

"The chips aren't orange," said Mum. "And have you offered Daniel a drink?"

"They are *so* orange," protested Dad hotly. "And no I haven't."

"Daniel, would you like a drink?" asked Mum, standing up.

"Well, if they're not orange, what colour would you say they are?" demanded Dad of the table in general. "Pink? Green?"

"No thanks, Mrs Sullivan," said Daniel nervously. "I wouldn't like a drink."

"You're not getting one," said Dad belligerently. "Unless you say the chips are orange."

Mum and Dad stared at Daniel, both willing him to be on their side.

"They're more a kind of a golden colour," he finally suggested, ever the diplomat.

"They're orange!"

"Golden," said Mum.

Daniel said nothing. He just looked embarrassed.

"All right then." Dad roared and slammed his hand down on the table, causing all the plates and cutlery to jump and rattle.

"You drive a hard bargain. Goldeny orange, and that's my final offer. Take it or leave it. But you can't say I'm not a fair man. Give him a drink."

Dad cheered up again in no time. The dinner worked wonders on his lugubrious mood.

"There's only one thing to bate a fish finger," he said, delightedly, smiling around the table. "And that's six more of them."

"Look at that," he said admiringly, lifting the entire fish finger up onto his fork and twiddling it around so that he could view it from all angles. "Beautiful. That's craftsmanship, you know. You'd need a university schooling to know how to make one of these lads properly."

"Jamsie, stop making an exhibition piece of your dinner," Mum said, ruining the fun.

"I'd like to meet this Captain Birds eye character and shake him by the hand and congratulate him on a job well done," declared Dad, ignoring her. "So I would. Maybe they'll have him on *This is your Life*. What do you think, Lucy?"

"I don't think he's a real person, Dad," I giggled.

"Not real?" asked Dad. "But I've seen him on the telly. Great white whiskers on his face and he lives on a ship."

"But . . ."

I wasn't sure whether Dad was joking or not. I thought he was – I certainly hoped he was.

"He should be given the Nobel prize, so he should," declared Dad.

"The Nobel prize for what?" asked Mum, sarcastically.

"The Nobel prize for fish fingers, of course," said Dad, sounding surprised. "What kind of Nobel prize did you think I meant, Connie? The prize for literature? Sure, that wouldn't make any sense at all!"

Then Mum gave a little laugh and the two of them looked at each other in a funny way.

After the dinner plates were cleared away, Dad retreated to his armchair in the corner while Daniel, Mum and I stayed at the kitchen table and drank oceans of tea.

"I suppose we'd better go," I said idly at about half past ten. I had spent the previous half-hour trying to pluck up the courage to make the suggestion. I knew it wouldn't go down too well with my mother.

"Already?" she shrieked. "But you've barely got here."

"It's late, Mum, and it'll be later still by the time I get home. I need my sleep."

"I don't know what's wrong with you at all, Lucy. When I was your age I could stay up dancing until the sun rose."

"Iron tablets, Lucy," shouted Dad from the corner. "That's what you need. Or what's that other thing all the youngsters take to give them energy?"

"I don't know Dad. Sanatogen?"

"No," he muttered. "It had a different name."

"We really must go. Mustn't we, Daniel?" I said firmly.

"Er, yes."

"Cocaine! That's what it is," shouted Dad, delighted that he had remembered. "Go down to the Medical Hall and get yourself a dose of cocaine and you'll be lepping around the place in no time."

"I don't think so, Dad," I giggled.

"Why not?" he demanded. "Or is cocaine one of those illegal ones?"

"Yes, Dad."

"That's a bloody outrage," he declared. "Them legislators go and ruin everything on us, with their taxes and 'this is illegal', 'that is illegal' carry-on. What harm would a drop of cocaine do you now and then? They've no bit of fun in them, at all, so they haven't."

"Yes, Dad."

"Why don't you stay the night?" suggested Mum. "The bed is made up in your old room."

I was filled with horror at the idea. Stay under her roof? Feel like I was trapped here again? Like I'd never escaped?

"Er, no, Mum, Daniel has to get home so I may as well go back up to town with him . . ."

"But Daniel can stay too," said Mum excitedly. "He can stay in the lads' old room."

"Thanks very much, Mrs Sullivan . . ."

"Connie," she said, leaning across the table and placing her hand on his sleeve. "Call me Connie, it seems a bit silly for you to call me 'Mrs Sullivan' now that you're all grown up."

Good God! She was acting, as though . . . as though, she was *flirting* with him. I could have thrown up.

"Thanks very much, *Connie*," repeated Daniel, "but I'd really better get back. I've got a very early meeting in the morning . . ."

"Well if you're sure. Far be it from me to interrupt the wheels of industry. But you'll come and see us again soon?"

"Certainly, I'd love to."

"And maybe you'll both stay the next time?"

"Oh, I'm invited too, am I?" I asked.

"Lucy," tisked Mum. "You don't need an invitation. How do you put up with her?" she asked Daniel, "she's very touchy."

"She's not too bad," mumbled Daniel. His innate politeness made him want to agree with Mum, his innate sense of survival reminded him that he would be foolhardy to annoy me.

It must be hard being Daniel, I thought, and feeling like you had to try and please everyone all of the time. Being charming and amenable twenty-four hours a day must take it out of a body.

"You could have fooled me," said Mum sharply.

"Er, can we phone for a taxi?" asked Daniel, keen to change the subject.

"What's wrong with getting the tube?" I asked.

"It's late."

"So?"

"It's wet."

"So?"

"I'll pay."

"Fine."

"There's a minicab firm down the road," said Mum. "If you're that keen to get going, I'll give them a ring."

My heart sank. The minicab firm down the road was staffed by an ever-changing assortment of Afghani refugees, Indonesian asylum seekers and exiled Algerians, none of whom could speak a word of English and who, to judge by their sense of direction, had just arrived in Europe. I had every sympathy with their various causes, but I wanted to get home without having to go via Oslo.

Mum rang them.

"Fifteen minutes," she said.

We sat round the table and waited. The atmosphere was strained, we were trying to pretend that this bit was the same as the rest of the evening and that we were happy to be there and that our ears weren't straining to hear the sound of a car's brakes outside the front door. None of us spoke. I certainly couldn't think of anything light-hearted to say that might dispel the tension.

Mum sighed and said stupid things like "well". She was the only person I knew who could say "well" and "another cup of tea?" bitterly.

After what seemed like ten hours I thought I heard a car outside the house so I ran out to have a look.

Their cars were always awful old wrecks, mostly Ladas and Skodas.

Sure enough, an ancient filthy Ford Escort had pulled up, and even through the gloom I could see that it was covered in rust.

"Here's our minicab," I said. I grabbed my coat, hugged Dad and hopped into the car.

"Hello, I'm Lucy," I said to the driver. As we would be spending a lot of time together, I thought we might as well be on first name terms.

"Hassan," he smiled.

"Can we first go to Ladbroke Grove?" I asked.

"Not much English," said Hassan apologetically.

"Oh."

"Parlez-vous français?" he asked.

"Un peu," I replied. "And do you *parlez* any *français*?" I asked Daniel as he got into the car.

"Un peu," he replied.

"Daniel, this is Hassan. Hassan, Daniel."

They shook hands and Daniel patiently tried to negotiate directions.

"*Savez-vous* the Westway?"

"Er . . ."

"Well, *savez-vous* the centre of London?"

A blank look.

"Have you *heard* of London?" Daniel asked gently.

"Ah, yes, London." Understanding dawned on Hassan's face.

"Bien!" said Daniel, pleased.

"It is the capital city of the United Kingdom."

"That's the one."

"It has a population of . . ." Hassan went on.

"Can you take us there please?" asked Daniel. He had begun to sound anxious. "I'll give you directions. And lots of money."

And off we went, Daniel occasionally shouting *"A droit,"* or *"A gauche"*.

"Thank God that's over," I sighed, as we drove away, Mum waving down the darkened road after us.

"I thought it was a nice evening," said Daniel.

"Don't be ridiculous," I said scornfully.

"I *did*."

"How could you? With that . . . that . . . mean old woman there?"

"I presume you're talking about your mother. And I don't think she's mean."

"Daniel! She never misses a chance to put me down."

"And you never miss a chance to rile her."

"What? How dare you? I am such a good and dutiful daughter and I let her away with so many insults."

"Lucy," Daniel laughed. "You don't. You wind her up and you say things to deliberately upset her."

"I really don't know what you're talking about. And anyway, it's none of your business."

"Fine."

"And isn't she *boring*?" I continued almost immediately. "Going on and on about the bloody dry-cleaners. What do we care about it?"

"But . . ."

"What?"

"I don't know . . . I think she's lonely. She mustn't have anyone to talk to . . ."

"If she's lonely, it's her own fault."

" . . . stuck in that house with only your Dad to talk to. Does she ever get out? Apart from going to work?"

"I don't know. I don't think so. And most importantly, I don't care."

"There's an awful lot of fun in her, you know?"

"I don't know."

"No, really, Lucy, there is. She's still a youngish woman."

"She's an old hag."

"You're unbelievable!" said Daniel. "You are *so* unreasonable. She's not an old hag. She's very pretty. You look a lot like her."

"Daniel," I hissed, "that is the worst thing you've ever said to me. It's the worst thing anyone has ever said to me."

He just laughed.

"You're daft."

"It was lovely to see Dad, though."

"Yes, he was quite nice to me," said Daniel.

"He's always nice."

"The last time I met him he wasn't."

"Wasn't he?"

"No. He called me a Sassenach bastard and accused me of stealing his land and oppressing him for 700 years."

"He didn't mean you personally," I said soothingly. "You were just a symbol to him."

"It still wasn't nice," said Daniel stiffly. "I've never stolen anything in my life."

"Never?"

341

"Never."

"Not even when you were a little boy?"

"Er, no."

"Are you sure?"

"Yes."

"*Really* sure?"

"Well, *fairly* sure."

"Not even sweets from a shop?"

"No."

"Sorry, I didn't catch that?"

"No!"

"There's no need to shout."

"All right then! Yes! I suppose you're thinking about that time in Woolworth's when Chris and I stole those knives and forks."

"Er . . ."

This was all news to me, but Daniel was racing ahead.

"You never let me away with anything, do you?" he demanded angrily. "You just ferret everything out of me, I can't have any secrets from you . . ."

"Why knives and forks," I interrupted, puzzled.

"Why not?"

"But . . . what did you want with them? Why did you steal them?"

"Because we could."

"I don't understand."

"Because we could. We took them *because* we *could*. Not because we wanted them," he explained to me. "The prize wasn't what we acquired, it was the acquiring itself. The act of acquisition was the important bit, not what we actually acquired."

"Oh."

"Do you understand?"

"Yes, I think so. And what did you do with them?"

"I gave them to my mother for her birthday."

"You mean pig!"

"But I got her something else also," he said hurriedly. "An egg-timer. No, no, I *paid* for the egg-timer. Don't look at me like that Lucy!"

"It's not because I thought you stole the egg-timer. It's because it's an egg-timer at all! What kind of present is that for a woman?"

"I was young, Lucy. Too young to know better."

"What age were you? Twenty-seven?"

"No," he laughed. "I was about six."

"You haven't changed much, have you, Daniel?"

"How do you mean? That I still steal cutlery from Woolworth's to give to my mother for her birthday?"

"No."

"How then?"

"By taking things just because you can."

"I don't know what you're talking about?" he said huffily.

"Oh yes, you do," I sang, happily.

"I don't."

"You do. Am I annoying you?"

"Yes."

"I'm talking about women, Daniel. Women and you, Daniel. You and women, Daniel."

"I thought you might be," he said, trying to hide a little smile.

"The way you take them just because you can."

"I don't."

"Yes, you do."

"Lucy, I bloody well *don't*."

"Well, what about Karen?"

"What about her?"

"How much do you like her? Or are you just amusing yourself with her?"

"I really like her," he said earnestly. "Lucy, I do. She's very clever and great company and lovely looking."

"Honestly?" I asked sternly.

"Honestly."

"Are you serious about her?"

"Yes."

"God."

A little pause.

"Er, are you, you know . . . *in love* with her?" I asked cautiously.

"Lucy, I don't know her long enough to be in love with her."

"Fine."

"But I'm trying to be."

"I see."

Another peculiar little pause.

I really couldn't think of one thing to say. And that had never happened with me and Daniel before.

"Dad was quiet tonight," I said eventually. "Very well behaved."

"Yes, he didn't even sing anything."

"Sing?"

"He usually treats me to several rousing choruses of 'Carrickfergus' or 'Four Green Fields' and makes me sing along with him."

I had an uncomfortable feeling that Daniel was

laughing at Dad, but I didn't want to find out for certain, so I said nothing.

A long time later we arrived at my flat.

"Thanks for coming with me," I said to Daniel.

"Don't be silly. I enjoyed it."

"Well, er, goodnight."

"Goodnight, Lucy."

"I'll see you soon. You'll probably be round to see Karen."

"Probably." He smiled.

I felt an unexpected rush of annoyance, the childish feeling of "He's supposed to be *my friend*".

"Bye," I said shortly, turning to get out of the car.

"Lucy," said Daniel.

There was something unusual, something new in his tone, *urgency* perhaps, that made me turn and look at him.

"What?" I asked.

"Nothing . . . just . . . goodnight."

"Yes, goodnight," I said, trying to sound exasperated. But I didn't get out of the car. There was a funny tension that told me I was waiting for something, but I didn't know what it was.

We must be having a row, I decided, one of the silent but deadly types.

"Lucy," said Daniel, again in that funny, urgent voice.

But I didn't say anything, I didn't sigh and demand "what?" like I usually would have.

I just looked up at him and, for the first time in my whole life, I felt *shy* with Daniel. I didn't want to look at him, but I couldn't stop myself.

He put his hand up and touched my face and I

watched him, like a rabbit caught in a car's headlights. What the hell was he doing?

He gently pushed my hair back out of my eyes while I sat rigid, staring at him.

Then I came to life again.

"Goodnight," I yelled cheerfully, gathering my bag and moving towards the car door. "Thanks for the lift. See you soon."

"Oh, and *bonsoir*," I called to Hassan. "*Bon chance* with the Home Office."

"*Salut,*" he called back.

I ran towards the house and put my key in the door. My hands shook. I couldn't get inside fast enough. I just wanted to get to my room and be safe. I felt really scared. What was the sudden tension between Daniel and me? There were so few people that I felt comfortable with, so few people that I considered to be friends. I couldn't bear it if things went wrong with Daniel.

But something *was* wrong, things had taken a turn for the very weird. Maybe he was cross with me for being mean about his girlfriends. Maybe he'd fallen in love with Karen and was coming over all protective about her.

Maybe he wouldn't need me anymore if he had fallen in love and found a soul mate – because that was what happened sometimes. How many friendships came a cropper when one of the parties fell in love? Hundreds, probably. I shouldn't be surprised if it happened with Daniel and me.

Anyway, I had Gus. I had other friends. I would be fine.

Chapter Thirty-Eight

It was about six weeks later, on a Sunday night, *late* on Sunday night.

We had been back from the Cash'n'Curry for a while, Gus had left about an hour before. Karen, Charlotte and I were limply draped over various pieces of the living-room furniture, eating crisps, watching telly and recuperating from the weekend. Karen suddenly sat up straight, looking as though she had come to a major decision.

"I'm having a dinner party on Friday," she declared, "and you two and Simon and Gus are invited."

"Gosh, thanks, Karen," I said, nervously.

I had known she was plotting something. She'd been staring at the fire for the last-half hour with a funny, determined look on her face.

"Is Daniel coming?" asked Charlotte, naïve to a fault.

Of course Daniel was coming. Daniel was the reason that Karen was *having* it.

"Of course Daniel is coming," said Karen. "Daniel is the bloody reason I'm *having* it."

"I see," nodded Charlotte.

I saw too.

Karen was going to cook a very elaborate, double-figure-course dinner, serve it stylishly, graciously and without spilling anything on her dress or getting a red, shiny face. She would look beautiful, be witty and entertaining company, all in an attempt to show Daniel how indispensable she was to him.

"We'll have a lovely dinner," she said. "And you're all to dress up."

"That sounds like fun," said Charlotte. "I can wear my cowgirl outfit."

"Not that kind of dressing up," said Karen in alarm. "I mean glamorous dressing up, nice frocks, jewellery, high heels."

"I'm not sure if Gus has a nice frock," I said.

"Ha, ha," said Karen, unamused. "Very funny. But make sure he turns up in something decent and not in his usual Oxfam rejects."

"And now," continued Karen, "I'll need, let's say . . . ooh . . . thirty pounds from each of you now and we'll sort the final sum out later."

"Wha-at?" I asked, flooded with alarm.

I hadn't been expecting that. Neither had Charlotte judging by the way her jaw had fallen open.

Oh no! I had partied hard with Gus all weekend and I felt far too fragile to have a "discussion" with Karen.

"Yes," she said, annoyed. "You don't expect me to pay for all the food, do you? I'm masterminding the whole thing and I'm doing all the cooking."

"Oh, well, fair enough," said Charlotte, trying to sound cheerful and giving me a "let's try and look on the bright side of this" look. "We can't expect her to feed us and our blokes out of the goodness of her heart."

How right she was.

"Good, that's settled," said Karen firmly. "And I'll have it now, if you don't mind."

There was a stricken pause.

"Now," repeated Karen.

There was a half-hearted reach for bags, followed by lacklustre excuses.

"I don't think I have it just now."

"Can I give you a cheque?"

"Will tomorrow evening do?"

"Honestly, Karen," I said, "how can you possibly expect us to have any money left on a Sunday night? Especially after the weekend we've just had."

She said something really annoying about wise virgins and foolish virgins, but I said that there weren't any virgins, wise, foolish or otherwise in the flat so I didn't know what she was talking about.

We all laughed and the tension lifted momentarily until Karen started again.

"I *do* actually need the money now," she warned.

"Why?" I asked – foolishly. "I didn't think Waitrose was open on a Sunday night at ten-thirty."

"Don't try and be funny, Lucy," she said witheringly. "It doesn't suit you."

"Actually, I wasn't," I stuttered. "I really did wonder why you need it now. Tonight. Late on Sunday."

"Not for tonight, stupid. For tomorrow. I'll do the shopping on the way home from work tomorrow, so I need the money now."

"Oh."

"We'll all walk down to the cash point now," said Karen in a voice that brooked no argument.

Charlotte attempted a brave protest, but it was doomed to failure.

"But it's raining and it's Sunday night and I'm in my nightie . . ."

"You don't have to get dressed," said Karen kindly.

"Thanks," sighed Charlotte.

"Just put a coat on over your nightdress," continued Karen. "And a pair of leggings and boots, and you'll be fine. It's dark, no one will see."

"OK," said Charlotte, meekly.

"And both of you don't have to go," continued Karen. "Lucy, give your card to Charlotte and tell her your PIN number."

"You mean you're not coming?" I said faintly.

"Lucy, *honestly,* at times you can be so daft, why do I need to go?"

"But, I thought . . ."

"You *didn't* think, that's your problem. Anyway, Charlotte is going, there's no need for you to go."

I didn't bother getting annoyed with her. One of the features of successful flat-sharing is the ability to let other people be completely horrible from time to time. So that when you feel like behaving like an antichrist they'll return the favour.

"I can't let Charlotte go on her own," I said.

"Charlotte isn't bloody well going on her own," called Charlotte from her bedroom.

Karen shrugged. "If you're going to be noble about it . . ."

I put on my coat over my pyjamas and tucked my pyjama bottoms into my boots.

"My umbrella's in the hall," sang Karen.

"Stick your umbrella," I said, but from the safety of the far side of the closed front door.

Of course, another feature of successful flat-sharing is recognising an opportunity to let off steam.

Charlotte and I battled through the rain to the bank.

"Bitch!" said Charlotte.

"She's not a bitch," I said grimly.

"Isn't she?" asked Charlotte, sounding surprised.

"No! She's a *fucking* bitch," I corrected.

Charlotte stamped along through the puddles. "Bitch, bitch, bitch, bitch, bitch, bitch, bitch, bitch, *bitch*!" she shouted.

A man out walking his dog crossed the road when he got a good look at us, this pair of foul-mouthed lunatics, marching along, the frills of Charlotte's pink nightdress flouncing wildly beneath her coat with each stride she took, the legs of my powder-blue winceyette pyjamas flapping in the wind.

"I hope she gets the clap from Daniel," I said. "Or herpes, or genital warts or something really horrible."

"Or crabs," agreed Charlotte, viciously. "And I hope she gets pregnant. And the next time Daniel is over, I'm going to walk around the flat with no clothes on, so that he can see that I've got bigger tits than her. She'd hate that, the bossy old bitch."

"Do!" I said fervently. "In fact, you should try to snog him."

"Yes," she agreed, enthusiastically. "I'd love to."

351

"In fact, you should try and have sex with him. And in her bed, if you could possibly manage it," I suggested with malicious pleasure.

"Great idea!" squealed Charlotte.

"And then tell her that he said that she was crap in bed and that you were far better."

"I don't know, though," said Charlotte doubtfully. "It mightn't be that easy to get off with him, you know, he seems to really like her. Why don't you try?"

"Me?"

"Yes, you'd have a better chance" she said. "I think Daniel has a soft spot for you."

"Maybe he does," I said gloomily. "But this is sex we're talking about, Charlotte. It's no good if Daniel's spot for me is soft."

We both laughed and felt better. Except that it made me think of Daniel – Daniel was barely speaking to me. Or maybe I was barely speaking to Daniel. Something odd was going on at any rate.

We got the money and returned home, wet and resentful and handed it over to Karen in surly fashion.

"So I can stick my umbrella?" she asked archly, from her prone position on the couch.

I reddened with embarrassment. But when I looked at her she was grinning.

"Yes," I laughed, the tension dispelled.

"I'm going to bed. Goodnight," I said.

"Goodnight," called Karen to my back. "Oh and Lucy, I'll need you and Charlotte to be here on Thursday night for the cleaning and the preparations."

I paused in the doorway and realised that another feature of successful flat-sharing is the ability to imagine your flatmate being beaten about the head with a stick that has a nail stuck in it.

"OK," I mumbled, without turning around.

I spent the night fantasising about putting all Karen's clothes in black bin-liners and leaving them out for the rubbish men.

On Thursday night, the Night of the Long Preparations, I thought I had died and gone to Hell.

Karen had decided to prepare most of the food the night before, so that on the actual night of the dinner she would have very little to do, other than look beautiful and cool and calm and in control.

Except that Karen was so nervous about it and so determined that it would impress Daniel that she seemed to be more, how would I put it? . . . difficult, than usual. She had always been dynamic and strong-willed, but there was a fine line between being dynamic and strong-willed and being a bossy bitch. Karen seemed to have successfully made that leap.

She had decided that Charlotte and I would do the actual hands-on preparation and she, herself, would be more in the role of an Artistic Director, overseeing us, advising, guiding and managing us.

In other words, if there were potatoes to be peeled, she had no intention of doing them.

Charlotte and I were barely in the door from work before she set about organising us.

"You," she shouted at Charlotte, pointing a pen

and reading from a list, "are on carrot, pepper, aubergine and courgette preparation, coriander and lemongrass soup and asparagus soufflé duty."

"And you," she shouted at me, "are on duchesse potato, kiwi fruit purée, cranberry jelly, whipping cream, stuffing mushroom and Viennese biscuit duty."

Charlotte and I were terrified. We had barely heard of most of these things, let alone knew how to cook them. Charlotte's culinary speciality was toast, mine was supernoodles and anytime we tried to make anything more complicated than that, it ended in tears and rows and recriminations. Outside incineration, inner rawness, raised voices, hurt feelings, spillages and slippages. You can't make an omelette without breaking legs – or at least *I* had certainly never managed it.

That evening the kitchen was a scene from Dante's Inferno. The circle where sinners were tormented with fruit and vegetables. All four rings and the oven were in constant use, steam billowing, lids rattling and hopping, water boiling over. There were mounds of grapes, asparagus, cauliflower, potatoes, carrots and kiwi fruit everywhere. The heat was intense and Charlotte and I were the colour of tomatoes. Karen wasn't.

There was no room to put anything, because Karen had made us move the kitchen table down to the sitting room.

"Just put them down over there. No, no, not on the meringue base, for Christ's sake!" she screeched when I had to empty the fridge of its normal contents to make room for the twenty or thirty desserts she seemed to be expecting us to make.

Everywhere there was food. On the top of the fridge, on the draining board, most of the floor was covered in bowls of pork that was marinating and jelly that was setting and garlic bread that was wrapped in tinfoil. I was afraid to move my foot half an inch in case I ended up ankle-deep in olive oil, red wine, juniper, vanilla, cumin and "Karen's secret ingredient" marinade. And as far as I could see Karen's secret ingredient was nothing other than ordinary brown sugar. I was itching to slap her for being so "third secret of Fatima" about it.

I peeled fourteen million potatoes. I sliced seventeen thousand kiwi fruit. Then I chopped them. And then I had to shove them through a sieve – whatever that was all about. I skinned my knuckles carrying the kitchen table down the hall. I cut my thumb when I topped and tailed the mangetout. Chilli got into the cut. Karen said I should be more careful, that she didn't want blood in the food.

Every so often she came around and "jokingly inspected" what we were doing and, even though I knew it was ridiculous, I felt nervous. She was like a sergeant-major examining the young soldiers on parade.

"No, no, no," she said, and to my disbelief, she rapped me on the knuckles with a wooden spoon! "That's not the way to peel potatoes. You're taking half the potato off with the skin. It's wasteful, Lucy."

"Fuck off with the wooden spoon," I said angrily, wishing my peeler was a flick-knife.

The bossy bitch had gone too far and the wooden spoon had hurt.

"Oooooh, we *are* bad-tempered this evening," she laughed. "You'll have to learn how to accept constructive criticism, Lucy. You'll never succeed with that attitude."

I could taste fury in my mouth. But I was trying – I had to understand that she was crazy about a man. Even if he was Daniel. It wasn't my place to judge.

"And what on earth is this?" she demanded. She had moved on to where Charlotte was scraping carrots, and held up a carrot from the "done" pile.

"It's a carrot," said Charlotte. Surly. Defensive.

"What kind of a carrot?" asked Karen slowly and meaningfully.

"A peeled carrot."

"A *peeled* carrot!" said Karen in triumph. "A *peeled* carrot, she tells me. Might I just ask you, Lucy Sullivan, does this carrot looked peeled to you?"

"Yes," I said stoutly, loyally.

"Oh no, it does not! If this is a peeled carrot it's a very badly peeled one. Start again, Charlotte, and get it right this time."

"Knock it off, Karen," I blurted out, too angry to care. "We're doing you a favour."

"Excuse me?" said Karen archly. "But run that one by me again – *you're* doing *me* a favour? I think not, Lucy. But, by all means stop if you want, just don't expect a place set at the table for Gus and yourself tomorrow night."

That shut me up.

Gus had been very excited when I had told him

about the dinner, especially the dressing up bit. He'd be bitterly disappointed if he couldn't come. So I swallowed my rage. Another instalment on my road to ulcerdom.

"I'm having a glass of wine," I said, angrily, reaching for one of the bottles that were in the fridge. "How about you, Charlotte?"

"No, you are not!" declared Karen. "They're for tomorrow ni . . . oh go on then. I'll have one while you're at it."

On and on into the night we worked, peeling, scraping, slicing, grating, stuffing, whipping, piping, baking.

We did so much work that Karen was almost grateful, but only for about two seconds.

"Thanks, both of you," she said, bending down to take something out of the oven.

"Sorry?" I asked, so tired that I thought I was hearing things.

"I said 'thanks'," she said. "You're both very goo . . . Oh Christ! Move, move," she roared, kicking me out of the way, throwing down a tray of what must have been the Viennese biscuits, sending them skittering into the bowl of ratatouille. "I'm burnt to a crisp!" she gasped. "These bloody oven gloves are useless."

I finally got to bed at about two o'clock, my hands raw and cut, stinking of garlic and Drambuie. My prize nail, that I'd nurtured since it was only a piece of quick, snagged and broken.

Chapter Thirty-Nine

It was a good job I got a seat on the tube to work the next morning because I was so tired that I would have lain down on the floor otherwise. Charlotte and I spent our journey wearily discussing how much of a stupid bitch we thought Karen was.

"I mean, who does she think she is?" asked Charlotte, yawning.

"Exactly!" I yawned back, slumped in my seat. I noticed that my shoes were filthy and scuffed and that made me feel depressed. I sat up straight so that I wouldn't see them, but then I had to look at the horrible man in a suit, sitting opposite me, who had his eyes trained on Charlotte's breasts, his eyes glazing with lust every time she yawned and her chest expanded. I wanted to hit him, to batter him around the head and neck with his *Daily Mail*.

I thought I had better close my eyes for the rest of the journey, it was safer.

"And it won't last with Karen and Daniel," declared Charlotte, uncertainly. "He'll get sick of her."

"Ummm," I agreed, opening my eyes for a moment. I clamped them shut again, but not before I had seen an ad on the wall asking for donations for animals that had been mistreated, and a heart-rending picture of a skinny, miserable-looking dog.

It was almost a relief to get to work, where I had to endure taunts from Meredia and Megan who insisted that I'd been out on the beer the night before.

"I *haven't*," I protested feebly.

"Course you have," snorted Megan. "Just look at you."

The moment I put my key in the door on Friday evening, Karen was in the hall. She had taken Friday afternoon off work so that she could get her hair done and tidy the flat. She immediately set about organising me.

"Wash yourself and get dressed *now*, Lucy. I need to run through the arrangements with you."

In fairness to her, the flat looked beautiful.

There were fresh flowers everywhere. She had laid a crisp white tablecloth on the nasty Formica kitchen table and placed an exquisite candelabra, with eight red candles, in the middle of it.

"I didn't know we had that candelabra," I said, thinking how nice it would look in my bedroom.

"We don't," she said shortly. "I borrowed it."

While I was in the bathroom she hammered on the door and shouted, "I've put clean towels on the rail, don't even *think* of using them."

It was eight o'clock. The three of us were ready.

The table was laid, the candles were lit, the lights turned down low, the white wine was in the fridge, the red wine was opened and ready in the kitchen, and pots and pans and containers of food stood on the stove, poised for the off.

Karen switched on the stereo and strange noises came from it.

"What's that?" demanded Charlotte in shock.

"Jazz." Karen sounded slightly embarrassed.

"Jazz?" snorted Charlotte derisively. "But we hate jazz. Don't we, Lucy?"

"Yes." I was happy to confirm.

"What do we call people who like jazz, Lucy?" asked Charlotte.

"Weirdo anoraks?" I suggested,

"No, not that."

"Goatee-beard, beatnik art students?"

"That's it," she said in glee. "Lads who wear black French polos and ski-pants."

"That's as maybe, but we like jazz now," said Karen firmly.

"You mean, Daniel does," muttered Charlotte.

Karen looked exquisite – or ridiculous, depending on your point of view. She wore a pale green, off-the-shoulder, Grecian type of frock. Her hair was up, but lots of it was falling down in little curls and tendrils. She shone, she looked so much more glamorous and soignée than Charlotte or I. I was wearing my gold dress, the one I had worn the night I had met Gus because it was the only dressy-up dress I had, but it looked tatty and bedraggled compared to Karen's splendour.

Charlotte, to be frank, looked a bit of a mess, even worse than me. She wore the only formal dress that she had, the one she had worn when she was her sister's bridesmaid, a huge red taffeta meringue. I think she must have put on some weight since the wedding because her chest fairly exploded from the strapless bodice.

Karen looked very doubtful when Charlotte rustled out from her bedroom, said "Da, daaah!" and did a little pirouette. She probably wished she had allowed Charlotte to wear her cowgirl outfit after all.

Karen had given frantic instructions. "Now when they arrive, I'll keep them talking in the front room, Lucy, you turn on the oven at a very low heat to warm the potatoes and Charlotte, you stir the . . ."

She paused suddenly, a horrified look on her face.

"The bread, the bread, the bread," shrieked Karen. "I forgot to buy the bread. Everything's ruined! Totally ruined. They'll all have to go home."

"Karen, calm down. It's on the table," said Charlotte.

"Oh. Oh. Oh, thank God. Is it really?" She sounded close to tears. Charlotte and I exchanged longsuffering looks.

Karen was quiet for a moment, then she looked at the clock.

"Where the fuck are they?" she demanded, lighting a cigarette. Her hand shook.

"Give them a chance," I said soothingly. "It's just gone eight."

"I said eight o'clock on the dot," said Karen aggressively.

"But no one takes that seriously," I murmured. "It's considered bad manners to arrive on time."

It was on the tip of my tongue to remind her that it was only a dinner party and that the guest of honour was just Daniel, but I stopped myself in time. Waves of aggression came from her.

We sat in tense silence.

"No one's coming," said Karen tearfully, gulping back a glass of wine. "We may as well throw it all out. Come on, let's go down to the kitchen and fling it all in the bin."

She banged her glass down on the table and stood up.

"Well, come on," she ordered.

"No!" said Charlotte. "Why should we throw it out? After all the trouble we've gone to? We can eat it ourselves and we'll freeze what we don't eat."

"Oh, I see," said Karen, nastily. "We can eat it ourselves, can we? What makes you so certain that no one's coming? What do you know that I don't?"

"Nothing," declared Charlotte in exasperation. "But you said . . ."

The doorbell rang. It was Daniel. Relief was written all over Karen's beautifully made-up face. My God, I thought with a little jump, she really is bonkers about him.

Daniel was wearing a dark suit and a dazzling white shirt, which set off the faint tan he still had from his holiday in Jamaica in February. He looked tall and dark and handsome, he smiled a lot, his hair flopped over his forehead and he had brought two bottles of chilled champagne – the ideal guest. I couldn't help smiling. Perfectly turned out, beautifully behaved, and just ever so slightly clichéd.

He said all the things that nice polite people say when they come to dinner at your house, like, "Mmmm, something smells delicious" and, "You look wonderful, Karen. And you, Charlotte."

Only when he got to me did his impeccable manners slip a little. "What are you laughing at, Sullivan?" he demanded. "My suit? My hair? What is it?"

"Nothing," I protested. "Nothing at all. Why should I laugh at you?"

"Why change the habit of a life time?" he muttered. Then he moved away from me and said more of those polite guest things like "Can I do anything to help?" knowing that the answer would be an avalanche of "Nos" and "Not at alls" and slightly hysterical "Everything's under controls!".

"Have a drink, Daniel," said Karen graciously, as she swept him into the front room. Charlotte and I attempted to follow them but Karen stuck her head back out at us. "Get stirring," she hissed, blocking our entrance, as I ran into the back of Charlotte.

The doorbell rang again. Simon this time. As always he was dressed to kill, wearing a dinner suit and a red satin cummerbund that looked really stupid. He had brought a bottle of champagne also.

Oh dear, I thought. Gus was going to be the odd man out – more than usual, that was. Gus wouldn't bring champagne, Gus probably wouldn't bring anything.

Not that it would embarrass me, but I was worried that it might embarrass him.

I wondered if I could run out to the off-licence to

buy some champagne and slip it to Gus when he arrived, but I was on potato-heating duty so I was confined to barracks.

Simon said, as Daniel had moments earlier, "Mmmm, something smells delicious".

Gus wouldn't. Gus would say, "Where's me spuds, I'm starving".

"How's it all going?" asked Karen, appearing at the kitchen door. She had obviously left Daniel and Simon to do some awkward male bonding in the front room.

"Fine," I said.

"Watch that sauce, Lucy," she said anxiously. "If there are lumps in it, I'll kill you."

I said nothing. I felt like throwing the saucepan across the kitchen at her.

"And where's your mad Irishman?"

"On his way."

"He'd better hurry up."

"Don't worry."

"What time did you tell him to get here at?"

"Eight o'clock."

"It's a quarter past now."

"Karen – he'll be here."

"He'd better."

Karen swished back to the front room, with a bottle of something under her arm.

I kept stirring the sauce, a tiny little flutter of anxiety coming to life in my stomach.

He *would* be here.

But I hadn't spoken to him since Tuesday and I hadn't seen him since Sunday. That suddenly seemed like an awful, long time. Time for him to have forgotten me?

A little while later Karen was back.

"Lucy," she yelled. "It's half past eight!"

"So?"

"So where the hell is Gus?"

"I don't know, Karen."

"Well," she spluttered. "Don't you think you had better find out?"

"Why don't you ring him?" suggested Charlotte. "Just to make sure that he hasn't forgotten. He might have got the day wrong."

"He might have got the *year* wrong," said Karen, nastily.

"I'm sure he's on his way," I said, "but I'll give him a ring just in case."

I sounded a lot more confident than I felt. I wasn't at all sure that he was on his way. Anything could have happened to Gus. He could have forgotten, he could have got delayed, he could have fallen under a bus. But I wasn't going to let anyone know how worried I was.

I was embarrassed. I felt ashamed. Both their boyfriends had arrived on time. *With* bottles of champagne. My boyfriend was already half an hour late and he wouldn't even have a bottle of Babycham, he wouldn't even have a bottle of *tap water* with him when he did eventually turn up.

If he turns up, said a little voice in my head.

Panic rushed through me. What if he didn't arrive? What if he didn't come and didn't ring me and I never heard from him again? What would I do?

I tried to calm myself down. Of course he would come. He was probably outside right now. He really liked me and he obviously cared about me, of course he wouldn't abandon me.

I didn't want to phone him, I had never phoned him. He had given me his phone number when I had asked for it, but I had got the feeling that he wasn't that keen for me to ring him. He said that he hated phones, that they were a necessary evil. And there had never been any need for me to ring him because he always rang me, and now that I thought of it, they always seemed to be brief calls from a phone box, somewhere noisy. Or else he called round to my flat or collected me from work.

We certainly didn't spend hours and hours on the phone whispering and giggling to each other, the way Charlotte and Simon did.

I found his number in my purse and dialled it. His phone rang and rang for ages and no one answered.

"No answer," I said in relief. "He must be on his way."

Just then someone picked up the phone at the other end.

A man's voice said "Hello".

"Er, hello, can I speak to Gus?"

"Who?"

"Gus. Gus Lavan."

"Oh, him. No, he's not here."

I put my hand over the mouthpiece. "He's on his way." I smiled at Karen.

"When did he leave?" she asked.

"How long ago did he leave?" I parroted.

"Let's see, ooh, about two weeks ago, I suppose."

"Wha . . . at?"

My horror must have shown on my face because Karen burst out, "I don't believe it! I bet the little bastard just left five minutes ago. Well, tough for him because we're going to start without him . . ."

Her voice trailed away as she marched down the hall no doubt to galvanise Charlotte into finalising the starters.

"Two weeks?" I asked quietly. Horrified and all as I was, I knew that this was something best kept to myself. It would be far, far too humiliating to broadcast it to my flatmates and their boyfriends.

"About two weeks," said the voice, considering. "Ten days, something like that."

"Oh, well, er, thanks."

"Who's calling anyway? Is that Mandy?"

"No," I said, feeling as if I was going to burst into tears. "It's not Mandy."

Who the fuck was Mandy?

"Can I give him a message if I happen to see him again?"

"No. Thank you. Goodbye."

I hung up. Something was wrong. I knew it. This was not normal behaviour. Why hadn't Gus mentioned that he was leaving his flat? Why hadn't he given me his new phone number? And where on earth was he now?

Daniel had come out to the hall.

"Christ, what's wrong with you?"

"Nothing," I said, attempting a smile.

Karen came back down the hall.

"Sorry, Lucy, we'll wait a little bit longer for him."

Oh no. No, no, *no*. I didn't want any waiting to be done. I had a horrible feeling that he wasn't going to come. I didn't want us all to sit watching the door because then it would be so *obvious* when he didn't arrive. I wanted the evening to proceed without him. And then, if he arrived, it would be a bonus.

"Er, no, Karen, we may as well start."

"No, honestly, another half hour won't matter that much."

It was typical. Karen was being nice, which didn't happen very often, and for once I didn't want her to be.

"Come in and sit down and have a glass of wine," suggested Daniel. "You're as white as a ghost, you look exhausted."

We trooped into the front room and I took a glass of wine from someone's hand and tried to act normal.

The others were acting relaxed and happy, chatting, lolling about, sipping wine, but I was rigid with tension, white-faced, silent, straining to hear the sound of the doorbell, praying to hear the phone.

"Oh, please, Gus, don't do this to me," I begged silently.

"Please God, please God, make him come."

In what seemed like thirty seconds later, it was nine o'clock.

Time was such a contrary bastard. When I wanted it to gallop along, which is what I wanted it to do while I was at work, it slowed to a standstill. It could take up to twenty-four hours for an hour to pass.

And now that I wanted time to stop, it was racing past. I had wanted it to linger around the eight-thirty mark for at least a couple of hours, so Gus wouldn't be terribly late. While he was only half an hour late, there was still hope, there was still a chance that he would arrive. I wanted the time to go oh-so-slowly to keep me in the timescale within which he could still arrive. Every second that passed, every second that made the time later was my enemy. Every tick of the clock took Gus further and further away from me.

Whenever there was a lull in the conversation – and there were a few, because we were all slightly uncomfortable with so much formality in our own home and enough wine hadn't yet been drunk – someone would say, "What's keeping Gus?" or "Where's he coming from? Camden? He might have trouble on the tube," or "I'm sure he didn't realise that you meant eight o'clock so literally".

Nobody seemed terribly worried. But I was.

I was scared.

It wasn't just the fact that he was late – although that was deeply embarrassing after all the fuss Karen had made about the dinner – but his lateness, taken in conjunction with his having moved out of his flat without telling me. Now *that* was ominous. No matter what way I looked at it, I felt it was not A Good Thing.

I kept having little stabs of despair.

What if he didn't come?

What if I never saw him again?

And who was Mandy?

I made attempts to join in with the slightly self-conscious camaraderie in the front room, tried to listen to what they were saying, to force a smile onto my rigid, white face.

But I was so agitated, I could hardly sit still for a moment.

And then the pendulum swung back in the other direction and I calmed down. After all he was only an hour, well an hour and a quarter – damn, was it an hour and a quarter already? – late. He would probably arrive along in a moment, a little bit drunk, with some hilarious, outlandish excuse. I was always overreacting to things, I told myself sternly. I was certain that he would come and I was slightly amused at how easy it was for me to think the worst.

Gus was my friend, we'd become so close over the past couple of months, I knew he cared about me and that he wouldn't let me down.

Chapter Forty

By ten o'clock the crisp bowls were all emptied and everyone seemed to be drunk.

"I'm not listening to any more of this shite," announced Charlotte, turning off the stereo. "Jazz, my arse."

"You're such a pleb," said Karen.

"So what if I am?" she demanded, her face flushed and shiny. "It's still shite, there's no tune to it, every time I try to sing along to it, it goes all funny. Now where's my Simply Red?"

Karen allowed Charlotte to change the tape, which meant that she too must have had enough of John Coltrane's later meanderings.

"Right then," announced Karen, changing the subject. "Gus or no Gus, it's time to eat. I want you to have the delicious food before you're all too drunk to appreciate it."

"Dinner is served. Charlotte, Lucy." She motioned us towards the door.

That was our cue to become serving wenches.

I couldn't eat anything. I was still hoping desperately that Gus would show up. Just arrive along with some fantastic, outrageous excuse. I won't be cross with you, Gus, I promised fervently. Honestly, just get here and I won't say a thing.

After a while everyone stopped saying things like "I wonder what's keeping Gus," and "What could have happened to Gus," and looking out the window to see if a taxi was coming up the road with Gus inside it.

In fact, everyone took great care not to mention Gus at all. It had become clear that Gus wasn't merely late, but that he wasn't coming.

They all knew that I'd been stood up and, in their awkward, embarrassed way, they were trying to pretend that I hadn't been and if I had, that they certainly hadn't noticed.

I knew they were just trying to be kind, but their kindness was humiliating.

The evening was interminable. There was so much food, so many courses, I thought it would never end. I would have given anything to go to bed, but pride forbade me.

It was only much, much later when everyone was *really* drunk – as opposed to just very drunk – that the subject of Gus was brought up again.

"Dump the fucker," slurred Karen. Her hair-do was keeling over to one side. "How dare he treat you like this? I'd kill him."

"Let's give him a chance." I smiled tensely. "Anything could have happened to him."

"Oh come *on*, Lucy," scoffed Karen. "How can you be such an idiot? It's *obvious* that he's stood you up."

Of *course* it was obvious that he'd stood me up,

but I was hoping to hang on to a remnant of my dignity by pretending that he hadn't.

Daniel and Simon looked uncomfortable. Simon said heartily to Daniel, "Well, how's work?"

"He could have phoned," said Charlotte.

"Maybe he forgot," I said miserably.

"Well, he shouldn't have," slurred Karen.

"Have you checked the phone?" Charlotte shouted suddenly. "I bet the phone is broken, the lines are down or something, that's why he hasn't called."

"I doubt it," said Karen.

"Maybe you didn't hang it up properly," suggested Daniel. "Maybe it's off the hook and he hasn't been able to get through."

Because Daniel had suggested it, it was given a bit of credibility. There was a surge towards the hall, me at the head of it, hoping against hope that Daniel was right. Of course he wasn't. There was nothing wrong with the phone and the receiver had been replaced perfectly.

How embarrassing.

"Maybe something's happened to him," I suggested hopefully. "Maybe he's had an accident. He could have been knocked down and killed," I said, fresh hope surging through me. Far better for Gus to be lying broken and bloodied beneath the wheels of a juggernaut than for him to have decided that he didn't fancy me anymore.

Karen was having a passionate but hard-to-follow argument with Simon about Scottish Nationalism when the knock on the door came.

"Quiet," shouted Daniel. "I think someone's at the door."

We fell silent – surprise, rather than the desire to hear, robbed us of the power of speech.

We held our breath and listened. Daniel was right.

Someone *was* knocking on the door.

Thank God, I thought fervently, relief making me dizzy.

Thank you God, thank you God, thank you God! Pencil me in for charitable work, kindness to the poor, contributions to church funds, bad skin, anything you like, but thank you God for giving me back Gus.

"I'll answer it, Lucy." Charlotte swayed to her feet. "You don't want him to think you've been worried. Just look casual."

"Thanks," I said, rushing to the mirror in panic. "Do I look OK? Is my hair all right? Oh no, look at how red my face is! Quick, quick, someone give me lipstick!"

I ran my fingers through my hair and flung myself onto the couch, trying to look unconcerned, and waited for Gus to roll into the room. I was so *happy* I couldn't sit still. I was looking forward to hearing whatever elaborate and imaginative excuse he might make. No doubt it would be hilarious.

But a while passed and he didn't appear. I could hear voices in the hall.

"What's keeping him?" I hissed, anxiously perched on the edge of my seat.

"Just relax." Daniel rubbed my knee. He stopped abruptly when Karen stared pointedly at his hand, then at him, then at his hand again. She had a peculiar expression which kind of slid off her face. I realised that she had been trying to arch her eyebrows quizzically, but it had lost something in the inebriation.

More time passed and still Gus didn't appear. I realised that something was wrong – perhaps he hadn't come in because he was injured – and after a few minutes I couldn't bear it anymore and, throwing my veneer of unconcernedness to the wind, I went out to have a look.

There was no Gus.

Just Neil from downstairs.

Neil in a bad mood, complaining about the music and wearing a very short dressing-gown.

I was certain that Gus was on the premises and it took a great leap of imagination for me to grasp that, actually, he wasn't. I squinted drunkenly past Neil, wondering why I couldn't see Gus hovering behind him.

And when it hit me that Gus hadn't arrived after all, I could hardly believe it.

The disappointment was so intense that the ground literally rocked beneath my feet. Then again, it might have been all the wine I'd drunk.

" . . . you don't have to turn the music down," Neil was saying. "But for pity's sake, change the tape. If you have any compassion, any feeling for a fellow human being, you'll change the tape."

"But I *like* Simply Red," said Charlotte.

"I *know!*" said Neil. "Why else would you play it for eight weeks non-stop? *Please*, Charlotte."

"OK," she agreed sulkily.

"And would you mind playing this instead?" he asked, handing her a tape.

"Get lost!" spluttered Charlotte. "The nerve of you, this is *our* flat, we'll play *our* music."

"But I have to listen to it too, you know . . ." whinged Neil.

I lurched back into the front room.

"Where's Gus?" asked Daniel.

"Don't know," I muttered.

I got very drunk, and at some late hour, I think it was about half past two, I decided that I would find Gus. Maybe I could get his new number from the man I had spoken to in his old flat.

I sneaked out to the hall to the phone. If Karen and Charlotte knew what I was doing they would have tried to stop me. Luckily they were all really drunk. They had stopped playing strip Trivial Pursuit because Charlotte had insisted on putting on some Spanish music. Then she demonstrated the steps that she had learnt at her flamingo dancing lessons and made them all join in.

I knew what I was doing had desperation stamped all over it, but I was drunk, I had no willpower. I had no idea what I would say if I did get though to him. How could I explain that I'd found his new number and tracked him down without seeming like a woman obsessed? But I didn't care.

Surely I had every right to find him and speak to him, I reasoned drunkenly. I *deserved* an explanation.

But I wouldn't be angry with him, I decided. I would be friendly and would calmly ask why he hadn't come.

There was a tiny sober little part of me that said I shouldn't ring him, that I was behaving like a mad person, that I was compounding my humiliation by trying to trace him, but I didn't listen. I was in the grip of a compulsion and I couldn't stop myself.

But no one answered the phone. I sat on the hall floor and let it ring until I got the recorded message telling me that my number wasn't being answered – hey, thanks, I would never have noticed otherwise – and in frustration I slammed the phone back on the receiver. I was barely aware of the tumbling and commotion in the front room.

"No answer?" asked someone. I jumped.

Damn! It was Daniel, en route to the kitchen, probably looking for more wine.

"No," I said, angry that I'd been caught.

"Who were you ringing?" asked Daniel.

"Who do you think?"

"Poor Lucy."

I felt terrible. It wasn't like the old days when Daniel laughed at me and made fun of my misfortunes. Things had changed and I didn't feel as if Daniel was my friend any more. I had to hide my feelings from him.

"You poor, little thing," he said again.

"Oh shut up," I said sulkily, looking up at him from my position on the floor.

We had somehow crossed a line. All that light-hearted sparring had become real and nasty.

"What's wrong, Lucy?" Daniel crouched down to where I was slumped on the floor.

"Oh, don't start," I spat. "You know what's wrong."

"No," he said. "I mean, what's wrong with us?"

"There is no 'us'," I said, partly to hurt him and partly to avoid the confrontation and plain speaking that I felt was imminent.

"Yes, there is." He gently put his hand on my neck and began stroking the area under my ear with little circles of his thumb.

"There is," he said again. His thumb sent odd shivers through my neck and down into my chest. Suddenly I couldn't breathe too well and then, to my disbelief, I felt my nipples begin to harden.

"What the fuck are you doing?" I whispered, staring up into his handsome familiar face.

But I didn't pull away. I was drunk, I was rejected and someone was being nice to me.

"I don't know," he said, sounding shocked. I could feel his breath on my face. Oh Christ, I thought in horror, as Daniel's face came closer to mine. He's going to kiss me. Daniel! *Daniel*'s going to kiss me, even though his girlfriend is only two yards away and I'm so drunk or upset or whatever that I'm going to let him.

"What's keeping Dan?" said Karen's voice, as she flounced out into the hall.

Saved by the belle!

"What are the pair of you doing down there?" she screeched.

"Nothing," said Daniel, getting to his feet.

"Nothing," I gasped, clambering to mine.

"You were supposed to be getting the basin of water for Charlotte's ankle," said Karen in a fury.

"Why, what's happened?" I asked, glad of the diversion, *any* diversion, as Daniel made for the kitchen.

"She tripped doing her flamingo dancing," said Karen coldly. "And she's sprained her ankle. But it would appear that Daniel would rather sit on the floor and chat to you than help poor Charlotte."

I went back into the front room. Charlotte was stretched out on the couch, giggling and saying "ouch" as Simon massaged her foot and looked up her dress.

There was almost no wine left, just dribs and drabs in the bottom of bottles but I made my way round the table drinking everything in my path, until it all ran out. I was desperate for something to drink and suddenly there seemed to be nothing.

An argument broke out because Charlotte insisted that her ankle was broken and that she should go to the hospital and Simon said that it definitely wasn't broken, it was only sprained. Then Karen said that Charlotte should stop whinging and then Simon intervened and told Karen to shut up and not to say nasty things to his girlfriend, and if Charlotte wanted to go to the hospital then to the hospital she would go. Karen asked Simon who had made his dinner for him that evening and Simon replied that he had heard all about Karen and the work she had made Charlotte do and that if anyone deserved thanks for the food that evening it was Charlotte . . . and on and on.

I was gulping a half-bottle of red wine that I had found abandoned behind the couch and I sat, swinging my legs, enjoying the row.

Karen then shouted at Charlotte for telling Simon that she had done all the cooking because Charlotte had done nothing. Nothing! Just peeled a few carrots and that was all . . .

I smiled over at Daniel, forgetting for a moment what had happened, or nearly happened, in the hall. He grinned back, then I remembered what had happened, or nearly happened, in the hall, so I blushed and looked away.

I found some gin and finished that. And I still wasn't drunk enough. I was sure that I had a bottle of rum in the cupboard in the front room but search as I might I couldn't find it.

"Gus probably stole it," suggested Karen.

"He probably did," I said grimly.

Eventually I admitted defeat and I went to bed, alone, and passed out.

Chapter Forty-One

I jerked awake at about seven o'clock – it *was* Saturday, after all, and immediately knew that something was wrong. What was it?

Oh yes! I remembered.

Oh no! I wished I hadn't.

Luckily I was badly hungover so I was able to go back to sleep.

I woke again at ten and the realisation that I had lost Gus hit me like a clunk on the head from a frying pan. I got up and dragged myself down the hall and found Charlotte and Karen in the kitchen clearing up. There was so much leftover food that I could have cried but I didn't because they would have thought that I was crying about Gus.

"Morning," I said.

"Morning," they replied.

I waited. I held my breath, hoping that one of them would say "Oh, Gus rang."

But they didn't.

I knew there was no point in asking if he had rung. They both knew how important it was to me. If Gus had called they would have excitedly told me immediately. In fact, they would have come to me with the news, they would woken me up.

But even knowing that, I still found myself asking tentatively,

"Did anyone ring for me while I was asleep?"

I couldn't stop myself. In for a penny, in for a pound. I was hurt – why stop now?

"Er, no," muttered Karen, not meeting my eye.

"No," agreed Charlotte. "No one."

I had known that was the case, so why did I still feel so disappointed?

"How's your ankle?" I asked Charlotte.

"Fine," she said, looking sheepish.

"I'm just running out to buy the paper," I said. "And then I'll be back to help with the cleaning. Does anyone want anything?"

"No thanks."

I didn't even want the paper. But a watched pot never boils and if I did a vigil round my phone, Gus wouldn't call. I knew of old that if I was out of the house there was a better chance he might ring me.

When I let myself back into the flat I held my breath, waiting for Karen or Charlotte to run down the hall and say, breathlessly, "Guess what? Gus rang," or "Guess what? Gus is *here*. He was kidnapped last night and they just let him go a few moments ago."

But no one ran down the hall and breathlessly told me anything. I was forced to go, cap-in-hand, to the kitchen, where I was handed a tea towel.

"Did anyone ring for me?" I found myself asking, hollowly.

Again, Karen and Charlotte shook their heads. I shut

my mouth grimly. I'm not going to ask again, I decided. I was tearing myself apart with disappointment and I was embarrassing them.

I followed the advice of thousands of women's magazines and Kept Busy. Keeping Busy is supposed to be very good for taking your mind off runaway men and, as luck would have it, there was an alarming amount of cleaning up to be done after the excesses of the previous evening – although I hadn't expected that *I'd* have to do any of it. I thought that I'd be given compassionate leave, that because Gus had dumped me, everyone would be nice to me, that I'd be given a special dispensation and Karen would let me off my chores.

Not a chance.

Karen wasted no time in setting me right.

"Keep busy," she said cheerfully, as she loaded me up with filthy plates. "It'll take your mind off him."

That made me feel even more upset – I wanted sympathy, I wanted kid-glove treatment, I wanted to be treated like a convalescent invalid. What I didn't want was to do the washing-up.

And anyone who says that Keeping Busy is a distraction from heartbreak is mistaken, because I Kept *very* Busy that day, and I thought about Gus constantly – how cleaning up the sick in the bathroom was supposed to make me feel better about Gus disappearing had me baffled. All that happened was that one form of misery was temporarily exchanged for another.

I hoovered the entire flat, I washed the unbroken

plates and glasses, I put the broken plates and glasses into a bin-bag and attached a nice little note for the binmen so that they wouldn't cut themselves. I emptied mountains of ash-trays, I covered bowls of untouched food with clingfilm and put them in the fridge, where they would take up valuable low-fat yoghurt space for three weeks and grow wispy beards of mould before they would be eventually thrown out. I tried to get the candle wax out of the carpet and couldn't, so I moved the couch to cover it. And I thought continually about Gus.

My nerves were *shot*. The phone rang all day long and every single time I jumped and twitched and frantically prayed, "Please God, let it be Gus." I didn't dare pick it up, just in case it was Gus. Answering the phone was tantamount to admitting I cared and that would have been unforgivable. Karen or Charlotte had to leave their pot scrubbing (in Charlotte's case) or their dancing around spraying air-freshener (in Karen's case) and do it for me.

And, as befitted a rejected woman, I insisted that they observe a five-ring interval before answering.

"Not yet, not yet!" I begged, time after time. "Let it ring a bit longer. We can't let him think that we're waiting for him to call."

"But, we are." Charlotte looked puzzled. "At least you are."

It made no difference. Only one of the calls was for me, and that was from – of all people – my mother.

"What took you so long to answer?" she demanded, when Charlotte sadly handed me the receiver.

And suddenly it was Saturday night.

Saturday night had always played a starring role in my life. It had been a thing of beauty, a bright spot in a dark world, but an *empty* Saturday night, a Gus-free Saturday night – well, I was shocked to find that I was almost *frightened* of it.

Every Saturday night for the previous – had it only been six weeks? – had been taken care of because I had been with Gus. Sometimes we had gone out, and other times we stayed in, but whatever we had done, we had done it together. And now I felt as if I had never, ever had a free Saturday night before in my life, so alien did it feel to me.

It had taken on a certain malevolence, as though someone had flung a snake at me and told me to amuse it for a few hours.

What was I supposed to *do* with it? And with whom? All my friends were paired up with someone. Charlotte was with Simon, Karen was with Daniel, Daniel was with Karen and anyway Daniel wasn't my friend anymore.

I could have called Dennis but that was a ridiculous idea. It was a Saturday night, he was a gay man, he would be at home shaving his head and revving up for a night of unbridled hedonism.

Charlotte and Simon invited me to go to the cinema with them – as Charlotte said, the cinema was about all she could stomach after the imbibing of the previous evening – but I didn't want to go.

It wasn't that I was afraid of being a gooseberry – I had no problem with that, after all I'd done it many times in the past, and the first ten thousand times are the worst – but I'm ashamed to say I was afraid to leave the flat in case Gus arrived.

Like a fool, I was still hoping that I might hear from him. In fact, what I actually hoped for was that, at around eight, he would arrive in a borrowed, too-big jacket and a badly knotted tie, having made the mistake of thinking that Saturday night was the night for the dinner and not Friday.

It was possible, I told myself weakly.

Things like that happened sometimes. Maybe it would happen to me and I would be saved. I could draw back from the edge of the abyss laughing because I hadn't needed to be there at all.

Karen and Daniel didn't invite me to join them in whatever they were doing. Somehow I hadn't expected them to. Anyhow I didn't want them to. I felt so uncomfortable around Daniel that we were barely speaking to each other. And I went crimson when I remembered how I had thought that he was going to kiss me the previous evening, when he was only being nice because Gus had stood me up. How could I have thought such a thing? I asked myself in mortification. And worse again, how could I have thought that it was a nice idea? It was Daniel, after all. It would have been like thinking that snogging my dad was a nice idea.

Everyone left and I was alone in the flat on a bright, Saturday evening in April.

Somewhere in between Gus entering and exiting my life, winter had changed into spring, but I had been too busy enjoying myself and falling in love to notice.

I found rejection that much harder to cope with when the evenings were bright.

At least when it was dark I could draw the curtains and light the fire and snuggle and hide and feel quite cosy in my aloneness. But the brightness of the spring evening was embarrassing. It highlighted what a failure I was – my rejection was too visible. I felt as if I was the only person in the whole world sitting in, alone, on a Saturday night.

Winter was a much better time to be abandoned – it was so much more *discreet*.

After eight o'clock came and Gus didn't, I moved down one more step on the stairs of misery. Why couldn't I have just tumbled straight to the bottom in one go and got it over and done with? I understood the wisdom of pulling a plaster off a cut with a single, flamboyant, eye-watering rip, but when it came to matters of the heart, I removed things from me with painful slowness.

I decided to go out to get a video. And a bottle of wine because there was no way I'd get through the evening without a drink.

"Gus won't ring anyway, Gus will be out with Mandy," I said, playing "it really doesn't matter" with the gods. If you can play that well, if you can convince the gods that you really don't want what you really do want, then you'll probably get it.

At the video shop Adrian greeted me like a long-lost sister. "Lucy! Where've you been?" he roared the length of the shop. "I haven't seen you in *ages. Ages!*"

"Hi, Adrian," I mouthed at him, hoping to lower his volume slightly by my good example.

"So what do we owe this pleasure?" he yelled.

"On your own on a Saturday night? He must have dumped you!"

I smiled tightly and picked up *Reservoir Dogs*.

When Adrian had turned around to find my video, I gave him a half-hearted vetting. I owed it to myself, I told myself. Now that I was single again I had to keep my eyes peeled for the potential husband that Mrs Nolan had predicted for me. He wasn't bad, I thought wearily. Nice bum, nothing wrong with it, couldn't fault it except for one thing, it wasn't Gus's bum. Nice smile, but it wasn't Gus's smile.

It was a total waste of time, my head was filled with Gus and I couldn't look at another man.

Anyway I didn't really believe that it was over with Gus – it was too soon. I needed to be thumped over the head with proof, battered into the ground by it, before I could truly believe it. Giving up on things didn't come easily to me. Letting go was not one of my strong points.

On the one hand I knew for certain that I'd never see Gus again, and on the other hand I just couldn't stop hoping that there would be some explanation, no matter how unlikely, and that we could start again.

I went next door to the off-licence. It was full of young, happy people, buying bottles of wine and cans of lager and hundreds of cigarettes. I was suddenly pierced with the old familiar feeling that life was a party to which I hadn't been invited. A feeling of belonging had made a guest appearance in my life while I'd been with Gus, but now it was back to feeling like the spectre at life's feast.

As I walked slowly back to the flat, trying to waste time, I was suddenly overcome with panic, convinced that Gus was ringing me at that instant. I rushed up the road and back into the flat and breathlessly ran to see if the little red light on the answering machine was blinking, but it wasn't. It stared and stared and stared at me and didn't blink once.

It took forever for the day to inch painfully slowly towards darkness, for other people to come home from their nights out, for other people to go to bed, for the gap between me and everyone else to narrow, for me to stop feeling like the *only one* . . .

I got drunk and once again I rang the number that Gus had given me. Nobody answered – luckily. Although I didn't feel that it was lucky at the time, I was furious, beside myself with frustration and loneliness. I just wanted to talk to him, if I could have spoken to him I knew he would make it all right.

I even, in my drunken state, thought about getting a taxi to Camden and walking around and seeing if I could find him and going to the pubs that he had taken me to there, but thankfully, something stopped me – maybe the awfulness of the idea of stumbling across him with the mysterious Mandy. A little bit of sanity pierced my armour of obsession.

I woke to the stillness of Sunday morning. I knew, even before I got out of bed, that I was the only person in the flat, that Karen and Charlotte hadn't come home the previous night. It was only seven o'clock and I was completely awake and completely alone.

How was I supposed to fill my head to keep the loneliness away? How was I supposed to stop myself from going mad thinking about Gus?

I could have read but I didn't want to, there was nothing I wanted to read. I could have watched telly but I knew I wouldn't be able to concentrate. I could have gone for a run, that might have taken away some of the terrible anxiety, but I could barely get out of bed. I was buzzing with nervy adrenaline but I couldn't face getting up. I could ring the Samaritans, but it would sound so feeble – "My boyfriend has abandoned me and we were supposed to be getting *married*!" when they had real people with real problems to deal with.

It wasn't just Gus that had deserted me, but my dreams of marrying him had also gone for the milk. Letting go of the fantasy was almost as hard as letting go of the man.

Of course, it was my own fault. I should never have taken Mrs Nolan's predictions seriously. I was the one who had berated Meredia and Megan for believing her. No sooner were their backs turned, than I had believed her also.

So, instead of treating it like a casual fling, I had thought that Gus was the one for me and that we'd be together forever.

It wasn't *really* my fault, I tried to convince myself. Mrs Nolan had sensed my insecurity and loneliness and told me what I wanted to hear. And, while I could take or leave the actual getting married bit – you know, the white dress, rows with my mother, ham salad, all that – I was very pleased with the promise of a soul mate.

I only had myself to blame for falling for a load of nonsense.

I lay in bed, my head whirring, blaming myself, absolving myself, blaming myself again, listening for the phone, seized by murderous jealousy towards the unknown Mandy, hoping that she might only be a friend, thinking that Gus might still ring, telling myself not to be so stupid, then thinking that, no, really, he *might*, warning myself that I was a masochist, then protesting that I was merely a romantic and so on . . .

I was sure that the void of Sunday morning had never been so bad before. Tumbleweed blew up and down the dusty streets of my ghost-town psyche.

How had I coped before I met Gus? I wondered. How had I filled all that empty space? I didn't remember it ever feeling quite this empty, but it must have done, because I had lived for Sunday after Sunday without Gus.

Then I realised what had happened – he had come, filled the gap and, when he left, he took more than he had arrived with. He had charmed his way into my heart, made me trust him and, then when I wasn't looking, had stolen my emotional fixtures and fittings, leaving my interior sitting-room stripped bare. He had probably gone to a pub in Camden and sold the lot for way under their market value.

I had been suckered and not for the first time.

Sunday took an eternity to pass. Charlotte and Karen didn't come home. The phone never rang. At about nine o'clock I brought back the video, got another one and a bottle of wine. I drank the wine, I got drunk, I went to sleep.

And then it was Monday morning. The weekend was over and he hadn't rung.

Chapter Forty-Two

Hetty's replacement started work with us that morning.

It had been six weeks since she had left, a long time for three people to spend trying to do the work of one.

But Ivor had begged Personnel for a stay of execution, a couple of weeks grace before they advertised for a new person. The poor fool had held out hope that Hetty might return to his short, pudgy, pink, freckled arms.

But she was now living in Edinburgh with her brother-in-law – very happily, by all accounts – so he had finally come to terms with it.

Our new colleague happened to be a young man. That wasn't the random stroke of luck that it might, at first glance, appear to be. Oh no!

Meredia had arranged for it to be that way.

And the only reason that I knew about it was because I had caught her at her machinations.

A couple of Mondays before, because of a series of unfortunate accidents – my train rushed in as I reached the platform, my connecting train was actually waiting for me, etc., etc. – I had arrived early for work.

Meredia was actually in *before* me. That was surprising in itself, but what was more surprising was that she was already working, feverishly sorting through a pile of papers, discarding some and feeding others into the paper shredder.

"Morning," I said.

"Shut up, I'm busy," she muttered.

"Meredia, what are you doing?"

"Nothing," she said, continuing to cram documents into the shredder.

I was intrigued, because she was obviously up to something. I should have known that there was no way that she'd be working at a quarter to nine on a Monday morning on *work* work.

I took a closer look at the pile of papers on her desk. They were job applications.

"Meredia, what are these and where did you get them?"

"They're the applications for Hetty's replacement. Personnel sent them down for Smelly Simmonds to look at."

"But why are you shredding them? Don't you want a new person in?"

"I'm not getting rid of them all."

"I see." I didn't.

"Just the married women," she continued.

"Might I ask why?"

"Why should they have a husband and a job?" asked Meredia, bitterly.

"You're joking?" I said weakly. "Are you trying to tell me that you're destroying all the applications from the married women just because they're married?"

"Yes," she said grimly. "I'm simply evening up the good fortune in the world. You can't depend on karma to work properly so, if you want something done right, you have to do it yourself."

"But Meredia," I protested, "just because they're married doesn't mean that they're happy. They could be married to a man who thumps them or who has affairs or who's really boring. Or they could be widowed, or separated, or divorced."

"I don't care," sniffed Meredia. "They've still had their big day, they've still had their waltz up the aisle wearing their fancy frocks."

"But if you don't want them to be happy surely the best possible thing you could do is ensure that one of them gets the job. Look at how miserable we all are!"

"Don't try and get round me, Lucy," she said scrutinising another. "What do you think this Ms L Rogers is? Married or not married?"

"I don't know. You're not *supposed* to know. That's why she put 'Ms'."

"Not married, I bet," continued Meredia, ignoring me. "She's only put 'Ms' to hide the fact that she doesn't have a man. OK, she gets an interview."

"Well, look at it another way," I suggested. "What if we get a single woman in here? Doesn't that just increase the competition for the few available men out there?"

I had only been joking, but a spasm of horror wobbled across Meredia's face.

"Christ, you're right, you know," she said, "I never thought of that."

"In fact," I said, feeling a bout of mischief-making coming on, "you'd be much better off getting rid of the applications from all the women and just keeping the men's."

She liked the sound of that.

"Brilliant!" she exclaimed, hugging me. "Brilliant, brilliant, brilliant!"

I was pleased – any kind of subversion in the workplace lessened the tedium.

So she frantically flicked through the bundle of applications, and set about weeding out *all* the women before Ivor came in.

But the purge didn't end there because the power of life and death over people had gone to her head.

"Why should we put up with some old codger?" she demanded. And then proceeded to cull all of the men over thirty-five.

The once fat pile was emaciated by then and she whittled it down even more by checking under their hobbies and interests section.

"Hmmm, this one likes gardening. Say 'bye bye'," she said, flinging it to one side.

"And this one's in the territorial army," tossing another one away. By the time she was finished there were only four left. Four men, between the ages of twenty-one and twenty-seven, who listed their hobbies variously as "partying", "working out", "socialising", "holidaying in Ios", and "drinking".

I had to say, it looked promising.

If I hadn't been living in a fool's paradise, thinking everything was blissfully wonderful with Gus, I would have been quite excited myself.

All four of them came for interviews over the course of that week. As each one arrived, Meredia, Megan and I loitered by reception to get a good look at them before they were whisked away to Personnel so that Blandina could ask them where they saw themselves in five years time. ("Swinging from a noose if I'm still working here," was the correct answer, although they weren't to know. Never mind – if they got the job, they'd find out quick enough.)

We gave them marks out of ten for good-lookingness, niceness of bum, size of packet, etc., not, of course, that Meredia, Megan and I actually had any say in the final outcome.

But that didn't stop us discussing them with passionate interest. "I liked number two," said Megan. "What did you think, Louise?"

"My name is Meredia" said Meredia hotly. "And number three was by far the cutest."

"I preferred two," I said. "He looked really *nice.*"

Megan liked the sound of number four, the one who put "working out" as one of his hobbies, but, when he arrived, we were all saddened to observe that he was terminally homosexual. And naturally he wasn't picked because Ivor was about as homophobic as you could get. When he came back to the office after interviewing him, he told us many jokes along the lines of, "If I had dropped fifty pence on the floor, I wouldn't have bent down to pick it up," and, "Backs to the wall, eh? Guffaw, guffaw."

"But seriously, girls," he continued, "we couldn't have a gay man in here."

"Why not?" I demanded.

He went all coy. "What if he . . . er . . . *fancied* . . . me."

"You!" I spluttered.

"Yes, me," said Ivor, smoothing back what remained of his hair.

"But he didn't *look* mentally retarded," I said, while Megan and Meredia sniggered.

Ivor narrowed his eyes at me but I didn't care, I was furious.

"What do you mean, Miss Sullivan?" he asked coldly.

"I mean that just because he's gay and just because you're a man doesn't mean that he'll fancy you."

The cheek of him to think that *anyone*, man, woman, child or farmyard animal, might find him attractive.

"Of course he'd fancy me," muttered Ivor. "You know what they're like. Promiscuous."

There was a chorus of outrage from Meredia, Megan and me.

"How dare you!" and "You fascist!" and "How the hell would you know?"

"What if he already has a boyfriend?" demanded Megan. "What if he's in love with someone?"

"Don't be ridiculous," stuttered Ivor. "And you can all shut up because we're not hiring him. He can go off and get himself a job hairdressing, or in one of those Terence Conran restaurants. He'll be much better suited to that."

He went into his office and slammed the door, and left the three of us positively seething.

Number two, the nice, smiley, twenty-seven-year-old drew the short straw. He was offered the job, and he compounded his misfortune by accepting it.

His name was Jed and, although he hadn't been the best looking of the bunch, I had a good feeling about him. He never stopped smiling, lovely big beams. The corners of his mouth disappeared into his hairline and his eyes were nowhere to be seen – it would be interesting to see how quickly the job wiped the smile off his face.

Mr Simmonds was very excited. "It'll be great to have another man around the place," he kept saying, sloughing his hands together with glee, visualising lunch-time pints of lager and manly chats about cars and being able to throw his eyes to heaven and snort "Women!" and get an empathetic response.

Jed started work the Monday after Gus had disappeared on me.

I surprised myself by my resilience that morning. I got up, showered, dressed myself, went to work, wondered where I had gone wrong with Gus, but mostly felt not too bad, although in a dead kind of a way.

Megan was in before me, just back from a weekend in Scotland. She had been all Australian about it – why fly when you can spend twelve hours in a rattley old bus and save a fiver? She had taken in about ten cities in the course of her forty-eight hours and climbed a few mountains and met a couple of kiwi blokes and got plastered in a Glasgow pub with them and slept on the floor at their hostel and found time to send postcards to everyone she had ever met and hadn't slept a wink and still looked beautiful and was raring to go. She even brought us back a present, a slab of Scottish toffee, the good old-fashioned type that's harder than diamond and glues your teeth together and renders you speechless.

Next to arrive was Meredia. She bustled in wearing her best curtain in honour of our new employee and pounced on the toffee, ripping off the tartan cellophane. We all tucked in.

Then Jed arrived, looking shy and nervous, but still grinning like a loon. He was wearing a suit and shirt and tie but we'd soon knock that out of him.

Poison Ivor arrived hot on his heels and did his Important Businessman routine. He shouted and made lots of manly physical contact and threw his head back a lot and barked with laughter. He'd copied it from the bosses upstairs. He loved to do it but didn't often get the chance.

"Jed!" he barked, sticking out his hand and shaking Jed's. "Good to see you! Glad you could make it! Sorry I wasn't here to greet you – got caught up in something, you know how it is? I hope this lot of reprobates, ha ha, have been looking after you, ha ha." He slung his arm paternally across Jed's shoulder, and steered him over to my desk. "Ladies, ha ha, I'd like you to meet the latest addition to our team, ha, ha, Mr Davies."

"Jed, please," murmured Jed.

A silence followed. None of us could speak because our jaws were glued together with toffee. But we smiled and nodded in an enthusiastic way. I think we made him feel welcome.

Ivor had decided that he would be Jed's Svengali and was delighted to have someone to impress – he knew that we women didn't have an ounce of respect for him – and he showed off shamelessly.

He bored on and on about the importance of his office in the structure of the company, and about the career opportunities for Jed, "if you work hard". He flashed the rest of us a bitter look when he said that. "Someday," he said, "you could even end up at my level."

Then he finished by saying, "Well, I can't stand here all day chatting. I'm a very busy man." He gave Jed a rueful, I-work-so-hard, one-man-to-another smile, and self-importantly sailed into his office.

There was a moment of silence. We all smiled awkwardly at each other.

Then Jed spoke.

"Wanker," he said, to the closed door.

The relief – Jed was one of us! Megan, Meredia and I exchanged proud, delighted smiles. Such promise! And he had only been in the office ten minutes. We would painstakingly mould him and guide him until he was as sarcastic and cynical as, well, maybe even, *Meredia*.

Chapter Forty-Three

I tried very hard not to think about Gus, and it worked. Apart from a constant feeling of slight nausea, I would barely have known how miserable I was. The sensation of having swallowed a lump of lead and not having the energy to drag the extra weight around with me was another little clue.

But that was all.

I didn't cry, or anything like that. I didn't even tell the girls at work. I just couldn't be *bothered* to, I was too disappointed.

It was only when the phone rang that I wasn't quite in control. Renegade Hope managed to give me the slip and escape from its container to play hopscotch on my nerve endings. But never for long. By the third ring I'd usually caught up with it, forced it back into the container, and sat on the lid.

The only phone call of note that I got that week, wasn't. It was from my brother, Peter.

I couldn't for the life of me understand why he was ringing me. He was my brother and I loved him, I suppose, but it wasn't as if we *liked* each other very much.

"Have you been out home recently?" he asked.

"A few weeks ago," I admitted, hoping that his

question wouldn't be followed with, "Well, don't you bloody well think it's time that you went?"

"I'm worried about Mammy," he said.

"Why?" I asked. "And do you have to call her 'Mammy'? You sound like Al Jolson."

"Who?"

"You know – I'd walk a million miles for one of your smiles?"

There was a silence.

"I worry about you, Lucy, I really do. But, listen to me, Mammy's gone a bit funny, strange like."

"In what way?" I sighed, trying to be interested.

"Forgetting things."

"Maybe she has Alzheimer's."

"Oh, you have to make a joke about everything, don't you, Lucy?"

"I wasn't joking, Peter. Maybe she does have Alzheimer's. What kind of things has she started forgetting?"

"Well, you know the way I hate mushrooms?"

"Um, do you?"

"Yes! You know I do. *Everyone* knows I do!"

"All right, all right, calm down."

"Well, when I was out there the other night she gave me mushrooms on toast for my tea."

"And . . . ?"

"What do you mean 'and?' Isn't that enough! And I said it to her. I said, 'Mammy, I hate mushrooms' and she just said, 'Oh, I must be mixing you up with Christopher'."

"That's shocking, Pete," I said drily. "We'll be lucky if she sees out the month."

"Jeer all you like," he said, sounding hurt. "But there's more."

"Do tell."

"She's done something funny to her hair."

"Anything would be an improvement."

"No, Lucy, it's funny. It's all kind of curly and blonde, she doesn't look like Mammy any more."

"Ah! Now it all makes sense," I said solemnly. "There's no need to worry, Peter, I know exactly what's up."

"Well, what is it?"

"She's got a boyfriend, silly."

Poor Peter got very upset. He thought that our mother was like The Blessed Virgin, only more chaste and saintly. But at least I got rid of him and hopefully he wouldn't bother me with any more ridiculous phone calls. God knows, I had enough real things to worry about.

Chapter Forty-Four

Megan and her housemates were having a party that Saturday night.

She shared a three-bedroomed house with twenty-eight other Australians, all of whom did shift work, so there were actually enough beds to sleep whoever needed to sleep at the time. It just meant that the beds were used on a time-share basis, round the clock, twenty-four hours a day.

Apparently Megan shared a single bed with a roofer called Donnie and a night porter called Shane, neither of whom she ever saw. In fact, she liked to make it sound as if they had never actually met.

She promised me that there would be thousands of single men at the party. (On Thursday, I had sheepishly come clean to my colleagues about Gus's disappearance.)

I was miserable on Saturday. Without Gus, and Mrs Nolan's promise of imminent marriage, my life was so, so, *nothingy*. There were no added extras, no human accessories, no soft-focus future, no soaring magic, nothing at all to enhance me. Me, on my own, was colourless, dull, earth-bound, unadorned. I had become the Amish frock of personalities and even *I* had lost interest in myself.

I didn't want to go to the party because I was having much too good a time feeling sorry for myself, but I had to go because I'd arranged to meet Jed. I couldn't stand him up because he wouldn't know anyone else there.

Meredia wouldn't be there (a subsequent engagement), but that was handy because the house was quite small.

Of course Megan would be there but she was the hostess, and she'd be too busy breaking up fights and having yard-of-lager competitions to look after Jed.

Jed and I met at the tube station at Earls Court, or Little Sydney, as it should have been called.

Now, going for drinks with work people after work is one thing, but I always drew the line at having them spill over into my weekend.

But Jed was different – he was wonderful, *exceptional*. By the end of his first week he'd already coined the name "Mr Semens" for Mr Simmonds, been late once, rung a friend in Madrid twice, and could fit a whole chocolate digestive into his mouth. He was much more fun than Hetty had ever been. I think Ivor had already begun to feel as let down and betrayed by Jed as he had once been by Hetty.

As Megan had promised, the party was packed with men – huge, drunk, boisterous, Antipodean men. It was like being in a forest. Jed and I got separated when we arrived and I didn't see him again for the rest of the night. He was just too short.

The giants were called things like Kevin O'Leary and Kevin McAllister and shouted drunkenly at each other about the time they'd got drunk and gone white-water rafting in the Zambia. Or when they'd got drunk and gone sky-diving in Jo'burg. Or when they'd got drunk and gone bungee jumping off some Aztec ruins in Mexico City.

They were very foreign to me, a different breed of man from what I was used to. They were too big, too sun-bleached, too enthusiastic.

And worst of all they all wore strange jeans – they were trousers made of blue denim, but the resemblance ended there. (They're jeans, Jim, but not as we know them.) There were no recognisable brand names and I think Jed was the only man in the house who had a button-fly, all the others had zips. One bloke had a parrot embroidered onto his back pocket, another one had a seam sewn down the centre of his legs, a kind of built-in crease. Another one had pockets all down the side of his legs and yet another one had jeans that were made up entirely of little squares of denim. It was horrible. There were even a couple of stone-washed pairs. They didn't seem to care.

I had thought that I didn't mind how a man dressed, that it didn't matter if he just threw on any old thing, but I realised that night that I did care a lot. I liked a man to look devil-may-care and casual, but it had to be a very specific type of devil-may-care and casual.

All of them tried to get off with me – some of them tried twice and three times – using the same chat-up lines.

"Fancy a shag?"

"No thank you."

"Well, would you mind lying down while I have one?"

And, "Do you sleep on your stomach?"

"No."

"Well, do you mind if I do?"

After I had been thus approached for about the fifth time, I said, "Kevin, ask me how I like my eggs in the morning."

"Lucy, mite, how do you like your eggs in the morning?"

"Unfertilised!" I shouted. "Now fuck off!"

They were impossible to offend.

"OK," they shrugged. "No haaaaaad foilings." They just moved on to the next woman who strayed into their line of vision, propositioning her in the same charming way. At about one-thirty I had drunk four million cans of Castlemain and I was stone cold sober. I hadn't seen one attractive man and I knew that things wouldn't get any better. If I stayed any longer I'd be throwing good time after bad. I decided to quit while I wasn't ahead.

No one noticed me leave.

I stood alone on the road, trying to flag down a taxi, and wondered in despair – was that it? Was that all I could expect from life? Was that the best I could expect from being a single woman in London?

Another Saturday night over and nothing to show for it.

My flat was silent when I got in. I felt so depressed that I vaguely contemplated suicide, but couldn't muster the enthusiasm for it. Maybe in the morning, I promised myself, maybe I'll feel more able for it when I'm not so depressed.

"You rotten bastard, Gus," was my last thought before I went to sleep. "This is all your fault."

Chapter Forty-Five

A couple of weeks had passed and Gus still hadn't phoned me.

Every morning I thought I had come to terms with it and every evening when I went to bed I realised that I had been holding my breath all day, hoping, almost *expecting*, to hear from him.

I discovered that I had become an embarrassment.

By allowing myself to be dropped by Gus I had upset the delicate tripartite balance that had existed between my flatmates and I. When the three of us had had boyfriends, things had been fine. If one couple wanted to have the sitting-room to themselves – for whatever reason – all the other couples had to do was go to their respective bedrooms and make their own entertainment.

But now that I was on my own, the couple who wanted the sitting-room would feel guilty about banishing me to the sensory deprivation of my bedroom and then they'd feel annoyed with me, because annoyance is much more pleasant than guilt. Being dropped by Gus was regarded as being my own fault, a result of careless, slipshod behaviour.

Charlotte decided that it was time for me to get a new boyfriend. She had a childish desire to help and a not-so-childish desire to get me out of the house once in a while so that she and Simon could play doctors and nurses or whatever it was they got up to.

"You really should forget about Gus and try and meet someone else," she said, encouragingly, one evening when just the two of us were in.

"Give it time," I said.

Surely *she* was supposed to say that to *me* and not the other way round, I thought in confusion.

"But you'll never meet anyone if you never go out," she said.

And, of course, she would never get to have sex with Simon on the hall floor, either, if I never went out. But she was nice enough not to say it.

"But I do go out," I said. "I went to a party on Saturday night."

"We could put an ad in the paper for you," suggested Charlotte.

"What kind of an ad?"

"An ad in the personal columns."

"No!" I was horrified at the suggestion. "I may be in a bad way, all right, I *am* in a bad way, but I hope I'll never sink that low."

"No, Lucy," protested Charlotte, "you've got it all wrong. Lots of people do it. Lots of normal people meet people through the lonely hearts pages."

"You must be out of your mind," I said firmly. "I am not about to enter that twilight world of singles bars, singles laundrettes, men who say on the phone that they look like Keanu Reeves and then when they turn up they're more like Van Morrison without the dress sense, men who say they want an equal loving partnership when what they really want is to bludgeon you to death and then carve stars with a bread knife all over your stomach. No way. Absolutely not."

Charlotte found that hilarious.

"You've got it all wrong," she wheezed, wiping her eyes. "It's not a bit like that anymore. It used to be sleazy . . ."

"Would you do it?" I asked, cutting to the heart of the matter.

"Well, it's hard to say," she stuttered. "I mean, I *have* a boyfriend . . ."

"Anyway, it's not just the sleaze that I object to," I interjected angrily, "it's being tarred with the 'Sad Lonely Bastard' brush that upsets me. Don't you understand Charlotte – if I go down the lonely hearts path, I might as well be dead. My hope will die with my few remaining ounces of self-esteem."

"Don't be silly," said Charlotte, sitting up straight on the couch and reaching for a pen and a piece of paper which turned out to be the Chinese takeaway menu.

"Come on," she said happily. "Let's make up a lovely description of you and lots of lovely lads will answer and you'll have a great time!"

"No!"

"Yes," she said nicely, but firmly. "Now let's see, how will we describe you? . . . Hmmm, how about 'short'? . . . no maybe not 'short'."

"Definitely not 'short'," I found myself agreeing. "That makes me sound like a dwarf."

"You're not allowed to say 'dwarf' anymore."

"Vertically challenged, then."

"What's that?"

"A dwarf."

"Why didn't you just say that?"

"Bu . . ."

"OK, how about 'petite'?"

"No, I hate 'petite'. It sounds so . . . so . . . girly and pathetic. Like I can't change a plug."

"You can't change a plug."

"So? It doesn't mean I have to go public about it, though."

"Fair enough. Maybe I'll ask Simon to write an ad for you – after all he's in advertising."

"But, Charlotte, he's a graphic designer."

She looked blankly at me.

"What do you mean?"

"I mean that he does the, er, drawings, for the ads. Not the writing bits."

"So *that's* what a graphic designer does," she said, as if she'd just found out the earth was round.

Sometimes Charlotte really scared me. I wouldn't have liked to live in her head, it must have been a dark, lonely, frightening place. You could walk for miles and miles without meeting a single intelligent thought.

"I know, I know, I've got it! How about 'pocket Venus'?" Charlotte turned to me, her eyes shining with delight at her creative powers.

"No!"

"Why not? That's a good one."

"Because I'm not a bloody pocket Venus, that's why!"

"So what? They won't know and by then they'll have met you and seen how nice you are."

"No, Charlotte, it's not right. And it could turn nasty – they might ask for their money back."

"Oh gosh," agreed Charlotte, dismay on her face, "you've got a point."

"Please forget it," I pleaded.

"Well, why don't we just run through the ones here in *Time Out* and see if there's anyone nice for you."

"No!" I said in despair.

"Oh listen, here's a good one," squeaked Charlotte. "'Tall, muscular, hirsute, oh . . . oh dear . . .'"

"Yuk," I squirmed. "That's not my type at all."

"Just as well," said Charlotte, a bit deflated looking. "She's a lesbian. Such a pity. I was starting to like the sound of her myself. Oh well, so it goes."

Charlotte continued reading. Every now and then she'd make an enquiry of me.

"What does it mean when they say they've got a soh?"

"That they've got a sense of humour."

"So what's gsoh then?"

"Good sense of humour, I suppose."

"Oh, that's nice."

"No, it's not, Charlotte," I said annoyed. "It just means they think they're hilarious and they laugh at their own jokes."

"What does w/e mean?"

"Well endowed."

"No!"

"Yes."

"Gosh! That sounds really sort of showy-offy, doesn't it? That would put you right off, wouldn't it?"

"It depends. It would certainly put me off. But maybe not everyone."

"You wouldn't be interested in weekday afternoon romps in Hampstead with a married couple?"

"Charlotte!" I said outraged. "How could you make such a suggestion?"

"You know I can't get the time off work," I added grumpily and the pair of us cackled a bit at that.

"How about 'caring, affectionate man with so much love in his heart to give to the right girl'?"

"No way! He sounds like a *total* loser. A male version of me."

"Yes, he does sound a bit wet," agreed Charlotte. "Well, how about 'virile, demanding hunk seeks classy, athletic, supple woman for adventures'?"

"Supple?" I shrieked. "Athletic? Adventures? How vile and awful. Could he be a bit more *overt* about what he wants from a relationship? Jesus!"

I was getting upset. It was terribly depressing. Sordid and sad. For as long as I lived I would never go out with a man that I'd met through the personal ads.

"You look lovely," said Charlotte, adjusting my collar.

"Is that supposed to make me feel better?" I asked bitterly.

"I bet you'll have a great time," she said, tentatively.

"I know for a fact I'll have a horrible time."

"Think positive."

"Think positive indeed! Why the hell don't you go?"

"I don't need to go. I already *have* a boyfriend."

"Rub it in, why don't you?"

"But he might be nice," suggested Charlotte.

"He *won't* be nice."

"No, really, he might."

"I can't believe you're doing this to me, Charlotte," I said, still stunned.

I really couldn't believe it – Charlotte had betrayed me. The cow had set me up with some man she had found in a lonely hearts column. Without even consulting me she had arranged a date for me and some American man. And of course when I found out, I was outraged.

Although my reaction wasn't as extreme as Karen's. When she heard about "my blind date", as Charlotte insisted on calling it, she laughed until she cried. She managed to stop laughing just long enough to ring Daniel to tell him all about it and then she convulsed for another twenty minutes.

"Christ, you really *are* desperate," she said as she hung up the phone and wiped tears from her cheeks.

"It's nothing to do with me," I protested angrily. "And I'm not going."

"But you have to go," said Charlotte. "It wouldn't be fair to him."

"You're out of your daft little mind," I said.

She stared at me, her big blue eyes filling with tears.

"Sorry, Charlotte," I said awkwardly. "You're not daft."

Simon had called her daft a few days before and her boss called her daft quite a bit, so she was a bit sensitive about daftness allegations.

"But, Charlotte, really," I blustered, trying to be strong, "I'm not going out with him. I don't care how nice or normal he sounds."

"I was only trying to help," she sniffed, tears trickling out of the corners of her eyes. "I thought it would be nice for you to meet a sweet man."

"I know," I stretched up and guiltily put my arm around her. "I know, Charlotte."

"Don't be cross with me, please, Lucy," she sobbed.

"I'm not cross," I said, hugging her. "Oh, Charlotte, please don't cry."

I hated to see anyone cry – with the possible exception of my mother – but I promised myself, no matter what happened, no matter how much she cried, I was not giving in to Charlotte, I was not going to meet this Chuck bloke.

I gave in to Charlotte and agreed to meet this Chuck bloke. I'm not really sure how or why I agreed, but I agreed.

Although I retained a small remnant of self-esteem by complaining bitterly about it.

"He'll be completely vile," I assured Charlotte as I prepared to leave. "Do I look all right?"

"I keep telling you, you look lovely. Doesn't she Si?"

"What? Oh yes, yes, lovely," agreed Simon, heartily. He was just dying for me to go, so he could have sex with Charlotte.

"And, Lucy, he might be nice," she said.

"He'll be awful," I promised.

"You never know," said Charlotte darkly and wagged a finger at me, "he could be The One."

And to my horror, I found myself agreeing with her, or at least hoping that she was right. She had a point – he *might* be nice, he could be the exception that proved the rule, he mightn't be an anal-retentive, axe-murdering, astonishingly ugly, emotional cripple.

Hope, that fickle foolish creature, that emotional prodigal son, was making a guest appearance in my life.

In spite of all the times hope had let me down in the past, I had decided to give it one more chance.

Would I ever learn?

Am I addicted to disappointment, I wondered.

But then there was a surge of excitement through me – what if he was lovely? What if he was like Gus, only more normal and not so dippy and without the minimalist approach to phone calls? Wouldn't it be wonderful? And, just supposing that I did like him and it all worked out, I could still be within Mrs Nolan's timescale. I would have time to go to America to meet his family and organise a wedding within six months.

Chapter Forty-Six

I was meeting him at eight o'clock outside one of those boring steakhouse type restaurants that proliferate in central London, to cater for the masses and masses of Americans who visit the city every year.

Chuck had said – for a moment my head swam because I could hardly believe I was having dinner with a man called Chuck – Chuck had said I would recognise him by his navy raincoat and a copy of *Time Out*. By his navy raincoat and copy of *Time Out* so shall he be known!

I had no intention of loitering outside the restaurant waiting for him to arrive, thus leaving myself at his mercy if he turned out to be a total horror. Instead I cased the joint from across the road and pretended to be waiting for a bus. With the collar of my coat up I kept my eyes trained on the doorway opposite.

I had butterflies in my stomach because, while I fully expected him to be untouchable, there was always a small chance that he might be nice.

At five to eight my subject arrived, navy raincoat and copy of *Time Out* all present and correct.

From my lookout perch he seemed fine. Well, at least he *looked* normal enough. Only one head, no obvious disfigurements, no extra limbs, no missing limbs – at least none that I could see. I couldn't speak for his toes or his penis on such short acquaintanceship.

I crossed the road for a closer look.

Not bad, not bad, at all.

In fact, he could even be described as handsome. Medium height, tanned, dark hair, dark eyes, nice bones, a *strong* face. There was something about him that reminded me of someone . . . who could it be? It would come to me later.

Hope buzzed around in my chest. He wasn't my usual type, but things had never worked out with any of my usual types, so what the hell, I might as well give this a chance.

Maybe I owe you one, Charlotte, I thought.

He had seen me. He had clocked my matching copy of *Time Out*.

He spoke. No spit landed on my face. This was looking good.

"You must be Lucy," he said. Nil points for originality, minus several million for the dodgy trousers – but that's Americans for you – and ten out of ten for no hare lip or stutter or dribble.

Yet.

"And you must be Chuck?" I asked, not exactly breaking any new conversational ground there either.

"Chuck Thaddeus Mullerbraun the Second, all the way from Redridge, Tucson, Arizona," he grinned. He

419

stuck out his hand and gave me a hefty, hearty handshake.

Oh, oh, I thought.

Quickly I pulled myself up short. It wasn't his fault – Americans always did that. Ask them anything, *anything*, from "is there a god?" to "Can you pass the salt, please?" and the first thing they do is tell you their full name and address. As if they're afraid that, if they don't keep reminding themselves who they are and where they come from, they'll just disappear.

I *did* find it a bit odd. What if someone stopped me in the street and asked me the time and I replied, "Lucy Carmel Sullivan, the First, all the way from the top floor flat, 43D Bassett Crescent, Ladbroke Grove, London W10, UK, Yurrup, sorry I don't have a watch, but I think it's about one-fifteen."

It was just a different custom, I reminded myself, like Spaniards having their dinner at two in the morning, and I should be embracing this contact with a different culture. *Vive la difference!*

Lucy Mullerbraun?

I think I liked Lucy Lavan better, I thought wistfully, but there was no point pursuing that line of enquiry at this particular juncture.

Or at any juncture, ever.

"Shall we?" he suggested politely, indicating the door into the restaurant.

"Why not?"

We went into the vast restaurant where a small Puerto Rican man showed us to a window table.

I sat down.

Chuck sat down opposite me.

We gave each other halting, nervous smiles.

I went to speak, and he went to speak at the same time. Then we both stopped and neither of us said anything, then at the same time we both said, "You first, no really," then we both laughed, then we both said "Please, you go first."

It was kind of endearing. It broke the ice.

"Please," I said, taking charge, afraid that the double act could continue all night, "You go first, really, I insist."

"OK." He smiled. "I was just going to tell you that you've got beautiful eyes."

"Thank you." I smiled back, flushed with pleasure.

"I love brown eyes," he said.

"So do I," I agreed. So far so good. We'd obviously got a couple of things in common.

"My wife has brown eyes," he said.

What?

"Your wife?" I asked faintly.

"Well, ex-wife," he corrected. "We're divorced now, but I keep forgetting."

What was I supposed to say to *that*? I didn't know he'd been married. But so what, I decided, getting a firm grip on myself, everyone has a past and anyway he never said he *hadn't* been married either.

"I'm over it now," he said.

"Er . . . good, good," I said, trying to sound encouraging.

"I wish her well."

"Marvellous," I said, heartily.

A little pause.

"I'm not bitter," he said bitterly, staring bitterly at the tablecloth.

Another little pause.

"Meg," he said.

"S . . . sorry?" I said.

"Meg," he said again. "That's her name. Well, it's actually Margaret, but I always called her Meg. A little nickname, I suppose."

"That's nice," I said weakly.

"Yes," he said, giving a very whimsical, faraway smile. "Yes, it was."

An awkward silence followed.

I was aware of a faint sinking noise. It took me a moment or two to realise that it was the sound of my heart. The sound of it on an express-lift, no-stops-allowed, one-way-ticket, to my boots.

But perhaps I was being negative.

Maybe we could help mend each other's broken hearts. Perhaps all he needed was the love of a good woman. Perhaps all I needed was the love of Chuck Thaddeus Mullerbraun from – where was it? – somewhere in Arizona.

The waitress came to take our drinks order.

"A glass of your finest English tap water for me," said Chuck, leaning back in his chair and slapping his stomach. I had a horrible feeling that his shirt was nylon.

And what was that about tap water? He was *drinking* tap water? Had he a death wish?

The waitress gave Chuck a filthy look. She knew a cheapskate when she saw one.

Surely he wasn't expecting me to have tap water also?

Well, I was sorry, but he could go to hell, because I wanted a drink. A proper drink.

Start as you mean to go on.

"A Bacardi and diet coke," I said, trying to sound like it was a reasonable request.

The woman went away and Chuck leaned across the table. "I didn't know you drank *alcohol*," he said.

Maybe we wouldn't be mending each other's broken hearts, after all.

He might as well have told me he didn't know I had sex with small children, he said it with so much distaste and disgust.

"Yes," I said a little defiantly. "Why not? I enjoy a drink now and again."

"OK," he said slowly. "OK. OK. That's cool with me. That's OK."

"Don't you drink yourself?" I asked.

"Yeah, I drink," he said.

Thank God.

"I drink water," he continued. "I drink sodas. That's all I need to drink. The best goddam drink in the world – a glass of ice-cold water. I don't need alcohol."

I braced myself. If he tells me he's just high on life, I'm leaving, I promised myself.

But, alas, it was not to be.

And on with the conversation, such as it was.

"Your . . . er . . . Meg doesn't drink?" I asked. "Alcohol," I added hurriedly, before he started playing semantics with me again.

"Never touched alcohol, never needed to," he bellowed.

"Well, it's not as if I need to," I said, wondering why I was bothering to try and defend myself.

"Hey." He stared at me intently. "You gotta ask yourself – who are you trying to convince? Me? Or you?"

You know, now that I looked at him properly, he wasn't so much bronzed as *orange*.

Not so much tanned, as tangerine.

Our drinks arrived. Chuck's glass of water and my Instrument of the Devil and diet coke.

"Are you ready to order?" asked the waitress.

"Hey, we just got here," said Chuck rudely.

The woman slunk away. I wanted to run after her and apologise but Chuck engaged me in what could laughingly be called conversation.

"Have you ever been married, Lindy?" he asked.

"Lucy," I corrected him.

"What?" he asked.

"Lucy," I said. "My name's Lucy."

A blank stare from Chuck.

"Not Lindy," I said, by way of explanation.

"Oh, I *see*," he said, with a big, jovial burst of laughter. "Excuse me, excuse me. I gotcha. Yeah, yeah, *Lucy*."

He laughed again. A big, thigh-slapping bellow.

It took him quite a while to stop laughing, actually.

He kept shaking his head in disbelief and saying things like "Lindy! Well, how about that?" and "Ha, ha, ha. Lindy! Can you truly believe it?"

Then he put on a down-South in-bred red-neck accent and said something that sounded like "Waall, tie me down you hog and whup ma hide with molasses!"

At least I *think* that was what he said.

And the face that looked so *strong* on first meeting was actually *immobile*, unmoving, rigid.

I sat with a fixed smile on my face and waited for him to calm down and then said, "In answer to your question, Brad, no, I've never been married."

"Hey, hey, *hey*," he said, his face darkening with annoyance. "The name's Chuck. Who's this Brad guy?"

"It was a joke," I explained quickly. "You know . . . you called me Lindy. I called you Brad."

"Yeah, right." He stared at me as if I was completely mad. His face was like a slide show – one static image after another, with little gaps of nothingness while he cleared one emotion and waited for the new one to arrive.

"Hey, lady," he demanded. "Are you some kind of wacko? Because I got no room for wackos in my life right now."

I clamped my mouth shut to stop myself from asking him just *when* he might have room for wackos in his life, but it was difficult.

"It was a joke," I said nicely. I thought I had better appease him because I was just a little bit alarmed at his abrupt change of mood.

He probably belonged to a gun club. There was a slightly odd, kind of manic look in his eyes that I hadn't spotted when I first met him. And there was something weird about his hair . . . what was it?

He stared at me and nodded his head slowly (I couldn't help noticing that while his head moved, his hair seemed to stay in the same place) and said, "Right, I get it. This is humour, right?"

He flashed a mouthful of teeth at me. To let me know he appreciated my humour.

. . . It wasn't just that it was obviously blow-dried and flicked . . .

"That was an example of humour, hey? Yeah, pretty good."

. . . And of course it was thick with hairspray . . .

"I like it, yeah, yeah, I like it. You're one funny little lady, arencha?"

. . . Could it be a wig? . . .

"Mmmm," I murmured. I was afraid to open my mouth to speak in case I spewed all over him, right into his brushed-denim lap.

. . . Although it was more like a helmet, actually, all rigid and sticky . . .

He picked up a bread roll and shoved it into his mouth in one go and chewed and chewed and chewed, like a cow chewing the cud. It was disgusting.

I could hardly believe what he did next.

It was not so much that he broke wind. It was more like he took a hammer to it and shattered it into a million pieces.

Yes, he broke wind, long and loud and unapologetically.

While I was still reeling from the shock of that, the poor waitress came back to take our order, although I was sure I would vomit if I was required to eat anything. But there was nothing wrong with Chuck's appetite.

He ordered the biggest steak on the menu and asked for it rare.

"Why don't you just get the entire cow brought along to the table and you can get it to climb up onto your plate?" I suggested.

I had nothing against people eating red meat, but it was so nice to be mean to him that I wasn't able to pass up the chance.

But unfortunately he just laughed.

Such a pity, a waste of good nastiness.

Then he decided that it was time that we got to know each other better, time to share life experiences.

"Hey, ya ever go to the Caribbean?" he barked at me. And, without waiting for my answer, launched straight into a description of the white sands, the friendly natives, the great tax-free shopping, the wonderful cuisine, the cut-price all-inclusive deals he could get because his brother-in-law worked for a travel agent . . .

"Well, he's not technically your brother-in-law anymore, now that Meg has divorced you, is he . . . ?" I interrupted, but he elected not to hear me. All his attention was focused on himself.

On and on went the lyrical description. The beautiful cabana he had stayed in, the phosphorescence from the tropical fish. I was patient for as long as I could, until I couldn't take anymore. I very rudely interrupted a description of the clean, clear, blue water on which he went sailing in a glass-bottomed boat.

"Let me guess," I said sarcastically, "you went there with Meg."

He looked up at me quickly, as suspicion clanked onto his immobile face.

Then I gave him a dazzling smile, just to confuse him.

"Hey, how d'ya guess?" He grinned at me.

I sat on my hand to stop myself punching him in the face.

"Oh, feminine intuition, I guess." I giggled daintily, certain I could feel vomit lapping at the back of my teeth.

. . . *And speaking of teeth, what was wrong with his? Was he wearing a gumshield?* . . .

"So you'd like to have a relationship with me, Lisa?"

"Er . . ." How could I tell him I'd rather have a relationship with a leper without offending him?

The leper, that is.

"Cos I gotta warn you," he grinned, "I'm a pretty choosy guy."

Where was my dinner?

I no longer cared.

"But you're kinda cute."

"Thanks," I muttered. Don't bother, please.

"Yeah, on a scale of one to ten, I'd give you a . . . let's see, yeah, I'd give you a seven. No, let's say a six point five. I gotta deduct a half a per cent because you drank alcohol on the first date."

"I think you must mean half a point, not half a per cent, you're talking about tens, not hundreds, and what's wrong with drinking it on the first date, as opposed to any other time?" I demanded coldly.

He frowned slowly at me. "You got a big mouth on you. You ask a whole lot of questions, ya know that?"

"No, really Chuck, I'm very interested in knowing why I've lost half a point with you."

"OK. OK. I'll tell ya, I'll tell ya. Sure, I'll tell ya. You realise the signals that drinking alcohol on a first date gives out, Lisa? You see the kind of statement you're making about yourself?"

I stared blankly at him.

"No," I said sweetly. "But please do enlighten me."

"Huh?"

"Enligh . . . , er, please do *tell* me."

"A, V, I, L, A, B, L, E," he spelt out slowly.

"Sorry?" I said, confused.

"Available," he said impatiently. "It says to me that you're available."

"Oh, *available*," I said, understanding. "Well, perhaps if you had spelt it properly I might have realised what you were trying to say."

His eyes narrowed.

"Hey, what are you trying to say here? That you're smarter'n me or something?"

"Nothing of the sort," I said politely. "I was just letting you know that there are three 'A's in available."

God! He was nasty!

"No man has any respect for a woman who is a drunk," he said, looking with narrowed eyes at my Bacardi and then at me.

This had to be a joke. It had to be some kind of set-up. That was the only explanation. I looked round the room, half expecting to see Daniel sitting at one of the other tables, or Jeremy Beadle lurking with a cameraman.

But I recognised no one.

Oh dear, I sighed to myself, I wish this was over. What a waste of an evening. Especially a Friday evening, when there were such good things on telly.

"You know, you don't actually have to put up with this," a rebellious little voice whispered in my head.

"But of course I do," a dutiful little voice whispered back.

"No, honestly, you don't," replied the first voice.

"But, but . . . I agreed to meet him, I have to stay the allotted time. I can't leave. It wouldn't be *polite*," protested my dutiful part.

"*Polite,*" spluttered the rebellious voice, "*polite!* Is he polite? The Americans who nuked Hiroshima were probably more polite."

"Yes, but, I hardly ever meet men and I shouldn't look a gifthorse in the mouth and . . ." explained my dutiful part.

"I don't believe what you're saying," said the rebellious part, sounding genuinely shocked. "Do you really have such a low opinion of yourself that you'd rather be with a man like this than on your own?"

"But I'm so lonely," said the dutiful voice.

"Desperate, you mean," snorted the rebellious voice.

"Now that you put it like that . . ." said the dutiful part reluctantly, loath to turn away a man, *any* man, even a truly awful man.

"I *do* put it like that," said the rebellious part firmly.

"Well, OK then, I suppose I could pretend to be sick," said the dutiful voice. "I could fake a broken leg or a burst appendix, or something."

"No, you damn well won't," said the rebellious part. "Why spare him? If you're leaving, do it properly. Let him know how objectionable he is, how obnoxious you find him. Stand up for yourself – make a statement."

"Oh, I couldn't . . ." protested the dutiful part.

The rebellious voice was silent.

" . . . Could I?"

"Of course you could," said my rebellious voice warmly.

"But . . . but . . . what am I to do?" asked the dutiful part, excitement beginning to burn in the pit of its stomach.

"I'm sure you'll think of something. And, might I just remind you, that if you leave now, you'll be home in time for Rab C Nesbitt," advised my rebellious voice.

Chuck was droning on again.

"I was on the tube today and no kiddin' here, Lizzie, I was the only white guy on it . . ."

Right! Enough! No more.

"But I'm afraid of him," realised my dutiful part. "What if he tracks me down and tortures me and kills me – let's face it, that's the kind he seems to be."

"Don't be afraid," said the rebellious voice. "He doesn't know where you live, he doesn't even have your phone number. All he has is a PO box number. Go on! You've nothing to worry about."

Feeling light-headed with unaccustomed power I stood up, gathering my coat and my bag.

"Excuse me." I smiled sweetly, interrupting Chuck's speech about how there should be tighter controls on emigration and how only white people should have a vote. "I'm just going to the little girls' room."

"You gotta take your coat to the rest room?" enquired Chuck.

"Yes, Chuck," I said sweetly.

"You got it."

Dickhead!

I walked away from him, my legs shaking. I was afraid but I was also happy.

I passed our waitress clearing a table and I had so much adrenaline throbbing through me I could barely speak properly.

"Excuse me," I said, my words tripping over each other, my tongue far too big for my mouth. "I'm at the table by the window and the gentleman would like a bottle of your most expensive champagne sent over, please."

"Certainly," said the woman.

"Thank you," I smiled, and moved past her.

As soon as I got home I would ring the restaurant

to make sure that none of the staff were out of pocket, I decided.

I reached the Ladies, hesitated for only a moment, then kept on walking. I felt as if I was dreaming. It was only when I crossed over the threshold from the restaurant into the rainy street, that I really believed that I had done it, that I had left.

My initial plan had been to just leave and go home, letting the passage of time be Chuck's indicator that I was never to return. But that would be a mean thing to do. His dinner would get cold while he was waiting for me to get back. And waiting, and waiting . . .

Always assuming the revolting man would have the manners to wait for me to get back before tucking into his barely dead animal.

Nevertheless I decided to give him the benefit of the doubt.

I pulled my coat on, and even though it was a wet, Friday evening, I got a taxi immediately.

The gods were smiling on me. That was the kind of sign I needed to feel that I had done the right thing.

"Ladbroke Grove," I told the driver excitedly, as I clambered in. "But before that can you do me a favour?"

"Depends," he said suspiciously. But that's London cab-drivers for you.

"I've just said goodbye to my boyfriend. He's going away forever and he's sitting by the window in this restaurant here and I wonder if you could drive slowly by until he sees me so that I can wave farewell one last time."

The taxi-man seemed genuinely moved by my request.

"Just like Frank Sinatra and Ava Gardner. And I thought that romance was dead," he said hoarsely, a catch in his voice. "No problem, darling. Just tell me which one he is."

"That, er, tanned, handsome man just up there," I said, pointing to where Chuck was sitting, admiring his reflection in his knife, as he waited for me to come back from the loo.

The taxi-driver drove up right beside Chuck's table and I rolled down my window.

"I'll turn the light on, love, so he can see you better," said the driver.

"Thank you."

Chuck twiddled the knife backwards and forwards, catching his reflection in different lights.

"Likes 'imself," commented my driver.

"He certainly does."

"You sure that's 'im, love?" asked the driver doubtfully.

"Certain."

Chuck was starting to look annoyed now. I had obviously spent more time than Meg used to in the Ladies and he didn't approve.

"Should I 'oot the 'orn, love?" asked my faithful driver.

"Why not?"

The driver beeped the horn and Chuck looked out into the street to see what all the commotion was about. I leant out of the taxi window and waved energetically.

He smiled in cheery recognition when he saw me and raised his hand to wave back at me.

But then confusion began to inch its way painfully slowly across his stupid face when he noticed that the familiar looking person he was waving to was actually his date for the evening, the woman he was supposed to be having dinner with, the woman whose scampi-in-the-basket was, as we speak, being placed reverently in front of her empty chair, and that she was sitting in a taxi about to depart the scene. The fledgling cheery wave halted abruptly in its tracks.

He wrinkled his orange forehead. He didn't understand. This does not compute.

And then the penny dropped.

The look that appeared on his face was worth it all. When he realised that I was not in the little girls' room but was in fact doing a runner in a taxi, it was nothing short of beautiful. It had been worth the whole vile evening just to see the disbelief and rage and fury on his smug, weird, tanned face. He leapt up from his chair, and dropped the knife that he had so admired himself in.

I couldn't stop laughing.

"What the . . . ?" he mouthed out the window, his face contorted with fury. He looked almost animated.

"Fuck you!" I mouthed back in at him. Then I thrust both my hands out into the wet night and raised the first two fingers of each hand in a 'V' gesture at him, just in case his lip-reading wasn't too good. I made short, sharp upward motions with both my hands for about ten seconds while he stared at me in an impotent fury from the window.

"Drive," I ordered.

The driver put his foot on the accelerator just as two waiters appeared behind Chuck, one with an ice bucket and a white napkin, the other with a bottle of champagne.

In the cab I realised who Chuck had reminded me of. It was *Donny Osmond*!

Donny Osmond singing "Puppy Love".

Orange, sincere, soulful Donny Osmond with puppy dog eyes to match his puppy love. But a Donny Osmond for whom the glitter had faded, who had had a hard life, a Donny Osmond who things hadn't worked out for, a bitter, humourless, right-wing Donny.

Long before I reached home, I felt guilty about Chuck and the bottle of champagne. It wasn't fair that he should have to pay for it. Just because he was a nasty, horrible person didn't mean that I had to behave like one too. So the minute I got into the flat I rang the restaurant.

"Er, hello," I said nervously. "I wonder if you can help me. I was in your restaurant earlier and I had to leave suddenly, and before I left I ordered a bottle of champagne for my companion. It was an . . . er . . . surprise, and I don't think he would have wanted to pay. And I want to be sure that the waitress didn't have it docked from her wages or anything . . ."

"An American gentleman?" a man's voice asked.

"Yes," I reluctantly confirmed. Gentleman, my foot!

"And you must be the woman with the mental illness?" enquired the voice.

The cheek of him! How dare the voice imply that I was mad.

"The American man explained how you often do this kind of thing, that you can't help yourself."

I swallowed my rage.

"I'll pay for the champagne," I muttered.

"There's no need," said the voice. "We have agreed to overlook the damage he's caused to the furniture if he pays for the champagne."

"But it hardly seems fair for him to have to pay for it when he didn't drink it," I said.

"But he did drink it," said the voice.

"But he doesn't drink," I protested.

"Yes, he does," said the voice. "Come and look for yourself, if you don't believe me."

"You mean he's still there?"

"Oh, yes! And that's not alcohol-free tequila he's drinking."

Oh God! So now I had turning Chuck into a drunkard on my conscience. But what the hell – it might be the best thing that ever happened to him.

Right, now for the telly!

To my great dismay, Karen and Daniel were in the front room. They were sharing a bottle of wine and were sickeningly holdy-handy, watching *my* programmes on *my* telly.

"You're home early," said Karen, annoyed.

"Mmmmmm," I said non-committally.

I was annoyed also. That meant no Rab C Nesbitt for me. I couldn't stay in the same room as Karen and Daniel while they were cuddling and canoodling.

I would have to go and sit in my bedroom while they stretched out on the couch and Karen put her head in Daniel's lap and Daniel stroked Karen's hair, and Karen stroked Daniel's . . . well, whatever else they got up to, which I didn't really want to think about.

They were so lovey-dovey, they were disgusting.

Charlotte and Simon never made me feel awkward, I just didn't know what it was about Daniel and Karen.

"How are you?" asked Daniel, looking all smug and superior.

"Fine," I said airily.

"And how was your blind American?" asked Daniel.

"Mad."

"Really?"

"Really."

"Oh Lucy, not again," sighed Karen. "You're beginning to make a habit of this kind of thing."

"I'm going to bed," I said.

"Good," said Karen, winking lasciviously at Daniel.

"Ha, ha," I said, keen to seem like a good sport. "Goodnight."

"Lucy, don't feel you have to leave just because we're here," said Daniel, polite as ever.

"Do," corrected Karen.

"Stay," urged Daniel.

"Don't," laughed Karen.

"Karen, don't be so rude," said Daniel, looking embarrassed.

"I'm not being rude," smiled Karen. "I'm just being honest. I'm letting Lucy know where she stands."

I went, feeling inexplicably tearful.

"Oh, by the way, Lucy," called Karen after me.

"What?" I asked, standing by the door.

"There was a phone call for you."

"Who was it?"

"Gus."

Chapter Forty-Seven

A great load tumbled from me and I breathed out, a long, delicious sigh – I'd been waiting to do that for three weeks.

"Well, what did he say?" I demanded, excitedly.

"That he'd ring again in an hour and that if you weren't back then he'd call every hour until you got home."

Happiness flooded through me. He hadn't abandoned me, I hadn't done anything wrong, my position hadn't been usurped by Mandy.

A thought struck me.

"Where did you say I was?" I asked breathlessly.

"Out."

"Out with a man?"

"Yes."

"Great! That might worry him. What time is he calling back at?"

Karen sat up straight and stared at me.

"Why?" she asked. "Surely you're not going to *speak* to him?"

"Er, yes, I am," I said sheepishly, shifting from one foot to the other.

Daniel shook his head in a "will she ever learn" kind of way and gave an exasperated little smile. The cheek of him! What would he know of the agonies of unrequited or semi-requited love?

"Haven't you any self-respect?" asked Karen disbelievingly.

"No," I said absently, wondering what tone I should adopt with Gus — amused? cross? stern?

I knew I was going to forgive him – it was only a question of how hard I was going to make him work for it.

"Well, it's your funeral," said Karen, turning away from me. "He should call in about twenty minutes."

I went to my room and ran on the spot with delight. Twenty minutes – how could I contain myself?

But I had to be calm, I couldn't let him know how thrilled I was so I forced myself to take deep breaths.

But I couldn't stop smiling – at five to ten, I'd be speaking to Gus, Gus whom I thought I'd lost forever, and I could barely wait.

When my digital alarm clock said nine fifty-five, I placed my feet in the starting blocks and waited for the off.

And waited.

And waited . . .

He didn't ring.

Of course, he didn't ring.

How could I have possibly thought he might?

So that I wouldn't cry, I fed myself all the usual excuses.

My clock could be fast. Gus couldn't tell the difference between five minutes and an hour, he was probably in a pub where, if there was a phone at all, it was probably broken and if it wasn't broken it was probably being hogged by some young woman from Galway on a marathon tearful call home.

But after eleven I admitted defeat and went to bed.

"The little bastard," I thought angrily. "He had his chance and he blew it. When he does ring, I'm not going to speak to him. And if I do speak to him, it'll only be to tell him that I'm not speaking to him."

Some time later I heard the doorbell ring and I sat up in bed in horror. Oh no! He was here, on the premises and I'd taken my make-up off! Christ, what a disaster. I leapt out of bed and heard Karen or Daniel pressing the buzzer.

"You keep him talking," I hissed at Karen, sticking my head out of my bedroom door. "I'll be ready in five minutes."

"Keep who talking?" she asked.

"Gus, of course."

"Why, where is he?"

"On his way up – you've just buzzed him in."

"No, I haven't," she said.

"Yes, you have," I insisted. "Just now."

She was behaving very oddly, but she didn't *look* drunk.

"No, I haven't," she insisted. She looked at me closely. "Are you all right, Lucy?"

"I'm fine," I said. "It's you I'm worried about. If it wasn't Gus, then *who* did you open the door for?"

"The pizza-man."

"*What* pizza-man?"

"The pizza-man delivering the pizza for me and Daniel."

"But, *where?*"

"Here," she said, flinging open the front door, revealing a man in a red plastic boiler suit and a crash helmet, with a cardboard box in his hands.

"Daniel," she shouted. "Make with the readies."

"I see," I whispered, and slunk back to bed.

Why had Gus ever bothered phoning at all, I wondered tearfully. What good had it done me? None whatsoever. Just caused upset and upheaval.

Hours later, when everyone was in bed and the flat was in darkness, the phone rang. I woke immediately – even in my sleep my nerves were still on full alert, hoping for Gus's call. I stumbled out into the hall to answer it because I knew it had to be Gus – no one else would call at such an hour, but I was too asleep to be happy about it.

Gus sounded drunk.

"Can I come over, Lucy?" was the first thing he said.

"No." I said, as I wondered, "Whatever happened to 'Hello'?"

"But I must see you, Lucy," he shouted passionately.

"And I must get my sleep."

"Lucy, Lucy, where's your fire, your passion? Sleep indeed. You can sleep anytime. But it's not every day we get the chance to be together."

I knew that only too well.

"Lucy, please," he said. "You're cross with me, is that it?"

"Yes, I'm cross with you," I said evenly, trying not to sound so cross as to frighten him away.

"But, please Lucy, I've got an excuse," he promised.

"Let's hear it."

"The dog ate my homework, my alarm clock didn't go off, my bike got a puncture."

I didn't think it was funny.

"Oh oh," he sang. "She's gone all quiet on me, that must mean that she's cross again," he said. "Seriously, Lucy, I do have an excuse."

"Please tell me it."

"Not over the phone. I'd rather come and see you."

"You won't see me until I hear your excuse," I said.

"You're a hard woman, Lucy Sullivan," he shouted sadly. "Hard! Cruel!"

"The excuse?" I asked politely.

"It's really better if I explain it in my full three dimensions. Disembodied voices aren't half as good," he said wheedlingly. "Please, Lucy, I hate the phone."

I was well aware of that.

"Come over tomorrow, then. It's far too late now."

"Late! Lucy Sullivan, when did the time ever matter to the both of us? You're like me – a free spirit who is not bound by time, as issued to us by that crowd of meanies beyond in Greenwich. What's happened to you? Has your soul been stolen by the goblins of clock-watching?"

He paused for a second and then said in tones of hushed horror, "Jesus, Lucy – you haven't gone and bought a *watch*!?"

I laughed – the little swine. How could I scare him if he made me laugh?

"Come over tomorrow morning, Gus." I tried to sound crisp and authoritative, "and we'll talk then."

"No time like the present," he said cheerfully.

"No, Gus. Tomorrow."

"Who knows what tomorrow will bring, Lucy? Tomorrow is another day and who knows where we might be?"

Whether or not he meant it as one, I knew a threat when I heard it – he might not call me tomorrow, I might never hear from him again, but right then, at that very moment, he wanted to see me. He was *mine*, and I would be well advised not to look a gift horse in the mouth, to catch the ball on the hop, and to learn the difference between birds in the hand and birds in the bush.

Do you really want him on these terms? asked a little voice in my head.

Yes, I replied wearily.

But, haven't you any self-respe . . . ?

No, I haven't! How many times do I have to tell you?

"OK, Gus." I sighed, pretending that I had just given in, although, of course, the outcome had never been in doubt. "Come over."

"I'm on my way," he said.

That could have meant anything from fifteen minutes to four months, and my dilemma was should I put my make-up on or should I just stay as I was.

I knew about the dangers of tempting fate – if I

put my make-up on, he wouldn't come. If I *didn't* put my make-up on, he would come, but would be so shocked at what I looked like that he would immediately leave.

"What's going on?" whispered a voice. It was Karen. "Was that Gus?"

I nodded, "Sorry for waking you."

"Did you tell him to go and fuck himself?"

"Er, no, you see I haven't heard the full story yet. He's, er, coming over now to tell me it."

"Now!? At two-thirty in the morning?"

"No time like the present," I said weakly.

"In other words, he was at a party and didn't score with anyone and he's in the mood for a shag. Nice one, Lucy, you certainly put a high price on yourself."

"It's not like that . . ." I said, my stomach lurching.

"Goodnight, Lucy," she sighed, ignoring me. "I'm going back to bed."

"With Daniel," she added smugly.

I knew she was going to tell Daniel all about it, because she told him *everything* about me, well, all the embarrassing and shameful stuff, at any rate. I had no privacy, and I hated him knowing so much about me and being smug and judgemental.

He was always in the flat, I almost felt like we lived together. Why couldn't the pair of them go to *his* flat and leave me alone in peace?

"I wish they'd split up," I thought fiercely.

I decided that I'd hoodwink Fate, I was sick of it having all the power so, while I did put on some make-up, I didn't get dressed.

And, in no time at all, the sound of the buzzer boomed through the flat in a manner that would wake the dead. It stopped and gave some welcome peace for a few seconds before starting again and continuing for what seemed like hours – Gus had arrived.

I opened the door of the flat and waited for him to appear, but he didn't. And then I could hear raised voices from a few floors below. Eventually he stumbled up the stairs, looking cute, sexy, dishevelled and drunk.

I was lost, hopelessly, completely lost. It was only when I saw him that I realised how much I had missed him.

"Jesus, Lucy," he grumbled, as he wriggled past me and into the flat, "that neighbour of yours has a ferocious bad temper. It was a mistake anyone could make."

"What have you done, Gus?" I asked.

"I rang the wrong bell," he said sulkily, clumping straight into my bedroom.

Now, now, wait a minute, I thought. He's being too forward altogether. He can't just waltz up here after no contact for three weeks and expect to jump straight into bed with me.

Apparently he could. He was already sitting on my bed, taking off his boots.

"Gus . . ." I said tentatively, about to embark on my lecture. You know, the usual – how dare you treat me like this, who do you think you are, who do you think I am, I've too much respect for myself (a lie), I'm not putting up with this (another lie), etc., etc.

447

"And I said to him, Lucy, I said, 'I only woke you up, it's not like I invaded Poland'. Ha, ha, I knew that'd give him something to think about. German, isn't he?"

"Sorry, Gus, no. He's Austrian."

"Sure, it's all the one. Aren't they all big and blond and forever eating sausages."

Then he focused his dancey, bloodshot eyes on me, seeing me for the first time since he had barged in.

"Lucy! My darling Lucy, you're looking beautiful."

He jumped up and ran over to me and the scent of him triggered a longing and lust that surprised me with its intensity.

"Mmmmmmm, Lucy, I've missed you." He nuzzled my neck and slid his hand under my pyjama top. The touch of his hand on my bare skin made me shiver with lust that had slumbered undisturbed for three weeks, but with supreme self-control I pushed him away.

Get off! I thought – I haven't given you my lecture yet.

"Oh, Lucy, Lucy," he murmured, as he relaunched his attack. "We must never be apart again."

He slid one arm tightly around my waist and opened the top button of my pyjamas with the other. I fumbled with it, trying to close it again, but it was mere tokenism.

I couldn't help myself – he was too sexy. Beautiful and dangerous and roguish. And he *smelt* so nice, so like Gus.

"Gus!" I wrestled with him as he tried to get my top off, "you didn't ring me for three wee . . ."

448

"I know, Lucy, I'm sorry Lucy," he said, tugging hard. "But I never wanted it to be that way. Jesus, you're beautiful."

"I deserve an explanation, you know," resisting hard as he pushed me towards the bed.

"Indeed you do, Lucy, indeed you do," he agreed vaguely, as he pushed down on my shoulder, trying to get me to buckle at the knees. "But will it do in the morning?"

"Gus, do you solemnly promise that you have a good excuse and that you'll tell it to me in the morning?"

"I do," he said, staring sincerely into my eyes and at the same time tugging hard, trying to get my pyjama bottoms down.

"And you can give out shite to me. You can even make me cry," he promised.

So we went to bed.

I remembered what Karen had said, but I disagreed with her – I didn't feel used. I *wanted* Gus to want to have sex with me. That would prove that he still fancied me, that he hadn't gone off me that, although he had run away for three weeks, it hadn't been my fault.

I decided that the lecture could wait until the morning. So I gave into my desire and Gus and I had sex. But I had forgotten that Gus was a bit of a wham, bam, thank you ma'am merchant – the sex was over almost as soon as it started. As in the past, Gus came in a matter of minutes. Which left plenty of time to hear his excuses. But he fell sound asleep immediately afterwards. And eventually I feel asleep too.

Chapter Forty-Eight

The following morning Gus wasn't any easier to pin down for his lecture.

Considering how drunk he had been the previous night, he was surprisingly full of energy. By rights he should have been stretched on the flat of his back, begging for a bucket and swearing never to drink again, like any normal person. Instead he was awake at the crack of dawn, eating biscuits. And when the post arrived, he bounced out to the hall to get it, and then, with much rustling of paper and ripping of envelopes, opened mine and told me what was in it.

"Oh, good girl, Lucy." He sounded proud. "I'm glad to see that you owe them Visa lads loads more money. Now all you have to do is move house and not tell them."

I lay in bed and wished bleakly that he would calm down. Or at least stop reminding me how much money I owed.

"What goes on at Russell & Bromley?" he asked. "Is it your old trouble again?"

"Yes." A pair of black suede knee boots and a pair of sexy, snakeskin sandals, to be precise.

"Now, Gus!" I tried to be firm and get his attention. "We really must . . ."

"What about this one, Lucy?" He waved an envelope at me. "It looks like Karen's bank statement. Should we . . . ?"

God, it was tempting. Charlotte and I suspected that Karen had thousands salted away and I would have *loved* to know.

But I had work to do.

"Never mind Karen's bank statement, Gus." I tried again. "You said last night that you had an excuse and that . . ."

"Can I have a shower, Lucy?" He interrupted. "I fear I pong a bit."

He lifted up his arm and put his nose to his armpit.

"Pooh," he said, making a disgusted face. "I stink, therefore I am."

He smelt fine to me.

"You can have a shower in a little while. Give me that envelope."

"But we could steam it and she'd never know . . ."

It was obvious that, despite his passionate promises the previous night, he had no intention of explaining anything to me.

And I was so delighted he was back that I didn't want to scare him away by pushing for explanations and apologies.

But, at the same time, he had to realise that he couldn't get away with treating me badly.

Of course, he *could* get away with treating me badly, in fact, he just had. But I had to, at least, lodge my protest, go through the motions of acting as if I had self-respect. In the hope that, even though I couldn't fool myself, perhaps I could fool him.

I would have to trick him into having the Serious Talk. It would have to be coaxed out of him, wheedled out of him, so that he wasn't even aware that he was doing it.

He wouldn't cooperate if he was approached full-frontal, as it were.

I would have to be very, very pleasant, but with an undercurrent of firmness.

I turned to Gus who was stretched out on the bed, reading a pension offer thing from my bank.

"Gus, I'd like to talk to you," I said, striving to sound pleasantly firm, or failing that, firmly pleasant.

I must have overdone the firmness because he said, "Oh oh," and made an "Oh oh" face. And he jumped off the bed and huddled in a cringing manner in the space between the wardrobe and the wall. "I'm afeerd."

"Come on now, Gus, there's no need to be afraid."

"I'm not afraid, I'm afeerd."

"Afeerd, then. There's no need to be."

But he wasn't taking it seriously at all. He kept poking his head of black curls out and I'd catch a glimpse of his bright eyes, before he'd whisk his head back in and I would hear him muttering, "Oh, no, I'm planking it, I'm bricking it, I'm done for, she's going to make mince-mate of me."

Then he started singing a song, something about whenever he felt afraid, he'd hold his knob erect and whistle a happy tune, so no one would suspect . . . "I'm AFRAID!"

"Gus, come out, please, there isn't anything to be afraid of."

I tried to laugh to show how good-humoured I was, but it was hard work being patient. It would have been lovely to shout at him.

"Come on, Gus, I'm not scary, you know that."

"The only thing I have to fear, is fear itself, is that it?" asked his disembodied voice.

"Exactly." I nodded to the wardrobe.

"But, the thing is, Lucy," it continued. "I actually fear fear an awful lot."

"Well, you must stop. There's nothing to be afraid of with me."

He slunk out, looking cute. "You won't shout at me?"

"No." I was forced to agree with him. "I won't shout at you."

"But I do want to know where you've been for the last three weeks."

"Has it been that long?" he asked innocently.

"Come on, now Gus. The last time I heard from you was the Tuesday night before Karen's party. What have you been up to?"

"This and that." He was vague.

"You can't just disappear for three weeks, you know?" But I said it very gently so that he wouldn't get annoyed and tell me to get lost and that he could disappear for as long as he liked and there wasn't anything I could do about it.

"All right then," he said. I leaned towards him eagerly, hoping to hear stories of natural disasters and acts of God. That neither I nor Gus were responsible for the three-week severance.

453

"The brother came over from th'Emerald Isle and we had a bit of a session."

"A session that lasted three weeks?" I asked disbelievingly. I didn't like the fact that I kept calling it three weeks, I should have been vaguer about it. I didn't want him to think that I'd counted the days since he'd been gone, which is of course, exactly what I *had* done.

"Yes, a session that lasted three weeks," he said sounding surprised. "What's wrong with that?"

"What's wrong with that?" I echoed mockingly.

"I've often been missing in action for lots longer than three weeks," he said, sounding confused.

"You're trying to tell me that you've been out drinking for three weeks?"

And suddenly I was appalled at myself. I sounded just like my mother, the tone of voice, the accusation, even the words.

"Och, I'm sorry, wee Lucy," said Gus. "It's not as bad as it sounds. I forgot about Karen's party and by the time I remembered I was too afraid to ring you, because I knew you'd be hoppin'."

"But why didn't you ring the next day?" I asked, cringing with pain as I remembered the agony of waiting that I had endured.

"Because I was in a right oul' shtate about missing the party and annoying you, so Stevie said to me, 'There's only one thing that'll sort you out, wee son, and that's . . .'"

" . . . Another drink, I'm sure," I finished for him.

"Exactly! And the next day . . ."

" . . . You felt so bad about not ringing me the

previous day that you had to go and get drunk to feel all right about it . . ."

"No," he said, sounding surprised. "The next day there was a big party in Kentish Town that started at eleven in the morning and we went along to that and got good and hammered, Lucy. Hammered! You never saw anyone so drunk, I hardly knew me own name."

"That's no excuse!" I exclaimed, and then shut up abruptly as, once again, I heard my mother.

"You know I don't mind you getting drunk." I tried to sound calm. "But it's not on to simply disappear and then come back and act like nothing is wrong."

"Sorry," he exclaimed. "Sorry, sorry, sorry."

Then I braced myself for the hardest question of all.

"Gus, who's Mandy?"

I stared hard into his face so that I could draw conclusions from his reaction.

Was it my imagination or did he look alarmed?

It *could* just have been my imagination. After all, his jaw didn't drop open and he didn't bury his face in his hands and sob, "I knew this day would come."

In fact all he did was look sulky and say "No one."

"She can't be no one. She's someone." I smiled tightly to convey that I wasn't accusing him of anything, that my fire was strictly friendly.

"She's no one special. She's just a friend."

"Gus," I said, my heart beating fast. "There's no need to lie to me."

"I'm *not*." Aggrieved, pained.

"I'm not saying you are. But if you're seeing someone else, I'd rather know."

I didn't say, if you're seeing someone else you can go and fuck yourself, which is what I *should* have said. But I didn't want to commit the cardinal sin of seeming to care. Popular myth has it that women are desperate to trap men, that men are afraid of being trapped, so the best way to trap them is to pretend that you don't want to trap them. However, that had backfired more times than I'd care to mention, with me saying, "I don't own you. But if you are seeing someone else, I'd like to know." And then meeting my so-called-boyfriend at a party wrapped around another woman and wanting to fling a drink over the two of them. And then being told, "But you *said* you didn't mind.

"Lucy, I'm not going with any other girls," said Gus. He had lost the defensive look and there was the light of sincerity in his green eyes.

He looked as if he cared about me. And although I was afraid of seeming ungrateful, I pushed ahead.

"Gus, *were* you seeing someone else, you know, before, when we were, er, you know, seeing each other?"

He looked puzzled for a moment while he translated my question into his vernacular. Then he got it.

"Was I two-timing you?" He sounded horrified. "I was NOT."

There was always the chance that he was telling the truth. In fact he probably was because he didn't have the organisational skills to live a double life. As it was, it was a triumph that he remembered to keep breathing when he woke up every morning.

"How dare you?" he demanded. "What kind of person do you think I am?"

The combination of his passionate denials and my desperate desire to believe him, meant that I did. Relief made me joyous and slightly light-headed.

Then he kissed me and I felt even more light-headed.

"Lucy," he said. "I would never do anything to hurt you."

I believed him. It would have been churlish to bring up the fact that he *had* hurt me. The important thing was that he hadn't meant to.

"Now can I hose myself down?" He asked meekly.

He went and had his shower and I thought about my mother. It had scared me a lot to hear me sounding like her. I would try even harder to be more and more liberal, I promised myself.

I heard Daniel and Karen greet Gus, as Gus came out of the bathroom.

"Morning, Gus," said Daniel. Was there something amused in his tone, I wondered defensively.

"Morning, Danny Boy. Morning, Morag McVitie," said Gus jovially, as if he'd never been away.

"Morning, Paddy O'Paddy," said Karen to Gus.

"Morning, Heather McShortbread," said Gus to Karen.

"Morning, Pisshead O'Bricklayer," said Karen to Gus.

"Morning, Skinflint McSeanConnery," said Gus to Karen.

"Morning, Rosarybeads O'Semtex," said Karen to Gus.

"Morning, Ronald McDonald," said Gus to Karen.

I heard roars of laughter. Outside the bathroom door was obviously the place to be.

Flatmates and boyfriend had successfully rebonded, and no one seemed embarrassed except me.

Chapter Forty-Nine

So Gus and I became an item again.

And I tried to relax and give him a longer leash.

Gus was a free spirit, I constantly reminded myself. Normal rules didn't apply to him. Just because he was late, or talked for hours to someone else at a party to which he'd taken me and where I knew no one, didn't mean that he didn't care about me.

I wasn't lowering my expectations, I decided. I was simply changing my perspective.

I knew he cared about me because he had come back, after the three-week hiatus. He didn't have to do that, no one forced him.

And with my new attitude Gus and I got on beautifully. He behaved impeccably. Well, as impeccably as he could without ceasing to be Gus.

It was summer and for once it acted it.

The weather in London was so unusually warm and sunny that many people took it as a sign that the world was about to end.

Day followed day of golden, blue-skied heat, but the population of London had been betrayed by the weather so many times that they expected the heatwave to disappear at any moment.

Everyone shook their heads and said gloomily, "It won't last, you know." But it did last and it seemed that the sun would shine forever.

I remember the time as idyllic.

Weeks and weeks where life seemed heavenly, where I felt as if I was living in a little golden cocoon.

My bedroom was flooded with yellow light every morning, so that it was nearly a pleasure to get up and live my life.

My depression always abated in the summer, and even work didn't seem so gruelling. Especially after we had the mini-mutiny and the maintenance department had to buy us a fan.

Most lunchtimes, Jed and I went to Soho Square where we scrambled with several thousand other office workers for a square inch of grass on which to lounge and read our books.

Jed was the best person to do that with because if he tried to talk to me, I could just tell him to shut up and he would. We could lie there in companionable silence.

At least, I found it companionable.

Meredia wouldn't come with us because she hated the sun. She spent her lunch-times hidden in the office, with the blinds down, trying to cast a spell on the weather, so that it would rain. Every day, she anxiously read the forecast, hoping for news of a drop in the temperature, raging as big black clouds that were coming from Ireland bypassed the UK and made straight for France.

Throughout the day, she treated us to the sight of

her hoiking up her skirt to shake containers of talcum powder between her gargantuan thighs. "Warm weather isn't kind to the larger woman," she would say bitterly and then ask if we wanted to see her red chafe marks.

The only thing that cheered her up was reading the temperatures of places in the world that were hotter than London. "At least I'm not in Mecca," she often sighed. And, "Think of what it must be like in Cairo", was another.

Megan wouldn't come to the park either.

Like a true Australian, she revelled in the warm weather, and took her sunbathing seriously. Far more seriously than Jed and I did.

She made great mock of me and all the other people who sat on the grass and pulled our skirts up above our knees and thought that we were daring and unfettered. She was in a different league – she went to the open-air pool and sunbathed topless.

Her contempt for Meredia was even more energetic than usual. "Listen, Pauline," she hissed. "If you don't stop whinging about your thighs, I'm going to show you all my tanned nipples."

"Keep talking, keep talking," said Jed eagerly to Meredia. She bestowed a sour look upon him and muttered, "My name is Meredia."

Megan blossomed in the heat. She was totally at home with it. She wore cut-off jeans to work – it wasn't her fault she looked like something out of *Baywatch*. She didn't mean to be provocative, she couldn't help being beautiful.

But I was very glad I wasn't Australian. I would

461

have been far too self-conscious to walk around half-naked. I thanked God that I had been born in a cold country.

Most afternoons we had an ice cream run and even Ivor joined us. Like the soldiers that played football in no-man's-land at Christmas, the unusual weather made us suspend our work-a-day hostilities.

Although it was far from pleasant to watch Ivor nibbling all the chocolate off his Magnum and then seeing his fat red tongue swirling around the ice cream bit.

Megan was eventually dragged up to Personnel because there had been complaints about her shorts. The complaints must have been lodged by some of our female employees, because they certainly weren't made by the hordes of men who came to our office on the flimsiest of pretexts, to inspect her long, golden thighs.

Meredia was thrilled. She hoped that Megan would be sacked. But Megan came back with a mysterious, yet satisfied smile.

"Should we help you clear out your desk?" asked Meredia hopefully.

"Maybe, Rosemary, maybe," smirked Megan.

"What are you looking so pleased about?" Meredia was confused and suspicious.

"And it's Meredia," she added vaguely.

"I may be moving *up*." Megan punctuated this with a point of her finger towards the ceiling. "Up, in the world."

Meredia looked stricken. "What do you mean?" she gasped.

Then she rallied. "Up to the dole queue?"

"Oh no," said Megan. That mysterious, satisfied, sphinx-like smile again. "Just up a few floors."

Meredia looked as if she was going to pass away.

"How many?" she managed to ask hoarsely. "One?"

Megan smiled and shook her head.

"Two?"

Another smile and another shake of the head.

Meredia barely managed to squeak "Three?"

And Megan, cruel, cruel Megan, waited a few, breathless, unbearable seconds before once again shaking her head.

"Not . . . *not* the fourth floor?" whispered poor Meredia.

"Yes, fatgirl, the fourth floor."

It appeared that Megan in her shorts had appealed to Frank Erskine, one of the flabby, bald, soft old codgers in Management. And in the god-like way that these men seemed to have, Frank had promised to create a position for her.

"What position might that be?" asked Meredia, with bitter innuendo. "The flat on your back position?"

The news spread like headlice in a primary school because Megan's shorts to riches story captured the imagination of the entire staff. It was everyone's fantasy to be plucked from the ignominy of Credit Control on the ground floor and suddenly elevated to the heights of the fourth floor. With the commensurate elevation of stipend, of course.

People sighed and said, "And to think I didn't believe in fairytales."

Meredia took it bad, she was a broken woman. Eight years she'd been there, she moaned, eight years. And that Australian slut was barely off the plane. And she was probably the direct descendant of a sheep-stealer. Or even a sheep-shagger, the whore . . .

Whenever anyone said to Meredia, "I hear Megan's going up in the world," she said, "She's going up because she goes down, if you follow me." Then she would purse her lips and nod her head self-righteously.

It wasn't long before word of Meredia's scurrilous allegations made its way back to Megan.

Megan, flint-eyed with rage, took Meredia aside. I'm not sure what she said to her, but it was enough to ensure that Meredia looked pale and terrified for a couple of days. And, thereafter, she energetically stressed that Megan had got the promotion entirely on her professional merits.

At least in public.

Chapter Fifty

Thinking back to that summer, I remember that Gus would collect me after work, just as the burning heat of the day was starting to abate. And we would sit outside pubs on balmy evenings, drinking cold lager, talking, laughing.

Sometimes there were lots of us, sometimes just me and Gus. But always there was the still, warm air, the clink of glasses, the hum of conversation.

The sun didn't set until late and the sky never really became night. The blueness just intensified and changed to a darker shade, then only a few hours later, the sun rose again on another dazzling day.

And the heat changed people, it made them so much nicer.

London was full of chatty, friendly people, the same people who slunk around miserably the rest of the year. Their mood was rendered open and Mediterranean by being able to sit in the street at eleven o'clock at night wearing a T-shirt and not freeze to death.

And when you looked around at a beer-garden full of people, it was obvious who had a job and who was unemployed. Not just because the unemployed ones never bought a round, but because they had brilliant tans.

It was always too warm to even think about eating until ten or eleven in the evening, when we would wander languidly along to some restaurant that had all its doors and windows opened onto the street, and drink cheap wine and pretend that we were abroad.

Every night we went to bed with the windows open, covered only by a sheet and it was *still* too hot to sleep.

It was impossible to imagine ever being cold again. One night I was so warm that, in desperation, I poured a glass of water over myself in bed. Which was very pleasant. And the height of passion that it incited Gus to was even more pleasant.

There was always too much to do. Life was a non-stop parade of barbecues, parties and nights out or at least that's how I remembered it. There must have been *some* nights when I stayed in and watched telly and went to bed early but, if there were, I can't recall them.

And not only was there loads to do, but there were loads of people to do it with. There was always someone to go out with. I mean, quite apart from Gus – he was available for outings every night.

There was never any danger of wanting to go for a drink and having no one to go with.

The people from my office often came out with Gus and I. Even poor Meredia lumbered along and sat and gasped and fanned herself and talked about how faint she felt.

Jed and Gus got along very well – at least after a while. When they first met they were like two shy little boys who wanted to play with each other but didn't know how to go about it. But eventually they both emerged from behind the folds of my skirt and made overtures. Gus might have offered to show Jed his new lump of hash, something like that. Then there was no stopping them. I barely got to speak to Gus on the nights that Jed came out. The pair of them had long, heads together, sotto voce conversations which I suspected had something to do with music. Boys often talked about that kind of thing. Where they tried to out do each other by remembering the name of some obscure group that someone played guitar with before he left and played guitar for another. It could keep them occupied for *days*.

But whenever anyone asked Jed and Gus what they were talking about they would just say mysteriously, "It's a bloke thing, you wouldn't understand."

Which earned them indulgent smiles until the night they said it to Charlotte's Simon.

The two of them constantly bitched about Simon and his ever-changing array of slick, fashionable clothes and his electronic personal organiser and the copy of *Arena* or *GQ* he always had about his person. But there was no need for them to be so obvious about it.

They never missed a chance to upset poor Simon.

"Is that a new T-shirt?" Gus asked Simon one night. Gus had a butter-wouldn't-melt-in-his-mouth expression that signalled trouble.

"Yeah, it's from Paul Smith," said Simon proudly, holding out his arms for us all to get a good look at it.

"We're twins!" said Gus engagingly. "It's just like the ones I got in Chapel Street market, five for a fiver. But I don't think the fella who sold it to me was one of the Smiths, I thought they were all banged up last month for receiving stolen goods. Are you sure it was a Smith?"

"Yes," said Simon, tightly. "I'm sure."

"Maybe they're out already," said Gus vaguely. And then moved onto something else, happy that he had ruined Simon's enjoyment of his new T-shirt.

The long-awaited evening rolled around when Dennis finally met Gus. Dennis shook hands with Gus and smiled politely. Then he turned to me and made an anguished face and put his knuckles in his mouth. "A word in private," he said and dragged me across the pub.

"Oh Lucy," he moaned.

"What?"

He put his hands on his face in distraught manner and whispered dramatically, "He's an angel, an absolute *angel.*"

"You like the look of him?" I was suffused with pride.

"Lucy, he's DIVINE!"

I had to agree.

"It's so rare to come across a good-looking Irishman," went on Dennis, "but when they get it right, they *really* get it right."

Not that Dennis would know. At least, not if he was relying on the mirror for his information.

Dennis commandeered Gus that evening, which made me quite edgy. Dennis constantly insisted that all was fair in love and war. At least when he fancied someone else's boyfriend, he did. And later that night, when Gus and I were going home on the bus, Gus said, "That Dennis is a lovely, friendly fellow."

Could Gus really be that innocent?

"Has he got a girl?"

"No."

"That's a shame, a dead nice lad like him."

I braced myself for Gus to tell me that he was meeting Dennis for a boys-only drink later in the week, but thankfully he didn't.

"We must fix him up with someone," said Gus. "Have you any single friends?"

"Only Meredia and Megan."

"Well, it can't be that poor craythur, Meredia," said Gus sympathetically.

"Why not?" I asked, all defensive.

"Well, isn't it obvious?" said Gus.

"Isn't what obvious?" I sneered, getting ready to push him out of the seat and onto the floor of the bus.

"Come on now, Lucy, don't tell me you haven't noticed," he said reasonably.

"That she's overweight?" I demanded hotly. "That's a lovely attit . . ."

"No, you big eejit," he said. "I don't mean that. Jesus, Lucy, that's a shocking thing to say, I wouldn't have expected that from you."

"What are you talking about?"

"Meredia and Jed, of course."

"Gus," I said earnestly. "You're fucking mad."

"That's as maybe," he agreed.

"What do you mean 'Meredia and Jed'?"

"I mean that Meredia is very fond of Jed."

"We're all very fond of Jed," I said.

"No, Lucy," said Gus. "I mean she's fond of the idea of Jed in his pelt, of getting Jed into the scratcher."

"No, she's not," I scoffed.

"Yes, she is."

"But how do you know?" I asked.

"Isn't it obvious?"

"Not to me."

"Well, it is to me," said Gus. "And you're the woman, you're the one who's supposed to have the intuition."

"But, but . . . she's too old for him."

"Well, you're older than me."

"Only by a couple of years."

"Anyway, love knows no age," said Gus wisely. "I read that in the fall-out from a Christmas cracker."

Well, well, well. How thrilling. The romance! The intrigue! Love among the threatening letters.

"And does *he* fancy her?" I asked eagerly, suddenly very interested.

"How do I know?"

"Well, you must find out. You talk to him, he talks to you."

"Yes, but we're men, we don't talk about that kind of a caper."

"Promise me that you'll try, Gus," I pleaded.

"I promise," he said. "But it still doesn't solve the problem of Dennis not having a girl."

"What about Megan?"

Gus made a face and shook his head. "She has notions, that one. She thinks she's it. She'd think she was too good-looking for Dennis, even though he's a lovely fellow."

"Gus! Megan isn't a bit like that."

"She is," he muttered.

"She isn't," I insisted.

"She is," he insisted back.

"Have it your way," I said.

"That'd make a welcome change," he said gloomily.

When I debriefed Dennis afterwards, first of all he told me that Gus was gorgeous, then he told me that Gus was gay – no surprises there. But then he defused the celebratory tone of the conversation by asking about Gus and his money situation.

"Oh that," I said dismissively. "It's not a problem."

"But has he any money?"

"Not much."

"But you two go out all the time."

"So what?"

"Have you been to any of his gigs?"

"No."

"Why not?"

"Because he gets most of his work in the winter."

"Just be careful, Lucy," warned Dennis. "He's a heartbreaker, that one."

"Thanks for the advice, Dennis, but I'm well able to look after myself."

"No, you're not."

I saw a lot of Charlotte and Simon over the summer. When the usual suspects were rounded up for a post-work drink, they were nearly always to be found in the thick of things.

Then they went to Portugal for a week. They asked Gus and I to go with them. Or rather, Charlotte asked me to come and said that I could bring Gus along, if I wanted. And not to worry about him and Simon squabbling.

But Gus and I didn't have enough money to go – not that I minded, because my life felt like a holiday anyway.

Gus, Jed, Megan, Meredia, Dennis and I went out to the airport to see them off, because we all had become so attached that we couldn't bear to be parted.

For the week they were away, we had lots of conversations like "What do you think Simon and Charlotte are doing now?" and "Do you think they're thinking about us?"

Even Gus missed Simon. "I've no one to make sport of," he complained.

The night that they came back, everyone was so ecstatic that there was a wild celebration. We drank all the duty-free vinho verde that they had brought home. The evening was deemed to be a great success when Charlotte vomited and had to be put to bed.

During that summer, the only people who didn't come out and play were Karen and Daniel.

I barely saw them.

Karen spent most of her time in Daniel's flat. She

stopped by at our flat occasionally to collect a change of clothes, just running in and out while Daniel waited in the car.

Daniel and I *never* saw each other on our own anymore. In fact we didn't even ring each other.

Which I felt a sense of regret about, because that was the kind of sentimental, emotional fool I was. But I didn't know what to do about it, there was no road back.

So I tried to focus on the good things in my life – namely Gus.

I realised just how serious Daniel and Karen had become when the news broke that they were going to Scotland together in September. From the gleam in Karen's eye, she thought she was home and dry with Daniel. It was only a matter of time before she could start fighting with her mother about the inviting of fifth cousins, four times removed and comparing the respective merits of lemon meringue pie and baked Alaska.

I wondered if she would ask me to be her bridesmaid. Somehow I thought not.

One Saturday night, all of us – me, Charlotte, Simon, Gus, Dennis, Jed, Megan, even Karen and Daniel – went to an open-air concert in the grounds of a stately home in north London.

Even though it was classical music, we had a wonderful time. Stretched out on the warm grass, listening to the rustle of the leaves in the still evening air, sipping champagne, eating Marks and Spencer's sausage rolls and mini-eclairs.

After the concert was over, we decided we had had enough of behaving like adults and we hadn't yet wrung enough debauched enjoyment out of the evening. It was only midnight and going to bed before the sun rose was regarded as a wasted night.

So we bought lots of wine from a twenty-four-hour shop that was happy to break the law and piled into several taxis and went back to our flat.

Where there were no clean glasses, so Karen volunteered me to wash some.

While I was in the kitchen dashing cups under the running tap, resenting every moment that I was away from the fun in the front room, Daniel came in searching for the corkscrew.

"How are you?" I asked. Before I knew what had happened I'd smiled because old habits die hard.

"Fine," he said, looking bleak. "And you?"

"Fine."

An awkward pause.

"I haven't seen you for ages," I said.

"No," he agreed.

Another pause. Talking to him was like trying to get blood out of a turnip.

"So you're off to Scotland?" I said.

"Yes."

"Looking forward to it?"

"Yes, I've never been to Scotland before," he said tersely.

"And it's not just that, is it?" I teased gently.

"What do you mean?" He stared coldly at me.

"Well, you know, meeting Karen's family and all that." I nodded eagerly. "So what's next?"

"What are you talking about?" he said, tight-lipped.

"You *know*," I said, smiling uncertainly.

"No I don't," he snapped. "It's just a bloody holiday, OK?"

"Christ," I muttered. "I remember when you used to have a sense of humour."

"Sorry, Lucy." He tried to grab my arm, but I shook it off and walked out of the kitchen.

My eyes filled with tears, which was really scary because I *never* cried. Except when I had PMT, and that didn't count.

Or whenever there was a programme about Siamese twins who had been separated and one of them died. Or whenever I saw an old person hobbling down the road on their own. Or whenever I went into the living-room and everyone shouted at me for coming back without the clean glasses. The bastards.

But despite the high-profile presence of Meredia, Jed, Megan, Dennis, Charlotte and Simon in my life, there was no denying that it was The Summer of Gus.

From the moment he returned from the three-week absence, we were hardly ever apart.

I made occasional perfunctory attempts to spend evenings on my own – not because I wanted to, but because I felt that it was expected of me.

I had to pretend that I was independent, that I had a life of my own, but the truth of it was that anything I enjoyed without Gus, I enjoyed even more with Gus.

And he was as bad.

"We won't see each other tonight," I said a few times. "I've got my washing and things to do."

"But, Lucy," he wailed, "I'll miss you."

"But I'll see you tomorrow," I said, pretending to be exasperated, but, of course, I was delighted. "Surely you can survive without me for one night."

But each time, Gus arrived at my flat by nine o'clock, trying to look shamefaced, but not pulling it off.

"Sorry, Lucy." He grinned. "I know you want to be on your own. But I had to see you, just for five minutes. I'll be off, now that I've had my fix of you."

"No, don't go," I said every time, as he must have known I would.

It was alarming to find that I considered any time away from Gus a waste.

Although I tried not to be obvious about it, I was crazy about him. And he seemed to be crazy about me, too, if the amount of time that he spent with me was any indication.

The only trouble, if trouble it was, was that he hadn't told me that he loved me. He hadn't actually said the words, "I love you, Lucy." Not that I worried – well, not much anyway – because I knew that normal rules didn't apply to Gus. He probably did love me but it might have slipped his mind to mention it. After all, that was the kind of man he was. But nevertheless, I thought it was best that I didn't tell him that I loved *him* – even though I did – until he told me.

No point in any premature jumpings of guns.

Besides, there was always a small chance that he

didn't love me, and there is *nothing* more embarrassing.

I would have liked to talk to him about our relationship, like where we were going and our future. But he never brought it up and I felt too awkward to.

I had to be patient, but it was hard to play the waiting game. The few times that I had any fears or doubts, I referred myself to Mrs Nolan's prediction, and remembered that I had seen the future and it was Gus. (Or that I had seen the future and it drank, as smug-arse Daniel put it.)

I consoled myself that patience is a virtue, that all things come to he – or she – who waits, that softly, softly, catchee monkey. And ignored the adages that urged me to strike when the iron is hot, not to let the grass grow under my feet, and that to stand still is to die.

I don't remember having great concern about my future with Gus throughout the magical, golden summer. At the time I *thought* I was happy, and that was good enough for me.

Chapter Fifty-One

The twelfth morning in August didn't seem any different from all the other golden mornings that had preceded it.

Except for one important detail – Gus got up before me.

It was impossible to stress just how unusual that was. Every morning when I left for work, Gus was still sound asleep. And at some stage, much, *much* later in the day he let himself out, pulling the door behind him. (After first eating anything in the fridge that wasn't actually moving, then making a couple of phone calls to Donegal.) This meant that the flat wasn't Chubb-locked and was thereby at the mercy of roving burglars, which caused several rows between Karen and I, on the rare occasions when Karen came home.

But I couldn't bring myself to give Gus a set of keys because I didn't want to scare him with a "Let's live together" message.

And I consoled Karen that the flat was so untidy that if any burglars *did* break in, they'd think a rival gang had gone over the place just a few minutes previously. We could even come home to find a *new* telly and stereo in the front room, I suggested enthusiastically to a sceptical raise of Karen's eyebrows.

That morning Gus got up before me, which started distant alarm bells ringing in my brain.

He sat on the bed and, as he put on his shoes, he commented casually, "D'you know, this is getting a bit heavy, Lucy."

"Mmmm, I s'pose," I said, still too sleepy to notice that I was alarmed.

But it was the work of an instant for me to realise that he wasn't just making idle conversation when he said, "I think we should slow down a bit."

The "this is getting a bit heavy" – particularly his use of the word "heavy" – had started Alsatian dogs barking by the perimeter fence. But the "I think we should slow down a bit" had the sirens whining and the searchlights swooping back and forth over the grounds.

While I scrambled around in the bed, trying to sit up, a voice in my head announced, *This is an emergency, boyfriend trying to escape, repeat, boyfriend trying to escape.*

I had the sensation of being in a lift that was dropping dangerously quickly, because every woman knows that talk of slowing down or seeing less of each other is actually bloke-speak for, "Take a good, long look at me, you will never see me again."

I hoped that I would be able to tell what was going on from the expression on his face. But he wouldn't look at me, his black curly head was bent over his feet as he laced his shoes with unprecedented diligence.

"Gus, are you trying to tell me something?"

"We might take a little break from each other," he muttered.

It sounded as if he'd been coached, as if he was clumsily reading from an autocue. In fact, it looked as if he was reading his lines from his shoe. But at the time I was so shocked by the import of what he was saying that I couldn't be bothered worrying that these weren't the kind of things he normally said.

I should have noticed that the very fact that Gus had even bothered to tell me that he was ending things was wildly out of character.

"But why?" I asked, in horror. "What's happened? What's gone wrong? What's changed?"

"Nothing."

Finally and nervously he lifted his head. He must have laced and unlaced his shoes forty times.

When his sidelong glance found my face, he looked guilty for a split second, then burst out, "It's your fault, Lucy, you shouldn't have got so involved, you shouldn't have let it get so serious."

I hadn't realised that Gus was from the attack-is-the-best-form-of-defence school of ending relationships. I had though that hit-and-run was more his style.

I was too stunned to remind him that he hadn't left me alone for a single night, that I hadn't even been able to de-hair my legs without having him camped outside the bathroom door, roaring that he missed me, asking me to sing to him, demanding to know how much longer I was going to be.

But I couldn't afford the luxury of being angry with him. That would have to wait until later.

As I stuttered and stumbled and tried to get out of bed, Gus backed towards the door and raised a hand in farewell.

"I'm going now, Lucy. Good luck! May the road rise with me." He sounded upbeat and cheerful. And more so with every inch he moved away from me.

"No, Gus, wait, please. Let's talk about this. Please, Gus."

"No, I've got to go now."

"Why, why in such a hurry?"

"I just do."

"Well, could we meet later? I don't understand this, please talk to me, Gus."

He looked sulky and surly.

"Will you meet me after work?" I asked, trying to sound calm, striving to keep the edge of hysteria out of my voice.

Still he said nothing.

"Please, Gus," I said again.

"OK," he muttered, sliding out of the room.

Then there was the bang of the front door. He was gone and I was still half-asleep, wondering if I was at large in a nightmare.

It wasn't even eight o'clock.

I had been too dazed to think of flinging myself in front of the door in an attempt to stop him from leaving. And when it occurred to me, instead of being grateful I was furious.

Somehow I got to work, not that I was much use when I got there. I felt as if I was wading around under water – everything was muffled, fuzzy, happening in slow motion. Voices came from a long way away, stretched and distorted. I couldn't really hear them and I couldn't concentrate on what they wanted from me.

The day was a slow agony of inching towards five o'clock.

Now and then, like the sun breaking through the clouds, I could think clearly. When that happened, waves of panic swept over me. What if he didn't come, I asked myself in appalled horror. What would I do?

But he *had* to come, I reasoned desperately. I *had* to talk to him, to find out what was wrong.

The worst part was that I couldn't tell anyone at work what was wrong. Because Gus wasn't leaving just me, he was leaving Jed, Meredia and Megan too, and I was afraid that they'd be hurt. I was also afraid that I'd get the blame.

I spent the day in a daze.

When I should have been ringing customers and threatening to sue them if they didn't pay us soon, I was in another world, where the only thing that meant anything was Gus.

Why did he think we were getting too serious, I wondered. Apart from the obvious fact that we were. But what was wrong with that?

I struggled to do some work, but it mattered so little.

Who cared if Spare Tyres had exceeded their ninety-day credit period by about two years? I didn't give a damn. I had bigger, more important things to worry about. So what if Wheel Meet Again had gone out of business owing us thousands of pounds? What did any of it matter when my heart was aching?

The pointlessness of my job was always highlighted when my heart was broken. Being abandoned brought out the nihilist in me.

I miserably made phone calls, wishy-washily threatened to sue people and take them for every penny they had, and thought, "In a hundred years time, *none* of this will matter."

Several millennia later the day finally dragged itself to its sluggish close.

And when five o'clock came, Gus didn't.

I hung on desperately until half past six, because I was at a complete loss as to what I should do with me, my time, my life.

Waiting for Gus was all I was good for.

But he didn't come.

Of course he didn't come.

And as I wondered what my next move should be, something that had been shimmering ominously at the back of my mind crystallised into a conscious fear.

I didn't know where Gus lived.

If he didn't come to me, I couldn't go to him. I had no phone number, no address for him.

He had never taken me to his house, everything we did together – from sleeping to sex to telly-watching – happened at my flat. I had known it wasn't right, but whenever I had suggested going home with him, he fobbed me off with a selection of surreal excuses. Which were so bizarre that I shuddered at the ease with which I had swallowed them.

I shouldn't have been so pliant, I thought in despair. I should have *insisted*. If I had been more demanding, I wouldn't be in such a mess. At least I'd know where to find him.

I couldn't believe how docile I had been – hadn't I even been *suspicious*?

In fact, as I remembered it, I *had* been suspicious. But because it threatened to ruffle the calm surface of my happiness, I forced myself not to be.

I had let Gus get away with an awful lot, with the vague, catch-all explanation that he was unusual and eccentric. And now that he had disappeared, I could hardly credit my naïveté.

If I had read about me in the newspaper, about a girl who had been going out with a bloke for five months (nearly), (if you count the three weeks in May that he'd been missing), and that she didn't even know where he lived, I would have dismissed her as a half-wit who deserved everything she got.

Or didn't.

But the reality had been so different. I had been afraid to force anything because I didn't want to drive him away.

And anyway, I had thought there was no need to force anything because he behaved as if he *cared* about me.

But the frustration of not being able to contact him was unbearable. Especially because it was all my fault.

Over the next few interminal, hellish days Gus

didn't reappear, and I didn't hold out any hope that he would.

Because I had realised something awful – I had been *expecting* him to leave me. All the time that I'd been with him, I had been waiting for it.

My idyllic summer had been nothing but a sham. Although it was only in retrospect that I could see tensions beneath the balmy, sunny surface.

I had never felt safe after his three-week disappearance. I *pretended* that I did, because it felt nicer that way. But things had never been the same. It had tipped the balance of power completely in Gus's favour – he had treated me with a lack of respect and I had told him that it was perfectly all right to do so. I had given him *carte blanche* to treat me badly.

He had been quite gallant about it, never openly reminding me just how much of a hostage I was. But it was always there in the subtext – he had left me once and he could do it again, any time he liked. He wielded his ability to disappear like a weapon.

A covert power struggle had gone on between Gus and me. He played brinkmanship, and I played stoicism. How long could he abandon me at a party before I got angry? How much money could he "borrow" from me before I refused to "loan" him any more? How flirtatious could he get with Megan, how many times did he have to touch her hair, before it wiped the fixed smile off my face?

All that fear had burnt up so much of my energy – I was continually nervy around him. Edgy. Every time he said he'd collect me or meet me, my nerves were zinging until he turned up.

But I had stuffed all my questions beneath the surface, I couldn't let them pop their heads up and ruin things.

I had papered over cracks, suppressed fears and swallowed insults, because I thought it was worth it.

And it had seemed to be, because – at least on the outside – Gus and I were happy.

But now that he had gone, I realised that any time I had been with him there was a fear that it might be the last. There was a kind of desperation in me, a need to get my money's worth. A need to cram as much Gus into my life as I possibly could to store against the time when he would run away again.

Chapter Fifty-Two

I eventually had to tell the others in the office that Gus and I were no more. It was horrible. Jed and Meredia were distraught – they looked like children who had just found out that there was no Santa Claus.

"Doesn't Gus like us anymore?" asked Meredia in a small voice, her head bent, plucking at her marquee of a skirt.

"Of course he does," I assured her warmly.

"Is it our fault?" asked Jed, looking as woebegone as a four-year-old. "Have we done something wrong?"

"Of course it's not your fault," I said heartily. "Gus and I can't be together anymore, but . . ."

I stopped myself before I sat down and put my arms around the two of them and gently explained that, "Sometimes grown-up people stop loving each other and it's very sad, but it doesn't mean that Gus doesn't love both of you very much, still . . ."

Instead I exclaimed tearfully, "Oh for God's sake. You're not the children of a divorcing couple, so stop acting it!"

"This is *my* tragedy," I reminded them, in more reasoned tones.

"Maybe we can still see him." Jed turned to Meredia. "Lucy doesn't have to be there."

"Thanks, you mean pigs," I said. "Next you'll be asking me to talk to him about visitation rights."

Megan was abrupt and unsympathetic. "You're better off without that loser," or, "You're bitter off weethout thit loy-zee," she said, with a dismissive wave of her hand.

She was right of course. But it was hard to feel grateful.

I was punch-drunk, reeling from the sudden loss.

The unexpectedness of his departure had thrown me into a state of shock. Because there had been no warning that his interest in me was waning – right up to the last few minutes he had certainly *acted* happy.

And well he might, I thought with a tinge of self-righteousness – I had put enough effort into making it all wonderful for him.

Naturally, because I had the double handicap of being a woman, and having low self-esteem, I sought to blame myself. Why had he left? What had I done? What hadn't I done?

If only I had known, I thought helplessly. Then I could have tried harder. Although, quite frankly, that was debatable.

The worst thing about Gus exiting from my life was the thing I *always* found hardest about rejection – the amount of time I suddenly had. Like the last time he left me, there was so bloody much of it. An entire fourth dimension had been handed to me, a bottomless pit of never-ending evenings, and I couldn't get rid of them fast enough.

I didn't remember it ever being so bad before. But I supposed I thought that every time my heart was broken.

To try to offload some of my surplus hours and minutes, I went out all the time, trying to party away my misery, to burn it off. I *had* to – I was too agitated not to. Just to do *nothing* was impossible.

But it didn't work, the awfulness never left me. Even as I sat in pubs with lots of happy, laughing people, I still felt the frantic, panicky fear racing around in my veins.

There was almost no escape from it. I could only sleep for a few hours a night. The falling asleep bit wasn't hard, but I woke really early in the morning, at four or five, and stayed awake. I couldn't bear to be on my own. But there was no one that I wanted to be with. And no matter where I was, I wanted to be somewhere else.

No matter who I was with, no matter what I was doing, no matter where I was, it was wrong, I didn't want it.

Every night, I sat with crowds of people and I felt totally alone.

A couple of weeks passed, and perhaps I had got slightly better, but the change was too small for me to see.

"You'll get over him," everyone said sympathetically.

But I didn't want to get over him. I still thought he was the funniest, cleverest, sexiest man I had ever met, or would ever meet.

He was my ideal. And if I got over him, if I didn't want him anymore, I would have lost part of myself.

I didn't want to let the wound heal.

Anyway, despite what everyone said, I *knew* that I'd never get over him. I was in so much pain that I couldn't imagine not feeling it.

Besides, Mrs Nolan and her bloody prediction were still on my mind. I found it hard to accept all the signs that were *screaming* that Gus wasn't the man for me, because it was nicer to believe that it was written in the stars that we'd be together.

"That Gus – what a bastard, eh?" Megan cheerfully remarked, one day at work.

"I suppose," I agreed politely.

"You're not going to tell me that you don't hate him?" Megan sounded outraged.

"I don't hate him," I said. "Maybe I should, but I don't."

"But why not?" she demanded.

"Because that's the way Gus is," I tried to explain. "If you love him, you've got to accept that you love the unreliable part of him also."

I waited for Megan to scoff and mock and call me a wimp and a girl. And she did.

"Don't be such a drongo, Lucy." She laughed. "It was your fault, you shouldn't have stood for any nonsense from him. With animals like Gus, you have to show them who's boss, you've got to *break* them."

"I always do," she added.

It was all right for Megan, she'd been brought up on a farm, an *Australian* farm, at that. She knew all about tethering and spancelling and breaking spirits.

"I didn't want to *break* him," I said. "If he'd been well behaved, he wouldn't have been Gus."

"You can't have it both ways, Lucy," said Megan.

"I haven't got it *any* way," I reminded her.

"Come on, cheer up. You don't really care, do you?" she asked brightly.

"I do," I said humbly, because such lack of self-respect is not something to be proud of.

"No, you don't," she scoffed.

"I do."

"Do you really?" She looked at me anxiously.

"Yes."

"But why?" she asked.

"Because . . . because," I floundered. "Because he's so special. I've never met anyone like him. And I'll never meet anyone like him . . . *sniff* . . . ever again."

My voice wobbled dangerously when I said "ever again", but I managed not to fling myself on my desk and sob bitterly.

"So if he arrived on your doorstop, begging you to take him back, you'd forgive him?" asked Megan, continuing to press me.

I didn't like the sound of that. I had a vague picture in my head of a terribly unfortunate woman, whose bloke beat her up and stole her money and had affairs with her friends.

"Megan," I said, anxiously, "I'm not one of those women who get treated badly by their man, but still take them back time after time after time."

"That's funny," said Megan. "Because you certainly act just like one."

"Only for Gus," I explained. "Only for Gus. I wouldn't do it for every man I ever met. This is a one-off."

"Gus is worth breaking rules for," I added.

"So it seems," she said.

I felt a strange desire to thump her.

"But so what?" she boomed, determinedly upbeat. "You'll get over him. In two weeks time you won't even remember his name, you won't know what all the fuss was about!"

Chapter Fifty-Three

I could hear the screaming from three floors below, the dreadful sounds of an animal in pain or a woman giving birth or a child being scalded.

Something terrible had happened and as I ran up the stairs, I realised that the wails were coming from our flat.

"Oh, Lucy," gasped Charlotte, as I fell in the front door. "I'm so glad you're here."

She was lucky. It was only because there was no one to go for a drink with after work, except Barney and Slayer, the two Neanderthals from the post room, that I was home.

"What's wrong?" I asked in horror.

"It's Karen," she said.

"Where is she? Is she hurt? What is it?"

Karen burst out of her bedroom, her clothes askew, her face red and blotchy with tears and threw a glass at the wall which shattered around the hall.

"The bastaird, the bastaird, the bastaird!" she shrieked.

Something was very wrong with Karen, but at least there didn't seem to be anything wrong with her physically, although her hair could have done with a comb. There was a strong smell of alcohol coming from her.

Then she noticed me.

"And it's all your fault, you stupid bitch, Sullivan," she shouted.

"What's my fault? I haven't done anything," I protested, feeling guilty and frightened.

"Yes, it is. You introduced me to him. If I'd never met him, I'd never have fallen in love with him. Not that I *am* in love with him, I hate his guts!" she roared, running back into her room and flinging herself face-downwards on her bed.

Charlotte and I followed.

"Is this something to do with Daniel?" I muttered to Charlotte.

"Don't say his name!" screeched Karen. "I never want to hear his name spoken in this flat ever again."

"You know the way you're the Spinster of this Parish?" muttered Charlotte to me.

I nodded.

"Well, you're not the only one now."

So there had been a breakdown in the Daniel/Karen alliance.

"What's happened?" I asked Karen, gently.

"I finished with him," she gulped, reaching for a bottle of brandy that she had beside her bed and swigging from it. Over half of it was already gone.

"Why did you finish with him?" I asked, intrigued. I had thought she really liked him.

"Just never forget it, Sullivan. *I* finished with *him*, not the other way round."

"Fine," I said nervously. "But why?"

"Because . . . because . . ." Tears began rolling down her face again.

"Because . . . I asked him if he loved me and he said, he said . . . he . . . he . . . he . . ."

Charlotte and I waited politely for her to get to the point.

" . . . he . . . DIDN'T," she finally managed and started that awful wailing again.

"He doesn't love me," she said, staring at me with unfocused, miserable eyes. "Can you believe it? He said he doesn't love me."

"If it's any help, Karen, I know what it's like. Gus broke it off with me only two weeks ago, remember?"

"Don't be so fucking stupid," she said thickly, through her tears. "Gus and you weren't serious, Daniel and I were."

"I took Gus very seriously," I said stiffly.

"More fool you," said Karen. "Anyone can see that he's mad and unreliable and flighty. But Daniel has a, a . . . a GOOD JOB!"

She became incoherent with sobbing again and I couldn't really make out what she was saying. Something about Daniel owning his own flat and having an expensive . . . *yard*, was it? No, no, sorry, an expensive *car*.

"Things like this don't happen to me," she sobbed. "It wasn't part of the plan."

"They happen to everyone," I said gently.

"No, they don't. They don't happen to me."

"Karen, really, they happen to everyone," I insisted. "Look at me and Gus . . ."

"*Don't* compare me to you," she screamed. "I'm nothing like you. Men finish with you, and you," she said nodding at Charlotte. "But they don't finish with me, I don't permit it to happen."

That shut Charlotte and I up.

"Oh God." Karen, commenced a fresh bout of weeping. "How can I go to Scotland now? I've told everyone about Daniel and how rich he is. And we were going to drive up and now I'll have to pay my own fare and I was going to buy that jacket in Morgans and now I won't be able to. The bastaird!"

She reached for the brandy bottle again.

It was a very old, rare brandy, the type that rich businessmen give to each other at Christmas, the type that you're not really supposed to drink. It's meant to be a decoration piece, more an ostentatious display of wealth than something you mix with ginger.

"Where did you get this?" I asked Karen.

"Took it from that bastaird's flat when I was leaving," she said viciously. "Only sorry that I didn't take more."

Then came more tears.

"And it's such a lovely flat," she howled. "And I was going to decorate it, I was going to make him buy this wrought iron bed that I saw in *Elle Decoration*. He's such a bastaird."

Yes, yes, yes, quite.

"We must sober her up," I said.

"We could make her eat something," suggested Charlotte. "I could do with something myself."

But as always there was nothing in the flat except some gone-off low-fat yoghurt.

496

So we went to the Cash'n'Curry and caused consternation and confusion among the staff because we only ever, ever went there on a Sunday.

"Here, I could have sworn that today was Monday," said Pavel in Bangladeshi to Karim when the three of us walked in and sat at our usual table.

"Christ, me too," agreed Karim. "But it must only be Sunday. That's great, we close an hour earlier tonight. Right, you get their wine and I'll tell the chef they're here and he can get the chicken tikka masalas on. They've caught us on the hop tonight and no mistake."

"Can we have a bottle of house white, please?" I asked Mahmood, but Pavel was already behind the bar opening it for us. We always had exactly the same thing at the Indian – they no longer even brought us menus. It was always one vegetable biryani, two chicken tikka masalas, pilau rice and white wine. Only the number of bottles of wine varied, but it was always at least two.

While we waited for the food we managed to piece together exactly what had happened with Karen and Daniel.

It seemed that Karen was certain that Daniel had fallen in love with her and decided she was ready for a declaration to that effect. That would have given them enough time to buy an engagement ring before they went to Scotland, where they would break the happy news to Karen's parents. But Daniel was annoyingly reticent with his declaration, so Karen decided that she had better take events into her own hands, what with the date of their departure for

497

Scotland drawing nearer. So, fully certain that the answer would be in the affirmative, she asked Daniel if he loved her. And Daniel put the cat among the pigeons, good and proper, by telling her that he was very fond of her.

And Karen said, very good, but did he *love* her?

And Daniel said that she was a joy to be with and a very beautiful woman.

I know all that, Karen scornfully told him, but do you love me?

Who's to say what love is? asked Daniel, no doubt getting increasingly desperate.

Answer me, yes or no, demanded Karen, DO-YOU-LOVE-ME?

I'm afraid that my answer would have to be no, said Daniel.

Cue shattered dreams, violent row, theft of bottle of expensive brandy, calling of a taxi, hope by Karen that Daniel would burn in hell, departure of Karen from Daniel's flat and arrival at ours.

"He's a bastaird," sobbed Karen.

Mahmood, Karim, Pavel and the one who said his name was Michael all nodded in sympathy. They had been hanging on Karen's every word. Pavel looked close to tears.

Karen gulped back a glass of wine, spilling some of it down her chin and immediately filled up her glass again.

"'Nother bottle," she called, waving the empty one at the cluster of waiters.

Charlotte and I exchanged a glance which said "She's had quite enough to drink already," but neither of us dared say it to her.

Karim brought us more wine and, as he placed the bottle on the table he murmured, "This one's on us, with our commiserations."

Charlotte and I ended up getting drunk also, because we were trying to save Karen from getting any drunker by drinking as much of the wine as we possibly could. Not that it worked, because Karen roared for another bottle as soon as the second was finished and the whole process began all over again.

Although by then I was starting to enjoy myself.

Karen got drunker and drunker, she lit the wrong end of her cigarette twice, rested the cuffs of her jacket in her dinner, knocked a glass of water into my vegetable biryani and slurred "Looked disgustin', anyway."

And then, to my absolute horror, her eyes glazed over and she slowly keeled forward until she was face downwards in her plate of chicken tikka masala and pilau rice.

"Quick, quick, Charlotte," I said in panic. "Lift her up, get her face out of her dinner, she'll drown!"

Charlotte yanked Karen's head up by the hair and Karen turned a drunken, confused face to Charlotte.

"Whatta fucker you doin'?" she demanded. She had some red masala sauce on her forehead and grains of rice in her hair.

"Karen, you passed out," I gasped. "You just collapsed into your meal. We'd better get you home."

"Fuck off," she slurred. "No, I didn't. I just dropped my cigarette and I had to pick it up off the floor."

"Oh," I said, both relieved and embarrassed.

"Stupid fuck," muttered Karen aggressively. "Are you trinta say I can't hold my drink?"

"C'mere you," she beckoned Mahmood. "D'you think I'm 'tractive? Eh, well?"

"Most attractive," he agreed warmly, thinking for a second that his luck was in.

"'Course I am," said Karen. "'Course I am."

"You're not," she added as an afterthought.

He looked hurt so I gave him a bigger than usual tip when we left. I had to pay because Charlotte had forgotten her purse in the excitement and although Karen tried to write a cheque, she was too drunk to even hold the pen.

We carried Karen home, undressed her and put her to bed.

"Drink some water, Karen, good girl, so you won't feel so bad when you wake up in the morning," said Charlotte, shoving a pint glass under Karen's nose. Charlotte was far from sober herself.

"I nevr, nevr want to wake up again," said Karen.

She made some funny, little whiney noises and I realised after a while that she was singing. Sort of.

"You're so vain . . . bet y'think thissongs aboucha. Doancha, doancha . . ." she whined.

"Come on Karen, *please*," begged Charlotte, advancing again with her pint of water.

"Doan interrupme whem singin'. Singin' 'bout Daniel. Join in! You're so vain . . . betcha . . . think . . . thissongs . . . Come on," she said aggressively, "Sing with me."

"Karen, please," I murmured soothingly.

"Doan patronise me," she said. "Sing the fuckin' song. You're so va . . . come on, everybody!"

"Er, you're so vain," sang Charlotte and I, feeling very foolish. "Ahem, I, er, bet, you, um, think this song is about, ah, you . . ."

She passed out before we got to the second verse.

"Oh Lucy," wailed Charlotte. "I'm so worried."

"Don't be," I said soothingly, with a confidence that I didn't feel. "I'm sure she'll be fine. She'll bounce back in no time."

"Not about her!" said Charlotte. "I'm worried about me."

"Why?"

"First Gus goes, then Daniel, what if Simon is next?"

"But why on earth should he? It's not a contagious disease."

"But bad things always happen in threes," said Charlotte, her soft pink face crumpled with anxiety.

"Maybe they do in Yorkshire," I said kindly. "But you're in London now, so don't worry."

"You're right," she said, cheering up. "Anyway, Gus has dumped you twice, so with Daniel breaking it off with Karen, that's three already."

"Well, what a pity that Gus couldn't have finished with me one more time and I could have saved Karen all this upset," I said a little tartly.

"Don't worry, Lucy," said Charlotte. "You weren't to know."

Chapter Fifty-Four

And then there were three.

Daft and all as she usually was, Charlotte's instinct had been entirely correct. Simon did not ring her at work on Tuesday, and he normally rang her every day, sometimes twice a day.

When she rang him on Tuesday evening he wasn't in and his normally friendly flatmate was awkward and uncommunicative as to Simon's whereabouts.

"Lucy, I have a very bad feeling about this," Charlotte said.

She rang him at work on Wednesday and Simon didn't answer his phone. Instead a woman did and asked Charlotte "Who's calling?". When Charlotte said "Charlotte," the woman immediately said "Simon's in a meeting".

Charlotte rang back about an hour later and exactly the same thing happened.

So, straight away, Charlotte got her friend Jennifer to ring and Simon was suddenly home to callers because he was able to take the call from "Jennifer Morris".

Jennifer handed the phone to Charlotte when

Simon said "Hello" and Charlotte said "Simon, what's going on? Are you trying to avoid me?".

And Simon laughed nervously and jovially and said, "Indeed not, indeed not, indeed not!".

Charlotte said that was when she really knew something was wrong because Simon would normally never say "Indeed not."

"Meet me for lunch, Simon," said Charlotte.

"Would love to, would love to," said Simon. "But no can do."

"Why are you talking like that?" asked Charlotte.

"Like what?" asked Simon.

"Like a dickhead with a mobile phone," said Charlotte.

(Which I thought was quite ironic because I had *always* thought that Simon was like a dickhead with a mobile phone, but I didn't say so because I didn't want to upset Charlotte any further.)

"No idea what you're talking about," said Simon.

Charlotte sighed. "OK, tonight then."

"'Fraid that's impossible," said Simon.

"Why?"

"Business, Charlotte, business," he drawled.

"But you've never had to do that before," said Charlotte.

"First time for everything," said Simon smoothly.

"Well, when *can* I see you?" asked Charlotte.

"Bad news, Charlie," said Simon, "but you can't."

"Until when?" she asked.

"You're not making this easy for either of us, are you?" he asked lightly.

"What are you talking about?"

"I mean, Charlotte, that you can't see me."

"Why not?"

"Because it's O,V,E,R, over."

"Over? Us? You mean *we're* over?" she asked.

"Bravo," he laughed. "The message finally hits home."

"And when were you going to tell me?" she asked.

"I've just told you, haven't I?" he said in a reasonable voice.

"But only because I rang you. Were you going to ring me? Or were you just going to let me find out myself?"

"You would have got the message soon enough," he said.

"But why?" asked Charlotte, her voice wobbling. "Don't you, don't you . . . *like* me anymore?"

"Oh Charlotte, don't make a fool of yourself," he said. "It was fun, we both enjoyed ourselves and now I've found someone else to have fun with."

"But what about me?" asked Charlotte. "Who will I have fun with?"

"That's not my problem," said Simon. "But, anyway, you'll meet someone else. You're bound to, with those tits."

"I don't want to have fun with anyone else," pleaded Charlotte. "I want to have fun with you."

"Tough!" he said cheerfully. "Your time is up. Don't be selfish, Charlie, let some of the other girls have a go."

"But I thought you cared about me," she said.

"Well, you shouldn't have taken it so seriously," he answered.

"So this is it?" she asked tearfully.

"This is it," he agreed.

"Lucy, he was like a total stranger," she said later. "I thought I *knew* him. I thought he cared about me, I just can't believe he could drop me so suddenly."

"I just don't understand *why!*" she said over and over again. "What did I do wrong? Why did he go off me? Maybe I've put on some weight? Have I, Lucy? Or did I go on too much about the bad time I was having at work? If only I knew."

She shook her head in bewilderment. "There's nowt so queer as blokes," she sighed.

At least she wasn't tortured by the images of that boyfriend-stealing mythical woman who coloured the imaginations of us small-breasted, rejected women – A Girl With Bigger Tits, because Charlotte was That Girl With Bigger Tits.

But she doubted herself in every other area.

She forced him to see her. She stalked him with a tenacity and a determination that you wouldn't have believed she was capable of when you first saw her round, innocent face. She waited outside his office for a couple of days at his going-home time, then he finally agreed to have a drink with her, in the hope that she might leave him alone.

One drink led to several more and they both got very drunk and went back to Simon's and had sex.

Then in the morning Simon said, "That was very pleasant, Charlotte. Now stop hanging round outside my office. You're embarrassing yourself."

Charlotte was rather taken aback by all of this. She was inexperienced enough in the arena of love to assume that because he had slept with her, it meant that their romance was back on track.

"But . . . but," she said. "What about last night? Didn't it . . . ?"

"NO, Charlotte," interrupted Simon impatiently. "It didn't mean a thing to me. A shag is a shag. Now please get dressed and collect your P45 as you leave."

"And the worst thing is, Lucy," she complained afterwards. "I *still* don't know why he ended it with me."

"But why not?" I asked.

"I forgot to ask."

"What were you *doing* all that time?" I asked in surprise. "No, no, don't tell me, I can guess."

"I'm too young to be a Spinster of this Parish," said Charlotte gloomily.

"You're never too young," I said wisely.

Chapter Fifty-Five

Megan was due to start her new job that week, but there were complications. Well, only one actually.

To wit: Frank Erskine's mental health.

The MD wasn't too pleased with the behaviour of one of his Directors.

Frank's offer to create a new job for an attractive, tanned young woman, who wore shorts, was regarded as the embarrassing act of a middle-aged man who should have known better. The company buzzed with the rumour that he was having a combination of mid-life crisis and a nervous breakdown and wasn't capable of rational thought.

He was persuaded – quite forcibly, according to my sources in Personnel – to take an extended period of sick leave. Luckily his wife agreed to stand by him, and the press were kept out of it.

When he returned – although no one really thought he would – then Management would be only too happy to talk to Megan about her promotion.

But until then, Megan was condemned to fester in Credit Control. Meredia nearly vomited with glee.

Chapter Fifty-Six

Three hearts were heavy.

It was as if we had all been struck down by the plague. The flat should have been draped in black crêpe and have had a black cross on the front door. All about us was an air of terrible gloom, sickness and death.

Whenever I came home I expected to hear the sounds of a funeral dirge being played on an organ, coming from the attic.

"There is a blight upon this house," I said, and the other two miserably agreed.

Then Charlotte asked what a blight was.

Even though it was still high summer, once you crossed the threshold into our flat, it was loveless, bleak winter.

One Sunday lunch-time Karen and Charlotte went to the pub to get drunk and hiss venemously at each other about how small Simon's and Daniel's penises had been really. And how the sex had been crap with them and that they had never actually had any orgasms, but had faked every single one of them.

I would have loved to go with them but I had placed myself under voluntary house arrest.

I was slightly worried about how much I had

been drinking, both during and especially post Gus, so I was seeking to escape by another route.

I was reading a great book that I had found in the local Oxfam, about women who love too much. I was amazed that our paths had never crossed until now, but it had been published a good ten years earlier when I was a mere novice at being neurotic, only barely getting the hang of things.

The phone rang.

"Daniel," I said – for it was he. "And what do you want, you philandering fucker?"

"Lucy," he said in a low, urgent tone. "Is she there?"

"Is who here?" I asked coldly.

"Karen?"

"No, she's not, I'll tell her you rang. Although don't hold your breath if you're expecting her to call back."

"No, Lucy." He sounded frightened. "Don't tell her I rang. I want to talk to you."

"Well, I don't want to talk to you," I said.

"Please, Lucy!"

"No, get lost," I spluttered. "I've got my loyalties, you know. You can't just mess my friend around, break her heart, and still expect me to be your bosom buddy."

I expected him to say something about my bosoms, but he didn't.

"But, Lucy, you were *my* friend first," he said.

"Tough," I said simply. "You know the rules – boy meets girl, boy breaks it off with girl, boy has contract on life put out by girl's flatmates."

"Lucy," said Daniel, sounding very serious. "I've got something to say to you."

"Say it then, but be quick about it."

"Well, I never thought I'd hear myself saying this, but . . . well . . . I *miss* you, Lucy."

I felt a stab of sadness. But that was nothing unusual.

"You didn't call me all summer," I reminded him.

"You didn't call me either."

"Well, how could I? You were going out with someone and she would have killed me."

"You were going out with someone also." Daniel pointed out.

"Hah! Gus was hardly a threat, was he?"

"I wouldn't have said that."

"I know what you mean," I said, going all dewy-eyed at the memory of Gus. "Even though he's not very tall, I bet he can stand his own in hand-to-hand combat."

"I didn't mean that," said Daniel. "He doesn't need to hit anyone. He could have paralysed me with five minutes of his boring conversation."

I was outraged. The idea of *Daniel* calling *Gus* boring. It was too ludicrous to even bother arguing about.

"Sorry," said Daniel. "I shouldn't have said that. He's a great laugh, really."

"Do you mean it?"

"No. But I'm afraid that you'll slam the phone down and refuse to see me."

"You're quite right to be afraid," I said. "Because I've no intention of seeing you."

"Please, Lucy?" he asked.

"What for? You're so pathetic – you're momentarily without a woman and your ego can't handle it, so you ring up good old Lucy and . . ."

"Jesus," he complained, "if I needed an ego boost, you'd be the last person I'd go to."

"Then why do you want to see me?"

"Because I miss you."

I'd momentarily run out of insults for him, and Daniel saw his opening.

"I'm not bored," he said earnestly, "I'm not lonely, I don't just want female company, I don't need an ego boost. I want to see you. No one else but you."

There was a pause. The air reverberated with his sincerity and for a moment I nearly believed him.

"Listen to you," I said with a little laugh. "You think you can charm every girl who crosses your path, don't you?"

But despite my bluster, there was a small flicker of something else. Relief, maybe? Although I couldn't give in just yet, it would disappoint him.

"You know that your usual smooth, slick lines don't work on me," I reminded Daniel.

"I know," he agreed, "And I know that if you meet me, you'll be horrible."

"Oh yes?"

"You're going to call me a flirt and a . . . a . . ."

"A slimebucket?" I supplied helpfully.

"Yes, a slimebucket. And a womaniser?"

"Of course – you can't even imagine what I have in store for you."

"That's OK."

"You're a sick man, Daniel Watson."

"But you'll meet me?"

"But . . . but, I like it here."

"What are you doing?"

"Lying down . . ."

"You can lie down here."

"Eating chocolate . . ."

"I'll buy you as much chocolate as you want."

"But I'm reading a brilliant book and you'll want me to talk to you . . ."

"I won't. I promise."

"And I've no make-up on and I look horrible."

"So what?"

And when I asked, "How will I get over to your flat?", my capitulation was complete.

"I'll drive over and fetch you," offered Daniel.

At that I threw back my head and laughed mirthlessly.

"What's so funny?" he asked.

"Daniel," I said. "Be realistic. How do you think Karen's going to feel if she sees your car outside our flat?"

"Oh yes, of course," muttered Daniel, sounding shamed. "How could I have been so insensitive?"

"Don't be daft," I scoffed. "We all know that you're insensitive – after all, you're a man, aren't you? No, I mean if she finds out that you've come to see me and not her she'll kill you."

"And me," I added, suddenly touched by the cold hand of fear.

"Well, we'll have to think of something else then," said Daniel.

I waited for him to acknowledge that we couldn't see each other.

"I know!" he said eagerly. "I'll collect you down by the traffic-lights. She'll never see me there."

"Daniel!" I shouted, outraged. "How could you . . . ? Oh all right then."

As I got ready, I was aware of a feeling of subterfuge that I found both frightening and exciting.

Karen hadn't forbidden me to see Daniel. Not forbidden, as *such*. But I knew that she expected me to hate him for what he had done to her. That female flatmate solidarity dictated a "One out, all out" stance whenever our blokes dumped us. If they broke it off with one of us, they had to forgo the pleasure of the company of all three.

But, once I had spoken to Daniel, I realised how much I had missed him. Now that we seemed to be friends again, it was safe to admit it. I had that bittersweet feeling that happens after you make it up with someone.

He was fun and fun was a commodity that had been fairly thin on the ground around that time.

I'd had enough of Karen, Charlotte and I going round with pinched faces and almost never eating – picking up a biscuit, nibbling a tiny corner of it and then putting it down again and completely forgetting about it.

And I was worn down by the violent films that Karen kept getting out. *Carrie* and *Dirty Weekend* and anything else that she could lay her hands on about women extracting revenge in a bloody and brutal fashion.

And Charlotte had regressed badly – we thought that we had said goodbye forever to Christopher Plummer and his thighs. But no, she had relapsed with a vengeance, watching *The Sound of Music* whenever Karen wasn't filling the screen with images of blood and pain. *Men's* blood and pain, if at all possible.

I was tired of living in a house of mourning. I wanted to put on a red dress and go out and party.

But I wasn't being fair. It was only sheer good fortune that my boyfriend had tired of me sooner than Karen's or Charlotte's, which meant that I was a couple of weeks further along the recovery process than they were.

How quickly we forget.

In fact it was only ten days since I had sat sniffing on the couch, the remote control in my hand, and watched the bit in *Terminator* where he says "I travelled through time for you". Then rewound it and watched it again. Then rewound it and watched it again. Then rewound it and . . .

It's scary, the things heartbreak makes us do.

But at least it meant that business was booming for Adrian.

Daniel looked shifty and nervous as he waited in his car by the traffic-lights.

"Don't expect me to talk to you," I said, as I clambered in.

I had to admit that Daniel was looking quite attractive, if you liked that kind of thing.

I thanked God I didn't.

Instead of the work suits that I normally saw him

in, he was wearing faded jeans and a really nice grey jumper.

A *really* nice grey jumper, I thought, maybe he'd let me borrow it.

And I'd never noticed before how long and thick his eyelashes were – like the grey jumper they would have looked much nicer on me.

I felt a bit shy and awkward. It had been so long since I had seen him like this, on our own, that I'd forgotten how I was supposed to behave.

But by the warm rush of affection I felt for him, I must have been glad to see him.

"Do you want to drive?" he asked. The rush of affection intensified.

"Can I?" I breathed with excitement.

I had taken driving lessons and passed my test about a year before, even though I didn't have a car, couldn't afford a car and didn't need a car.

I had done it to feel empowered – yet another thing that I had done to try and make me satisfied with my life. Of course it hadn't worked. But one of its side effects was that I loved driving. And Daniel had a gorgeous car, sporty and sexy. I didn't know what *kind* of car it was, because, after all, I was a girl. But I knew the important things – that it looked great and went really fast.

Women loved it.

To upset Daniel I called it "the shagmobile" or "the fuck truck" and told him that girls only went out with him because of his wheels.

So we got out and swapped sides and he threw me the keys over the roof of the car.

I drove through the London traffic to Daniel's flat, and had the best time I'd had since the last night I had sex with Gus.

Although I didn't mean to, I drove like a maniac. It had been a long time since I'd been behind the wheel of a car. Too long, probably.

I did all kinds of reckless things that look great if you're driving a fast car. I pulled away from traffic lights with a roar, leaving the other drivers staring bitterly after me – that was called "burning them up" said Daniel. I drove out in front of other cars – Daniel said that was called "cutting them up" and while we were stuck in a traffic jam, I winked and smiled at attractive men in other cars – Daniel said that was called "being a brazen trollop".

I was slightly shocked when other drivers called me names and gesticulated angrily at me, when I burned them up and cut them up – at least at first. But I soon got the hang of the driving etiquette. So when one man cut in front of me, I furiously yelled "Wanker!" and tried to roll down the window so I could make rude gestures at him, but I couldn't find the handle.

He drove away with a look of fear on his face. And suddenly, like a mist clearing, I saw myself as I must have appeared to others, not least the wanker in the car. I was shocked – I hadn't realised that I could be so aggressive. Worse, I hadn't realised that I'd enjoy it so much.

I was afraid that Daniel would be cross with me – after all, the man could have got out and road-raged us. Road-rage was so en vogue that people thought that they were almost *obliged* to feel it. That they weren't getting value for money from their driver's licence, if at least once a week, they didn't find themselves stripped to the waist, in a traffic jam, squaring up to a fellow motorist.

"Sorry about that, Daniel," I muttered, and flicked a nervous, sidelong look at him, but he was laughing. "The look on that man's face," he wheezed. "He couldn't *believe* it."

He laughed until tears ran down his face and finally managed to say, "And by the way, the switch for the electric windows is over there."

When we got to Daniel's road and I had parked about four feet from the kerb, I said, "Thank you, Daniel. That's the best fun I've had in weeks."

I wasn't a bad driver but I wasn't too good at parking.

"You're welcome," he said. "You look good in it. You and the car suit each other."

I blushed and smiled, feeling happy and embarrassed.

"But it wasn't long enough," I complained.

"Well, if you like," he said. "Next weekend, I'll take you out into the country and you can burn up everyone else on the motorway."

"Mmmmm," I said non-committally. There was something about the way he said "I'll take you" rather than "We can go" that made me feel funny. Not exactly nervous . . . well, maybe not *just* nervous.

"Er, Lucy . . ."

"What?"

"Would you be very offended if I parked the car a bit, um, closer to the kerb?"

"No." I suddenly felt the need to smile at him. "No, not at all."

Chapter Fifty-Seven

I hadn't been to Daniel's flat for ages and ages. The last time I'd been there it had looked like a building site, because Daniel had been trying to put up shelves and most of the wall had fallen off onto the floor. You could hardly see the carpet because there was so much plaster on it.

But this time you'd barely have known it was a boy's flat – it didn't look like a scrapyard or the inside of a sports bag. There were no broken motorbike engines on the kitchen table, no stray pieces of chipboard cluttering up the hall, no badminton racquets on the sofa, no row of shuttlecocks on top of the telly.

Having said that, I don't want to give the impression that Daniel's flat was *nice*. The furniture was a bit weird because he got some of it from his older brother Paul when his marriage broke up and he went to work in Saudi Arabia, and some of it from his granny when she shuffled off her mortal coil. I suppose the best thing that could be said about Daniel's furniture was that it hadn't enough character to be offensive.

Here and there, like oases in the desert, were a couple of things that were actively *nice* – a red giraffe compact disc holder, a free-standing candlestick – the sort of things that Simon's flat was packed with. But if you said to Simon, "nice shelf", he wouldn't just say "Thanks", he'd reel off, "Conran shop, Ron Arad, limited edition, be worth a fortune one day soon." Which was all probably true, but it somehow struck me as, well, *unmanly*. All Simon's inanimate articles had pedigrees and lineages, he liked to be able to trace them right back to Le Corbusier or the Bauhaus.

Simon never said, "Stick on the kettle". Instead he said, "Gently flick the turquoise enamel genuine fifties reproduction switch on my stainless steel Alessi pyramid kettle, if you damage a hair on it's sleek, silver head, I'll kill you with the largest from my full set of Sabatier knives."

If I hadn't known better, I would have sworn that Simon was gay.

He had a passion for home-making that I associated – rightly or wrongly – with members of the homosexual community.

Daniel's Nice Things were an odd mixture – some looked like antiques and others were shiny and new and modern.

"Oh, I love this clock," I said, picking it up off a disgusting sideboard that had been part of his inheritance. "I'd love one like this, where did you get it?"

"Er, Ruth gave it to me."

"Oh." And then I saw something else I liked.

"Look at this lovely mirror," I breathed, and ran to touch the green wooden frame with covetous desire. "Where did you get this?"

"Um, Karen gave it to me," he said sheepishly.

That explained the hotch-potch of different styles in the flat – Daniel's women must have each sought to make their mark on his furnishings but they seemed to all have had different tastes.

"I'm surprised Karen hasn't asked for it back," I said.

"Actually she has," admitted Daniel quietly.

"So why is it still here?"

"She hung up on me after she told me she wanted it and she's refused to take my calls since, so I don't know when I should deliver it to her."

"*I* could take it home this evening," I suggested eagerly, as a vision of the mirror hanging in my bedroom appeared before me.

"But, no . . . I can't. She'd know I'd been here and I don't think she'd be too pleased."

"Lucy, you have every right to be here . . ." said Daniel. But I ignored him. *I* knew I had every right to be there, but I knew that Karen would see it differently.

"Let's see the most important room in the house," I said, making for his bedroom. "What new things have you bought?"

I flung myself on Daniel's bed and bounced around a bit. "So this is where it all happens?" I asked.

"I don't know what you're talking about," he muttered. "Unless you mean sleep."

"But what's this?" I demanded, plucking at his duvet cover. "This looks suspiciously like it came from Habitat – I thought *lurve* machines like you had fur coverlets on your beds. Not that I know the difference between a cover and a coverlet."

"We do, but I took off the fur coverlet when you said you'd come over. And I unscrewed the mirror off the ceiling. But I didn't have time to switch off the video camera."

"You're disgusting," I said idly.

He smiled slightly.

"Imagine," I said, looking up at him, from where I was stretched out on his bed. "I'm in Daniel Watson's bed, well, *on* it, which will have to do. I'm the envy of hundreds of women."

"*Two*, anyway," I said, thinking of Karen and Charlotte.

Then I did what I always did when I was in Daniel's bedroom.

"Guess who I am, Daniel," I said. Then I wriggled around on his bed and made pretend noises of ecstasy.

"Oh Daniel, Daniel," I moaned.

I waited for him to laugh like he normally would, but he didn't.

"Have you guessed?" I demanded.

"No."

"Dennis," I said triumphantly

He gave a weak smile. Maybe I'd done it once too often.

"So, who's your current bed-mate?" I asked, changing the subject.

"Never you mind."

"*Is* there a current?"

"Not exactly."

"What? You mean you've fancied a woman for more than four hours and you haven't managed to seduce her with your "I'm so innocent, I'm not a lech, I'm a really nice bloke," brand of charm. You must be losing your touch," I exclaimed.

"I must be."

He didn't smile the way he always did. He just walked out of the room. That was alarming so I jumped off the bed and ran after him.

"And how come your flat is so clean and tidy?" I asked suspiciously, when we got back to his living-room.

I felt ashamed because despite the frequent rotas that Karen and Charlotte and I drew up our flat was a tip.

We always started off full of good intentions but after a day or so our resolve slackened and we said things like, "Charlotte, if you do my bathroom duty, you can borrow my suede dress for that thing you're going to on Friday night," and "Fuck off Karen, I *did* clean it . . . yes, well, how could I use a brillo pad? – Charlotte used them all on herself after sleeping with that Danish bloke . . . well it's not my fault that it didn't all come off, it's not for want of trying," and "I know it's Sunday evening and we're stretched out watching telly and we're all so relaxed that we're nearly comatose, but I have to do the vacuuming so I'm sorry but you're all going to have to move and you'll have to turn off the telly because I need the plug socket . . . hey, don't shout! Don't shout! If it's that much of a disruption, I suppose I could leave it, I don't want to, but if you're certain that you'd rather I didn't . . ."

What we really needed was to pay someone to come in and clean for a couple of hours a week, but Karen vetoed the suggestion every time. "Why should we pay someone to do something that we can do ourselves?" she demanded. "We're young and fit and well able to do it."

Except that we didn't.

"Have you got some poor Filipina child-bride slave that you pay way under the minimum wage, coming in and 'doing' for you," I asked Daniel.

"I have not," he said, all affronted.

"Not even a bit player from *Eastenders*, with an apron and a headscarf and a bad back and red knees, coming in to dust and drink tea and complain?"

"No," said Daniel, "I do all my own cleaning, actually."

"Sure," I said disbelievingly. "Well I bet you get your current victim of a girlfriend to iron your shirts and clean the bathroom."

"I don't."

"Well, why not?" I asked. "I'm sure they'd love to. If someone offered to do my ironing in return for sexual favours, I wouldn't be able to turn it down."

"Lucy, I'll do your ironing in return for sexual favours," said Daniel, deadpan.

"Anyone apart from you, I think I must have forgotten to mention," I corrected.

"But, Lucy, I actually like doing housework," he said.

I threw him a scornful look. "And you say *I'm* weird."

"I don't actually, Lucy," he said, looking hurt.

"Don't you?" I asked surprised. "Well, you should
. . . Now me – I absolutely *hate* doing housework. If
there's a hell being prepared for me – and I see no
reason to think that there isn't – it'll involve me
having do to all of Satan's ironing. And vacuuming –
that's the worst, that's my room 101 of housework,
I'll be forced to vacuum all of hell every day."

"I'm like Nature," I added.

"How so?" asked Daniel.

"Nature abhors a vacuum, but not as much as I
abhor one."

Daniel laughed. Thank God for that, I thought. He
had been uncharacteristically mirthless.

"Now come over here, Lucy," said Daniel, and put
his arm around me. I felt a little leap of fear, until I
realised that he was only steering me across the room
to the sofa.

"You wanted to be horizontal?" he enquired.

"Yes."

"Here's the very place to do it."

"What about the chocolate you promised me?" I
demanded, not about to be fobbed off. Lying down
was no good without the chocolate. And chocolate is
at its best when eaten lying down.

"Consider it done." He left the room to get it.

That was the day that the weather broke.

It was the end of August and although it was no
longer sweltering, it was still warm enough for all the
windows to be open in Daniel's front room.

Suddenly, like a switch being flicked, the breeze

picked up, the rustling of the leaves intensified, the sky darkened and we heard the first ominous growl of the storm.

"Was that thunder?" I asked hopefully.

"It sounded like it."

I raced to the window, and leant out. A crisp bag that had probably lain undisturbed all summer skittered along the pavement, whipped by the breeze. And in seconds the rain had started and the world was transformed.

The roads and gardens changed from beige and dry and dusty to dark and sleek, the bright green of the trees was instantly almost black.

It was beautiful.

The air smelt green and fragrant and cool. The scent of the wet grass rushed up to me as I lent precariously out of the window.

Now and then my face got splashed with raindrops so big that they nearly concussed me.

I loved thunderstorms – the only time I ever really felt at peace with myself was during a storm. All the turmoil and exuberance seemed to calm me.

Apparently that wasn't just because I was weird – there was a scientific explanation for it. Thunderstorms filled the air with negative ions, although I'm not sure what they are, I know they're supposed to make you feel good. When I had found that out, I had even *bought* an ioniser to try to recreate the effect of a storm all the time.

But nothing compared to the real thing.

There was another rumble of thunder and the room was zapped by silver juddery light.

In the momentary flash of silver, Daniel's table and chairs and things looking startled, like people who had been unexpectedly woken up by the bedroom light being switched on.

The rain cascaded down and I could feel the bumping of the thunder deep within me.

"Isn't it amazing?" I said, and turned, smiling to Daniel.

He was standing a couple of feet away from me, watching me. Staring at me with hard intensity, curiosity on his face.

I immediately felt awkward. He thought I was a nutter to enjoy the downpour.

Then the funny, intense look disappeared and he smiled.

"I forgot that you always loved the rain," he said. "You told me once that when it rains you feel that your insides match your outsides."

"Did I?" I was embarrassed. "No wonder you think I'm certifiable."

"But I don't," he said.

I smiled at him. He smiled back, a funny little twist of a smile.

"I think you're incredible," he said.

That threw me.

There was a long pause. I tried to think of something light and insulting – either to him or to me – to say. Anything to dispel the tension. But I couldn't say a thing. I was mute. I was pretty sure that he had meant "incredible" in a complimentary way but I didn't know how I should respond.

"Come away from the window," he eventually said. "I don't want you getting struck by lightning."

"Let's face it, if it could happen to anyone, it could happen to me," I said and we both laughed extra heartily.

Although we kept well out of each other's way.

He closed the windows, muffling the sounds of the storm.

And still the thunder complained and roared and bumped above us. The rain torrented down and by five o'clock in the afternoon, it was almost as dark as night. Except for when there was a flash of lightning and the room was lit up for a dazzling second. Water cascaded down the windows.

"That looks like the end of summer," said Daniel.

I felt sad for only a moment.

I always knew that it wouldn't last forever and it was time to move on.

Anyway I liked autumn. Autumn – the season of new boots.

Eventually all the emotion of the storm was spent and the rain settled down into a steady beating, calming, hypnotising, cosy. I lay on the couch under a duvet, luxuriating in feeling snug, comfortable and safe.

I read my book and ate chocolate.

Daniel sat on the armchair, eating twiglets, reading the papers and watching the telly with the sound turned down.

I don't think we spoke one word to each other in two hours.

Now and then I would sigh and wriggle and say "God, this is gorgeous," or "Peel me another grape, Copernicus." And Daniel would smile at me when I said these things, but I don't think they counted as conversation.

It was only hunger that eventually forced us to communicate.

"Daniel, I'm starving."

"Well . . . "

"And don't tell me that I've been eating chocolate all afternoon and that I can't be hungry."

"I wasn't going to." He sounded surprised. "I know that you have a different stomach for biscuits and sweets. Would you like me to take you out for something to eat?"

"Does it mean I have to get off the couch?"

"Oh, I see the problem," he said. "Would you like a pizza?"

"And garlic bread?" I asked hopefully.

"With cheese?" he asked smoothly.

What a man!

He opened a drawer on one of his fancy shelf units and took out mounds of pizza leaflets and brochures.

"Have a look through these and decide what you want."

"Do I have to?"

"Not if you don't want to."

"But then how will I know about the different types?"

So he read aloud to me of pizzas.

"Thin crust or deep crust?"

"Thin crust."

"Normal base or wholewheat base?"

"*Normal!* Wholewheat – what a disgusting idea."

"Small, medium or large?"

"Small."

He was silent.

"All right then, medium."

Once the food order was established, conversation stopped again.

We watched telly, we ate, we barely spoke. I couldn't remember feeling as happy in ages.

Not that that was saying much, considering that I'd been suicidal for weeks.

During the evening the phone rang twice, but when Daniel answered it, the person hung up. I suspected that it was probably one of his hundreds of ex-girlfriends. Which made me feel uncomfortable, because it reminded me of when *I* used to do that to men who had broken *my* heart. If Gus had had a phone I'd probably have done it about ten times a day.

Later, Daniel drove me home. I insisted that he drop me at the traffic-lights.

"No," he said. "You'll get soaked."

"Please, Daniel," I begged. "I'm afraid that Karen will see your car."

"And what's wrong with that?"

"She'll make my life a misery."

"We have every right to see each other."

"Maybe," I agreed. "But I'm the one who has to live with her. You wouldn't be so brave if she was *your* flatmate."

"I'll come in with you and *I'll* deal with her," he threatened.

"Oh no!" I exclaimed. "That would be awful."

"Look," I said, more calmly. "I'll talk to her, it'll be OK."

Chapter Fifty-Eight

As I ran along the puddled road, the rain pelting down on me, I agonised about what I would say to Karen when she asked me where I'd been. The easiest thing would be to lie, of course, except that she was bound to know I was lying.

And, anyway, why should I lie? I hadn't done anything wrong, I told myself.

I had every right to see Daniel, he was my friend, he had been my friend for years, long before he had ever met Karen, long before I met Karen, for that matter.

It all sounded terribly reasonable when I said it like that.

But as soon as I put my key in the door, my courage deserted me.

"Where the fuck have you been?"

Karen was waiting for me, her face like thunder, an ash-tray a yard high on the table in front of her.

"Er . . ."

I would have quite happily lied but it was obvious that she knew.

How did she know? Who grassed?

I found out later from Charlotte that it was Adrian. After the pub had shut, Karen and Charlotte decided to get a video to kill a couple of Sunday afternoon hours and Adrian asked them who "the flash bastard in the poncey car" that I had left with was.

"He looked like he was going to cry," said Charlotte. "I think he fancies you."

My fault of course. If I had met Daniel at my flat, instead of engaging in subterfuge, I wouldn't have been found out. Honesty was the best policy. Either that or covering my tracks properly.

"So what's going on?" she demanded, in a shrill voice. Her face was really pale except for two red blotchy patches on her cheeks. She looked *demented* with fury or nerves or something.

"Nothing's going on," I said, anxious to reassure her. Not just out of concern for my personal safety, but because I knew what a living hell it is when you suspect that the man you love has found someone else.

"Don't give me that."

"Really, Karen, I just went over to his flat. It was totally innocent."

"Innocent! Nothing that man does is innocent. And do you know who told me that – it was *you*, Lucy Sullivan."

"It's different with me . . . "

She laughed bitterly. "Oh no, it's not, Lucy, don't flatter yourself."

"I'm not . . . "

"Yes, you are. That's the way he operates – he made *me* feel like the only girl in the world."

"I don't mean that, Karen. I mean, it's different because he doesn't fancy me and I don't fancy him and we're just friends."

"Don't be so naïve – anyway, I've always suspected you, you've always made far too much of a point of how you don't think he's lovely . . . "

"I was only being the voice of reason . . . "

" . . . and he wouldn't be bothered spending time with you if he didn't intend to get you into the sack – he can't resist a challenge. He'll try to shag you just because you act like you don't want to."

I opened my mouth but nothing came out.

"And is it true that he let you drive his car?"

"Yes."

"The bastard – he never let me. In six months he never once let me."

"But you can't drive."

"Well, he could have taught me, couldn't he?! If he had any decency he would have given me driving lessons."

"Er . . . "

"So is he going out with someone else, yet?" she asked, her face twisting as she tried to smile.

"I don't think so," I said soothingly. "Don't worry."

"I'm not worried," she sneered. "Why would I be worried? After all I ended it with him."

"Of course." It was hard to know what the right thing to say was.

"How can you be so pathetic?" she demanded. "Find your own bloke, stop satisfying yourself with my leavings."

Before I could defend myself against that she moved on to a different accusation.

"And how could you be so disloyal, how would you feel if I went out with Gus?"

"I'm sorry." I was humbled. She was right and I felt ashamed, a traitor.

"You're *not* to see him again, you're not to bring my ex-boyfriend into my own home."

"But I wouldn't." I had thought I was being sensitive and mindful of her feelings, but she made me sound callous and selfish.

"And I suppose he talked all about me . . . "

I didn't know what to say – I was afraid I would hurt her if I said that he hadn't.

" . . . well, I don't want him to know anything. How can I have any privacy, with my flatmate going out with my ex?"

"It isn't like that."

I felt torn apart with guilt and remorse. I hated myself for causing her pain, and I couldn't understand how it had ever seemed justifiable to do it.

Then came the thunderbolt.

"I forbid you to see him." She stared me right in the eye.

That was my cue to square my shoulders and swallow hard and tell her that she couldn't forbid me to see anyone.

But I didn't.

I felt too guilty to stand up to her. I had no right to. I was a bad friend, a bad flatmate, a bad human being. I wanted to make it all right. I didn't think what it would be like if I didn't see Daniel because I wanted to make things up to Karen.

"OK." I bowed my head and left the room.

Chapter Fifty-Nine

I went out with Daniel the following night – I couldn't understand what was happening to me. I knew I was forbidden to see Daniel, and I was *terrified* of Karen, petrified.

But when he rang and asked if he could take me for something to eat after work, for some reason I decided to say yes. Probably just because it had been ages since someone had taken me out and fed me.

Although perhaps it was a form of rebellion, I thought, albeit a secretive, private form. A flicking of two fingers at Karen, even though I was wearing metaphorical oven gloves.

Just before Daniel arrived at my office I decided to reapply my make-up – even though it was only him I was going out with, a night out was a night out and I never knew who I might meet. But as I wobbled on my eyeliner I was alarmed to discover that I felt a bit fluttery and shaky. Surely to God I didn't fancy Daniel, I thought in horror. Then I realised that it was just good plain old-fashioned fear. Fear of Karen and what she'd do to me if she ever found out. What a relief! How much better it was to feel sick with terror, not sick with anticipation.

When Daniel walked into my office at five o'clock

(wearing his Visitor's pass, Daniel would never do a Gus) I was so pleased to see him, even though he was wearing his suit, that I felt a lurch of self-righteous anger towards Karen. I even toyed with the idea that I might confront her. Although not seriously.

"We're going to the pub before our dinner," I said to Meredia, Megan and Jed. "You're welcome to join us."

But they declined. Meredia and Jed wore their "He's not Gus" faces, and watched me with narrowed, judgemental eyes as I put on my coat. Mummy had a new boyfriend, they wanted Mummy to be with Daddy.

Stupid fuckers.

Mummy wanted to be with Daddy also, but what could Mummy do about it? Would refusing a free meal from Daniel bring Gus rushing back?

Megan declined by cheerfully telling Daniel, "Thanks for the offer, and I hope you *will* be offended if I decline – I'm not in the mood for a smoothie like you. I've got a date with a *real* man."

Like me, Megan felt the need to punish Daniel for being good-looking and turning intelligent women to mush. All the same, that sounded a bit harsh. And who was this *real* man of whom she boasted? Probably one of the giant sheepshearers, who hadn't shaved for days or changed his underpants in as long.

So Daniel and I went to the pub alone.

"Karen rang me," he said, as we sat down.

"Oh." I felt a belly-flop of alarm. "What did she want?"

Were they going to get back together?

"She told me to keep away from you," he said.

"The cheek of her." I exploded in relief. "And what did you say?"

"I said that we're both adults and we can do what we like."

"What did you have to go and say that for?" I wailed.

"But why not?"

"It's OK for *you* to be an adult and to do what you like – you don't have to live with her. If I try to be an adult and do what I like, she'll kill me."

"But . . ."

"So what did she say when you said that?" I asked him.

"She sounded annoyed with me."

"How do you mean?" My heart sank.

"She said – let me see if I can remember exactly what she said – she said that I was awful in bed. And, of course, she told me that my penis was one of the smallest she'd ever seen."

"Naturally," I agreed.

"And that the only time she'd seen a smaller one was on her two-month-old nephew and it was no wonder I'd had so many girlfriends because it was obvious I was trying to prove that I was a man."

All the usual small member allegations that were par for the course from a woman scorned, but there was a danger that Daniel could be upset by Karen's version of the No Fury that Hell Hath. From the way he grinned, he didn't *look* upset.

"And what else did she scream at me?" He stared

thoughtfully. "I wish I could remember because it was really good, but I can ask everyone else in the office because they heard it too."

"I thought you said she rang you." I was puzzled.

"She *did* ring me. But everyone in the office *still* heard. Oh I remember – she swears she saw two grey ones in my pubic hair and that she only went out with me because I drove her to work most mornings and saved her having to buy a travel card, and that my hair is thinning at the back of my head and I'll be as bald as Right Said Fred by the time I'm thirty-five and no girl will go near me."

"The bitch!" I said. The Right Said Fred allegation was low.

You had to hand it to her.

"And what nasty stuff did she say about me?" I tried to brace myself.

"Nothing."

"Really?"

"Really."

He was lying. When Karen was inflamed, she attacked indiscriminately.

"I don't believe you, Daniel. What did she say?"

"Nothing, Lucy."

"I know you're lying. I bet she told you that sometimes I stuff my bra with cotton wool."

"She did but I knew that anyway."

"How?! No, don't tell me, I don't want to know. OK, I bet she told you that she reckons I must be hopeless in bed because I'm too inhibited. She knows that would upset me."

Daniel looked mortified.

"Was that it?" I demanded.

"Something like that," he muttered.

"Exactly what did she say?!"

"She said we'd be well matched, because we're probably as bad as each other in bed," he admitted.

"The fucking bitch," I said in admiration. "She's so good at knowing what hurts most."

"But she didn't mean what she said about you," I continued, anxious to reassure him. "She always told me that you were great in bed, and that your penis is lovely and big."

The two builders at the next table stared at us with open interest.

"Thanks, Lucy," Daniel said warmly. "And I have it on good authority that you're good in bed, also."

"Gerry Baker?" I asked. Gerry Baker was a colleague of Daniel's that I'd had a short-lived fling with.

"Gerry Baker," confirmed Daniel. Foolishly.

"I *told* you not to talk to Gerry about what I was like in bed," I said angrily.

"I *didn't*," protested Daniel nervously. "All that happened was that he said that you were good in bed and . . ."

One of the builders winked at me, and said, "I can well believe it, darling."

The other builder looked appalled and hastily said to Daniel, "Sorry, mate, sorry abat 'im. 'E's 'ad a few. No disrespect meant to you or your lady."

"It's OK," I said quickly, before Daniel was forced to defend my honour. "I'm not his girlfriend."

Which meant it was fine to insult me.

The builders smiled with relief but it took a little while to persuade Daniel that I hadn't been offended by them.

"*You're* the one I'm pissed off with," I explained.

"I didn't *ask* Gerry, you know," muttered Daniel. He looked suitably shamefaced. "It just slipped out accidentally and he said it without even . . ."

"Shut up," I said. "You're in luck. I'm too upset about what Karen said to worry about you and Gerry discussing my knickers."

"He didn't even mention your knickers," Daniel reassured me.

"Good."

"From what I heard they weren't on you long enough for him to even notice . . ."

"I'm joking," he said hastily, as I turned a face burning with rage upon him.

Back to Karen.

"She doesn't really think anything's going on with us," I said. "She knows we're only friends."

"Exactly," Daniel said eagerly. "That's just what I said to her, that you and me are only friends."

And we both laughed heartily.

Chapter Sixty

If I hadn't been so pissed off with Karen I'd never have taken part in the Great Bitching Session which followed.

It wasn't an honourable, noble thing to do, to bitch about my friend, flatmate and fellow female, and especially to do it with a *man*, but I was only human.

Crap in bed, indeed! The bloody nerve of her.

Of course, no good ever came of gossiping. I'd hate myself later, what goes around comes around, my bad karma would be returned to me three-fold, and so on and so on. But I decided I could live with it.

Gossiping was a kind of McDonalds for my psyche. Irresistible at the time, but I always felt sort of disgusting afterwards. And hungry again ten minutes later.

"Tell me about you and Karen. What have you done to make her hate you so much?" I asked him.

"I don't know," he said.

"I suppose it's because you're an egocentric, selfish bastard who broke her heart."

"Am I, Lucy, is that what you think?" He looked upset.

"Well . . . yes, I suppose."

"But, Lucy," he insisted. "I'm not, I didn't. It wasn't like that."

"So what *was* it like? I want to know why you didn't tell her that you loved her," I said, rolling up my bitching sleeves.

I'd teach her to suggest that I was useless in bed!

"I didn't tell her that I loved her because I didn't love her." He sighed.

"*Why* didn't you love her?" I asked. "What was wrong with her?"

Then I held my breath. In spite of what Karen had said about Daniel – and me – it was very important that he didn't say mean things about her, that he treated her with respect, that he behaved like a gentleman.

I hadn't forgotten that he was a man, and so was basically the enemy.

It was fine for *me* to destroy Karen's reputation with the airing of a few well-chosen secrets, but Daniel wasn't allowed to treat her with anything other than the utmost respect. At least not until I said otherwise.

"Lucy," he said carefully, choosing his words slowly and watching my face for my reaction, "I don't want to say anything about Karen that could be misconstrued as nasty."

Right answer.

We both smiled with relief.

"I understand that, Daniel." I nodded gravely.

That was enough of that. He had observed the formalities, and now I wanted to hear *everything* about Karen. The more awful the better.

"That's fine, I won't misconstrue anything." I was brisk. "You can tell me all about it."

"Lucy," he said awkwardly. "I'm not sure . . . it hardly seems right . . ."

"It's OK, Daniel, you've convinced me that you're really a nice guy," I reassured him.

"Really?" he asked.

"Yes," I promised insincerely. "Now bloody well tell me!"

Daniel, like all men, had to be coaxed. They like to pretend that it isn't in their nature to be bitchy, but of course, they love a good character assassination, the bloodier the better.

Men make me laugh when they throw their eyes to heaven and sanctimoniously say, "Meeee-*yoww*!" whenever a woman makes an unkind comment. Men are *worse* gossips than women.

"Lucy, *if* I tell you anything – and I'm not saying that I will, mind – it's to go no further," he said sternly.

"Of course." I nodded earnestly. I wondered if Charlotte would still be up when I got home.

"Not even Charlotte," he added.

Bastard!

"Oh go on, let me at least tell Charlotte," I said sulkily.

"No."

"Please."

"*No*, Lucy. If you don't promise, I'm not going to tell you anything."

"I promise," I said in a sing-song voice.

No problem. Talk was cheap and I wasn't under oath.

I took a quick look at him and he had trouble maintaining the straight, stern face. He tried not to smile, but he couldn't stop himself. I felt a surge of pleasure that I could still make him laugh.

"OK, Lucy," he took a deep breath and finally started. "You know I don't want to say anything bad about Karen."

"Good," I said stoutly, "I wouldn't want you to."

Our eyes met and again his mouth twitched. He looked sideways over his shoulder, pretending to look around the pub, but I knew he was trying to hide his grin.

It had been a mistake on Karen's part to insult Daniel and me together because it had united us against her. Until the sting of her allegations stopped smarting, we would be close allies. Nothing unites two people as warmly and lovingly, as a shared grievance against a third party.

Eventually Daniel cleared his throat and spoke.

"I know it sounds like I'm trying to shove all the blame onto her," he said. "But Karen didn't really care about me. She didn't even like me very much."

"It sounds like you're trying to shove all the blame onto her." I eyeballed him steadily.

"But it's true, Lucy, honestly! She didn't care about me."

"You lying bastard!" I scoffed. "She was besotted with you."

"No she wasn't," he said, with a bitterness that surprised me. "She was besotted with my bank balance – at least what she thought my bank balance was. She must have mistaken my overdraft for savings."

"Oh Daniel, no woman goes out with a man for his money. It's an Old Husband's Tale," I said.

"Karen did. Size mattered to her – the size of my wallet."

I would have laughed except he looked so miserable.

"And she kept trying to change me," he said miserably. "She didn't like me the way I was. She was disappointed because she got a pig in a poke."

"A pig who gave her a poke, more like." I was unable to resist the cheap joke.

"I'm not a pig," he said huffily.

"In what way did she try to change you?" I asked kindly. I didn't want him to get so huffy that he would stop telling me things.

"She told me that I didn't take my job seriously enough. She said that I should be more ambitious. And she was always on at me to learn to play golf, she said that more deals are done on the golf course than in the boardroom."

"But you're a research person thingy." I was confused. "You don't *do* deals, do you?"

"Exactly!" he said.

"And do you remember when I took her to that work thing at the end of July?"

"No," I said, managing to bite my tongue and not shout at him, "How the bloody hell would I know *what* you took her to, it's not as if you rang me or anything to keep me abreast of what was going on in your life."

"Well, you should have seen the way she carried on at that!"

I felt a cheap thrill and drew nearer, all the better to hear whatever awful thing he was about to tell me.

"The way she behaved with Joe . . ."

"Joe, your boss, *that* Joe?" I asked.

" . . . Yes. It was horrible, Lucy. She practically offered to sleep with him if it would enhance my promotion prospects."

"God, that's awful," I said, blushing for her. "Joe, of all people! But didn't you try to stop her?"

"Of *course* I tried to stop her, but you know what she's like, she's so headstrong."

"How excruciating." I squirmed.

"Lucy, I was badly embarrassed for her," said Daniel. He looked pale and sweaty at the memory. "I felt awful for her."

"I bet."

Joe was gay.

We sat in silence. Our thoughts occupied by a mental image of poor Karen, as she flashed her tits, but flashed in vain.

"But apart from the career stuff and the money, did you have fun?" I asked. "Did you like her?"

"Oh, yes," he said firmly.

I was silent.

"Well, she was all right, I suppose." He sighed. "She didn't have much of a sense of humour. None, in fact."

"That's not true." I felt I *had* to say it.

"No, you're right, Lucy. She did have a sense of humour, the kind of one where you laugh at people who slip on banana skins."

Guilt wrestled with my desire to really trash her.

Guilt won.

"She's beautiful though. Isn't she?" I asked.

"Very," he agreed.

"She has a lovely body, hasn't she?" I asked, pressing him.

He looked at me oddly. "Yes," he said. "I suppose she has."

"Then why have you given all that up?"

"Because I just didn't fancy her anymore."

I laughed mirthlessly. "Ha! As if. A large-breasted blonde."

"But she was cold," he protested. "It's a terrible turn-off if you feel your shagee doesn't even *like* you. Lucy, contrary to the terrible things you think about me – and all men, from what I can gather – big breasts and lots of sex aren't the highest things on my list of priorities. There are other things too."

"Like what?" I asked suspiciously.

"Well, a sense of humour. And it would have been nice if I hadn't had to pay for everything."

"Daniel, why are you suddenly so weird about money?" I was surprised. "It's not like you to be stingy."

"It's not the principle, it's the money." He grinned. "No, Lucy, I don't really care about the money, it was the way she never even offered to pay that pissed me off. It would have been nice if *she* had taken *me* out for a change."

"But maybe she doesn't have much money," I suggested doubtfully.

"It didn't have to be some place that cost lots. Just the gesture would have been enough."

"But she had a dinner party for you."

"No, she didn't. You and Charlotte did most of the work."

Suddenly I had a very vivid memory of the Night of the Long Preparations. "*And* we each had to pay a third of the cost," I said, my integrity a shadow of its former self.

"So did I," he said.

"What?" I screeched. "I don't believe you!"

You had to admire her nerve, all the same.

"She probably got Simon and Gus to pay a third each also," I exclaimed. "She must have made a huge profit on the bloody thing."

"She'd have had a long wait trying to get any money out of Gus," said Daniel.

But I didn't tell him to fuck off and leave Gus alone. We had just spent the last hour destroying his ex-girlfriend's character. It was only fair that Daniel got a go at my ex-boyfriend.

"And she never read anything except that stupid magazine that has photos of lady this and countess that and Ivana Trump," he added.

"That's bad," I agreed.

"I prefer the one with the articles about men who have babies and 'I married a child molester', what's that one called, Lucy?"

"*The National Enquirer?*"

"No, Lucy, a girl's one."

"*Marie Claire?*"

"That's it!" He was enthusiastic. "I love that. Did you see the report about the women who were imprisoned for having abortions? I think it was the February one. Jesus, Lucy, it was . . ."

I interrupted. "But Karen does read *Marie Claire*," I exclaimed in her defence.

"Oh." That brought him up short. He was silent and thoughtful for a while.

"No," he finally said.

"No, what?"

"I still don't think I love her."

I laughed. I couldn't help it. God would punish me.

"I suppose," Daniel said sadly, "what it comes down to is I was bored with Karen."

"Again?" I exclaimed.

"What do you mean, Lucy? Again?"

"That's just what you said about Ruth – that she bored you. Maybe you have a very low boredom threshold."

"No, I don't. You don't bore me."

"Neither does motor racing. But that's not your girlfriend either," I said smartly.

"But . . ."

"This mysterious new woman that you haven't managed to get into bed yet – she doesn't bore you?" I asked nicely.

"No."

"Give it time, Daniel. I bet in three months time you'll be complaining to me about how tedious you find her."

"You're probably right," he said. "You usually are."

"Good. Now take me somewhere and feed me. Anything; except a pizza."

That had been one of Gus's greatest handicaps,

his fear of fancy foreign muck. The only thing he hadn't been afraid of was pizzas.

We went to the Indian restaurant next to the pub.

I wanted to be serious and offload onto Daniel about Gus. But I couldn't nail him down for a serious conversation. Every time I asked him a question, he sang songs about the food. Which, no doubt, was very endearing, but I wanted to talk about matters of the heart. *My* heart. *And* he couldn't sing. Not like Gus. But there was a good chance that Daniel wouldn't fleece me for every penny I had. There was a bright side.

"Do you think Gus and I saw too much of each other?" I asked, as the waiter put the pilau rice on the table.

"Lay your head upon my pilau," sang Daniel tunelessly, "Ah, here's the bhajees. Lay your warm and tender bhajee close to mine." He lined up our onion bhajees side by side. "I don't know, Lucy, I really don't."

Such high spirits were a bit out of character. Although maybe they weren't. Daniel *used* to be fun, before my flatmates started to fancy him. In fact he was still fun, but I had no time to have fun with him, it was my job to discipline him. Let's face it, no one else would do it.

"But I really don't think we did, you know. If anything I wanted to see him less than he wanted to see me . . ."

"Your turn," he interrupted. "You have to sing something."

"Er, popadom, don't preach, I'm in trouble deep,"

I half-sang awkwardly. I pointed to my popadom so that he'd know what I was singing about. "So do you think I'll ever get over him?"

"Here's the chicken korma," he said, as he saw the waiter coming.

"Korma, korma, korma, korma, kor-ma, chameleon! You come and go, you come and go," Daniel sort-of-sang, moving the dish close to me and then moving it away again, moving it closer, moving it away. "Course you will. Your turn."

I pointed to the bowl of aloo gobi on the next people's table and sang absently, "Aloo, is it me you're looking for? But when?"

"Let me see," he said carefully. "I'll have to think about this one, Lucy. Oh yes, I know!"

My heart leapt. Daniel *knew* when I'd get over Gus?

"Tikka chance, tikka chance, tikka, tikka, tikka chance, tikka chance on me," he sang.

"That was a good one, wasn't it?" He beamed.

"Chicken *tikka*," he explained kindly to my puzzled face. "You know, tikka chance on me – Abba sang it."

"But what about me and Gus?" I asked faintly. "Oh fuck it! I can see it's pointless trying to have a serious conversation with you. What's this?"

"Vegetable curry."

"OK. You can't curry love, you just have to wait. Your turn."

It took him a moment or two before he thought of one.

"It's my paratha, and I'll cry if I want to, cry if I want to, cry if I want to," he tone-deafed at me.

I stopped a passing waiter and asked him to bring me a bowl of dhal tarka, then I turned to Daniel.

"Got myself a crying, walking, sleeping, talking, living dhal!" I sang.

"Stand by your naan," he replied.

We spent the rest of the evening in convulsions. I know we had fun because the people at the next table complained about us. I couldn't remember the last time I'd had such a laugh. Well, it had probably been one night with Gus.

And when I got home Karen wasn't waiting up for me.

That was one of the great advantages of her having no respect for me. It meant that I could fly in the face of her orders, actively disobey her and it would never even *occur* to her.

Chapter Sixty-One

The next morning when I arrived at work, Megan said, "That slime-merchant Daniel just rang, he said he'll call back later."

"What's he ever done to you?" I asked in surprise.

"Nothing." It was her turn to sound surprised.

"So why are you calling him names?" There was a defensive edge to my voice.

"But that's what *you* always call him," she protested.

"Oh." I was shaken. "I suppose I do."

Technically she was right, yes, of *course*, I was nasty to Daniel all the time but it wasn't as if I really *meant* it.

"It's what we both call him, Lucy," she reminded me. She sounded concerned and well she might. When Megan had first met Daniel and she said that she didn't fancy him and couldn't see what all the fuss was about, I had been thrilled. I held her aloft as an example of intelligent womanhood to anyone who would listen. "She says that Daniel wouldn't stand a chance in Australia," I gleefully told everyone, including Daniel. "She says he's too slimy and she likes her men to be rougher and tougher than him."

And now Megan was concerned that I had changed the rules. It was no longer open season on Daniel.

I *hadn't* changed any rules, I thought uncomfortably, but it sounded funny to hear Megan call Daniel a slime-merchant. Horrible, actually. I felt as if I was being disloyal to him, especially after he'd been so nice and paid for my dinner.

But then Meredia lumbered in, followed by Jed. And I forgot about Daniel because Jed was so funny. He hung up his coat, stared around at Megan, Meredia and I, rubbed his eyes and said, "Oh no, so I didn't dream it, it wasn't a nightmare! It's horrible, HORRIBLE!"

He did that most mornings. We were so proud of him.

The day proceeded.

I barely had my computer switched on (which meant that it was about ten to eleven) when my mother phoned and said that she was on her way up to town, it would be nice to meet me.

I couldn't have agreed less, but she was insistent.

"I've something to tell you," she said mysteriously.

"I can't wait," I said patiently. Her "somethings" were usually about the next-door-neighbours stealing our dustbin lid, or the birds continually pecking the tops of the bottles of milk even though she had repeatedly told the milkman to close the gate after him, or something equally earthshattering.

It was odd that she was coming up to town. She didn't ever, even though she was only twenty miles from central London.

Twenty miles and fifty years.

I didn't really feel up to meeting her but I felt that I should because I hadn't seen her since the start of the summer. Not that that had been my fault – I'd been out to the house *loads* of times – well, once or twice anyway – but only Dad had been there.

I agreed to meet her for lunch, although not in those words because I didn't think she was au fait with the concept of "lunch".

She was more of a "cup of tea and ham sandwich" kind of woman.

"Meet me in the pub across the road from my office at one o'clock," I said.

But she was appalled at the suggestion that she sit in the pub on her own and wait for me.

"What would people think?" she asked in alarm.

"OK." I sighed. "I'll get there first and you won't have to wait on your own."

"But no," she said, sounding panicked. "Sure, that's just as bad, a single woman in a public house . . ."

"What's wrong with that?" I scoffed and began to tell her that I was always going into pubs on my own, but stopped myself in time, before she started wailing, "Oh, what kind of corner girl have I reared?"

"Some place where we can have a cup of tea," she suggested, again.

"All right then, there's a café near . . ."

"Nothing too fancy," she interrupted anxiously, terrified that she might be caught in a "which one of these five forks should I use" scenario. But she needn't have worried, I wasn't too comfortable in those kind of places either.

"It's not too fancy," I said. "It's nice, relax."

"And what kind of things have they there?"

"Normal food," I reassured her. "Sandwiches, cheesecake, that kind of thing."

"Black Forest gâteau?" she asked hopefully. She knew about Black Forest gâteau.

"Probably," I said. "Or something very similar, anyway."

"And do I ask for my tea at the counter or do I . . . ?"

"You sit down, Mum, and the girl takes your order."

"And can I just march on in there and sit wherever I like, or should I . . . ?"

"Wait until they seat you," I advised.

When I arrived she was already sitting at the table, looking like a hick up from the sticks for a day, all awkward, as if she felt she had no right to be there. She was wearing a nervous "I'm just fine" smile and had her handbag clenched tightly against all the muggers that she had heard London was full of. "They won't get the better of me," her grim little hands seemed to say.

She looked slightly different – slimmer and younger than usual. For once Peter had been right – she *had* done something funny to her hair. But it suited her, I grudgingly admitted.

And there was something strange about her clothes, they were . . . they were . . . what was it? They were *nice*.

And, to top it all, she was wearing red lipstick. She never wore lipstick, except to weddings. And sometimes to funerals, if she hadn't liked the person who died.

I sat down opposite her, smiled awkwardly and wondered what it was she wanted to tell me.

Chapter Sixty-Two

She was leaving my father.

That was what she wanted to tell me. (Although it was probably overstating the case to say that she *wanted* to tell me, it was more accurate to say it was what she *had* to tell me.)

The shock was nauseating, literally. I was surprised that she waited until after I had ordered a sandwich to break the news to me, because she deplored waste.

"I don't believe you," I croaked, searching her face for a sign that it wasn't true. But all I saw was that she was wearing eyeliner and she had it on crooked.

"I'm sorry," she said humbly.

My world felt as if it was falling apart, and that confused me. I had thought I was an independent twenty-six-year-old woman who had left home and established her own life, one who had no interest in whatever sexual shenanigans her parents might get up to. But right at that moment I felt afraid and angry, like an abandoned four-year-old.

"But why?" I asked. "Why are you leaving him? How could you?"

"Because, Lucy, it's been a marriage in name only

for years and years. Lucy, surely you know that?" she asked, urging me to agree with her.

"No, I didn't know that," I said. "This is all news to me."

"Lucy, you must have known," she insisted.

She was overdoing the calling me "Lucy" bit. She kept trying to touch my arm in a pleading sort of way.

"I didn't know," I insisted back. She wasn't going to get me to agree with her, no matter what.

What's going on, I wondered in horror – other people's parents split up, but mine didn't. Especially because mine were *Catholics*.

A stable home life was the only reason I had put up with Catholic parents and their nonsense for so long. It had been an unspoken deal. My part involved, among other things, going to Mass every Sunday, not wearing patent shoes on a date and abstaining from confectionery for forty days every spring. In return for which, my parents were supposed to stay together even though they might have hated each other's guts.

"Poor Lucy." She sighed. "You could never face up to anything unpleasant, could you? You always ran off or stuck your nose in a book when the going got rough."

"Just fuck off," I said angrily. "Stop picking on me, you're the one in the wrong here."

"Sorry," she said gently. "I shouldn't have said that."

Now that really shocked me, it was one thing for her to tell me that she was leaving my father, but this was another thing entirely. Not only had she not shouted at me for using bad language, but *she'd* apologised to *me*.

I stared at her, sick with dread. Things must be very serious.

"Lucy," she said, even more gently. "Your father and I haven't loved each other for years. I'm sorry this has come as such a shock."

I couldn't speak. I was witnessing the destruction of my home, and me with it. My sense of self was amorphous enough as it was. I was afraid I would completely vanish into thin air if one of my main defining features disintegrated.

"But why now?" I appealed to her, after we had sat in silence for a few moments. "If you haven't loved each other for years, which I don't believe anyway, why have you picked now to leave him?"

And suddenly I knew why – the hair-do, the make-up, the new clothes – they all made sense.

"Oh Christ," I said. "I don't believe it – you've met someone else, haven't you? You've got a . . . a . . . boyfriend!"

She wouldn't meet my eyes, the bitch, and I knew I was right.

"Lucy," she implored. "I've been so lonely."

"Lonely?" I asked in disbelief. "How could you be lonely when you've got Dad?"

"Lucy, please understand," she begged. "Living with your father was like living with a child."

"Don't!" I said. "Don't try and make out that it was his fault. You've done this, it's *your* fault."

She stared unhappily at her hands and didn't say anything to defend herself.

"So who is he?" I spat, the taste of bile in my mouth. "Who is this . . . this . . . *boyfriend* of yours?"

"Please, Lucy," she murmured. Her gentleness unsettled me, I was much more comfortable when she was scathing and sharp-tongued.

"Tell me," I demanded.

She just stared mutely, tears in her eyes. Why wouldn't she tell me?

"It's someone I know, isn't it?" I said in alarm.

"Yes, Lucy. I'm sorry, Lucy, I never meant for it to happen . . ."

"Just tell me who it is," I said, my breaths coming short and quick.

"It's . . ."

"Yes?"

"It's . . ."

"WHOOOO?" I almost screamed.

"It's Ken Kearns," she blurted.

"Who?" I thought, dizzily. "Who's Ken Kearns?"

"Ken Kearns. You know, Mr Kearns from the dry-cleaners."

"Oh, *Mr* Kearns," I said, vaguely remembering a bald old codger with a brown cardigan and plastic shoes and false teeth that seemed to have a life of their own.

The relief! Ludicrous as it seemed, I had been gripped with fear that her boyfriend was *Daniel*. What with the way he'd been boring on recently about his mysterious new woman, and the way Mum had flirted with him when he came to visit, and the way that Daniel had said that Mum was pretty . . .

OK, so I was glad it wasn't Daniel, but, honestly, *Mr Kearns from the dry-cleaners* – she couldn't have picked anyone more awful if she had tried.

"Tell me if I've got this right," I said, in a daze. "Mr Kearns, with the false teeth that are too big for him, is your new boyfriend."

"He's getting new ones," she said tearfully.

"You're disgusting," I said, shaking my head. "You are truly disgusting."

She didn't shout at me or berate me like she would normally have done when I said something disrespectful to her. Instead she acted all martyrish and humble.

"Lucy, look at me, please," she said, tears jostling at the corners of her eyes. "Ken makes me feel like a teenager, can't you see – I'm a woman, a woman with needs . . ."

"I don't want to hear about your disgusting needs, thanks very much," I said, shutting out the appalling mental image of my mother and Mr Kearns rolling around amongst the coat hangers.

And still she made no move to defend herself, but I knew her. Sooner or later she'd run out of cheeks to turn.

"Lucy, I'm fifty-three years of age, this could be my last chance of happiness. Surely you can't deny me that?"

"You and your happiness! Well, what about Dad? What about *his* happiness?"

"I've tried to make him happy," she said sadly. "But nothing works."

"Rubbish," I spluttered. "You've always tried to make his life a misery! Why the hell didn't you just leave years ago?"

"But . . ." she said feebly.

"Where are you going to live?" I interrupted, feeling sick.

"With Ken," she whispered.

"And where's that?"

"It's the yellow house across from the school." She tried, but failed, to keep the hint of pride out of her voice. Ken, the Dry-Cleaning King, obviously had a few bob.

"And what about your wedding vows?" I asked. I knew that would really hit her where it hurt. "What about the promises you made, in a church, that you'd stay with him for better, for worse?"

"Please, Lucy," she said in a little voice. "I can't tell you how I've wrestled with my conscience, I've prayed and prayed for guidance . . ."

"You're such a hypocrite," I exclaimed – not that it mattered to me on any moral ground, but I knew it would upset her, and that was my highest priority. "You've rammed the teachings of the Catholic Church down my throat all my life and stood in judgement over unmarried mothers and people who've had abortions, and now you're no better yourself! You're an adulterer, you've broken your precious seventh commandment."

"Sixth," she said, her usual sparky self making a guest reappearance.

Hah! I knew I'd break her.

"What?" I asked in disgust.

"I've broken the *sixth* commandment, seventh is stealing, didn't they teach you anything in catechism classes?"

"You see, you see!" I crowed in bitter triumph. "There you go again, standing in judgement, setting yourself up as a moral watchdog. Well, let he who is without sin cast the log out of his own eye!"

She hung her head and twisted her hands. Back to being a martyr.

"And what has Father Colm to say about all of this?" I demanded. "I bet he's not so pally with you now, now that you've become a . . . a . . . a *home wrecker*."

"Well?" I asked again, when she didn't answer.

"They've told me not to do the flowers for the altar anymore," she finally admitted. A single tear ran down her cheek, leaving a little white line as it washed through her inexpertly applied foundation.

"Quite right," I snorted.

"And the committee wouldn't take the apple tart that I'd made for the sale of work," she said, more tears streaking down her face. She looked like a deckchair.

"Quite right too," I said hotly.

"I suppose they thought it might be catching," she said with a little smile. I stared coldly at her and, after a few seconds, her smile vanished.

"*And* you picked a great time to tell me," I said nastily. "How am I supposed to go back and do an afternoon's work after hearing this?"

That was unfair of me because Ivor was out and I wouldn't have done anything anyway, but it wasn't the point.

"Lucy, I'm sorry," she said quietly. "But I wanted to tell you straight away. And I couldn't have you finding out from someone else."

"OK," I said briskly, picking up my bag. "You've told me. Thanks a lot and goodbye."

I put no money on the table. She could pay for my sandwich as she was the reason that I hadn't been able to eat it.

"Wait, please," she urged. "Don't go yet, Lucy. Please just give me a chance to say my piece, that's all I ask of you."

"Go on then," I said. "This should be good for a laugh."

She took a deep breath and started.

"Lucy, I know you've always loved your dad more than you've loved me . . ."

She paused, in case I needed to contradict her. I stayed silent.

" . . . but it was very hard for me," she continued. "I had to be the strong one, I had to be the disciplinarian, because he wouldn't. And I know you thought that he was a great laugh and that I was mean and miserable, but one of us had to be a parent to you."

"How dare you," I spluttered. "Dad was twice, *ten* times, the parent you ever were."

"But he was so irresponsible . . ." she started to protest.

"Don't talk to me about irresponsible," I interrupted. "What about your responsibilities? Who's going to take care of Dad?"

Although I already knew the answer to that one.

"Why should anyone need to take care of Dad?" she asked. "He's only fifty-four and there's nothing wrong with him."

"You know he needs to be taken care of," I said. "You know he can't look after himself."

"And why's that, Lucy?" she asked. "Lots of men live alone, men much older than Dad and they're well able to mind themselves."

"But Dad's not like other men, and you know it," I said. "Don't think you can get off the hook that way."

"And why isn't your dad like other men?" she asked.

"You know why," I said angrily.

"No, I don't," she said. "Tell me why."

"I'm not having this discussion with you any longer," I said. "You know Dad needs looking after and that's that."

"You can't face it, can you, Lucy?" she said, looking at me with this infuriating saint-like, doe-eyed expression, all faux-compassion and social-workeresque concern.

"Can't face what?" I asked. "There's nothing I can't face, you're talking even more nonsense than you usually do."

"He's an alcoholic," she said gently. "*That's* what you can't face."

"Who's an alcoholic?" I asked, disgusted by her manipulations. "Dad is *not* an alcoholic. I see what you're up to, you think you can call Dad names and say terrible things about him just so people will feel sorry for you and say that it's OK for you to leave him. Well, you can't fool me."

"Lucy, he's been an alcoholic for years and years, probably before we even got married, but I didn't know the signs then," she said.

"Rubbish," I snorted. "He's not an alcoholic, you must take me for a complete fool. Alcoholics are those men in the street with dirty coats and big beards, who talk to themselves."

"Lucy, alcoholics come in all shapes and sizes, those men in the street are men just like your Dad, except they were a bit more unlucky."

"They couldn't have got more unlucky than being married to you," I threw at her.

"Lucy, do you deny that your father drinks a lot?"

"He drinks a bit," I admitted. "And why wouldn't he? You've made him miserable all these years. You know, my earliest memory is of you shouting at him."

"I'm sorry, Lucy," she said, tears spilling down her face. "But it was so hard, we never had any money, and he wouldn't get a job, and he'd take the money that I had put aside to buy food for you and your brothers and he'd drink it. And I'd have to go down to the local shop and give them some made-up story about not getting to the bank on time and would they give me a bit of credit. And they knew damn well, and I had some pride, Lucy, you know. It didn't come easy to me to do that, I was brought up to expect more from life than that."

She was crying good and proper now, but it meant nothing to me.

"And I loved him, so I did," she sobbed. "I was

twenty-two and I thought he was gorgeous. He kept telling me that he'd give it up and I kept hoping that things would get better. I believed him every single time, and every single time he let me down."

On and on she went, a catalogue of accusations. How he was drunk the morning of their wedding, how, when she went into labour with Chris, she had to make her own way to the hospital because he was missing, presumed drunk, how he stood at the back of the church at Peter's Confirmation and sang "The men behind the wire" . . .

I didn't even listen. I decided that it was time for me to go back to work.

When I stood up to leave, I said, "Not that you're worried about it, but I'll take care of him, and I'll probably do a far better job than you ever did."

"Is that right, Lucy?" She sounded unimpressed.

"Yes."

"Good luck," she said. "You'll need it."

"What do you mean?"

"Are you any good at washing sheets?" she asked cryptically.

"What are you talking about?"

"You'll see," she said wearily. "You'll see."

Chapter Sixty-Three

I went back to work in a state of shock.

The first thing I did was ring Dad to make sure he was OK, but he sounded incoherent and dazed, which worried me sick.

"I'll be out to you straight after work this evening," I promised. "Everything will be all right, please don't worry."

"Who will take care of me, Lucy?" he asked, sounding very, very old. I could have killed my mother.

"I will," I promised fervently. "I'll always take care of you, don't worry."

"You won't leave me?" he asked pathetically.

"Never," I said, meaning it as I'd never meant anything before in my life.

"You'll stay the night?" he asked.

"Of course I will, I'll stay with you always."

Then I rang Peter. He wasn't at work, so I presumed that Mum had already broken the news to him and, Oedipal idiot that he was, had gone home to lie down in a darkened room, waiting to die of a broken heart. Sure enough, when I rang him at home, he answered the phone in a hoarse, grief-sodden voice. He, too, said that he hated our mother.

But I knew it was for an entirely different reason and that he and I didn't share any common cause. Peter was devastated, not because my mother had left Dad, but that she hadn't left Dad for him.

Then I rang Chris and discovered that Mum had informed him of her news that morning. I was annoyed with Chris because he hadn't rung and tipped me off. So we had a brief argument which was nice because it took my mind off Dad for a while. Chris was wildly relieved when I said that I was spending the evening with Dad. ("Jesus, thanks, Lucy, I owe you one.") Chris and Responsibility weren't on the best of terms, they had never really seen eye to eye.

Then I rang Daniel and told him what had happened. He was a good person to tell because he was so sympathetic. And besides, he'd always been fond of my mother. I was glad to give him an opportunity to see what a bitch she really was.

He didn't comment on my runaway mother. He suggested that he'd drive me out to dad.

"No," I said.

"Yes," he said.

"No way," I said. "I'm very upset, I'm no company, it's a long, boring drive and, when we get there, I just want to be with my dad."

"Fine," he said. "But I'd still like to be with you."

"Daniel." I sighed. "It's obvious that you need to seek psychiatric help, but I really don't have the time at the moment to deal with your mental problems."

"Lucy, be sensible," he said firmly.

We both had a little laugh at that.

"Daniel, you're asking the impossible," I said. "Stop building failure into your expectations of me."

"Now listen," he shouted. "I have a car, you have a long way to go, you'll have to stop at your flat to get clothes and things. I'm not doing anything else this evening, I will drive you to Uxbridge and I want to hear no more about it!"

"Woooh!" I said, amused and slightly impressed, despite the awful circumstances. "It's Mills and Boon Man! Check your thighs, I bet they've gone all muscular."

He didn't really know what I was talking about.

It was odd, I'd never thought about Daniel's thighs before. I had a vague suspicion that they were already muscular. I felt a bit funny, sort of nervous, so I stopped.

"Thank you, Daniel." I gave in. "If you really don't mind, then it would be a help if you could take me."

The awfulness of Mum leaving Dad hadn't overridden my fear of Karen, and what she would do to me if she found out that Daniel was escorting me to Uxbridge. But luckily she hadn't come home from work by the time Daniel and I left my flat.

We stopped at a supermarket on the way to buy supplies for Dad. I spent a fortune, buying everything I could possibly think of that he had ever liked – hobnobs, bakewell tarts, alphabetti-spaghetti, mini-trifles, sugar puffs, coloured polo mints and a bottle of whiskey. I didn't give a damn about what my mother had said about him being an alcoholic. I didn't believe it. And even if I did, I didn't care. I would have given him *anything*, to help him feel better, to feel that someone still loved him.

I would create a loving home for him, I thought with missionary zeal.

I was quite looking forward to it. I'd show my mother how it should be done.

When Daniel and I arrived, we found Dad slumped in his armchair, drunk and crying. I was shaken to see how upset he was because, in a way, I'd thought he would be pleased that Mum had gone and left him in peace. I had almost expected him to be relieved, that it was just me and him.

"Poor, poor Dad." I dumped the bags on the table and rushed to his side.

"Oh Lucy," he said, shaking his head slowly. "Oh Lucy, what will become of me?"

"I'll take care of you. Now, have a drink, Dad," I urged, gesturing at Daniel to bring the bottle of whiskey.

"I might as well, Lucy," agreed Dad, sadly. "I might as well."

"Are you sure, Lucy?" asked Daniel quietly.

"Don't you start," I hissed quietly. "His wife has just left him, let him have a bloody drink."

"Calm down, Lucy," he said, picking up an empty bottle of Jameson from the floor beside Dad's chair and thrusting it at me. "I just don't want you to kill the man."

"One more can't hurt him," I said stiffly.

Suddenly I felt very sorry for myself and Dad. Before I knew what was happening I was in the midst of throwing a mini-tantrum. "Oh for God's sake, Daniel," I screeched. Then I marched out of the kitchen and slammed the door behind me.

I shoved open the door of the "good" front room and flung myself in a tantrumy rage on the "good" metal and brown corduroy couch. The room had always been kept for visitors. But as we had never had many visitors, it was in pristine, 1973 condition. It was like being in a timewarp.

I sat and cried, at the same time feeling daring for sitting on the good furniture that only priests and visitors from Ireland were permitted to sit on. And, in a few moments Daniel came in as I had known he would.

"Did you give him a drink?" I asked accusingly.

"Yes," he said, and skirted the smoked glass coffee table. He sat beside me on the fossilised couch. He put his arm around me as I had known he would. Daniel was good at that kind of thing, Daniel was nice and predictable, I could always rely on Daniel to do the right thing.

Then he pulled me onto his lap, one hand around my shoulders, the other under my knees. I hadn't been expecting that, but I was quite happy to go along with it. Lots of affection was just what I needed.

I indulged myself and snuggled up to him and cried a little more. Daniel was a great person to cry on, there was something very reassuring and protective about him. I really got into it and snuffled around with my face on the shoulder of his suit, while he put a hand up and gently stroked my hair and said comforting things like, "Shush, Lucy, don't cry." It was very nice.

He smelt lovely – my nose was stuck in his neck, his scent was overwhelming. Manly and sweet.

Quite sexy, actually, I thought in surprise – at least it would have been sexy if it wasn't Daniel's.

Idly, I wondered what he tasted like. Lovely, probably. In fact, I was so close to him that all I had to do was stick out my tongue and touch the smooth skin of his neck with it.

Quickly I stopped myself. I couldn't just go round licking men, not even if they were Daniel.

He continued caressing my hair with one hand and slipped the other under the hair at the nape of my neck, where he did some kind of funny manipulation with his thumb and index finger.

I sighed and relaxed closer to him. It felt gorgeous, really soothing.

Mmmmm, I thought, soothing in a shivery kind of way. Soothing and sort of . . .

Suddenly I became aware that I was no longer crying. I panicked, realising I had to extricate myself from Daniel's arms immediately. I was only allowed to cuddle up to men if we were romantically involved, or if one of us were comforting the other. As neither was the case with Daniel, I was in his arms under false pretences, my tenancy had run out with my tears.

Hoping that he didn't think I was ungrateful, I tried to jerk away from him.

He smiled at me, his face close to mine, as if he

knew something that I didn't. Or perhaps something that I *should* know.

Sometimes his clichéd good looks really get on my nerves, I thought, annoyed. And surely his teeth looked whiter than usual, he must have just been to the dentist. That annoyed me too.

I felt hot and uncomfortable. I wasn't sure why.

It must have been because we had reached the awkward stage of an emotional outburst. The flash flood of happiness or misery had passed, and the hand-holding or hugging or tear-shedding or whatever suddenly became excruciatingly embarrassing. *That* was probably why I felt as if I had to escape from him, I thought, scrambling around for a reason.

I wasn't at my most comfortable with displays of affection.

At least not sober ones.

But Daniel didn't seem to realise I wanted to break up our clinch. I tried to push myself out of the circle of his arms but nothing happened. Another wave of panicky fear swept over me.

"Thanks," I sniffed up at him, hoping that I sounded normal. As, once again, I made another attempt to wrench myself free from him. "Sorry about that."

I *had* to get away from him, I thought, frantically. I felt embarrassed and awkward in his arms, but it wasn't the usual sort of embarrassed and awkward.

He was *disturbing* me.

I was aware of all sorts of things about him that I hadn't noticed when I'd been busy crying.

Like, he was so *big* – I was used to small men. It felt funny to be held by someone as big as Daniel.

The scary kind of funny.

"Don't be sorry," he said.

I waited, expecting him to flash me his usual slightly mocking smile, but he didn't. He stared down at me, his eyes dark and serious, and didn't move.

I stared back at him. A stillness settled on us. A waiting. Moments before, I had felt safe, now I felt anything but. And I couldn't seem to catch my breath, it wouldn't go the whole way down.

Daniel moved slightly, and I jumped. But he was only stroking my hair back off my forehead. The touch of his hand sent a little thrill through me.

"But I have to be sorry," I managed to blabber nervously, unable to look him in the eye. "You know me – I love to feel guilty."

He didn't laugh.

A bad sign.

And he didn't let me go either.

A worse sign.

To my horror, I felt a powerful rush of sexual attraction for him which nearly knocked me off his lap.

I made another attempt to scramble away from him.

I suppose it wasn't a very diligent effort.

"Lucy," he said, putting his hand on my chin, and gently moving my face, so that I had to look at him. "I'm not going to let you go, so stop trying."

Oh God, I thought. The gloves were off. I didn't like his tone. Well, actually I liked it very much. If I

575

hadn't been so scared of what it meant, I would have loved it.

Something very weird was going on – why was Sexual Attraction calling to see if Daniel and I were coming out to play? Why now?

"Why won't you let me go?" I stammered up at him, trying to buy time. I was vaguely distracted by his eyelashes – they were so long and thick it was indecent. And had his mouth always been that sexy? He was such a lovely colour, slightly tanned against the whiteness of his shirt.

"Because," he said, staring down at me, "I want you."

Fuck it! My insides lurched with a scary thrill. We were approaching a border, about to cross into unknown territory. If I had any sense, I would stop us.

But I didn't have any sense. I couldn't stop myself.

And, even if I had wanted to, I certainly couldn't stop *him*.

For ages before it happened, I knew he was going to kiss me.

We hovered in space, our mouths almost touching, moving infinitesimally closer.

For years his face had been so familiar to me, but now he looked like a stranger, a very attractive one.

It was horrifying.

In a very nice way.

Finally, when my nerves were stretched to screaming point and I was sure that I couldn't wait another second, he bent his head and put his lips to mine and kissed me. His kiss flooded through me like a sparkling drink.

I kissed him back.

Because – shameful admission – I *wanted* to kiss him back.

I hated it because it was gorgeous.

It was the nicest kiss I'd ever had in my entire life and it was from Daniel. How awful – if he ever found out, his ego would go into orbit. I had to make sure that he never knew, I thought urgently.

I noticed all kinds of things that I'd never noticed before. How big and hard his back felt as I ran my hands along the grown-up-person's fabric of his suit.

No wonder he's such a lovely kisser, I thought, trying to put myself off him, he's had so much practice.

But then he kissed me again and I thought, well, the damage is done, hung for a sheep as for a lamb, might as well have another one.

He was delicious. He had such a perfect mouth and the smoothest *skin*. He tasted musky and sexy.

He was a *man*, a real man.

Oh Christ, I thought, I'll never, ever live this one down.

He'll never let me forget this. The shame! After all the abuse I've hurled at him and his philandering ways.

If I hadn't been so turned on, I might almost have laughed at myself.

Karen would kill me, I realised. I was as good as dead.

How could I do this? I asked myself in shock.

But how could I not?

All these thoughts rushed through my head, and then out the other side as I became overwhelmed with desire for him.

Every now and then a little voice would go, Do you know who this *is*? This is *Daniel*, in case you hadn't noticed. And have you noticed *where* you are? Yes, exactly, you're in your mother's good room. On Father Colm's *couch*.

I was shaking because I fancied him so much. I wanted to have sex with him there and then, on Father Colm's couch, with Dad in the next room. I didn't care.

And all he was doing was *kissing* me. Kissing and caressing me in totally chaste places. I didn't know whether to be impressed or annoyed that he wasn't trying to grope me, that he hadn't tipped me back on the couch and inched his hand up my skirt.

Finally he pulled away from me and said, "Lucy, you don't know how long I've waited to do this."

I had to hand it to him – he was good. He sounded intense and passionate. He *looked* great. His pupils were dilated. His eyes were nearly black and his hair was all messy and sexy, very different from its normal well-groomed look. The expression on his face was the best – he looked like a man in love, or in lust, at the very least.

No wonder so many women fell for him.

"Yes, Daniel," I said, in a shaky voice, trying to smile, "I bet you say that to all the girls."

"I'm serious, Lucy," he said in a serious voice with serious undertones, looking at me seriously.

"So am I," I said lightly.

Sanity, such as it was, had started its reluctant return to my wayward head. Although my whole body still shook with unsated desire.

I looked at him, wanting to believe him, knowing I couldn't.

We sat beside each other, close but separate, him looking sad, me looking sad, me still in his arms, having overstayed my welcome but loath to leave.

"Please, Lucy," he said, and put both his hands on my face, holding it as gently and carefully as if my head was a brimming bucket of sulphuric acid.

Then the door opened. Dad shambled in. Even though Daniel and I sprang apart with the high-jump ability of spring lambs, he still saw what was in progress and looked shocked and annoyed.

"Good God," he roared. "Ye'er all at it, it's like Sodom and Begorrah around here."

Chapter Sixty-Four

My life changed very quickly in the following days. Suddenly I had a new home, or an old one, depending on how you looked at it. I was keen to hand in the notice on my flat immediately, eager to begin my new life, anxious to show how committed I was to it.

Someone had to move in to take care of Dad. I was the obvious candidate.

If Chris or Peter had offered to, I would still have insisted on doing it myself. Not that they *did* offer, the lazy bastards. They were both appalled at the prospect. It wasn't as if they'd have been any good at it either – my mother had done everything for both of them since the day they were born, so they hardly knew how to run a bath, never mind run a house. It was a miracle that they'd ever even learnt how to tie their own shoes. Not that I was much better myself at housekeeping, but I knew I'd manage somehow. I would *learn* how to cook fish fingers, I thought passionately, it would be a labour of love.

Everyone tried to talk me out of going back to live in Uxbridge. Karen and Charlotte didn't want me to leave – and not just because of the hassle of having to find a suitable new flatmate either.

"But there's nothing wrong with your dad," said Karen, puzzled. "Lots of men are on their own. Why do you have to go and actually *live* with him? Can't you just visit him every couple of days, you know, get a neighbour to look in on him, get your brothers to take turns, that kind of thing?"

I couldn't explain why to Karen. I felt that nothing less than the whole hog would do. I had to do it properly. I would move back and look after Dad, as he'd never been looked after before, as he should always have been. I was *glad*, glad to have him to myself, that it would be just the two of us. I was bitter and angry with my mother for her fickleness, but it was nothing more than I expected from her. I was relieved that, finally, she was out of the picture.

"But how awful for you, moving back home to live with your parents," said Charlotte, sounding horrified. "Parent, I mean," she added quickly. "Think about it, Lucy – when will you be able to have sex with boys? Won't you be afraid of your dad bursting in and catching you at it, telling you that you can't do that kind of thing under his roof?"

"And will he tell you what time you must get home at?" she chattered on, not noticing me squirm. "And say 'you're not going out in that' and 'you look like a prostitute with all that make-up' and things like that?" she exclaimed. "You're bonkers!"

Charlotte's problem was that she had made her

escape from her familial home too recently. The memory of being under her father's thumb was very fresh in her mind. She still revelled in her new-found freedom. On the days that she wasn't suicidal with guilt about it, that was.

"Or what if your dad gets a new girlfriend?" she demanded. "Won't it be disgusting if you burst in and catch *him* having sex?"

"But . . ." I tried to interrupt. The idea of poor Dad having a girlfriend was laughable. Almost as funny as the idea of me having a boyfriend.

A boyfriend was not on the cards. Daniel's kiss had been a one-off. A never-to-be-repeated, once-in-a-lifetime opportunity. Hurry now, while stocks last.

After Dad had caught us taking a snog-breather, he glared at us both for a little while. We cringed, as befitted us, under his disapproving look. Then he withdrew from the room and Daniel and I rearranged ourselves. I waited for my heartbeat to slow down and my breathing to return to normal. Daniel waited for his erection to subside and his gait to return to normal (I found that out some time later).

We sat side by side on the couch, a vision of mute sheepishness.

I wanted to die.

It was all so awful.

Snogging Daniel! *Snogging* Daniel. Snogging *Daniel*. And getting caught by Dad – the mortification! There was a part of me that would always be fourteen.

I was in a state of shock anyway, what with Mum having left Dad. And, in a way, I was *beyond* being shocked by Daniel snogging me.

It was too weird to think about.

I didn't know why he'd had such an effect on me – I decided I was probably feeling vulnerable because of the disintegration of the familial unit.

And as for Daniel's motives, well, who knows? He was a man, I was a woman (well, sort of, more of a girl, really, I felt). Basically, I had been *there*.

Everything was topsy-turvy I'd had enough upheaval for one day and I wanted Daniel and I to be back to normal. And the best way to do that was to *act* normal. So I insulted him.

"You took advantage of me," I grumbled.

"You stupid bastard," I added, just in case.

"Did I?" he asked in surprise.

"Yes," I said. "You knew I was upset about poor Dad. And then you insult me by feeding me your usual smoothie big-hit-with-the-girls-stuff and snog me."

"Sorry," he said, sounding horrified. "That wasn't my intention . . ."

"Forget it." I sighed self-righteously. "Let's just forget it. But don't let it happen again."

Mean of me, I know. It takes two to tango etc., etc., but I had enough on my mind, without wondering if I fancied Daniel.

I wouldn't think about it, I decided. I was good at not thinking about unpleasant things.

At the time, I didn't know just how good I was.

After about ten minutes, Daniel shamefully slunk off. Dad stood at the front door, almost shaking his fist after him and watched until he was sure Daniel was gone. We hadn't even given him a valedictory cup of tea. My mother would turn in her grave.

I wished.

Chapter Sixty-Five

Daniel came to Uxbridge to see me a couple of nights after the great snogging episode. I was so embarrassed and confused that I would have been quite happy never to have seen him again, but he had pestered me.

First he rang me at work the day afterwards and asked me to meet him for lunch. I told him I didn't want to.

"Please, Lucy," he said.

"Why?" I asked. "Oh no."

"Oh no, what?"

"If you say we have to talk, I'll kill you," I said.

Megan, Meredia and Jed nearly gave themselves whiplash looking up with interest.

"Actually, we do have to talk," said Daniel. "About your flat."

My flat?

"What about it?" I was surprised.

"Just let me talk to you."

It was obviously an excuse, but I decided to go along with it.

"Come out to the house tomorrow night," I finally agreed.

To my alarm, I felt warm and glad at the thought of seeing him. A stop would have to be put to that.

"I'll come and meet you after work," he offered.

"Oh no!" I said quickly. There was no way I could bear an entire train journey with him. I would spontaneously combust from unspoken embarrassment.

When I hung up the phone, Megan, Meredia and Jed descended on me like vultures.

"Who was it?"

"Was it Gus?"

"What's going on?"

"Are you and him shagging again?" they clamoured.

I was frighteningly nervous as I waited for Daniel to arrive.

My head raced with the pros and cons – well, actually, the cons and cons – of it all. Snogging Daniel had been a big mistake. Any further snogs would be careless in the extreme.

OK, so I felt as if I fancied him, but I knew that I didn't really.

The shock of my mother leaving my father had addled my emotions and I just *thought* I did.

Daniel kissing me had been the product of an unusual set of circumstances.

Let's look at it dispassionately, I thought, as I frantically brushed my hair. Dad watched me benignly. He wouldn't be quite so benign when he realised who I was brushing my hair for.

On the one hand, I thought dramatically, there was me. Confused, vulnerable, needy, a child from a freshly broken home, ready to love the first person who showed her affection.

On the other hand, there was Daniel – a man who was used to a lot of sex, and who hadn't had it in a couple of days. So naturally he wasn't choosy about who he interfered with. I had been there. He had interfered with me.

See. Not choosy.

And Daniel was a man who loved a challenge. What Karen had screeched at me on Sunday night had confirmed what I had always known. Daniel would probably try to get off with his own mother if he thought she'd put up enough of a fight.

But I would not succumb, I thought grimly.

For once I would resist the impulse to self-destruct. I would not fancy Daniel. I would be different.

As soon as I opened the front door to him, my resolution to not fancy him wavered, then dissolved. He looked handsome and attractive, which came as an unpleasant shock. How come he looked so sexy all of a sudden? He never had before – at least not to me. To my great disappointment I came over all girlie and simpery and shy.

"Hello," I said to the knot of his tie.

He bent to kiss me and a roar came from the kitchen.

"Hi you!" yelled Dad. "Layve my daughter alone, you scut."

Daniel backed off hurriedly. I felt like a starving person who'd had a bag of chips waved under her nose and then whisked away.

"Come in," I invited the collar of his shirt.

I was horribly awkward. As I led him through the hall, I banged my hip-bone on the telephone table and then had to pretend it didn't hurt. I didn't want him to offer to kiss it better. Because I might have let him.

"Take off your coat." I stared his breast-pocket in the eye.

I was disgusted by the effect he was having on me. It was obvious that I was way out of my depth, only temporarily, of course. Only because my parents had split up. But all the same I had to protect myself.

I decided that I wouldn't be alone with him and, after he left that evening, I wouldn't see him again, *ever*. Well, maybe not ever, but for a while at least. Until I was back to normal, whatever that was.

As part of my cunning plan, I forced Daniel into the kitchen, where Dad sat glaring.

"Hello, Mr Sullivan," Daniel said nervously.

"Haven't you the brass neck?" growled Dad. "Coming back here after you treating my home like a . . . like a . . . like a *hoor-house*."

"Shush, Dad." I was mortified. "It won't happen again."

"A neck like a jockey's bollix," muttered Dad.

Then, thankfully, he shut up.

"Would you like a cup of tea?" I asked Daniel's shoulder.

"When are we getting the crispy pancakes?" Dad interrupted rudely.

"What crispy pancakes?"

"We always have crispy pancakes on a Wednesday."

"But today's Thursday."

"Is it? Well, when are we getting the stew?"

"Do you always have stew on Thursdays?"

He looked at me mournfully.

"Sorry, Dad, I'll get into a routine next week. Can you make do with a pizza for this evening?"

"A pizza that you ring for?" He suddenly perked up.

"Yes." What other types were there? I wondered.

"Not one from the freezer?" The look of hope on his face was heart-rending.

"God, no."

"Great," he said with glee. "And can we get beer?"

"Of course."

I suspected that he was fulfilling a life-long ambition. My mother would have frowned on such extravagance.

When I rang the pizza company, Dad insisted on speaking personally to the man who made the pizzas to discuss what toppings he should have.

"What are anchovies? Go on, sure I'll have a couple. What are capers? Sure, you might as well fling a few on. Now do you think them anchovy (he pronounced it 'anne-chovie') yokes will go with the pineapple . . . ?"

I had to admire Daniel's patience, although I still couldn't look him in the eye.

When the pizzas and beer arrived the three of us sat around the kitchen table. As soon as the food was eaten, Dad recommenced glaring at Daniel. The tension was dreadful.

Dad wouldn't look directly at Daniel. He stared

589

viciously at him whenever Daniel was looking at something else, but looked away quickly whenever Daniel flicked a glance at him. Daniel suspected that Dad was giving him dirty looks, so then *he* started to try and catch Dad at it. One microsecond he'd be idly drinking his beer, then, in a blur, he'd whip his head round to where Dad was gurning at him. Then, in another blur, Dad whipped *his* head away and slurped *his* beer with a face as innocent as an angel's.

It went on for hours. At least, that was how it felt.

The atmosphere was so loaded that, when we finished the beer, we started, with gusto, on the Jameson.

The few times that Dad turned away to shout insults at a politician on the television, ("stick out your tongue, till we see the black line down the middle from all them lies you're telling!") Daniel made all kinds of energetic gestures with his face and head, winking and jerking his head towards the door, indicating that we should exit by it and go to another room. Probably the sitting-room, for a repeat of the previous time.

I ignored him.

But finally Dad decided to go to bed.

We were all quite drunk by then.

"Are you going to be here all night?" he demanded of Daniel.

"No," said Daniel.

"Well, off with you, so," he said, standing up.

"Would you mind if I had a word with Lucy in private, Mr Sullivan?" Daniel asked.

"Mind? Mind!" Dad spluttered. "After the way ye two were carrying on the other night, you can be damn sure that I mind."

"I'm sorry about that," said Daniel humbly. "And I can assure you it won't happen again."

"Do you promise?" Dad asked sternly.

"I promise," said Daniel solemnly.

"All right, so," said Dad.

"Thanks," said Daniel.

"Now, I'm trusting the two of you, mind," said Dad, waggling his finger at us. "No high jinks, right?"

"None," promised Daniel. "Not a jink of any level, low, medium or high."

Dad shot him a suspicious glare, as he wondered if Daniel was taking the piss. Daniel put on his ultra-earnest, you-can-trust-me-with-your-daughter-Mr-Sullivan face.

Not quite convinced, Dad shuffled off to bed.

Of course, I expected Daniel to try and jump me the minute the door closed after Dad. I was most put out when he didn't. I had been looking forward to fighting him off and calling him a pervert all evening.

But he confused me by tenderly taking my hand and speaking gently.

"Lucy," he said. "I want to talk to you about something important."

"Oh yes," I said sarcastically. "About my . . ." – little snigger – "flat."

I knew a pretext as well as the next woman.

"Yes," he said. "I hope you don't think I'm interfering – actually I *know* you'll think I'm

591

interfering – but please don't hand your notice in just yet."

That floored me – I hadn't *really* expected him to want to talk about my living arrangements.

"But why not?" I asked him.

"All I'm saying is, don't rush into something that you can't get out of," he said.

"I'm not," I said.

"You are," he said. The cheek of him.

"You're too upset at the moment to make a rational decision."

"No, I'm not," I said as my eyes filled with tears.

"Yes, you are," he said. "Just look at you."

Maybe he had a point, but I couldn't give in without a fight.

I gulped a mouthful of whiskey.

"But what sense does it make?" I asked him, "to live with my dad and pay rent on a flat?"

"But you may not *want* to stay with your father after a while," he suggested.

"Don't be silly," I said.

"Well, your mother may come back. She might make it up with your dad," he said.

That thought filled me with alarm.

"Unlikely," I blustered.

"Well, what about when you go into town and you've missed the last tube home and you don't want to spend a thousand pounds on a taxi back to Uxbridge? Wouldn't it be sensible to have a little *pied-à-terre* in Ladbroke Grove?" he suggested.

"But Daniel," I said desperately, "there won't be

any nights out on the town anymore. That part of my life is over. More whiskey?"

"Yes please. Lucy, I'm very worried about you," he said, putting on his concerned face.

"Don't be," I said, annoyed and frustrated. "And don't give me that cute face, I'm not one of your . . . your . . . *women*. You obviously don't realise the seriousness of what's happened to my family. My mother has left my father and I have responsibilities."

"People's mothers leave people's fathers every day of the week," said Daniel. "And the fathers cope. They don't need their daughters to give up everything and act as if they've entered a nunnery."

"Daniel, I *want* to do this, it's not a sacrifice. I have to do it, I have no choice in it. I don't care if I can't go out and have fun anymore. Besides I wasn't having fun anyway."

I was nearly in tears at the idea of such goodness, such daughterly devotion.

"Please, Lucy, just wait a month or so." He didn't look as moved as I felt.

"Oh, all right then," I agreed.

"Is that a promise?"

"I suppose it is."

And then I caught Daniel's eye. Christ, he was good-looking! I nearly knocked over my glass.

I was impatient for the molesting to begin. I was so sure that he'd arranged to see me just so he could try to snog me that I was damned if he was leaving without trying.

Chapter Sixty-Six

What I did next was very out of character for me.

I blame it on the amount I'd had to drink. Combined with the trauma. Plus the fact that I hadn't had sex in ages.

The sort of willpower, where you really fancy someone but keep away from them because you know that they're bad news, doesn't exist in real life. Not in my version of it anyway. My heart ruled my head.

My lust ruled my head.

"Maybe it's time I started," I said slowly.

"Started what?"

"Fun. Having it."

Purposefully – if a bit unsteadily – I stood up, holding his gaze, and made my way around the kitchen table to Daniel. While he sat staring uncertainly at me, I coaxed a piece of my hair seductively over one eye and then wantonly wriggled onto his lap and put my arms around his neck.

I moved my face closer to his.

God, he was gorgeous. Just look at that beautiful mouth, and any second now it would be kissing me.

What I needed was a good seeing to, some wild abandoned sex, lots of affection. And who better to do it than Daniel?

Of course I wasn't in love with him. I was in love with Gus. But I was a woman. And I had my needs. Why should it only be men who're allowed a zipless fuck? I wanted one too, whatever it was.

"Lucy, what are you doing?" he asked.

"What does it look like?" I tried to make my voice husky and sexy.

He didn't put his arms around me. I wriggled a bit closer to him.

"But you promised your dad." He looked worried.

"No I didn't. You did."

"Did I? OK, *I* promised your dad."

"You lied," I said. More low, sultry tones. This seduction carry-on was great fun, I decided. And remarkably easy.

I was looking forward to this. I was going to enjoy myself like I hadn't enjoyed myself in ages.

"Lucy, no," he said.

No? *No?* Was I hearing things?

He stood up and I sort of slid off his lap.

I landed on the floor, swaying slightly. Scorching humiliation hadn't arrived yet. It was held up by my intoxication. But it was definitely on it's way.

How excruciating. Daniel would shag *anyone*. What was wrong with me? Surely I wasn't that revolting?

"Lucy, I'm flattered . . ."

Now, that annoyed me.

"Flattered!" I roared. "Fuck off, you patronising

595

fucker. You can give it but you can't take it. You flirt with me then, when I call your bluff, you can't deliver the goods."

"Lucy, it's not that at *all*. But you're too upset and confused and I would be taking advantage . . ."

"*I'll* be the judge of that," I said.

"Lucy, I'm very attracted to you . . ."

"But you don't want to shag me," I finished for him.

"You're right, I don't want to shag you."

"God, how embarrassing," I whispered.

Then I rallied.

"Well, what were you playing at the other night?" I demanded. "That wasn't a pistol in your pocket – you certainly acted like a man after his jump, *then*."

His face twisted in what I initially thought was distaste, until I realised that he was trying not to laugh.

"Where did you hear that expression, Lucy?"

"From you, as I remember."

"Really? I suppose you're right."

There was a pause and I looked at my feet. I seemed to have four. No, two. No, it was four again.

"Lucy, look at me," coaxed Daniel. "I want to tell you something."

I turned a face burning with shame to him.

"I'd like to make it clear that I don't want to *shag* you," he said. "But, when things are different and you're not so upset and your life isn't in such upheaval, I *would* like to make love to you."

Now *that* was funny.

I laughed and laughed.

"What have I said?" He looked confused.

"Oh Daniel, *please*. What a slimy, smooth-bastard thing to say. 'I'd like to make *lurve* to you,' but not at the moment. Please credit me with a little bit of nous – I know when I'm being rejected."

"You're *not* being rejected."

"Let me see if I've got this right. You'd like to make *lurve* to me," I cruelly mimicked him.

"That's right," he said quietly.

"But not just now. If that's not rejection, I don't know what is."

I laughed again.

He had hurt me and humiliated me and I wanted to do the same to him.

"Please, Lucy, listen to . . ."

"No!"

Then I either sobered up or calmed down.

"I'm very sorry about all of this, Daniel. I'm not in the fullness of my mental health. It's all been a terrible mistake."

"No, it hasn't . . ."

"And now I think it's time you left, you've a long journey home."

He looked sadly at me.

"Are you OK?" he asked.

"Fuck off, don't flatter yourself," I said grumpily. "I've been rejected by much more attractive men than you. As soon as the killer mortification wears off, I'll be fine."

He opened his mouth to begin a fresh stream of platitudes.

"Goodbye, Daniel," I said firmly.

He kissed me on the cheek. I stood as if made of stone.

"I'll phone you tomorrow," he said at the front door.

I shrugged.

Things would never be the same again.

God, I felt depressed.

Chapter Sixty-Seven

The following day I took official leave of my Ladbroke Grove residence. Charlotte and Karen waved me off, after Karen had forced me to leave a handful of post-dated cheques for the rent.

"Goodbye, I may never see you again," I said, hoping to make her feel guilty.

"Oh don't, Lucy." Charlotte was nearly in tears. She was so sentimental.

"We'll contact you when the phone bill comes in," said Karen.

"My life is over," I said coldly.

"But," I added. "If Gus rings, make bloody sure you give him my number."

Chapter Sixty-Eight

Living with Dad wasn't the way I thought it would be.

I thought that we wanted the same things – I would devote my life to taking care of him and making him happy, and he would reciprocate by letting himself be taken care of and being happy.

But something had gone wrong, because I didn't make him happy. He didn't even seem to *want* to be happy.

He always crying and I couldn't understand why. I thought he should be glad to be rid of my mother, that he was much better off with me.

I didn't miss her and I couldn't see why *he* did.

I brimmed with love and concern for him and I was quite prepared to do anything for him, spend time with him, cosset him, cook for him, get him anything he wanted or needed. Except I didn't want to listen to him tell me how much he had loved her.

I wanted to take care of him only if he was going to be happy about it.

"Maybe she'll come back," he said over and over.

"Maybe," I muttered, thinking *What's wrong with him?*

Although, luckily, he never did anything practical

to try and win her back. He made no great displays of passion, like standing outside Ken's yellow house and shouting neighbour-waking abuse at him in the middle of the night. Or daubing "Adulterer" in green fluorescent paint on Ken's front door. Or emptying the rubbish bins of the neighbourhood in Ken's driveway, so that when he left in the morning for a hard day's dry-cleaning, he would sink ankle-deep in rusty tin cans and potato peelings. Or picketing the dry cleaners with signs saying "This man stole my wife. Don't get your shirts cleaned here."

Although I couldn't understand his pain, I tried to lessen it. But all I knew to do was to force food and drink on him and treat him like a convalescent invalid and point out the (few) amenities and diversions offered by our home. Like asking him in gentle tones if he would like to watch telly. Football? *Coronation Street*? Or suggesting that he get some rest.

Bed and telly was about the extent of our recreational facilities.

He barely ate, no matter how hard I coaxed him. Neither did I. But while I knew that I'd be OK, I was afraid that he had started on his terminal decline.

Even before the end of the first week I was exhausted.

I had thought my love for him would give me limitless energy, that the more he asked of me the better I would feel, that the more I did for him, the more I would *want* to do for him.

I tried too hard to please and that burnt up an awful lot of energy.

601

I eagerly watched him, anticipated his every need and did things for him even when he said that I didn't need to.

And then I was surprised to find that I was shattered.

The mere practicalities, alone, took their toll.

Like the fact that it took me at least an hour and a half to travel to work every morning. I had become spoiled by the thirty-minute journey from Ladbroke Grove, where I had numerous tubes, buses and taxis to choose from.

I had forgotten what it was like to commute from the suburbs, where there was only one train at my disposal and if I missed that there was a twenty-minute wait until the next one.

I had once been a master of the ancient art of commuting, but I had lived in the city for too long and had lost many of my skills. I had forgotten how to sniff the air and stare at the sky (and the electronic noticeboard) and feel that the train was leaving in about one minute and that I had no time to buy a paper. I was no longer able to sense the vibes of a packed platform and realise that three trains in a row had been cancelled and, if I fancied my chances of getting on the next one, I should start kicking and squeezing my way to the front immediately.

I used to *know* such things instinctively. I used to commune with the trains, almost merging into one being with the Underground system, man and machines working in synchronicity, perfect harmony.

But not anymore.

And even though I had always been late for work

in the past, I *could* have been on time if I had wanted. Now I really had no choice. I was at the mercy of London Underground and their various delaying mechanisms, leaves on the track, bodies on the track, signal failures, someone leaving their cheese sandwiches on the train, causing a bomb scare.

I had to get up so early. And before the first week was over, I discovered that Dad had a little problem and it became obvious I would have to get up even earlier.

At work I worried all day long about him, because it soon became clear that he couldn't be left on his own for any length of time. Taking care of Dad was like taking care of a child. Like a child, he had no fear, no sense of the consequences of his actions. He thought it was no big deal to go out leaving the front door open. Not just unlocked, but swinging open. Not that we had much to steal, but nevertheless.

As soon as work finished I rushed home. Anything could have happened. Almost every day there was a crisis of some kind. I lost count of the times he'd fallen asleep, either leaving the bath running, or the gas on. Or with a pot bubbling and burning, forgotten on the hob, or with a cigarette slowly burning its way through the cushion he was sitting on.

I often came home from work, exhausted, to find hot water leaking through the kitchen ceiling. Or to the smell of burning and find a blackened, burnt-out pot on the ring while Dad lay slumped asleep in his chair.

There were no more nights out on the town for me. I had thought I wouldn't mind and I was ashamed to find I did.

And the early nights didn't mean that I got plenty of sleep, because Dad usually woke me in the middle of the night and I had to get up to help him.

Dad wet his bed the first night I was home.

The heartbreak that I felt very nearly pushed me over the edge to insanity.

"I can't bear it, I can't bear it," I thought desperately. "Please God, help me to live through this pain."

To see my father so stripped of his dignity was almost more than I was able for.

He woke me up at about three in the morning to tell me. .

"I'm sorry, Lucy," he said, looking mortified. "I'm sorry, I'm sorry."

"It's OK," I hushed, "stop saying sorry."

I had a quick look at his bed and realised that there was no way he could sleep there.

"Why don't you go and sleep in the boys' room and I'll, you know, tidy, er, up your bed," I suggested.

"I will so," he said.

"Do," I urged.

"And you're not cross with me?" he asked meekly.

"Cross?" I exclaimed. "Why would I be cross with you?"

"You'll come and say 'good night' to me?"

"Of course I will."

So he got into Chris's single bed and pulled the covers up to his chin, his slack old person's chin rough with white stubble. I smoothed down his wispy grey hair and kissed him on the forehead and I was filled with a fierce pride, a sense of how well I took care of him. No one would ever look after anyone as well as I would look after Dad.

When he went back to sleep I pulled the sheets off the bed and put them in for the laundry. Then I got a basin of hot, soapy water and dettol and scrubbed and rinsed the mattress.

The only thing that worried me about the whole episode was that the next morning, when Dad woke up in Chris's bed, he was confused and frightened. He didn't know how he'd got there because he couldn't remember anything of the night before.

When he wet his bed on the first night I was there, I thought it was because he was so upset, and that it was an isolated event.

But it wasn't.

It happened nearly every night. Sometimes more than once.

Sometimes in Chris's bed, too.

When that happened, I got him to move to Peter's bed. Luckily – because there was nowhere else for him to move to except mine – he managed not to wet Peter's bed.

He always woke me up to tell me and at first I got up and comforted and relocated him.

After the first few nights I was so exhausted that I decided to leave my nocturnal cleaning-up until the morning, before I left for work.

605

I didn't, *couldn't* leave it until the evening, and it was out of the question to ask Dad to help.

Instead, I reset my clock to half an hour earlier than the already horribly early time it was set for, so I could clear up whatever needed to be cleared up each morning.

When he woke me to tell me that he had wet his bed, I just told him to move to another one and tried to go back to sleep.

But it was so difficult, because he was racked with guilt every time it happened and wanted to talk about how sorry he was and to make sure that I wasn't cross with him. Sometimes he would ramble on for hours, crying and saying he was a failure and that he'd try to make sure it never happened again. And because I was so tired I found it hard not to get impatient with him. And that would upset him and I'd feel destroyed with guilt, which meant I got even less sleep, which made me more impatient the next time . . .

And, always, like little whispers in the corner of my head was the memory of what my mother had said about him being an alcoholic. I watched everything he drank. And it seemed to be an awful lot. More than I remembered from when we were young. But then I wasn't sure if I was overreacting to what she had said, so I tried to put it out of my mind.

Maybe he was drinking a lot, but so what? His wife had just left him, so why shouldn't he?

Chapter Sixty-Nine

My life quickly developed a routine.

In the evenings I had to run to the laundrette to dry the sheets I'd left in before I went to work. Then I made his dinner, then there was usually some small crisis to deal with because he was forever burning things or breaking them or losing them.

I don't know when the tiredness turned to resentment. I kept it hidden for ages because I was ashamed of it. Through guilt and misplaced pride, I even managed to hide it from myself for a while.

I began to miss my other life.

I wanted to go out and get drunk and stay up late and swap clothes with Karen and Charlotte and talk about boys and the size of their penises.

I was tired of having to be constantly vigilant, of always having to be there for Dad.

A big part of the problem was that I had wanted to be perfect for Dad. I had wanted to be the one who took care of him better than anyone else.

But I couldn't and then I didn't even want to. It wasn't a challenge anymore, it was a burden.

I was aware that I was a young woman, that looking after Dad, wasn't my responsibility.

But I would have died rather than admit it.

Looking after the two of us seemed an awful lot harder than looking after just me. A lot more than twice as hard.

And a lot more than twice as expensive.

Before long, money became a real worry. In the past, I had *thought* it was a problem, I never felt as though I had enough to buy essentials like new shoes and clothes. But now I was horrified to find I was afraid that I wouldn't have enough to cover essentials like *feeding* the two of us.

I couldn't figure out where it was all going. For the first time in my life I was afraid of losing my job. I mean, *really* afraid.

Everything had changed, now that I had a dependent. I suddenly understood why they say in marriage ceremonies, "Till debt do us part."

Except, of course, that I wasn't married to Dad.

It was easy to be generous with money when I had plenty of it. I had never imagined that I would begrudge my father anything. That I wouldn't have given him the cut-off lycra shirt off my back.

But it wasn't true. As money got tighter, I resented having to give him any. I resented him saying to me every morning before I dragged myself off to work, "Lucy, love, could you leave some money on the table? A tenner if you can manage it."

I resented the worry. I resented having to ask for an overdraft. I resented having no money for myself.

And I hated what it did to me – the pettiness, the watching of every bite that went into his mouth, the watching of every bite that *didn't* go into his mouth.

608

If I go to the trouble of buying food for him and cooking it for him, the least he could do is eat it, I thought angrily.

Dad got dole money every two weeks, but I wasn't sure what he did with it. I ran the household on my salary alone.

"Couldn't he even buy a pint of milk?" I sometimes thought, in impotent rage.

I felt increasingly isolated. Apart from the people at work, the only person I ever saw was Dad.

I never went out with any of the people I used to see. I didn't have time, because it was so important to get home immediately after work. Karen and Charlotte kept saying they'd come out to visit me, but they made it sound like a trip to a foreign country. Anyway it was a relief that they didn't come – I didn't think I'd be able to act happy for an entire two hours.

I missed Gus terribly. I fantasised about him coming to rescue me. But I had no chance of running into him while I lived in Uxbridge.

The only person I saw from my old life was Daniel. He was always "dropping by" and I hated it.

Every time I answered the door to him my first thought was how big and sexy and attractive he was. Then my second thought was of the night that I threw myself at him and he'd refused to bed me. I burned with shame at the memory.

And, as if that wasn't hard enough to cope with, he constantly asked awkward questions.

"Why are you always so tired?" and, "You're going to the laundrette, *again*?" and, "Why are all your saucepans burnt to pieces?"

"Can I do anything to help?" he asked over and over again. But my pride wouldn't let me tell him how bad things were with Dad.

I just said, "Go away, Daniel, there's nothing for you to do here."

The money situation got worse.

The sensible thing would have been to hand in my notice on the flat in Ladbroke Grove. After all, what did I gain by paying rent on a place I never stayed in? But, suddenly, I realised that I didn't want to, that I was terrified of having to do that. My flat was my last link with my old life. I that went, it would be a sign that I was never going back, that I was stuck out in Uxbridge forever.

Chapter Seventy

In the end, out of desperation, I went to see our local GP, who happened to be Dr Thornton, the same man who had prescribed antidepressants for me all those years before.

Ostensibly I went to get advice about Dad's bed-wetting, but in reality it was a good plain old-fashioned cry for help. In the hope that he would tell me what I knew to be true wasn't really.

I hated going to Dr Thornton. Not only was he a cranky old man who should have been put out to grass years before, but, because I knew he thought our entire family was nuts. He'd already had to deal with me and my depression. And there had been that time when Peter was fifteen and he'd got his hands on a medical encyclopaedia and became convinced that he had every disease he read about. Mum was up and down to the surgery almost daily with him as he worked his way alphabetiacally and hypochondriacally through the book, exhibiting symptoms of Acne, Agoraphobia, Alzheimer's, Angina, Angst and Anthrax until finally someone blew the whistle on him. Even the Acne wasn't real. Although the Angst was by the time Mum had finished with him.

The waiting room was like the day of judgement, packed to the rafters (figuratively speaking, because Portakabins don't have rafters) with fighting children, screaming mothers and consumptive geriatrics.

When I was finally granted an audience with His Healingness, he was slumped across his desk, looking exhausted and bad-tempered, his pen poised over the prescription pad.

"What can I do for you, Lucy?" he asked wearily.

I knew what he really meant was, "I remember you, you're one of those mad Sullivans. So? Losing it again, are you?"

"Well, it's not about me," I began hesitantly.

He immediately looked interested.

"A friend of yours?" he asked hopefully.

"Well, sort of." I agreed.

"Thinks she might be pregnant?" he asked. "Hmmmm, is that it?"

"No, it's . . ."

"Has a mysterious discharge?" he interrupted eagerly.

"No, nothing like that . . ."

"Very heavy periods?"

"No . . ."

"Lump in her breast?"

"No," I said, almost laughing. "It really *isn't* me. It's my dad."

"Oh him," he said, annoyed. "Well, why isn't *he* here? You can't just send someone else along, I don't do virtual diagnosis."

"What do you mean?"

"I'm sick of it," he burst out. "It's all mobile

phones and internets, and computer games and simulated flights. None of you want to do anything real!"

"Er . . ." I said, shocked, not knowing how to respond to his outpourings of Luddite vitriol. He'd become slightly more eccentric since our previous encounter.

"You all think you needn't do anything," he went on in a high voice. His face was flushed. "You can just sit at home with your modems and your PCs and think you're living, that you needn't get off your lazy behinds and interact with other human beings. You just E-mail me your symptoms, is that it?" Physician, heal thyself! Dr Thornton seemed to be cracking up.

Then, as suddenly as it had arrived, the fight went out of him.

"Well, what about your father?" he sighed, slumping back over his desk.

"It's a bit embarrassing," I said awkwardly.

"Why?"

"Well, he doesn't think there's anything wrong with him . . ." I started to delicately pick my way through the complicated story.

"Well, if he doesn't think there's anything wrong with him, and you do, then you're the one with the problem," said Dr Thornton bluntly.

"No, listen, you don't understand . . ."

"I do understand," he interrupted. "There's nothing wrong with Jamsie Sullivan. If he cut out the booze, he'd be fine."

"Although maybe he wouldn't be," he added, as if

he was talking to himself. "God alone knows what shape his liver is in by now. Probably hexagonal."

"But . . ."

"Lucy, you're wasting my time. I've got a waiting-room full of sick people out there, *really* sick people, who need looking after. And instead I get the female Sullivans plaguing me, looking for cures for a man who has decided to drink himself to death."

"What do you mean, female Sullivans?" I asked.

"You. Your mother. Your mother is almost a permanent fixture here."

"Really?" I hooted with surprise.

"Well, actually, now that you mention it, she hasn't been here in a while. Sent you instead, has she?"

"Er, no . . ."

"Why not?" he asked. "What's happened?"

"She's left Dad," I said, expecting sympathy.

Instead he laughed. Kind of. He really was behaving oddly.

"So she finally did it," he chuckled, while I stared at him, my head on one side, wondering what was wrong with him.

And what was he talking about, saying that Dad was drinking himself to death? Why did everything come back to Dad and drink?

Somewhere in my head, something had started its slow descent into place and I was frightened.

"And now you've taken over where your mother left off, have you?" asked Dr Thornton.

"If you mean, am I looking after him, then, yes," I said.

"Lucy, go home," he sighed. "There's nothing you can do for your father, we've tried everything. Until he decides to stop drinking, nobody can do anything for him."

More things slotted into place in my head.

"Look, you've got it all wrong," I said, fighting against what I knew to be true. "I'm not here about his drinking. I'm here because there *is* something wrong with him and it's got nothing to do with drink."

"Well, what is it?" he asked impatiently.

"He wets his bed."

There was a silence. That's shut him up, I thought, nervously, hoping that it really had.

"Bed-wetting's an emotional thing," I went on, hopefully. "It's nothing to do with drink."

"Lucy," he said grimly. "It's got everything to do with drink."

"I don't know what you mean," I said, feeling sick with apprehension. "I don't understand why you're saying all these things about Dad and drink."

"Don't you?" he frowned. "But you *must* know, of course you know. How can you live with him and not know?"

"I *don't* live with him," I said. "At least I haven't for years, I've just moved back."

"But hasn't your mother told you all about . . . ?" he asked, looking at my sick, anxious face. "Oh. Oh. I see. She hasn't."

I could feel a trembling in my lower thighs, I knew what he was about to tell me. This was the disaster that I'd been avoiding all my life and now

615

here I was face to face with it. This was the big one. There was almost a sense of relief, I could stop evading and avoiding now.

"Well," sighed Dr Thornton. "Your father is a chronic alcoholic."

My stomach lurched. I had known and yet I hadn't known.

"Are you sure?" I asked.

"You really didn't know, did you?" he asked, a bit less bad-temperedly.

"No," I said. "But now that you tell me, I can't understand how I didn't know until now."

"It happens a lot," he said, wearily. "I see it over and over again, where there's something very amiss in a home and everyone acts as if there's nothing wrong."

"Oh," I said.

"It's as if they have an elephant in their living-room and they all tiptoe around pretending not to see it."

"Oh," I said again. "Well, what can I do?"

"To be quite frank, Lucy," he said. "This isn't really my area, I only know about physical ailments. If your father had, let's say, an ingrowing toenail or maybe an irritable bowel, I could suggest all kinds of treatment. But this family therapy, psychodrama, confrontation kind of stuff isn't something I'm familiar with. It came after my time."

"Oh."

"But are *you* feeling all right?" he asked hopefully. "Has all of this come as a shock? Because I can do shock, that's something I *do* know about."

"I'll be fine," I said, getting up to leave. I had to get away to deal with what he'd told me, I couldn't get out fast enough.

"No wait," he said urgently. "I could give you a prescription."

"What for?" I asked. "A new father? One that isn't an alcoholic?"

"Don't be like that," he said. "Sleeping tablets? Tranquillisers? Antidepressants?"

"No thanks."

"Well, I've another suggestion that might be of help," he said thoughtfully.

Hope ricocheted in my chest.

"Yes?" I asked breathlessly.

"Plastic sheets."

"Plastic sheets?" I asked faintly.

"Yes, you know, to save the mattress from . . ."

I left.

I went away in a state of shock. When I got home, Dad had fallen asleep in his chair, leaving a cigarette burning into the arm-rest. He jerked awake when I came in.

"Will you run down to the off-licence for me, Lucy?" he asked.

"OK," I said, too shell-shocked to argue. "What do you want?"

"Whatever you can afford," he said humbly.

"Oh," I said coldly. "You want me to pay for it?"

"Weeelll," he said vaguely.

"But you got your giro only two days ago," I said. "What have you done with it?"

"Oh Lucy," he laughed, kind of nastily. "But you're your mother's daughter and no mistake."

I left the house, subdued, feeling sick. Was I just like my mother? I wondered. At the off-licence I bought him a bottle of proper whiskey instead of the funny cheap stuff from Eastern Europe that he usually got. But I was still edgy, still desperate to spend money on him, so I bought forty cigarettes and four bars of chocolate and two bags of tortilla chips.

When my expenditure hovered around the twenty pound mark, I was able to breathe easy again, secure in the knowledge that my extravagance had destroyed any similarity to my mother.

I couldn't stop thinking about what Dr Thornton had told me. I didn't want to believe him, but I couldn't help it. I tried looking at Dad in the old way and then in the light of him being an alcoholic and the alcoholic light fitted better. Fitted perfectly.

Dr Thornton's revelation had knocked down the first domino, the rest were hitting the deck at high speed.

Like red wine spilt on a white tablecloth, the knowledge poured through my life, back to my earliest memory, tainting everything.

And it *should* be tainted. It *was* tainted.

I had been looking at my life, my father, my family from upside-down and suddenly it had come upright. I couldn't cope with the way everything really was.

The worst thing was that Dad *looked* different to me. Like someone I'd never met before. I tried not to let it happen. I didn't want the man I loved to waver and disappear right before my eyes. I had to love him. He was all I had.

I kept sneaking looks at him, at all the things that had happened, all the signs. I tried to control it, just to look at a little bit of my life at a time, to dole out the unpleasantness in easy-to-manage, bite-sized pieces. I tried to protect myself, not to overwhelm myself with the loss of it all.

But I couldn't stop seeing him differently.

He no longer seemed loveable and cute and cuddly and great fun. But drunk and lopsided and slurred and incapable and *selfish*.

I didn't want to think that way about my father, it was unbearable. He was the person I'd loved most, maybe the only person I'd ever really loved. And now I found that the person I had adored didn't even exist.

No wonder he was always such fun when I was young. It's easy to be playful if you're drunk. No wonder he sang so much. No wonder he cried so much.

The one thing that stopped me going round the bend was the hope that maybe I could change him.

I could reluctantly admit that he had a drink problem, only if I could say that it was a solvable problem.

I'd heard that people with drink problems got better. All I had to do was to find out how to go about it. I'd fix him. My father would be back and everyone would be happy.

Chapter Seventy-One

So I made another appointment to see Dr Thornton. I was full of hope, convinced that there would be a way to save Dad.

"Can you prescribe something for him so that he won't want to drink?" I asked, confident that there would be something on the market for that.

"Lucy," he said. "I can't prescribe anything for *you* to give to *him*."

"OK," I said eagerly. "I'll get him down here in person and then you can give him a prescription."

"No," he said annoyed. "You don't understand, there's no cure for alcoholism."

"Don't call it that."

"Why not, Lucy? That's what it is."

"So what's going to happen?"

"He'll die if he doesn't stop drinking," he said.

Fear made me dizzy.

"But we've got to make him stop," I said desperately. "I'm sure I've heard of heavy drinkers who've managed to stop. How have they done it?"

"The only thing I've ever heard of that works is AA," he said.

"What's tha . . . ? Oh, you mean Alcoholics Anonymous," I said understanding. "Well, I don't

think he needs to go there. I mean, it's full of . . . of
. . . *alcoholics*."

"Exactly."

"But seriously." I almost laughed. "Smelly old
men, with strings around their coats and plastic bags
around their feet? Come on now, my father is nothing
like that."

Although on second thoughts, he *was* fairly
smelly, he never seemed to actually *have* the
numerous baths that he ran, but I wasn't going to tell
Dr Thornton that.

"Lucy," he said. "Alcoholics come in all shapes
and sizes, men and women, young and old, smelly
and fragrant."

"Really?" I asked with scepticism.

"Yes."

"Even women?"

"Yes. Women with homes and husbands and jobs
and children and nice clothes and high heels and
perfume and lovely hair . . ." he trailed off sadly, he
seemed to be thinking of someone in particular.

"So they go to this AA place and what happens?"

"They don't drink."

"Ever?"

"Never."

"Not even at Christmas and at weddings and on
holidays and things like that?"

"No."

"I'm not sure he'd go for that," I said doubtfully.

"It's all or nothing," said the doctor. "And with
your father, it'll be nothing."

"OK," I sighed, "if it's our only option, let's tell him about this Alcoholics Anonymous thing."

"Lucy," said Dr Thornton, sounding annoyed again. "He *knows*. He's known for years."

I broached the subject that evening. Eventually. I kept putting it off and in the end Dad was drunk before I brought it up.

"Dad," I quavered nervously. "Did you ever think that maybe you were drinking too much?"

He narrowed his eyes at me. I'd never seen him like that before. He looked different. Like a nasty, vicious, drunk old man, one you'd see on the street, flailing about, shouting slurred insults and trying to hit someone, but being too drunk to do any real damage.

He was watchful, eyeing me as if I was the enemy.

"My wife has just left me," he said aggressively. "Are you going to deny me a drink?"

"No," I said. "Of course not."

I wasn't very good at this.

"You see, Dad," I went on cautiously, hating every second of it. I wasn't his parent. I was his *daughter*, he was supposed to tell me off, not the other way round.

"It's a question of money," I forged ahead, wimpily.

"I see, I see," he said in a raised voice. "Money, money, money. Always whining about money. You're just like your mother. Well, why don't you leave me too. Go on, get out. Go on, there's the door."

That put an end to that conversation.

"Of course I won't leave you," I whispered. "I'll never leave you."

I was damned if I was going to admit that my mother had been right.

But shortly after that Dad seemed to get far worse. Or maybe it was just that I was aware of it now. That he drank in the mornings became obvious. And that he caused fights in the local pub. And a couple of times the police brought him home in the middle of the night.

But still I held myself together. I couldn't go to pieces because I had no one to help me pick them up.

I went to Dr Thornton again and he just shook his head abruptly when he saw me and said, "Sorry, no miracle cures have been invented. Unless it's happened since ten o'clock this morning."

"No, wait," I said eagerly. "I've been reading about hypnosis – couldn't Dad be hypnotised to stop drinking? You know, the way people are hypnotised to stop smoking or eating chocolate?"

"No, Lucy," he said, sounding annoyed. "There's no proof that hypnosis works and, even if there was, the person being hypnotised has to *want* to give up the cigarettes or whatever. Your father won't even admit that he drinks to excess so there's no chance that he'll decide that he wants to give up."

"And if he says he wants to give up, then he's ready for AA," he added smugly.

I rolled my eyes. Him and his bloody AA.

"OK." I wasn't disheartened. "Never mind hypnosis. What about acupuncture?"

"What about it?" he asked wearily.

"Couldn't he have that done? Couldn't he have a little pin stuck in his ear? Or someplace?"

"Someplace indeed," he muttered. Quite nastily, actually.

"No, Lucy."

So, as a last resort, I found the number for Alcoholics Anonymous in the phone book and rang to ask them what I should do with Dad. And although they were very nice and sympathetic, they told me that I could do nothing for him, until he himself admitted that he had a problem. That rang a vague bell with me, I'd picked that up from popular culture at some stage. And something else. If the person admits they have a problem, that's half the battle. But I didn't believe it.

"Come on," I said annoyed. "You lot are supposed to stop people drinking, so stop him drinking."

"I'm sorry," said the woman I was speaking to. "No one can do it except him."

"But he's an alcoholic," I burst out. "Alcoholics aren't supposed to be able to stop by themselves."

"No," she said. "But they must want to stop for themselves."

"Look, I don't think you understand," I said. "He's had a very hard life and his wife has just left him and, in a way, he *has* to drink."

"No, he doesn't," she said. Nicely.

"This is ridiculous," I said. "Can I speak to your boss? I need to speak to an expert here. He's a very special case."

She laughed. And that made me even more annoyed.

"We all thought that we were special cases," she said. "If I had a pound for every alcoholic who said that to me, I'd be a rich woman."

"What are you talking about?" I asked coldly.

"Well, I'm an alcoholic," she said.

"Are you?" I asked in surprise. "You don't sound like one."

"What did you think I'd sound like?" she asked.

"Well, . . . drunk, I suppose."

"I haven't had a drink for nearly two years," she said.

"*Nothing?*"

"Nothing."

"I mean, nothing at *all?*"

"No, nothing at all."

She can't have drunk very much, I thought, if she's been able to abstain for two years. She was probably a four-spritzers-on-a-Friday-night type of person.

"Oh, well, thank you," I said, getting ready to hang up. "But I don't think Dad is anything like you. He drinks whiskey and he drinks it in the mornings." I said it almost boastfully. "He'd find it very hard to stop. He'd never be able to go without a drink for two years."

"I drank in the mornings," said the woman.

I swallowed. I didn't believe her.

"And my favourite drink was neat brandy," she went on.

"A bottle a day," she added when I still didn't say anything. "I was no different from your dad."

"But he's old . . ." I said desperately. "You don't sound old."

"There's people of all ages in AA. Lots of old people."

"I can send someone round to talk to him," she suggested.

But I thought of how angry he'd be, how humiliating he would find it and thought better of it.

Then she gave me the phone number of another lot of people called Al-Anon and said that it was for friends and families of alcoholics and that they might be able to help me. So, as a last resort, I rang them. I even went to one of their meetings, expecting to be given all kinds of tips to help Dad stop drinking – how to hide the booze in the house, how to water the drinks, how to persuade him not to drink until after eight in the evening – that sort of thing.

And I was outraged to find that it was nothing like that.

Everyone there talked about how they were trying to leave their alcoholic husband or boyfriend or wife or daughter or friend or whatever to their own devices and simply get on with their own lives. One man talked about his mother being a drunk and how he always fell in love with helpless women who had drink problems.

They were all talking about something called "co-dependency", which I knew about, because I'd read so many self-help books, but I couldn't see how it applied to me and my father.

"You can't change your dad," one woman said to

me. "And by trying to, you're just avoiding your own problems."

"My dad is my problem," I said huffily.

"No, he isn't," she said.

"How can you be so heartless?" I asked. "I love my father."

"Don't you think that you're allowed to have a nice life?" she asked.

"I couldn't just abandon him," I said stiffly.

"It might be the best thing that you ever did," she said.

"The guilt would kill me," I said self-righteously.

"Guilt is a self-indulgence," she said.

"How dare you," I said. "You haven't a clue what you're talking about."

"I was married to an alcoholic," she said. "I know exactly what you're going through."

"I'm just a normal person who happens to have a father with a drink problem. I'm not like you lot of . . . of . . . losers who have to come to these stupid meetings and talk about how you're managing to *detach* from the alcoholic in your lives."

"That's what I said in the beginning too," she said.

"God!" I said, angrily. "I just want to help him to stop drinking. What's so wrong with that?"

"Because you *can't* help," she said. "You are powerless over him and his alcohol. But you're not powerless over your own life."

"I have responsibilities."

"To yourself. And it's never as simple as someone stopping drinking and the other person suddenly being fine."

"What do you mean?"

"Well, what kind of relationships do you have with other men?"

I didn't answer.

"Lots of women like us have a really hard time having successful relationships," she said.

"I'm not a woman like you," I said scornfully.

"You'd be amazed how many of us have the wrong kind of relationships with the wrong kind of men," she said gently. "Because our expectations of the relationship is based on what we learnt from dealing with the alcoholic in our lives."

"Here's my phone number," she said. "Ring me if you ever need to talk. Any time."

I walked away before she gave it to me.

Another avenue explored. Another dead end.

Now what was I going to do?

I tried to give him less money. But he begged and cried and the guilt was so awful that I gave it to him, even though I really didn't have it.

I swung from feeling furious to feeling so sad I thought my heart would break. Sometimes I hated him and sometimes I loved him.

But I felt increasingly trapped and desperate.

Chapter Seventy-Two

Christmas was horrible. I couldn't go to any of the hundreds of piss-ups or parties. While everyone else was putting on short, black, glittery dresses (and that was just the men) I was on a train home to Uxbridge. While everyone else was puking or snogging their boss, I was begging Dad to go back to sleep, telling him it really didn't matter that he'd wet his bed again.

I think my Fairy Godmother must have misheard her instructions, because instead of her saying, "You *shall* go to the piss-up!" she said, "You *shall* clean the piss up!"

Even if there was someone else to take care of Dad, I still couldn't have gone because I was too broke to buy a round of drinks.

Dad's drinking got even worse in the run-up to The Festive Season. I didn't know why – it wasn't as if he needed an *excuse* to drink.

To compound my self-pity, I only got two Christmas cards. One from Daniel and one from Adrian in the video shop.

Christmas Day itself was truly awful. Chris and Peter didn't come to see Dad and me.

"I don't want it to look as if I'm taking sides," was Chris's excuse.

"I don't want to upset Mammy," was Al Jolson's, I mean, Peter's.

It was a horrible day. The best thing about it was that Dad was comatose by eleven in the morning.

I was so desperate for someone else to talk to, anything to dilute Dad's presence, that I almost looked forward to going back to work.

Chapter Seventy-Three

Because Christmas had been so awful, I foolishly approached the new year with hope.

But on the fourth of January, Dad went on a massive bender. He had obviously planned it because when I tried to buy a packet of wine gums at the station on my way to work, all my cash had disappeared. I could have run home and tried to stop him, but somehow I just couldn't be bothered.

When I got to town, I tried to get money from a cash point and it swallowed my card. "You are heinously overdrawn, contact your bank," the flashing message advised. I will not, I thought. If they want me, they'll have to come and get me. (They'll never take me alive, etc., etc.)

I had to borrow a tenner from Megan.

When I got home from work, there was a scary-looking official letter just inside the front door. It was from my bank instructing me to return my cheque-book.

Things were moving out of control. I tried to suppress the icy fear. Where would it all end?

As I made for the kitchen, something crunched under my foot. I looked down and the hall carpet was covered in broken glass. And so was the kitchen floor. The kitchen table was scattered with broken plates and saucers and bowls. In the front room, the smoked-glass coffee table was in smithereens, books and tapes scattered all over the floor. The whole downstairs (such as it was) was in a shambles.

Dad's handiwork.

He'd done some drunken breaking and smashing in the past, but nothing as spectacular as this.

Naturally, he was nowhere to be seen.

I went from the kitchen to the front room and back again, unable to believe the extent of the damage. If it was breakable, he had broken it. Even if it wasn't breakable, he had *tried* to break it. There was a yellow plastic basin in the kitchen that he had obviously attempted to smash the living daylights out of, judging by the number of dents there were in it. In the front room there was a whole shelf of disgusting china boys and dogs and bells that my mother had doted on, that he had wiped out. I felt a spasm of sadness for my mother. He knew what they meant to her.

I didn't even cry. I just began to clear it up.

While I was on my knees picking shards of broken china boy out of the carpet, the phone rang. It was the police to say that Dad had been arrested. I was cordially invited to come to the police station and bail him out.

I had no money and no more energy.

I decided to cry.

Then I decided to ring Daniel.

Miraculously he was in – I don't know what I would have done if he hadn't been.

I was crying so much he couldn't really make out what I was saying.

"It's Dad," I wailed.

"What's dead?"

"Nothing's dead, it's Dad."

"Lucy, either it's dead or it's not, it can't be both at once."

"Oh for God's sake, just get over here, will you?"

"I'll be with you as soon as I can," he promised.

"Bring lots of money," I added.

He arrived two china dogs, a china bell and half a coffee table later.

"Sorry, Lucy," he said, as soon as I opened the front door. "I figured it out. It's your Dad?"

He went to put his arms around me but I skipped nimbly away. The last thing my melting pot of emotions needed was sexual attraction.

"Yes," I said, as tears poured down my face. "But he's not . . ."

"Dead," he finished for me. "Yes, I'd gathered that much. Sorry, I couldn't hear you very well. Christ, has there been an earthquake out here?"

"No, it's . . ."

"You've been burgled! Don't touch a thing, Lucy."

"We haven't been fucking well burgled," I wept. "My stupid, drunk bastard of a father has done all this."

"I don't believe you, Lucy." He looked genuinely horrified, which made me feel even worse.

"But why?" he asked, running his hands through his hair.

"I don't know. But it gets worse. He's been arrested."

"Since when can they arrest you for breaking things in your own house? God, this country becomes more and more like a police state every day. Next it'll be illegal to burn the toast and to eat ice cream straight from the carton and . . ."

"Shut up, you *Guardian* reading, bleeding-heart liberal." I laughed despite myself. "He hasn't been arrested for breaking his own ornaments. I don't know *why* he's been arrested, but I dread to think."

"So he needs to be bailed out?"

"He does."

"OK, Lucy, to the chick-mobile. Let's go and rescue him!"

Dad had been charged with about a million things – being drunk and disorderly, causing a public affray, causing damage to property, intention to cause actual bodily harm, obscene behaviour and on and on. It was horrific. I had never imagined that the day would come when I'd have to bail my father out after he'd been arrested.

When Dad was led from the cells, he was as meek as a lamb – the fight had gone out of him. Daniel and I took him home and put him to bed.

Then I made Daniel a cup of tea.

"Right, Lucy, what are we going to do about this?" he asked.

"Whose 'we'?" I asked defensively.

"You and me."

"What's it got to do with you?"

"For once, Lucy, just for once, Lucy, could you try not to fight with me? I'm only trying to help."

"I don't want your help."

"You do," he said. "You wouldn't have rung me if you didn't."

"There's no *shame* in it," he added. "Lucy, there's no need to be so touchy."

"You'd be touchy if your Dad was an alcoholic," I said, as tears splashed down my face – *again*. "Well, maybe he's not an alcoholic . . ."

"He's an alcoholic." Daniel was grim.

"Call him what you bloody well like," I sobbed. "I don't give a shit whether he's an alcoholic or not. All I care about is he's a drunk and it's ruining my life."

I sobbed a good bit more, the burden of months and months of worry spilled down my cheeks.

"Did you know?" I asked. "You know, about Dad?"

"Er, yes."

"But how?"

"Chris told me."

"Why didn't anyone tell me?"

"They did."

"Well, why didn't anyone help me?"

"They tried. You wouldn't let them."

"What am I going to do now?"

"How about moving out and letting someone else look after him?"

"Oh no," I said in fear.

"Fine, if you don't want to move out, you don't have to, but there's lots of people who can help you. Apart from your brothers, there's home helps and domiciliary care and social workers and all kinds of people. You'll still be able to look after him, but you won't have to do it on your own."

"Let me think about it."

At midnight, while Daniel and I were still sitting gloomily at the kitchen table, the phone rang.

"What now?" I asked in fear.

"Hello?"

"Might I have a word with Lucy Sullivan?" roared a familiar voice.

"Gus?" I asked, as joy flooded through me.

"The very fella," he shouted.

"Hello," I wanted to dance. "Where did you get my number?"

"I met the scary, blonde wan in McMullens and she said you were living out in the back arse of nowhere. And, sure, hadn't I been thinking about you and missing you, anyway?"

"Had you?" I was almost in tears with joy.

"Indeed I had, Lucy. So I sez to her, 'give us d'oul phone number, till I ring her and take her out.' So here I am, Lucy, ringing you and asking to take you out."

"Great!" I said in delight. "I'd love to see you."

"OK, give me the address and I'll be right out to you."

"You mean, *now?*"

"When else?"

"Oh, now isn't a good time, Gus." I felt very ungrateful.

"Well, when is?"

"The day after tomorrow?"

"Right you are. Thursday, after your work, I'll come and get you."

"Great."

I turned back to Daniel with shining eyes.

"That was Gus," I said breathlessly.

"I gathered."

"He was thinking about me."

"Was he?"

"He wants to see me."

"He's very lucky that you're so obliging."

"What are you pissed off about?"

"Couldn't you have made him work a bit harder, Lucy? I wish you hadn't given in so easily."

"Daniel, Gus ringing me is the nicest thing that's happened in months and months. And I don't have the energy to play games with him."

He gave a tight little smile.

"You'd better have plenty of energy for game-playing on Thursday night," he said curtly.

"And so what if I do?" I asked angrily. "I'm allowed to have sex, you know. Why have you gone all Victorian-dad on me?"

"Because you're worth more than him."

He got up to leave.

"Are you sure you don't need me to stay the night?"

"I'm sure, thanks."

"And you'll think about what I said about getting help for your Dad?"

"I'll think about it."

"I'll call you tomorrow. Bye."

As he bent to kiss me – on the cheek – I said, "Oh, er, Daniel, can you loan me any money?"

"How much?"

"Er, twenty, if you don't mind."

He gave me sixty.

"Have a nice time with Gus," he said.

"This money isn't for Gus," I said defensively.

"I didn't say it was."

Chapter Seventy-Four

I was *beside myself* about seeing Gus. Obviously, because I hadn't been out for about three months, some of the excitement was good plain old-fashioned cabin fever. But it wasn't just that – I was still crazy about him. I'd never given up hope that it might work out for us. I was so excited that I was able to put my worry about Dad on hold.

When I told the others in the office that I was meeting Gus, there was mayhem. Meredia and Jed gasped with delight, then linked arms and skipped around the office, knocking over a chair in the process. Then they changed direction and Meredia's generous hip sent a desk-tidy flying onto the floor, scattering paper clips and Tippex and pens and highlighters everywhere.

They were almost as excited as I was – probably because their social and romantic lives were as uneventful as mine, and they were glad of any diversion, personal or vicarious.

Only Megan looked disgusted.

"Gus?" she asked. "You're going out with *Gus*? But what happened? Where did you meet him?"

"I didn't, he rang me."

"The little bastard!" she exclaimed.

There was a chorus of disagreement from the rest of us.

"No, he's not," yelled Meredia.

"Leave him alone, he's a great bloke," shouted Jed.

"So what happened?" demanded Megan, ignoring them. "He rang you and then what?"

"He asked me to meet him," I said.

"And did he say why?" she quizzed. "Did he say what he wants from you?"

"No."

"And *are* you going to meet him?"

"Yes."

"When?"

"Tomorrow."

"Can we come too?" begged Meredia, as she crouched on the floor, scooping up handfuls of staples.

"No, Meredia, not this time," I said.

"Nothing nice ever happens to us," she said moodily.

"Oh, come on now," said Jed jovially, trying to cheer her up. "What about the fire drill?"

We had had a fire drill about a week before, and in fairness, it *had* been great fun. Especially as we got advance warning of it – Gary in Security leaked details of it to Megan in a fruitless attempt to advance himself sexually with her. So, for two hours before the bell went off, we had our coats on and our bags on our desks, ready for the off.

According to the memo that had been circulated, I was a Fire Monitor, but I didn't know what that was, and no one had explained it to me. So, instead, I took advantage of the bedlam and confusion and went to Oxford Street and took in a couple of shoe shops.

"Don't meet him, Lucy," said Megan. She sounded upset.

"It's OK," I reassured Megan, touched by her protectiveness. "I can look after myself."

She shook her head, "He's bad news, Lucy."

And then she was unusually silent.

The following day when Jed came into work, he said he hadn't been able to sleep the night before with excitement. Then he complained all day long that he had butterflies in his stomach.

He insisted on personally vetting my appearance before I met Gus. "Good luck, Agent Sullivan," he said. "We're all depending on you."

It had been a long time since I had felt this young and happy. As if life had possibilities.

Gus was waiting outside the building for me, swapping insults with Winston and Harry (which I later discovered were real). When I saw him my stomach did a flip – he looked lovely, his black, shiny hair falling into his green eyes.

The four months had done nothing to diminish his attractiveness.

"Lucy," he shouted when he saw me and lounged sexily over to me, opening his arms wide.

"Gus." I smiled breathlessly, hoping he wouldn't see that my legs were wobbling from exhilaration and nerves.

He threw his arms around me and wrapped me tight, but my soaring happiness came to a screeching halt as I got a whiff of alcohol from him.

It was nothing unusual for Gus to reek of alcohol – in fact it was more unusual for him *not* to reek of alcohol. That was one of the things I found attractive about him.

Or rather, *had* found attractive about him.

Not any more, it seemed.

For a moment I felt a flash of hard-done-by anger – if I'd wanted to spend the evening with a smelly drunk I could have stayed at home with Dad. My evening with Gus was meant to be The Great Escape, not more of the same.

He moved back slightly so he could look at me, but kept his arms around me and smiled and smiled and smiled. And I cheered up.

I felt dizzy to be within kissing distance of that sexy, handsome face.

I'm with Gus, I thought in disbelief, *I'm holding my dream in my arms*.

"Let's go for a drink, Lucy," he suggested.

There was that feeling again – a surge of annoyance.

"Well, surprise, surprise," I thought, pissed off. I had hoped he might have laid on something a bit more imaginative for our reconciliation. More fool me.

"Come on," he beckoned and started walking briskly. In fact, he almost broke into a run. He must be dying for a drink, I thought, as I traipsed behind him. He led us to a nearby pub, which we had been to lots of times in the past. It was one of Gus's favourite pubs, he knew the barman and most of the clientele.

As I passed over the threshold behind the speeding Gus, I suddenly thought – *I hate this pub*. I had never noticed before, but I always felt uncomfortable there.

It was dirty and no one ever wiped down the tables. It was full of men who all stared at me when I came in, and the staff were downright rude to girls. Or maybe it was just me.

But I tried to think positive.

I was with Gus and he looked beautiful. He was cute and funny and sexy. Even if he was still wearing that awful sheepskin coat that I was sure had fleas.

There was a momentous break with tradition when the time came to buy the first drink – it was bought by Gus.

And what an all-singing, all-dancing production he made of it.

Naturally, as soon as we were sitting down, I reached for my purse, as I always had to with Gus. With everyone, I thought gloomily. But instead of placing his order with me, like he usually did, he jumped up and practically roared, "NO, NO! I won't hear of it!"

"What?" I asked, slightly irritated.

"Put your money away, put your money away!" he urged, waving his arm in a "put your money away" fashion at me, like drunk uncles do at a wedding. "I'm getting this round."

It was like the sun coming out from behind the

clouds – Gus had money. It was a sign telling me that everything would be fine, Gus would take care of me.

"OK." I smiled.

"No, I insist," he said loudly, making flapping movements in the direction of my purse.

"Fine," I said.

"I'll be insulted if you won't let me. I'll take it as a personal *insult* if you won't permit me to get this round," he insisted, with great magnanimity.

"Gus," I said, "I'm not arguing."

"Oh. Oh. Right then." He sounded a bit put out. "What do you want?"

"A gin and tonic," I muttered humbly.

He arrived back with my gin and a pint of lager and a measure of whiskey for himself.

His face was dark with annoyance.

"Jesus," he complained. "It's daylight robbery! Do you know how much that gin and tonic was?"

Not as much as I'll have to spend on you for the next round, I thought. Why do you always have to have two drinks, when everyone else has just one?

But all I said was a meek "sorry" because I didn't want to cast a blight on the evening that I had looked forward to so much.

His bad mood didn't last long, they never did.

"Cheers, Lucy." He smiled, clinking his pint against my extortionate gin.

"Cheers," I said, trying to sound as if I meant it.

"I drink, therefore I am," he announced, with a grin, and drank half the pint in one go.

I smiled but it was an effort. Usually I was delighted by his witty remarks, but not this evening.

It wasn't going the way I had wanted it to.

I didn't really know what to talk to Gus about and he didn't seem to be bothered talking at all. In the past, we had always had so much to talk about, I thought wistfully. But suddenly it was awkwardness and tense silences – at least on my part.

I desperately wanted to make it all right, to push us through the tension barrier, but I hadn't the heart to kick-start the conversation.

Gus made no effort either. In fact he seemed oblivious to the silence. Oblivious to me too, I realised after a while.

He was a man at peace with himself and the world, settled in his armchair with his drinks and his cigarette, comfortable, pleased with himself, surveying the pub, nodding and winking at the people he knew, watching the world go by.

As relaxed as a newt.

He grinned and finished his two drinks in record speed, went back to the bar and got himself another couple.

He didn't offer me a drink. Not even one. In fact, now that I remembered, he hardly ever did. But I couldn't remember minding before. I certainly minded now.

We sat there in silence, me mute with unfulfillable expectation, while he drank his two drinks and smoked a cigarette. Then he threw the remaining half pint or so into him in one gulp and, before he had even finished swallowing, gasped, "Your round, Lucy."

Like a robot, I got out of my seat and asked him what he wanted.

"A pint and a small one," he said innocently.

"Anything else?" I asked sarcastically.

"Thanks very much, Lucy," he said, sounding delighted. "Fine girl you are, I could do with some smokes."

"Smokes?"

"Cigarettes."

"Cigarettes? What flavour?"

"Benson and Hedges."

"How many? A thousand?"

He seemed to find that hilarious. "Just the twenty will do, unless you really *want* to buy me more."

"No, Gus, I don't," I said coldly.

While I waited at the bar, I wondered why I was so pissed off.

It was my own fault, I decided. I had set myself up for disappointment. I had come carrying so much expectation. And too much need.

I yearned for Gus to be nice to me, to pay me attention, to tell me he'd missed me, that I was beautiful, that he was madly in love with me.

And he hadn't. He hadn't asked how I was, he didn't explain where he had been, why he hadn't contacted me for nearly four months.

But I was asking too much of him – I was so unhappy with the rest of my life that I hoped Gus would be my saviour. Someone to take care of me, someone that I could hand my life over to and say "Here, fix this."

I wanted the lot.

Relax, I advised myself, as I tried to catch the barman's eye, enjoy yourself. At least you're *with* him. Didn't he turn up? And he's still the same witty, entertaining person he always was. So what more do you want?

I came back to the table, loaded down with drinks and renewed hope.

"Good on you, Lucy," said Gus, and fell on the drinks, like a premenstrual woman on a walnut whip.

Shortly after that he announced, "We'll have another drink."

Almost as an afterthought he added, " And you're buying."

Something slipped from a shelf inside me and went crashing to the floor.

I was not a charity. At least, not anymore.

"Oh really," I said, unable to hide my anger. "Since when have they started accepting fresh air as legal tender?"

"What are you talking about?" he asked, looking at me warily. There was something about me that he wasn't at all familiar with.

"Gus," I said, with grim delight. "I've no money left."

That wasn't quite true, I had enough left to get me home and even to buy a bag of chips on the way, but I wasn't telling him that. He'd wheedle it out of me if he knew I had it.

"You're a terrible woman," he laughed, "trying to scare me like that."

"I'm serious."

"Go on out of that," he joshed. "You've got one of

those magic little cards that gives you money from the hole-in-the-wall, the drink-link thing."

"Yes, but . . ."

"Well, what are you waiting for – off with you, Lucy, there's no time to waste. Run down and get the loot and I'll wait here and mind the seats."

"What about you, Gus?"

"Well, I suppose I could manage another pint while you're gone, thanks very much."

"No, I mean, haven't you got a cash-point card, Gus?"

"Me?" he yelled and laughed and laughed. "Are you serious?"

He laughed and laughed again, and then made a face to convey that he thought I'd gone mad.

I sat in silence, waiting for him to finish.

"No, Lucy." He cleared his throat and finally calmed down, but his mouth kept twitching. "No, Lucy, I haven't."

"Well, neither have I, Gus."

"I *know* you have," he scoffed. "I've seen you use it."

"I don't have it anymore."

"Get away outa that."

"Really, Gus."

"Well, why don't you?"

"It was swallowed. Because I didn't have any money in my account."

"Didn't you?" He sounded stunned.

That's shown him, I thought with satisfaction.

Then I felt ashamed. It wasn't right to take it out on Gus just because I was annoyed with Dad.

I suddenly felt that I wanted to tell Gus all about it, to explain why I was being difficult and bad-tempered. I wanted understanding and forgiveness, sympathy and affection. So, without further ado, I launched into the whole saga about living with Dad and having to give him money and having none left for me and . . .

"Lucy," interrupted Gus urgently.

"Yes?" I said hopefully, looking forward to a bit of sympathy.

"I know what we'll do," he said with a brilliant smile.

"You do?" Great! I thought.

"You've a cheque book, right?" he said.

Cheque book, I thought? *Cheque book?* What's that got to do with how misfortunate I am?

"Well, I know the barman," continued Gus, eyes shining. "And he'll cash your cheque if I vouch for you."

I swallowed. That wasn't what I'd wanted to hear.

"So write the cheque, Lucy, and we're in business." He beamed.

"But, Gus." Even though I shouldn't have, I felt like a spoilsport. "I've no money in my account, in fact I'm overdrawn over my overdraft limit."

"Och, never mind that," said Gus. "Isn't it only a bank, what can they do to you? Property is theft, come on, Lucy, let's beat the system!"

"No," I said apologetically. "I really can't."

"Well, bad cess to you, Lucy, and the horse you rode in on, we might as well just go home," he said sulkily. "Bye, nice seeing you."

"Oh, all right," I sighed, reaching for my handbag and my cheque book, trying not to think of the terrifying phone call from my bank that was certain to follow.

Gus was right, I thought, it was only money. But I couldn't help feeling that I was always having to give and give and that, for a change, I wanted someone to give to me.

I wrote a cheque and Gus went to the bar with it. From the length of time he was gone and the expression on the barman's face, he wasn't finding it too easy to cash.

He eventually came back, loaded down with drinks.

"Successful mission." He grinned, stashing a handful of notes into his pocket. I noticed that the fly of his jeans was held together with a safety pin.

"My change, Gus," I said, trying to keep the anger out of my voice.

"What's wrong with you, Lucy?" he grumbled. "You've gone very stingy and mean on me."

"Really?" I was nauseous with inarticulated fury. "What's mean and stingy about me? Haven't I bought you nearly every drink this evening?"

"Well," he said, all indignant, "if you're going to be like that about it, just tell me what I owe you and I'll give it back to you when I get it."

"Fine," I said. "I will."

"Here's your change," he said, slamming a bundle of notes and coins down on the table.

That was the point where it was obvious that the evening was ruined, beyond redemption. Not that it had been a wild success before that. But at least before that, I still had hope that it would get better.

I knew it was a deeply insulting thing to do, but I picked up the bundle and began to count it.

I had written a cheque for fifty pounds and he had returned about thirty. A round of drinks for two – even a round including Gus – didn't cost twenty pounds.

"Where's the rest of my change?" I asked.

"Oh that?" He was annoyed, but tried not to show it. "I didn't think you'd mind, but I bought Vinnie – that's the barman – a drink for facilitating us, I thought that was only fair and decent."

"And what about the rest?"

"While I was up there, Keith Kennedy came along and I felt that I should see him right too."

"See him right?"

"Buy him a drink, he's been awful good to me, Lucy."

"That still doesn't account for it all," I said, admiring my tenacity.

Gus laughed, but it sounded a bit high-pitched and forced.

" . . . And I, er, owed him a tenner," he finally admitted.

"You owed him a tenner and you gave it to him out of my money?" I asked calmly.

"Er, yes. I didn't think you'd mind. You're like me, Lucy, a free spirit. You don't care about money."

On and on he went, and then he started to sing John Lennon's *Imagine*, except the only line he seemed to know was the one about imagining no possessions. He put on quite a show – stretching out his arms beseechingly and making meaningful faces at me. "Oh, Lucy, imagine no possessions, imagine no possessions, sing along! Imagine no poss-eh-SHUNS! Do, do, do, do, doo-oooooh-oooooooh!"

He paused and waited for me to laugh. I didn't, so he kept singing. "You may sa-aay I'm a cleaner, that I've got a hairy bum . . ."

In the past, I would have been touched and charmed by his singing. I would have laughed and told him that he was a terrible man and forgiven him.

But not this time.

I didn't say a thing. I couldn't. I really couldn't. I was beyond anger. I felt too much of a fool. I was too ashamed of myself to be angry. I didn't *deserve* to be angry.

The whole evening had been an exercise in damage limitation, with me trying to hide from myself just how upset I was. Now the awfulness of it all was right out in the open.

Why did I feel as if this was constantly happening to me, I wondered. So I did a quick scan of my life and realised it was because it *was* constantly happening to me.

It happened every day with my father. I got myself into financial trouble so that I could give money to him.

No wonder it felt so familiar.

Hadn't Gus always leant on me for money? He had never had a penny.

I had been glad to give it to him in the beginning. I had thought I was helping him, that he needed me.

The knowledge made me feel sick. I was a fool, a bloody idiot. Everyone knew it, except me. I was a soft touch. Good old Lucy, she's so desperate for love and affection that she's prepared to buy it. She'll give you the shirt off her back because she thinks that you deserve it more than she does. You'll never go hungry with Lucy, even though she might. But so what? What does she matter?

Gus hadn't been the only boyfriend that I had taken care of financially. Most of them hadn't had jobs. And the ones that had jobs still managed never to have any money.

The rest of the evening, I felt as if I was outside my body, looking at me and Gus.

He got really drunk.

I should have got up and left but I couldn't. I was fascinated, repelled, appalled at what I was seeing, but I couldn't look away.

He burnt my tights with his cigarette and didn't even notice. He slopped his pint on me and didn't notice that either. He slurred, he talked rubbish, he started stories and meandered and forgot about them. He talked to the man and woman at the next table and kept on talking to them even when it became obvious that he was annoying them.

He got a five pound note out of his pocket, when he had told me that he didn't have any money left and interrupted the people at the next table again by waving it at them and shouting, "Come here till I show you a picture of my girlfriend. It was taken on her twenty-first. Look, isn't she lovely?"

That was the kind of thing that would have had me in stitches in the past. Now it was embarrassing and, in the end, just plain boring.

The drunker he got, the more sober I became. I barely spoke and he either didn't notice or didn't care.

Had he always been like this, I wondered.

And the answer was, of course, yes.

He hadn't changed. But I had. I saw things differently.

It barely mattered to him that I was there. I was merely a source of money.

Daniel had been right. As if I wasn't feeling bad enough, I had to admit that that smug pig had been right. He'd never let me forget it. Although maybe he would – he wasn't as smug as he used to be. He wasn't really smug at all. He was nice. At least he bought me an occasional drink. And an occasional dinner . . .

I sat with an empty glass in front of me for over an hour. Gus didn't notice.

He went to the Gents and was gone for twenty minutes and didn't explain or apologise when he eventually returned. There was nothing unusual in such behaviour. Nights out with Gus were always like that.

Somehow I was surrounded by men who drank a lot and took advantage of me and I couldn't understand how it had happened.

But I knew I'd had enough.

At closing time, Gus had an argument with one of the barmen – it was a fairly regular occurrence. The barman shouted "Have you no homes to go to?" and

Gus decided that was a terrible thing for him to say because there had been an earthquake in China a few days previously. "What if a Chinese person heard you?" shouted Gus. To describe the rest of the incoherent drivel that he came out with would be too tedious for words. Suffice it to say that the barman physically hustled him towards the door, as Gus struggled and shouted, "I hope you die roaring for a priest."

To think I once *admired* that kind of behaviour, that I'd thought Gus was a rebel.

We stood in the street as the door slammed behind us.

"Right, Lucy, home we go," said Gus, swaying slightly and looking bleary.

"Home?" I asked politely.

"Yes," he said.

"Fine, Gus," I said smoothly.

He smiled the smile of a victorious man.

"And where are you living now?" I asked.

"Still in Camden," he said vaguely. "But why . . . ?"

"Well, off to Camden with us," I said.

"No," said Gus in alarm.

"Why not?" I asked.

"Because we can't," he said.

"Why can't we?"

"Because we just . . . can't."

"Well, you're not coming out to my father's house."

"But why not? I'd say your old man and I would get along just fine."

"I'm sure you would," I agreed. "That's what I'm afraid of."

Something was up, I'd known it all along. He probably had a girlfriend in Camden, one that he lived with, something like that.

But I didn't care. I wouldn't have touched him with a bargepole. I couldn't see how I had ever fancied him. He looked like a little gnome, a little, drunk leprechaun. With his stupid sheepskin jacket and his filthy brown jumper.

The spell was broken. Everything about him revolted me. He even smelt funny. Disgusting, like a carpet the morning after a really rowdy party.

"Save your excuses," I said. "Don't tell me why you won't take me to your flat. Why you never did, in fact. Save your ridiculous stories."

"What ridiculous stories?" he asked. He had difficulty saying "ridiculous".

"Let's see," I said. "You might tell me that you're taking care of a cow for your brother and that it has nowhere to stay except in your bedroom and that it's shy and afraid of strangers."

"Might I?" he asked, thoughtfully. "Well, you might be right, that sounds like me, so it does. You're an exceptional woman, Lucy Sullivan."

"Oh, I'm not," I smiled. "Not any more."

That confused his already alcohol-addled head.

"So you see," he said, "we have to go back to your place."

"*I'm* going," I said. "You're not."

"But . . . " he said.

"Goodbye," I sang.

"No, wait, Lucy," he said in alarm.

I turned and smiled benignly on him. "Yes?"

"How am I going to get home?" he asked.

"Do I look like I can foretell the future?" I asked innocently.

"But Lucy, I've no money."

I put my face up to his and smiled.

He smiled back.

"Frankly my dear," I beamed, "I don't give a damn."

I had always wanted to say that.

"What do you mean?"

"I mean, in language that you'll understand," I paused for impact and put my face right into his, "FUCK OFF, GUS!"

A little pause while I took another deep breath. "Extort money from someone else, you drunken little bastard. I'm no longer open for business."

And I swung off down the road, smirking like a cat, leaving Gus staring after me.

A few seconds later I realised I was going the wrong direction for the tube station and slunk back the way I had come, hoping that the little swine wasn't still there to see me.

Chapter Seventy-Five

I was exhilarated with anger.

I went to Uxbridge, but only to pick up my things. The other passengers on the train looked at me oddly and kept their distance. I kept remembering how mean I'd been to Gus and a triumphant voice in my head reminded me that *you've got to be cruel to be cruel.*

With bitter amusement, I wondered what my father had managed to destroy in my absence. The drunken fool had probably burnt the house down. And, if he had, I just hoped that he'd managed to burn himself with it.

I thought of what a conflagration there'd be, and in spite of everything, I laughed. More funny looks from the other passengers. It would take about a week to put him out. He'd burn so brightly he'd probably be visible from outer space, just like the Great Wall of China. Maybe they could harness him up to an electricity generator and he could power the whole of London for a couple of days.

I hated him.

I had seen how badly I let Gus treat me and it was an exact copy of the way my father treated me. I only knew how to love drunk, irresponsible, penniless men. Because that's what my father had taught me.

But I didn't feel as if I loved him anymore. I'd had enough. He could look after himself from now on. And I wouldn't give him any more money – either of them. Gus and Dad had merged into one in the melting pot of my anger. Dad had never stroked Megan's hair, but, nevertheless, I was furious with him for doing it. Gus hadn't cried all over me when I was a little girl and told me that the world was a pit, but that was still no reason to forgive him for it.

I was actually grateful to both Dad and Gus for being so horrible to me. For pushing me into a place where I didn't care about them anymore. What if I'd never found out? If they'd been a bit nicer, it could have gone on forever. With me forgiving them again and again and again.

Memories of other relationships rushed back, ones that I thought I'd forgotten. Other men, other humiliations, other situations where I'd made it my life's work to look after a difficult, selfish person.

With the unfamiliar anger, another strange emotion had surfaced. This new one was called Self-Preservation.

Chapter Seventy-Six

"You're so lucky," sighed Charlotte enviously.

"Why?" I asked in surprise. I couldn't think of anyone less lucky than me.

"Because you're all sorted out now," she said.

"Am I?"

"Yes, I wish *my* dad was an alcoholic, I wish I hated *my* mother."

This bizarre conversation with Charlotte took place the day after I had left my dad's and returned to my flat in Ladbroke Grove. It was nearly enough to make me consider moving back in with Dad.

"If only I could be like you," Charlotte went on. "But my father can hold his drink and I love my mother."

"It's not fair," she added bitterly.

"Charlotte, please tell me what you're talking about."

"Men, of course." She was surprised. "Boys, blokes, lads, fellas, the ones with the love truncheons."

"But what about them?"

"You're going to meet Mr Right and live happily ever after."

"Am I?" That was nice to hear, but I wondered where she was getting her information from.

"Yes." She waved a book at me. "I read it here. It's one of your mad books. About people like you, how you always pick men just like your dad – you know, ones that drink lots and don't want any responsibility and all that."

I felt a twist of pain, but I let her go on.

"It's not your fault," she said, consulting her book. "You see, the child – that's you, Lucy – senses that the parent – that's your dad, Lucy – is unhappy. And because – well, I don't really know why – because children are thick, I suppose, the child thinks it's her fault. That it's up to her to make him feel better. See?"

"I suppose so." She *had* a point. I had so many memories of Dad crying, and I never knew why. But I remembered the overwhelming need to know that it wasn't my fault. And the fear that he'd never be happy again. I would have done anything to help him, feel better.

Charlotte continued blithely to slot my round life into the round hole of her theory.

"And as the child – that's you again, Lucy – grows older, she is attracted to situations where the feelings of childhood are . . . what the fuck's this? Re . . . re . . . rep . . . ?"

"Replicated," I supplied helpfully

"Wow, Lucy, how did you know?" She was impressed.

But of course I knew. I had read that book loads of times. Well, at least once. And I was fully conversant with all the theories in it. It was just that I had never thought they applied to me before now.

"It means 'copied', doesn't it, Lucy?"

"It does, Charlotte."

"OK, so you sensed that your dad was an alkie, and you tried to make him better. But you couldn't. Not that it was your fault, Lucy," she added hurriedly. "I mean, you were only a little girl and what could you do? Hide the bottles?"

Hide the bottles.

I heard a bell ring, it was a long way away, more than twenty years. And suddenly I remembered a day when I was very young, maybe four or five, and that's what Chris said to me. "Come on, Lucy, we'll hide the bottles. If we hide the bottles then they'll have nothing to fight about."

A wave of heartbreak washed over me, for the little girl who hid a bottle of whiskey that was almost as big as herself in the dog's basket. But Charlotte kept chattering, so I had to file it away for later.

"So the child – that's still you, Lucy – grows into adulthood and meets all kinds of blokes. But the ones she's attracted to are the ones with the same problems as the child's parent – that's still your dad. See?"

"I see."

"The grown-up child feels comfortable and familiar with a man who drinks to excess or is irresponsible with money or who routinely uses violence . . ." she read aloud.

"My father was never violent." I was nearly in tears.

"Now, now, Lucy." Charlotte calmly wagged her finger at me. "These are only examples. It means that if the father always ate his dinner wearing a gorilla suit, then the child feels comfortable and familiar with boyfriends who wear fur coats or have hairy backs. See?"

"No."

She sighed with exaggerated patience.

"It means that you met lads who were always pissed and hadn't got jobs and sometimes were Irish and they reminded you of your dad. But you weren't able to make your dad happy, so you felt like you'd been given a second chance and you thought 'oh good, I can fix *this* one, even if I wasn't able to fix my dad'. See?"

"Maybe." It was so painful I nearly asked her to stop.

"Definitely," said Charlotte firmly. "Not that you did it on purpose, Lucy. I'm not saying that it was your fault. It was your conscience that did it."

"Do you mean my *subconscious*?"

She consulted the book. "Oh yes, your *sub* conscience. I wonder what the difference is?"

I hadn't the energy.

"And that's why you always fell in love with mad piss-heads like Gus and Malachy and . . . who was the one that fell out of the window?"

"Nick."

"That's right, Nick. How is he, by the way?"

"Still in the wheelchair, as far as I know."

"Oh, that's terrible." She spoke in suddenly hushed tones. "Is he *crippled*?"

"No, Charlotte." I was brisk. "He's completely better, but he says the wheelchair is much handier for getting round, seeing as he's pissed the whole time."

"That's OK." Charlotte sighed with relief. "I thought his willy was kaput."

It wouldn't have made any difference if Nick *had* lost the use of his genitals. Most of the time I'd been with him he'd been too drunk to even get it up. If his wallet hadn't been stolen early one Saturday evening, I don't think we'd ever have consummated the relationship.

Charlotte continued.

"And now that you know why you always pick the wrong men you won't do it anymore." She beamed at me. "You'll tell all the drunk spongers like Gus to get lost and you'll meet the right man and live happily ever after!"

I couldn't return her dazzling smile.

"Just because I know why I pick the wrong men doesn't mean that I'll stop doing it, you know." I laughed in exasperation.

"Nonsense!" she declared.

"I might become mean and bitter and hate men who drink."

"No, Lucy, you will allow yourself to be loved by a man worthy of you," she quoted. "Chapter Ten."

"But first I'll have to relearn the habits of a lifetime . . ." – Let's not forget that I had read the book too. "Chapter Twelve."

My ingratitude upset her.

"Why are you being so awkward?" she said. "You don't know how lucky you are. I'd give *anything* to have a dysfunctional family."

"Believe me, Charlotte, you wouldn't."

"Yes, I would." She was firm.

"For God's sake, why?" I was becoming more and more upset.

"Because if there's nothing wrong with me and my family, how can I explain why all my relationships are disasters? I've nothing or no one to blame, except me."

She stared at me again, with resentful envy.

"You don't think my father's a bully, do you?" she asked hopefully.

"No," I said. "I don't know him well, but he seems to be a very nice man."

"You don't think he's weak and ineffectual and a poor leader, inviting disrespect?" she asked, reading aloud from the book.

"On the contrary," I said. "He seems to command a lot of respect."

"Would you say he's a control freak?" She begged. "A melagomaniac?"

"It's megalomaniac, and no, he isn't."

"Sorry," I added.

She was annoyed.

"Well, Lucy, I know it's not really your fault, but you invented all these things . . ."

"Invented what?" I demanded, poised to be annoyed.

"OK, well, not invented them exactly," she backtracked. "But I wouldn't know about them if it wasn't for you."

"You've put ideas in my head," she added sulkily.

"In that case I should get a medal," I muttered.

"That's mean," she said, her eyes bright with tears that were under starter's orders.

"Sorry," I said. Poor Charlotte. How awful to be just bright enough to know how stupid you are.

But she never stayed down for long.

"Tell me again how you told Gus to fuck off," she demanded excitedly.

So, not for the first – or last – time, I told her.

"And how did you feel?" she exclaimed. "Powerful? Victorious? I'd love to be able to do that with that pig Simon."

"Have you spoken to him lately?"

"I had sex with him on Tuesday night."

"Yes, but have you spoken to him recently?"

"No, not really."

That made her laugh.

"Oh, I'm so glad you're back, Lucy," she sighed. "I've missed you."

"I've missed you too."

"And now that you're back we can have lovely talks about Frood . . ."

"Who? Oh, *Freud.*"

"Wha . . . ? Say it again, how does it go?"

"Like 'fried', but in an Australian accent. Froyd."

"Froyd," she murmured. "Yes, I was reading about Froyd . . . Now, Froyd says that . . ."

"Charlotte, what are you doing?"

"Practising for the party on Saturday." She was suddenly bitter. "I'm sick to death of men thinking that just because I've got big tits, I'm stupid. I'll show them. I'll go on and on about Frood, I mean, Froyd. Although they probably won't even notice, men never listen to me, they just have conversations with my chest."

She was gloomy for only a moment.

"What are you wearing to the party? It must be ages since you've been out properly."

"I'm not going to the party."

"What?"

"Not yet. It's too soon."

Charlotte laughed and laughed.

People getting over leaving their alcoholic father was obviously up there with people tripping on a hose and falling into swimming-pools fully clothed or getting locked out in the middle of the night while wearing a rabbit outfit and having to ask their neighbour – who already thinks they're mad – if they can use their phone.

"You big silly," she roared. "You make it sound as if you're in mourning."

"I am," I replied primly.

Chapter Seventy-Seven

The anger that I felt the night I went out with Gus propelled me out of my father's house, with the minimum of anguish and soul-searching. I moved back in with Karen and Charlotte and waited for normal life to resume.

I don't know how I thought I'd get off so lightly.

It took less than a day for the hired gun of Guilt and his henchmen to track me down. They worked me over good and proper and continued to do so every day. I was almost unrecognisable, beaten to a pulp by Grief, Anger and Shame.

I felt as though my father had died. In a way he had – the man that I thought had been my father no longer existed. Had never existed, in fact, except in my head. But I couldn't mourn him because he was still alive. Worse than that, he was alive, and I had chosen to abandon him. I had surrendered my right to grieve.

Daniel was wonderful. He had told me not to worry about a thing, that he would sort something out. But I couldn't let him do it. It was my family, my problem and I had to be the one to fix it. First of all, I yanked Chris's and Pete's heads out from where they were buried in the sand, and in fairness to the pair of lazy bastards, they said that they'd help to look after Dad.

Daniel had suggested contacting the social services and there was a time when I would have thought that that was the most shameful thing I could do to Dad. But I was beyond feeling shame, I was all shamed out.

So I rang lots of local authority numbers. The first number I rang told me to ring a second number and when I rang the second number they told me it was the people at the first number that should help me. Then when I rang the first number again they told me that the rules had been changed and it really was the people at the second number that should be helping me.

I spent about a million hours of my employer's time on the phone and heard the words, "That's not our area" over and over again.

Eventually, because Dad was such a danger to himself and others, they made him a priority case and allocated him a social worker and a home help.

I felt wretched.

"He's OK, Lucy," Daniel promised me. "He's being taken care of."

"But not by me." I was lacerated by a sense of failure.

"It's not your job to take care of him," Daniel gently pointed out.

"I know, but . . ." I said miserably.

It was January. Everyone was broke and depressed.

No one went out much, but I didn't go out at all. Apart from with Daniel.

I thought about my father constantly, trying to justify what I had done.

It had come down to a choice between me and him, I decided. One of us could have had me, but there wasn't enough of me to be shared between two.

I chose me.

Survival was an unpleasant thing to witness. Survival at someone else's expense was an unpleasant thing to do. There had been no room for love or nobility or honour or feeling for my fellow man – in this case, Dad. It was about me and only me.

I had always thought I was a nice person, a kind, generous, selfless person. It was a shock to find that when the chips were down, the kindness and generosity were only a veneer. That I was a snarling beast just like everyone else.

I didn't like myself very much – although that was nothing new.

Meredia, Jed and Megan were intrigued by my state of mind. Or rather, my states of mind. Every day I had a different emotion and they were keen to know all about it and offer advice and opinions.

As I said, it was January and no one got out much.

"What is it today?" they chorused when I walked into the office.

"Anger. Anger at not having had a proper father when I was a little girl."

Or . . .

"Grief. I feel like the man I loved, the man I always thought my father was, has died."

Or . . .

"Inadequacy. I should have been able to take care of him."

Or . . .

"Guilt. I feel so guilty for abandoning him."

Or . . .

"Jealousy. I'm jealous of people who had a normal childhood."

Or . . .

"Grief . . ."

"What, again?" demanded Meredia. "We had grief only a couple of days ago."

"Yes, I know," I said. "But it's a different kind of grief, this time it's grief for me."

We had all kinds of wonderful, metaphysical discussions.

I instigated a lot of conversations about survival in extreme circumstances.

"Remember those boys that were in the plane crash in the Andes?" I asked.

"The ones who ate the other passengers?" asked Meredia.

"And the survivors were shunned by the rest of the town when they got home for eating their neighbours?" asked Jed.

As an office, we had never stinted on reading the tabloids.

"That's right," I said. "So do you think it's better to die with honour or to get your hands good and dirty in the base, ignoble struggle for survival?"

We argued it back and forth for hours, and pondered vital moral issues.

"What do you think human flesh tastes like?" asked Jed. "I think I heard someone say it was a bit like chicken."

"Chicken breast or chicken thigh?" asked Meredia thoughtfully. "Because if it was chicken breast I wouldn't mind, but if it was chicken thigh I don't think I could."

"Me neither," I agreed. "Not unless it was in barbecue sauce."

"Did they have anything to put on it? Mayonnaise or ketchup or something?" Jed wondered.

"I wonder if the pilot had a different flavour to the passengers?" I asked.

"Very probably." Meredia nodded her head knowledgeably.

"Do you think they cooked it or ate it raw? asked Megan.

"Probably raw," I said.

"Jeez, Oi moight puke," said Megan.

"Really?" We all looked at her in surprise. Megan wasn't the squeamish type.

"But you weren't out on the piss last night." I was confused.

She *did* look pale. But that could have just been because her tan had finally faded.

She placed her hand on her chest and made heaving kind of actions.

"Are you really going to puke?" I asked in alarm. Jed thoughtfully placed a wastepaper basket on her lap.

The three of us stared at her, delighted with the drama, hoping that she might throw up and add some excitement to our day. But she didn't. After a few minutes she flung the basket on the floor and said, "Roight, Oi'm foine. Let's have a show of hands. All those in favour of eating them?"

Three hands shot up.

"Come on, Lucy," said Jed. "Put your hand up."

"I'm not sure . . ."

"Lucy, who did you allow to survive? You or your father? Eh?"

I shamefacedly put my hand up. Then while Meredia still had her hand up, Jed tickled under her arm. She squealed and giggled and said, "Ooooh, you little . . ." Oblivious to their audience, they called each other names and pretended to wrestle. I raised my eyebrows meaningfully at Megan, and she raised hers back at me.

Grey January limped along. And my social life remained barren.

I recommenced my close relationship with Adrian in the video-shop.

I tried to take out *When a Man Loves a Woman* and came home instead with Krzysztof Kieslowski's *The Double Life of Veronique*. I wanted to hire *Postcards from the Edge* and somehow ended up with *Il Postino*, (the undubbed, unsubtitled version). I begged Adrian to give me *Leaving Las Vegas* but instead he gave me something called *Eine Sonderbare Liebe*, which I didn't even bother to watch.

I didn't really need to go out because there was a real life soap opera taking place in my office.

Meredia and Jed had become very close. Very close *indeed*. They always left at the same time – although that was no great surprise because every employee in the building bolted from their desks the second it was five o'clock. But, more tellingly, they always *arrived* at the same time. And their behaviour in the office was very loving and couply. Giggly and coy and constantly simpering and blushing – Jed seemed to have fallen hard. And they had a private little game that no one else was allowed play, where Meredia threw Maltesers or Rolos or grapes in an arc across the office at Jed and he tried to catch them in his mouth, then flapped his arms together and made seal noises.

I envied them their happiness.

I was delighted that *they* were falling in love before my very eyes. Because I could no longer depend on Megan to provide me with romantic drama. She had changed. She didn't look like Megan anymore, as the sharp fall-off in the number of young men hanging round the office was testament to – now we could get out the door without having to push and shove grimly and say, "Excuse me, do you *mind?*" I couldn't figure out what was different about her and then I realised. Of course! The tan – it was no more. Winter had finally run her to ground and stripped her of her golden, lit-from-within translucence. It had faded her from a magnificent goddess to an ordinary, sturdy girl whose hair sometimes looked greasy.

But I realised that it wasn't just her good looks that had been muted. She wasn't the breezy, happy, energetic person she used to be. She no longer tried to find out Meredia's real name. She was often sullen and snappy, and it worried me.

That was quite an achievement, considering how busy I was feeling sorry for myself, but I cared about her.

I tried to find out what was wrong – and not just out of morbid curiosity either. I drew blanks until the day I tentatively asked her if she missed Australia. She turned to me and yelled, "OK, Lucy, I'm bloody homesick! Now, *stop* asking me what's wrong."

I knew how she felt – I had spent my whole life feeling homesick. The only difference between the two of us was that I didn't know what or where home was.

As soon as I realised that Megan's happiness was solar powered, I was anxious to give her some sun. Although I couldn't buy her a trip to Australia, I *could* buy her a gift voucher from the sunbed place near work. But when I gave it to her, she looked appalled. She stared at it like it was a warrant for her death, then finally choked out, "Noi, Loicy, Oi couldeent."

And then I was *really* worried about her – it's not that Megan was a stingy woman, but she had a great deal of respect for money and especially for things that were *free*. But, no matter how hard I tried, she continued to insist that it was far too decent of me and that she couldn't possibly accept.

So, in the end I went myself and all it did was give me eight million more freckles than I already had.

Chapter Seventy-Eight

The only person I saw in any kind of a social sense was Daniel. He was always available for outings with me because he was still without a girlfriend, which must have been the longest gap since the day he was born. I didn't feel guilty about the time he spent with me – I reckoned I was keeping him out of harm's way and saving some poor woman from falling in love with him.

I always felt really glad to see him, but I knew it was just because he filled the fatherless vacuum in my life. And I thought it was very important to tell him that – I didn't want him to get the idea that I might, God forbid, *fancy* him. So every time I met him, the first thing I said was, "I'm very glad to see you, Daniel, but only because you're filling an empty space in my life." And he showed unusual restraint by not making some vulgar comment about which one of my empty spaces he'd like to be filling. Which made me sad for the days when he made suggestive remarks to me all the time.

I said the empty space thing so often, that in the end he used to beat me to it. Whenever I said, "Hi Daniel, it's lovely to see you . . ." he'd interrupt,

"Yes, yes, Lucy, I know, but it's only because I'm filling the father figure gap in your life."

We went out two or three times a week, and somehow I never got round to telling Karen about it. I *meant* to, of course, but I was so concerned with trying to ration the number of times I saw Daniel that I didn't have the energy to tackle Karen.

At least that was what I liked to believe. And it *was* hard work trying to not see Daniel every night.

"Stop asking me out!" I scolded him, one evening while he cooked dinner for me at his flat.

"Sorry, Lucy," he said humbly, as he chopped carrots.

"I can't let myself become too dependent on you," I complained. "There's a danger it could happen, you know, because without Dad there's a big gap in my life . . ."

" . . . and your immediate instinct is to fill it," he finished for me. "You're very vulnerable right now and you can't afford to become too close to anyone."

I looked at him with admiration.

"Very good, Daniel. Now finish the sentence. Especially not who? Who should I especially not become too close to?"

"Especially not a man," he said proudly.

"Correct," I beamed. "Top marks."

I was delighted with him for knowing so much psychobabble. Especially when you considered that he was a good-looking man who enjoyed great success with women and didn't need to read up on pop psychology.

"Oh, while I think of it," I said. "Will you come to the pictures with me tomorrow night?"

676

"Of course I will, Lucy, but didn't you just say you can't get too close to a man . . ."

"I don't mean *you*," I said airily. "*You* don't count as a man."

He threw me a hurt look.

"Oh, you know what I mean." I was exasperated. "Of course you're a man for *other* women, but you're *my* friend."

"I'm still a man," he muttered. "Even if I'm your friend."

"Daniel, don't sulk. Think about it – isn't it far better for me to be with you than with some other bloke that I might fall for? Well, isn't it?"

"Yes, but . . ." he trailed away. He sounded confused.

He wasn't the only one. I didn't know whether it was safe to be with Daniel because it was keeping me out of harm's way or whether I was putting myself in mortal danger of becoming too close to him. On balance I thought I was safer with him than not with him. And I kept the barriers up simply by constantly reminding him that they were there. It was OK to be with him as long as I reminded us both that it wasn't OK. Or *something* like that. All in all, it was easier not to think about it.

Occasionally I remembered the time he had kissed me and I was more than happy, *delighted* in fact, to skirt round the memory of it. Because whenever I remembered it – and it really was very rarely – quick as a flash, I immediately remembered the night when he *wouldn't* kiss me, and the rush of shame that followed put an end to my reminiscences good and fast.

677

Anyway, Daniel and I were back on our old footing, so relaxed with each other that we could laugh together at our brief romantic/sexual encounter.

Well, almost.

Sometimes when he said to me, "Would you like another drink?" I forced a laugh and lightly replied, "Oh no, I've had enough. After all we don't want a repeat of that night out in Dad's when I tried to seduce you."

I always laughed heartily, hoping to laugh away any residual shame and embarrassment. He never really laughed at all, but then again, he didn't need to.

Chapter Seventy-Nine

January became February. Crocuses and snowdrops started to appear. People emerged from their cocoons, especially around the time they got paid and had money for the first time since the financial holocaust of Christmas. Meredia, Jed and Megan lost interest in my personal life now that they had money to go out on the piss and create lives of their own. Which was a terrible shame because I still had so much to offer – not a day passed that I wasn't tortured by self-loathing and shame.

I went to see Dad once a week. Every Sunday because I always felt suicidal on Sunday *anyway*, and it seemed a shame to waste it. And, acute and all as my self-loathing was, it was nothing compared to the hatred that Dad had for me. Of course, I warmly welcomed his disgust and venom because I felt that it was all that I deserved.

February edged into March and I was the only living thing still in hibernation. Even though Dad was being well looked after in a physical sense, I felt *filthy* with guilt. And Daniel was the only person left that I felt comfortable whinging to. No matter what people say, there *is* a time limit to the amount of time you're allowed to be in mourning, be it for a father, a boyfriend or a pair of shoes that they didn't have in your size. And Daniel's time limit was a lot longer than everyone else's.

No one at work even *listened* to me anymore. On Mondays when someone asked, "Hi, nice weekend?" I usually replied, "Awful, I wish I was dead," and no one turned a hair.

I think I would have gone mad without Daniel. He was just like a therapist, except he didn't charge me forty pounds an hour, or wear beige cords or socks with sandals.

It wasn't always doom and gloom when I met him but, when it was, he was great. Time after time he listened to me covering the same ground, going over the same anguish again and again.

I could meet him for a drink after work and flop onto the seat beside him and say, "Don't stop me if you've heard this, but . . ." and launch into yet another saga of – let's just say – a sleepless night, or a tearful Sunday, or a miserable evening I'd had worrying or feeling guilty or ashamed about Dad. Daniel never once complained about my lack of new material.

He never held up his hand like a policeman stopping traffic and said, "No, hold on! Wait a minute, Lucy, I think I know this one!"

And he would have been perfectly entitled to. Because if Daniel had heard my story of woe once, he had heard it a million times. Sometimes the wording was slightly different but the punch line was always the same. Poor him.

"Sorry, Daniel," I said. "I wish my misery was a bit more varied. It must be very boring for you."

"It's OK, Lucy." He grinned. "I'm like a goldfish, I've a very short memory span. Every time I hear it, it's as if it's for the first time."

"Well, if you're sure," I said awkwardly.

"I'm sure," he said cheerfully. "Come on and tell me again about the imaginary bargain that you've made with your father."

I flicked him a quick glance to see if he was making fun of me, but he wasn't.

"OK," I said awkwardly, trying (once again) to find the right words to say how I felt. "It's like I've made a bargain with Dad."

"What kind of bargain?" Daniel asked, in the same kind of voice that music hall comedians said, "But how does he smell?" Straight man to my funny man. We made a great double act.

"It's all in my head," I said. "But it's like I've said, 'It's OK, Dad, I know I abandoned you, but my life isn't worth living because I hate myself so much for saving me instead of you. So, we're equal. Quits.' Am I making any sense, Dan?"

"Absolutely," he agreed, for the umpteenth time.

It surprised me to realise how highly I thought of Daniel. He had been so good to me through the whole Dad crisis.

"You're a good bloke," I told him, one evening, when I had paused for breath.

"No, I'm not, I wouldn't do it for anyone except you." He smiled.

"But, even so, I mustn't become too dependent on you," I added hurriedly. I hadn't said it in at least five minutes and his smile had unnerved me. I had to neutralise it. "I'm on the emotional rebound, you know."

"Yes, Lucy."

"I'm getting over the loss of my dad, you know."

"Yes, Lucy."

I wanted that twilight life to continue forever, where I didn't have any real contact with anyone except my therapist – by which I mean Daniel. Until Daniel decided that he'd had enough, which threatened to destroy the nice safe world I'd created.

He gave me no warning.

One evening we met and I said the usual, "Hi Daniel, it's lovely to see you but only because you're filling a gap in my life," he held my hand and very gently said, "Lucy, isn't it about time that this stopped?"

"Wh-what?" I asked, feeling as if the ground had swayed beneath my feet. "What are you talking about?"

"Lucy, the last thing I want to do is upset you, but I've been thinking and I wondered if the time has come for you to try and get over this," he said, in an even *more* gentle tone. The expression on my face was on the rigor mortis end of the stricken scale.

"Maybe I shouldn't have indulged you so much," he said. He looked sick. "Maybe I've even been bad for you."

"No, no," I hastened to say. "You've been *good* for me, *brilliant*."

"Lucy, I think you should start going out again," he suggested in gentle tones which did nothing but scare me.

"But I'm out now." I was apprehensive. Not to

mention defensive. I sensed that my days in the safe haven were coming to an end.

"I mean, *out*, out," said Daniel. "When are you going to start living properly again? Seeing other people? Going to parties?"

"When the guilt about Dad goes away, of course." I looked at him suspiciously. "Daniel, you're supposed to *understand*."

"So you can't have a life because you feel guilty about your dad?"

"Exactly!" I hoped that meant that the subject was closed. But it wasn't.

Daniel said, "Guilt doesn't go away on its own. You've got to make it happen."

Oh no! I didn't want to hear that.

I decided to sway him with my womanly charms so I gave him a coy little glance from under my eyelashes.

"Please don't look at me like that, Lucy," he said. "It won't work."

"Fuck you," I muttered, then I sat in embarrassed, sullen silence.

I tried a nasty glare, but no luck with that either. I could see he meant business.

"Lucy," he said, "I don't want to upset you, so please let me help you." In fairness to him, he *did* sound as if he was in terrible anguish.

I sighed and gave in. "OK, you mean bastard, help me then."

"Lucy, your guilt will probably get less, but it won't ever disappear completely. You'll have to learn to live with it."

"But I don't want to."

"I know, but you're going to have to. You can't just opt out of life until some time in the distant future when you don't feel guilty – it mightn't ever happen."

I had been quite happy to.

"You're like the Little Mermaid," he said, suddenly changing the subject.

"Am I?" I glowed with pleasure. This conversation was much more to my liking. And my hair *did* look long and curly and sleek, now that he mentioned it.

"She had to suffer the agony of walking on blades in exchange for being able to live on dry land. You've made the same kind of bargain – you've paid for your freedom with guilt."

"Oh." No mention of my hair.

"You're a good person, Lucy, you haven't done anything wrong and you're allowed to have a nice life," he explained. "Think about it, that's all I ask."

So I thought about it. And thought about it. And thought about it. I smoked a cigarette and thought about it. I drank my gin and tonic and thought about it. While Daniel was at the bar buying me another one, I thought about it. I finally spoke.

"I've thought about it. Maybe you're right, maybe it's time to move on."

The whole truth was that perhaps I was finally becoming bored of so much unadulterated misery. *Bored* of being so self-indulgent. And I could have gone on for a lot longer than I already had – years probably – if Daniel hadn't pulled me up short.

"Great, Lucy." He was delighted. "And while I'm

being mean to you, maybe you could give some thought to visiting your mother."

"What are you?" I asked sharply. "My bloody conscience?"

"And seeing as you're already pissed off with me," he grinned, "I think I might as well tell you that it's about time you stopped taking any more abuse from your dad. Stop punishing yourself. You've repaid your debt to society and your sentence is at an end."

"I'll be the judge of that," I said angrily. Stop punishing myself, indeed! It was obvious that *he* hadn't been brought up as a Catholic. I couldn't even *begin* to contemplate a life that didn't involve lots of self-flagellation.

Although now that I thought about it, maybe going easy on myself was a good idea, a very pleasant option, in fact. And, as I wavered on the brink, Daniel said something that changed everything for me.

He said, "You know, Lucy, if you feel that guilty, you can always go back to your father. Anytime you like."

The suggestion appalled me. I wouldn't do that. Not ever. And it was only *then* that I realised what Daniel had been talking about. I'd chosen freedom because that was what I had wanted. I might as well use the bloody thing.

I stared at him as realisation dawned.

"You're right, you know," I said faintly. "Life is for living."

"God, Lucy." He sounded shocked. "There's no call for clichés."

"Bastard." I smiled.

"You can't be afraid forever," he said, making the most of my good humour. "You can't hide from your feelings, from other people."

He paused for emphasis, "Lucy, you can't hide from men."

Now, that was going too far. He was trying to make me run before I could walk.

"A *boyfriend*!" I said in alarm. "You want me to get a boyfriend after all the disasters I've been through."

"Christ, Lucy, hold on," said Daniel. He grabbed my arm as if I was just about to run out into the street and proposition the first man I met. "Not immediately. I mean *sometime*, not now . . ."

"But Daniel," I wailed. "I'm such a bad judge of men. You, of all people know how hopeless I am."

"No, Lucy, I only want you to *think* about it . . ." he said anxiously.

"I can't believe you think I'm ready for a boyfriend," I said in surprise.

"Lucy, I don't mean . . . all I'm saying is . . ."

"But I trust your judgement," I said doubtfully. "If you say it's the right thing for me, then it must be."

"It's only a suggestion, Lucy." Daniel sounded nervous.

But something had tickled the back of my brain, the memory of the fun of being in love. I vaguely remembered how nice it had been. Maybe, along with being bored by my misery, I had also become bored of being without a man.

"No, Daniel," I said thoughtfully. "Now that you mention it, maybe it's not such a bad idea."

"Wait, Lucy, I only said . . . Now that I think

about it, it's a bad idea, a very bad idea, I'm sorry I ever mentioned it."

I held my hand up authoritatively.

"Nonsense, Daniel, you were right to say all this to me. Thank you."

"But . . ."

"No buts, Daniel, you're quite right. The next time there's a party on, I'll go!" I finished decisively.

After a few triumphant minutes I said in a little voice, "But we'll still see each other, won't we? Not all the time, or anything, but you know . . . ?"

And he replied stoutly, "Of course we will, Lucy, of course we will."

It never occurred to me, not even for a moment, that Daniel might have had another reason for wanting to ease me away from him, for setting me free to fly on my own. That his concern for my independence mightn't have been entirely altruistic. That, perhaps he might have had a new girlfriend impatiently fidgeting in the wings. Anxiously waiting for me to take my final bow and exit stage left so that she could take her rightful place in the spotlight. I never doubted that his concern for me was genuine and sincere and selfless. I trusted him utterly. And because of that, I decided to go along with what he suggested.

Chapter Eighty

The new me. Oozing strength. Independent. Reborn. Back out there. Fighting fit. Firm handshake. Meeting new people. Social interaction. Flirting. Strong woman. Knows her own mind.

God, it was *exhausting*.

And so *boring*. As far as I could see, what Learning to Live Again *really* meant was just staying away from Daniel. Or at least cutting down drastically on the amount of time I spent with him. And I missed him terribly. No one was as much fun as he was. But it was for my own good, even *I* could see that, and rules were rules. Anyway, it wasn't the awful cold turkey that I'd expected because he still rang me every day. And I knew that I'd see him the following Sunday because I was taking him out for lunch for his birthday.

This Learning to Live Again business was easier said than done – I'd been out of circulation for too long and I had no one to play with. I gatecrashed a post-work drink with Jed and Meredia and what a mistake that was. They both behaved as if I was invisible.

The following night I went out with Dennis and, even though he had promised me a wild night, that was also a disaster. First of all he refused to go to any pubs except gay ones and I spent the night desperately trying to make eye contact with him as he twitched in his seat, watching young boys in tight white T-shirts over my shoulder. I could barely get a word of conversation out of him. And when he *did* bother to talk to me, all he spoke about was Daniel. Which was very irresponsible of him – he was feeding my habit, instead of weaning me off it.

Megan was still laid low with her Seasonal Affective Disorder because, when I suggested going out and getting pissed and picking up men, she just sighed and said she was too tired.

So that left Charlotte and Karen. And with all due respect, flatmates were a bit of a last resort. I could have got drunk with them *anytime*.

"Can't you think of anything better for us to do than go to the Dog's Bollix and have drinks spilled on us by Scottish builders?" I complained.

"Not that there's anything wrong with Scottish builders," I said quickly, as Karen's face darkened.

"Leave it to me." Charlotte mysteriously tapped the side of her nose. And, with the flair of a magician pulling a rabbit out of a hat, she produced a party for us to go to on Saturday night. Her workmate's flatmate's boyfriend's brother's colleague's cousin was having a party because he hadn't got off with a girl in ages. For this very reason Charlotte, Karen and I were extremely welcome.

On Saturday night the preparations for the party were just like old times. Charlotte and I opened a bottle of wine and got ready together in my bedroom.

"I wonder if there'll be any nice blokes there tonight?" asked Charlotte, as she tried to put mascara on her bottom lashes with a slightly drunken hand.

"I wonder if there'll be any blokes there at *all*," I said doubtfully. "Especially if the guy is only having the party so that he can get off with a girl."

"Don't worry," said Charlotte, her hand wobbling. "There'll *have* to be some lads, and one or two of them will probably be nice."

"I don't care as long as they're not like Gus," I said.

Karen marched into the room and opened my wardrobe.

"You mean the days of you bringing home drunk, penniless lunatics, who steal our bottles of tequila are over?" she demanded as she efficiently flicked through my hangers.

"Yes."

"Oh fukkit!" exclaimed Charlotte. "Give me a tissue someone, it's gone all over my face."

"And it's all because of this business with your dad?" asked Karen, ignoring Charlotte.

"Who knows? Maybe I would have grown out of penniless musicians anyway," I said.

"Hardly," said Charlotte, as she licked a tissue and dabbed it at the mascara streaks on her cheekbones. She was loath to give up on her theory. "Let's face it, Lucy, you weren't getting any younger. Froyd says . . ."

"Oh shut up, Charlotte," snapped Karen. "Go back to reading your Enid Blyton's. Lucy, where's your suede jacket, I want to wear it tonight."

I resentfully handed it over.

Eventually we were ready.

"Lucy, you look *beautiful*," said Charlotte.

"No, I don't."

"You *do*. Do I look like I'm wearing grey blusher?"

"Not really. Anyway, you're beautiful."

Actually, you *could* still see faint traces of where she'd rubbed the mascara into her face, but the taxi was on its way and we didn't have time for Charlotte to redo her make-up. I'd send her to the bathroom when we arrived at the party.

"Karen, we must watch Lucy in action tonight," said Charlotte. "She'll find the best-looking, richest man in the room and get off with him."

"No, I won't." I didn't want to disappoint Charlotte. My transformation couldn't be the immediate, miraculous one that she expected. "Decent men are in short enough supply as it is – why should I suddenly meet a gorgeous one who worships the ground that I walk on just because I've found out my father's an alcoholic?"

"You will." She was adamant.

"Listen to me," said Karen. "If there's a rich, good-looking man there, he's got my name on him."

The word "Daniel" hovered unspoken between Karen and me.

Then fearless Karen spoke it.

"Do you remember when I thought there was something going on with you and Daniel?" she asked with a menacing laugh. "Although I'm still not convinced that you haven't secretly got the hots for him."

691

"Not that it'll do you any good," she continued. "Let's face it, Lucy." She flicked her sophisticated blonde glance over my short, flat-chested body. I automatically obliged her by feeling ashamed and worthless. "You're not exactly his type, are you?"

Indeed I wasn't. It was official – he had told me so. The memory of the night he had turned me down was in the forefront of my mind.

Chapter Eighty-One

At the party I spotted him immediately – the one I would have picked in my former existence. He was young, with sun-bleached surfer's hair, which was long enough to indicate that he wasn't a stockbroker. He was handsome and unreliable looking with bright sparkly eyes. The sparkliness of his eyes had probably been achieved by chemical means. You could tell, just by looking at him, that he had never been on time for anything in his life.

His jumper was what I would have once described as individual and unique, when the word horrible would have sufficed. He was loud and lively and in the middle of telling a story that involved great sweeps of his arms. The group of people around him were all laughing uncontrollably but then again they all looked like drug-addicts. He was probably telling them about one of the times he was arrested, I thought uncharitably.

I pulled myself up short. When did I get to be so bitter? It wasn't right to lump every badly dressed, long-haired young man in the same category as Gus. This blond bloke might be kind and generous with a good heart and lots of money.

I stared at him, and thought, "You know, he *is* cute."

He caught me looking at him, and winked and grinned at me. I turned away.

A few minutes later, someone tapped me on the shoulder. I turned round and it was him – the cute, loud, sun-bleached jail-bird.

"Hello," he said loudly. His eyes were an amazing glittery silver colour. The pattern on his jumper could have brought on an epileptic fit.

"Hello." I smiled. I couldn't help it, it was completely automatic.

"I spotted you from across the room." He grinned. "And I spotted that you were spotting me too. I wondered if you'd like to come out to the conservatory with me to smoke a spliff or twenty . . .

His voice trailed away as I just stared at him. I didn't mean to be rude but I had to check my vital signs to see if I was attracted to him. But nothing happened, I was stone cold.

"Er . . . maybe not . . . just a suggestion." He backed away from me, his smile replaced by a look of nervous apprehension. "Stupid thing to say, because I haven't any drugs, never touch them – 'just say no', that's my motto . . ."

He bolted back to his mates and I heard him telling them that I was an undercover policewoman. They looked collectively ashen and, as a single body, shuffled from the room.

Whatever he thought he had seen in me – the signal that I used to give out to attract men like him –

had gone. It was only the ghost of it that had flickered briefly and lured him in error.

Pity, though, because he really was very cute.

Later on, I heard someone complain that there was no one at the party to buy any drugs from. I had the grace to feel guilty.

It was an awful party, the neighbours didn't even call the police. The music was terrible, there was almost nothing to drink, and not a single attractive man.

None that I liked the look of anyway.

Karen got her knickers all in a twist because of some big, beefy bloke whose dad was rumoured to be loaded. And, in her usual determined manner, she found someone who knew someone who knew someone who knew the big, beefy bloke and ended up speaking to him.

Charlotte and I sat on the sofa while all the people milling around completely ignored us. I was bored out of my skull. Charlotte kept up a running commentary on everyone there. "See him, Lucy, the way he's got his arms by his side – a classic anal tentative," and, "See her, Lucy, desperate for affection – probably wasn't breast-fed."

And I muttered, "It's retentive," and, "That's her husband she's holding hands with."

How I rued the day Charlotte had ever got her hands on my Psychology for Miserable Women books.

The tedium continued. But at least there was the walk to the minicab office and the kebab to look forward to.

Karen swanned by with the human steak.

"Girls," she said to Charlotte and I, in her put-on, I'm-so-charming voice, "this is Tom. He wanted to be introduced to the two of you – God knows why!"

Charlotte and I laughed. Because we knew there would be trouble later if we didn't.

"Tom, this is Charlotte and this is Lucy."

Up close he wasn't so bad, really. Brown eyes, brown hair, quite a kind face. It was just that I couldn't stop imagining him covered with pepper sauce.

The person beside me on the couch got up because their friend had collapsed in the bathroom. And Tom asked Karen if she wanted to sit down.

"No," she said. Because she wanted to stand beside him, of course.

"Are you sure?" he asked puzzled.

"Quite." She laughed gaily up at him. "I love to stand."

"OK," he said, *really* puzzled by then. And, to Karen's slack-jawed horror he sat down beside me.

Quick as a flash, in a damage limitation exercise, Karen perched on the arm of the sofa, beside Charlotte. Actually, she really sat *on* Charlotte. Then she leant across us so that she could talk to T-bone, almost obscuring Charlotte and I.

But she was wasting her time.

"I'm so glad I met Karen," said Tom to me.

I smiled politely.

"Because," he continued. "I've been watching you all evening and I've been trying to pluck up the courage to come and talk to you."

I smiled politely again.

Christ! Karen would *kill* me.

"So I couldn't believe my luck when I ended up speaking to your friend."

"What's all this?" smiled Karen.

"I'm just telling Lucy how glad I am that I got talking to you," said Tom.

Karen tossed her hair back in a gesture of triumph.

"I've spent the whole night wondering how I could get to meet Lucy," he continued.

Karen froze mid-toss. Even the strands of her hair were rigid.

She turned a Lucy-you-will-die-for-this-you-bitch face on me.

I shrunk back into the couch. A few days later I heard that all the plants in the house died that night.

And it wasn't as if I found Tom even remotely attractive – after all, I was almost vegetarian.

"I'm glad I was of use to you, Tom," said Karen corrosively. She stood up and stalked across the room.

Tom and I looked at each other, him in shock, me in fear. Then we both burst out laughing.

It was typical that Tom fancied me. Because I didn't fancy him. I hadn't even noticed him. I had always found that the best way to get men interested in me was not to fancy them. But I had to mean it – faking it never worked. Men always knew that when I ignored them and lifted my chin haughtily, I was actually gagging for it. (I quote.)

Charlotte – obviously on a death wish – ran after

697

Karen, so I talked to meaty Tom. I was touched by his little confession about being too nervous to talk to me etc., etc. And he seemed nice. But of course he did – he wanted to get me into bed. I almost shuddered at the thought – he was so *big*, it would be like having sex with a bull.

Not like Daniel – *he* was big, but nice big. Idly, I wondered where he was that evening. I suddenly had a horrible thought – maybe he was at another party, doing a Tom, trying to persuade a girl to come home with him. My stomach clenched in fear and I had a panicky urge to ring him in the hope that I might find him at home in bed – alone.

"Oh no," I said to myself in horror, "I *warned* you this might happen."

After all I'd said, had I become too dependent on Daniel?

I forced myself to sit still – I couldn't just ring him and ask if he was in bed with someone. And, while I was on the subject, why did I want to?

That scared me into calming down. I had *never* been possessive about Daniel. I had never minded who he chatted up, who he seduced, who he took home to his bed and took their clothes off and . . .

The panicky fear began to rise again. He had been without a girlfriend for a long time – and it couldn't go on forever. He was bound to meet some nice woman at some stage. But if he started going out with someone, what would happen to me? Where would I fit into his life?

What was going on, I wondered in fear. I was acting as if I was jealous, as if . . . as if . . . as if *I fancied him.* No, no, I wouldn't think it! I WOULD NOT THINK IT. I nearly screamed it out loud.

My mind lurched back to the present. I tried to focus on poor Tom because he had asked me a question and seemed to be eagerly waiting for an answer.

"What?" I asked. I felt slightly sick.

"Lucy, can I take you out some night?"

"But I don't fancy you, Tom," I blurted out. In fact, what I actually said was, "I don't fancy *you.*"

He looked a little bit taken aback.

"Sorry," I said. "I wasn't thinking . . ."

But I *had* been thinking. I had become too possessive of Daniel and Daniel obviously knew it. He probably thought I fancied him. The cheek of him.

"I only want to take you out for dinner, Lucy," Tom said humbly. "Do you have to fancy me for that?"

"Sorry, Tom."

I could barely speak to him. Daniel wanted to get rid of me, I realised. That was what all that about me having to start living again was about. Little mermaid, indeed! He was just trying to prise my clinging hands from him, finger by finger. I felt a fierce burst of humiliation, which quickly became anger. Fine then, I thought in fury, I'd have nothing further to do with Daniel. I'd get a new boyfriend and that'd show him. I'd go out with Tom and we'd fall in love and be really happy.

"Tom, I'd be delighted to go out with you," I said. I wished that I was dead.

"That's great." Tom beamed. If I hadn't felt so sorry for him, it would have been nice to give him a thump.

"When?" I tried to force some enthusiasm into my voice.

"Now?" he asked hopefully.

With a scathing raise of an eyebrow I managed to convey that Tom was in danger of dying shortly.

"Sorry," he said in fear. "Sorry, sorry, sorry. Tomorrow night?"

"OK."

It was a done deal. And just in time, for the party keeled over and died.

Chapter Eighty-Two

I had every intention of never seeing Daniel again. The only problem was that the following day I was supposed to take him out for his birthday lunch. I felt that I couldn't cancel it – not only had it been arranged for weeks, but it was his *birthday*.

Perhaps I felt relieved, but I tried not to think about it. That was easy because the atmosphere between Karen and I was terrible. She wouldn't speak to me and she did regular tours of the flat where she went to the time and trouble to open all the doors just so she could slam them shut again.

It was very unpleasant. And I bitterly regretted having said that I'd go out with Tom. I must have been out of my mind – he was *awful* and Karen was welcome to him. I knew for a fact that I wouldn't fall in love with him and prove anything to Daniel.

The terrible fear that Daniel had met a new woman had come sneaking back while I slept. I was sure that the terror that I'd felt the previous night had been a premonition. It was no longer just a thought – it had mutated into a *premonition*.

I tried to talk sense into myself as I got ready to go out. I was fairly sure that I didn't fancy Daniel, *as such*. It wasn't a romantic or sexual thing that I felt for him. Immediately, memories of The Kiss flooded back uninvited but I blanked them out. (I was still so good at blanking things out – it really was a wonderful ability.) But perhaps I had come to depend on him too much as a friend? In the aftermath of the disintegration of my family had I become too fond of him?

Well, if I had, it must stop.

I was pleased with myself for being so sensible. Although it only lasted a moment. The panic started again immediately.

But what if he's in bed with her *right now*? I thought.

In the end I rang him. I simply couldn't stop myself. I pretended that I had rung to check where I was meeting him – even though I knew it was Green Park tube at two o'clock. And, to my relief, it didn't *sound* as if there was a woman in bed beside him. Although it was hard to be certain – Daniel's life wasn't a Carry On film where women shriek and giggle while they're in bed.

It was a godsend being in the doghouse with Karen because I didn't have to make up some elaborate excuse when I left to meet Daniel. If she had been speaking to me she would have definitely been suspicious because, in an attempt to show Daniel that I wasn't a clingy loser, I was dressed to the nines. My very short shift dress and matching swingy coat were hardly appropriate protection from the bitterly cold March day, but I didn't care. Pride would keep me warm.

He was waiting outside Green Park tube at the appointed time. As I wobbled, shivering, towards him on my high snakeskin sandals he gave me a smile of such dazzling intensity that it nearly sent me over on my ankle. I was annoyed – and very suspicious. What was he grinning about? Was it the delight of having a new girlfriend that made his smile so broad? Was it a post-coital glow that made him look so gorgeous?

"Lucy, you look beautiful," he said. Then he kissed me on the cheek and my skin tightened and tingled. "But aren't you cold?"

"Not at all," I said vaguely, as I discreetly examined him for lovebites, chapped lips, scratches, etc.

"Where are we going, Lucy?" he asked.

I couldn't see any obvious signs of recent sexual activity on him, but as most of him was bundled up in a winter coat, that was no reason for me to breathe a sigh of relief.

"It's a surprise," I said, as I wondered if he had his coat collar up to hide a neckful of hickeys. "Come on, let's hurry, I'm freezing!"

Damn! Our eyes met and his mouth twitched as he tried not to laugh.

"Don't even think about it," I threatened.

"I wouldn't," he said humbly.

I led him to Arbroath Street and when we reached the glass front of Shore, I said "Dah, daah!"

He was impressed and I was happy. Shore was one of London's newest, grooviest restaurants, frequented by models and actresses. Or so the magazines said – this would be my first and probably my last visit.

As soon as we walked in, I realised that I had gravely underestimated *just* how groovy and happening a place Shore was. The rudeness of the staff gave it away.

The greeter, a young saturnine man, stared at me as if I had just squatted down in the entrance and urinated.

"Yes?" he hissed.

"A table for two in the name of . . ."

"Have you booked?" he snapped.

Immediately I wanted to say, "Look, you little asshole, you're only a *receptionist*, you know. I'm *sorry* that I'm going to spend more on a meal than you get paid in a week, but ruining our lunch isn't going to bring about a redistribution of wealth. Have you thought about night classes? You could go back to school and try passing a couple of exams. Then you might get a proper job."

But because it was Daniel's birthday and I wanted everything to go beautifully, I humbly said, "Yes, I've booked. The name is Sullivan."

But I spoke to thin air. He had emerged from behind his little podium and was air-kissing a woman in Gucci flares who had come in after us.

"Kiki, darling," he fawned. "How was Barbados?"

"You know – Barbados." She pushed past me. "We're just off the plane. David's parking the beemer."

She surveyed the restaurant. Daniel and I obligingly pressed ourselves back against the wall.

"Just the two of us," she said. "A window table would be nice."

"Have you . . . er . . . booked?" He discreetly coughed.

"Oh, naughty me." She smiled icily. "I should have called you on the car phone. But I have every faith in you, Raymond."

"Er, it's Maurice," said Raymond. He pronounced it "Mor-eece."

"Whatever." She waved a hand dismissively. "Just get us a table and fast. David's starving."

"Don't worry, ducks, we'll squeeze you in somewhere." He giggled. "Leave it to Mor-eece."

He consulted his book. Daniel and I merged with the wallpaper. Even though there wasn't any.

"Let's see," muttered Maurice anxiously. "Table ten should be just about leaving . . ."

He continued to ignore Daniel and me.

I hate you, I thought.

If I had been on my own I would have waited forever. But because we were there for Daniel's birthday, and I wanted him to have a good time, I decided to take matters into my own hands.

"Excuse me, Maurice," – I pronounced it "Morris" – "Daniel's starving, in fact he's nearly as hungry as David. We'd like to go to our table, please. The one we *booked*."

Daniel burst out laughing. Maurice glared at me, snapped up two menus and gave Kiki a, "Christ, can you believe it?" look. He set off across the restaurant at high speed. For some reason he seemed to have a ten-pence-piece between his tiny buttocks, and he took great pains not to drop it. Clenched. Very clenched.

705

He slung the menus on a little table and disappeared. He couldn't get away from us quickly enough. Ordinary people, ugh!

Daniel and I sat down. Daniel laughed and laughed.

"That was great, Lucy," he said.

"Sorry about that, Daniel." I felt quite tearful. "I want you to really enjoy this because it's your birthday and you've been very good to me and I've so much to thank you for and what did you do last night?"

"Sorry?" He looked confused. "What did I do last night?"

"Um, yes," I said. I hadn't meant to blurt it out like that.

"I went for a couple of pints with Chris."

"And who else?"

"No one else."

Phew.

The relief was great for about thirty seconds. Until I realised that there were thousands more Saturday nights in the future, stretching out into infinity. And on every single one of them there was a chance that Daniel would meet a woman.

That subdued me so much that I could barely listen to him. He was saying something about us going to see some comedian that evening.

"No, Daniel, wait," I said quickly. "I can't go out with you tonight."

"Can't you?"

Was he disappointed? I wondered hopefully.

"I've got a hot date," I said.

"Really? That's great, Lucy." Did he have to sound so bloody pleased for me?

"Yes, it *is* great." I felt defensive and angry. "He's not a drunk, penniless layabout. He has a job and a car and Karen fancied him."

"Great," he said – again!

I nodded curtly.

"Well done," he said enthusiastically.

Well done? I thought angrily. Have I been that pathetic?

The day had suddenly clouded over. I sat in silence. Birthday or no birthday, I felt much too angry to be nice to him.

"So I won't be seeing quite so much of you from now on," I said.

"I understand, Lucy," he said nicely.

I wanted to cry.

I sat and sullenly stared at the table. Daniel must have picked up on my mood because, unusually for him, he also became very subdued.

Despite the rudeness of the staff, the lunch was not a success. The food was nice, but I didn't want to eat it. I was too pissed off with Daniel. How dare he be glad for me? As if I was handicapped or something.

Luckily, the horribleness of the staff gave Daniel and I something to talk about. Every single one of them was so patronising, condescending and good, plain, old-fashioned rude that towards the end of the meal we began to tentatively communicate again.

"Wanker." Daniel gave me a little smile as our waiter ignored us when we wanted to order coffee.

"Stupid bastard," I smilingly agreed.

When the bill came we scuffled over it.

"No, Daniel," I insisted. "This is on me, for your birthday."

"If you're sure?"

"I'm sure." I smiled. But not for long when I saw how much I had to pay.

"Let me pay half," suggested Daniel when he saw my appalled expression.

"No way."

More scuffles. Daniel tried to grab the bill from my hand, I pulled it away from him, etc., etc. In the end he graciously let me pay.

"Thanks for a lovely lunch, Lucy," he said.

"It wasn't lovely, though, was it?" I asked sadly.

"Yes it was," he said stoutly. "I wanted to come here and now I know what it's like."

"Promise me something, Daniel," I asked fervently.

"Anything."

"That you will never knowingly, willingly come here again."

"I promise, Lucy."

I walked him to the tube station, then I walked to the bus stop. I felt very depressed.

Tom was the perfect gentleman.

He rang my doorbell at seven exactly, as arranged. And, as arranged, he didn't come up to the flat. What he lacked in graceful, elegant, emaciated good looks he more than made up for in the instinct of self-preservation. He was no fool, and he suspected that Karen was a sore and vengeful loser.

I ran downstairs to where he waited in his car. I got a slight shock when I saw him sitting behind the wheel. There was nothing wrong – it was just that he looked as if he'd be more at home hanging from a butcher's hook. He made it worse by wearing a red shirt. I hoped he would never get his nose pierced.

He took me to a restaurant – the *same* Emperor's New Clothes restaurant that I'd taken Daniel to for lunch. Maurice was still on duty. He stared with loathing and disbelief when Tom stampeded through the door and pawed the ground with me at his side.

Tom wined and dined me, then tried to get me to go back to his flat, with a view to sixty-nining me, I suppose.

He hadn't a chance.

Nice bloke, but I wouldn't have bedded him if he was the last man on the planet. And he *loved* me for it.

His eyes shone with admiration as I turned him down.

"Would you like to go out during the week?" he asked eagerly. "We could go to the theatre."

"Maybe," I agreed doubtfully.

"Well, it doesn't have to be the theatre," he said anxiously. "We could go bowling. Or go-karting. Whatever you like, really."

"I'll see," I said. I felt bad. "I'll ring you."

"OK," he said. "Here's my number. And here's my work number. And here's my mobile. And here's my fax number. And here's my e-mail address. And here's my real address."

"Thank you."

"Ring anytime," he said, fervently. "Anytime at all. Day or night."

Chapter Eighty-Three

Charlotte dropped the bombshell on Thursday evening. She rushed in from work, all agog.

"Guess who I met?" she screeched.

"Who?" Karen and I asked in unison.

"Daniel," she beamed. "And he was with his new girlfriend."

I couldn't see my face, but I *felt* myself go pale.

"His new what?" hissed Karen. She didn't look too hot herself.

"Yes," said Charlotte. "And he looked gorgeous. And he seemed really glad to see me . . ."

"What's she like, the bitch?" hissed Karen.

Thank God for Karen. She asked all the awful questions that I couldn't.

"Beautiful!" enthused Charlotte. "Really tiny and dainty, I felt like an elephant next to her. And she has loads of dark, curly hair. She's like a little doll, a bit like Lucy. And Daniel is *crazy* about her, you should have seen his body language . . ."

"Lucy isn't like a little doll," Karen interrupted.

"Yes, she is."

"No, she isn't. There's a difference between being short and being a little doll, you fool."

"Well, her face looked like Lucy. And her hair," shouted Charlotte.

"I thought you said she was beautiful," sniffed Karen.

At first I thought she was sniffing dismissively. But when sniff followed sniff, followed by heaving shoulders, followed by outright sobbing, I realised that she was crying.

Lucky her. In her position of ex-girlfriend she was allowed. I had no rights.

"The rotten, stinking, lousy bastard," she fumed. "How dare he be happy without me? He wasn't supposed to meet someone else, he was supposed to find out that he couldn't live without me. I hope he loses his job and that his house is burnt to the ground and that he gets syphilis, no wait . . . AIDS, no wait . . . *acne*, he'd hate that, and that he's in a car crash and his fuck-truck is a write-off and that his dick gets caught in a mincing machine and that he's arrested for a crime he didn't commit and . . ."

The usual kind of things that you say when your ex-boyfriend has the audacity to meet someone new.

Charlotte patted and shushed her, but I just walked away. I felt nothing for her, I was too busy feeling for me.

I was in shock.

I had just realised that I was in love with Daniel.

I could hardly believe my stupidity, not to mention my poor judgement. I had suspected for some time that I fancied him. That had been very careless of me. But to be in love with him, to *love* him – that was nothing short of criminal negligence.

And to think of how I had laughed at all the other women who had fallen for him over the years. Little did I think it would happen to me. Doubtless there was a great lesson to be learnt from it – don't mock lest ye be mocked yourself, or something like that.

I couldn't think straight because the sharp tearing pain of jealousy was driving me demented.

Worse than the jealousy was the fear that I had lost Daniel forever. It had been such a long time since he'd been out with anyone, that I had started to think of him as *mine*.

Big mistake.

I did the most foolish thing I could think of – I rang him.

He was the only one who could comfort my pain, even though he was the one who had caused it.

It was an unusual situation to cry on a friend's shoulder about my broken heart, when the person whose shoulder I was crying on was actually the one who had broken my heart. But I never seemed to do things normally.

"Daniel, are you on your own?" I expected him to say no.

"Yes."

"Can I come over?"

He didn't say, "It's late" or "What do you want?" or "Can't it wait until tomorrow?"

He just said, "I'll come and collect you."

"No," I said. "I'll get a taxi, I'll see you shortly."

"Where are you going?" Karen caught me trying to sneak out the front door.

"Out," I said, with a soupçon of defiance. Misery had made me less afraid of her.

"Out where?"

"Just out."

"You're going to see Daniel, aren't you?"

She was either very perceptive or else highly paranoid and obsessed.

"Yes." I met her eyes.

"You stupid bitch, you haven't a hope with him."

"I know." I made for the stairs.

"Are you still going?" she asked in angry surprise.

"Yes."

"You-are-not-to-go," she barked in staccato fashion.

"Says who?" By then I was half-way down the stairs, where it was a lot easier to be brazen.

"I forbid you to," she said.

"I'm going."

She was incandescent with rage. She could barely speak.

"I don't want to make you see a fool of yourself," she finally managed to splutter out.

"Maybe not, but you'd love to see me make a fool of myself."

"Come back here!"

"Get lost," I said bravely and bolted.

"I'll wait up for you!" she screamed. "You'd better come home . . ."

Chapter Eighty-Four

In the taxi, on the way over, I decided that the only thing I could do was tell Daniel why I was so upset – despite the Greek chorus in my head begging me not to.

"You know that the last thing you should ever do is tell the man you're in love with, that you're in love with him!" they sang and clamoured. "*Especially*, when he's not in love with you."

"I know," I said in exasperation. "But it's different with me and Daniel. He's my friend, he'll talk me out of it. He'll tell me how horrible he is to his girlfriends."

"Get someone else to talk you out of it," they sang. "There's a world full of people – why pick on him?"

"He'll take away the pain, he'll make me feel better."

"But . . ."

"He's the only one who can," I said with firm finality.

"You're not fooling us," the chorus sang. "We know you're up to something."

"Shut up, I'm not," I protested.

I understood that Victorian stuff about, "He must

715

never know how much I love him, I could not bear his pity." Especially if the man wasn't very nice and would laugh and tell his friends about it when they went shooting grouse. But it didn't apply to me, I decided. I didn't need my dignity with Daniel.

When he opened the door to me, I was so happy to see him that my heart leapt.

Dammit, I thought, so it's true, I really *am* in love with him.

I ran straight into his arms – being his friend had lots of advantages that I had no intention of giving up just because he had got himself a new girlfriend.

I clung to him tightly and – fair play to him – he clung on to me pretty tightly also.

He must have thought that I was behaving most oddly but, being the decent kind of bloke he was, he went along with it. I would explain in a little while, I decided. But for the moment I was staying where I was. He was still my friend, I was still allowed to be hugged by him. And for a few moments I could pretend that he was my lover.

"Sorry about this, Daniel, but I need you to be my friend."

A lie of course – but I couldn't really say, "Sorry about this, Daniel, but I want to marry you and have your children."

"I'll always be your friend, Lucy," he murmured as he stroked my hair.

Thanks for nothing, I thought uncharitably. But only briefly. He was a great friend – it was hardly his fault that I'd been foolish enough to fall in love with him.

After a while I felt strong enough to disentangle myself from him.

"So what's wrong?" he asked. "Is it your dad?"

"Oh no, nothing like that."

"Tom?"

"Who? Oh no, poor Tom, not him. Why do the ones we don't love always fall in love with us, Daniel?"

"I don't know, Lucy, but they do."

"You don't know the half of it," I thought nervously.

I took a deep breath. "Daniel, I need to talk to you."

But when I actually tried to tell him what was wrong with me, it wasn't as easy as I had thought it would be. In fact, it was really awkward and embarrassing.

The romantic idea I had harboured of flying to him and expecting him to magically kiss away my pain had evaporated. He had a girlfriend, for God's sake. I was only his friend. I had no rights over him. What could I say? – "Daniel, I want you to break it off with your new girlfriend." Hardly.

"Er, Lucy, what do you want to talk to me about?" he asked, after the seconds had ticked by and I still hadn't said anything.

I looked at my hands for ages before I found the right words.

"Charlotte said she met you with a girl and I was, er, jealous," I finally managed to blurt out. I couldn't meet his eyes, and I *cringed*.

Maybe telling him wasn't a good idea.

Maybe it was a very bad idea.

I shouldn't have come, I realised, I must have been mad. I should have just gone to bed and waited it out. The pain would have gone eventually.

"Only because she was short with dark hair," I added quickly, in an attempt to recover lost ground and lost dignity. I had been wrong about the dignity – I *did* need it with him. "I've no problems with you shagging big blonde girls, but I keep remembering that night out in Dad's when you turned me down and I thought it was because I wasn't your type. And it didn't feel very nice when Charlotte said that the girl she met you with looked a bit like me, because what was wrong with me . . . ?"

"Oh, Lucy." He kind of half-laughed. At me or with me? Was it good or bad?

"I suppose Sascha does look a bit like you," he said. "I hadn't noticed, but now that you mention it . . ."

Sascha. It would be. Why couldn't she have been called Madge?

"Anyway, that's all that was wrong with me," I said briskly, in a very belated attempt to recover lost ground. "Nothing at all the matter, I've overreacted as usual. You know me. Well, it's been good to get it off my chest. But I must be off now . . ."

I stood up to leave and if I had left then, that second, I would have missed the arrival of my anger. But no, I met it at the door as it staggered in, gasping and panting, worn out from the crosstown journey. "Sorry, I'm late," it wheezed, clutching its chest. "Awful traffic. But I'm here now . . ." And with that I rounded on Daniel with sudden fury.

"You could have just told me, you know, that you had a new girlfriend. Instead of giving me all that . . . that . . . *crap*," I spat, "about me needing to get out more. You only had to tell me that I was cluttering up your life and that *Sascha* needed you more than I did. I would've understood, you know."

He opened his mouth to say something but I beat him to it.

"If you wanted me out of the way, then you only had to say. Did you think I'd mind, did you think I'd be jealous? The cheek of you! You think you're gorgeous, don't you? That every woman is mad about you."

Once again he tried to say something, it seemed to be some sort of denial, but he didn't stand a chance.

"We're supposed to be friends, you know, Daniel. So how could you pretend that you were *concerned* about me? That you cared about me?"

"But . . . ."

"When it's obvious that the only person you care about is yourself!"

That was the part in most arguments when the angry shouting changes into tearful wobbling. This one was no exception – you could have set your watch by it. My voice veered off the trembly end of the scale and I realised that I was dangerously close to crying. But still I didn't leave. Like a fool I was waiting in the hope that he might be nice to me, that he might say something to make me feel better.

"I wasn't pretending," he protested. "I really *was* concerned for you."

719

I hated the look of pity on his face.

"Well, there's no need," I said nastily. "I can look after myself."

"Can you really?" He sounded pathetically hopeful.

How dare he! "Of course, I can," I threw at him.

"That's great," he said.

How could he be so cruel, I wondered, as pain tore through me.

Easily, I realised. Very easily. He'd done it lots of times to lots of other women, why should I get special treatment?

"Goodbye, Daniel. I hope things work out for you and the beautiful Sascha," I said sarcastically.

"Thanks, Lucy, and the best of luck with rich Tom." He matched my sarcasm.

"What are *you* being so nasty about?" I asked in angry surprise.

"What do you think?" His voice had suddenly gone up several decibels.

"How the fuck should I know?" I shouted back.

"You're not the only one who's jealous?" he yelled. He looked furious.

"I know I'm not!" I said. "But, to be quite honest, Daniel, Karen isn't really my concern right now."

"What the hell are you talking about?" he asked. "I'm talking about *me*! I'm fucking jealous too! I've spent months waiting for the right time, waiting for you to get over your Dad. I did everything I could think of to stop myself making a pass at you. I was so patient, it nearly killed me."

He paused for breath. I stared at him, unable to

speak. Before I could take it all in he began shouting again.

"And then!" he roared into my face. "And then, when I finally manage to convince you to start thinking about having a relationship with a man, you go and get off with someone else. I meant *me*, I wanted you to think about having a relationship with *me*, and instead some rich, lucky bastard gets you!"

My head raced as I tried to take it all in.

"Wait a minute, wait a minute, why is Tom a lucky bastard?" I asked. "Because he's rich?"

"No!" Daniel shouted. "Because he's going out with you, of course."

"But he's not going out with me," I said. "I only went out with him once and that was just to annoy you. Not that it worked."

"Not that it worked!" spluttered Daniel. "Of course it worked. I got so drunk on Sunday night that I was too sick to go to work on Monday."

"Really?" I asked, momentarily sidetracked. "Were you throwing up? That kind of sick?"

"Couldn't eat a thing until Tuesday evening," he said.

There was a little silence and for a moment we were just Daniel and Lucy again.

"What was that bit that you said about wanting to make a pass at me?" I asked.

"Nothing, forget it," he said sulkily.

"Tell me!" I shouted.

"Nothing to say," he muttered. "It was just that I could hardly keep my hands off you, but I knew I had to because you were so vulnerable. If anything had happened with us I'd always be afraid that you had only done it because you were all mixed-up."

"That was why I gave you that talk about coming back to the land of the living," he said. "I wanted you to know your own mind and be able to make decisions so that when I asked you out and if you said yes, I wouldn't feel like I was taking advantage of you."

"Ask me out?" I said, carefully.

"Out, *out*," said Daniel, sheepishly. "As in boyfriend and girlfriend out."

"Really?" I asked. "Are you serious? So all that stuff about me meeting people wasn't just to get me out of the way to make room for Sascha."

"No."

"Who's this Sascha anyway?" I asked jealously.

"A girl from work."

"And does she look like me?"

"I suppose there's a superficial resemblance. Although she's not half as beautiful as you," he said idly. "Or as funny or as sexy or as cute or as clever."

I sat very still. That sounded promising. But not promising enough.

"How long have you been going out with her?" I asked.

"But I'm not going out with her." He sounded annoyed.

"But Charlotte said . . ."

"Please!" Daniel put his hand to his forehead, as if he had a headache. "I'm sure Charlotte said plenty and you know how fond of her I am, but she doesn't always get things right."

"So, you're *not* going out with Sascha?" I asked.

"No."

"Why not?"

"I didn't think it was fair to go out with her when I'm in love with you."

My brain went into shock. The words hit home long before the feelings arrived.

"Oh," I said in surprise.

I couldn't think of anything to say. I would have settled for him fancying me.

God, this was great.

"I shouldn't have said that." Daniel looked miserable.

"Why not? Isn't it true?"

"Of course it's true. I don't go round telling women I love them at the drop of a hat. But I don't want to scare you. Please, Lucy, forget I said it."

"I will not," I said irritably. "That's the nicest thing anyone has ever said to me."

"Really?" he said hopefully. "You mean you . . ."

"Yes, yes." I waved my arm distractedly. I wanted to think about what he had said to me. I had no time to bother with him.

"I love you too," I added. "I think I must have for ages."

Happiness and relief began to trickle through me, increasing to a steady flow, then gushed as though from a broken pipe. But I had to be sure.

"Are you really in love with me?" I asked him suspiciously.

"Oh, God, yes."

"Since when?"

"For a long time."

"Since Gus?"

"Since long before Gus."

"Why didn't you ever tell me?"

"Because you would have screeched with laughter and humiliated me . . ."

"I would *not* have!" I was outraged.

"Yes, you would."

"Would I?"

"Oh yes, Lucy."

"Well, maybe I would," I reluctantly agreed.

"Oh, sorry, Daniel." I was passionately apologetic. "But I *had* to be mean to you, because you were just too attractive."

"And that's actually a compliment," I added.

"Really?" he asked. "But all the blokes you went out with were completely different from me – how could I compete with someone like Gus?"

He was right – until recently I couldn't have coped with a boyfriend who didn't have a terrible credit rating and a drink problem.

I thought about it some more.

"Are you really, *really* in love with me?"

"Yes, Lucy."

"No, I mean *really?*"

"Yes, really."

"In that case, can we go to bed?"

Chapter Eighty-Five

Astonished by my brazenness, I took him by the hand and led him into his bedroom

I was torn between acute lust and acute embarrassment. Because I was afraid that it could still go horribly wrong.

It was all very well for him to go round telling me he loved me, but the real test, the real issue was the bed one.

What if I was crap in bed?

What about the fact that we'd been friends for more than ten years? The potential cringe factor was high. How could we possibly be all gooey and romantic about each other and not laugh?

What if he thought I was hideous? He was used to women with huge breasts. What would he say when he saw my fried eggs?

I was so nervous that I almost changed my mind.

But not quite.

I had a chance to sleep with him and I fully intended to avail of it. I loved him. But I also fancied him.

However, after the flying start where I brazenly took his hand, I ran out of trollopy steam. Once I got him into the bedroom, I didn't really know what to do. Should I drape myself seductively on his Habitat duvet? Should I shove him onto the bed and jump on top of him. But I couldn't, it was too mortifying.

I perched on the edge of his bed. He sat down beside me.

God, this was so much easier when I was drunk.

"What's wrong?" he whispered.

"What if you think I'm hideous?"

"What if you think *I'm* hideous?"

"But you're gorgeous." I giggled.

"So are you."

"I'm so nervous," I whispered.

"I am too."

"I don't believe you."

"But I am, honestly," he said. "Here, feel my heart."

That made me edgy. In the past I had submitted my hand for the alleged feeling of a heart and instead my hand had been placed on the young man's erect member and then rubbed up and down said member at high speed.

But Daniel really did place my hand on his heart. And, yes, there did seem to be a fair amount of commotion going on in his chest.

"I love you, Lucy," he said.

"I love you, too," I said shyly.

"Givvus a kiss," he said.

"OK." I turned my face up to his, but I closed my eyes. He kissed my eyes, and my eyebrows, and along my hairline and all the way down to my neck. Light, tantalising kisses that were almost unbearably pleasurable. Then he kissed the corner of my mouth and gently pulled at my lower lip with his teeth.

"Knock off the arch-seducer stuff," I complained, "and kiss me properly."

"Well, if my form of kissing is not to Modom's satisfaction . . ." He laughed.

Then he did the smile thing that he did so well. And I kissed him – I couldn't help myself.

"I thought you said you were nervous," he said.

"Shush." I put a finger to my lips. "I nearly forgot about it for a second."

"How about if I lie down on the bed and you lie here next to me in my arms?" he asked as he pulled me down next to him on the bed. "Is that too arch-seducery for you?"

"No, that was nice and clumsily done," I said to his chest.

"Any chance that you might kiss me again, Lucy?" he whispered.

"OK," I whispered back. "But I don't want any slick moves from you – like you taking my bra off in one go."

"Don't worry, Lucy, I'll fumble."

"And you're not to say 'what's that, Lucy?' and take my knickers out from behind my ear. Do you hear?" I said grumpily.

"But that's my party trick," he said. "It's the most spectacular thing I do in bed."

I kissed him again and I relaxed a bit. It was wonderful lying so close to him, inhaling the Daniel smell, touching his beautiful face. God, he was sexy.

"Do you really love me?" I asked again.

"Lucy, I love you so much."

"No, I mean, do you really, *really* love me?"

"I really, *really* love you," he said, looking into my eyes. "More than I've ever loved anyone, more than you can imagine."

I relaxed for a second. But only for a second.

"Really?" I asked.

"Really."

"No, Daniel, I mean, really, *really*?"

"Really, *really*."

"OK."

There was a little pause.

"You don't mind me asking, do you?" I asked.

"Not at all."

"It's just that I've got to be sure."

"I completely understand. Do you believe me?"

"I believe you."

We lay smiling at each other.

"Lucy?" asked Daniel.

"What?"

"Do you really love me?"

"Daniel, I really love you."

"No, but, Lucy," he said awkwardly. "I mean do you *really* love me? As in really, *really*?"

"I really, *really* love you, Daniel."

"Really?"

"Really."

Very, very slowly, he took off my clothes, skilfully managing to snag zips and yank things that shouldn't have been yanked. Every time he opened a button he kissed me for about an hour before he opened the next one. He kissed me everywhere. Well, almost everywhere, thankfully he left my feet alone. Fergie had a lot to answer for – men seemed to think that they had to suck toes before they had fulfilled their bedtime duties. A few years ago, it had been cunnilingus – the watching paint dry of sex, I always felt. I didn't like men going near my feet, not unless I'd had plenty of warning – enough of a warning to have had a pedicure. He kissed me and opened buttons, kissed me and peeled my shirt off one shoulder, kissed me again, peeled my shirt off my other shoulder, kissed me again, didn't comment on the greyness of my white knickers, kissed me again, said my breasts weren't like fried eggs, kissed me again, said they were more like hamburger buns, kissed me again. "You're so beautiful, Lucy," he said, over and over again. "I love you."

Until I had nothing on.

There was something very erotic about being naked while he was still dressed.

I clamped my arms around my chest and wrapped myself up in a ball.

"Get your kit off," I giggled.

"You're so romantic, Lucy," he said, peeling one arm off my chest, then the other.

"Don't hide yourself," he said. "You're too beautiful."

He gently forced my knees away from my chest.

"Get lost," I said, trying to hide my excitement. "How come I'm not wearing a stitch and you're still fully dressed?"

"I can take my clothes off, if you want," he teased.

"Do it then," I said, trying to be brisk.

"Ask me."

"No."

"You'll have to do it, in that case."

I took off his clothes. My fingers were trembling so much that I could hardly open the buttons of his shirt. But it was worth it.

He had such a beautiful chest, such smooth skin, such a flat stomach.

I traced the line of hair from his bellybutton with my fingernail, as far as the waistband of his trousers, and a shiver ran through me when I heard him gasp.

Out of the corner of my eye, I had a quick look at the groin area of his trousers, and was appalled and thrilled when I saw the way the fabric strained.

Eventually I plucked up enough courage to slowly start opening his trousers. But I wasn't used to men in suits. Daniel's trousers had a system of buttons and zips that could rival Fort Knox.

Eventually we liberated his straining erection.

He passed the underpants test. Which was more than could be said for me. My knickers had seen better days, most of them inside a washing machine, mistakenly put in with a black wash.

He was gorgeous – and something that made him even more attractive to me – he wasn't perfect. Although his body was beautiful, it wasn't one of those muscular elaborately patterned ones that Chippendales seem to have.

The feel of his skin on my skin was indescribable. Everything felt so sensitive, the skin on the inside of my arms tingled as I wrapped them around his back.

The feel of the roughness of his thighs against the softness of mine was weak-making, his hardness against my wetness was explosive.

All embarrassment had gone. Only desire remained. When I caught his eye I no longer felt a hysterical urge to laugh. We'd passed over the line – we were no longer Daniel and Lucy, we were a man and a woman.

We hadn't mentioned birth control, but when the time came we were both responsible adults living in the HIV positive nineties.

He produced a condom and I helped him put it on. And then, we . . . er, you know . . .

He came in about three seconds. It was mind-blowingly erotic to see Daniel's face scrunched up in ecstasy, ecstasy that I'd caused.

"Sorry, Lucy," he gasped. "I couldn't stop myself, you're so beautiful and I've wanted you for so long."

"I thought you were supposed to be brilliant in bed," I complained teasingly. "I never heard that you were a premature-ejaculation merchant."

"I'm not," he protested anxiously. "I haven't done that since I was a teenager. Just give me five minutes and I'll prove it to you."

I lay in the circle of his arms and he kept up the constant volley of kisses and stroked my back and my thighs and my stomach.

And in an admirably short time, he made love to me again.

The second time lasted for ages and he did it achingly slowly and tantalisingly and with all the attention focused on me and what I wanted. No one had ever been as selfless and giving in bed to me before. And I climaxed as I never had before, shuddering and trembling, my eyes wide with shock and pleasure.

This time when he came, he kept his eyes open and looked at me. I nearly dissolved, it was so erotic.

We hugged each other fiercely, we couldn't get close enough.

"I wish I could unzip my skin and put you inside me," he said. And I knew what he meant.

We lay in silence for a while.

"There now, that wasn't too bad, was it?" asked Daniel. "What were you afraid of?"

"Lots of things," I laughed. "That you might think I had a horrible body. That you might make me do weird stuff."

"You have a *beautiful* body. And what kind of weird stuff? Plastic bags and oranges?"

"Well, not really, because you're not a Tory MP, but other things."

"Now I'm intrigued, what am I missing out on?"

"You know," I said awkwardly.

"No," he said.

"Well," I explained, "there are some men who say things like, 'can you just stand on your head, here, don't worry about the pain, I'm told it gets easier to bear after a while. Now, keeping your legs at a 130 degree angle to each other, I'm going to enter you from behind, now can you move your entire body in a kind of pincer like movement, approximately eight inches, no, I said *eight* inches, that's more like ten – stupid bitch, are you trying to kill me?' – that kind of thing."

He laughed and laughed, and that felt wonderful too.

And then, more sleepily, more relaxed, we made love again.

"What time is it?" I asked later.

"About two."

"Have you work in the morning?"

"Yes, have you?"

"Yes, I suppose we should get some sleep," I said. But we didn't.

I was starving, so Daniel went to the kitchen and came back with a packet of chocolate biscuits, and we lay in bed and ate them and hugged each other and kissed each other and talked about nothing in particular.

"I should join a gym," he said ruefully, poking a finger into his stomach. "If I had known that this was going to happen, I would have joined months ago."

That, more than anything, endeared him to me.

When we finished the biscuits, he commanded me, "Sit up."

I sat.

He brushed the sheets with vigour.

"I can't have my woman sleeping on chocolate biscuit crumbs," he said.

As I smiled at him, the phone rang and I jumped about a foot. Daniel answered it.

"Hello, oh hello, Karen, yes, I *am* in bed actually."

A pause.

"Lucy?" he asked slowly, as if he'd never heard such a name. "Lucy *Sullivan*?"

Another pause.

"Lucy Sullivan, your *flatmate*? *That* Lucy Sullivan? Yes, she's right here beside me."

"Yes, right here beside me in bed," he said. "Would you like to speak to her?"

I made all kinds of frantic denial actions and made a cross of my two index fingers and held them towards the phone.

"Oh yes," said Daniel cheerfully. "Three times. Wasn't it three times, Lucy?"

"Wasn't what three times?" I asked.

"The number of times I've made love to you in the last couple of hours."

"Er, yes, three," I said faintly.

"Yes, it was definitely three, Karen. Although we might do it again before the night is out. Is there anything else you need to know?"

I heard screaming and ranting from Karen. Even *I* heard the crunch when she banged down the phone.

"What did she say?" I asked.

"She said she hopes we give each other AIDS."

"Is that all?"

"Er, yes."

"Come on, Dan, what else did she say?"

"Lucy, I don't want to upset you . . ."

"You've *got* to tell me now."

"She said that she slept with Gus when you were going out with him."

He looked at me anxiously. "Have I upset you?"

"No, I'm kind of relieved. I always felt that there was someone else. But are *you* upset?"

"Why would I be upset? I wasn't going out with Gus."

"No, but you were going out with Karen when I was going out with Gus. If she slept with Gus, then . . ."

"Oh, I *see*," he said cheerfully. "It means that she two-timed me."

"Do you mind?" I asked anxiously.

"Of course I don't mind. I couldn't care less about Karen sleeping with him. It was *you* sleeping with him that bothered me."

We lay in silence, the circle of bliss ruptured.

"I'll have to move out," I said finally.

"You can move in here," he offered.

"Don't be ridiculous," I said. "We've only been going out with each other three and a half hours. Isn't it a bit soon to be talking about living together?"

"Living together?" Daniel sounded shocked. "Who mentioned living together?"

"You did."

"No, I didn't. I'm far too frightened of your mother to suggest living in sin with her only daughter."

"Well, in that case, what *are* you talking about?"

"Lucy," he said sheepishly, "I was, er, you know wondering if . . ."

"What?"

"Would there be any chance . . . ? You know . . . ?"

"Any chance of what?"

"You'll probably think I have an awful nerve asking, but I love you so much and . . ."

"Daniel," I begged. "*Please* tell me what you're on about."

"You don't have to give me your answer straight away, or anything."

"My answer to what?" I pleaded.

"Take ages to think about it, as long as you like."

"To think about WHAT?" I yelled.

"Sorry, I didn't mean to annoy you, but, it's just that, um, well, er . . ."

"Daniel, what are you trying to say?"

He paused, took a deep breath and blurted out, "Lucy Carmel Sullivan, will you marry me?"

Epilogue

Hetty never came back to work, she divorced Dick, left Roger, got rid of the tweed skirts, bought lots of leggings, enrolled in Women's Studies and is now happily romantically involved with an earnest Swedish woman called Agnetha. According to Meredia neither of them shave under their arms.

Frank Erskine never came back to work either, he took early retirement and left without fanfare. Apparently he plays a lot of golf.

Adrian now only works weekends at the video shop because he's got a place on a film-making course, where I hope he meets a nice girl who knows her Walt Disney from her Quentin Tarantino.

Daniel's Ruth, the woman he was going out with before Karen, was in the *News of the World* for having sex with a politician.

Jed moved in with Meredia and they both seem to be blissfully happy. Despite his small stature he is very protective of large Meredia, and gets many opportunities to prove it.

Meredia's real name is Valerie and she's thirty-eight. I found out by accident when I was called to

Personnel for being late once too often. Her record file was just lying open in Blandina's filing cabinet and I couldn't help but see.

I haven't told Megan. In fact, I haven't told anyone.

Charlotte still hasn't found a man to take her seriously and is talking about having a breast reduction. She is going to apply to study psychology. Just as soon as she's learnt how to spell it.

Karen started going out with Simon shortly after Daniel and I got together, and the pair of them have matching His'n'Hers lifestyles. They buy a lot of expensive clothes and go to bars that have only been open a week and that are photographed for architectural magazines.

Dennis still hasn't found Mr Right, although he's having a lot of fun looking. He had a bad knock when Michael Flatley left the cast of Riverdance, but he's over it now.

Megan is pregnant.

And Gus is the father. Apparently they've been together since the summer that I was allegedly going out with him. Megan even wrote Gus's farewell speech to me. Although I haven't seen Gus, I gather that imminent fatherhood hasn't made him any less irresponsible. Poor Megan looks constantly exhausted and miserable. I feel really sorry for her and I'm not saying that in the way that you do when you don't feel sorry for the person at all and instead you really hate them. My heart genuinely goes out to her.

My mother is still living with Ken Kearns and

they're like love-struck teenagers. Ken has got new false teeth, they look like expensive, de luxe, top of the range ones. My mother looks younger and younger every time I see her. Soon they won't serve her in pubs. Mum and I have had a tentative reunion. And although we're not the best of pals yet, we're working on it.

My father is still drinking, but he's being looked after. He has a social worker and a home help. Chris, Peter and I take it in turn to visit him. Whenever it's my turn, Daniel comes with me, which is great because it means that Dad has to divide his insults between the two of us. I still feel guilty, I suppose I always will, but it's only guilt and it's not going to kill me.

Daniel keeps asking me to marry him. And I keep telling him to get lost. "Be practical," I say. "Who would give me away? Even if Dad didn't hate me he still wouldn't be sober enough to lurch up the aisle with me." But the real reason that I won't agree to marry Daniel is because I'm afraid of being jilted at the altar. I obviously haven't got used to a bloke being nice to me yet. But Daniel says that he'll always love me and never leave me and that, short of lopping off his penis and presenting it to me in a jar of preservative, getting married is the most extreme thing he can think of to convince me of his unending devotion.

I've told him I'll think about it. The getting married bit, I mean. Not the lopping off of his . . . oh, you know what I mean.

And if we do get married I want Mrs Nolan as my matron of honour.

Daniel swears he loves me. He certainly *acts* as if he does.

And, you know, I'm halfway to believing him.

One thing I'm sure of, I love Daniel.

So, watch this space . . .